GLAMARA

The day after we moved into our new home we were introduced to Mr Hardcastle, who had brought some disquieting news from the city. Queen Victoria was dead. He told us that many of the buildings in Leeds were already draped in black and all the flags were flying at half mast. People were crying in the streets and in the villages too the people seemed stunned.

I couldn't imagine England without Queen Victoria. It seemed to me that she had always been there, that old plain sad lady who had stamped her personality upon our world. To her subjects it was as though a dearly loved grandmother had suddenly died, leaving them lost and bewildered.

I was ten years old when the Queen died and I thought about her death in relation to my life. It was 1901, a new century, and my mother and I had been given a new start in life. From now on, I told myself with the supreme optimism of youth, everything was going to be perfect.

GLAMARA

Sara Hylton

**THE SHERIDAN
BOOK COMPANY**

This edition published in 1994 by
The Sheridan Book Company

First published in Great Britain
by Century 1986
Random House, 20 Vauxhall Bridge Road, London SW1V 2SA
Arrow edition 1988

Printed and bound in Great Britain by
Cox & Wyman Ltd, Reading, Berkshire

ISBN 1-85501-468-8

I dedicate this novel to members of
my family and friends in gratitude for
their encouragement and the faith
they have shown in my ability to
write it.

THEY ARE NOT LONG

They are not long, the weeping and the
laughter,
    Love and desire and hate:
I think they have no portion in us after
    We pass the gate.

They are not long, the days of wine and
roses:
    Out of a misty dream
Our path emerges for awhile, then
closes
    Within a dream.

ERNEST DOWSON
(The Bodley Head)

PART ONE

PROLOGUE

We always return to Glamara at Eastertime. For months I try
not to think of it, and then, I only have to see daffodils piled
high on street barrows and feel the new warmth in the sun for
the old longing to take hold of me. In my dreams I return
often, and always on awakening I have been aware of the
tears drying on my cheeks and my heart has been heavy with
remembered pain.

Those dreams are too powerful to be ignored, and now,
even after all these years I know that for the first few days my
heart will be plagued with memories, haunting and
tormenting, until I find reassurance in remembering that
although I encountered sorrow at Glamara, for the first time
I became aware of the tenderness and power of love.

The road twists and winds as it follows faithfully the river
Wharfe's meanderings through the lonely yet beautiful
Yorkshire Dales. It is a beauty that leads us over undulating
moorland where limestone crags rise in rugged splendour
towards the windblown clouds, through peaceful, timeless
stone villages where ancient churches and ruined abbeys
have weathered the stern winds that sweep down upon them
from the lofty fells. At times the river is wide and peaceful, at
others it is turbulent, swirling between the stones, and here
and there along its banks the willows dip their graceful
feathery branches.

We seldom speak as we travel northward, but my eyes are
ever searching for the sight of the dark dismal pines on the
hill above the house, and the shadows cast by the clouds give
the Pennines a gentleness they do not really possess. It is
dusk as we approach the village of Lambreck and the lights
from the Chalfont Arms shine warmly through the gathering
gloom in a street that has remained unchanged since I first
walked along its cobbled length as a girl. Soon we will take

3

the right fork out of the village with the fourteenth-century church with its square Norman tower standing high above the road.

The old excitement is with me now as we climb the road leading up to the great iron gates which have been left open in anticipation of our arrival. Before us stretches the long drive across the park with Glamara in the distance, the lights from the windows illuminating the forecourt and gardens.

There will be warm greetings from the few old servants who remain there. When they have gone who knows what will happen, for the young people leave the villages now and no longer bind their lives and their memories to families and great houses.

I know that for a long moment I will stand in the hall, my heart plagued with memories. That hall which I have so often seen decked with holly and mistletoe for the Christmas festivities, with a log fire burning in the great stone fireplace and groups of people drinking hot punch before they went out into the wintry cold. In my imagination I will people the hall with those I have once known. Sir Godfrey Chalfont with his handsome weather-beaten face and his robust laughter, relating his ribald hunting stories to his special cronies, and Abigail, plain and tender, worshipping him with her gentle smile and her shy doe eyes. The twins, Adam and Robert, good-looking and carefree, drinking the night away in spite of Aunt Hetty, dear Aunt Hetty who was always the butt for their banter.

I know every picture, every portrait, every piece of furniture in those lofty rooms and I wonder how long it is since music was played in the ballroom. Dancing in that ballroom had been a joy. With Alec in his new uniform, so young and attractive and full of life, and Julian who filled my young heart with its first dream of love, dark and remote with his sudden sweet smile that robbed his handsome face of its accustomed severity.

I never felt that Roxanne had any part in our life at Glamara, she was an intruder, just as she was an intruder into my life, and yet why must I always think of her gypsy-dark beauty and her green eyes like pieces of chipped jade?

Roxanne is a phantom conjured up by my own fears but her face is tormentingly real. She obtrudes into my conscious thoughts unbidden and alien.

Roxanne on that Christmas night with the scent of burning logs filling the air, the glow from their leaping flames playing on tinselled tree and glossy holly leaves, standing at the head of the stairs in a scarlet gown, her beauty as glowing and rich as a poppy, or dancing in Julian's arms, his dark head inclined to listen to her words as her eyes flashed tantalizingly in her exquisite face. Two people cut from the same mould and with the power still to fill my heart with immeasurable pain.

Laura alone has escaped from Glamara with few regrets and I find it hard to believe that except for Robert and me Glamara will know them no more, yet I know that as I walk through the empty rooms the dear friends will come trooping back bringing memories of old summers when the crags stood golden bright in the sunlight and I shall hear again the gay jingle of bridle bits and laughter as we rode our horses across the lonely fells.

How could I know then that Glamara would shed her impossible magic across all the years of my life? The house was never mine, for I was only a passenger in its long and chequered history.

My life is full and warm with contentment. Surely it is unfair and dangerous to prejudice the present with memories which stir my heart with the glamour of old loves and times gone. Life has taught me that nothing is for ever, that joy, sorrow, hatred and even love are transient, so why do I insist on coming back year after year to stir the embers of old emotions and bitter-sweet memories? Strangers now walk entranced through the rooms of Glamara, whispering and exclaiming over things I once accepted as part of everyday living, whilst the family merely occupies a modest apartment within the house.

Tonight my eyes will meet Robert's eyes across the dining table while the others smile indulgently as we tantalize our thoughts with the words: 'Do you remember, oh do you remember?'

Perhaps next Easter I will listen to the persuasions of others and we will drive south to Tuscany, follow the Rhone in its peaceful meanderings towards the sun and the sea. Let others try to capture the haunting tenacity of Glamara so that they too will feel this painful urge to return again and again; but they should pause before they do, for Glamara will never belong to them. When the last footfall has left the hall and the last car has disappeared along the drive, Glamara will be at one again with the rugged crags and the pines and the haunting beauty of the eternal hills.

CHAPTER ONE

It seems strange that I who have loved Glamara the most had the least right to be there. I must tell you something of my mother's life, for it is she who closed the gates of Glamara for ever behind her.

My grandfather, Sir John Chalfont, had three children: Henrietta, from his first marriage to Maria Lancaster, and Godfrey and Diana from his second marriage to Louise Frazer who lived only two days after the birth of my mother. He never married again and his children were brought up by a changing stream of nursemaids and nannies.

Henrietta was a sweet though plain child, not given to tantrums or the more wild escapades of her sister. The two girls were educated by governesses although Godfrey was sent away to school. Diana was the one who could twist her father round her little finger, largely because she reminded him of her mother and perhaps because he recognized in her some of his own high-spirited pride and arrogance.

It was Diana Chalfont who wore the most beautiful ball gowns and captivated the most eligible bachelors, Diana who splendidly rode her father's fine horses and Diana who filled Glamara with an army of her friends so that Sir John was always entertained and enlivened by her.

He was exceedingly gratified when she fell in love with a man he most heartily approved of, a young man whose father owned vast acres in the West Riding of Yorkshire and whose family home was only a little less grand than his own. Edward Chalmers was welcomed cordially and it seemed for a time that the young couple were happy; until one Christmas when he arrived in the company of his cousin, Nigel Lorival. Diana had never met a man like this before. Nigel Lorival was an adventurer. He had already served as a mercenary in several of the world's trouble spots and he was handsome, reckless and impoverished. Unfortunately these were attributes that made him in Diana's eyes the most exciting person in the world.

That her father disapproved of the infatuation only fanned the flame. She had always managed to persuade him into her way of thinking but for the first time in her life she was denied something she desperately wanted. My grandfather was adamant that Nigel Lorival was not the man for his daughter. He forbade her to see him again and he made it plain to Nigel that he would not be welcome at Glamara. Diana wrote long impassioned letters dutifully carried by Hetty, in which she assured her lover that once they were together her father would swallow his pride and forget his animosity. He had always forgiven her indiscretions.

Together they hit upon a daring plan. My grandfather was visiting friends in Scotland. Diana planned to leave the house as usual on Sunday morning with her sister and some of the servants, for the church service. During the service she would feign illness and one of the servants would drive her back to Glamara, giving her enough time to gather her clothes and jewellery together before Nigel came for her. She took everything that would go conveniently into the trap he was driving – furs, clothes, jewels, indeed everything of value that she possessed. When Henrietta arrived home from church there was simply a letter to say she had gone, and another for her father and the man she had promised to marry.

It was a story like so many others in an age when parents chose the men and women their children should marry, but not all such stories had the same tragic ending.

At first they were madly, deliriously happy in a richly appointed house in Chelsea. She discovered that he was a gambler, but as he was enjoying a run of unprecedented good luck, it didn't worry her overmuch. They were the beautiful exciting Lorivals, she gay and beautiful, a charming delightful hostess, he handsome, charming and something of a rake. They were welcomed everywhere: in the homes of high-living friends, at grand balls and race meetings. They went for long weekends to fashionable country houses, and

8

the story of their elopement only added to the pleasure of entertaining them. Then my father began to lose money and things dramatically changed. Instead of an asset my mother became a drain and very soon the furs and the jewels began to go to settle his gambling debts.

He begged her to write to her father, a thing she was reluctant to do since she had received no word from him since she left Glamara, and she possessed all of his stubborn pride. Instead she wrote to her sister Hetty who replied that Sir John would not allow her name to be mentioned in his house. All her portraits had been removed from the walls and burned.

Perhaps the worst time of all was when she realized she was going to have a child, and then my father began to feel like the rat trembling in the circle before the dogs were released. The fashionable house had to go and something less pretentious took its place, then a few months later something smaller still, and always further away from the more fashionable part of the city.

The friends of their heyday began to drift away. They were no longer welcome, they had become an embarrassment; and while my father was at his clubs trying to revive the luck that had deserted him, my mother was alone in cheap lodgings, unhappy and bewildered, shabby and ailing, her once-beautiful face pinched by the first pangs of poverty.

The only jewellery she wore now was her plain wedding band, and the fashionable clothes had long since found their way into the local pawnbroker's.

My father was so sure that his luck must turn. There was to be a gambling session in a country house and he was determined to go. Although she pleaded, nothing she could say would deter him. In despair she watched him drive away in the trap he had hired that morning with money from the sale of his silver-topped cane and gold cigarette case.

In that country house he was accused of cheating at cards, and the following morning he saddled one of the horses and rode madly across the downs, pursued I have no doubt by the devil which drove him to disaster. He was found in the early afternoon with his neck broken after the horse had returned lame to the stable. On the night my mother was told of his death I was born six weeks prematurely and it seems to me now that I have only ever known of my father's bad qualities, not those others he must have possessed to make my mother love him.

I remember nothing of my early life in London. My first memory is of the tiny room at the top of Mrs Caxton's three storey house in Pimlico. I remember that the hall and stairs always smelled vaguely of cabbage and that Kitty, the cockney maid of all work hated me. She was not averse to pinching me whenever I passed her on her hands and knees scrubbing the stairs and she resented us because her employer had taken a liking to my mother who she regarded as fallen gentry. Because of this liking we acquired the room in exchange for the services my mother did for the old lady, like shopping, changing her library books and reading to her in the evenings. Crippled with arthritis she spent her life sitting in a shabby armchair enveloped in thick blankets.

When she died quite suddenly one morning the son who had never called to see her in all the time we had lived in her house suddenly arrived and began stripping it of everything he thought might be of value, and it was only when he decided my mother might be part of the furnishings that she made up her mind to leave London.

My mother had never had to live with poverty. She had never been called upon to earn her own living and her mind flew immediately to her old friends in the North of England. She swallowed her pride and wrote to Sir John telling him of our plight and begging him to care for me even if he couldn't find it in his heart to forgive her, but again there was no reply. Indeed the only person who did reply to her impassioned letters was a Mrs Joan Southeby living in the West Riding of Yorkshire, one of my mother's old friends and Edward Chalmer's cousin.

I was four years old when we finally left London.

Mrs Southeby had sent a trap to the station to meet us and in a short while we were driving through rhododendrons towards a large bright red-brick house. A neat maidservant opened the door and we were shown into a room where a pretty dark-haired lady came forward to embrace my mother. The maid took our outdoor clothing and for the first time I felt conscious of my darned dress and I saw the woman look at my mother in well-bred surprise.

'How thin you are,' she said, 'and to think that once you were the girl with a figure to drive men mad.'

'What is gone is gone, Joan. My sister has told me Father was very bitter and will never forgive me. He will never receive us and if we are to survive I shall have to find some way of earning a living.'

'What lines are you thinking on?' Mrs Southeby asked, pouring tea from a silver teapot into transparent china cups, and handing round plates filled with tiny iced cakes and thinly cut bread and butter.

'I honestly don't know. I can do needlework. I can speak French fairly well and write good English. I have been wondering if some family in the area were looking for a teacher, to encourage a delicate child, perhaps. You know that I ride well, I could even teach horsemanship, but it must be somewhere where I can have Tessa with me.'

'I'd like to help you but there are more than enough impoverished governesses around the area and not enough sick children. Perhaps riding would be a better idea. The gentry are already catered for in that direction but there could be the others, of course.'

'What do you mean by the others?'

'Well, there are the farming families and now there are industrialists who have moved into the country, having made their money in the cities. They are buying up properties at a ridiculous rate, you would be surprised how many old-established families have moved away because they couldn't afford to keep their estates. I expect the new people aim to be the gentry of the future. If breeding can be taught they certainly have the money to pay for it.'

My mother looked at her eagerly, the first faint flush of hope colouring her cheeks. 'Please, Joan, I'd be so grateful if you would ask, I'll work hard, I'll try anything, I'm not afraid of hard work.'

'No, I don't suppose you are. I never thought I would ever

11

see the day when Diana Chalfont would be asking if I could find her work. You always had everything Diana, beauty, money, adoration, and look how easily you threw it away. I suppose you know you were the talk of the county?'

'I must have been. It was all going to be so wonderful. We believed we were two people fate had meant for each other and we were going to show everybody how wrong they had been about us.'

'You hurt a great many people, Diana.'

'Yes. My father most of all.'

'And Edward.'

'Of course. Poor Edward, I once thought you and he would marry, you were always very close.'

'There was no chance of that. We are first cousins you know and neither side of the family has a history of robust health. Edward married Dora Rakesby and they have had two children. Richard is a little older than your daughter but Millicent died in infancy.'

'I'm sorry. When did they marry?'

'Not long after you left Glamara. People said he'd married Dora on the rebound but she came to him with a fair-sized dowry and she had always wanted him.'

'Does Edward visit you? I don't really feel I'm ready to see him again just yet.'

'We meet very seldom and he's not likely to visit me today. There are horse sales at Doncaster.'

'Horse sales! How remote it all sounds and yet I used to love going to horse sales with my father. I missed the horses and the dogs so much, although at first life in London seemed so exciting after the country. It is only now that I am really beginning to see how much I gave up.'

'Have you given any thought where you are to live, Diana?'

'We could stay at the inn for a little while, I have enough money to tide us over if it isn't too expensive.'

'I would ask you to stay here but Maurice and I are dining out this evening.' I felt this was a lame excuse not to have us stay. 'There is a woman who comes up from the village to help with the cleaning, I know she takes in boarders. If you like I'll ask her – Mrs Elliott – if she can take you and Tessa for a few days.'

'I shall be very grateful to you.'

'Tomorrow I will start to ask around. It might be a few days before I can let you know anything, shall we say Thursday if you can call here?'

'Of course, Thursday will do very well.'

My mother's face was very pale, pale and proud, and as if Mrs Southeby thought so too she turned abruptly away.

Mrs Elliott said she could take us in and we walked with her to the village. She was a small cheerful woman who kept up a steady stream of conversation which needed no concentration or replies from us. Her cottage was the end one of a row, with long gardens and a stone path leading up to the front door. Almost immediately we were standing in a room bright with firelight shining on polished brass and copper. The black-leaded firegrate occupied almost the whole of one wall and a kettle was already simmering on the hob. An old man dozed in a chair before the fire and the woman clicked her tongue impatiently as she shook his shoulder.

'Dad, wake up, we've got visitors an' you promised to 'ave the table laid.'

He roused himself and studied us through bleary, sleep-laden eyes. Then without a word he shuffled to his feet and stirred the coals on the fire.

''Ere, Mrs Lorival, give mi yer coat an' 'at, an' the little girl's too. I'll soon make a meal. Now move back a bit an' let the visitors see the fire, Dad.'

'Perhaps I can help you, Mrs Elliott,' my mother proffered.

'Nay, bless ye, it's all ready in the kitchen, it only needs bringin' in 'ere.'

Soon we were eating new bread and country butter and rich crumbly cheese and she was cutting into a huge fruit cake. I was hungry and the old man twinkled at me over his steel spectacles, saying, 'Tuck in little 'un, it's plain ter see tha's not bin used to good country food.'

13

My mother too was urged to eat and I was delighted to see the colour return to her cheeks as she helped herself to the proffered plates.

At just after seven o'clock Mr Elliott arrived home. He was a fat man with big gnarled hands, and immediately a large mug of strong tea was placed in front of him. He looked at me with friendly eyes.

''Ello, little 'un, 'ave not seen thee afore.'

I smiled at him shyly and his wife explained, 'This is Mrs Lorival an' 'er daughter Tessa. The lady's 'opin' ter find work i' these parts.'

'Work is it, what sort o work?'

'Teaching perhaps, or stable work. I was a good horsewoman when I was younger,' my mother answered.

He shook his head lugubriously, 'Works 'ard to come by. Widder woman are ye?'

'Yes.'

'Wi a little 'un to raise. Well, a wishes yer luck Mrs, but times is 'ard.'

Between then and Thursday we walked the country lanes and climbed over the stiles that led across the moorland between one hamlet and the next. To me it was a time of enchantment and I discovered that I loved the country and was desperately praying that we would be allowed to stay in it.

We watched the blacksmith shoeing horses and were invited to join him in strong brews of scalding tea, and I was thrilled with the cleverness of the black and white border collies as they marshalled the sheep on the fells. Although it was winter the scents of the countryside were warm and potent. The clean scent of the rich brown soil after a shower of rain was as heady in my nostrils as the perfume in a rose garden and the forests of dark green conifers and the golden brittle bracken made me feel strangely strong and alive.

'Was it like this when you were growing up at Glamara?' I asked my mother during one of our walks.

'Yes, only wilder, more rugged, more splendid. The hills were higher, the rivers were deeper. Oh Tessa, I wish that one day you could see Glamara. Why have I never realized

14

until now how desperately I hungered for the sight of those hills and the closeness of old friends that I threw away so unthinkingly?'

I wished I weren't a child. I wished I understood the pain in her eyes and the yearning in her voice, but more and more now she was speaking to me of the past and I was seeing Glamara with her eyes and wishing we could go there with all her longing.

As I trudged besides her on the long drive up to Mrs Southeby's house on Thursday afternoon I was repeating my prayers, entreating silently, 'Please God; please let us stay here, please let Mrs Southeby help us.'

Once more we were shown into the drawing room where tea was set in front of the fire and Mrs Southeby, gracious in a pretty tea gown, came forward to kiss my mother's cheek.

They talked pleasantries until I thought I would scream with frustration and my mother's hand gripped mine to tell me that she was feeling it too. At last Mrs Southeby assumed a more businesslike air.

'None of this has been easy for me, Diana,' she began. 'I talked first to the women you knew as a girl. Naturally they don't feel very kindly disposed towards you after you let Edward down so badly, but they are not entirely lacking in compassion and for the main part they are prepared to forget the past. They are sorry you have fallen on hard times and together we have been able to come up with something.

'Josephine Mallory's husband breeds horses and at the moment he does have a string of docile mounts he is prepared to place at your disposal in order to start a riding school at his stables. It is an undisputed fact that you were the best horsewoman in the county and Hugh is a businessman if nothing else. He will pay you a wage for handling the teaching side of the agreement and the people who make use of the stables will pay him for the hire of his horses and your services. He will advertise the proposition and he has no doubt that many local people will come forward.'

'I would have thought that most of the people around here already ride.'

'Hugh is thinking of the people who have moved here from

the cities and towns. Most of them are terrible social climbers, indeed many of them have already made approaches to join the local hunt, but I shouldn't think they have had anything to do with horses prior to living in the country.'

'Would it be such a terrible thing for them to join the hunt?'

'Not really, we need some new blood and their money would come in useful.'

My mother was thoughtful and I was wondering impatiently why she hadn't jumped at the offer. I thought Mrs Southeby was also surprised at her doubts because somewhat sharply she said, 'You're not saying anything, Diana, I'm afraid it was the only thing we could come up with.'

'And I am more than grateful, Joan, but there is the question of where we are to live. The Mallory place is some distance outside the village, would there be a cottage we could rent on the estate?'

'There is one, I went into that. It's not very grand, and it's unfurnished, but he's promised to do some work on it before you move in.'

'When will he want me to start these lessons?'

'Well, give him a week or two to get the feeling of the people round here and do the work required on the cottage. You can stay on at Mrs Elliott's and I can let you know when things are ready.'

Mother assured Mrs Southeby that she was grateful for her help and that she would try her best to fit in with any of Mr Mallory's plans. Before I realized what was happening we had said our farewells and were walking quickly down the drive.

I wanted to jump for joy but when I looked up at my mother's face expecting to find happiness there, I discovered instead that it was wet with her tears and her eyes were bleak with misery.

In the next few days we visited second-hand shops in neighbouring villages until we acquired enough badly made and badly painted furniture for our needs. Mother wrinkled up her elegant nose at its cheap ugliness but shrugging her shoulders philosophically said she could live without Chippendale and Hepplewhite. One shouldn't build one's life around bricks and mortar or pieces of polished wood.

I did not know it then but I came to know over the years how much my proud, beautiful mother suffered at the hands of her old friends: the slights, their patronizing air of indifference to one who had once been their idol, their condescending assumption that because she was no longer one of them she had ceased to feel the pain of their rejection.

She did not expect to be invited to their balls and weekend parties. She learned how to take a back seat when they showed off their children's riding skills which she had patiently taught them. But how galling it must have been to sit quietly in our cottage while the carriages came trundling down the lane after a late-night party or ball.

For my part I would sit at the table poring over my crayoning book, watching her hands lying idle on the book she was supposed to be reading. But the pages never turned and I knew she was suffering, her mind on the happy days that seemed to have gone for ever.

She was happiest riding across the fells with her little band of children, me included. I rode well, she told me, pleased with my prowess in this respect. As I grew older I helped with the grooming and saddling of the horses and ponies. Hugh Mallory was a constant visitor to the stables. He seemed well pleased with the success of the riding school and that each week more and more children joined us.

He was a tall jovial man with a red weather-beaten face and a loud laugh. He invariably tweaked my hair on arrival but wasted no time in singling out my mother, who seemed not to care for his attentions. She would busy herself with tightening girths and adjusting saddles, anything to put distance between them, making excuses not to chat on the grounds that more and more of the children's mothers were asking her to teach them, too.

They recognized her air of refinement and copied her style of dress, because although she did not have many clothes she chose them for practicality and simplicity, her inborn sense

17

of style dictating classical clothes that did not date.

It seemed to me that my life would go on uninterruptedly in this happy vein. I attended the village school and in the evenings my mother worked over my schoolbooks with me, so that I very quickly left the other children behind. I knew that my mother was putting aside every penny she could for my schooling later on, but for the present I was content.

Then one day I was late home from school and was rushing madly towards the stables where I knew my pony would be waiting to be fed. I could hear voices in the stableyard, my mother's and the deeper tones of a man. I recognized Hugh Mallory's voice, but it was the urgency of his tones that slowed my run into a walk. Then I heard my mother's footsteps running across the cobbles, followed by his. I stood in the gateway and saw him swing her round to face him, and his voice was rough, his face flushed and angry.

'Oh come on Diana, how is it you're suddenly so pure and untouchable? Anybody who lived with Nigel Lorival knows what it's all about.'

'What is that supposed to mean?'

'Well you knew he was married when you went off with him. That put you immediately outside the pale. People haven't forgotten what you did.'

'You don't know what you're saying,' my mother cried. 'Nigel Lorival was my husband, we were married in London. How dare you say he was already married?'

'Then I suggest you check it out with Joan Southeby, or Edward Chalmers. He was a cousin of theirs although I doubt if Edward would give you the time of day after what you did to him.'

'You are being cruelly vindictive Hugh, just because I won't have you near me. If you persist in pestering me I shall have to leave here.'

'Where would you go, look for another Lorival? Oh come on, Diana, I'm not blaming you, you were a girl with her head in the clouds and Lorival was always a plausible rogue. I've always admired you. You were the best looker in the county and I'm a man of the world, not one of your country bumpkins. We'll make something of these stables Diana, and

18

I'll be generous. That girl of yours can be educated and we would be discreet. There'll be many an opportunity for us to slip away together and heaven knows Josephine is too wrapped up in her good works to care what I do.'

He reached out for her, his red face cruelly determined. Without pausing I rushed into the stableyard shouting, 'Leave my mother alone, leave my mother alone,' but he seemed not to hear me. His arms were round her, hurting her as he struggled to kiss her lips. I saw her raise her riding crop, then with an enraged screech of pain he let her go so abruptly she tottered, while he stood facing us with his hands up to his face and the blood from the wound made by her riding crop streaming through his fingers.

'You little hell-cat! You can get out of my cottage tonight and take your brat with you. I'll see you get no more work around these parts.'

Without a word she took hold of my hand and we ran together out of the stableyard and down the lane. Inside the cottage she sank on to a chair and I busied myself making tea. I was frightened because we had to leave the cottage and we had nowhere to go, and I was miserable because I would never see my pony again. Then I suddenly remembered the enormity of the thing Hugh Mallory had said. If I was not Tessa Lorival and my mother had not been married to my father, who was I?

We stayed that night in the cottage, dozing fitfully in chairs over a dying fire. Before first light there was a loud knock at the door: Hugh Mallory's bailiff stood there, a loud-mouthed boastful man who had always resented my mother's success at the stables.

'Ye've to vacate the cottage afore noon ma'am,' he said. 'Master's orders, an ye've to take all yer sticks o' furniture wi ye.'

'Very well, Mr Oates, I'll see to it,' my mother answered him.

'Leave it exactly as ye found it Mrs Lorival, them's mi orders,' was his parting shot.

Mother was trembling as we faced each other across the table. 'What are we to do Tessa?' she asked. 'How can we

19

move the furniture ourselves and where are we to put it?'

'Somebody will move us, Mother, they don't all work for Mr Mallory and perhaps Mrs Elliott will take us in until we find something else.'

'Oh Tessa, it's the rest of our lives that I am worrying about now,' she cried.

Jed Birkett the blacksmith helped us by sending a boy up with a handcart for our furniture. He had to make three trips before the cottage was empty but the blacksmith promised he would store it at the back of the smithy until we had found somewhere to go.

''Ave ye thowt where yer goin', Mrs Lorival?' he asked quietly.

'We thought perhaps Mrs Elliott might take us in for a few days, just until we've had time to think quietly about things.'

'I'll bring thi luggage o'er later on, yer could walk to Grindale across the fields, it's noan so far that way.'

We both thanked him warmly for his help but he waved our thanks aside saying, 'A doan't know rightly what's gone on ma'am, but if I were yer I'd get as far away fro't squire as yer con. He's a vindictive mon, an a should know whose shod is 'orses for nigh on ten year.'

Mother smiled a little and extended her hand. 'Thank you again Mr Birkett, we are very indebted to you.'

We set off across the fields, muddy in the early-morning dew, so that very soon our shoes were caked in mud and our feet squelched uncomfortably in the tracks made by the cattle. It was mid-morning when we reached Grindale and I asked curiously, 'Will you visit Mrs Southeby again, Mother?'

'Right at this moment I don't know what I shall do, Tessa.'

Mrs Elliott welcomed us with some surprise and immediately started to ply us with questions until her father said sharply, 'Con ye noan see woman that their shoon an stockins are wet through, catch their death o' cold they will afore you've given 'em a bite to eat or a cup o' tea.'

After that she bustled round brewing tea, buttering fresh home-made scones and seeing to it that we took off our wet shoes and stockings, while in turn we washed our cold feet in hot water in a kitchen bowl.

'Can we stay here a few days Mrs Elliott, at least until I can see my way clear?' my Mother asked.

'O course yer can, I've nobody else in. Do you want me to say anythin' to Mrs Southeby? I'm due up there this afternoon.'

'I'd rather you didn't, Mrs Elliott, word will get to her soon enough, although I'm pretty certain there will be no truth in the things she hears.'

'Well then, she should be put reet,' the good woman asserted staunchly.

'Perhaps, but not by you, Mrs Elliott. You and your husband work for the Southebys, the less said about the matter by you the better.'

Mrs Elliott sniffed perceptively. 'Hugh Mallory's well known round these parts, Mrs Lorival. There's monny a servant girl bringin' up a child of 'is. Oh, 'ee might think 'ee's a gentleman cause 'ee lives in a fine 'ouse and owns a string o' fine 'orses, but 'is wife's money 'ad sommat to do wi' that. She were an only child an' that 'ouse were old Albert Ridgeway's. Fell on 'is feet proper did Mallory when 'ee wed Josephine Ridgeway.'

For the first night in our old familiar bedroom I know that my mother didn't sleep and every sound in the street outside our window made my eyes fly open. I dreaded hearing a beating on the door and voices asking the Elliotts if they were harbouring us.

After breakfast Mother stated her intention of going up to see Mrs Southeby after all and I prepared to accompany her.

'I want you to stay here,' she said firmly, 'I shan't be long.'

'But why Mother? I won't be any bother.'

She looked at me for a few moments as if she needed to make up her mind about something, then she took hold of my hand and pulled me down on to the edge of the bed besides her.

'You heard what Hugh Mallory said yesterday about your father and me not being truly married, Tessa?'

'Yes Mother,' I murmured unhappily. 'Is it true?'

'I don't know, but Joan Southeby will be able to tell me.

She and your father were cousins. I intend to ask her.'

'If he was married to somebody else then I shan't be called Lorival, will I?'

'No darling, and neither shall I. Our name will be Chalfont, but I don't intend to use it while we are living here. There are some very unkind people in the world, Tessa, who might one day call you something else. If ever they do will you try to understand that I truly believed your father and I were married, that I did not know about his wife and that I did not willingly bring a child into the world without being able to give her a name? And when you are older I hope you will forgive me.'

'I'd rather be Tessa Chalfont anyway,' I asserted stoutly. 'I don't care if they do call me a bastard.'

She looked at me with startled, tear-filled eyes, then she hugged me close to her. 'Oh my darling, how very quickly you are having to grow up and what a wretched life I am giving you.'

'But you're not, Mother, I love it here in Yorkshire and I loved the Mallory place but I'm not sorry we've left it now that I know how hateful Hugh Mallory was to you.'

'You're a good child Tessa, and I don't know what I would do without you. But you must realize that whatever I do now or in the future is for your welfare. Now I must go. Stay near the house if you go out, and don't go on to the fells. It is far too cold.'

I watched her leave, walking briskly with the wind against her face. She walked with the tall lithe grace that I loved and I thought to myself that one day I wanted to walk like her and look like her, but I knew I never would. Our colouring was different. My mother had green eyes and dark red hair, while I had fine silver-fair hair. She told me that my father had been very dark, and I was fiercely glad that I did not resemble him in any way. I had unusual blue-grey eyes which were fringed by long straight lashes, but my mouth was like my mother's, generous and warm, and I was glad that I possessed her long-legged grace.

Two hours later she returned, and in answer to the question in my eyes she nodded. 'It's true, Tessa. Nigel

Lorival went through a form of marriage with a woman in Mombassa. She was half-English, half-Negress, and for a time he lived with her in Durban, but he deserted her. They were never divorced.'

She made the statement baldly and I listened to her just as calmly. I didn't care. I had never known my father and the mere matter of a name troubled me not at all. I was now Tessa Chalfont, and I vowed then and there that one day I would return to Glamara. My grandfather had no right to cast us off as though we were driftwood. I would live to ride fine horses and dance in stately halls, and I would see with my own eyes the dark pines on the rolling hills above Glamara. I too would stand in those gardens surrounded by the dark Pennine hills and watch the wild geese flying inward with the sun on their wings to find their resting place on the sunlit waters of the tarn.

During the days that followed, Hugh Mallory's version of our flight from his stables became known and now the children and their parents looked at us in uncomfortable silence when we met them in the lanes and on the fells. Whenever this happened I would see my mother's face grow pale and her lips begin to tremble.

After one such occasion I burst out angrily, 'How I hate them, why don't you tell them what really happened, why should he get away with it?'

'This is a lesson I have to learn Tessa, but you remind me of myself when I was young. In those days when I was Diana Chalfont living at Glamara I believed that money could buy everything – respect, friendship, even love. Now I know that it wasn't true. These things have to be earned, they are not things to be paid for like merchandise over a shop counter. Hugh Mallory is a part of a society that thinks as I used to think. His money has bought the friendship of those people who will always prefer to believe him rather than a woman who is alone and without money.'

I knew that she suffered, that her proud independent spirit was being crushed with every new day, but the ultimate pain came on the day Joan Southeby and her husband passed us in the lane. They were driving in their carriage and we had to step quickly aside to allow them to pass. They turned their heads away as though they hadn't seen us.

Mother stared after their carriage and, although I put my arms around her and held her close, I believe on that day she finally and irrevocably realized she had become an outcast from everything she had once known.

We had been at Mrs Elliott's for almost two weeks and I was sitting in our bedroom watching my mother counting her money.

'How much have we got?' I asked her fearfully.

'Enough to pay Mrs Elliott for two more weeks, but we should think of moving on, while we have enough money to pay our fare and find rooms. It is no use staying on here until we are without means altogether.'

'But where shall we go, back to London?'

'No, we shall go to Leeds. Surely there must be some work I could do in the city, I'm not too stupid to learn to do the things other women do. I'll tell Mrs Elliott after supper this evening,' she said, putting the money back in her purse. 'Who knows, she might know somebody in Leeds who could find a room for us.'

We were clearing away after supper when we heard the sound of carriage wheels and Mrs Elliott said, 'P'raps it's Mrs Southeby come to 'er senses at last,' and in answer to the sharp rap on the door she took off her apron and bustled to answer it.

We heard the sound of voices then she came back into the kitchen, her eyes bright with curiosity. 'There's a Mrs Hardcastle askin' for ye, Mrs Lorival. I've shown 'er into the livin' room. Go wi' yer mother, Tessa,' she added, 'I'm sure the lady won't mind.'

Mrs Hardcastle was a plump lady, exceedingly stylishly dressed: wearing a large hat lavishly bedecked with bunches of artificial cherries and veiling, a fox fur and fine kid gloves. She had a high colour which my mother told me later was the result of too much powder and paint and she spoke in a businesslike clipped voice as though she was a lady who knew what she wanted and had every intention of getting it.

She and my mother shook hands then Mrs Hardcastle

said, 'You don't know me Mrs Lorival but me and my husband have just bought Briarcrag, the big red-brick house on the hill at the end of the lane. We've always lived in Leeds and we've 'ad our eye on that house for many a year. We've come from the city at the weekends just looking for something in the country and we snapped Briarcrag up as soon as we saw it was for sale. You've been teaching riding to some of the folks around here?'

'Yes that is true, Mrs Hardcastle.'

'But you're not teaching them now?'

'No. I have left Mr Mallory's employment.'

'Are you looking for work?'

My mother looked at her, not a little taken aback by her directness. 'My daughter and I have been talking about going to Leeds only this evening. I should find something soon and there is very little in the country.'

'And the folk round here are not very charitable when it comes to choosin' between you an' folk like the Mallorys.'

'What exactly have you heard, Mrs Hardcastle?'

'Well it's going about that you set your cap at him an' expected more from the stables than 'ee was prepared to give you. I'm not concerned with whether it's true or not, it won't make any difference to what I want.'

'But I am concerned, Mrs Hardcastle, and it's not true, not a word of it. I was happy enough with my work at the stables and quite satisfied with the money he paid me. As for Mr Mallory, I have known him a long time as the husband of an old friend of mine, I never regarded him as anything else.'

She looked at my mother long and hard, then nodding her head she said, 'I believe you, Mrs Lorival. Now let me tell you what I have in mind. My husband's a businessman. He started in a small way making his own furniture, then he took on others when it began to sell, and now we've got two factories in Leeds and two more in Bradford. Have you ever heard of Castle Furniture?'

'No, I'm afraid not.'

'No, well you wouldn't have. It's my guess you've bin used to better things, not that my Joe's furniture isn't good mind, but I'd like to bet that the sort o' things you've bin used to had been in your family for years. Not up-to-date stuff like Castle Mills produces.'

My mother smiled a little but offered no comment.

'Well my Joe has prospered. Those uppity folk you were workin' for'll look down on the likes of us, an' they won't much like it that we've bin able to buy Briarcrag. Anyway we're not concerned with the likes o' them, we 'as our own friends and the folks round here'll come to our way of thinkin' before we comes to theirs.'

'How can I help you, Mrs Hardcastle?'

'You'll call it social climbin', Mrs Lorival, but I've two girls and a boy to bring up an' I don't want any of them to have to work like their dad and me. When I were little older than yer daughter 'ere I worked in a factory in Bradford. I had to get up at five in the mornin' an' go to work before it were properly light. We slept four in a bed, me and mi three sisters. I were that glad to marry Joe an' get a tumble-down cottage of our own. He were only a carpenter's apprentice then but he had a good 'ead on his shoulders and he believed in himself.'

My mother smiled, waiting patiently for Mrs Hardcastle to come to the reason for her visit, and I marvelled how broad her speech had become in her enthusiasm to talk about her past.

'Over the past few months since we came 'ere I've had my eyes on you, Mrs Lorival. I said to Joe, there's a real lady if ever I've seen one, she sits her horse like a queen and I've heard you talkin' to folk. I wants my children to learn to speak properly and I want 'em to learn to ride a horse and drive the trap. I'd like you to 'elp mi.'

'Do I understand, Mrs Hardcastle, that you are offering me employment to teach your children to ride and help with their education?'

'That's right. Alec is nearly thirteen and the girls are eight and ten.'

'But aren't they all in school?'

'We've got Alec in at a boys' school with a very good name and in the autumn the girls are goin' to a school in Harrogate. Very expensive it is but I'd like 'em to speak a bit better before they go. Joan's the eldest and Susy's the youngest. We've no horses at the moment but Joe thought you could go to the horse sales with him and give him the benefit of your advice.'

'Are you aiming to ride yourself, Mrs Hardcastle?'

'Bless you no. I don't know one end of a horse from the other, but I wouldn't mind learning how to handle the pony that pulls the trap.'

'When the children are away at school I doubt if I shall be fully occupied, Mrs Hardcastle, and there is the question of somewhere for us to live. I do really need permanent employment.'

'You'll be fully employed, Mrs Lorival. I'd want you to come to sales with me, sales in big old houses where we could pick up real old and good furniture, not like the mass-produced stuff Joe makes. We've bought ourselves a real nice house, now we wants some nice ornaments, vases and bowls and mirrors, you'll know the sort o' thing we want, and money bein' no object you can have a free 'and.'

Still my mother looked doubtful, and Mrs Hardcastle urged, 'You can help me too, Mrs Lorival, I don't always speak the Queen's English. I don't want mi children to be ashamed of their mother when the time comes for them to bring their posh friends home. I'll pay ye more than ever Hugh Mallory paid and there's a lodge house at the end of the drive for you an' your daughter. It's a nice little house, bone dry, an' there's two bedrooms, a nice-sized parlour and a kitchen. You can take a look at it tomorrow if you like.'

I watched my mother sink trembling into a chair while the tears rolled slowly down her face.

Mrs Hardcastle stared at her for a moment in silence. 'I don't see I've said anything for you to cry about, Mrs Lorival.'

My mother rose to her feet and took both Mrs Hardcastle's hands in hers. 'Oh Mrs Hardcastle, don't you see I am crying with relief? An hour ago I didn't know what was to become of us. I'll do my best to help you in any way I can.'

'Well that's that then,' Mrs Hardcastle said practically,

evidently unused to such displays of emotion. 'Here's the key to the lodge house and when you've seen it perhaps you'd like to take a walk up to Briarcrag and give me some idea what's needed there.'

'Of course I'll be glad to.'

Together we showed her out to where a smart pony and trap waited in the lane. A young man was driving it and Mrs Hardcastle said, 'This is Ned. Mi husband's brought him from the factory at Bradford. He has asthma and can't stand the dust so he'll be workin' for us here. There'll be plenty for him to do.'

Back indoors, we clasped hands and danced for joy around the table. The Elliotts too were delighted with our news and Mrs Elliott remarked shrewdly, 'That's one woman who cares nowt for Hugh Mallory or 'is like. They might look down their noses at 'em now, but mark my words, a lot o' the money'll be in different 'ands an' you'll see 'ow they kowtows to the likes o' Mrs Hardcastle then.'

I loved the lodge house the moment I saw it and I helped my mother to stitch curtains for the windows from material Mrs Hardcastle found – remnants, she said, from the cotton mills in Lancashire. The blacksmith sent our furniture, and by the time we had placed our bits and pieces in the rooms the little lodge had a cosy, lived-in air.

When Mrs Hardcastle saw it she said, 'You've nothin' worth much, Mrs Lorival, but you have a knack of makin' it all seem much better than it is. I expect you might be lookin' for a few things yourself to brighten up the place.'

'Yes, I shall be keeping my eyes open for a few good pieces of porcelain and a decent mirror, a few pictures too if I am lucky.'

'How long have you bin a widow?'

'He died before my daughter was born and Tessa is ten years old.'

'Had you no family to help you, no parents or kin of any kind?'

'None that could help me, I'm afraid.'

'Ah well, you'll settle in 'ere all right and I don't see any reason why you and me shouldn't get along very well. I'd like to think we can be friends.'

'I feel sure we shall be very good friends, Mrs Hardcastle.'

'What's your Christian name, Mrs Lorival?'

'Diana, and my daughter's name is Tessa.'

'Well mine's Madge. There's no way o' shortenin' it but you 'as my permission to use it if you wants to.'

The day after we moved into our new home we were introduced to Mr Hardcastle, who had brought some disquieting news from the city. Queen Victoria was dead. He told us that many of the buildings in Leeds were already draped in black and all the flags were flying at half mast. People were crying in the streets and in the villages too the people seemed stunned.

I couldn't imagine England without Queen Victoria. It seemed to me that she had always been there, that old plain sad lady who had stamped her personality upon our world. To her subjects it was as though a dearly loved grandmother had suddenly died, leaving them lost and bewildered.

The Queen's funeral took place amid much pomp in London, to be followed by the weeks of state mourning; and then suddenly gaiety, which England had lacked for so long, returned to the streets. The fashions were more daring but infinitely more elegant, and the sober standards Victoria had imposed upon her subjects gave way to a freer, more extravagant society.

I was ten years old when the Queen died and I thought about her death in relation to my life. It was 1901, a new century, and my mother and I had been given a new start in life. From now on, I told myself with the supreme optimism of youth, everything was going to be perfect.

CHAPTER TWO

In the next two years my life changed substantially. For the first time we had real money in our pocket and the bloom came back into my mother's cheeks and the sparkle into her eyes. That the gentry looked at us with undisguised hostility didn't worry her at all and she seemed to enjoy going to sales with Mrs Hardcastle where they could bid for works of art which her old associates could no longer afford.

She transformed Briarcrag into a beautiful house that was the envy of their neighbours and she advised Mr Hardcastle on horse purchasing so that very soon he had two thoroughbreds in his stables and four stalwart Welsh ponies. I liked the Hardcastle children but strangely enough it was Alec who became my closest friend. The two girls did not take kindly to horses and Joan, who was nearest my own age, failed to respond to my overtures of friendship.

I had never had a close friend before and Alec seemed to fill every lonely corner of my life. I told him about our troubles before his mother came to our rescue. Indeed there was little left out during our rides together, and in turn he told me how much he hated the thought of going into his father's business and how he wanted to make the army his career when he left school.

'But then you'd have to go to war and perhaps get killed,' I cried with astonishment.

'I'm not afraid to go to war, but wars don't happen all the time. I want to see the North West Frontier and the Sudan, I want to see the Rockies and all those places where the British Army have outposts. There are so many things to see Tessa, why should I spend my life working in a dusty old factory in Leeds?'

'If you did work in the factory you could make enough

money to see all those wonderful places without getting shot at,' I said astutely.

'It wouldn't be the same, Tessa. I say, you won't tell my mother will you? She'd tell my father and he'd not want me to join the army.'

'Of course I won't tell them,' I said stoutly. All the same I hoped he would change his mind – he was my friend and I felt he would be safer and closer in Leeds.

'What do you want to do when you're old enough?' he asked me curiously.

'I want to live at Glamara, it's the only thing I want.'

'But what would you do there?'

'I don't know, I've never even seen it, but I could do the things my mother used to do, ride and go to balls and have a wonderful time.'

'Sounds a pretty useless sort of life to me.'

'Not when you've never had that sort of life, not when your grandfather's ignored your existence since you were born. I never did anything to hurt him, that was my mother, why should he ignore me?'

'You can't make him change his mind, Tessa, he'll be old and stubborn.'

'You think I should forget about Glamara, don't you Alec?'

'Yes Tessa, I do, I think you should go forward, never backward.'

'Then you are happy with your life, your school, everything?'

'Yes. It's a good school, it'll give me a better chance of going to Sandhurst when the time comes.'

'Why do you think it's so right for you to go to Sandhurst and so wrong for me to think about Glamara?'

It was always the same when Alec and I rode together, the arguments, the disagreements, but our friendship was never in doubt.

When the Hardcastle children went back to school in the autumn Mother found a school for me. It was run by a retired private governess in a nearby hamlet. Her name was Mrs Randall and she had an invalid husband who needed a great deal of her attention, so she had set up a private school in two rooms of a rambling old house. She told us she intended taking around twelve pupils, in order to devote individual attention to their needs. She had no hesitation in accepting me.

I thought her fees quite exorbitant. 'Can we afford it?' I asked Mother after we had left Mrs Randall's.

'Of course, Tessa. I am able to put a little money on one side now, and education is very important.'

'I don't want my education to take all our money,' I protested, but my mother merely smiled down at me confidently.

'Let me worry about that, Tessa. Our circumstances have changed, life is much happier for us now.'

Looking back I believe the years that followed were among the happiest of my life. At first I was not a popular pupil in Mrs Randall's school. Much of my earlier history was known, and I worked too hard to think of socializing. However Mrs Randall often held me up as the sort of example the others should follow and one by one the girls came over to my side. They were largely the daughters of the new people in the area and they regarded me as the daughter of a paid servant; at the same time they couldn't disregard my mother's air of refinement or my prowess in many of the subjects they found so difficult.

Mother too was enjoying herself. She was now invited out to race meetings and tea dances. She had an entire new wardrobe and once more she became the centre of attraction. It is true she was mingling with a very different society, but she seemed happy enough. Now we rode along the lanes on expensive mounts, wearing perfectly fitting riding habits, and even the gentry began to acknowledge our existence.

Although Mr Hardcastle was a hard-headed businessman he was also the soul of generosity and in no time the gentry were begging him to join the hunt and sit on charity committees. Mrs Hardcastle too was invited to judge flower shows and open church bazaars and they gave generously to the church and to the poor in the village.

Mother had done her duty very well with Mrs Hardcastle. Now she dressed more elegantly in plainer clothes, and her make-up was less evident. She had learnt to speak correctly, even if her voice still bore its city accents and her forthright manner persisted.

I can see her now dressed to attend one of her various meetings, attired in a plain brown jacket and skirt, sable ties round her shoulders and a becoming hat, eyeing herself in the long mirror in the hall of Briarcrag.

'My mother used to say you can't make a silk purse out of a sow's ear but you've done your level best with me, Diana. Even Joe says you've worked wonders with me. He respects your opinion about most things and he's proud of what you've done with Briarcrag.'

'I'm glad you have been so well received in the area,' my mother said, smiling. 'It's never easy to fit in with people who have been settled here for ages.'

'Oh we've no illusions about that,' Mrs Hardcastle snapped. 'It's our money that's brought them round.'

It was Mr Hardcastle who decided that Alec and I should go to the point-to-point meeting during the Easter holidays, and he insisted that my mother should ride in the ladies' race. At first she was reluctant, knowing that many of the women who had once been her friends would be riding.

'Ride Blackamoor,' Mr Hardcastle encouraged her, 'he's a better mount than any they'll be riding. Let 'em all see you're back in the saddle and in control.'

She smiled at his enthusiasm, then with a nod she said, 'All right, I will ride Blackamoor. I had no difficulty in beating them in the old days, I can beat them now.'

Later in the evening, in our own home, I said, 'Suppose they don't speak to you, Mother, won't you feel awfully alone out there?'

'No more alone than I have felt these last few years, Tessa. We must both do well on the day, if only to show Mr Hardcastle that he hasn't wasted his confidence.'

It was a beautiful spring morning when we arrived at the meeting. Large tents had been erected for refreshments and the hunt committee, and the bookmakers were busy putting up their boards. The children's races were to be run on the lower slopes of the fells, before noon, with the boys riding first.

Alec was riding Taffy, a large white Welsh pony who jumped well and had a great burst of speed. Alec rode well but Mother maintained that he was too impulsive and the pony should not be given his head. When I watched Alec with the other riders I remembered something his mother had said about rags to riches in three generations. Now with his superior education he could hold his own with any of them. He spoke like them and already had their air of timeless superiority. At that moment I knew for a certainty that there would be no going back for the Hardcastles. In three generations they would be gentry.

I was cheering wildly as he swept into the lead and then they were approaching the last fence and I could see that the pony was fighting him, galloping with his head up while Alec was striving desperately to keep him straight. They took off too soon, ending with the pony sitting astride the fence and Alec rolling nimbly out of the way of his threshing hooves. I heard his mother's cry, his father's sharp intake of breath, then Alec was picking himself up ruefully while he went forward to help the pony out of his predicament.

'The young fool!' his father said, more in relief than anger. 'He never had a hope of clearing that fence.'

'No,' my mother said softly, 'he has lost the race but he has learnt a valuable lesson.' Turning to me she said, 'You've no time to worry about Alec now Tessa, it's time for you to go to the paddock.'

I too was riding a Welsh pony, Jonesey. He was a smaller animal than Taffy but he was strong and wiry and I knew he was capable of winning the race because I had already ridden him over territory more wild and arduous than that morning's course.

As we rode slowly round the paddock before the race I looked around to see who my competitors were, and I recognized a good many I had ridden with during our time at the Mallory stables. They chattered among themselves without paying much attention to me, but I did not have my

34

mother's memories of happier days so I did not care whether they acknowledged me or not.

Mrs Southeby came to chat to her daughter. As she left she spoke to me saying, 'Good morning Tessa, are you looking forward to the race?'

I was surprised after being ignored by her for so many months, but I answered her politely. 'Yes Mrs Southeby, I am.'

'That is a nice pony you have there. Mr Hardcastle's mounts seem to be in excellent condition.'

'Yes, that is why they were chosen. My mother is an excellent judge of horseflesh.'

I saw the rich red colour rise up into her face and I was fiercely glad that she was discomfited. I had only told her the truth. Next moment my name was called and with a brief smile I wished her good morning and rode away.

Winning that race was easy for me. The pony was fresh and he jumped the hurdles so cleanly and easily I felt he could have jumped hurdles twice the height.

I went up to the prize tent proudly, to receive the silver cup Mr Hardcastle had donated, and was greeted ecstatically by Alec. 'You were marvellous, Tessa. I made an awful hash of things but I'll win next year, you'll see.'

'Yes, I'm sure you will,' I answered him confidently. 'Is the pony no worse for wear?'

'My father's having a vet look him over but he seems all right. I couldn't hold him, Tessa. He was fighting me all the way. I suppose I'll get a long lecture from your mother.'

'I expect so. Oh Alec, I am enjoying myself, it's so lovely here on the fells.'

He admired my cup and then my mother joined us. 'You will be the first person to have your name engraved on the cup,' she told me proudly, then turning to Alec with a half smile she said, 'And I hope yours will be the second name on the boys' cup next year Alec. Promise me.'

He grinned, unabashed. 'I've just been telling Tessa I shall win next year, I mean it.'

'I believe you Alec. Your mother and Susy have gone to the refreshment tent, perhaps you should join them there.'

'I'm far too excited to eat,' he said laughing, 'but I suppose I'll have to go.'

'Why didn't your sister Joan come with you?' she asked him curiously.

'Oh she's hopeless. She's frightened of horses, that's why she'll never make a rider. She's probably got her head stuck in a book somewhere.'

Mother said thoughtfully, 'I must try to get your mother to see that there are other things in life for Joan.'

'My mother thinks she'll be out of things if she doesn't ride. She says all the girls are mad keen on horses here in the country.'

We watched him shouldering his way through the crowds and then we started slowly towards the paddock, my mother's arm around my shoulder. Suddenly a man came to stand in front of us and looking up I saw the colour fade from my Mother's face.

'Why Edward,' she breathed in little more than a whisper.

He was only slightly taller than my mother and stockily built, but his tweed jacket was expertly cut and there was an air of refinement about him. A boy, perhaps a little older than myself, stood beside him, and when our eyes met he looked nervously away. I thought he must be very shy.

'How are you, Diana? I heard you intended to ride today,' he said calmly and unsmilingly.

'I am well Edward. Is this your son?'

'Yes, Richard, and this I suppose is your daughter?'

'Yes, her name is Tessa. Tessa, this is Sir Edward Chalmers, we knew each other a long time ago.'

'I've heard about you from time to time, from Joan Southeby and a few other people. I hear you are giving riding lessons.'

'Yes. My daughter has just won the cup for her class, we were busy admiring it. Does your son ride?'

'Yes, but he hasn't hunted his horse this season so he wasn't eligible to enter.'

'How is your wife? Is she here with you?'

'Yes, she's around somewhere. We lead a very quiet life in the country but Dora seems content enough. She has never

36

been a woman who has longed for the fleshpots.'

I felt that there was a personal accusation in his words and I believe my mother thought so too because she murmured, 'Oh Edward, please. Not after all this time.'

Just then a small thin woman came to stand beside him and I guessed that this was his wife. She looked at my mother unsmiling but my mother said graciously enough, 'How are you, Dora? I have just been introduced to your son, and this is my daughter Tessa.'

The woman inclined her head the merest fraction, then taking her husband's arm she said sharply, 'I want to get a good place for the next race Edward, we had better go.'

Sir Edward bowed but his wife moved on with the briefest nod of her head. The boy however had blushed scarlet at his mother's rudeness and I felt sorry for him.

I could tell that their meeting had unnerved my Mother, but when I asked if it had upset her she merely said, 'I hadn't expected a ghost to walk over my grave today, Tessa.'

'That is the man you could have married isn't it?'

'Yes, and I feel he still hasn't forgiven me, even though he is married and they have a son. I feel that he would make me suffer for what I did to him if he could.'

'The boy looked nice.'

'Yes. Dora never liked me when we were young. I was always the one with a string of admirers and she was plain even in those days. She always wanted Edward, she never wanted me to have him, but surely after all these years you'd think she'd be a little grateful to me for running off and leaving the way clear for her.'

'Perhaps she thinks he's still in love with you.'

'That is very unlikely, Tessa. Now I must go to the stables; the ladies' race is the event after this one.'

I went down to the paddock to watch them saddling the horses for the next race, then I stayed to watch my mother parading her horse. I left before they walked down to the starting post because I wanted a good position where I could see the finish.

Mother had looked so elegant in her black riding habit. It fitted her perfectly and the white lace ruffles at her throat and cuffs showed off her beautiful colouring and her long slender hands. She was riding Blackamoor, a stallion, as black as her riding habit, his proud arched neck and high-stepping grace a perfect foil for her beauty. I was so proud of her.

As my eyes followed the riders up to the start I felt somebody gently touch my arm. I turned quickly to find Sir Edward Chalmers' son at my elbow. His face was suffused with blushes and he blurted out, 'My mother was rude to your mother, I'm very sorry.'

'Oh please don't be, it wasn't your fault.'

'I don't want them to see me talking to you, I'd better get back, but I just wanted you to know.'

'Where are your parents now?'

'My mother doesn't want to watch the ladies' race, my father's over there.'

I saw Sir Edward with his binoculars trained on the horses waiting for the starter's orders. When I looked back the boy had gone.

The race was run over open fell country, hedgerows and narrow streams. They would go twice round this circuit, then finish on the straight in front of the tents where higher jumps had been erected.

Most of the large crowd had gathered round the rails and soon we could see the horses leaving the start for the sharp climb towards the ridge of the fell where they were lost to us for several minutes. Then they were coming downhill with a considerable distance between the foremost rider and the rest.

When they passed us the first time round my mother was in fifth place while the leading horse appeared to be tiring, and as they climbed the fell the others were gaining on him. Again they disappeared and then they were coming downhill and a new leader was in front. At the water jump I recognized her as Mrs Southeby on her bright chestnut gelding.

She was jumping well and the horse that had led first time round was now nearer the back and almost spent, while the rest were grouped in a tight little band in the centre, then one horse left the rest and followed Mrs Southeby, jumping the fences cleanly and bravely. For a moment as they turned into the long stretch before the winning post I lost sight of them, but then they were at the last fence and I saw Blackamoor reach it first. He jumped it better and with greater impetus, and now my mother was in the lead and there was no chance of the chestnut catching them.

I leapt up and down in my excitement and there were wide smiles on the bookmakers' faces. Joan Southeby had been highly fancied and I heard people saying she had won the race for the last five years. Then I saw Mr Hardcastle hurrying up the hill to lead in his horse with my mother in the saddle, and when I felt a firm hand placed on my shoulder I looked up to see Hugh Mallory smiling down at me. Memories of our last meeting left me flushing furiously under his regard. He on the other hand seemed completely unperturbed.

'I knew when your mother entered the others didn't stand a chance,' he said shortly. 'Tell your mother what I said, she'll bear no grudges or she's not the girl I used to know.'

As I turned away I caught sight of Sir Edward staring down the stretch. There was a bleak, haunted look in his eyes: like a man who was facing his past while the world around him had ceased to exist.

That night there were celebrations at Briarcrag. I wore my first grown-up party dress, a pretty thing in pale blue crêpe de chine, my favourite colour. It suited my pale hair and blue-grey eyes, but I thought my mother was the most beautiful woman there. She wore jade green, which emphasized her green eyes and dark red hair and I had never seen her looking lovelier. Men flocked to her side, and one man in particular.

I had seen him many times before, driving up to Briarcrag, a red-faced stocky man with little hair but long steel-grey sideboards along his face. Now he was being attentive to Mother's wants, bringing her food and seeing that her glass was filled. I did not like him. I felt he was coarse and that he could have little in common with my charming beautiful mother.

She was enjoying herself, it was like the old days when she was always the centre of attraction at Glamara.

'Who is he?' I asked Alec who came to sit with me on the stairs where we could watch everything in the hall.

'He's called Bryant, Jack Bryant I think.'

'Is he a friend of your parents?'

'Business associate more likely. His mills produce a lot of the material my father uses. I've heard Father say he has a finger in a few pies.'

'Do you like him?'

'I don't really know him. Why all the questions?'

'I don't like the way he monopolizes my mother.'

'You're jealous, Tessa, there's just been the two of you for so long.'

'No Alec, it's not like that, I'm sure it's not. He's so wrong for her, he's far too old and he's not even attractive. Look at the man she's dancing with now, he's attractive and they look good together. Why can't my mother see that Bryant's fat and bald and that he has small piggy eyes? I hate the way he looks at her, I hate the way he looks at me. He undresses me with his eyes.'

Alec stared at me in surprise and I felt at that moment that I was at least a generation older than he, then with that unusual perception of his he said, 'The man your mother is dancing with is one of my father's salesmen. He hasn't any money.'

'Oh money, always money. Why has everybody to be so preoccupied with money?'

'Probably because it's so miserable when you haven't any.'

'I don't want my mother to think about Jack Bryant as a way out, that way we'll never get back to Glamara.'

He stared at me with a wry smile. 'Oh Tessa, stop thinking about Glamara. It's never going to happen for you.'

Back at home that night I asked my mother about Jack Bryant, lightly, as if it was not very important. 'I've seen him before but I don't know who he is.'

'He has mills in the city, Tessa, woollen mills I think. He is very rich, or so they tell me.'

'Is he a nice man?'

'I've never thought about it. He is always very polite and attentive. You are a funny little thing, why are you asking?'

'You are not going to be any more friendly with him than you are now?' I insisted.

'Well I don't know darling, I shouldn't think so.' She looked down at me thoughtfully, then putting her arm round my shoulders she said, 'I know we have always been very close, Tessa, but I must have friends of my own just as you must. One day you are going to fall in love with some young man and leave me, so you see how I must have something of my own for the time when you're not here.'

'I shall never leave you, Mother, never.'

'Oh my darling you will, and perhaps sooner than you think. Try not to worry about the things I do, everything is for your good in the long run.'

I didn't argue with her, but I couldn't see that being friendly with the man I disliked so intensely could possibly be for my good or hers.

More and more I was becoming afraid.

She began to wear jewellery I had never seen before: a string of beautifully matched pearls and diamond earrings. A velvet wrap edged with white fox fur arrived, and one evening she happily produced a wide gold bracelet.

My mother too was changing. From being vulnerable and gentle she was becoming harder. The girlhood friends had made her feel inferior and miserable, but now she had other friends who were richer and who were able to give her the things she yearned for.

Jack Bryant came openly to the house for her, nodding to me only briefly as I pored over my homework. I would watch them drive off in his fine carriage to race meetings or evening parties and balls in the houses of people he knew, then I would lie awake until the small hours waiting for her return. Sometimes he came into the house with her and I would hear their voices and laughter.

My schoolwork suffered as a result of my lack of sleep and one morning my mother faced me after she had watched me lethargically collecting my schoolbooks. 'What is the matter, Tessa, why are you so silent this morning?' she asked shortly.

How could I tell my mother I didn't approve of the company she was keeping? I feigned a headache and went to my bedroom, but she followed me. I can still see her, wearing an elegant grey silk gown, eyeing me sternly.

'You are sulking, Tessa, and I really don't see why. On the day you bring a young man into this house I doubt if I shall sulk at you.'

Tears welled, and I blurted out, 'It's just that I think he's so wrong for you, Mother. I don't like the way he looks or his voice, and I don't like all those rings he wears.'

'But they do advertise the fact that he is rich, Tessa. I'm tired of being looked down on by people who were once envious of me. I'll never replace the old life at Glamara but I can marry a rich man so that neither of us will ever want for anything again.'

I stared at her, aghast. 'You're not going to *marry* him, Mother!'

'I'm thinking about it.'

'Has he asked you to marry him?'

'Several times, and on each occasion I've said I would think about it. Now I really am doing just that. Don't you want to live in a beautiful house and have lots of servants? Don't you want to go away to finishing school and meet eligible young men who can give you a good stable future?'

'I don't want you to throw yourself away on Mr Bryant so that we can have those things.'

'Oh Tessa, don't be such a child. I shan't be throwing myself away. And what's more, I won't have you talk to me like this. Nobody knows better than you what the last few years have been like. In time you will come to thank me for seeing that we both have a future.'

She stalked away with an angry swish of her skirts. It was the first time we had ever quarrelled. Ours had been a sympathetic and close relationship but with the advent of this man we were drifting apart. Indeed there were whole days when I felt she was more like a stranger than the mother I adored, and other days when I hardly saw her.

For the first time in years she was being courted and fêted and I began to see in her the old Diana Chalfont before Nigel Lorival took her away from a secure and wealthy background, the wilful headstrong Diana Chalfont who had grasped life with greedy fingers like a spoilt child who believed she had a heaven-sent right to the good things in life, and I became desperately afraid.

On the day she flashed her large diamond engagement ring in front of my eyes I embraced her swiftly, with tears in my eyes. Then I made myself take Jack Bryant's plump limp hand on which the heavy gold rings seemed so incongruous.

A few weeks later I was in my bedroom when I heard Mrs Hardcastle's voice in the living room. In what she called polite society she always took her time so that she would speak correctly, but when she was agitated her voice always reverted to its sharp city tones, and this morning was no exception.

'I've said nothin' afore, Diana, but I hope you knows what you're doing,' was her opening gambit.

'I'm sorry Madge, I don't know what you mean.'

'Jack Bryant, that's what I mean. He's not good enough for the likes of you and I've known him a good number o' years. He's always bin a hard drinker and if rumours are to be believed he's also been somethin' of a womanizer. Oh I know you met him in my house, he's a businessman like Joe and business is business, but he's not a gentleman an' you've bin brought up to expect somethin' better than him.'

'Why Madge, I can't really think that any of this is your business.'

'You're right, it's not. I just think if you marry him you'll regret it.'

'I don't think so, Madge. I've decided to turn my back completely on the old life, Jack Bryant can give us a good home and enough money to buy the best things in life. I've swallowed my pride once, I can do so again.'

'It's not just your pride you'll be swallowin', it's decency and respectability too. I've heard things said about Jack Bryant that no decent self-respecting woman would repeat.'

'If you are not prepared to repeat them Madge, how am I to judge whether they are true or not?' my mother snapped, and I could tell that she was coldly angry.

'You're in no mood to listen to reason Diana, it's gone too far. Well, if you wed him you'll be leavin' us and I'd like to be able to wish you joy, I can't in all honesty do that, but if you needs a friend, you or your daughter, you know you can find us at Briarcrag.'

'Thank you Madge. You have been a good friend. But don't you see I need to make my future so secure that what happened to us in the past could never happen again?'

'I see, I only wish you'd built your future on a more solid foundation. It's like buildin' a house on sand pinnin' all your hopes on somebody like Jack Bryant.'

I heard the front door close firmly behind her, then my mother slamming about in the next room. After a few minutes she came into my room.

'I suppose you heard all that, Tessa,' she began. 'Madge has absolutely no right to interfere in my life simply because she pays my wages.'

'I'm sure she only wanted to be kind, Mother,' I murmured unhappily.

'You mean she said what you wanted to hear. People have interfered in my life since the day I was born. Well, I'm sick of it. And look at me when I'm talking to you, Tessa. I'm going to marry Jack Bryant and we are all going to live in his house in Leeds until we can find something better. It is in a good quarter, he intends keeping his housekeeper, and other help. Think of it Tessa, we'll be able to see the opera and the ballet and we'll find a proper school for you.'

Her voice changed suddenly, becoming cajoling, and I was not proof against the appeal in her eyes. 'I've got my wedding dress, do you want to see it?'

I followed her into her bedroom to find it stocked with cardboard boxes of all shapes and sizes. She brought out a most beautiful gown in pale apricot watered silk which she held against her. It had a demure mandarin collar and the bodice was made in tiny tucks to the narrow waist, then the flowing skirt fell to the ground.

She looked so beautiful that I threw my arms round her and she laughed, saying, 'Not now darling, you'll crease the gown. I have a hat somewhere if I can just find it.'

She put several boxes on her bed and hunted through them, then with a gay flourish she produced a hat in the same

44

material as her gown. It was a dream in the fashionable boater style with osprey feathers in the same pale cream as her gloves and shoes.

'Do you like them?' she asked superfluously.

'Oh mother, you'll look so beautiful, there's nobody as lovely as you are.'

'Now see what I have for you,' she said, bringing out a silk gown in pale rose-pink silk which she made me hold against me so that I could see it in the mirror. I had never owned such a gown. It swept to my feet in long delicate folds and there was a softly pleated fichu to swathe my shoulders. While I was admiring the dress she produced a large cream straw hat trimmed with pink chiffon roses.

There were tears in my eyes as I turned to face her, she was so like a child waiting to be praised for her cleverness, and I could not even find it in my heart to wish her happiness. Misinterpreting the tears she said, 'What a strange child you are Tessa, I can see you like the dress, there's no need to cry about it.'

'Oh mother they're all so lovely, you'll be the most beautiful bride ever.'

Her face grew suddenly wistful and still holding my hat she sank down on to the edge of her bed.

'When I was a little girl I always used to imagine myself in yards and yards of tulle walking on my father's arm towards the village church at Lambreck. It was to be the wedding of the year, with six bridesmaids and hundreds of guests. Neither of my weddings will have been like that.'

'Did you ever imagine what the bridegroom would be like?' I asked her curiously.

'He was a vague creature because in those days I was only concerned about me, but when I first saw your father he seemed like the man I had imagined falling in love with all my life. Have you never dreamed of the sort of wedding you will have?'

'Yes, but I don't think it has any chance of coming true.'

'Whyever not, child? You're going to have a very rich stepfather and I'm going to see to it that he indulges his stepdaughter as often as possible.'

I smiled at her. I could not tell her that I had only ever dreamt of holding my wedding reception in the great hall at Glamara after my wedding in the village church at Lambreck.

Everything seemed to happen so quickly after that. We spent days packing boxes with our clothes and ornaments.

'What are we to do with our furniture?' I asked. 'Shall we have room for it in Mr Bryant's house?'

She looked round at our shining little home, her face thoughtful. Then as if making up her mind quickly she said, 'I think we will wipe the slate clean, Tessa, and take none of it. I'll ask Mr Birkett the blacksmith if his wife would like any of our things, if she doesn't want them then I'm sure Mrs Elliott will be glad of them.'

In the end it transpired that Mrs Elliott and Mr Birkett shared our things and both seemed delighted with the arrangement.

'Are the Hardcastles coming to your wedding?' I asked her.

'They've been invited, I don't really see how they can refuse to come.'

'Will there be a lot of people at the wedding?'

'At the reception. Jack and myself and you and Jack's friend Mr Lowrie are going to the church, then after the ceremony we go straight back to the hotel for the reception.

'We are going to the coast for about four days, that's the most Jack can spare from his business, but you won't mind being in the Leeds house while we're away. The housekeeper will be there to look after you and it's for such a short time.'

I would have preferred to stay alone at the lodge house but I knew that would not be possible.

I said my goodbyes to the girls at the school and to the Randalls and I hoped my face looked more cheerful than I felt because I had come to love that improvised little schoolroom whose windows looked out towards the fells.

I said goodbye to the blacksmith and his two assistants and then I walked slowly across the fields to Mrs Elliott's cottage. She made me sit in front of the fire while she plied me with home-make cakes and scones.

At the door she embraced me clumsily, for she was not given to displays of affection. 'Tha mun look after thiself lass, an' yer know yer can allus come to us if things don't work out.'

I kissed her and thanked her warmly then I ran down the lane, aware that she watched me until I turned the bend in the road.

It was our last night in the lodge house and my mother asked, 'Have you said goodbye to the Hardcastles? Alec is at home. There's an infection at the school and they have sent the boys home for the rest of the week. It's stopped raining, a walk would do you good.'

All the way up to Briarcrag I was saying to myself, This is the last time I shall walk along this lane, the last time I shall see the soft country twilight, the last time I shall see Alec, and my heart felt immeasurably sad.

I dawdled along the lane until I felt calmer. It would not do for Mrs Hardcastle to see me so distressed after the things she had said to my mother.

I was shown into the drawing room where Mrs Hardcastle sat with her knitting while her husband read the evening paper. Alec was at a table with his schoolbooks.

'Well Tessa,' Mrs Hardcastle said in her usual forthright manner, 'and are you all ready to go off to Leeds in the morning?'

'We're all packed up and Mr Birkett will be going for the furniture as soon as we've gone. Will there be anybody else coming to live in the lodge house?' I asked her.

'Well not immediately. One of these days we might get somebody to work for us who hasn't got a place to live, it'll come in very useful then. I reckon you and your mother have been happy enough living there.'

'Oh yes, more than happy. It's the best home I've ever had, I'm sorry to be leaving it.'

She looked at me keenly over her spectacles. 'Where are you staying in Leeds until the wedding?'

'In some hotel, then I'm to stay at his house when they're away. Mr Bryant has a housekeeper so I won't be alone.'

'No. I've heard all about Mr Bryant's housekeeper.' There

was something in her tone which made me look at her sharply, and Mr Hardcastle shook his head as though to warn her to say nothing more.

Alec closed his schoolbooks and came to sit on the sofa beside me. 'Will you be able to ride in Leeds, Tessa? It's a pity if you have to give that up.'

'I don't know. It isn't the same in a city and you know more about Leeds than I do.'

He smiled a little at that. 'I do, don't I? But we never kept horses in Leeds. Don't you remember your mother gave me my first riding lesson?'

How could I have forgotten that afternoon when he rode Taffy for the first time, and I had been so much more knowledgeable than he as we rode across the fells.

I stayed with the Hardcastles until the shadows lengthened and the lamps had to be lit. Alec suggested that he should walk home with me and I readily agreed – I wanted to say goodbye to him alone.

As we sauntered down the drive he suddenly took hold of my hand saying, 'You're not happy to be leaving, are you Tessa?'

'No. Why does everything have to change?'

'You're not happy about your mother marrying Mr Bryant?'

'No, I hate him.'

'It could be jealousy. You're not really giving him much of a chance are you?'

'I'm not jealous of him. There's something about him I don't like.'

'Perhaps he's made up his mind to be different when he's married to your mother.'

'My *father* wasn't different. He spent his money and hers too. Oh, wouldn't you just think she'd have learnt her lesson with him?'

'Well, you heard what my mother said, we'll be your friends, Tessa. I'd like you to write to me at school.'

'I will, I will. Oh Alec, I'm going to miss you so.'

I threw my arms around him and laid my cheek against his. I felt him hold back for a moment. He was a boy living in a boy's world and he was unused to demonstrations of affection from girls, but then his arms came round me and he was kissing my lips and cheeks with sympathetic fervour.

We were standing in each other's arms when the door opened to reveal my mother silhouetted against the light, and although our embrace had been youthfully innocent we sprang apart and for a few moments there was silence. Then Alec held out his hand to her. 'Goodbye Mrs Lorival, I hope you will be very happy in Leeds,' he said calmly enough.

'Thank you Alec, and thank you for walking Tessa home.'

I stood in the doorway until his slight boyish figure disappeared round the bend in the drive, then my mother pulled me gently inside the house.

'You are too young to be in love,' she chided me softly.

'I'm not in love with Alec, Mother. I shall miss him, he's been my one true friend.'

She smiled gently. 'And you found it good to have a boy's arms around you when you felt lonely and sad. Can you not try to understand that I too have needs?'

I did understand, but why did they have to be Jack Bryant's arms? Why couldn't they have belonged to somebody more worthy of her?

CHAPTER THREE

We chatted only spasmodically in the train that was taking us to Leeds and a new life. My mother's thoughts were elsewhere and I sat gazing out at the disappearing countryside. It was a grey day with a chill wind that stirred the grass and played among the weeds on the railway embankment, a day when the moors looked wild and unfriendly, as though by showing me their most lonely and eerie aspect the memories of their beauty would be obliterated.

I found the outskirts of the city depressing with the mean

little streets and rubbish dumps, the tall mill chimneys and the pall of grey smoke which seemed to hang there permanently. Mother too seemed to find it depressing but after a while she said, 'Cities are all like this as one approaches them, even London. Leeds is a very fine city and we shall be living in an extremely good area.'

'When are we going to see Mr Bryant's house?' I asked without really caring.

'Perhaps we could go up there tomorrow. We could walk through the park if it's a nice day.'

'Is the park close by then?'

'Right across the road. The house needs a lot doing to it and it needs a woman's touch. It is some years since Jack's mother died and you can't really expect a man to take much interest.'

'But he has a housekeeper.'

'Yes, but she probably hasn't a lot of ideas. I've never met her, she's always been out when he's taken me to the house. We'll make wonderful changes Tessa, and if we don't settle there we can always move into something else.'

I didn't share her optimism about our life in the city but I was impressed by the wide streets in the centre and the fine buildings. I couldn't reconcile what I was seeing with Alec's stories of poverty and deprivation until I remembered the mean cobbled streets we had seen from the train. One day, I decided, I would find out for myself what life was like in those streets.

Our hotel was new and luxurious by any standard and I cheered up considerably as I lay in the scented water of my bath. I dawdled over my toilet and was still sitting in my dressing gown when mt mother came into my room. She was wearing a coat I hadn't seen before, a light beige wool trimmed with sable, and a soft beige felt hat. She presented such a picture of elegance that I laughed with delight.

'It's lovely Mother, but then you always look so beautiful in everything.'

'Well I shall see that you are well dressed too. I'm going to set out your stall so that one day some rich and handsome young man will come along and snap you up before anybody else has a chance.'

'I'd much rather he snapped me up for myself.'

'Darling don't be tiresome, or bourgeois. Only the poor people in this country can afford to marry for love. We are going to be rich Tessa and you will learn to love where money is.'

'Well you haven't any money, so Mr Bryant can't be marrying you for that.'

'Jack Bryant is a self-made man and he wants his wife to give him status, in other words Tessa he wants to marry a lady because like the Hardcastles he's on his way up, not down.'

'But what do *you* want, Mother? You're always telling me what he wants. Do your wants and his mean the same thing?'

She stared at me thoughtfully while she pulled on her thin leather gloves, then in her firmest voice she said, 'I want security for both of us.'

'But do you love him, Mother?'

Her eyes wavered, then airily she said, 'You're far too young to know very much about love. I was in love once, just a silly young girl with stars in her eyes. Well the stars went out and the only things that will ever light them again are riches and position. Trust me Tessa, in time you will come to see how right I have been.'

We stared at each other for several moments without speaking, then in a lighter voice she said, 'I have to go out for a little while. If you like you can go down to the tea lounge for afternoon tea. Tell them to put it on the bill.'

With one brief smile she was gone and disconsolately I turned to look through the window. The pavements were crowded with shoppers, and horsedrawn cabs moved slowly along the wide thoroughfare. I saw my mother walk quickly across the road and along the pavement opposite. People turned to look at her, she was so tall and graceful, but it was her air of well-bred elegance that made them stare. As she reached the corner she looked up at the hotel, and although I waved my hand I was not sure that she had seen me.

51

I dressed in my favourite skirt and silk blouse and for a few moments stood looking at myself in the mirror. I would never be as tall as my mother, but I had inherited her slender figure and grace. My fair hair fell in heavy waves on to my shoulders and my large candid blue-grey eyes stared back at me with critical awareness. I saw a new maturity in the tender swell of my small breasts and felt a strange awareness of my own beauty where before I had seen beauty only in my mother's face. Now I stared at the gold-tipped lashes against the tender curve of my cheek and the proud sensitive mouth, faintly pink against the creamy warmth of my face. For the first time I was glad that I was not going to be like my mother; I would have my own sort of beauty and my own values which could never be hers.

I had all a girl's dreams of love. The handsome prince and the beggarmaid, the princess in her ivory tower and the knight who rides to her rescue, but now I became aware of a strange sort of cynicism which I blamed my mother for putting into me.

It is the city, I told myself angrily, I never felt like this in the dales. There I could stand with the wind in my hair, whipping my face into rosy colour while I listened to the cries of the moorland birds and dreamed my unreal dreams. My mother hated the past but it was all I had to hold on to, and the future was clouded with shadows and uncertainties.

I locked the bedroom door behind me and went down to the tea lounge which was already almost full.

If people looked at me curiously, thinking it strange to see a girl alone in such a public place, I didn't let it worry me. I chose a table next to the wall which was already occupied by two ladies quietly chatting, both of them quietly but expensively dressed.

One of them looked at me curiously but I averted my eyes, hoping I could catch the eye of the waiter who was hovering at a table nearby. I ordered tea and cakes and sat back to enjoy this feeling of adult freedom. When the tea arrived I began to feel quite grown up and matronly, pouring out tea and selecting sugar with the tiniest of silver tongs. The cakes were delicious, filled with cream and decorated with icing sugar. I helped myself to two, hoping they would not put too great a strain on our bill.

Once again my eyes met those of the woman sitting across from me and I surprised an awareness in hers that momentarily startled me for I had never seen her before.

She was small and slender, and although her face was pretty it was quite unremarkable. She was dressed quietly in brown, with a small pull-on felt hat covering her light brown hair. A pair of sable ties rested on the seat beside her, together with soft brown kid gloves and a plain handbag. She wore a single strand of pearls and her narrow brown shoes had only a moderate heel, yet there was about her an undefinable aura of class, and her voice too was softly pitched and cultured.

Her companion was a larger lady altogether and considerably more talkative, so it was hardly surprising that their conversation was forced upon me.

'I hope it's not going to be twelve months before I see you again Hetty,' she was saying.

'Well I'm not sure, I've had an invitation to visit Nancy Richmond in Oxfordshire but it's becoming more and more difficult to get away these days. Father doesn't like me to be away for too long.'

'You spoil that man, Hetty. Couldn't he go to Godfrey and Abigail for once? After all you should have some sort of life of your own.'

'Abigail hasn't been too strong since Laura was born and Father can be difficult.'

'I thought they were quite wrong to buy that house in the North Riding, surely Glamara is big enough for all of you.'

'It is, and they'll be returning to it in the autumn. It was natural for Abigail to want her own home when the children were small.'

'Well the children are all away at school now and are hardly children any more. I've met Godfrey quite often at race meetings in Yorkshire but she never seems to be with him.'

'No. Abigail doesn't care for racing but she doesn't seem to mind what Godfrey does as long as he's happy.'

'Abigail is a fool. A handsome fine-looking man like that. I've seen the women looking at him. One of these days she could be sorry she hasn't put herself out to accompany him on his racing jaunts.'

I waited with bated breath for the magic word Glamara to enter their conversation again. Meanwhile Hetty was saying, 'We shouldn't criticize Abigail, Gertrude, she's a very sweet person.'

'I'm not disputing it, but it's you I'm thinking of. Look at you Hetty, you're over forty and you've never had a soul to call your own. Neither your father nor Glamara will run away if you absent yourself for a week or two. The house is full of servants anyway, and he hardly speaks a civil word to you when you're there.'

My eyes devoured them as they chatted away together. Hetty! My mother's sister. And Glamara. Oh, it just wasn't possible that she wasn't my Aunt Hetty, and nowhere in Yorkshire could there be another Glamara. I wondered what she would do if my mother were suddenly to come through the door. Would they recognize one another after seventeen years?

'Ah, here it is,' said Gertrude, producing a notebook and pencil from the copious handbag she had been rummaging through. 'Give me Nancy Richmond's address. I'd like to drop her a line and I hope she goes on insisting that you visit her.'

Hetty smiled gently, 'If she does I'll have to speak to Father in one of his more mellow moods, after one of his horses has done particularly well at a race meeting, perhaps.'

'Oh well if you have to wait for that you could be waiting a long time. Horses are unpredictable creatures and I should know.'

'You mean Martin is still gambling heavily?'

'Yes, but I've put a stop to him gambling with my money. I've tied up most of it in government stock. I'm not sure I've done the right thing but he'll have to learn to cut his coat according to his cloth.'

'Well Father does have considerable success with his

horses, I think sometimes it's the only thing that keeps him going.'

'He should have forgiven your sister, Hetty. I think it's quite stupid to nurse his grievances all these years, besides it would have been kinder to you. Diana was always his favourite, she could have done her share of looking after him. I don't suppose he ever mentions her name.'

'No. Godfrey mentioned her one Christmas Eve and my father ordered him out of the house. He came to apologize the next day.'

'That's what I mean, it's absolutely ridiculous in this day and age. I don't suppose you ever hear from her?'

'No. She could be dead for all I know.'

I wanted to tell her that my mother wasn't dead, that she was in Leeds waiting to be married and that I was her daughter, but instead I looked away, aware that my face was burning. I wanted to stay and listen to more but the Gertrude woman had noticed my interest and had started to whisper. I left the table as nonchalantly as I could, and immediately discovered that behind a pillar there was an empty chair and table. I had to listen to their conversation, I had to know more about Glamara, and I was prepared to stay there as long as they did.

'I could swear that girl was listening to our conversation,' Gertrude was saying. 'Young people have absolutely no manners these days.'

'I'm sure she wasn't listening deliberately. She reminded me of someone but I can't remember who. I've been puzzling about it.'

'Well I wasn't paying her much attention until I caught her listening. She was far too young to be taking tea alone, there are all sorts of strange men in a place like this simply looking for girls on their own.'

'She seemed quite a nice girl. There was something about her ... but then my memory isn't what it was.'

'I'm not surprised,' sniffed Gertrude. 'Living in that great house with your cantankerous old father. He's stopped you marrying, you've always put him first.'

'He hasn't stopped me marrying. I didn't care enough for the only man who proposed to me and he didn't care enough to ask me again. Things will be different when the family comes back to Glamara. I'm very fond of the boys and I adore Laura.'

'Doesn't Laura remind your father of Diana? I see your sister in her every time we meet.'

'Their colouring is similar it's true, but their features are not at all the same.'

'I know the boys are at Oxford, but where is Laura now?'

'Switzerland, Vevey, finishing her education. We don't expect to see her at all this summer, she's to spend the holidays near Seville with relatives of a schoolfriend.'

'And Godfrey is allowing her to go!'

'Of course. I'm sure they will be properly chaperoned, the Spanish are very strict with their girls.'

'This schoolfriend, is she English?'

'No. Roxanne is an orphan, both her parents died in a rail crash on the continent several years ago. Her guardian lives in England and they have both been visitors at Glamara. Sir Julian is really quite young, extremely handsome and remotely charming.'

'Tolerant too if he's allowing his ward to spend the summer in Spain with a schoolfriend for company. Too much freedom makes it impossible for girls to settle down, they are simply not ready for marriage when the time comes.'

'Well Laura and Roxanne are only seventeen so there is plenty of time to think about marriage. I am sure Sir Julian is well aware how much freedom his ward should have. Now don't you think we should be leaving if we are to catch that train for Harrogate?'

When they left the tea lounge I skipped adroitly round the back of the pillar so that they wouldn't see me, then followed. I prayed that my mother would not come in through the door as they went out. For some quite unknown reason I didn't want them to see her and I had no intention of telling her what I had overheard.

As she crossed the foyer I thought again how Hetty's understated elegance proclaimed her class. It was not the elegance of my mother but of a country gentlewoman, perhaps a little unfashionable, but quiet and restrained.

Less than five minutes later Mother walked into the foyer and I hurried across the thickly carpeted space to meet her.

'Did you have tea darling?' she said, smiling. 'I had hoped to be back to join you but I was held up in the traffic.'

'What have you been buying?' I asked, indicating the packages she was carrying.

'Silk stockings for both of us, oh and two lace tablecloths for the house. They seemed such a good buy and I expect most of the table linen at Jack's house belonged to his mother and she's been dead ages.'

We ran lightly up the shallow stairs. She seemed to be in high spirits and I couldn't help comparing her vivid loveliness with the colourless gentility of Aunt Hetty. I could understand more easily now how my grandfather must have adored her.

She ordered tea to be sent up and I watched as she undid her purchases, laying them out on the bed for my inspection.

'Are they real silk stockings?' I asked her breathlessly, fingering their fragile beauty.

'Absolutely real. Two pairs each, both the same colour in case you ladder one of them. They were terribly expensive but we can't go to my wedding in anything less than silk stockings.'

'Nobody is going to see them under our long dresses.'

'Perhaps not but *we* shall know what we're wearing. It's how we feel about things that matter darling, not what other people can see.'

'By the way, Jack is coming for us after dinner so you'll be able to see the house and a little more of the city.'

'Is he joining us for a meal?'

'No, afterwards, but he's paying our hotel bill so it really doesn't matter whether he eats with us or not.'

That my mother was becoming increasingly mercenary made me unhappy. She came to sit beside me on the bed. 'Now then,' she began brightly, 'I'm sure you have lots of questions to ask me about the city.'

'No Mother, I'll find out about the city when you're away

in Scarborough. I'll be able to explore. Mother, do you suppose I have cousins living in Yorkshire?'

She stared at me in surprise. 'Well of course it's possible, but never having heard from the family how could I know?'

'Your brother's children or Aunt Hetty's perhaps?'

'Well I'm sure Godfrey would marry and probably he does have a family. Hetty too could be married but she was always such a retiring shy little thing I never knew her even friendly with a boy. Why is it that you're always thinking about Glamara, Tessa? Even if my father had forgiven me years ago, even if I had never left it, it will belong to Godfrey one day and after him to his eldest son. Any child of mine would naturally have grown up in my husband's house and not at Glamara.'

'I know. I can't help wondering about my relatives, though. Wouldn't it be strange if one day we simply ran into them? You could meet one of them in Scarborough perhaps on your honeymoon.'

'Heaven forbid, darling. I don't wonder about them all the time like you do and I don't think I ever want to meet any of them again. The past is over for me Tessa.'

CHAPTER FOUR

I was glad that Mr Bryant would not be joining us for dinner. Mother said he had last-minute matters to attend to at the mill. 'One would think the entire place was going to grind to a halt just because he is going away for a few days.'

I made no comment. I felt sure the times when we dined alone would be pitifully few after this evening.

He was waiting in the foyer as we left the restaurant. 'You're late,' he said curtly, 'it's past eight o'clock.'

'I'm sorry Jack, the service was rather slow. It's only just after eight,' my mother answered in a placatory tone.

'The cab's waiting, and cabs cost money here in the city,' was his reply.

She made a little grimace at me behind his back but we hurried behind him nevertheless. My spirits sank into my shoes. If he could get so disgruntled on the eve of their marriage, it didn't augur very well for afterwards.

As we turned off the main thoroughfares the streets became much darker and narrower and I could see very little. The horse cantered at a brisk trot and soon we were driving alongside the iron railings of a park. Opposite were large Georgian houses, most of them double fronted but all alike, with short paths leading to the front doors, the paths lined with rhododendron bushes, their leaves dusty from the city smoke, their flowers faded by rain.

The front door was slightly ajar and behind it was a square vestibule, its floor tiled in black and white. Before us was another door, the top half of stained glass, and through this we could see the light in the hall.

I have seen this hall many times since that first evening but I never lost the feeling of depressing dinginess. The wallpaper was an insipid fawn, the two gas lamps did little to expel the general gloom. The stairs ran off at right angles and at one end stood a giant dresser with two very large bronze horses and a bronze pot containing a dejected aspidistra. Over the chest hung a stag's head and in the corner was a large hallstand.

He took us first of all into the sitting room and went immediately to the gas lamp, which he pulled down from the ceiling to light. It was a large room, well furnished with a three-piece velvet suite and there was a skin rug in front of the black and grey marble fireplace.

On one wall was a large china cabinet and a bookcase occupied the whole of one alcove. The suite and carpet were in shades of brown and fawn and there was a large oil painting, but I couldn't see it properly in the dim light.

'My mother chose the furniture,' he announced. 'It's all good stuff, well made and solid, I don't see any reason to alter any of it. She 'ad very good taste.'

My mother didn't speak, she only gripped my hand a little

tighter. Turning off the gas lamp he said, 'We'll go into the dining room next, it's just across the hall.'

Again he lit the gas lamps and this time the light fell on a huge dining table and eight chairs, two of them carvers. There was a ponderous sideboard and small buffet sideboard, all in the same dark mahogany, and this time the carpet was a thick red Turkey which gave the room some semblance of cheerfulness.

Next we were shown into the morning room at the back of the house.

'Is there a garden?' I asked.

'No, it overlooks the coalshed, the laundry room and the stables.'

My eyes lit up and I said enthusiastically, 'I didn't know you kept horses, Mr Bryant.'

'No more I do. Horses are only for the gentry and the would-be gentry. The former have them to keep up appearances, the latter to make them feel like gentry. The stables in this house are used for storing old furniture and there's one or two old looms in there that we no longer use at mill.'

I bit my lip and lapsed into silence.

Again dark mahogany furniture took pride of place, and because this room was smaller than the others it looked considerably more cluttered and gloomy.

I hated the house. It was the home of a man who had furnished it with expensive things regardless of either good taste or beauty. Expensive ornaments which should have been proudly displayed on their own were pushed side by side with inferior bric-a-brac and the thick velour curtains at the windows looked dusty. Overall there was a stale smell, as in a museum where old things are displayed, old dead things.

The bedrooms were no more welcoming. Again mahogany was predominating. In the master bedroom was a massive four-poster bed, but the curtains and bed hangings in dark ruby-red damask did nothing to lighten the room.

We were next taken down a corridor where he flung open a door saying, 'This is to be your room. It's not been used for many years so I had it decorated, that's probably what you can smell.' Indeed it did smell of decorator's paste but at least the walls were clean and the furniture, what there was of it, was not so heavy. It consisted of a small chest of drawers across one corner, and a table near the single bed. But the carpet was that same hateful shade of fawn and the brown curtains looked as though they had hung there for centuries.

I stared round without comment and my mother said, 'We'll be able to do something about the curtains and carpets when we have more time, darling. Mr Bryant is a very busy man and we can't expect him to spend all his time looking after the things in his house. Things at the mills are far more important I'm sure.'

He gave her a hard stare but didn't answer her, and on the way down the stairs she said, 'I've never seen the kitchens Jack, perhaps you could show me now.'

'It's not necessary. Mrs Howlett uses the kitchen for her sitting room and she'll like as not have visitors.'

'Oh well, then of course I wouldn't want to intrude. You realize of course that I've never met her?'

'There's time enough for that when you move in here.'

'Does she have any help to manage the house?'

'She'll 'ave help. Her niece is coming to work with her and as lady of the house I've no doubt there's many a task you'll be taking off her shoulders, you and the girl here.' He looked at me standing dismally at the foot of the stairs. 'Well young miss, and what do you think about the house, you've said very little?'

'It's very nice, Mr Bryant, I'm sure we shall settle down here very happily.' I didn't mean it.

Mother looked at me doubtfully. 'You can't go on calling your new stepfather Mr Bryant, Tessa, we shall have to think of something else,' she said, looking at him for inspiration.

'I don't care what she calls me,' he put in sharply, 'Jack if she has a mind to.'

'Uncle Jack would be better and more respectful from one so young,' she said firmly.

I didn't argue. I knew that the term 'Uncle Jack' would stick in my throat and I determined that I would try not to address him as anything at all, that is if ever the time came when we felt the need to converse. I didn't like him and he didn't like me. To him I was an encumbrance. His next words seemed to prove the point.

'I suppose a school is the next thing I shall be expected to come up with?'

Before my mother could say a word I said, 'I can try to find work, I know that girls younger than me are already working in the factories here, why should I be any different?'

Mother looked scandalized, but before she could speak he said shortly, 'I daresay they are but I won't have folk saying I've put mi wife's daughter out to work rather than pay for her education. There's a girls' school not far from here. It's run by nuns but I know for a fact they takes Protestant girls because I know some of the folk that sends their daughters there. Your mother can take you round as soon as we get back.'

I wanted to be grateful, I wanted to smile at him and express my gratitude in words but they refused to come.

I realized afterwards that I remembered little of my mother's wedding to Jack Bryant. I recall that the day was fine because it was the first thing she remarked upon that morning.

She looked very beautiful if a trifle pale and I felt terribly grown up in my beautiful pink gown with the big hat decorated with roses and pale pink streamers.

I listened to the brief ceremony as if in a dream and the reception too seemed as though everything was happening in a different dimension and to other people.

The reception was an expensive affair in the banquet room of the hotel. The champagne flowed and the food was over-plentiful and tasteless in my mouth. I listened to the toasts and speeches with the one thought: life would never be the same, ever. My mother would never be the same now that she belonged to somebody else.

I saw Mrs Hardcastle sitting beside her husband, somewhat grim-faced, and once I saw him nudge her gently, after which she smiled a little and seemed to relax. She complimented me on my dress, saying, 'You look lovely, Tessa, quite grown up. Are you going to be happy, lass?'

I smiled at her brightly. 'I think so, Mrs Hardcastle. I shall be starting a new school soon so I'm looking forward to that.'

'Well, I can see Joe looks as though he's here for the rest of the afternoon so I'm going to drag him away. To tell the truth I'm getting to be quite a country bumpkin, I hates being away from Briarcrag.'

'Oh Mrs Hardcastle, how I can understand that. Please give my love to Alec and the girls.'

'I will, and you're welcome to visit any time you wants to.'

I thanked her warmly, and she had only just left me when Mother came hurrying across. 'I'm going to get changed now Tessa, will you come upstairs and help me?'

The rest of our clothes were already packed and the gowns we had worn for the wedding were packed carefully in layers and layers of tissue in a separate suitcase. Hatboxes were found for the hats and then I helped my mother to dress in the things she had bought new for the journey: a long cornflower-blue skirt and neatly fitting jacket, worn with a delicate pale pink chiffon blouse and a pretty blue hat decorated with pale pink flowers. For my part I was glad to don my plain navy-blue skirt and white shirt blouse which seemed at once to divorce me from the events of the day.

'A cab has been ordered for you for six o'clock, and a boy will be coming to take all these cases down to the foyer. I'm leaving you sufficient money for everything you might need; tip the boy and if you tip the cabby well he will carry your luggage to the front door. You're not worried about going to the house alone, I hope?'

'No mother, I'm not worried. I'm sure I shall manage very well.'

I clenched my hands firmly together. I must not cry at our parting. It was her wedding day and no tears of mine should ruffle her happiness.

She embraced me warmly and for a few moments we clung together and when we fell apart the tears were in her eyes, not mine.

'Do you realize darling, it's the first time we've ever been separated?' she asked tremulously.

'You are not to worry about me, I'm practically an adult.

Just go along to Scarborough and enjoy yourself.'

She dabbed her eyes for a few moments, then she smiled bravely. 'I *shall* worry about you Tessa, but I'll bring you back a lovely present and next week we'll go and look at this new school.'

Once more we embraced, then arm in arm we went down to the foyer and the waiting guests.

I watched my mother and her new husband depart in a flurry of good wishes and loud laughter, then one by one the others went their separate ways, leaving me alone.

It was the first time I had travelled in a cab on my own, and as it was only just dusk I saw rather more of the city than I had before. As I looked out at the mill chimneys and dimly lit factory windows I felt sure that behind those windows people younger than I were still working at their looms, waiting for the shrill whistles which would end their toil for the day.

My stepfather's house looked no more prepossessing in the failing light than it had in the darkness. By any standard it was solid and well built but it possessed neither grace nor charm and I hesitated on the step before I dared ring the bell. The house was in complete darkness and the cabby who had brought my luggage to the door stared up at the house.

'Are yer sure tha's expected, lass?' he asked in some concern.

'Well yes. There must be somebody in.'

'Mebbe the bell's off. 'Ere, let mi knock on the door fer yer.'

Suiting his actions to his words he pounded on the door. 'Well if that isn't enough to waken the dead a don't know what is.'

Not a light showed and I began to tremble with dread. If I was not welcome in this house I had nowhere to go. Some of my anxiety must have conveyed itself to my companion who said, 'I'll go round the back miss. If there's a light in't kitchen I'll knock on't winder, mebbe she's deaf.'

I watched him go down the narrow entry that separated the house from the next and waited. I saw a woman walking up the path of the house next door but she never once looked in my direction and I was reluctant to involve her in my dilemma, particularly when she inserted a key in the lock and went quickly inside.

The cabby returned. 'There's a light in't kitchen so a banged on't winder an shouted out fer somebody to attend to't front door. Cum on lass, we'll ring agin.'

At long last we heard some movement behind the door and I thanked the cabby warmly for his help, tipping him far more than my mother had advised, but feeling that it was worth it.

He touched his cap respectfully, 'You'll be all reet now lass, I'd best get on.'

I heard bolts being drawn back, then a woman stood staring at me, barring my path and saying in an unwelcoming voice, 'Well?'

'Are you Mrs Howlett, Mr Bryant's housekeeper?'

'I am. Was it you bangin' on the door rousin' all't street?'

'I'm sorry but the house looked empty. I'm Tessa Chalfont, I thought you would be expecting me.'

'O' course, the daughter. You'd best come in.'

I struggled with the luggage and she made no effort to help me until I got the largest suitcase stuck in the door. 'Ere,' she said impatiently, 'if yer not careful it'll scratch the woodwork, let me 'ave that end. Where do yer want all this stuff puttin'?'

'My mother said to leave it in the morning room until they get back.'

'Well then we'd best do as she said. Clutterin' the place up. Yer can 'ang yer coat on that 'atstand. I suppose yer know where yer bedroom is?'

It was so dark in the hall I still hadn't seen her properly, and the stairs too were shrouded in darkness. I doubted if I could find my way up to my bedroom without a light of some sort.

'Are there any lights upstairs?'

'I'll light this in the 'all, yer can light the others as yer come to 'em. Ave yer got matches?'

'No.'

'Well then yer'd best take these,' she said, turning to hand the matches to me.

I had pictured Mrs Howlett as a small motherly sort of woman, plump and apple-cheeked, and now I stared at the woman facing me with the utmost surprise. She was tall like my mother but considerably stouter and although it was only late afternoon she was wearing a colourful silk wrap and her hair was a bright flaming red surrounding a face that was heavily made up. Her eyes were puffy, either from sleep or tears, and she wore dangling gold earrings. So incongruous did I find the sight of her that I stared at her stupidly until she said, 'Well yer'll know me the next time, that's fer sure.'

'Oh Mrs Howlett, I'm so sorry, it's just that I expected a much older woman.'

She smiled but her smile was without any trace of mirth. 'Did 'ee tell yer that I was old?'

'He?'

'Mr Bryant.'

'Why no. I just imagined it.'

'Well now yer knows different. I'll be in the kitchen if yer wants me. I 'ave a visitor at present.'

At that she left me, closing the kitchen door firmly behind her. I stood disconsolately in the hall for several minutes and I could hear the sound of laughter from the kitchen. I didn't know how many visitors she had in there but I could hear a man's voice and I wondered how long he would be staying.

There were no fires in any of the downstairs rooms although one had been laid in the sitting room, and I debated with myself whether I should put a match to it. I decided against it however and wandered dismally upstairs, so depressed I could easily have dissolved into tears. I put a match to the gas jet on the landing which enabled me to find my bedroom, where I unpacked. I found hooks hidden behind a curtain across an alcove, and I realized this was expected to serve as a wardrobe.

The odours of paste and paint persisted and I turned the bedclothes back to expose the sheets. They were clean but they felt icy cold. I was convinced the bed had never been aired and I dreaded having to sleep in it. A wicker chair had appeared in the room since my last visit so I decided if the worst came to the worst I would sleep in that with a blanket wrapped around me.

It had started to rain. I could hear it hammering with staccato insistence against the window and I shivered with the increasing cold that seemed to eat into my bones. There was a small iron fireplace but the chimney had been stuffed with newspaper and the bottom half was covered with brown paper which told me that a fire was never intended to be lit in it. All the same I could hear the wind echoing mournfully in the chimney and the paper rattled noisily in keeping with the mounting gale.

A glass shade would have improved the appearance of the one gas jet, but that was a concession not afforded my functional little room and I wondered miserably what I would be expected to do for the rest of the evening. I heard Mrs Howlett's visitors leaving with much talk and laughter and then the house was quiet.

I wasn't hungry, but I thought I should find her and ask for a cup of tea. I manoeuvred the stairs cautiously, surprised that Mr Bryant with all his affluence hadn't seen fit to replace the carpet, which was quite threadbare in places. I could see that the kitchen light was still burning but I was reluctant to face Mrs Howlett again. Then something of my mother's aplomb came to my rescue. After all she was supposed to be the housekeeper, I had a right to some civility, even a little comfort.

I knocked timidly at first, then more assertively and a loud voice bade me enter.

Mrs Howlett was at the kitchen table with a newspaper spread in front of her and a thick pint pot in her hands. A bright fire burned in the grate and two gas lamps had been lit over the fireplace. The kitchen presented the brightest most homely piece of warmth in the entire house.

She stared at me without speaking and I made myself stare back so that after a few moments her stare wavered and she said, 'Unpacked, 'ave yer?'

'Yes. None of the fires have been lit so I didn't know what to do.'

'I 'ad no instructions to light the fires, only to lay 'em.'

'It is very cold in the sitting room.'

'That's right, it's allus a cold room. Faces north, that's why.'

I stood uncomfortably at the other side of the table and she continued to eye me over in between sips from the mug in her hands. 'I suppose the weddin' went off all right?'

'Yes, very well. Did you watch it?'

She threw back her head and laughed, then seeing my surprise she said, 'I didn't watch it, what made yer think a should 'a done?'

'Oh I didn't, Mrs Howlett, I just thought that perhaps you would have been interested, I suppose you've worked for Mr Bryant quite a long time.'

She scowled but didn't answer. Instead she rose to her feet and poured herself another mug of tea from a large earthenware teapot standing on the stove, then she pulled the cork off a bottle and poured a fair amount of its golden liquid into her tea before adding milk and spooning sugar into the concoction.

''Elp yourself,' she said. 'There's a mug on the dresser but the tea'll stand some 'ot water. The kettle's full.'

When I didn't immediately go for the tea she said sharply, 'I've 'ad no instructions that I'm to wait on yer, Miss Chalfont, there's food and drink in the 'ouse, yer welcome to take what yer wants so long as yer don't get under mi feet.'

I got the tea, it was either that or I did without.

'Do you mind if I sit with you? It's much warmer here than the rest of the house.'

'Sit where you wants,' she answered with a sweeping gesture at the chair facing her. Then with a most unladylike belch she pushed the bottle towards me, saying, 'This'll warm you up, 'elp yourself.'

When I refused with a little shake of my head she snorted, 'Oh well, I don't suppose your lady mother would approve, but she's not the one bein' asked to sleep in that back bedroom which is as cold as charity.'

'The bedclothes felt damp. Shouldn't they have been aired?'

68

'I've only one pair of 'ands and this is a big 'ouse.'

'I know, perhaps you should have more help.'

'Ay well, I shall be 'avin' fro' next Monday, Annie mi sister's girl is comin'. Yer grumblin about yer room, yer should see the one Annie'll be expected to sleep in.'

'You mean it's worse?'

'Worse! It's up in the attic wi'out a gas jet an' no drawers, she'll 'after keep all 'er clothes in 'er suitcase.'

'But that's inhuman,' I cried.

'It's inhuman when yer thinks the girl's already got asthma fro' workin' in the mills an' all that lint gettin' on 'er chest. She's allus bin a sickly girl, I'm not sure she's doin' the right thing comin' 'ere but it's either this or back ter the mill.'

'How old is Annie, Mrs Howlett?'

'She'll be around yer age, but I'll bet you've never bin asked to work in a factory or be a skivvy in a 'ouse like this.'

'That's true. We've lived in the country since I was four years old and there aren't any factories where we lived. We have very little money but life has been kind to us in other ways.'

'No money did yer say? I understood fro' Mr Bryant that yer mother were a lady, fro' the gentry 'ee said.'

'She was, and she is, a very great lady. Money has nothing to do with that. She did something to offend my grandfather and he never forgave her, that's why we never had any money, but you'll see, she is a lady.'

She helped herself to more whisky from the bottle, then she said, 'Well Annie's comin' 'ere on Monday, you'll see 'er fer the sick child she is.'

'Don't you hate Mr Bryant for employing those children in his mills, and for what he's going to do to Annie?'

Her eyes narrowed in her painted flace. 'Oh I 'ates 'im all right, but not fer any reason yer'd think a should 'ate 'im fer.'

She lapsed into silence and I saw that her lips were trembling as if she were about to cry. Hurriedly I said, 'Would you mind if I put one of the oven-plates into my bed? It would air it before I have to sleep in it.'

'Oven-plates! In the bed!'

'Why, yes. I'll wrap it in a towel so that it won't soil the bedclothes.'

'Do as yer thinks fit, but if yer set's the bed on fire don't expect me to come up and put it out.'

'There's no danger of that,' I answered her, busying myself wrapping the oven-plate – which fortunately felt quite hot.

I groped my way up to my bedroom without bothering to light the gas, clutching the towel-wrapped oven-plate. I pushed it down between the bedclothes, hoping it would still be warm by the time I got to bed, then groped my way back to the kitchen.

Mrs Howlett was sitting with her face on the newspaper and her arms spread across the table, snoring gently.

I tiptoed about the kitchen, finding what I needed to make an omelette. I was washing up afterwards when Mrs Howlett woke.

'I'm sorry if I woke you Mrs Howlett,' I said.

'Well yer can clear away an' leave everythin' decent, I'm goin' to bed.' She swayed drunkenly towards the door carrying the bottle with her, then with a little titter she thought better of it and slammed it back on the table.

'Don't forget to turn the lights out,' she said, 'an' don't expect me to be an early riser.'

I had finished tidying when my eyes fell on the whisky bottle. I had never tasted the stuff but the thought of that bleak bedroom made me reckless. I took out the stopper and applied the bottle to my lips. It brought tears to my eyes and warmth to my entire body.

It was the rain pattering against my window and the grey daylight that awakened me the next morning.

My mouth felt dry and there was a strange hammering in my head, but I struggled to my feet. Then I heard the church bells. It was Sunday morning and people were going to church. It was the day after my mother's wedding and it felt like a thousand years.

CHAPTER FIVE

I hated the taste of stale whisky on my breath, I felt somehow depraved.

I shrugged into my dressing gown and wandered out into the passage. After opening several doors, most of them showing rooms filled with junk and evidently not in use, I came upon a bathroom. It was a dingy place. The bath was stained brown but the washbowl was intact and to my surprise the water was reasonably warm. I washed hurriedly and scrubbed my teeth energetically to ged rid of the taste of whisky, then I hurried to get dressed.

The kitchen was exactly as I had left it the night before except that the whisky bottle had gone. It was almost eleven o'clock and I decided first of all to put a match to the sitting room fire, then I found a duster and went from room to room until I was satisfied that the house looked more presentable. There was still no sign of the housekeeper. I heard the clatter of the milk cart outside so I went to the front door to meet the milkman. He stared at me in surprise. 'Is 'er ladyship away then?'

'Do you mean Mrs Howlett?'

'Ay, the 'ousekeeper. Who are you then?'

'I'm Tessa Chalfont, I shall be living here from now on.'

'Wi' 'er ladyship do yer mean?'

'Mrs Howlett will still be here, but Mr Bryant married my mother yesterday and she will be the lady of the house.'

'Will she indeed? Well, 'ere yer are luv, will a pint o' milk do yer?'

'No, we'd better have another.'

He trotted off to his cart returning with another bottle which he handed to me saying, 'Well, she didn't tell mi there was goin' ter be a weddin', I reckon things'll alter round 'ere.'

'I reckon they will,' I answered him, then with a brief smile I went back inside.

I made some tea and toast, then tidied up. The day stretched ahead of me interminably. I decided to sit in the sitting room with my book. I dreaded the scenes in store when my mother arrived back. She would not tolerate Mrs Howlett's slipshod ways for a single moment but the woman had looked as though she could give a good account of herself and I didn't know how much Mr Bryant valued the services of his housekeeper.

It was early afternoon when I heard Mrs Howlett shuffling downstairs. I waited a few minutes, then I too went into the kitchen. She looked up and I had never seen such an unprepossessing sight.

Her makeup of the night before was stale on her face and her bright red hair was tangled. The colourful silk wrap had gone and in its place she wore a dark skirt and fawn blouse which she had not bothered to fasten and which hung loosely, showing her underclothes and a fair expanse of bosom.

She stared at me uncomprehending for several moments then she seemed to collect her thoughts. 'You've bin mighty busy a can see. Lit the sittin' room fire?'

'Yes.'

'Well I 'ope yer don't think I'm carryin' coal in an' out fer yer. When that in the 'od's bin taken yer'll 'ave to go outside fer more. Yer didn't see fit to light a fire in 'ere then?'

'No. I thought you would do that. This is your kitchen and you know where everything is kept.'

'That I do, an' I told yer last night I wasn't 'ere to wait on yer.'

'That's all right, Mrs Howlett, I can look after myself, but I don't intend to look after you as well.'

'You're a cheeky young madam, I'll say that fer yer.'

'I'm not in the least cheeky, Mrs Howlett, but I did expect some sort of welcome in this house and I haven't received any.'

She stared at me open mouthed.

Without giving her a chance to reply, I continued, 'I'm

72

going out for a while. I haven't a key to get back in the house.'

'I don't expect to be goin' out but I might 'ave a visitor. Yer'll find a key under the last stone in the garden. That's where I leaves it regular if I has to go out.'

I couldn't help wondering as I crossed the road towards the park gates if she would address my mother in the same take it or leave it tones. If so she was in for a shock.

The park was not a large one. I came across a crowd of boys and girls standing round the pond watching the ducks. They were younger than I and poorly clad against the chilly wind. They set up a chorus of whistles and catcalls but I walked past without glancing at them. A park-keeper stopped me by saying, 'Are yer alone in the park, lassy? Take no notice o' that lot, little 'ooligans they are, but yer really shouldn't be on yer own, a young lady like yerself.'

I smiled at him. 'I'm just on my way home, good afternoon.'

So it would seem that I too had an air, like my mother's, that set me apart from those children in the park. I didn't know if it was a good thing or not in my case. Times would change, indeed they were already changing, and what went for gentry in my mother's day might be very different in mine.

The next day I rose early. I laid the fire in the sitting room and took out the ashes, then I cooked bacon and egg and ate a hearty breakfast, once again being sure to clear everything away so that Mrs Howlett would have no cause for complaint. I was embarked upon an adventure as I joined the people waiting at the tram stop and we didn't have long to wait before the clanging noisy monster arrived.

It was the first time I had ever travelled on a tram. I loved the noisy clamour of it and after paying my fare to the terminus I sat back to enjoy the ride.

As we moved out of the city the roads became narrower and the houses smaller, but for the most part they were in neat terraced rows, either of stone or red brick. At every window hung clean lace curtains and every doorstep had been well scrubbed and donkeystoned. A forest of mill chimneys rose up behind them and whenever the tram stopped I could hear the looms.

Filled with curiosity I spoke to the woman sitting next to me. 'Are all of these woollen mills?'

'Oh ay, those are Prescott's mills, weavers o' woollen cloth, plaids and the like.'

'And those others in the valley?'

'One of 'em is Prescott's Fernbank mill where they weave suitings an' 'igh-class stuff. That other's an engineerin' mill where they make looms.'

'Do Bryant's have any mills in this area?'

'I don't think so, lass. Bryant's is nearer the city. This is a better-class area.'

'Do young people work in those mills?'

'Prescott's 'ave never bin keen to employ the little 'uns, cheap labour it is, but then again if it's stamped out their folks are goin' to miss the bit o' money they earn.'

'Have you ever worked in a mill?'

'That I 'ave, but not a woollen mill. I come fro' Burnley, that's i' Lancashire at th'other side o' them 'ills there. I married a Yorkshireman an came to live i' Leeds. Mi husband's a tackler at one o' the Prescott mills.'

'A tackler? What's that?'

'A tackler's the chap as mends the looms when someat goes wrong wi' 'em. Different sort o' looms they are fro' the cotton looms. I worked in a cotton mill til a got married, av'e never worked in a mill since.'

'Are you sorry about that?'

'Nay lass, I'm reet glad. They're cold dark places an' now an' again yer can have mice runnin' round yer feet if the mill's an old un.'

I bade my travelling companion good morning at the terminus, and set off along the road in the direction of the countryside. I felt suddenly free as I climbed towards the hills where I could look down on the city sheltering under its permanent umbrella of grey smoke.

The cobbled road gave way to a dirt track and still it climbed towards a hamlet in the shelter of a gentle hill. For a while I sat swinging my legs against a five-barred gate, looking for landmarks. Surrounded by formal parkland stood a large stone mansion and I thought it probably belonged to some factory master. How I wished that my stepfather had chosen to live in the country instead of that cold draughty house opposite the park.

The tower of Leeds Town Hall was an easy landmark and there were church towers and spires in plenty, incongruous beside those towering mill chimneys belching out volumes of black smoke. Wide thoroughfares cut through the centre of the city but from the hill overlooking it I could see where the narrow straggling streets lay and I knew that was where I would find the real city, where the brass was made to adorn all that was gracious and noblest in Leeds.

The mills held a strange fascination for me. I felt I would like to go inside and see how the looms worked but I had no wish to go into the Bryant mills, I could only think they would be as depressing as his house.

I continued my walk, upwards to a village with a swift stream running alongside the main street. It was pretty. Cottage gardens came right down to the stream and could only be reached by crossing bridges which appeared at intervals along the street. The cottages on the other side came right on to the street and did not have gardens, but they all looked spotlessly clean.

I stopped to talk to a plump black and white cat who sat washing his face at one of the doorsteps and on hearing my voice a woman came to the door. She was quite old, but her smile was warm and friendly.

'Good afternoon,' I said. 'He's a lovely cat isn't he?'

'Ay, 'is name's 'Enry. Do yer like cats then?' she asked smiling. 'I can get yer a kitten if yer'd like one.'

'Thank you, I'd love one, but I would have to ask.'

'Would yer like to come in and 'ave a cup of tea?' she invited. 'It's not offen I get's company in the daytime.'

I followed her into a neat front parlour, and she brought out home-made fruit cake, buttered scones, jam and teapot.

'What do they call yer, lass?'

'Tessa, Tessa Chalfont.'

'Well isn't that funny now. I knew some Chalfonts once, but it were up i' Wensleydale. It's not a name yer ere much i' these parts.'

'Were they friends of yours?'

'Nay lass, the Chalfonts were gentry. A were born i' Lambreck, an mi mother were a laundrymaid at the big 'ouse. She used to take mi wi' 'er when a weren't at school, eh but I luved goin' to the 'all. Wi got to play in the park an' cook used to make buns fer us. It were such a lovely 'ouse an' if yer met one o' the family they allus 'ad a kind word fer yer.'

'The Chalfonts?'

'Ay. Sir Edward Chalfont was the owner then. 'Ee only 'ad one son, John. My but 'ee were a 'andsome lad, mi mother said all the servant girls an' the village girls were i' love wi' 'im.'

'What was the name of the hall?'

'It's funny yer should ask that, luv. 'Ave never forgotten it. Glamara, that's what it were called.'

I stayed at the cottage with the old lady until halfway through the afternoon and I had to run all the way down the hill because I wanted to get back to the house before the factories came out. But I was deep in thought for most of my journey. It seemed that Glamara would never let me be, that every time it seemed most remote something or someone would remind me of it.

In all this I saw the hand of fate. It was not merely chance that I was not being allowed to forget Glamara.

CHAPTER SIX

The house smelled of furniture polish and the fire burned brightly in the sitting room. I began to think that Mrs Howlett had overcome her animosity towards me but she appeared out of the kitchen, favouring me with a cool stare. 'I thowt yer'd gone fer good. Yer didn't see fit to tell me yer'd be out all day. Annie's laid yer fire an lit it an there's some hash on the stove if yer'd like some.'

I was too surprised to thank her, and by the time I had gathered my scattered wits she had returned to the kitchen. I was hungry, and the very thought of hot potato hash sent me hurrying after her.

She was busy at the sink washing the dishes, and drying them was a girl of about my own age. She was smaller than me and painfully thin, with a mop of frizzy brown hair, and she was wearing one of her aunt's aprons which was several sizes too large for her. She stared at me with wide dark eyes, then quickly busied herself with the dishes.

'Hello Annie,' I said. 'Thank you for lighting the sitting room fire, it looks cosy in there and everything's so nice and clean.'

She bobbed me a quaint curtsey which surprised me because I had never been curtsied to before.

'I'd love some hash, Mrs Howlett,' I said, grabbing a dish from the table and hurrying to the stove. The hash was warm and thick with potatoes and onions. There was very little meat in it but it tasted good and I sat at the kitchen table to eat it. As soon as I had emptied the dish Annie came to the table to take it away and I noticed that her hands were red and swollen with chilblains and she sniffed constantly as though she had a head cold.

'Are yer goin' out again?' Mrs Howlett said shortly.

'No, I'm going to read in the sitting room.'

'Well, the fire'll need bankin' up, I'll send Annie in when we've finished in 'ere.'

'May Annie stay and talk to me for a little while?'

'Annie 'as 'er work ter do an' I won't 'ave yer fillin' 'er silly 'ead wi' all sorts o' fancy things that'll make 'er discontented an' do no good to a lass in 'er station.'

I was determined to talk to Annie when she came in to bank up the fire but I hadn't thought how difficult that would be.

She came struggling in with a bucket of coal, panting a little, and I stood up quickly to help her.

But she shook her head. 'I can manage on mi own,' she

whispered, 'mi aunt says if I don't try, out I go.'

She put the coal on the fire with her fingers, wiping them on her apron which was none too clean to begin with.

'Are you going to be happy doing this sort of work, Annie?' I asked her.

She stared at me, sweeping her hair back from her face with the back of her hand and leaving a sooty smear. 'I 'as to work at someat, this is as good as any other.'

'When did you leave school?'

'When I were eleven, but I've worked in't factory since then. I 'ad to leave cause I've got asthma. I were glad to leave, I were that frightened o' them shuttles, I've seen 'em fly off right inter a girl's face, dangerous they are.'

'I wish your aunt would go out so that you could sit in here and talk to me.'

'If she catches me talking ter yer miss she'll be that mad.' She bobbed one of her quaint curtseys and fled.

I heard her aunt shouting to her, 'It's taken a 'ell of a time to stoke up that fire. Bin chattin' to 'er 'ighness, 'ave yer?'

'No aunt, 'onest I 'aven't, leastways only when I was stokin' up the fire.'

I heard Annie give a frightened squeal and I surmised her aunt had slapped her.

Suddenly the tears rolled down my cheeks and my throat felt tight and sore from a grief I couldn't at first recognize. I was crying for Annie and all those like her who would spend their lives in servitude to some master or other. For people like Annie there would always be a Mrs Howlett to box their ears if they walked out of step.

Nothing I heard or saw the following day cheered me about life in the big city. I took a tram into the city centre but I had no idea how far I must walk before I came across the poor area I was looking for. I decided to follow two women wearing shawls and clogs, who seemed out of place beside the smart city shoppers. It was not long before I found myself in a maze of narrow streets and back-to-back houses without gardens and sharing long toilet blocks. Poorly clad and dirty children hung about outside the public houses.

'Why are you waiting here?' I asked one small boy with a dripping nose and threadbare coat.

'Am waitin fer mi dad, 'ee's in't pub. Mi mam sent mi, she's no money fer our dinner til me dad gets 'ome.'

I felt so angry that men should be drinking while their wives and families were short, I felt like hammering on the door and crying for them to come outside and give their money to their children.

A man emerged almost shamefacedly from the side door and immediately three children ran to his side with happy cries of welcome. Another man brought his son a smart slap on the side of his face which sent him reeling into the gutter, and further down the street I could hear a woman screaming abuse at her returning husband.

I walked along the miserable cobbled street. The houses were dirty and unkempt, but it was a dirt allied to despair, a dejected acceptance that life was meant to be like this, that there was nothing else, ever.

Abruptly mill whistles all around me started to shriek, and it seemed that out of every house in that shabby little street men, women and children hurried like an army of ants towards the factory gates.

Along that road I passed factory after factory until I came at last to a brass plaque proclaiming that these were the premises of J. Bryant & Co., Woollen Manufacturers, Croft Mills, Leeds.

So this was where my stepfather made his money. As I stood there a woman came out and started to give the brass plaque her complete attention. I watched her rubbing and polishing until it earned her approval. Becoming aware of my interest, she said, 'Do yer want to see somebody in the office, lass?'

'No. I was just watching you. That brass looks very nice.'

'Ay well, the weather plays havoc wi brass, it'll noan stay like that long, worse luck.'

'Do you work at the mills here?'

'I cleans the office, mi 'usband works in't mill, boilerman

'ee is. Works down there shovellin' coal into them great boilers over 'is 'ead. Man an boy ee's worked i' the boiler room.'

'Has he always worked here for Bryant's?'

'No. When a married 'im 'ee worked for Prescott's but wi couldn't afford the 'ouses up there so wi bowt one round 'ere. It's not a bad little 'ouse, not like them down't street, an' wi got taken on 'ere. It's nowt like Prescott's but we couldn't afford fares ter go up there every day.'

'I take it you're not too happy working for Mr Bryant then?'

Her voice sank to a conspiratorial whisper. 'Likes 'is pound of flesh 'ee does, worse than 'is father, an' '*ee* was bad enough. Prescotts were good masters. Old Sir Edward were a right gentleman, one o' the old school, an 'ee were generous to 'is workfolk at Christmas an' 'olidays.'

'It's a pity you had to leave.'

'It is, but work's work an' yer 'as to be glad of it. They do say the master got wed last Saturday ter a fine lady fro' the dales. 'Is secretary were at the weddin', very posh do it were an' she says Mrs Bryant looked right beautiful an' folk were right, she *is* a lady. Ee's done well to get somebody like 'er 'cause 'ee's not got a good name i' the town.'

At that moment the office door opened and a tall man came out. He was wearing a dark navy-blue suit and a shirt with a high winged collar. His large moustache had been carefully waxed and one strand of hair had been brought down over his nearly bald head to form some sort of quiff. 'Haven't you finished out here yet, Mrs Jenkins? You'd best get busy on Mr Bryant's office, 'ee's back on Friday.'

With a scarlet face she gathered her belongings together and scuttled past him saying, 'I was just comin', Mr Laycock.'

He favoured me with a stern look but I stared back at him unabashed.

Once again I was late back at the house and again the fire was burning brightly. I went to kneel on the rug, luxuriating in its warmth.

I was still pondering on all that I had seen in the town when there was a sharp knock and Annie poked her head round the door. 'There's bacon an' sausage on the stove, miss. Mi aunt's gone out, she's visitin'.'

I jumped to my feet and followed her into the kitchen. The table had been laid and she indicated that I should sit at it while she brought the food.

'Have you eaten, Annie?'

'Oh yes miss, I ate earlier wi mi aunt.'

'Have you been busy all day?'

'Ay, she finds mi plenty ter do but she were out this mornin' so I could work at mi own speed.'

I ate with relish and after I had cleaned my plate she brought me a cup of tea, suggesting that I drank it in the sitting room.

'I'd much rather stay here and talk to you, Annie. I get bored on my own in there.'

'Mi aunt wouldn't like it, miss.'

'Well she's not here, is she? And we don't need to tell her.'

'Supposin' she comes back an' finds yer 'ere?'

'I'll be gone long before she comes back. Where has she gone anyway?'

'To see Mona Gibbons. She were her friend 'afore she came 'ere, when she worked in't mill.'

'I didn't know she had ever worked in the mill.'

'Oh ay, she worked at Bryant's. She were an overlooker an' gettin' good money but 'ee brought 'er 'ere to 'ousekeep for 'im. Mi grandmother were agin' it fro' the start but mi aunt thowt it were a step up fro' workin' in a mill.'

'Did you hate it in the mill, Annie?'

'Oh yes, then a got this asthma wi' all the lint. I 'ave three sisters an' a brother all younger ner me, I 'ave to work at someat. A could 'a stayed on at school another year but mi money were wanted at 'ome.' She was silent for several minutes, standing near the table hiding her poor angry hands, her face reflective, then with a philosophical shrug she said, 'I reckon I've seen nowt and done nowt.'

Her next question surprised me: 'Is yer mother as nice as yer are, miss?'

'Oh yes Annie, she's quite lovely and you'll find she can be very kind.'

'Then a shan't mind workin' 'ere an' yer mustn't worry yer head about mi. I 'opes a suits yer mother, I'm not bothered about 'im.'

'You know Mr Bryant, Annie?'

'No. I've never laid eyes on 'im but I knows 'im fro' mi aunt an mi mother, mi grandmother too.'

'Did they all work at Bryant's mills?'

'Only mi mother an' aunt Josie.'

Something held me back. I didn't want to probe any further into Jack Bryant's history. I felt I would hear something I would rather not know, and I didn't want to be disloyal to my mother. Late tomorrow afternoon they would return from Scarborough and next week I hoped I would be out most of the day at my new school.

I expected my mother would have a very busy social life and I wanted desperately to make my own friends. Surely there would be somebody in that school who would be a special friend so that I could escape from the loneliness I was feeling now.

'Is it very cold upstairs in the attic Annie?' I asked.

'It's freezin', miss. I slept wi' mi clothes on last night, or I couldn't a' slept at all.'

I showed Annie how to wrap an oven-plate in a towel, and we went upstairs together, each clasping her warm bundle. She watched me put my oven plate in my bed, then hurried up to her own dreary room.

After a few minutes I called out to her, 'Are you up there, Annie?'

'Yes miss, I'm goin' to get inter bed 'afore it's got a chance o' gettin' cold. Goodnight miss.'

'Goodnight Annie. Sleep well.'

CHAPTER SEVEN

It was early next evening when I heard my mother's voice and from the window I saw her coming up the path carrying a good many parcels, while the cabby followed her husband with their luggage, I could tell that she was still filled with euphoria after her wedding and the honeymoon, and I hurried to the door, throwing it open wide and rushing into her arms.

'Darling let me look at you!' she cried. 'Gracious me but I declare you've grown, either that or you're thinner. Has Mrs Howlett been giving you enough to eat?'

'Yes of course, I've been doing lots of walking.'

'I do hope you're not going to be one of those long leggy girls like a young colt, entirely without shape. Help me with these parcels, darling.'

There were so many parcels and hatboxes, he must have spent extravagantly on her during their short holiday.

'We thought of having dinner at a hotel but it was difficult with all this stuff. I suppose Mrs Howlett will have something for us.'

I didn't know. After her performance of the last few days I doubted if Mrs Howlett was prepared for their homecoming, and although she must have heard their arrival she hadn't come out of the kitchen to welcome them.

I followed Mother into the sitting room where she threw her parcels in a heap on to the settee. The fire shed its glow on the furniture Annie had so enthusiastically polished and flowers I had bought, spring flowers that gave to the stolid room a feeling of unaccustomed gaiety.

She looked round, obviously pleased. 'There now,' she said, 'didn't I tell you this room could look charming?'

She held out her hands to the blaze. 'These early spring evenings are chilly and it was so cold at the coast. It rained solidly for the first two days and today when we were coming home the sun actually shone. . . . What is she like?'

She said the last sentence in a whisper but I knew she was referring to the housekeeper.

'You'll be surprised when you meet her, she's not at all what I expected.'

'Oh, why is that?'

'Well, she's much younger for a start, and she has vivid red hair and a great deal of make-up.'

'She sounds a positive hussy darling, but the house looks nice and clean, I'll say that for her.'

'You have Annie to thank for that, Mother. She only came on Monday but she works very hard. Her aunt puts on her, I'm quite sure of it. Annie's nice. She has asthma, that's why she had to leave the woollen mills and she has the most terrible chilblains on her hands. Will you let me have some cream to put on them? I told her I would ask as soon as you were home.'

She sat down among her parcels on the settee. 'You mean she isn't a trained housemaid?'

'Oh Mother, we don't want a housemaid, we want somebody like Annie to do the rough work.'

'We most certainly *do* want a housemaid, I expect to be entertaining and I shall want a girl to look attractive when she answers the door and brings in tea, not some waif with chilblains and asthma. Don't think I haven't heard those women talking about their coffee mornings and their tea parties. It will be expected of me, Tessa.'

But I was prepared to do battle for Annie. 'This room was miserable until she came,' I said stoutly, 'and one of your fancy housemaids wouldn't be prepared to sleep in that cold damp attic. Mother, this isn't Glamara, you must be practical.'

She glared at me, her cheeks pink, her eyes glittering with annoyance. 'One thing I am not prepared to do is argue with my daughter about my servants,' she snapped. 'Go into the kitchen and tell Mrs Howlett I would like to see her in here.'

'What is this then?'' came Jack Bryant's voice from the

doorway where he was standing eyeing first me and then my mother.

'Tessa tells me we have a girl from one of the factories to do the rough work, a girl with chilblains all over her hands and some sort of asthma. Surely what we wanted was a girl to wait on the table and answer the door, somebody who could do the light work and even some of the shopping.'

'You'd best have a word wi' Mrs Howlett, she's in charge of the work around here. I'll tell her to come in.'

I was more than glad that I didn't have to do it.

Mrs Howlett was cleaner and tidier than I had ever seen her. Her vivid hair was caught back in some sort of snood and her make-up had been toned down substantially. She stood in front of my mother without a smile of welcome and they seemed to me like two adult cats sizing each other up before deciding which way to pounce.

'Good evening, Mrs Howlett,' Mother said graciously enough, 'I regret that we haven't met before. I would like to thank you for looking after my daughter during my absence. I believe you now have more help in the house.'

'Yes, Mrs Bryant. Annie, mi sister's girl, is 'ere.'

I saw Mother raise her eyebrows slightly at the housekeeper's speech but she made no comment.

'Is Annie accustomed to working in service, Mrs Howlett?'

'No, she's worked in the mill, but she's used to 'ousework an' plenty of it. I don't think Annie'll give yer any cause for complaint.'

'But can she wait on table and look presentable at the door, Mrs Howlett? I don't expect you to wait on my guests but I shall expect it of somebody else.'

'She's not too dumb that she can't learn.'

'Have you the time to teach her? I'm sure I haven't.'

'I've bin askin' Mr Bryant for 'elp fer years an' just afore yer were married 'ee said a could 'ave Annie, 'ee'll not take kindly to a girl whose only job'll be waitin' on table an' answerin't door bell.'

'You can leave Mr Bryant to me, Mrs Howlett. In the meantime I hope we can expect a meal tonight?'

85

'There's roast lamb and vegetables and there's cheese and biscuits. Mr Bryant's not a great one for puddins.'

'Neither am I, Mrs Howlett, but there are more imaginative sweets. I can see you and I are going to have to put our heads together during the next few days. There will have to be changes, but then I am sure you expected that, didn't you?'

Mrs Howlett didn't say whether she had expected them or not, she merely edged nearer to the door. 'Well if that's all, Mrs Bryant, I must see to the meal.'

She left the room and I heard the kitchen door slam behind her. As for my mother, all the gaiety seemed to have left her and she was staring miserably after her.

She looked at me with a frown on her beautiful face but I kept my face stolidly without expression.

'Really Tessa, how can Jack have tolerated a woman like that all these years? He must never have had his friends to the house, how *could* he with a housekeeper of that sort?'

'Perhaps she's a very good cook?'

'Don't you know whether she can cook or not?'

'Annie's done most of the cooking, I think.'

'Well, something will have to be done. In the meantime you'd better help me upstairs with all these parcels. Don't you want to see what I've brought you?' she added, brightening a little.

'I didn't expect you to bring me anything, Mother. There was no need.'

'Don't be silly, darling, of course I had to bring you a present, and first thing in the morning you and I are going over to see the Mother Superior at that convent school across the park. I do hope they don't try to convert you, perhaps we should have looked elsewhere. Your grandfather would be horrified if he thought his granddaughter had turned Roman Catholic.'

'Mother, my grandfather doesn't want to know me, I'm sure he won't be interested in my religion.'

'Nevertheless you'll stay as you are. Old habits die hard, even when we are out of touch.'

Out of touch! If I turned Moslem or heathen Chinese my

grandfather wouldn't be interested because he wouldn't know. I helped her to collect her parcels and followed her straight-backed slender figure up to her bedroom. Once there she threw them on the bed and kicked off her shoes.

'My, but it's cold in here, one would have thought Mrs Howlett might have lit a fire.'

'Annie will light one if you ask her,' I answered, surprised at the sarcasm in the ordinary words. What was the matter with us? I loved my mother, I adored her, but the change I had noticed in her before her marriage was more pronounced now.

She hunted through the parcels, then tossed one over to me with a bright smile. 'Open it now, darling, and tell me what you think of it.'

It was a rose-coloured velvet cloak edged with swansdown, a beautiful thing which had evidently cost a great deal and I wondered if there would ever be an occasion to wear it.

'It's beautiful, Mother, but really you shouldn't have spent so much.'

'Just so long as you like it darling, but there are bound to be parties at the school and girls will invite you to their homes. I don't want you to say you haven't a cloak to wear over your party dresses.'

I hugged her warmly. She was wearing a new perfume, a far more exotic one than usual, and I commented on it.

'Do you like it dear? It's very expensive and French, far more sophisticated.'

My mother was more sophisticated, more unreal. She had come a long way from Mrs Elliott's cottage and the days of our poverty. I could begin to understand why Jack Bryant had been captivated by her. She was everything he was not.

The dining table had been laid, not very expertly from the look on my mother's face as she went about straightening the lie of a fork or napkin, but when Mr Bryant came to the table in his shirt sleeves it was too much.

'You are surely not going to sit down to dinner like that?' she snapped, her face a mask of outraged displeasure.

'Like what?' he asked, staring.

'Like that, in your shirt sleeves and without a tie on. No self-respecting gentleman would ever do so in the presence of ladies.'

'I've had a long day, Diana, and I'm more comfortable like this, surely you're not objecting to the way I dress in my own home?'

'Oh but I *am*, darling. You want the best from your wife, surely I'm entitled to ask the best from my husband.'

She smiled at him disarmingly and with a short grunt he went out of the room. She made a little face at me.

'Sit down, darling, we shall have to wait until he's presentable, but he must be made to see that I won't put up with anything.'

In a few minutes he was back wearing his tie and a velvet smoking jacket which had evidently seen better days. My mother smiled and if she thought the jacket shabby she made no comment.

I felt the pattern for what was to follow had already been set and all desire for food left me. Annie came in with a tray almost too large to pass through the door so I sprang up to open it wider for her. On the tray was a large oval plate containing a leg of lamb and there were several heavy tureens. She placed the tray on the table behind the door and then brought the dishes to the dining table. The lamb she placed in front of Mr Bryant, and the tureens in the centre. They were obviously very heavy and very hot and she allowed them to fall with something of a clatter on to the polished table top so that my mother winced and Annie attempted to pick up some of the spilled contents with one of the serving spoons.

'Leave it,' my mother commanded, and stepping back smartly, her face the colour of beetroot, Annie left it. Her appearance was startling. She was wearing a clean apron but it was several sizes too large. A mob cap sat on top of her frizzy hair rather than over it, and her hands were enclosed in white cotton gloves.

'I'm sorry, mum,' she apologized, 'but they're that 'ot an' 'eavy I couldn't 'old on to 'em.'

'That's all right Annie, you may serve the cheese later.'

'Cheese mum?'

'Yes, I believe there is cheese to follow. Mrs Howlett will instruct you.'

Gratefully she scurried out of the room and Mother's eyes met mine with resigned tolerance. My stepfather sat carving the lamb as though he had heard nothing. The meat was well cooked and succulent but the gravy was burnt and there was no mint sauce. The cabbage was hot but watery and the potatoes and carrots underdone.

Although he ate the meal with obvious relish Mother and I merely toyed with it and eventually he noticed. His eyes narrowed ominously. 'What's wrong with the food that you've left half of it?' he demanded.

'The lamb is very good, it's a pity it had to be spoiled by inferior vegetables,' my mother answered him calmly.

'What's wrong with the vegetables then?'

'They are underdone and the gravy is burnt. Really Jack, I can see that Mrs Howlett and I need to have a little talk. It's incredible that you should have put up with her for so long.'

'I won't have you upsetting the woman, she's done her best and she's had no other woman to tell 'er what to do. Now you'll go easy on her Diana, I mean it. If she gives in her notice through anything you've said it'll be you and that lass o' yours that suffers most.'

'You can rely on me to be tactful, I only hope she's willing to learn.'

He rose to leave the table. 'I'm goin' up to unpack my bag. I'm expectin' Miles Laycock from the factory with some figures for me. We shall be in the mornin' room for most of the night.'

'Don't you want any cheese?'

'No. When Miles comes have him shown into the morning room like I said.'

He left, and I felt a strong urge to laugh although there was no cause for mirth. Mother had put such store in Mr Bryant's wealth, surely she must now be wondering why it had seemed so important. He was uncouth and without a shred of charm, and I was sure my mother would become increasingly aware of the cruelty which I felt lived just below the surface. Those narrowed eyes of his could be vindictive, spiteful, and I thought again about those tumbledown houses surrounding the Bryant mills, with their rotting doors and dispirited tenants. I hoped Mother would never have to see the abject poverty in which those people lived.

She was sitting thoughtfully playing with a bracelet on her arm, as though her thoughts were elsewhere. Then: 'I am wondering if I should speak to Annie or to Mrs Howlett first,' she murmured.

The decision was made for her only a few moments later when Annie brought in the cheese. She bobbed her quaint little curtsey and was hurrying out when Mother called, 'Annie, come back. I want to speak to you.'

She came reluctantly.

'Let me see your hands, Annie.'

'Mi 'ands, mum!'

'Yes, my daughter tells me they are sore with chilblains. Have you seen a doctor?'

'No mum.'

'Whyever not?'

'Doctors cost money an' mi 'ands'll be better when the warm weather comes.'

'Let me see them, Annie.'

Reluctantly she pulled off one of her gloves and extended her hand towards my mother, who recoiled sharply. 'You should see a doctor at once, Annie, the chilblains have broken and could become infected. I hope you haven't been handling the food.'

'Oh no, Mrs Bryant. Only wi' mi gloves on.'

'That's a relief anyway. Now look Annie I have some ointment in my medicine chest that might help, but if they are not better in a week's time I shall call in the doctor to attend to them. Now my daughter will fetch the ointment for you. Wash your hands and smooth it on carefully, then wear your gloves so that it won't get on to your bedclothes.'

'Thank yer, mum,' she said, and with another wobbly curtsey escaped from the room.

Mother's beautiful face wore an expression of fastidious disenchantment. She was eyeing the cheese which sat in the middle of the table like a blob of yellow suet. 'That looks suspiciously like cooking cheese to me, and Yorkshire is the home of cheeses. I don't want any, do you Tessa?'

'No thank you mother.'

'Run into the kitchen, dear, and tell Mrs Howlett that we'll have our coffee in the drawing room.'

She swept out and I moved uncertainly in the direction of the kitchen. They were both busy at the sink but only Annie looked up with a little smile.

'We would like our coffee in the drawing room, Mrs Howlett. My mother likes it black but I prefer white.'

She spun round and stared at me as though I had lost my senses. 'Coffee!'

'Yes please, Mrs Howlett.'

'We don't usually 'ave coffee. Sometimes Mr Bryant likes a cup o' tea but more offen than not 'ee 'as a glass of ale. I 'aven't made any coffee.'

'Then perhaps you will do so,' I ventured unhappily.

She stood staring at me but then her eyes wavered, and she snapped at Annie, 'Fetch the milk, Annie, 'er 'ighness likes it white an' 'er majesty likes it black.'

I escaped with my cheeks flaming and if Mother noticed my discomfort she did not remark upon it. In due course Annie brought the coffee. There were two unmatched jugs, one containing cold milk, the other black coffee, and two enormous cups and saucers. The sugar was the usual white variety served with tea. Exasperated beyond her control my mother snapped, 'Annie will you please tell Mrs Howlett – no, I will tell her myself. Will you please ask her to come in here.'

This was the moment I had been dreading. I wanted to get out of the room and, making the ointment an excuse, I headed for the door. But Mother said, 'Stay here until I've dealt with Mrs Howlett, Tessa.'

Mrs Howlett took her time but she appeared at last minus her apron and with a look in her eyes that showed she was ready to do battle. My mother's voice was reasonable rather than hostile and I saw the uncertainty creep into Mrs Howlett's hard eyes.

'My daughter and I like to drink coffee after our evening meal, Mrs Howlett, and it should be served in two identical jugs, one containing hot milk and the other black coffee. If a small jug is used then it should contain cream. Haven't you any brown sugar?'

'No, we've 'ad no call fer it.'

'I suggest you get some, Mrs Howlett, and are these the only jugs you have, don't we have a coffee set?'

'Them's the only jugs I've ever seen.'

'Well, I'll see to it that we have others, either in china or silver. Surely there was one among our wedding presents?'

'Yer weddin presents are still in the mornin' room wrapped up, just as yer daughter brought 'em.'

'Then we'll unwrap them tomorrow. The lamb at dinner was very good, Mrs Howlett, but the vegetables were not to my liking. The potatoes and the carrots had not been cooked enough and the cabbage was too watery. You will come to know how I like things to be done in a little while, Mrs Howlett, it is natural that we should have these little upsets at the beginning. I understand you were not a housekeeper until you came here to Mr Bryant.'

'That's right, I worked in't mill.'

'What made you change, I wonder?'

'A bit more money an' mi own kitchen. I shared a cottage wi' mi mother, mi sister an' 'er 'usband and four children, yer can understand I didn't get much privacy wi' that lot.'

'I do understand, Mrs Howlett. I am no stranger to poverty although I have never been called upon to live so wretchedly. If you are willing to let me help you I can make you the kind of housekeeper the gentry would not be ashamed to employ.'

She stared at my mother in amazement, 'Nay Mrs Bryant, the gentry'd never employ me, not wi' their 'igh-class servants that'd look down their noses at the likes o' me.'

'I didn't say now, Mrs Howlett, I said in the future, if you will allow me to make something of you. There are times when you will be resentful but believe me in the end it will have been worthwhile, trust me.'

'I *do* resent yer, Mrs Bryant, I've 'ad mi own way around 'ere too long.'

'Yes, well I'm sure you are an intelligent woman so you will see things must change. I am the lady of the house now and you are the housekeeper. Our roles are different but we can help each other if you are willing to comply.'

'I'll give it a try but I'm not promisin' that things'll be different.'

'They've got to be, Mrs Howlett, either that or you and I are going to part company and I'm sure you have no desire to return to your work in the mill.'

Mrs Howlett's face grew bright red with anger but looking at my mother's calm, adamant face her eyes fell, and my mother knew that for the time being she had won. In her best conciliatory voice she said, 'We are going to get on very well Mrs Howlett, but there is the question of Annie, those hands of hers are quite terrible. Couldn't she keep them out of water for a few days until they are on the mend? It's surely the soda and cleaning soap that are doing so much harm.'

'Well it's either Annie or me, Mrs Bryant. She was supposed to be comin' 'ere to give mi a bit of 'elp, it's not goin' to be much 'elp if she 'as to stay out o' water.'

'I agree. Oh well, we will leave it for the time being and see what improvement my ointment brings about. Thank you Mrs Howlett, that will be all.'

After the housekeeper had left the room my mother looked at me with something of her old sparkle. 'You see Tessa, that wasn't really so bad. It's Annie I'm worried about, she certainly hasn't the makings of a parlour maid and she's not going to be much use as a scullery maid with those hands.'

In a sudden burst of anger I set out to defend Annie.

'You should go down those mean little streets near Mr Bryant's factory and see where people like Annie live: all those hundreds of shabby little houses with not even a bathroom or a lavatory to call their own. And the men all drink in the public houses while the children wait outside to be given money before they can eat. When you say Annie doesn't have the makings of a parlour maid, whatever could she be expected to have the makings of after being born in a hovel like those?'

'You had no right to go wandering those streets alone, Tessa. Good heavens, child, somebody could have murdered you for the bit of money you had.'

'I had a bar of chocolate which I gave to some children because they were hungry. Those poor dispirited people were not intent on murdering anybody. They were too busy answering the call of the mill hooters. Those noisy, dreadful mills.'

'You say they were Bryant's mills? I can't believe that Jack is a hard master. If they insist on drinking their wages away the children will suffer but the factory owner isn't to blame.'

'Oh Mother!' I cried in some exasperation. But at that moment I didn't feel equipped to argue further with her about the poverty in the world. I only wanted to fight for Annie, Annie whose job was threatened because of her chilblains and her inability to act the part of an upper-class servant.

'I don't know why you are so obsessed with saving Annie's job. She's only been here four days and here you are almost quarrelling with me because of her. What on earth can you possibly have in common with Annie?'

How could I tell her that we were both lonely, both crying out for something we couldn't have, both miserable and unhappy in an environment neither of us had sought? Instead I asked if I could look for the ointment and she told me where I might find it.

I felt miserably sad that I was unable to feel as close to Mother as I had once been. She was finding me difficult, hard to understand, and in my turn I saw that my championship of Annie was a personal thing but too important to be put aside.

While I was upstairs I heard the door bell and realized Mr Laycock had arrived. My stepfather opened the door to him and I heard their voices in the hall.

The long evening stretched ahead of me, but I was glad I didn't have to share it with my mother's husband. In the old days we had never found it difficult to be alone, there had been books to read, games to play. Surely we would be able to recapture something of those happy times? She went to her bed very early. I wondered if she thought I preferred to chat to Annie than to her, but dismissed such a notion immediately as being unworthy, then I cheered up by thinking that we would have most of tomorrow together.

My mother seemed in exceptionally high spirits the next morning as we stepped out across the park. The sun was shining, the birds were singing and the morning held all the promise of a fine spring day.

'This school has the best reputation in Leeds and I didn't want you to go away to school,' she remarked happily. 'I need you with me here, Tessa.'

'But you said you would have a very full social life, Mother, and would probably be entertaining a lot.'

'Yes, but I shall need you to help me. That way you will meet their sons and daughters and very soon we shall both be able to build up a wide circle of friends.... I can't say I like the house very much. This afternoon I must go into the city, there are things I need to buy.

'I got up very early this morning and opened our wedding presents. Really Tessa, you wouldn't believe that people with money can have such bad taste, there was virtually no decent china. The Hardcastles gave us some cut glass which was extremely nice but the only thing in silver was a salver for the hall table and there were some quite hideous ornaments which will be put away and only brought out when the people who gave them to us are visiting.

'Anyway as I was saying when I'd finished unwrapping the wedding presents I went into the kitchen to look round for myself. What is the use of keeping good china in the china cabinet when the china in the kitchen is in such a state? Nothing matches, and a lot of it is cracked. I know that Jack wouldn't like to see his mother's Crown Derby at the mercy of Mrs Howlett or Annie, but there are limits.'

'Have you talked to him about it?'

'I did tell him I was going to shop in the city but I don't think he was listening to me. Mr Laycock was at the house until well after midnight and, would you believe it, Jack had his account books spread all over the breakfast table.'

'Perhaps the mills are not doing too well,' I ventured.

She stared at me in some surprise. 'Why Tessa, what a little pessimist you are, of course the mills are doing well, why shouldn't they be? Darling, this park is really quite pretty, I like the pool and the weeping willows, if we could cut down those overgrown rhododendron bushes in front of the house we would be able to see into the park quite well.'

Nothing I could have said would have dampened her spirits that morning. She was going to the shops and she delighted in spending money, her interview at the convent was secondary.

The school was a square building behind high stone walls but when we had passed through the gate we found ourselves in a delightful garden with shallow stone steps leading to tennis courts and a croquet lawn. A neat maid in a long black dress, snowy white apron and white frilled cap showed us into the head mistress's study which overlooked the gardens, a tastefully furnished sunny room where we were asked to sit facing a wide mahogany desk.

'Did you see the maid?' my mother asked. 'Can you ever imagine that our Annie might turn out like that?'

I was saved from answering by the entrance of the Mother Superior who shook each of us by the hand. She was wearing the habit of a nun but instead of the sombre nun's veil she wore a wide snowy coif. She seemed to be quite old, but she had a wise sweet face and when she smiled her eyes crinkled with laughter lines.

I listened to my mother telling her that I had been privately educated in the country where I had had very good results from my work, but now that she had remarried and come to live in Leeds I needed to find somewhere nearby.

The Mother Superior listened without interrupting, occasionally nodding her head. My mother had never had any difficulty in making an impression on people. She was so composed, elegantly dressed and charming, but it was her voice that people listened to and which set her apart as if the dominance of lesser mortals lay in that clear, correct enunciation.

In less than an hour we were walking back across the park and my future at the Convent of St Clare was assured. I was to start the next day and my mother had been assured that no effort would be made to convert me from my Anglican faith. It transpired that Protestant girls attended St Clare's, and to my mother's utmost gratification she was assured that they were charming girls, the daughters of one of the city's most eminent lawyers, several millowners and city magistrates.

Over coffee my mother had spoken airily of her upbringing in the northern dales, of the beauties of Glamara and things she had not talked about for many years. The gulf that now divided us from them was never mentioned, indeed one could almost have believed that Glamara was our second home.

'Now where do we get this wretched tram into the city?' she asked as we neared the park gates. 'I do so hate those noisy things but I suppose like all young people you enjoy something new.'

'It doesn't cost much to ride on one,' I said astutely. 'The money we saved by not taking a cab will buy something at one of the shops.'

She laughed good-humouredly. 'You're right, Tessa, it will buy us lunch.'

The next few hours were a revelation. My mother bought silver and china, cutlery and material for curtains, ordering them to be delivered. She also dragged me round furniture shops to look at upholstery and bedroom furniture but those I was relieved to see were only jotted down in her notebook along with the prices.

We went to lunch in an elegant restaurant in the Headrow and as she swept towards our table heads turned to stare after her. Vehemently I wished I was older and walked with that same willowy grace.

As if she had guessed my thoughts she leaned across the table. 'When you are out of that gawky shyness, Tessa, I am going to dress you beautifully and you will learn all the things a woman needs to know about sitting gracefully, walking tall like a queen and knowing when to speak and when to remain silent.'

'Yes Mother,' was all I could think to say.

'I hope Jack will be in a good mood tonight when he gets home from the mills. I've spent a great deal of money, but they were all so necessary.'

'What is the material for?'

'Kitchen curtains dear.'

'I thought you had brought material for those from Scarborough.'

'I did, but this morning I gave that to Annie. She assures me that her mother can sew so I told her to ask her mother to run up a few little dresses or aprons for her, the child's a rag bag. She's not a pretty child, but she could look a whole lot better than she does.'

That was part of her charm, she could be so high-handed one moment and the next so incredibly sweet. How I adored her.

In the dining room that evening I was immediately aware of an atmosphere. My stepfather sat with a face like thunder at the head of the table and my mother sat opposite him, her face pink with annoyance, her right hand drumming impatiently on the table.

Mrs Howlett herself brought in the meal which was a steak pie and I was glad that the potatoes and vegetables were cooked this time to my mother's satisfaction. Mrs Howlett looked at my stepfather with grim amusement. She would know something of his moods, I felt sure, and would have little sympathy that my mother was learning something of them also.

Mother served the pie and passed the vegetable dishes along the table so that he could help himself. Unfortunately as he picked up the one containing potatoes the handle fell off and the potatoes cascaded on to the table top. He swore under his breath but instead of being annoyed my mother dissolved into laughter.

'What the hell's to laugh at?' he roared furiously.

'I thought all our china was in perfect condition, that it would last for years and that I had been wasting your hard-earned money.'

He glared at her then began to scoop up the potatoes from

the polished surface into the broken dish.

'Here, let me do it,' my mother said sharply. 'Tessa, please ask Mrs Howlett to wipe the table, these hot potatoes are not going to do much for the polished surface.'

I was glad to escape out of the dining room and when I went back with Mrs Howlett order appeared to have been restored. Mrs Howlett dealt with the sticky mess on the table top and I thought she was wearing a satisfied smirk.

'The meal is excellent,' my mother remarked. 'That little talk I had with Mrs Howlett seems to have worked wonders.'

'I told you to leave the woman alone,' my stepfather said gruffly.

'If that is all the thanks I get for trying to make your home more comfortable and your food more palatable I shall leave matters alone in future.' She stalked out.

My appetite had gone also but I made myself eat. I did not want to be accused for the second time of leaving good food on my plate. He was not enjoying his meal even though it was probably the best he had been served in that house for a considerable time. I could tell that he was worried by my mother's tantrum, and in a few minutes he left the table without a word.

I waited half an hour for them to come back and finish their meal, then decided to look for them. The sitting room was in complete darkness but from upstairs I could hear voices – my mother's tearful, his conciliatory. Just then Mrs Howlett came out of the kitchen carrying a tray.

'It would seem the 'oneymoon's on agin,' she said dryly. 'Ave they finished their meal? I made a special effort wi' that.'

'It was lovely, Mrs Howlett, I enjoyed it.'

'Well I'm glad somebody did. P'raps yer won't see 'em down 'ere again tonight,' she said, her eyes filled with sly amusement.

'Oh surely they won't have gone to bed, it's only just after eight.'

'Ay, well she's bin spendin' 'is money an' now she's thrown a tantrum that's put 'im in the wrong. 'Ee's up there apologizin an' in a while she's goin' to reluctantly forgive 'im.

No, you'll not see either of 'em down 'ere agin tonight.'

She laughed loudly, and her laughter followed me into the sitting room where I crouched in front of the fire hugging my knees and hating the thoughts of my mother in the arms of that man while his rough ugly hands explored her soft delicate body until she found it in her heart to forgive him.

CHAPTER EIGHT

Long before lunch time I knew I was going to enjoy being at St Clare's. The classrooms were pleasantly lofty and spacious and those of the senior students overlooked the pretty gardens and tennis courts. Tranquillity permeated the building, from the hall where we recited our morning prayers, through the classrooms and into the dining room. After lunch our time was our own for the next hour. We could read or study in the library or we could play tennis or croquet or simply watch others who were more energetically inclined.

I realized that I was a bit of a mystery. Most of the girls had been there since they were small. Many of them were boarders but only a few had gone to the school to finish the last two years of their education as I was doing. Until I knew the girls better, I realized, I would have to spend a lot of my time alone.

My form mistress was Sister Agnes and I was surprised to find her very young. She had a vitally alive face that always seemed to be smiling and I wondered how anyone so attractive could bear to spend all her life clothed in the sombre garb of a nun, never knowing what it was like to dance in a man's arms or visit concerts or theatres.

I realized after a time that the only pleasure sister Agnes and her colleagues missed was dancing in a ballroom with a man. They entered into the joys of country dancing with great enthusiasm and they took us to endless concerts and to the theatre when the play was one which would add lustre to our education.

At the end of that first day I walked home across the park with a jaunty step. I even made a face at a little boy who pulled out his tongue at me.

My mother was delighted to see me looking so happy. She was going to the theatre and was looking enchanting in a pale green gown over which she wore a long black velvet cloak lavishly trimmed with ermine. I watched her depart all in smiles, although my stepfather showed no interest in my first day at school and barely acknowledged my presence. I didn't care. So long as he was kind to my mother and to Annie he could ignore me all he wanted to.

I enjoyed eating alone, as I allowed my mind to wander back over the pleasures of the day. Perhaps tomorrow I would find a friend; several of the girls had smiled at me as we left the school and one of them had actually walked my way. She had kept well in front of me however and I had not hurried my steps to catch her up.

Annie came in to clear away and I asked about her hands.

'They're a bit better miss, leastways they've stopped itchin' as much. Yer mother's very kind, Miss Tessa. A were a bit frightened of 'er at first.'

'Why should you be frightened?'

'Well she talks so nice an' she's so stylish. You'll be like that one day, Miss Tessa. You don't look like yer mother but yer just as beautiful an' yer'll 'ave that air, yer'll see.'

I laughed. 'Oh Annie, you are funny. I always wanted to be like her but I'm thin and gawky.'

'Yer won't allus be thin, Miss Tessa, an' yer 'air's lovely, just like cornsilk, an' yer eyes are like the sea when it's angry.'

I stared at her, surprised. I had not known that there could be such poetry in Annie's soul, and as if she were ashamed of her outburst her cheeks blushed scarlet and she busied herself filling her tray.

'Annie, that was beautiful,' I said, 'when did you see the sea?'

'I never 'ave, but I did see a picture of it once in the art gallery. It were wild an' angry, wi' great waves an' there were little boats bein' tossed about. The North Sea it were, somewhere off Whitby, that's Yorkshire isn't it?'

'Yes Annie, that's Yorkshire.'

She smiled, that funny one-sided little smile that gave her gamin face a strange attraction, and I found myself wondering what St Clare's could have done with Annie if they had had her from childhood.

PART TWO

CHAPTER NINE

Spring passed into summer and I felt totally and gloriously happy. The long days meant that I could be out of the house often and the only times I saw my stepfather were during our meals. I was seeing less of my mother too because I had found a friend and now at weekends Susan Latchford and I would wander up in to the country.

Susan's father was an accountant and they lived beyond the tram terminus where the houses were beautifully built with large gardens and lawns. Mother was eager to know all I could tell her about Susan and her family. That Mr Latchford was a professional man gave her the utmost satisfaction and she inquired eagerly if there were other children, and particularly sons. I had not been to their home but I knew that Susan intended to invite me during the summer holidays, and Mother seemed perfectly happy to await developments.

I was never quite sure what Mother did with her time. She appeared not to visit friends and I was surprised that none came to the house, particularly as she had once said she expected to be entertaining extensively.

I felt strangely worried and I began to look for signs that my mother was lonely or unhappy, but always in my presence she seemed bright enough. One evening as we sat looking out across the park into the gathering dusk I said, 'Have you decided not to do any entertaining, Mother?'

She looked at me sharply and even in the twilight I could see the delicate colour in her cheeks.

'Why do you ask, Tessa?' she said, her eyes searching my face.

'Oh, just that I never see anybody here.'

'Well, Jack doesn't like entertaining so people are never invited in the evening.'

'He doesn't mind them coming in the daytime though?'

'Well of course not dear, but I find I really haven't a great deal in common with many of the women I meet. All they do is talk about their money, the latest fashion and scandal. Men are really much better company.'

'Do you visit any of them?'

'We prefer to go to the theatre and to race meetings. Why the inquisition darling? Don't worry about me, I'm perfectly happy, but when you visit your friend's home you must tell me about it and she must come here of course, Susan and her mother.'

My invitation to visit Susan's home came early in August after we had begun our five weeks' vacation. I was invited the first week because after that they had rented a cottage near the coast and the entire family were going there. Mr Latchford intended to join them for a fortnight and then at the weekends only. I realized I would miss her.

When I told my mother of the arrangement she said, 'What a good idea, but I know Jack would never agree to being away from Leeds for so long. The mills close for a week so that he could get away if he wanted to, but he seems not to care for the idea. I expect he'll go there as usual, just to keep an eye on things.'

'Couldn't we go, Mother, just you and I, to the coast or the country?'

'I'll mention it, but I don't think he'll like the idea.'

Whether she mentioned it or not I have no idea because she did not refer to it again.

I wore a new blue cotton dress on my visit to Susan's home and instead of tying my hair back with its customary ribbon I allowed it to fall around my face in its heavy waves.

'You look so pretty,' my mother said as she saw me off at the front doorstep. 'How can they help but find you perfectly enchanting.'

I was surprised that the Latchfords had another guest, Marylee Nelson. Although her family lived not far from Susan's she was a boarder at St Clare's and possibly the one girl I didn't really like very much. She was fair and pretty, with baby-blue eyes and a rosebud mouth that was capable of saying the most unkind things, and she was wearing a lavender silk dress decorated with tiny embroidered pink flowers. Her hair was caught back in a lavender silk ribbon and she was wearing high heels which prevented her from walking any distance. I was to learn later that she had invited herself, and when I met Susan's brother Lawrence I began to understand why.

Marylee ceased to have any time for either Susan or myself and she attached herself to Lawrence with a proprietory air. Susan's mother merely smiled.

'Do we have to have her to tea?' Susan hissed. 'After all she wasn't invited.'

'We must ask her, dear,' her mother replied, 'it would be terribly impolite not to.'

Susan and I took a walk, following the path I had taken on my first visit to the country here.

'Who does the big house belong to, that huge stone one with the long drive and the stables?' I asked.

'That's the Prescott house, Heatherlea. It's the home of Sir John Prescott and Lady Prescott, and they have two sons, Lionel and Alexander. Those are Prescott's mills you can see in the hollow.'

'Do the Prescotts entertain their friends in that big house?'

'My parents have been there several times – my father is Sir John's accountant. I've been riding with Alexander but I don't care for horses. Do you ride, Tessa?'

'I did when I was in the country. How many horses do the Prescotts have?'

'I'm not sure but Marylee might know. Her father is the sales manager for Prescott's. Did you see those high heels she's wearing? No wonder she didn't want to come walking.'

'I think she'd rather be with your brother.'

'I know, and he's flattered, the silly thing. If it was anybody but Marylee I wouldn't mind.'

'Where does she live?'

'At that big red brick house in the hollow. My father says it belongs to the firm, but nobody would ever think so by the way Marylee goes on.'

'Perhaps we should be starting back now,' I suggested, 'we have quite a fair walk.'

She sprang to her feet and pulled me up after her. 'I suppose we'll have Marylee with us all evening. Lawrence is going out.'

'She won't like that, couldn't he take her with him?'

'Not really. He already has a girl, a very nice girl.'

We chuckled over the fate of Marylee as we ran down the hill towards Susan's home.

Tea was served on the terrace above the lawn and the table was spread with all kinds of cakes, thinly cut sandwiches and warm scones with cream and jam. There were peaches and thick cream and home-made fruit cake and now and again as I helped myself to proffered plates I caught Marylee's eyes on me, vaguely speculating.

After the meal whilst we sat in the warm scented summer evening she informed us that her father now owned a new motor car which would be very helpful in his journeys across the country, and Susan whispered savagely in my ear. 'She means the *firm* owns it.'

'Has your father got a motorcar, Tessa?' Marylee asked.

'No, and he's not my father, he's my stepfather.'

'Oh really, I didn't know. Your mother's been married twice then.'

'Naturally when I am called Chalfont and she is called Bryant.'

I could have bitten off my tongue but it was too late. Her wide china-blue eyes narrowed and quite airily she said, 'And you live in those stone houses across from the park?'

'Yes.'

'I think my father knows your stepfather. It is a small world, isn't it?'

She dropped the subject but I felt sure her devious little mind was turning her new information this way and that, and one day soon I would find that she had twisted it to her own ends.

A little later Susan walked with me to the tram stop. It was still light and as we waited I put my arms round her and thanked her ecstatically for a lovely day.

'It would have been better without Marylee,' she said laughing, 'but you will come again, won't you Tessa?'

'I would love to but my mother wants you to visit us when you come back from holiday, both you and your mother.'

'Oh yes, that would be lovely Tessa. We'll look forward to it.'

That one week in August when the Bryant Mills were closed made little difference to my stepfather, who went there as usual. It made no difference to the rest of us.

I went with my mother to the shops and we walked in the park where there were innumerable band concerts. The atmosphere on these occasions was carefree and happy. The girls wore pretty floral cottons and the men white flannels and straw hats and blazers, and the children walked or ran alongside the bands as they marched from the gates to take up their positions in the bandstand. I loved the sound of the brass bands, and I wondered how these men who were employed in industry or in the mines every day of their working lives had discovered as a group the joy and enchantment of playing music.

On several days we took the tram as far as the terminus and climbed the low hills above the city and I was able to point out the landmarks Susan had showed me. Mother was very interested in the Prescott house and the mills they owned in the hollow.

'Have you met any of the Prescotts?' I asked her one day.

'No,' she answered me shortly, then as though she thought she should prolong her answer she said, 'I've seen Sir John and his wife at several race meetings.'

'What is she like?'

'Lady Prescott. Well she's about my age I should think, plump, quite pretty. I believe they have two sons.'

'Yes, Lionel and Alexander. Susan knows them.'

'Does she? Then perhaps you might meet them through Susan one day. That would be nice for you, Tessa.'

'I thought you might have met them through business, Mother, they have woollen mills like my stepfather.'

'You never have been able to call him uncle Jack, have you

Tessa? Stepfather sounds so cold somehow, one always associates it with unkindness or cruelty. Too much David Copperfield, I expect, when one was young and impressionable.'

'I wonder if any of those poor people in the city have been able to go away on holiday.'

'Not if the parks are any criterion. All those screaming children quite spoiled the band concert for me on Tuesday afternoon. There should be some sort of playground nearer their homes then they wouldn't be allowed to wander willy-nilly in our park.'

'It isn't our park, Mother. I expect the band concert was a rare treat.'

'Nonsense, they weren't even listening to the music, they were running screeching along the paths or swinging on the turnstiles. Nobody seemed to be in charge of them, I expect their parents were drinking in the public houses.'

'Perhaps if they got better wages they would be able to take their children away on holiday.'

It was out before I realized it and she turned her haughty stare on me in complete surprise. 'Really Tessa, you astonish me sometimes, what do you know about their wages or what they would do with the money if they had it? Don't let your Uncle Jack hear you saying anything about wages.'

'I'm not likely to discuss wages or his work people when he's there. Everybody should have enough money to be able to get to the sea or the country some time in their lives. Do you know that Annie has never seen the sea except on a painting in the art gallery.'

'Annie has been inside the art gallery?'

'Yes. She told me it was her favourite painting. There's so much more to Annie than you realize, Mother.'

She was staring at me, her green eyes thoughtful, her face remotely sad. 'She's such a quaint ragamuffin, but one day when I gave her some old curtains to take home she smiled and there was something strangely compelling and attractive about her face.'

'I know, I've seen it too.'

'When people smile often their smiles are seldom noticed,

but a smile on a face that is more often serious or grave can be quite beautiful, like the sun after rain, and so charming because its coming is so rare.'

I nodded eagerly. This was how I loved my mother best, when she was understanding and she could describe so beautifully the most mundane happening.

Because of her mood I felt I could ask the question I had been longing to ask every day since we arrived in Leeds.

'Are you happy Mother? Sometimes I wonder because you look so sad.'

She laughed a little. 'Well of course I'm happy darling, why shouldn't I be? I must improve my ways if you have caught me looking sad. I have absolutely nothing to look sad about.'

I wanted to believe her but I couldn't. Perhaps it was I who needed to improve my ways and think a little more of the man who was supposed to be making her so happy, but I had never been able to pretend.

At the beginning of September I returned to St Clare's and the familiar pattern of school life. I was now in the sixth form and our new form mistress was Sister Hilda. She was much older than Sister Agnes and she was strict, but she had a calm sad face and when we worked hard her patience was endless.

I greeted Susan joyously and she regaled me with happy stories of the days they had spent near the coast. Among the boarders I sensed a new coldness and where I had begun to make friends amongst them, now they clung together in tight little groups until the day girls and the boarders became two separate entities.

Susan too noticed the coolness that seemed to descend on us whenever we met them and I believed Marylee was at the centre of it. On several occasions I had caught her whispering to her friends whenever she saw me in the corridors or in the gardens but I put her from my mind. After all I had done nothing to offend Marylee.

My friendship with Susan continued happily and I did not mind about the others as long as I had her. One evening after dinner when my mother and I were sitting together in the drawing room she said, 'Isn't it time you invited your friend and her mother to the house, Tessa?'

'Yes of course Mother, but won't he mind?'

'If you mean your stepfather I don't imagine so. In any case he is away next weekend.'

'You're not going with him?'

'No. They are going to the races at Redcar and staying over until Sunday. I didn't want to go and I thought it would be a good idea to invite your friends.'

'I'll ask her in the morning, I'm sure they'll be glad to come.'

Susan received my invitation with her usual sweet smile and the following day she said they would both be delighted to accept.

During the week it seemed I was seeing less of Susan but I did see her in close association with Marylee and her cronies. She seemed remote, arriving late in the dining room so that we were not able to sit together and rushing off across the park in the evening before I could catch up with her. Friday came and I was determined to get close to her so that I could discover if everything was as we had planned for their Saturday visit.

I tracked her down in the library but she seemed evasive. 'My mother hasn't been well, Tessa,' she said, avoiding my eyes.

'But she will be well enough to come tomorrow? My mother will be so disappointed if neither of you can come.'

'Oh I'm sure she will be better by tomorrow.'

'But you *will* come won't you Susan, even if your mother can't?'

'Oh yes. I can't talk any more now Tessa, I'm searching for a book for Sister.'

I watched her hurrying away with my heart filled with doubt.

Next morning I met Mrs Howlett in the hall. 'Fine lot of fuss we're 'avin' this afternoon, yer'd think King Teddy and the queen were invited.'

'Has it been a lot of extra work for you, Mrs Howlett?'

'Nay, my bakin's not good enough. Yer mother's ordered

cakes an' scones fro' that posh baker's in the city an' she's decided she'll make the sandwiches. I'll not be cuttin' the bread thin enough fer 'er.'

I grinned at her. 'Well, why are you complaining? It's less work for you.'

'Oh ay, and that's not the end of it. Annie's bin given a fancy apron an' white frilly cap. She spent most o' last night preenin' through the lookin' glass. I told yer mother that Annie weren't cut out ter be a parlour maid, she'd come 'ere as a skivvy.'

'I must say you do a lot to give Annie confidence, Mrs Howlett.'

'And what good would that do 'er? She'd get ideas above 'er station an' I'd get little or no work from 'er.'

'Is my mother down yet?'

'Not yet, but 'ee's gone off afore six o'clock to Redcar. I doubt there'd 'a bin all this fuss if he'd 'a bin 'ere.'

'Well he isn't, is he?'

Several minutes later my mother arrived for breakfast looking happy and relaxed; indeed I hadn't seen her looking so fresh and sparkling for several weeks and I wondered if it was because we were expecting visitors or because *he* was away.

She told me details of the spread she had laid on for the afternoon and silently I prayed that nothing would prevent Susan and her mother from coming. I did however venture a small warning.

'Susan's mother isn't very well, I'm not sure that she will be able to come.'

She raised her eyebrows in surprise. 'She would have said, surely, that she wouldn't be coming, Tessa. If she didn't then she expects to be well enough. In any case your friend will be coming.'

'You mean if she can leave her mother.'

'Oh darling it's Saturday, her father will be at home and didn't you say she had a brother?'

'Yes, but perhaps they will be going out.'

'Is there a doubt about this visit, Tessa? Because if there is I think I should have been told about it sooner.'

'No mother, I'm sure there's not.'

I made myself get on with my breakfast but several times I felt her eyes upon me, puzzled and questioning.

As the day wore on my anxiety increased. It was still only midday when I went up to my room to change out of my blouse and skirt into a dress and I heard my mother quietly humming to herself in the bathroom.

How hard it was to sit patiently while the fingers of the clock on the mantelpiece hardly seemed to move. Neither the newspaper nor the magazines were capable of holding my interest and the anxiety mounted agonizingly. I prowled about the drawing room, at times going to look through the window, at others standing about helplessly and biting my nails, until Mother lost patience.

'If you are going to wander about looking restless I suggest you go to meet Mrs Latchford and Susan at the tram stop,' she said, and with alacrity I snatched my coat and ran down the path. I felt sick with apprehension and then I saw the tram rounding the bend beyond the park. It ground slowly to a stop and my eyes feverishly scanned the platform for those waiting to dismount. Susan and her mother were not among them and at that moment I felt I could have fainted with despair.

They had missed the tram, they would take the next, or better still Susan's father would drive them. My eyes scanned the road ahead for every vehicle that rounded the bend and then my hopes faded when it was not the vehicle I was looking for.

I watched the tram go upwards to the terminus and once more with my heart in my mouth I waited for its return. In ten minutes I would know for certain if they were coming. But what was ten minutes? I had often been ten minutes late for school and the world hadn't stopped. Susan would be full of excuses: a torn stocking, her mother's dissatisfaction with her hat, her gown. Ten minutes, and each one feeling like a year of my life.

I heard the tram's clanking long before it came into view and I stood with my heart in my mouth hardly daring to look at it. Only one person alighted, and then I watched the tram grinding away on its journey into the city.

Dejectedly I walked back towards the house. As I closed the front door my mother came out of the drawing room with a smile of welcome. It faltered when she saw I was alone. 'Isn't your friend with you Tessa?'

'No mother, I expect they missed the tram.'

'But you said three o'clock dear. They didn't come on that one and you waited for the next.'

'Yes, they weren't on either of them.'

I couldn't meet her eyes which were watching me closely.

'Come along, let me have your coat and I'll ask Mrs Howlett to make the tea.'

At that moment Annie came into the hall wearing her new apron and the white frilly cap which sat incongruously on her frizzy hair. Her expectant expression and quaint appearance brought a rush of tears into my eyes and I fled into my mother's arms, sobbing wildly. She drew me into the drawing room and we sat in front of the fire until my tears subsided, and then with a little smile she said, 'I'll bring in sufficient food for the two of us Tessa, you didn't eat very much lunch.'

In her absence I tried to control my tears but the misery remained.

I minded for my mother rather than myself. My friends were to have made up for all the lonely days when nobody came, when nobody invited her and for all those impossible dreams which were fading in the place of reality. Although she returned wearing a cheerful air, her eyes were bleak with disappointment. She was minding for me, ignoring her happy preparation for their visit, her desire that I should meet nice people, people who would be kind. Well so much for the nice people in Leeds, now I could only see their narrow-minded cruelty and prejudices. But why?

As if in answer to my unspoken question she sank slowly on to a chair and in a dull dispirited voice she said, 'Oh Tessa, what have I done?'

I stared at her without understanding her words and she stared back with the tears slowly sliding down her cheeks. I knelt at her feet and she put her arms around me. 'Tessa, what have I done?' she repeated unhappily.

'You haven't done anything, Mother, it's Susan and her mother who have done it. If they couldn't come why couldn't they have sent a message? They wouldn't like it if we'd done it to them.'

'No Tessa, it's my fault, I should never have married Jack Bryant and now because of my blindness you are paying for it too.'

'But you loved him, Mother.'

'No, I never loved him. I thought he was common and coarse, just like you said, and I hated this house and the people he mixed with at race meetings and at the theatre.'

'Then why did you marry him, oh Mother how could you marry him when you thought that about him?'

'I thought he would be kind. I thought he would pay for your education and when we first met he *was* kind. He bought me beautiful presents and he promised we would have a house nearer the country that I could choose for myself and furnish. He promised so many things he hasn't seen fit to fulfil. I've been a fool. I thought I could change Jack Bryant after we were married but I forgot that I could never change your father. He was a gambler when I met him and although he constantly promised that the next gamble would be the last it never was. But Nigel Lorival at least had great charm and he was a gentleman. Jack Bryant is a boor, a vulgarian, and perhaps we deserve each other.'

'Why do you say that?'

'Because I wanted to use him for my own ends, and now he is making very sure that he uses me.'

'But what has all this to do with the Latchfords staying away?'

'Why do you suppose all the other decent people in Leeds stay away? It is no use my lying to you any longer, Tessa. He does have a bad name in the city. He underpays his workpeople and they work and live in conditions that can only be described as terrible. I knew all this when I was defending him, but I couldn't bear for you to know it also, Tessa. I thought I could turn him into the sort of industrialist John Prescott is, a man who takes an interest in his workpeople and the cultural life of the city, a man who might donate a library or a park. But I have failed. I cannot turn Jack Bryant into that kind of man any more than he could turn me into one of those painted third-rate revue artists he admires so much.'

'If he is so fond of that type of woman why did he marry you?'

She raised her eyebrows cynically. 'Are you really suggesting he could have got your mother any other way, Tessa?'

The colour flooded my face but I didn't answer her and she went on. 'I suppose Joe Hardcastle bragged to his cronies about the upper-crust woman who was assisting him in the selection of his horses and his wife in the adornment of her home, and when Jack met me I was unlike any woman he had met before.

'He was generous as you know, now I suppose he is equally generous with the women he visits in the city since he is no longer generous with me. I didn't want to spend the rest of my life being a high-class servant to people like the Hardcastles. I wanted something better for both of us so I persuaded myself that I could change Jack Bryant and I persuaded him that I was what he was looking for, a stylish educated wife who would further his business ambitions and plant his feet firmly on a higher rung of the social ladder.

'It seems we deserve each other: I am not what he was looking for and he is not the sort of clay I could mould to my satisfaction. I wonder how you are going to bear the next few years, darling?'

'I shall,' I answered her, raising my head proudly. 'If the people here make judgements without knowing the truth then I don't particularly want to know them. In three months I shall be seventeen and I'm going to work so hard that I leave them all behind when the examination results are announced. I shall get myself a good job so that I can get away from Leeds, and in time you'll be able to leave him and come to live with me. You will, won't you Mother?'

'We'll see, darling. In the meantime how about having some of that lovely tea? And what is left we will give to Mrs

Howlett, and Annie can pack a basket and take some home. I'm sure it will meet with more appreciation than any your friends would have had for it.'

For the main part the food stuck in my throat. Mother too seemed to be making a noble effort but there was no doubt that Mrs Howlett and Annie enjoyed it, and later as we packed Annie's basket her bulging eyes and cries of rapture repaid us a little for the disappointments of the day.

When my mother went to the front door to lock up for the night she found a note pushed through the letter box. She came back into the hall staring at it curiously.

I watched her fingers tearing the envelope open, then after she had read the note she passed it over to me with a little smile.

'Dear Mrs Bryant,' I read, 'I am asking my son to deliver this note to your house giving my apologies that Susan and I were unable to visit you this afternoon as planned. I have not been too well all week and Susan felt she should stay with me. I hope our non-arrival did not put you to too much inconvenience. Yours sincerely, Grace Latchford.'

I stared at my mother in disbelief. What hypocrisy, I thought, what confounded presumption that put aside all our preparation, our anticipation and the disappointment their non-arrival had meant to us, and the mere supposition that this terse note would be sufficient apology, sent too late and simply pushed through the letter box.

It only stiffened my resolve to show them what I was made of, that I didn't care about their friendship or the lack of it.

CHAPTER TEN

On looking back I believe that weekend was the turning point in our lives, for my mother no longer felt the need to defend her husband to me and I began to see their marriage for the miserable sham that it was.

As for me I returned to St Clare's on Monday morning with my head held high and my determination to work to the exclusion of everything else still uppermost in my mind.

I saw the glances that passed from one girl to another when I walked into the classroom and the warm colour that crept into Susan's face when I gave her only a brief smile in her direction.

None of them seemed to have anything to say to me over lunch so I soon excused myself and went into the library where I sat with my head buried in a book.

As the weeks passed I missed Susan's friendship less and less, and I found that I was enjoying learning for learning's sake. I filled my whole life with knowledge but when Sister Hilda praised my efforts I was certain that it didn't add to my popularity.

I believe she sensed my anxieties and solitariness. One day when I was returning some books to her study she said, 'I am very pleased with your work Tessa and I admire your diligence, but you should make friends, all work and no play is not good for you. Are you unhappy about something Tessa? I see you sitting in the library reading when the other girls are out in the gardens.'

'I like reading, Sister Hilda, and I am quite happy.'

'I sense a desperation in you, a strange need to prove to yourself that only work is important and that people do not matter.'

'Perhaps I am not like the other girls. They have no need to find work when they leave here. I do.'

She raised her eyebrows slightly at my bluntness.

'When you first came here your mother made no mention of your needing to find employment. I admire your tenacity, but I would not like to think that you were sacrificing the friendship of other girls simply because they are not as ambitious as yourself.'

'No, Sister Hilda.'

'Work in this city is hard to come by, my dear, and those who do not have to work should not be too anxious to take it away from those who do. Make friends my dear, this should be a time of happiness for you to look back upon, life's problems overtake us whether we are ready for them or not.'

Her lecture both angered and distressed me, but I no longer spent so much time alone. I became a consummate actress, pretending a serenity I did not feel, but I stayed closer to the rest of them and always with a smile.

The late autumnal days grew cold. Susan and I spoke together now but the old camaraderie had gone. We no longer told each other secrets or laughed together over the vagaries of Marylee. Indeed the two girls now seemed very friendly together.

Marylee spoke to me on only one subject, and strangely enough it was religion. The Roman Catholic girls were celebrating a saint's day and I was curious so during the lunch hour I went into the chapel. I sat by myself at the back, listening to the music. The prayers were mostly said in Latin and I couldn't understand them. I felt for the first time the beauty and serenity, the mystical charm of the service as I looked at the rapt faces of the sisters and the devout bent heads of the girls, and when at last I slipped out of the chapel into the biting cold the charm and the warm glow were still with me.

Marylee and Susan were the first people I met as I reached the doors of the school and I was totally surprised when Marylee addressed me. 'I didn't know you were a Catholic.'

'I'm not.'

'But you were in the chapel.'

'Yes. It was beautiful.'

'You shouldn't be in there if you're not a Catholic. The Protestant girls never go in there, do they Susan?'

Susan shook her head but I could tell that she was embarrassed.

Marylee went on, 'We worship at St Margaret's where our parents worship, shouldn't you be doing the same?'

'My mother has found no church in Leeds and my stepfather worships money. Perhaps you can tell me where I can find a church that would be suitable for both of them.'

I turned my back on them, seething with anger. Religion was something that should draw people closer together, not tear them further apart.

One other incident stays in my mind, and that was the day I went with my mother to the shops in Leeds. I was standing at her side while she paid for something when I heard Susan's voice and saw her with her mother at the counter across the aisle.

They both smiled at me uncertainly as I went over to them. 'Good afternoon, Mrs Latchford,' I said quietly.

'Good afternoon, Tessa, are you alone?' she answered.

'No, I am with my mother,' and just then Mother left the counter and came to my side. I introduced them and Mother's charming smile enveloped them both. For a few moments the two women talked pleasantries while Susan and I merely looked on. My mother was the one to end the conversation by turning to me and saying, 'Come Tessa, it is growing late, if we don't pick up a cab now we shall find it very difficult later on.'

I had seen that surprise on the faces of other people at meeting a woman who had quality stamped all over her. People like the Latchfords had cut her dead because of her husband's misdemeanours but they could not fault her inherent air of breeding.

Life at home was far from tranquil. In Mrs Howlett's words, 'The honeymoon was finally over.'

My mother's tolerance of his habits was no longer evident. She found fault with his table manners, and his miserly approach to money both with her and with his workpeople. She disliked his friends and the doubtful plays and sleazy revues he relished. Now she no longer went to the theatre with him and very seldom to race meetings.

Her sarcasm stung him to foul language. She made him feel inadequate as a man and I knew that he was drinking heavily. He often kept her short of money and when he came in late his eyes were bleary and his speech slurred. I would pull the bedclothes over my head so that I didn't have to listen to their quarrelling and I knew by her cries that there were times when he struck her.

Mother too was drinking more than usual. I had never before seen her drink spirits but now in the evening she would often pour herself a glass of whisky and sometimes more than one. When I remonstrated with her she merely smiled, saying, 'It dulls one's senses, if one drinks enough of it.'

There were many times when she didn't come down to breakfast, and one morning Mrs Howlett said, 'Yer mother won't be down to breakfast, I saw 'er take the whisky bottle to bed an' 'ee didn't come 'ome at all last night.'

I glared at her, refusing to believe it, but when I went into Mother's bedroom she was sleeping heavily and the whisky bottle was empty.

That night our meal was a miserable affair. He sat glowering at his food while she talked airily to me about the curtains that hung dustily from the windows and the threadbare stair carpet. The food on our plates was burnt and uneatable and when Annie came in with the cheese the menacing atmosphere in the room made her so nervous she clattered the platter on to the table, then with a little cry she rushed from the room, leaving the door wide open.

Thoroughly exasperated, Mother cried, 'I'm tired of bad servants and badly cooked food. Those two will have to go, I can't tolerate them any longer.'

'They'll stay,' he growled at her. 'Unless you feel like soilin' your lily-white hands in the kitchen. If you want to get rid of Annie then that daughter of yours is going to have to do more. I don't see that that fancy convent education she's gettin 'll do her much good.'

'Never having had any education how could you?'

'But yer not ashamed to live on mi money in spite of mi lack of education. Where else would you be livin'? I'm tellin' you madam, Mrs Howlett stays. You can do what you like about Annie.'

He looked at me balefully and I wanted to run out of the room and keep on running until I didn't have to hear the sound of their voices ever again. Mother had provoked him but I could understand how she felt. She was tied irrevocably to this vulgar arrogant man who was now drinking his beer with great slobbering gulps and belching noisily.

He lurched to his feet. 'I shall be late, I'm going to the theatre.'

'I know which theatre,' she retorted, 'all Leeds is talking about that fourth-rate revue with its naked women and vulgar innuendos.'

'Ay well, if I didn't see the revue I'd a' forgotten what a naked woman looks like.'

With that remark he lurched out. Mother sat with glittering eyes and burning cheeks, while I looked down at my plate, my hands trembling on my knees.

Mrs Howlett came in to clear away and seeing the food congealing on the plates she said, 'Food not to yer likin' then.'

'No, Mrs Howlett, it isn't. The food is burnt and Annie has been particularly clumsy.'

'I'll talk to 'er,' Mrs Howlett snapped. 'Do yer want to get rid of 'er then?'

'Talk to her, Mrs Howlett, and please don't hit her. I suspect you do strike the girl from time to time.'

'Sometimes it's the only way ter make 'er 'eed me. I'd get more out of Annie if yer didn't keep givin' 'er things, Mrs Bryant, an' if Miss Tessa 'ere talked to 'er less. Givin 'er ideas, that's what yer both doin'.'

'You heard what she said, Tessa,' my mother said as soon as Mrs Howlett had gone. 'You had better stop treating Annie like a personal friend and I had better stop giving her things her family are badly in need of. One would have thought her aunt would have been pleased, after all Annie's mother is her sister.'

I didn't understand either. This terrible world with its boundaries of class, where even the poor set levels below which they were not prepared to go, nor let those below climb upwards. Joe Hardcastle had been more than competent when he had climbed out of his beginnings, he had been a magician.

Later that evening Mother sat in a big chair in front of the fire, gazing into the flames. Her face was pensive and she stared at me vaguely for a few moments.

'What were you thinking about? You were miles away,' I asked.

'I was thinking about Glamara.'

'Glamara!' I was surprised, for recently she never mentioned it at all. Why tonight of all nights did her thoughts return there?

With all my heart I longed for her to talk about Glamara and as if in answer she began, her voice so quiet I could hear the cinders falling on the hearth.

'In three weeks it will be Christmas, and I was thinking about those old lovely times at Glamara when the hall was gay with holly and I would wait until the very last moment before I ran down the stairs into the hall in my prettiest dress. There was always a crowd of laughing young men waiting to fill in my dance card.

'How we danced on those nights before Christmas when the park lay under its first carpet of snow. From the great windows in the drawing room, with the music from the ballroom filling the house, I would watch the long lines of carriages lumbering up the drive and there would be embraces and kissing and gaily wrapped packages thrust into our arms.

'Then on Christmas day after we had unwrapped our presents we would ride our horses across the fell or take sleighs into the villages where we would distribute food and drink to the tenants. Oh, I don't think I shall ever forget the sound of sleighbells or the sparkle in the eyes of those village people clustering around us.

'For years I have closed my heart and mind to Glamara, I have told myself constantly that I liked the new times better, the new glitter, the hurrying pace instead of the slow charm of the old days. I've been remembering long country twilights and cold frost-laden nights, the leaves turning red and gold on the beech trees in the park and primroses under the hedgerows in the early spring.

'I have always been my own worst enemy, Tessa, too headstrong, too spoilt. In those old days I listened to stories of city life and longed for its glamour. Now I see that glamour as a superficial thing and that the real glamour, the eternal glamour was the one I spurned. If tonight some great omnipotent God told me I could have the past back again, I *would* go back, except for one thing.'

'You would say no! But why?'

'Because of you, Tessa. Whatever wrongs I have done in my life you have given me so much joy, and you are young and warm and caring while Glamara is merely a heap of old stones.'

'Oh Mother,' I breathed, and knelt beside her chair. My heart felt dull with pain and weariness as I thought of the long road my mother had come.

For a long time that night I lay in my bed listening to the sounds outside: the clip-clop of horses' hooves, the barking of a dog and the sighing of night trains as they sped through the night. I was drifting into sleep when I heard laughter and women's voices below my window, and I hurried to peer out. Two carriages stood outside the house and men and women were alighting from them. There was much high-pitched chatter and loud laughter and I wondered what our neighbours were thinking of this outrageous behaviour in the middle of the night. They were walking up the path now, the men with their arms hugging the women, and I watched my stepfather following them, swaying up the path.

Then they were in the hall below, their voices echoing up the stairs. As I stood on the landing, doubtfully anxious, Mother's bedroom door was flung open and she stood there putting on her robe.

'Go back to bed, Tessa,' she said sharply. 'I will deal with this.'

Instead of going back to bed however I followed her at a distance down the stairs where she paused three steps from the bottom. I had never seen women like these, flashily dressed, the rouge standing out in great pink blobs on their cheeks. (I didn't know then that this was their stage make-up.) They had all been drinking. My stepfather was heading for the drawing room when he saw my mother on the stairs. He gave her a little bow, and to the company at large said, 'May I present my lady wife.'

One of the women giggled and one or two of the men looked slightly embarrassed, but my stepfather laughed uproariously, well pleased with his introduction.

'Come down and join us, mi dear,' he invited her, 'I know

125

you like your tipple, I've been measuring how fast mi whisky's bin disappearin' these last few weeks. But there's plenty more here, gin too if you likes that.'

'How dare you bring these people into my house?' she stormed. 'And at this hour. No wonder the neighbours refuse to speak to us. Get them out of here.'

'Get them out of *your* house,' he sneered. 'This is *my* house madam, and I'll ask you to remember it. Come and join us, you'll get an idea how real women behave.'

'If you don't remove those women at once I warn you I shall not be responsible for my actions.'

By this time Mrs Howlett and Annie had joined me on the landing, Annie with her eyes popping out of her head and Mrs Howlett with a smile of grim satisfaction.

For the first time I saw that my mother carried a riding crop and as Jack Bryant ushered them once more towards the drawing room she ran down and hit the nearest man across the side of his face.

The women started to scream and the man put his hand up to his face. My stepfather struggled to take the crop out of her hands whilst the others fled, leaving the door open. His face was convulsed with fury but so was hers. They stared at each other with hatred hanging like a spectre between them, then she turned and walked slowly up the stairs. With a howl of rage he came after her, pulled her round and brought her such a blow across her face that she fell senseless to the floor.

I rushed at him then, beating him with my inadequate fists while he cursed and swore as he struggled with my mother's body into the bedroom, then he dug his fingers into my shoulders and pushed me towards the door, slamming it behind me.

Annie stood at the bottom of the attic steps, her eyes starting from her head. Mrs Howlett had gone. I was shivering with vile anger and hatred, and I was frightened. Suppose he had killed her, suppose she was hurt so badly she needed a doctor? I slept no more that night but lay awake, listening. But all I could hear were his drunken snores.

CHAPTER ELEVEN

The following morning I waited till Jack Bryant had left the house before I went to see how Mother was. She lay on top of the bed with her eyes closed, looking as one dead, and I had to touch her to assure myself that she still breathed. She was cold, her breathing shallow, and where he had struck her there was a purple bruise. I pulled the eiderdown round her and rubbed her icy hands. She stirred, and in a soft voice I said, 'Mother it's Tessa, shall I call a doctor?'

She opened her eyes then and stared at me, but her expression was blank and it was several moments before recognition dawned.

'It's morning, isn't it Tessa?' She touched her face gingerly, and when I went to open the curtains she said, 'Leave them. The light hurts my eyes.'

'Let me go for the doctor, Mother, your face looks terrible.'

'No,' she said in a stronger voice. 'Bring me the witch hazel, my face will be better when I've bathed it. And I would like a cup of tea, Tessa.'

I ran to do her bidding. When I returned with the tea she was at the dressing table, looking at her face in the mirror. The dark ugly bruise looked worse and her eye was half closed.

'When did you say your Christmas party was to take place at St Clare's?' she asked me gently.

'The day after tomorrow.'

'You realize I won't be able to go looking like this, don't you Tessa?'

Disappointment flooded my entire being, to be followed by a deep hatred for Jack Bryant. I could have killed him at that moment. I never again in my life want to feel such a consuming, terrible hatred. I wished he was dead. I wished some accident would overtake him during the day so that I needn't set eyes on him again, and if he was dead then I would cheerfully dance on his grave.

'Have you had breakfast?' my mother asked.

'I'll only eat breakfast if you will join me.'

'There isn't time Tessa, you'll be late if you wait for me. I promise I'll eat something later, now do hurry dear and if Sister Hilda asks if I am going to the party tell her I am unwell.'

I muddled through my classes until lunchtime. I went to the library but couldn't concentrate on any book. I looked up impatiently when Marylee Nelson came in.

'Is your mother coming to the Christmas party?' she asked with a half smile.

'No, my mother is ill.'

'How unfortunate, but then it's hardly the sort of party she would enjoy anyway.'

I looked into her face, my eyes snapping dangerously. 'What exactly do you mean by that?'

'Well according to my father there was quite a party going on at your house last night. He passed it on his way home from his club. He said there was enough shouting and screaming to waken the whole neighbourhood and there was a crowd of painted women and several men coming from your house. Any party here would be tame by comparison.'

I sprang to my feet and shook her as hard as I could until her teeth chattered. When I released her she fell against one of the bookcases with a frightened cry. I turned to march out of the room, only to find Sister Hilda and the Mother Superior at the door.

'You will both come to my study at once,' the Reverend Mother said, and we had no choice but to follow.

She sat behind her desk with Sister Hilda standing beside her, and we were motioned to stand directly in front. I didn't look at Marylee again but I could hear her frightened sobs. I felt no emotion whatsoever, but I stood looking straight in front of me, uncontrite and impassive.

'That was disgraceful behaviour from two young ladies

128

who are about to take their place in the world of adults,' the Mother Superior said sternly. 'Whatever possessed you to attack Marylee, Tessa?'

I remained silent, staring above her head, and more urgently she said, 'I am waiting for your answer, Tessa.'

'Please, Reverend Mother, I would rather not say.'

'Then *you* shall tell me, Marylee. I saw Tessa attack you. What had you done or said to deserve it?'

'Why nothing, Reverend Mother, we were talking about the party tomorrow night.'

Marylee's voice was an appealing little girl's voice which might have disarmed a less discerning woman than the Mother Superior.

'There must have been something else, or why should she attack you?'

'I told her my father had seen a party going on at her house last night that was noisy, and there were a lot of people running about in the street.'

'And . . .'

'That her mother might find a party here too ordinary.'

'Marylee, it is no business of yours what sort of parties Mr Bryant wishes to have in his own home. Nor should you speculate on Mrs Bryant's taste in entertainment. On the other hand, Tessa, it was not necessary for you to shake Marylee.'

I accepted her rebuke with lowered head. She was right, but the Reverend Mother had not witnessed the scenes of last night or seen my mother's bruised face that morning.

'You may go,' she was telling us, 'but I want to see no more scenes, and in future, Marylee, do not provoke Tessa or any other of my girls with the sharpness of your tongue.'

We left her study and walked down the corridor together. Neither of us apologized. I had no regrets for what I had done and it would seem neither had Marylee. We were simply two girls who were never destined to be friends.

On the afternoon of the party I joined the others in decorating the hall with holly and streamers and setting up long tables which we covered with coloured paper. I had no heart for it. I didn't want to attend the party without my mother and by this time her poor face was a travesty of yellow and purple colour.

But she insisted.

'It's the only party you are likely to be invited to, Tessa, and you most certainly should go. Wear that lovely dress you wore for my wedding, nobody there will look so pretty.'

'But it's not that sort of a party mother, all the girls are just wearing their best winter dresses, I don't want to be overdressed.'

'Very well dear, wear the blue velvet, you look pretty in that.'

The blue velvet was a pretty dress, sapphire blue with a white lace collar and full, softly pleated skirt. There were lace ruffles at the wrists and when I wore it I always felt elegant and strangely adult. Mother insisted on hiring a cab to take me there.

The hall looked festive, and now the long tables were laden with food. Our music teacher was playing the piano, aided by an elderly gentleman playing the violin and a stout lady playing the cello. Some of the girls were dancing while others stood in happy groups chatting together. The parents sat round the hall balancing plates on their knees while the girls waited on them.

Sister Hilda came to me as soon as I had taken off my coat. 'Are you alone, Tessa?' she inquired, smiling.

'Yes, I'm afraid my mother wasn't well enough to come.'

'Well come along and I'll introduce you to some of the parents. After all you are my best pupil, you shouldn't go on hiding your light under a bushel.'

I blushed at this unaccustomed praise, gratified that she was taking the trouble to make me feel comfortable as we passed from group to group. I had not lived with my mother all these years without developing some of her charm, and I was determined to use it. I made myself respond to their smiles, their conversation, even their congratulations when Sister Hilda spoke of my academic accomplishments.

I joined in the country dancing and sang carols with the other girls, and we played musical chairs and party games where the parents were involved. Once I stood near a group of parents unobserved, and couldn't help hearing their conversation.

'What a beautiful girl Jack Bryant's stepdaughter is, and so charming,' one woman said as though she could hardly believe it.

'Yes, I must say I was surprised,' said another. 'Her dress must have cost a pretty penny and we all know what a reputation for meanness he has.'

'I should think the girl's mother has had a hand in that, she really is a very elegant woman, beautifully spoken and obviously upper class. How she ever came to marry that man I shall never understand.'

'Money, my dear.'

'I suppose Jack Bryant is educating the girl, it isn't cheap at St Clare's.'

'Well yes, that must be why she married him, and of course she never lived in Leeds before her marriage so she probably wasn't aware of what a bounder he is.'

'No, that must have come as a shock. They don't visit, you know, and I believe nobody visits them. It's him of course.'

'It seems a bit hard on her, and the daughter.'

'Well of course, but one couldn't really visit the Bryants.'

I had heard enough, I moved away slowly and escaped to the cloakroom where I picked up my coat and ran out into the frosty foggy air.

It was the first time in my life that I saw Christmas approaching without any feeling of joy. The shops in the city were filled with lovely things and tinsel and Christmas trees abounded, but not in the house across the park. When my mother suggested a tree my stepfather said they were a ridiculous extravagance, the needles would be all over the floor by the New Year and there was far too much fuss made about Christmas anyway.

When she asked him if there was anything special he would like he said, 'Since the money'll be comin out o' me anyway I'd prefer that you didn't bother.'

Mother and I had our own private party on Christmas Eve

and it was in his absence we exchanged our presents. He informed her he was going to his club and didn't expect to be home again that night.

'Is he really going to his club?' I asked in some surprise.

'To begin with perhaps, and then no doubt to some prostitute's house where he will be made welcome for the night.'

I stared at her dumbfounded. 'Don't you care?'

'Not in the least. She's welcome to him and in any case it means he makes fewer demands on me.'

He arrived home at noon on Christmas Day and went immediately to bed where he stayed until it was time for dinner. When he came downstairs he seemed more affable than of late and actually produced a bottle of burgundy to drink with our meal. The traditional turkey was served and for once the vegetables were properly cooked. My mother complimented Mrs Howlett on the excellence of the meal and went herself into the kitchen where she packed a large basket for Annie to take home. In it she put nuts and chocolates, dates and tangerines as well as several warm woollen scarves for her family, and Annie departed with that rare smile that made her face seem suddenly pretty.

Mrs Howlett's face blushed bright scarlet when my mother handed her a brightly wrapped package containing a pale pink bed-jacket edged with swansdown, and she stammered her thanks, obviously painfully embarrassed.

'I wonder if he ever gave her Christmas presents before we came?' I mused as we went into the drawing room.

'I shouldn't think so, money perhaps, but he doesn't have the insight to buy a present a woman would appreciate.'

'But he bought you presents, Mother, some of them quite beautiful.'

'Yes, and I always chose them. I could never rely on Jack's taste.'

He joined us in the drawing room on Christmas night, smoking a fat cigar and with a well filled glass of brandy. I sat with my head buried in a book while my mother worked on a tapestry firescreen.

'What's that you're doing?' he asked her curiously.

'A firescreen for the dining room.'

'What do we want that for?'

'For the summer when we shan't be burning a fire. There is nothing worse than a staring empty grate every time we sit down to a meal.'

He offered no further comment and it was several minutes before he spoke again, cheerfully, and evidently in high good humour.

'We shan't be here over the New Year, we've been invited to spend a few days at the Hardcastle place.'

My heart leapt with sudden joy and my eyes were shining as I looked up at him waiting for his next words.

As for my mother she put the tapestry down and stared at him in surprise. 'When did they invite us?'

'Last Wednesday in Bradford when I saw Joe comin' out of the Wool Exchange. Four days we're invited for, you and me and that girl of yours.'

'That is very civil of the Hardcastles, I take it Mrs Hardcastle has endorsed the invitation?'

'I reckon so, but it's enough if Joe's invited us. The day before New Year's Eve we're invited for until January second. You'll pack your best clothes because there's to be a dance on New Year's Eve and there'll be gentry there.

'I should take your riding habit too, there's a hunt meeting on New Year's mornin', Joe's ridin' and so is that lad of 'is.'

'It's a long time since I've been on a horse, I'm not sure I'm up to it these days.'

'Then you must make yerself feel up to it. I've told him you'll ride.'

Her eyes had narrowed and she was staring at him curiously, until he began to look uncomfortable, averting his eyes to stare into the fire.

'Why is it suddenly so important that I should ride on New Year's Day?' she asked him steadily. 'What exactly did you say to Joe Hardcastle.'

'He's got a new horse, a right beauty and up to now nobody's ridden him. He happened to say he wished you were back in the West Riding, you'd have showed him how to ride Jupiter.'

'He's expecting me to ride a horse nobody's ridden before?'

'Now then, stop getting excited. Naturally the horse has been ridden, but he's not bin hunted over moorland before. I told him you'd be glad to ride him.'

'Did you indeed? You had no right to tell him that. I shall need to see the horse myself before I agree to it. Is he expecting Tessa to ride also?'

'She wasn't mentioned, except to say that we could take her with us.'

My mother looked at me curiously. 'Do you want to go, Tessa?'

'Oh yes Mother, so very much. You know how I love the country and I would like to see Alec and all the other friends we had there.'

'I hadn't thought we were too well blessed with friends in the country?'

'But we were. There were the Elliotts and the blacksmith and Ned, besides I'd like to see Alec and his sisters again, all the Hardcastles in fact.'

'Very well then, we'll go.'

'It's evident you're more concerned with pleasin' that lass of yours than pleasin' me or the Hardcastles.'

'I want to please us all. A few days in the country will be very nice if the weather stays decent. January can be treacherous in the fells but perhaps you are not aware of it.'

'No. While you were actin' the fine lady in that great house you're so fond of talkin' about I were walkin' behind mi father on the factory floor learnin' how to work a loom an' keep an eye on the weavers.'

For once I didn't care about the sarcasm in their voices or the antagonism that distanced them irrevocably. We were going back to the stark hills and the misted moors, to trickling waterfalls and clear bubbling rivers, to forests of dark evergreens and white scudding clouds. Instead of chattering sparrows there would be the lonely call of the curlew and wild geese. We were going back to slow country voices and people as staunch and rugged as the rocky crags around which they lived, and I would see Alec again and

Briarcrag. If I could not have Glamara, Briarcrag was better than nothing.

CHAPTER TWELVE

Our train was met at the country station and we travelled up to the house in a smartly turned-out trap. My eyes devoured the moors and hills above the village, and as we passed Mrs Elliott's cottage I could see the play of firelight on the walls and a tiny Christmas tree decorated with silver balls and tinsel.

Nothing seemed to have changed, and I wondered, if I should come back in fifty years time, would it still remain the same? The pony trotted briskly up the lane and soon we were entering the gates leading to Briarcrag.

My mother looked steadily in front of her and in the strong light I could still see the fading bruise at the side of her face. She had tried to cover it with cream and powder but had not been completely successful.

The Hardcastles came into the hall to greet us and immediately Alec was at my side looking at me with a new awareness.

'Gosh you have grown up,' he said admiringly, 'you're hardly a schoolgirl any more.'

He too had grown tall and he had filled out surprisingly. Now I only came to his shoulder.

Servants came forward to take our coats but Alec said, 'Do you mind if Tessa and I have a walk round the estate? It's so long since she's seen it.'

His mother seemed to give her grudging consent, but then we were out in the gardens walking quickly towards the gates.

'Have you made many changes?' I asked him curiously.

'Well, the lodge house is occupied by father's new estate agent, and we've acquired several new servants, and much of the house has been knocked down and rebuilt. Every time I come home something has changed, I feel I can't keep pace.'

'But you didn't whisk me out here to tell me of these changes.'

'Well no, not entirely. In any case you'll soon see them for yourself. I'm in the dog house, Tessa. I finally told Father that I want to go to Sandhurst instead of the mills and of course he's furious. I've had it all over Christmas, how he's worked his fingers to the bone to give me the best possible start in life. How he's built up a fine healthy business so that I won't have to struggle like he had to struggle, and for what, so that I can join some fancy regiment then go to some benighted spot occupied by savages to get shot at. I once heard *you* say something very like that.'

'Yes, that's true.'

'Do you still think it's foolish of me?'

'I can see your father's point of view, but I can see yours too. You didn't ask to be a mill owner, you didn't ask to have your future planned for you and handed over like a dead fish on a platter. Couldn't you go into the army for a few years, say until your father didn't want to work in the business any longer? Would it be too late to come back into the factories then?'

'Perhaps I'll never get the army out of my system, it's all I've ever wanted. Gosh Tessa, I shouldn't be telling you all this now, but you're sure to notice the coldness between us and wonder what's wrong.'

'I'm glad you told me, Alec.'

'Are you riding tomorrow?'

'I don't think so. My stepfather didn't mention it and Mother wasn't sure if there would be a mount for me.'

'There's only old Ginger and he's getting a bit past hunting. Do you want to see Jupiter? He's a beauty. Father bought him to ride himself, now he's not so sure he's up to it. I think that's why he'd like your mother to ride him.'

I greeted old Ginger and the other horses I had known with affection, particularly the pony on which I had once won my point-to-point race and which was now ridden by Alec's youngest sister.

Jupiter was indeed a beautiful animal, pale beige with a black mane and tail. He refused to come to the stable door to be patted and stood pawing the ground. When Alec held out some little tit-bit he merely shied further away, glowering at us through his ridiculously long eyelashes.

'He's beautiful,' I admitted, but looking at the horse with his hostile eyes and trembling flanks, such a feeling of foreboding took hold of me that I turned away shivering.

'What is it, Tessa?' Alec asked, 'surely you're not afraid of him.'

'He doesn't like us, Alec, and I'm not so sure that I like him. Did your father receive advice when he bought him?'

'I'm not sure. He's learnt a lot in the past few years. I'm sure he knew what he was about when he bought Jupiter.'

Alec's voice was slightly resentful and I was wishing I hadn't posed that question when he said, 'When your mother sees him she will know immediately if she's going to be able to manage him.'

'Yes I suppose so,' I mumbled. I wasn't at all happy about the arrangement and I hoped my mother would see him today while he was in this particular mood. As we stood outside the stables I looked around at the bleak winter's landscape, breathing in the sharp frost-laden air appreciatively.

'Oh Alec, how I have missed all this,' I cried emotionally. 'Now in just four days I have to see as much as I can of it, I don't know how long the memories will have to last.'

He pointed to where the hills lay shrouded in mist against the winter sky and even as he spoke the dark purple clouds were thickening on Great Whernside and below the mass of cloud streaks of grey dragged downward, denoting rain.

'Do you want to go back, Tessa?'

'I'd rather walk a little while if you don't mind. Tomorrow we may not have the chance.'

He turned obligingly and hand in hand we walked towards the moors, climbing with the wind in our hair and our cheeks rosy and smarting in the first bluster of icy rain sweeping down from the hills.

'Oh Alec, don't you just love it,' I cried. I started to run to where from the top of the rise we could see down the entire valley with Great Whernside frowning omnipotently above us like a silent god with his grey and purple hair swirling around his shoulders.

Laughing, Alec caught me up and we stood together laughing in the wind until suddenly he put his arms around me and held me close, then he was kissing me, gently at first, and then with mounting passion.

I was not ready for passion. Alec was my good friend, my confidant, and as yet I only loved him with a girl's first tentative gentleness. At first I responded to the warmth of his ardour and then when I felt his thick boyish body become hard and taut against me I became afraid and struggled to be free.

'Why, Tessa, why?' he murmured against my hair, his voice thick and choked. 'I love you, I've always loved you. One day I shall marry you but it's years away. I want you now, please Tessa, don't be frightened, you know I love you.'

He was unbuttoning my coat, fumbling with the buttons on my blouse, and suddenly I became strong, pushing him away, afraid of his hungry eyes and clumsy fingers. With a great wrench I was suddenly free and taking to my heels I ran down the hill as fast as my legs would carry me, my hair released from its ribbon and streaming behind me. I heard him running after me as I reached the path.

'Tessa, please wait,' he gasped. 'Don't be angry.'

He reached my side, his eyes anxious, uncertain, and in answer to the appeal in them I said, 'I'm not angry Alec, I think we should go back to the house, that's all.'

We walked in silence and eventually he reached for my hand and held it trembling in his own. I allowed it to remain there and, reassured that we were still friends, he said, 'I do love you Tessa, one day I'll prove it.'

He had pulled me round to face him and although we were now in full view of the house he stared down into my face, his boy's face gravely sincere, pleading with me to have faith in his promises.

'I mean it Tessa, one day I'll marry you. There'll never be anybody else for me ever.'

'We're too young to make promises that time may not allow us to keep, Alec.'

'Time won't alter the way I feel about you. Why don't you believe me?'

'I do believe you mean it now Alec, but how do either of us know who we might meet in the future? You will be going to university or Sandhurst, there'll be other girls, sisters of your friends perhaps. Why don't we just wait and see what happens?'

'Oh we'll wait, we'll have to wait, but I shan't change my mind. I've always known what I want. I shan't change my mind about the army and I shan't change my mind about you.'

How stern and severe his young face looked at that moment. I knew that he meant every word he was saying and I felt strangely moved and comforted by his sincerity, then, as I turned away, I saw his mother watching us from the drawing room and I hurried towards the house.

She looked at us unsmiling as we entered the room and my mother too stared, first at Mrs Hardcastle and then at us standing blushing and windblown in the doorway.

When I was dressing for dinner Mother came into my room, closing the door sharply behind her so that I looked up at her uncertainly.

'You were out with Alec a long time this afternoon, Tessa, I think his mother was becoming anxious,' she said, staring at me curiously.

'There was no need for her to be anxious, we went to look at the horses and then we climbed the fell until it started to rain.'

'I told you before, Tessa, you are too young to be in love with Alec Hardcastle, too young and too artless.'

My eyes met hers through the dressing table mirror and I recognized the concern in them. 'Are you in love with him?' she persisted.

'I don't know, Mother. He told me he loves me, that one day he wants to marry me, but it is all so long away and many things could happen.'

'Well of course they could. He will meet other girls, and I

know for a fact his mother would like him to marry well. I don't think she was very pleased you were out together so long this afternoon.'

'I thought when you married Mr Bryant it was so that I would meet boys like Alec, that his money would open doors otherwise closed to me. You did say that, Mother.'

A spasm of pain crossed her face and I wished I could have bitten off my tongue.

'I believed those words when I said them Tessa, now I know how terribly untrue they were.'

'Why are they untrue? You taught Mrs Hardcastle how to speak and behave, how to be a lady, and now you say she might not care for Alec to fall in love with me. It's farcical.'

'Yes it's farcical, but it is a fact of life. Madge Hardcastle would like to see her only son married to one of those little ninnies she regards as gentry, not Jack Bryant's step-daughter. She made it very plain before we were married what she thought of him.'

'And she wouldn't have wanted him to marry me before I was Jack Bryant's stepdaughter because she looked upon you as a servant. That is the case, isn't it, Mother?'

My words were lashing both of us. The pain in her eyes mirrored the pain in my heart and then gently she said, 'Show them that you know how to conduct yourself, Tessa, that you are my daughter, and a Chalfont.'

I was never more aware of her proud, beautiful face, then abruptly she turned and walked swiftly towards the wardrobe, where she took out the gown I had worn for her wedding.

'I would like you to wear this, Tessa, it was expensive and it looks expensive. Would you like me to put up your hair?'

'You said I was too young.'

'For the convent yes, but tonight I think we might try it.'

She brushed it with a pad of silk she brought from her bedroom and I refrained from looking in the mirror until she stepped back to look at her handiwork, then she smiled, well satisfied.

'However many girls Alec Hardcastle meets in the years to

come he will find none more enchanting than you,' she said proudly.

I stared with amazement at the vision that confronted me. The graceful folds of the gown gave a new maturity to the blossoming curves of my figure, and the shining crown of my pale hair gave me added height. I might not possess the vivid beauty of my mother but there was beauty in the pale oval of my face and the gentle curve of my mouth. My eyes too shone with a strange new luminosity, blue-grey eyes, their dark lashes tipped with gold.

Suddenly I flung my arms around her until she cried out with pretended objection, 'Darling, you're crushing my gown.'

I released her and for the first time saw that she was wearing a gown I had always admired. It was jade, the colour that suited her colouring more than any other, and around her throat was a fine gold chain with one perfect emerald.

'I've never seen the emerald before,' I said curiously.

'It was my father's gift to me when I was twenty-one, the only thing I never allowed Nigel Lorival to get his hands on.'

I took the stone in my hand and turned it so that the light caught it and it seemed to glow with shafts of several shades of vivid green.

'One day it will be yours, Tessa, but you have my permission to part with it if you should ever need to.'

'I shall never part with it, Mother, never.'

She smiled a little sadly. 'Oh to be so young and so sure, darling.'

I couldn't help but be aware of the stir our walk down the staircase caused in the people gathered below. I saw Alec's eyes light up with pleasure and with my mother's hand grasping mine tightly I met those staring eyes and subtle whispers with all her unconcern.

Alec was dancing with his sister Joan, who was looking very grown up with her dark hair taken back from her face and held by a large watered silk bow to match her yellow dress.

I found Susy huddled on the bottom step of the staircase

staring disconsolately at the dancers, so I sank down beside her. She turned towards me with a scowl on her pretty face, and I was prompted to ask, 'Aren't you enjoying yourself, Susy?'

'Of course not. I didn't want to come, and nobody, just nobody is going to dance with me in this silly dress. Just look at it, it's awful.'

She spun round on her new dance slippers so that the white voile dress swirled above her ankles. It was a pretty dress with a broad blue sash to match the ribbon in her hair and the bows on the tiny sleeves. But it emphasized Mrs Hardcastle's taste, and her wish to keep her youngest daughter a child as long as possible.

'The boys look at me as though they think I'm too young to dance, and they're dancing with girls younger than me,' she complained. 'It's this wretched dress, I told my mother how much I hated it.'

'Alec and Joan are coming back, I'm sure Alec will dance with you.'

'He's my *brother*, for heaven's sake. You'll see, nobody else will ask me.'

With a toss of her head she ran quickly up the stairs, and Joan followed her.

'I'll bring her back,' she said to Alec, 'but you have to promise to dance with her.'

'Must I?'

'Well of course, Mother would be furious if you didn't.'

Unabashed, Alec pulled me on to the floor to dance.

My mother was dancing in the arms of the hunt master, Colonel Jeffries, favouring us with a bright smile as we danced close by. Alec's mother sat in a stiff-backed chair and although I felt her eyes upon us I deliberately averted my eyes.

My mother was charming to old acquaintances from whom she had once been estranged. She was gracious and poised and they were not proof against her serenity. She danced several times with Hugh Mallory and I couldn't help wondering what they were talking about and what they found to laugh about but I did not see my stepfather in the

142

ballroom until much later, when he stood near the door watching my mother with narrowed eyes and a strange expression that made me suddenly feel cold.

Later, as we stood at the buffet table, the talk turned to horses.

Hugh Mallory's voice raised above the rest, saying, 'So you're here to ride Jupiter, Diana? You can't be aware that the horse is pure vice.'

A sudden hush descended on the room which Joe Hardcastle hastened to break by urging those present to empty their glasses: there was plenty more.

'What does he mean?' I whispered urgently to Alec. 'Has he tried to ride Jupiter?'

'I don't know. My father always said he wanted your mother to ride Jupiter first.'

'Then why does Hugh Mallory know so much about him?'

'Honestly Tessa, I don't know.'

The question was answered for me when my mother said, 'If you know so much about the horse why don't you ride him yourself?'

'Not likely, my girl. I told Hardcastle if anybody could ride him you could, but I think too much about my skin to ride that devil.'

I pulled away from Alec sharply and in spite of all those present I cried, 'Don't ride him, Mother, he's highly strung and nervous.'

'You see,' Hugh Mallory said with a half-taunting smile. 'Out of the mouth of babes and sucklings comes a great deal of sense.'

'I shall take a good look at him in the morning before I decide whether to ride him,' she said.

'But it's not as simple as that, is it Hardcastle?' Hugh Mallory persisted. 'Didn't I hear something about a gentleman's wager and isn't there a substantial sum hanging on it?'

'A wager!' my mother cried sharply. 'What's this?'

Hugh Mallory's face took on an air of surprise which I felt sure was entirely feigned, while Joe Hardcastle looked uncomfortable and Mrs Hardcastle looked at him sharply, her face burning with colour. Another voice rang out and I turned to see my stepfather in the doorway, his face flushed and angry.

'You stand to gain as much as I do from that wager, Mallory,' he said, 'I should have thought you'd 'ave kept your mouth shut.'

Before Mallory could answer him Mrs Hardcastle stepped forward to face my stepfather and in a voice that all could hear said, 'If you men haven't any more sense than to wager money on a stupid horse and whether anybody's fit to ride him then that's up to you, but it's not going to spoil my party. Really Mr Mallory, I'm surprised that you thought fit to mention the subject at all in front of Mrs Bryant.'

'I beg your pardon Mrs Hardcastle, and yours too Mrs Bryant,' he said with a half-smile. 'Perhaps it would be better if I withdrew altogether from these proceedings.'

'There's no need for that if you promise to mend your manners.'

'I always thought my manners were adequate for the society I moved amongst.'

'You're an arrogant bastard,' Joe Hardcastle thundered at him. 'I think your room would be preferable to your company, but that's no reflection on you ma'am,' he said with a little bow in Mrs Mallory's direction.

Hugh Mallory strode towards the door where he waited, holding it open and looking at his wife, expecting her to leave with him. I felt sorry for her. She was very pale as she moved towards the door, turning to speak to Mrs Hardcastle as she went. There was a long silence after the door had closed behind them, then the talk was louder as though by its clamour the memory of the last few minutes could be erased.

My mother too was pale, her eyes strangely green and glittering as she strove to talk normally to those around her.

'Alec,' I said, pulling him to one side. 'I don't want my mother to ride Jupiter, I'm frightened.'

Alec's face was anxious as he looked towards my mother, who stood with her husband and his parents. They were speaking quietly but the conversation was not an amicable one. I saw my mother nod briefly to the Hardcastles then she walked quickly across the hall with a set pale face and ran quickly up the stairs.

I hurried after her, and those in my path parted quickly to make room for my flying feet. I found her pacing her bedroom, her face a white mask, green eyes glittering balefully.

She said sharply, 'I prefer to be left alone just now.'

'Mother, you *can't* ride that horse. I saw him this afternoon, he's wild and mean. What does it matter about their silly wager?'

Before she could answer, my stepfather came in. 'I'll thank you to keep out of this, young woman,' he said gruffly. 'It has nothing to do with you.'

'She's my mother.'

'And she's my wife so why don't you go back downstairs and leave matters alone?'

'I'm not going anywhere until I know what you're asking her to do.'

'I'm asking her to ride that horse and save me from losing more than I can afford.'

'How dare you make my mother the subject of a wager?' I stormed.

But Mother sat down calmly before the dessing table and said, '*I'd* like to know about that wager. I swear it, I won't ride that horse a yard until you've told me everything about that wager with Hugh Mallory.'

'There's not much to tell.'

'Then it will be of little consequence whether I ride him or not.'

'It was during that weekend when I came up here to play cards. Hardcastle had just bought the horse. Mallory took him out and got thrown over a hedge twice for his pains. Later we started talking about who could ride him and Major Goodchild said nobody could. Mallory said *you* could ride him. We'd all been drinking pretty heavily during the evening, and Goodchild, Mather and Linwood wagered against Mallory, Hardcastle and myself. If you don't ride him I stand to lose thirty thousand pounds.'

'Thirty thousand pounds!'

'If I lose I'll be in queer street, I can tell you.'

'You fool, Jack, you silly, *stupid* fool! Don't you see they were goading you into this because they know you're all talk and no substance?'

'If you don't ride him I stand to lose more than the money. The house will have to go for one thing. The mills haven't been doing well for years now, there's too much competition, and I've been selling shares for months. Number two mill'll have to go and there'll be a lot of talk.'

'And if you win the wager?'

'It'll pay my debts and we could probably move into one of those better areas you've been wanting ever since you married me. Mallory's a brute with his horses, he probably rode the horse badly.'

'How much does Joe Hardcastle stand to lose if I don't ride him?'

'The same as me. It's enough to make Madge leave him if he loses that much. He's always made the money but she's been at the back of him.'

Wearily Mother turned and started to take off her jewellery and catching sight of the emerald round her neck my stepfather snapped, 'That's worth a bob or two, I suppose some man gave it to you.'

'Of course, I wouldn't buy emeralds for myself,' she said with a cynical smile, and I knew she had not the least intention of telling him that it was a gift from her father.

'You didn't have it when I married you,' he accused angrily.

'I've had it for years. Why should I show you my possessions?'

He stared at her sullenly through the mirror and I shivered at the hostility that flared between them. I knew how he chafed with impatience as she dropped her jewellery into her casket and carefully locked it; then in the same unhurried fashion she slipped out of her gown and sauntered into the dressing room. We waited in silence, and she did not hurry. I longed, as he must have longed, to go into the dressing room and demand an answer from her.

At last she came back wearing her robe and with her bright

hair brushed loosely round her shoulders.

'The Hardcastles are holding a party for us,' he said angrily, 'the least you can do is to attend.'

'That is nonsense and you know it. The Hardcastles invited us because thirty thousand pounds rests on my riding Jupiter tomorrow. But for this stupid wager we would never have been invited.'

'People will want to know where you are, what shall I tell them?'

'You can tell them I have gone to bed. I need to prepare myself for tomorrow's ordeal.'

He watched her slide between the sheets, arranging her pillows with unhurried grace, finding her place in her book with maddening delay then settling down to read as though neither of us existed.

Thoroughly exasperated he snapped, 'Well. Are you going to tell me what you've decided?'

She looked up with some distaste. 'I've already told you. I will look at the horse in the morning. Now please, both of you, leave me in peace.'

He marched ahead of me down the stairs while I paused uncertainly, wondering if I should go in search of Alec who might offer some degree of comfort. I found him watching the festivities with a sulky frown. I took my place beside him and all at once the frown was gone and he was smiling again, inviting me to dance when I had never felt less like dancing.

I had no doubt that Mother would ride Jupiter. She knew that they could not afford to lose thirty thousand pounds but she was making Jack wait for her answer, making him suffer in the only way she could for his part in that stupid wager.

When I awoke the house was already astir with voices and footsteps along the passages.

It was a cold grey morning with the mist hanging heavily, but not too dense to disguise the ice which filled the puddles. I wished with all my heart that the fog would come down so densely that the hunt committee would decide it was unfit to ride.

I dressed in a warm tweed skirt and sweater. I intended to follow them on foot as so many others did when they had no mount. By taking part in even this small way I would somehow be keeping as close as possible to my mother. My stepfather did not ride and he was no walker, so cynically I thought he would occupy his time in drinking Joe Hardcastle's whisky until he heard the riders returning across the fields, living in anticipation that his wager had been won.

Breakfast was a silent meal with Mrs Hardcastle's face grim and uncompromising and her husband unusually glum. As an official of the hunt he was wearing the bright pink coat to which he was entitled, but he had neither the looks nor the figure of a horseman. His red face vied with the colour of his coat and he was too corpulent to do justice to it. Mother on the other hand looked completely elegant in her black riding habit, her dark red hair shining above the white lace ruffles on her blouse. She too was unusually silent, neither speaking to the Hardcastles nor my stepfather.

She smiled at my anxious face. 'If you like, Tessa, you can walk down to the stables with me and we will decide together if Jupiter is fit to be ridden.'

My stepfather scowled and even Joe Hardcastle permitted himself a troubled look in his wife's direction. Alec, like me, remained silent throughout the meal and none of us seemed to have much of an appetite.

Mother admonished me: 'Don't go tramping over the fields with the rest of them. Keep to the road if you must go down to the meet.'

'I wish you wouldn't ride him, Mother, I'm afraid for you.'

'My dear child, we can't afford to lose thirty thousand pounds. I shall mount him and ride him to settle the bet, but if I find he is playing up then I shall give up the chase and return on foot. I don't intend to break my neck.'

To my relief Jupiter, standing with the other mounts in the stableyard, appeared docile, even indifferent – unlike Blackamoor who was bucking impatiently as the groom walked him round.

Mother smiled at Joe Hardcastle. 'Perhaps you would

have stood to win twice as much if you had wagered on Blackamoor also. Are you quite sure you can ride him?'

There was sarcasm in her voice and fear in Joe Hardcastle's eyes, but my stepfather appeared well content. 'There you are,' he told her, 'the horse is docile enough this morning, I don't know why Mallory made all that fuss.'

'Hugh Mallory knows about horses,' she said quietly, 'you know nothing about them, which is why you were ill advised to place a bet.'

'Well no doubt you will remind me of my stupidity for ever more,' he snapped back.

Jupiter stood quiet while she mounted him, gracefully and unruffled as always. Joe Hardcastle had considerably more trouble with Blackamoor and set off in fits and starts, his face red with exertion, while my mother and Alec followed on more decorously. Joan's mount had injured his foot so she could not ride after all, nor did she seem upset in view of the mist and icy winds.

When we reached the village inn where the hunt met we could see that it was indeed a fair turnout. Hugh Mallory and his wife were both riding and there were others of our old acquaintances. Soon they were riding off along the road, the huntsman in front with the hounds trotting enthusiastically round him, eyes bright, tails carried proudly.

I hurried behind but it was so misty out there on the fell that I could single out no particular horse and rider. Soon they were swallowed up by the mist and I could follow them only by the baying of the hounds and the huntsman's horn.

My mother had asked me to stay on the road but the moors beckoned me as they always had, whatever my mood.

Today it was anxiety that drove me through the mist and across the frozen burns. At times I could recognize a farm or great house when the mist lifted and then the next moment it had come down again and all I could see were low stone walls and frozen hedgerows. Even as I stood peering the mist began to lift and I could see the rugged crags and the summit of Whernside.

There was no sign of the riders, the fell was empty and lonely. I knew I must go back. I had no way of knowing which way they had gone and I could hear nothing but the dismal cry of gulls.

I could see the village below me and the road where it climbed up to one of the farms set high above the tarn. I set off in that direction and soon found the bridle path that led to the village. The anxiety was still there. I wished the day was over, that it was the next day and we were in the train speeding back towards the city. At least I would know that my mother was safe.

I became aware of a solitary rider hurtling down the meadowland at breakneck speed – Alec, urging his horse ever faster. They were almost upon me before he saw me, pulling his horse up so sharply that it reared above me, whinnying shrilly in protest.

I knew that something was wrong, compassion, dread and fear were in his eyes, and I snatched at the bridle. 'It's my mother, isn't it? Where is she?'

'I must get help Tessa, stay here. I'll be back as quick as I can.'

'Where *is* she?'

'You'll never find her on foot. Wait for me.'

Brutally he wrenched the bridle from my grasp and took off down the hill, his horse steaming, its hooves throwing up great clods of frozen earth.

I waited with my heart thudding against my ribs, my eyes trained on the village where Alec had gone. Then I saw men with a horse-drawn cart leaving the village, while Alec raced back towards me.

He helped me, hampered by my long skirts, to clamber up behind him, and I held on to him for dear life, on a horse that was plainly spent.

Now when I think back on that journey I find I can remember nothing about the fell on which we found her or of the route we took to reach it.

We dismounted at a break in a fence and climbed through. I did not see her at first because the brambles and the bracken were so dense and it was only when Alec pulled me down a steep bank towards the frozen stream that I saw her lying in the undergrowth, her dark red hair vying with last summer's gold.

There was no sign of her horse. She lay on her side, her head twisted strangely, her face hidden as though she had tried to protect it from his flying hooves.

I ran to her, calling, finding her chilled hands, willing her to turn her head and look at me, but she lay quite still on the frozen ground. Alec knelt by me, his face tense and afraid.

'She isn't dead is she Alec? Oh please don't let her be dead!'

The tears rolled uncontrollably down my face and splashed on to her cold hands.

'We mustn't move her, Tessa. The men will bring the cart as near as they can and the doctor will be with them. They can't be long.'

'I can't see her breathing!'

'Don't panic, Tessa, it's difficult to see anything, the way she is lying.'

'Oh why don't they come? Suppose the doctor isn't there.'

'He'll be here.'

'What happened?'

'I was riding with her and suddenly Jupiter veered away. He was trying to unseat her. I thought she had him under control but then he started rearing up and took off like the wind towards the dell here.'

'And the rest of them just rode on, I suppose?'

'They didn't know she was in difficulties. I couldn't believe it myself, one minute they were so perfect together then it was just as though some devil took possession of him.'

We heard voices, then they were standing above us, a small group of men with strained faces, clutching their caps in gnarled rough hands, and the doctor was bending down to examine her.

I saw her face then, devoid of all colour except for a bruise at her temple, her eyes closed, the long lashes making dark crescents against her white cheeks.

I watched him with a desperation that made me feel sick and faint and when his eyes at last met mine he shook his head. His eyes saddened with sympathy at my scream of anguish, Alec put his arms around me and held me trembling while those rough hands lifted her on to the cart.

For two days I lived in a nightmare of pain. I too wanted to die. The one person that I had truly loved had gone and I couldn't believe that I would never see her again, hear her voice or join in her laughter.

It was Alec who told me about the inquest and who pleaded with me to eat, Alec who finally shook me out of my apathy by saying, 'If you go on like this Tessa you are not going to be able to attend your mother's funeral.'

That got through to me as nothing else had done, and that night I went down to dinner, no longer a girl but a woman with my youth for ever behind me and my future shrouded.

There was silence as I entered the dining room until Mrs Hardcastle rose hurriedly and came to put her arms around me.

'Sit here, Tessa, and get some food into you, you look like a ghost,' she admonished.

I accepted the food mechanically but it tasted of nothing.

My stepfather avoided looking at me and Mr Hardcastle ate his meal because it was there rather than because he was hungry.

When I finally found my voice I asked, 'When is my mother's funeral to take place?'

'On Saturday,' Mrs Hardcastle answered me, 'in Leeds.'

'Leeds! Why can't she be buried here in the country?'

'I have a family vault in Leeds,' my stepfather replied. 'Both my parents are interred there and I want my wife put there as well.'

I bit my lip but remained silent. I hated to think that my mother would be laid to rest with his parents but I would have no say in the matter, and as if she sensed my chagrin Mrs Hardcastle said briskly, 'If we've all finished we'll have coffee in the drawing room.'

We took our places in the drawing room and Mrs Hardcastle, leaning towards me, said, 'I've packed your mother's clothes and you can take them back to Leeds when you go the day after tomorrow. I don't think I've left anything out.'

'Perhaps you'll come to stay some other time when things are back to normal.'

'Thank you,' I murmured.

'What will you do now? Will you be all right in Jack Bryant's house without your mother?'

'I don't know, Mrs Hardcastle, I shall need time to think about it.'

'Yes of course. You know me and Joe'll give you any help you need.'

I nodded. I didn't want to discuss my future with her. She meant to be kind I felt sure, but my future was something I wanted to think about alone and unaided.

'If you want to see your mother she's in the church, Tessa. She looks very beautiful, as lovely as she did in life.'

'I think I would rather remember her as she was in life.'

'You don't want to look at her!'

'No.' My voice was sharp, filled with a strange resentment. Couldn't she understand that it was not my mother lying still and alone in the church? The vibrant being who had embraced life with such devastating fervour had gone.

She was staring at me in disbelief, but I was saved from further embarrassment by the arrival of Hugh Mallory. He took his place beside me, saying, 'I did my best to warn her, Tessa. The brute did the same thing with me. Just when I thought we were doing splendidly he seemed to go mad, as though some devil had got into him and I couldn't hold him.'

'And yet you wagered that she would be able to ride him, Mr Mallory.'

The warm red blood suffused his face and looking down at his hands he muttered, 'Yes, God help me, I did. I was drunk that night, and angry with the brute. How could I have known that it would come to this?'

'I had the horse shot when they brought him back,' Joe Hardcastle said, as though that deed of revenge would exonerate them all.

I felt nothing. The killing of that beautiful creature would not bring back my mother, nor did it erase their guilt.

As soon as it was possible I excused myself, saying I had things to do. I felt certain the rest of them would feel relief at my absence.

My bedroom felt cold. I do not know how long I had been lying sleepless when I heard a gentle tap on the door. The room was flooded with moonlight so that I could find my way easily to the door which I opened only a few inches to see who stood there, surprised to find it was Alec in his dressing gown, his eyes gentle and searching.

'Are you all right Tessa?'

Although he spoke in a whisper his voice seemed to carry in the stillness of the corridor and whispering in return I said, 'You'd better come in. I don't want your mother to find you here.'

His voice was low and matter of fact as he told me what arrangements had been made for us to return to Leeds. 'I expect all the villagers will turn out, and I know the hunt intend to gather at the station. Do you think you can bear it?'

'Why don't they just let us go? I can't stand to see Jack Bryant looking miserable and grieving when I know he cared more for his filthy money than he cared for her.'

'You don't really know how much he's suffering inside, Tessa. If he's anything like my father he's distraught.'

'He's not like your father. Your father is ashamed at what they've done. Jack Bryant doesn't know the meaning of the word.'

I had sunk trembling on the edge of my bed and he came to sit beside me, taking my cold hands in his and rubbing them gently.

'Heavens but you're frozen,' he said anxiously....

I had no thoughts beyond my own desperate need to be close to another human being, to be loved, and the warmth of his young body lying next to mine brought me a degree of comfort so precious that I found myself responding sensually to his caresses. His hands exploring my body were bringing the forgetfulness I yearned for. We were like two young animals, asking too much too soon, but the rhythm of our pulsating bodies was a sensation too desperate to be ignored.

It was demanding, urgent and yet so gradual that I was not prepared for the searing exquisite pain which seemed to fill my entire being until I screamed in agony.

Frightened, he buried my face in his shoulder to stifle the sound.

I held myself away from him, trembling with shame at what we had done. My mother lay dead in the church while my treacherous body had caused me to forget everything outside the passion that had consumed us both. Now I tore myself from his arms and stood glaring at him with a wild anger in my heart.

'Tessa, I love you,' he pleaded anxiously, 'you know I love you.'

I was in no mood for expressions of love. I felt soiled, unclean both in body and soul, and I wanted him to go. I couldn't bear to look at his young, pleading face.

'Please, Alec, leave me alone,' I muttered, and I ran to the door and held it open so that he had no option but to go.

In spite of the lateness of the hour I went into the bathroom and ran a bath, lying in the water until it went cold, brushing my skin with such vigour that it ached. It was as though I felt the need to scourge my tender body so that its pain would exonerate those moments of forgetfulness in Alec's arms.

I realized that I didn't hate him, I hated myself. I had allowed him to make love to me selfishly, wantonly. I didn't know if I loved him, not as he professed to love me. I had merely used him as a comforter, an opiate to ease my pain, unaware that my guilt would outweigh the feelings of sorrow.

Now as I lay shivering in my bed I only prayed that the next few days would pass quickly, even though they left scars that might never heal.

CHAPTER THIRTEEN

Dark leaden skies hung low over the vast cemetery and there was sleet in the air. Our feet slipped and slithered along the paths between the gravestones. The black coat and hat I was wearing had been my mother's. It was probably far too old for me but I didn't care, as I stood beside my stepfather in the gathering gloom.

I was surprised at the crowd that thronged the cemetery. Many of them were people who had attended the wedding reception but had not deigned to visit her or invited her to visit them. Now they stood with solemnly bent heads and I could not bear to look at them in case they saw how much I despised them.

Throngs of poorly clad people had stood round the cemetery gates, shivering in unsuitable clothing, the men with bared heads and caps held in red frozen hands, the women with shawls on their heads – workpeople from Bryant's mills. Expensive wreaths lined the paths and among the mourners I was surprised to see the Mallorys and their friends. Alec stood with his parents, white-faced and silent, and round the grave the huntsmen had gathered, their bright pink coats so much at variance with the sombre mourners and the black coaches and blacker horses wearing purple plumes on their headgear.

I was aware of Mrs Howlett standing with Annie, whose face was red with weeping as it had been ever since we returned to Leeds. It seemed that all my tears had been shed but when the huntsman raised his horn and blew the familiar 'Gone Away' I felt I could die in the searing pain that brought the sobs to my throat.

My mother was being buried in an impersonal cemetery in a city she had not really known or cared for and with people who were neither kith or kin, and at Glamara her father did not even know that the daughter he had adored was dead.

After that it was all a bewildering hotch-potch of words and farewells, and I went off to look at the flowers, not because I cared who had sent them, but because I wanted to be alone. I became aware of a man and a boy standing some little distance away beneath the trees. On the man's face was a despairing look of sorrow but the boy was looking at me searchingly, and I felt I should recognize him.

As they turned away the man raised his hat and bowed with grave courtesy and suddenly I recognized them as Sir Edward Chalmers and his son Richard. I remembered that afternoon as I went forward. 'I'm sorry, I didn't recognize you at first,' I said to Richard.

'I didn't want him to come alone.'

'No.'

Sir Edward was bending down to look at the cards on the wreaths.

'Will you stay in Leeds?' Richard surprised me by asking.

'I don't know. I haven't thought about it.'

'She rode well, your mother. All this is very difficult to believe.'

'Yes. The horse was unpredictable.'

'I suppose so.'

I was saved from further conversation by Alec, who stared hard at the boy, and to cover up an embarrassed silence I introduced them.

They merely nodded to each other, then Richard excused himself and turned away to join his father.

'Who is he anyway?' Alec asked petulantly.

'His father is Sir Edward Chalmers, he was once engaged to my mother.'

'Why didn't she marry him then?'

'It's a long story and best forgotten, I think.'

'I came to say goodbye. You will write to me won't you, Tessa? Let me know where you are and what you are doing, and perhaps you'll come to stay at Briarcrag at Easter. I want you to come.'

'We'll see.' It was all I could think to say. The future was uncertain, as though a dark curtain had been drawn against all the years ahead, and he did not know how much I was dreading returning to that lonely dark house so empty and impersonal without my mother's presence.

I returned to it with my stepfather. A fire burned in the drawing room but there were no flowers, and the coal seemed to have little life in it but spluttered in gassy spurts, throwing out lifeless cinders on to the hearth.

My stepfather went immediately to change his clothes and soon I heard the front door slam behind him.

Mrs Howlett came in to say that she would serve my meal on a tray as she too wanted to go out.

'Is Annie still here?'

'No, she's gone home for the rest of the day.'

'She'll be back in the morning?'

'I expect so, but 'e might not take to 'er stayin' on 'ere.'

'But what will Annie do if she loses her job?'

'She'll 'ave to look round for somethin' else like a lot of other folk.' With that she left, and I was alone.

I was awakened by voices and laughter. When I looked through the window the street was deserted. Struggling with matches I lit the gas lamp and looked at my watch. It was twenty past three and I returned to my bed thinking I must have been dreaming, but then I heard it again, a man's voice somewhere in the house and then a woman's laughter.

I opened the door a fraction and it came again, a man's rough muttering and a woman's shrill excited laughter.

I put on my robe and crept towards my stepfather's door. The voices came from inside and suddenly such a feeling of outrage overwhelmed me, I flung open the door, my eyes exploding with the sight that confronted me.

Jack Bryant and Mrs Howlett lay naked on the bed, two gross flaccid bodies threshing and heaving like floundering whales, her red hair standing out like a flaming halo against the white pillows, her eyes popping stupidly at the sight of me.

In my rage I seized a piece of heavy Victorian china from the dressing table and threw it with all my strength so that it struck his shoulders and bounced off to lie shattered against the wardrobe. He leapt up with a shriek of wounded anger and stood facing me, repulsive and obscene while she sat up against the pillow screaming.

'How I hate you,' I stormed at him, my voice thick with disgust. 'You're an animal, an ape, I hope you die and go to hell.'

I ran back to my room and slammed the door, standing with my back to it, afraid he would follow, perhaps even beat me. He did neither.

I could not stay in the house, and I set about packing my cases, taking everything from the drawers and makeshift wardrobe. There were things in the house that had belonged to my mother but I would have to leave them behind, even her emerald pendant, but all her jewellery was kept in the safe in the master bedroom and wild horses would not have dragged me in there again.

I sat in the chilly drawing room until the first tentative light of a new day lightened the room. Before either of them came downstairs I was standing outside on the frozen pavement with my luggage round my feet, helplessly wondering where to go.

A newspaper boy came past whistling cheerfully and soon after came the clatter of the milk cart driven by that same milkman I had seen on my first morning at my stepfather's house. He eyed me in amazement.

'What yer doin' out 'ere?'

Tears filled my eyes and rolled slowly down my cheeks, and he got clumsily out of his cab.

'What's all this then? I 'eard yer mother'd died luv, but yer can't just go off on yer own like this.'

'I have to go, I can't stay another minute in that house.'

He looked at me sympathetically but without surprise. 'No luv, it's no place fer yer now yer mother's gone. Where are yer goin'?'

'The convent? I could go there, I suppose.'

'That's right, the good sisters'll take care of yer. Come on then, give me yer luggage an' hop on the cart next to me. We can deliver the milk as we go.'

When at last he pulled the horse up outside the convent I hunted in my purse to give him some money.

'I don't want yer money luv, yer'll probably need all that afore yer've done. I'll just carry yer luggage to the door, yer'll be all right now, I'm sure.'

I watched him trundling off up the road in the early-morning mist before I pulled the bell. I didn't know how the sisters of St Clare's would receive me but at least there was hope in my heart.

CHAPTER FOURTEEN

The Mother Superior received me with great understanding and kindness, listening in silence until the whole sorry story was told, and if I had expected her face to register disgust or even horror at the previous night's events I was disappointed. It remained calm, as though the behaviour of mortals had ceased to surprise her.

When I had finished she said, 'Of course you must stay here, Tessa. Your fees are paid until the summer and a room will be found for you where you can study alone. I do not think it would be a good idea to place you in one of the dormitories unless you particularly wish it.'

'Oh no, Reverend Mother, I would prefer to be alone.'

'I think you are wise. The young can often be unkind, sometimes unwittingly, often deliberately, but then I suppose you have found that out for yourself.'

'Yes,' I murmured unhappily.

'Have you thought what you want to do when you leave St Clare's?'

'I shall need to find employment. Sister Hilda did tell me that people often approach you when they want to find a suitable girl to employ.'

'Yes that is true, and if something came up before it was time for you to leave would you be prepared to accept the position?'

'Yes Reverend Mother, particularly if it had your approval.'

'I have already had an inquiry from a gentleman in the West Riding. I propose to interview him quite soon.'

'I would rather not remain in Leeds.'

'That I can understand very well. I will send for you when I have had the opportunity of speaking to the gentleman.'

I settled down in my room happily enough but the first few days in the classroom were an ordeal. Although a great many girls expressed their sympathy, there were others like Marylee who seemed more interested in why I had sought shelter in the convent.

One afternoon after class there was a soft tap on my door. Susan Latchford stood there, her face pink with embarrassment, her attitude hesitant. She rushed in quickly with words of sympathy from herself and her parents, who begged me to visit them during the weekend.

Their kindness had come too late. I had no wish to be ungracious but I declined her offer and I could tell that my refusal hurt her. Later that evening the Mother Superior sent for me.

Although her eyes were kind there was an edge to her voice. 'Are you so well blessed with friends that you can afford to ignore their overtures of compassion? I am referring to Susan Latchford's visit to you. I happened to meet her in the corridor and she was crying.'

'I said nothing to make her cry,' I said defensively.

'But nor have you been able to forgive her for some hurt she caused you, Tessa. Let the bitterness go, child, there is no room in this life for nursed grievances and none of us can afford to toss aside the hand of friendship. Accept the olive branch that Susan has offered you.'

Next day I told Susan I would be happy to visit them over the weekend. I saw her face light up with pleasure and in spite of my reluctance to renew our old comradeship my heart warmed to her.

On the morning I set out for Susan's house I met Annie in the park. She was sitting on a form overlooking the pond. When I touched her shoulder she started up, frightened, and then she smiled and I went to sit beside her.

'Eh Miss Tessa but it's right nice to see yer. I couldn't believe it when mi aunt said yer'd gone right after yer mother's funeral. Where are yer stayin?'

'I'm at the convent. Are you still working at the house?'

'Ay, but I don't know fer 'ow long. 'E says as 'ow she should be able to manage now, wi' yer an' yer mother gone, 'sides I don't think they wants mi there.'

'No, I shouldn't imagine they do.'

'Yer knows about 'im an' 'er, then?'

'Yes Annie, I know.'

'I'll 'ave ter tell 'er where yer are, miss, she's bin anxious. There's things at the 'ouse belongin' to yer mother. She won't want someat as doesn't belong to 'er. An' mi aunt says she won't let mi go until 'e promises to find me a job at one o' the mills. Mi father's lost 'is job now so I'll be glad of anythin'.'

'Why has your father lost his job?'

'The firm's gone bust, an' there's little work about for somebody of 'is age. They'll take the young uns afore they takes the older men, that way they doesn't 'ave to pay out as much wages.'

'Oh Annie, I hate this city and its injustices. If I have the chance I shall go back to the country and if ever I can I shall help you find something better. You too should be in the country, breathing fresh clear air.'

Her face was suddenly rosy with blushes and I realized again how attractive her pinched face could be in the right environment. Rashly I took hold of her hand and said, 'Annie, promise me something. Promise me you'll look after yourself and not marry the first man who asks you just to get away from the miseries of your life. Surely you must have learned something from your mother's life. You can't just want a man, and a baby every year until you're too old to care.'

'I don't miss. I do want somethin' better fer miself, but where's ter find it?'

'I'll not forget you Annie, I swear it. One day I'll come for you.'

'Ey miss, but yer goin' ter 'ave a bad time looking out fer yerself, never mind about me. It's enough fer me to know yer want to 'elp mi.'

My talk with Annie had made me miss the tram to Susan's home and I had to wait for the next one. She was already walking down the road to meet me. There was an anxious look on her pretty face and for a moment I wondered if she had thought me capable of playing the same trick on them that they had played on me.

Her parents greeted me with a very special warmth. Mrs Latchford served us an excellent meal and Susan's brother was particularly attentive, then later in the evening we were taken to a concert. This is what it must be like to be part of a loving and caring family, I thought to myself, and on our departure for the convent on Monday morning I thanked them warmly.

'Have you really enjoyed it, Tessa?' Susan asked as we walked across the park.

'Very much. You have all been so kind.'

'We really are friends again then?'

'Yes of course.'

In the library the following afternoon Marylee put her head round the door saying, 'There's a woman asking for you downstairs, Tessa.'

'Asking for me? Did she say who she was?'

'I didn't ask. She's a rather common woman with bright red hair and a mangy fur.'

I found Mrs Howlett in the visitors' room, a suitcase and a smaller valise beside her. 'Them's yer mother's things. There's clothes and some of 'er china an' 'er jewellery. Don't think I blames yer for leavin' the 'ouse, I don't. I know 'ow it looked to yer an' I knows 'ow yer must 'a felt about it so soon after yer mother's death, but 'ow do yer think I felt on the day 'ee wed 'er.'

'I don't know what you mean.'

'I'll tell yer. 'Ee took me out o' the mill an' installed me in 'is 'ouse. 'Ee called me 'is 'ousekeeper but I were more than that. I lived wi' 'im, slept wi' 'im as well as cooked fer 'im, then one day 'ee told me to clear out, into mi own room, that 'ee were goin' to wed a lady 'ee said, a real lady. I broke mi 'eart that night. I'd bin good enough to sleep with but I weren't good enough to wed.

'I 'as mi feelings. I'm not dirt to be trampled on. I 'ated yer mother afore I ever saw 'er, but after a while I pitied 'er, when I saw the way 'ee treated 'er. They just weren't right together an' now 'ee knows it for 'isself, an' 'ee's glad ter get back to me.'

There was nothing to say, and not in the least surprised by my silence she walked towards the door. Then she turned and said, 'There's a chance 'ee'll wed mi now. I 'as the upper 'and at last.'

I stood at the window watching her stalk down the path. I knew I would not see her again and there was no hatred for her in my heart. All my hatred and resentment was for him. The words I had flung at him on the night I left his house were as potent now as they had been then. I hoped he would die, horribly and hurting, and go to hell.

CHAPTER FIFTEEN

It was a few mornings later when the Mother Superior told me that the potential employer she had mentioned was calling next day. Mr Chantry lived in the West Riding and was seeking a companion for his daughter.

'He is a widower,' she explained, 'but he doesn't tell me how old his daughter is or why she is short of companions. She could be an invalid, I suppose.'

Susan thought the widower with a daughter was an exciting proposition. 'He could be wildly handsome, a very young widower with a daughter about three years old. Besides he's rich and owns vast acres.'

'You've been reading too many romantic novels, Susan. At the moment all I want is to get as far away from Leeds as I can.'

'Did Mrs Howlett bring all your mother's things?'

'I don't know, I haven't felt able to face them just yet.'

'You could look in the smaller case, I'll stay until you've opened it, if you like.'

Susan sat on the edge of my bed watching me struggle with the lock. It was old and rusted and I guessed Mrs Howlett had found it in the attic since my mother would never have owned such a dejected affair. At last it was Susan who got it open with one of her hairpins and then began the heartbreaking task of handling my mother's possessions: her toilet things, silver-backed and heavily chased, articles of china and small pictures, and her jewellery case containing her watch, and the gold chain with its exquisite emerald. None of the jewellery Jack Bryant had given her was there and I imagined Mrs Howlett now had those. I fastened the pendant around my neck and vowed never to part with it.

'See, it wasn't so bad, was it Tessa?' Susan said brightly. 'Why don't you open the other one while I'm here and while you have the courage.'

The large case contained her clothes and even here I could see that only the gowns he had had no hand in purchasing were included. They were of inferior quality even though their cut was excellent, as all her clothes had been. Her underwear lay at the bottom of the case, delicately appliquéd with lace, soft gentle shades in heavy satin and crêpe de chine. I held one of her nightdresses against my face while her perfume brought the stinging tears to my eyes....

I made up a parcel of everything I thought might be of use to Annie's family and the following Saturday I set off with Susan in the direction of the pond. Sure enough Annie was there with her brother and sisters and after greeting me warmly she took the proffered parcel with eyes open wide in wonder.

'But yer can't want mi to 'ave all these Miss Tessa, yer mother allus 'ad the loveliest things. Don't yer want 'em fer yourself?'

'No. I couldn't wear her clothes. I'd much rather not have to look at them again.'

She hugged the parcel to her thin little body and after

calling to the children she said, 'I'll get off 'ome now, Miss Tessa, I can't wait fer mi mother to see what yer've sent 'er.'

We watched her half running along the path and, meeting Susan's eyes, I caught the suspicion of a tear which she hastily wiped away.

How strange it is to form an impression of a person and find in reality that they are totally different. I had imagined that Mr Chantry would be tall and dark, a very doting father of a small girl and a somewhat helpless widower. Instead he was of medium height with thinning grey hair and a pale severe face. He rose to shake hands with me when I entered the Reverend Mother's study the following afternoon and it was he who indicated where I should sit for the interview.

'The Mother Superior tells me you are an orphan, Miss Chalfont, that your mother has recently died and that you are needing to find a situation.'

'Yes, that is so sir.'

'I intend to be frank with both of you. I am a widower, my wife died when my daughter was only three weeks old and she is now fourteen. I have tried to bring her up correctly, to observe Christian teachings, to be obedient and chaste and I am telling you now that I have been doubly severe with Elizabeth because her mother's death caused me such bitter anguish.'

Neither the Reverend Mother not I spoke, and I felt confident he would elaborate on his words.

For several moments he sat silent and brooding with pursed lips, then he seemed to square his shoulders and, looking straight at me he said, 'My wife jumped from her bedroom window. A verdict of suicide while the balance of her mind was disturbed was brought in at the inquest. The doctors seemed to think she had been suffering from post-natal depression. There was no reason for her to do that dreadful thing. She had a beautiful home and I am a rich man. She had a baby to consider and she was both young and beautiful. You can imagine how carefully I have watched over my daughter for any signs of her mother's frailty.

'Elizabeth has been privately educated by several

governesses over the years but now I sense a restlessness in her. She needs a friend, an older girl, a girl she can ride with and walk with and no doubt chatter with on matters girls find so absorbing. There are extensive grounds to my house and I have furnished it with Elizabeth's future in mind. The library is filled with rare books and the gardens with rare plants and flowers. I consult her about the furnishings and she is amply supplied with clothes. A companion for her will live in a degree of luxury she has not perhaps been accustomed to in return for her loyalty and dedication.'

My eyes met his eagerly. To live in the West Riding in a beautiful house with horses and the chance to ride across the fells as I had in the old days filled my heart with hope. Without saying a word I silently promised to be a good friend to Elizabeth Chantry, to advance her knowledge if that was within my power and to enrich her life with my imaginings and taste for adventure.

'The Mother Superior tells me you have lived in the West Riding, Miss Chalfont, so I take it you have friends or acquaintances in the area?'

'Yes sir, I have friends in Grindale and neighbouring villages.'

He merely raised his eyebrows, so I said, 'I know the Hardcastles who live at Briarcrag and Sir Edward Chalmers.'

Why I mentioned Sir Edward I do not know, except that I believed Mr Chantry might think if I mentioned him, if only in passing, that I knew people in the area with some standing.

'I do not know the Hardcastles,' he said indifferently. 'Sir Edward Chalmers I know slightly. I do not socialize, I am far too busy on the estate and I have no doubt Sir Edward is equally involved in his.'

In some way I felt rebuffed, but I wasn't sure why. I was more than surprised however when the Reverend Mother said, 'Perhaps you should think of finding a girl of your daughter's age, Mr Chantry, perhaps a country girl from a good home and a Christian background, a girl who would appreciate her good fortune in finding herself with a young friend and a luxurious home.'

I stared at her askance. Surely I was that girl he was

looking for. I was just seventeen, three years older than Elizabeth, and I needed the job. What was the Reverend Mother thinking of in trying to put obstacles in my way? She went on to talk to him about an orphanage in the city where there were girls ready to go out into the world needing a home and friendship such as he offered. I could hardly believe it. What would I do if he rejected me in favour of one of these girls, where would I go?

As though aware of my thoughts he turned to me, saying, 'Perhaps you agree with the Reverend Mother, Miss Chalfont, that you are not the sort of young lady I am looking for?'

'I think I *am* the person you are looking for sir, I desperately want to return to the country, I need to get away from Leeds and I need to work for my living. I am sure if you employ me you will not regret it.'

The Mother Superior sat back resigned, and with a half smile he rose to his feet.

'Very well then, I offer you the post. When will you be able to come?'

'I could come to you almost immediately.'

'That suits me very well. Shall we say next Monday? I will send your ticket to you, and will meet the train myself. It is some little drive from the station.'

'Thank you sir, that is very kind.'

'All your meals will be provided and I will pay you ten pounds a year. Have you any questions to ask me?'

'No, Mr Chantry, except to thank you.'

He bowed briefly to the Mother Superior and after nodding to me curtly he left us. There was silence for several minutes after he had left, an uncomfortable silence. I made myself meet her troubled gaze calmly, though I felt disturbed by her attitude.

At last she broke the silence. 'You were impulsive, Tessa. Did nothing in our interview with Mr Chantry strike you as odd?'

'I'm not sure what you mean, Reverend Mother.'

'He spoke of his beautiful house and the extensive grounds. He spoke of his daughter's private education, that she lacked for nothing, and yet it seemed to me that she lacked everything, the warmth of companionship, the outside world, indeed everything except the watchfulness of her father.'

'But he said that there would be horses for us to ride, and books for us to read. I am sure he adores his daughter.'

'I felt he was cold, Tessa, cold and remote. He had never heard of your friends the Hardcastles and although he knew Sir Edward Chalmers he had been too busy to know him more intimately. I had a strong feeling that the man was a recluse, devoted only to his house and estate and with a daughter he hugged too closely to himself. Such an environment could be decidedly unhealthy where you are concerned, my dear.'

'Please, Reverend Mother, I am sure it will not be like that, but if it is I need not stay, though I'm sure I shall be able to write to you and tell you how happy I am.'

'I hope so my child, and I shall pray for you. There is something about you my dear which makes me feel you will need my prayers more intensely and longer than any other.'

As I walked back to my room I felt saddened by her words. What was it about me that made her feel so protective? I was no longer a child and even if I had lost my dear mother I had Alec who loved me....

Resolutely I thrust thoughts of Alec away from me. I could not rely on feelings of passion to obliterate every problem in my life, to lull my silent fears into a sense of false security when I didn't really know if I loved him or not.

I decided at that moment that even when I returned to the West Riding I would not tell Alec. The next time I allowed a man to possess me it would be because I loved him desperately and irrevocably, without thought of anything beyond the towering joys of the present.

CHAPTER SIXTEEN

I was glad to be leaving Leeds and yet I watched the receding vista of church towers, mill chimneys and ostentatious domes with a strange nostalgia. I was leaving the shelter of the convent and I was leaving Susan, who had cried a little on the station platform.

In my luggage were several farewell gifts from the Latchfords and an ivory-backed prayer and hymn book from the sisters.

My last visit had been to my mother's grave. There were no other flowers than mine on the marble vault, nor had her name been engraved alongside that of Jack Bryant's parents. It was as though she had never existed and I vowed that as soon as I could afford it I would make sure that her name appeared there.

When I stepped on to the platform I did so with the knowledge that this was indeed the first day of my new life, a life when all the decisions would be mine whether for good or ill.

I breathed in once more the fragrant moorland air and felt the cold moist wind against my cheek.

A solitary trap stood outside the station and I saw Mr Chantry approaching. 'I trust you had a pleasant journey.'

'Yes thank you sir, very pleasant.'

'Our drive to the house will take about twenty minutes, long enough I think for you to familiarize yourself with the area.'

I did not know the village we were passing through and yet it was all so familiar: the stone cottages and country gardens, the swiftly flowing streams and winding lanes, the lush farmland, and rising above it the wild sweeping moors. My heart was plagued by memories of other years and I had wilfully to turn my thoughts to other things or I was certain the treacherous tears would fill my eyes.

My companion seemed different to the man at our interview, more remote and severe.

He held the reins loosely and stared straight ahead as though driving the trap were something that needed to be done rather than a joy. The pony trotted smartly between the shafts, head up and tail gently swishing. He was a beautiful animal but I had the strangest feeling that the man beside me was unaware of his beauty and regarded him with no more enthusiasm than he would have regarded a plough, or one of those motor cars which were now becoming so popular.

Suddenly he slowed the pony and pointed across the fields. 'There is the house, Miss Chalfont, you can just see the chimneys behind the stone wall there.'

I looked and indeed I could see the chimneys but the stone wall was very high and I hoped we would have a better view of it when we rounded the bend in the road.

The high wall seemed to encircle the estate and we came at last to some very high iron gates which a man from the lodge house hurried to open. He touched his cap respectfully as we drove through and then I heard them clang to behind me with a terrible finality.

I recalled the Mother Superior's words. But no man would make a prisoner out of his daughter I told myself, surely he would want her to grow and blossom, make friends and eventually marry.

The house was a large red-brick building. I had imagined it would be built of stone, as were most of the large houses in the dales. Stone mellowed over the years until it blended exquisitely with the grey-green hills and forests, but this house stood out starkly red and harsh so that the scenery around it seemed muted and unimportant. I was surprised by the newness of it, and yet it wasn't new. A new house would never have sought such isolation and its design was undeniably Victorian.

'It's a very fine house, Miss Chalfont. My grandfather built it and used his imagination. One expects all the houses in this area to be built of Pennine stone. I am relieved that my grandfather decided this one should be different.'

'Yes indeed sir,' I murmured.

'He called the house Red Gables. Very appropriate, I think.'

'Yes sir. How far is it from the nearest village?'

'Well we have just passed through Browbeck which is little more than a hamlet. I expect Grindale is as near as anywhere.'

'I know Grindale quite well, we lived there for a time.'

'Tell me, Miss Chalfont, had you many friends in Leeds?'

'Not many, but I had friends I have promised to write to and who I hope to see again one day.'

'But for the time being you will confine your friendship to Elizabeth and not hanker too much over those you have left in the city.'

'I am here to carry out my duties to your satisfaction, Mr Chantry. I hope Elizabeth and I will be happy in each other's company.'

'When you have seen your room perhaps you will come down to my study and I will outline your duties for you, Miss Chalfont.'

'Very well sir.'

'Most of my servants are old. They were here in my father's time and are obviously loyal and devoted to Elizabeth and myself. Most of the villagers at Browbeck are employed on the estate in some form or another as were their fathers before them.'

'I understand sir, I think this is so with all the big estates in the area – the entire village revolves around the life of the great house and the family who employ them.'

He didn't speak again until we arrived at the front door and he was helping me down. Almost as though they had been standing inside waiting for us the door opened and an elderly maid hurried down the steps to take my luggage while immediately behind him came a tall thin woman clad in black with her grey hair pulled back severely from her gaunt face.

She bobbed a little curtsey before him and he said, 'This is Miss Chalfont, Mrs Holt. Has her room been prepared?'

'Yes sir, everything is in order.'

Indicating Mrs Holt he said to me, 'This is my

housekeeper. You may consult her about any matter regarding the house, the grounds and the staff generally. If you have any complaints about the food you should advise her and she will raise the matter in the proper quarter.'

How businesslike it all sounded, but nodding curtly in my direction she appeared not to think so. Instead she bustled in behind the maid carrying my luggage, and we followed more slowly. The hall was light and very lofty but it was also to my mind ungracious and spartan in the extreme. The floor tiles made it seem cold and the walls were panelled in light oak and unadorned with any pictures. The stairs ran up from the centre, dividing at the half landing.

Mrs Holt led me to a room at the side of the house on the first floor. It was the largest bedroom I had ever called my own but it was not a welcoming room. It is true that as yet none of my personal things lay around, but the grey carpet and blue curtains and bedcovers gave it a cold aspect.

Sharply I told myself not to be critical. There were two large wardrobes and a dressing table, the bed looked comfortable and there was a velvet chair drawn up before the fireplace, though instead of a welcoming fire the grate was covered by an embroidered firescreen and I realized how cold it was.

It was early February, a month when snow lay on the fells and the wind mourned round the house like a banshee. I shivered and the housekeeper said sharply, 'If you find it cold you may put a hot-water bottle in the bed. The master doesn't like fires in the bedrooms.'

'Not even on a day as cold as this one?'

'Not even then. The old gentleman would never allow them and Mr Chantry has followed on the tradition he knew as a child.'

'Have you been here long Mrs Holt?'

'I came to Red Gables as a kitchen maid and I have stayed on. My husband is the head groom. Only female servants serve in the house, apart from Jimmy that is, and he's not quite all there if you get what I mean. He's the gardener's son and Mr Chantry lets him make up the fires downstairs and run errands.'

'Where shall I find Mr Chantry's study?'

'On the right of the hall miss, the first door.'

When she had gone I went to stare out of the window. As far as I could see the high stone wall surrounded the grounds but beyond them the dark lonely hills stretched into the distance. My teeth were chattering in the cold wind that found its way through the side of the window and hurriedly I took off my coat and hat, smoothing my hair at the mirror. I was wearing a navy-blue skirt and white shirt blouse which I thought made me appear mature and businesslike, so squaring my shoulders I left the room, and marched briskly down the stairs. The house seemed so quiet. No sounds of voices or laughter, and I wondered what a fourteen-year-old girl found to do. Was Elizabeth out riding or was she waiting in her father's study to meet her new companion?

Mr Chantry was alone however, standing in front of the bright fire. 'Sit down, Miss Chalfont,' he invited. 'Do you find it cold in here, that you are shivering?'

'Not in here sir although I thought it was cold upstairs.'

'You will soon grow accustomed to the airiness of the bedrooms. You disapprove?'

'This is your house sir, it is not my place to agree or disagree with anything you do here.'

'I think you and I are going to understand each other very well. I think you should first be given a résumé of my daughter's daily activities. The mornings she spends with her governess in the library from nine until twelve and then she and I lunch together. You and Miss Allinson will lunch together. After lunch if the weather is fine she likes to go riding. You will have no difficulty in finding a suitable mount in the stables. Promptly at three o'clock she returns to the library for further tuition. You will be served tea at five and then you are free. At seven Elizabeth and I dine together. We always spend the evenings in each other's company, Miss Chalfont. Occasionally if Elizabeth wishes it you will be invited to dine with us but you will find that Miss Allinson is intelligent company. You may have the run of the house, and do not hesitate to borrow any book you require from the library.'

174

I felt confused and momentarily shaken, and sensing it he said sharply, 'You are troubled about something?'

'Yes, Mr Chantry. I understood I was to come here as Elizabeth's friend and companion and yet it seems we are to spend only a short time together during the course of a day.'

'You will spend all day together apart from luncheon and the evenings when I shall want Elizabeth to myself.'

'You mean I am to sit with Elizabeth during her lessons?'

'Yes, that is so.'

'But sir, I have been well educated by nuns at what is considered the best private school in Leeds, surely you do not think it necessary for me to continue my education with a private governess?'

'You are unwilling to learn more! I would have thought you would have grasped this chance to further your education.'

'Mr Chantry, your daughter is fourteen years old, I am seventeen. I am sure that anything your daughter is learning now I was taught three years before.'

'Of course if you do not wish to attend her studies you are free to walk in the park or read in your room. By sitting in with Elizabeth and her governess you would see more of each other, and I would have thought that to be entirely desirable.'

I bit my lip angrily. I must learn to be diplomatic instead of argumentative, but I was not happy with the prospect of going back to school. At that moment I knew I had made a mistake in coming here and it seemed to me that the years stretched ahead of me unrewarding and empty.

'If you would care to see the downstairs rooms I will be your guide, Miss Chalfont.'

'Yes indeed sir, I would like that very much.'

We went first to the library, a vast room, dark and very austere with its richly bound volumes and dark leather chairs. I was glad to see a fire in the grate.

'This is where you will study, at the table near the window and where Miss Allinson prefers to sit. The views over the park are particularly fine.'

My eyes were drawn to the large portrait above the stone

fireplace and I couldn't help feeling that it would have been more at home in the drawing room than in this severe and formal room.

It was the portrait of a young woman wearing a delicate white gown. On the grass beside her was a wide-brimmed straw hat and her dark hair hung in shining ringlets. Hers was a strangely haunting face, pretty yet insecure, her dark eyes questioning, her soft lips a shade petulant, yet the whole effect was charming and I wondered if she could be Elizabeth, small and delicate as porcelain.

As if in answer to the question in my eyes he said, 'You admire the portrait?'

'Yes, it is beautiful. Is it a portrait of Elizabeth?'

'No it is Caroline, Elizabeth's mother.'

'Of course, I should have known that she was older than fourteen.'

'She was eighteen when that picture was painted. We had been married just eleven months. My daughter resembles her mother very much, but she has a much stronger personality I am glad to say.'

'Your wife's story is a sad one.'

'It need not have been. She was too young, a child bride of whom my parents largely disapproved, mainly because of her youth, and because she had been spoiled by indulgent parents. One minute Caroline was playing with her dolls and the next with her baby daughter. She treated Elizabeth like a doll and when my mother chastised her she was far too foolish to accept it and strive to act more grown up. She jumped from the window overlooking this one. We found her outside that window there with her neck broken.'

He spoke so unemotionally, as though the death of his young wife had scarcely ruffled the calm waters of his life, that I began to wonder what event could stir the passions of this withdrawn, remote man.

As we moved from room to room and did not encounter Elizabeth I asked where we might find her.

'Elizabeth usually rests before dinner. She is at an age when acquiring knowledge tends to sap her energy and I encourage her to rest. She will no doubt have been walking in the park earlier this afternoon.'

I made no comment but I thought about the fourteen-year-olds at the convent who never rested before dinner and were never ready to go to their beds later.

At the end of our tour he remarked, 'It is already dusk and it will shortly be too dark to attend to your unpacking. You may have noticed that neither gas nor electricity have been laid on upstairs, all our lighting is by lamps or candlelight. I have given instructions that your evening meal is to be served in your room tonight. Tomorrow we shall be back to normal. You know where to find the library so please be there a little before ten. Are there any questions you wish to ask me?'

'Do Elizabeth's grandparents live close by, sir?'

'We are not in touch with her mother's family and both my parents are dead. Goodnight Miss Chalfont.'

'Goodnight sir.'

It was so gloomy in the corridors I made my way back to my room more by guess than recognition. It looked particularly depressing in the half light. There was one small candle in a holder on the dressing table.

I could have wept with disappointment, but then came a soft tap on the door and the entrance of an elderly woman bearing a tray.

The tray was set with my evening meal and a heavy brass candlestick containing a solitary candle already lit. Its flickering light shone feebly through the gathering dusk and I watched her close the curtains and fold back the bedcovers in silence.

These tasks completed she bobbed me a small curtsey saying, 'Will that be all miss?'

'I should like a hot-water bottle.'

'Yes miss, I'll bring one up for you.'

'Thank you, what is your name?'

'It's Martha, miss. I 'opes I've brought you enough dinner.'

She hurried away while I scanned the food without enthusiasm. There was a burnt piece of steak, a jacket potato

177

and sprouts, and doubtless the journey from the kitchens took some time, since the meal was only lukewarm. All the same I was hungry and I ate it.

When Martha reappeared with the hot-water bottle she brought a bowl of stewed apples and a cup of tea.

I pulled the curtain aside to look out across the park. It was pitch dark outside, without even a homely light from a nearby farmhouse to disturb the gloom, as though we existed in a vacuum, completely divorced from all forms of life. There was not a sound until an owl hooted mournfully and I jumped nervously because it seemed so impressively loud.

At Grindale I had loved the sounds of the night. The barking of foxes and the sighing of night trains, owls hooting and the rustlings of leaves, but here I could imagine that outside the window all the world was dead.

Although it was only six thirty I decided to climb into bed while the bottle was still warm. I did not expect to sleep for hours but lulled by the silence I drifted off, only to dream of Glamara: I was dancing in the ballroom in a shimmering white dress. I could smell flowers, and they were in my hair and on my dress, and a man's arms held me close. I expected to find Alec's face looking down at me, but the man I danced with wore a mask and all I saw was that he was dark and tall and danced divinely while below his mask his firmly chiselled lips formed a cool half smile I could not understand.

I presented myself in the library the following morning at five minutes to ten to find that Miss Allinson was already there. She was in her early fifties I imagined, busily engaged in stacking books in the centre of the table. She nodded to me brusquely but did not pause.

I stood beside the table uncertainly and eventually she looked up saying, 'Mr Chantry has informed me that you will be joining us for lessons, Miss Chalfont. I personally don't see the necessity for it – unless he feels your education has been inadequate?'

'I can assure you that isn't so, Miss Allinson.'

'Oh well. Elizabeth will be here directly.'

I found my eyes drawn again to the portrait of Caroline Chantry. In the light of day it took on a softness not evident before. She was so pretty and so absurdly young. I could imagine her with her dolls and that baby daughter she had treated like a doll.

I rose when Mr Chantry brought in his daughter, and I had to stop myself from staring at her, so closely did she resemble the portrait. Ringlets were no longer fashionable but that was how Elizabeth wore her hair. Only the dress was different: tartan skirt and fine white woollen blouse.

'This is Tessa Chalfont who is to be your companion and I hope your friend,' he said.

I held out my hand, surprised that the hand she placed in mine felt so limp and that in her eyes I read only apathy.

'I hope we shall be friends, Elizabeth. I am sitting in on your lesson with Miss Allinson. Where do you usually sit?'

'Anywhere, it does not matter,' she answered, then she turned to kiss her father's cheek before he left us.

Almost immediately Miss Allinson said, 'Did you manage to do your homework Elizabeth?'

She handed an exercise book to her governess. I was subjected to a history lesson but I found little interest in Miss Allinson's delivery. It was a singularly monotonous session on a subject I knew.

Elizabeth stumbled through it and I wondered if my presence contributed to her awkwardness. I thought about the nuns who had been so enthusiastic about teaching. Divided from the world they might have been but their lessons had had a freshness and vitality quite alien to Miss Allinson's stunted, unimaginative teaching. It was easy to allow my thoughts to wander and I was glad when Elizabeth left the room to lunch with her father.

'I believe you like to ride after lunch,' I said to her on parting.

'Yes, are you riding with me?'

'Yes of course. Shall I wait for you in the hall?'

'Yes, that will do very well.'

'You will be back here for three o'clock, Elizabeth,' Miss Allinson warned her.

The girl agreed, and I stared after her. She seemed so spiritless, so colourless and so very obedient.

Lunch was brought into the library for Miss Allinson and myself and in an attempt to make conversation I said, 'Have you worked here for some years?'

'Two years, that is all. Elizabeth has had a succession of governesses. She is a very withdrawn child, I can only hope she responds to you better than to me.'

'Perhaps she would have been happier at school with other girls,' I ventured, and instantly regretted it.

She snapped, 'When the royal family is educated privately, and most of the landed gentry, it is surely evident which form of education is to be preferred.'

'Private education for the royal family is perhaps understandable but for us lesser mortals I am not so sure,' I replied, astonished at my temerity, but this cold superior woman was annoying me with her patronizing air.

'May I give you a little advice, Miss Chalfont?' she said sharply.

'Of course.'

'You are very young, miss. I should refrain from making such remarks in the presence of Mr Chantry, who would not take kindly to them.'

'I would not dream of telling Mr Chantry how to bring up his daughter, but she seems so remote, so subdued.'

'She is dutiful. It is delightful to see a girl so obviously well brought up, adoring her father and obeying him.'

I was not so sure about that either. A girl might obey her father out of a sense of adoration, or she could be afraid of him. I didn't yet know Elizabeth Chantry well enough to judge.

'Perhaps you and I should be frank with each other,' the governess went on. 'You seem to think my pupil would have been happier in a school and I personally feel it was quite unnecessary to bring another girl into the house, particularly one who has spent her life in the company of other girls. I feel that Elizabeth would have had more in common with a similar type to herself, a girl who has been sheltered and protected from life's realities.

'You will find Mr Chantry a good employer if you perform your duties entirely to his satisfaction. If you require any advice I am here if you need me.'

She swept from the room with disapproval in every line of her thin angular body and in spite of her words I believed I had made an enemy. I should meekly have allowed her to lecture me without answering back, but more and more I was finding out that I was after all my mother's daughter, and that the blood of the man who had embraced life with such reckless assurance ran in my veins.

With the donning of my riding habit I assumed a new confidence. I knew that I rode well, and looked well in the severely cut black jacket and long skirt over shining riding boots. The black bowler made me look considerably older than my seventeen years.

Elizabeth came down to the hall eventually and I hoped she didn't notice my surprise at her old-fashioned velvet that might have been worn during the last century.

'You look awfully pretty, Elizabeth,' I said quickly. 'You make me feel very sombre.'

'This habit belonged to my mother,' she surprised me by saying. 'I know it is old-fashioned but since nobody is likely to see it except the grooms it doesn't matter.'

'You mean you usually ride alone?' I asked curiously.

'Yes, but that wasn't what I meant. I never ride outside the gates, my father does not allow it. The parkland is very large so the horses get enough exercise.'

'I see,' I murmured unhappily.

I didn't see. What was her father trying to do to her? What did he hope to attain by keeping his daughter a virtual prisoner? Surely he was pushing his daughter into a terrible rebellion.

It was difficult to make conversation although we had a long walk before we reached the stables. I tried to get her to talk about the gardens but she responded only briefly and the long silences were depressing.

Her stalwart Welsh pony was waiting for her at the mounting block but I was helped on my horse by one of the grooms who made a step with his hands. My horse was a grey and I was glad to see that he was spirited and fresh so that for the first time since I arrived I began to feel alive.

We walked our mounts slowly out of the stableyard and I asked casually, 'Which way do you wish to ride, Elizabeth?'

'It doesn't really matter. I keep to the paths in front of the house, you may ride wherever you please.'

'Within the gates? I said dryly.

'Yes. There are woods at the back of the house, but the undergrowth is very thick so I never go there.'

'Do you never ride towards the village?' I asked, trying hard to keep the dismay out of my voice.

'Only with my father in the chaise.'

'And where do you go then?'

'Occasionally to church, sometimes to visit my uncle in Deeply.'

'I suppose you enjoy that immensely.'

'I suppose so.'

Oh, the profound apathy in the girl's voice. It disturbed me so intensely I became unaware of my actions and allowed my horse to canter until I realized Elizabeth was trailing behind. I waited for her to catch up, surprised when she said, 'You ride well, Miss Chalfont. I am afraid I am not very experienced.'

'I would like you to call me Tessa, surely that will not be too difficult.'

'Very well Tessa.'

'Your pony needs to canter, Elizabeth. I will teach you and eventually you will allow him to gallop and perhaps even jump him.'

She stared at be doubtfully and I smiled to reassure her. 'You will love it, Elizabeth. Would you like to start now, just a little canter until you become more proficient.'

'Perhaps I should ask my father first, he may not allow it.'

'But he likes you to ride, doesn't he? He has provided you with a very handsome pony, I can assure you you will both enjoy the experience.'

She still looked uncertain and to encourage her further I said, 'You need not be afraid, Elizabeth, we will not go far and I am here to help you.'

'Behind the house then, away from the front windows.'

I agreed, and we walked our horses decorously until we reached a point behind the house where she assured me we would not be overlooked.

I showed her how to encourage her pony to canter gently and although at first she seemed afraid in a very short while the colour shone in her cheeks and she was laughing, more animated than I had as yet seen her.

The time flew by and suddenly she gave a little cry. 'Miss Allinson, Tessa! What time is it?'

I was horrified to see that it was after three o'clock and I knew that I would be blamed. I felt sure Elizabeth had never before been late for a lesson. We did not have time to change out of our riding clothes. Miss Allinson was waiting for us with a set frown of annoyance and Elizabeth rushed to apologize.

'We forgot the time, it was so lovely in the park.'

'I suppose you also forgot the time, Miss Chalfont?' she said, eyeing me with acute disapproval.

'Yes. It was entirely my fault, it won't occur again, Miss Allinson.'

'And you are still in your riding clothes. I dislike the smell of horses and Mr Chantry will not like their odour to linger in his library, I can assure you.'

One look at Elizabeth's unhappy face erased all the joy I had felt in the canter across the grass, but the lesson began and I tried to show my interest and not give Miss Allinson further cause to disapprove of me.

That night I sat by the library fire with a book but I was not reading. My thoughts were confused as I tried to understand how a man could condemn his child to a life of such sheltered inadequacy.

I too felt like a prisoner as I pulled the curtains aside and gazed out over the parkland glistening under a full moon. Somewhere out there the villages of the West Riding lay dreaming under the moonlight, the lamplight shining through cheerful curtains, and there would be warmth and the laughter of families after the day's toil. What was so sinful about that life that Elizabeth and I should be denied its innocent pleasures? But what troubled me the most was how long I was going to be able to bear such isolation, for I was not like Elizabeth. I had known freedom. Freedom of thought and speech, freedom to ride fearlessly across the lonely fells. And I had known the passion that could exist between a man and a woman, passion that had made my stunned heart forget, if only briefly. Now I was missing Alec desperately, his warmth and his laughter, the call of youth to youth, and there and then I decided to write and tell him so.

The following morning I asked Miss Allinson if I would be allowed to post my letter in the village, only to be informed that all letters were placed on the hall table where they would be collected by Mr Chantry who would post them personally.

At that moment I was convinced that Alec Hardcastle would never receive my letter.

CHAPTER SEVENTEEN

It seems incredible that a whole year passed in an environment that brought me little joy or contentment. I set foot outside the lodge gates only once in all that time, and that was to post a letter to Susan because I had received no letters in reply to the many I wrote: to the sisters at the convent, to Susan and to Alec and the Hardcastles. It was almost as though I only existed on some mysterious plane, divorced from human joys and sorrows, and yet the Hardcastles lived only a stone's throw away. They evidently had no desire to visit me, and I included Alec in their desertion.

I do not know who informed Mr Chantry that I had been outside the gates but one evening he invited me into his study where he indicated his extreme displeasure at my escapade.

'You know my thoughts on this matter,' he said gently, as if to lull my stunned mind into a feeling of security. 'What is so desirable about the hamlet you visited this morning when you have this entire estate to walk in? A few paltry cottages, a farmyard or two and a shabby-looking inn are surely insufficient incentives to disobey my orders.'

I remained silent, standing before him with heightened colour and my hands clenched in an anger he could not but be aware of.

'I trust you are not encouraging my daughter to be secretive or fractious,' he said sternly.

'Mr Chantry, I feel like a prisoner here. My life is unnatural, I do not understand what is wrong with companionship or closeness to people.'

'There is nothing wrong with it. Didn't I come looking for it for my daughter? Isn't her friendship enough?'

'*I* didn't go looking for it. I spoke to no one. I only went to post my letter.'

'You already know that all letters are posted by me.'

'Then why do I never receive replies to my letters, why do I feel so forsaken?'

'The sisters at the convent are busy people and a great many pupils pass through their hands. It is unrealistic to expect them to write to every one of their old pupils, and as for your friends they have evidently formed other associations. For a time friends are important and then when they go they are soon forgotten because others have taken their place. You must learn not to let these matters worry you my dear, it is a period of growing up, of weighing the good against the bad, the true against the false.'

'Mr Chantry, I cannot allow all my life to revolve around Elizabeth or hers around me. We need to make friends wherever we can, both of us, it does not mean that I shall care for Elizabeth less because I have other friends, they will only help to broaden my horizon as I hope they will in time broaden hers.'

'My daughter does not see herself as part of a merry throng. Elizabeth has always been a shy, withdrawn child. She is easily embarrasssed by too much attention and I do not want to see her changed.'

'Mr Chantry, I have only been to post a letter, I have not

been taking part in a witches' sabbath on Pendle Hill.'

His brow darkened and for one terrible moment I thought he would strike me. I had been inordinately rude to him but I felt it had been merited, he had spoken to me as though I had committed a cardinal sin instead of an innocent walk through the gates to post a letter. And then another thought occurred to me: If a reply came, he would keep it from me. I felt sure he was capable of such a thing.

He dismissed me curtly and I returned to the library. I thought the governess looked at me strangely, which made me feel that she had had a hand in telling him where I had been.

Strangely enough that evening I was invited to eat dinner with Elizabeth and her father, the first time since I had arrived at Red Gables. I put on a clean white blouse, deciding against wearing one of my more feminine dresses in case he did not approve, but I was surprised to see Elizabeth wearing a white lawn dress which was decidedly too young for her.

The meal was eaten in comparative silence, except to comment upon the tenderness of the chicken and the quality of the pudding. Over coffee he surprised me by saying, 'I have to go out this evening, Miss Chalfont, so perhaps you and Elizabeth would like to sit together in the drawing room. There is some very valuable china there, Elizabeth can tell you the history of most of the pieces.'

He went towards Elizabeth and put his arm round her shoulders, placing his cheek besides hers. I could not be sure but I thought she turned away with an inexplicable expression, then he began to stroke her arm in a teasing fashion, saying, 'My daughter is unfriendly this evening, I expect it is because I am going out.'

'You know it isn't, Father, you can go anywhere you like.'

He laughed, coaxing her to smile, and I felt acutely embarrassed, as though I watched a man coaxing the girl he loved into noticing him. Abruptly she pulled away from him so that the stroking had to stop.

'Oh well,' he said, smiling in a resigned way, 'If we are not to be forgiven I will let Miss Chalfont try to restore you to a better humour. Goodnight girls.'

186

The drawing room was the most pleasant room in the house, furnished in shades of blue and beige. I dutifully expressed my appreciation of the china figures she showed to me and the handsome tea services in the china cabinets.

'I don't suppose you have seen such beautiful china before,' she said, and I smiled a little at the condescension in her voice.

'Oh but I have, Elizabeth, my mother loved beautiful china and she bought several very lovely pieces in the early days of her marriage.'

'Why don't you have them with you now then?'

'I have some small pieces you can see if you like, the larger ornaments are still at my stepfather's house.'

'You didn't like him did you?'

'No.'

'Did you like your own father?'

'I never knew him, he died before I was born.'

'My mother died just after I was born. I never knew her.'

'That has been very sad for you, Elizabeth.'

'Not really, Father said my mother was a butterfly creature and I would have learned little from her.'

'You should not think of her like that, Elizabeth, in spite of what your father might say.'

'But you know I always obey him.'

There was something strange about our conversation and I felt that she was baiting me in some way. She seldom showed any interest in my life before I arrived at Red Gables.

Tonight for some reason she seemed different and I realized it was the first night we had spent together since my arrival. It is true we had ridden together but Elizabeth was no horsewoman and I devoted all my attention to keeping her safe.

'My father was angry with me before dinner,' she said, 'that is why he has gone out.'

I stared at her in some surprise. 'How could you possibly have made him angry – what on earth did you do?'

'He saw me talking to Jimmy the idiot boy at the morning room window.'

'It isn't very kind to call Jimmy the idiot boy, and in any

case why should your father mind so much? Jimmy is perfectly harmless.'

'My father was jealous.'

'Oh Elizabeth, how could he possibly be jealous of Jimmy? After all the boy usually runs away like a startled rabbit whenever he sees us.'

'He doesn't run away when I am alone.'

I was out of my depth. There was something sly and alien about Elizabeth, almost as though she were mocking me with her talk of her father's jealousy, and suddenly impatient with her I changed the subject.

'Does Mrs Holt take in the mail each morning, Elizabeth?'

'Yes.'

'And what happens to it then?'

'It is taken to my father's study so that he can deal with it. Are you expecting a letter?'

'I have been expecting several for a long time now but it seems everybody has forgotten my existence.'

'Have you asked my father?'

'Yes. He told me there haven't been any letters for me.'

I saw a flash of amusement in her eyes but immediately it was replaced by her usual demure expression. I found myself wishing it was time to retire but it was only eight o'clock. As though picking up my thoughts she said, 'You miss other people, don't you? What was it like being at school with other girls?'

'I enjoyed school most of the time, some of the girls were nice, others not so nice. One has to take the rough with the smooth.'

'Did you meet boys?'

'Why no, it was a girls' school.'

'But do you know any boys?'

'I knew boys when I lived at Grindale.'

'I only know Jimmy and he doesn't talk much, but he likes me Tessa, I can tell by the way he looks at me and the way he touches me.'

'He touches you, Elizabeth!' I said sharply.

'He strokes my face and my hands and he looks so sad, as though he would like to hold me like my father does.'

188

My mind was alert to all sorts of dangers. Her face was pensive and strangely innocent, and yet I saw something infinitely sinister in her words. What did I know of fathers?

'Elizabeth, you should not encourage Jimmy by being nice to him. It isn't fair.'

'Why ever not? I've known him all my life.'

'We don't know how intensely he feels things. We both know he isn't quite normal but we don't know anything about his emotions. I don't think your father is being jealous, simply protective.'

She laughed at that, not the open innocent laughter of a young girl but the cyncial laughter of a woman. 'You don't know everything do you Tessa?' she snapped spitefully.

'No I don't, but I know that I wouldn't encourage Jimmy if he started to touch me, and you shouldn't either.'

For several moments she sat with a sulky expression on her pretty face, then she went to the mirror where she stood rearranging her hair.

'I hate these silly ringlets,' she said angrily. 'I don't know why Father insists on me wearing them unless it's to make me look more like my mother.'

'You are very like her.'

'I know and she's dead. I want to look like me, to wear my hair how I like it and dress how I like. Look at this dress, it's years out of date, and that silly velvet riding habit makes me look like a girl out of a story book. Sometimes I hate my father, he keeps me looking like a child but expects me to behave like a woman.'

'You know you don't hate him at all Elizabeth, you're just unhappy because you've quarrelled.'

'I shall lock my bedroom door tonight so that he can't come in.'

'Does he always come into your bedroom?'

Her stormy eyes wavered before mine, and muttering she said, 'To say goodnight. I won't let him come in tonight, though.'

'Where shall we ride tomorrow?' I asked brightly, needing to change the subject with its sinister undertones and distasteful implications. 'Up to the woods, or would you like to try your hand at jumping? Just a very small fence.'

'I'm not ready for jumping yet. I'm not much good at riding anyway.'

'You're afraid of your pony Elizabeth, until you lose that fear you will never improve your horsemanship.'

'I don't enjoy riding. Where do we ever ride to? Round the park, up to the woods or along the path under the wall.'

'My, but we are in a rebellious mood tonight.'

She stared at me sullenly. 'I don't suppose I'll ever get away from here, but you could, you're not his daughter, you don't need to live here if you don't want to. Why don't you just run?'

'Because your father employs me to be your friend and companion, and I think perhaps you need me more than you know.'

To my dismay she burst into tears. Through the sobs which shook her dainty frame she choked, 'You won't ever leave me will you Tessa, you'll take me with you if you go, please?'

'Nobody's going anywhere Elizabeth, you're just upset tonight. You'll see, it'll all be different in the morning. Suppose we have some cocoa in here and then we'll go straight to bed.'

By the time the cocoa arrived she was kneeling on the rug in front of the fire staring into the flames while I was leafing through a magazine on field sports: a scene so normal the servant could never have guessed at the problems we were both troubled by.

The events of that night made me very watchful and as the weeks wore on I began to sense a terrible uneasiness. Beneath the Chantrys' superficial calm was tension, a pulsating antagonism, and I could not tell who was suffering most.

I wrote no more letters, there didn't seem much point when I received no replies. But then came the afternoon when a servant came into the library to tell me that I had a visitor.

I stared at her in amazement, saying stupidly, 'A visitor for me!'

'Yes miss, a young man.'

All eyes were upon me, and Elizabeth said, 'Well why don't you go and see who it is?'

I hurried towards the front door. For a few moments I stared at Alec in disbelief, then I ran laughing into his outstretched arms.

'Oh Alec I'm so glad to see you, but why didn't you write, why didn't you answer my letters?'

'I only received one letter and I did answer it, months ago.'

'I'm not sure where we can talk. I don't even know if Mr Chantry is in the house.'

'Can't we talk outside? It's a lovely day.'

He was right. Fluffy clouds sped across a deep blue sky and the hills looked beautiful, blue in the distance and pale green above us. The trees in the park were in heavy leaf and beneath our feet the grass was short and crisp. I felt so happy to be with Alec on such a day, and he took my hand as we sauntered towards the gates.

I found myself telling him eagerly about recent events of the last few months.

'I say,' he said, 'you don't think there's anything funny going on between this chap Chantry and Elizabeth, do you?'

'I'm not sure what you mean, Alec.'

'You know very well what I mean: like a nice juicy bit of incest for instance.'

'Oh Alec, trust you to put it into words. I honestly don't know and I don't want to think it either. There are whole days when I simply think they are a normal father and daughter and then something sparks off and I begin to wonder all over again.'

'What will you do if you find there is anything like that?'

'I don't know.'

'It's against the law, you should leave and then report it.'

'I'm afraid it wouldn't be as easy as that.'

'Because you need the job you mean?'

'That's one of the reasons.'

'It's a strange thing but nobody in these parts seems to know very much about Chantry and yet his family have been here for years. It's almost as though the house and even the village were no part of the West Riding at all, like a little private kingdom. Why have you never been to see us at Grindale?'

'Would you believe it if I told you we never ride outside the grounds?'

He stared at me askance. 'Heavens above, girl, that's not normal! Haven't you told him you had friends in the area, haven't you demanded to go out?'

'I did go out once to post a letter to Susan and I was severely chastised for it. There are things about this place I don't really know, Alec. His wife took her own life when Elizabeth was only a baby, perhaps that changed him somehow.'

'Perhaps it was his behaviour that caused her to do what she did.'

'I don't know Alec, I only wish I did. Elizabeth is extraordinarily like his wife ... surely he can't imagine that she is his wife come back to him?'

'He knows damn well she's not his wife. There's something very odd going on Tessa. I was hurt when you didn't write, I thought you no longer wanted anything to do with me. My parents too thought it strange that they hadn't heard from you. How many letters did you write to me?'

'About five.'

'Well I never received them, and the Mother Superior said she had heard from you only once since you left the convent and she has written to you several times.'

'I should have listened to her Alec, she warned me about taking this position. But why are we talking only about me, what happened to you? Did you go to university, or into your father's firm?'

'Neither Tessa, that's why I so desperately wanted to see you.' He was smiling down at me, his eyes bright, his entire demeanour filled with pride and joy and impetuously I said, 'You don't mean it Alec, you really got what you wanted?'

'Yes. I wore the old man down at last. I've been at Sandhurst now for over a year. In just over six months I'll be joining a regiment.'

'You don't know which one?'

'The Royal Horse Artillery I hope, it's what I've set my sights on.'

'Oh Alec I'm so proud of you, you'll make a wonderful officer, I just know it.'

'And when I've reached the exalted rank of first lieutenant in just a few years, you'll marry me?'

'So, it's ambitions you have is it? Who knows what beautiful women you might meet in the meantime.'

His face suddenly sobered. 'Don't stay here Tessa, cut and run. My mother'll be glad to have you at Briarcrag, she'll be able to find you plenty to do. She's chairwoman of this and that and the old man's a county councillor and aiming to be a Member of Parliament at the next election. The Hardcastles don't do anything by half, you should know that by now, my girl.'

'Oh I do, and I am more than honoured that the son of that illustrious family stepped off his pedestal long enough to seek out a little paid companion.'

He kissed me, then longer and more passionately he kissed me again until he released me blushing and breathless. Just then the gates ahead of us opened and Mr Chantry drove through. As he drew level he reigned in the pony and sat staring at us. I said haltingly, 'This is Alec Hardcastle, Mr Chantry, from Grindale.'

Neither of the men held out a hand in greeting. Mr Chantry merely nodded coldly while Alec said stiffly, 'How do you do, sir.'

'Shouldn't you be with Elizabeth at your lessons, Miss Chalfont?' Mr Chantry said sternly, ignoring Alec.

'I thought it more essential to see an old friend.'

'Very well Miss Chalfont, we will speak of it later. Good afternoon Mr Hardcastle.' With a crack of his whip he drove on.

'Supercilious blighter,' Alec exploded. 'What does he mean, "lessons"?'

'I sit with Elizabeth and her governess every day while she takes her lessons.'

He stared at me in disbelief. 'How utterly ridiculous. Does

he think you're an utter ignoramus?'

'I must always be with Elizabeth, Alec, unless he wants her to himself. Please don't mention any of this to your parents or to anybody else, it might get back to him and I don't want him to think I have been gossiping.'

'All right I won't say a word, but take my advice and get away as soon as you can. I don't like him and I don't like what you've told me about your life here.'

How I wished it was as simple as all that. And how could I make Alec understand what it was like to be alone and needing employment so desperately I was prepared to clutch at straws? Alec was on top of the world and I had no wish to burden him with my worries, or ruffle in any way the calm waters of his life.

I was called to Mr Chantry's study that evening. I sat clenching my hands. I was afraid but I was angry too. This man was my employer, nothing more, what right had he to order my life as strictly and narrowly as he ordered his daughter's? At last he looked up from his desk.

'Well Miss Chalfont, what have you to say for yourself?'

'I was not told that I could not have visitors, Mr Chantry. I have been here over a year and he is my first visitor.'

'May I ask if that young man is your lover?'

I choked in anger. 'Really, Mr Chantry, you have no right to ask such a question.'

'Oh but I believe I have. When I brought you here I wanted a companion for Elizabeth as pure and untouched as she herself, that is why I went to the convent, where I believed I could find such a girl. I saw myself as the protector of you both, nurtured in gentleness and needing no other companions.'

'That is an unnatural existence for both of us. People need people, all kinds of people, and you really have no right to withhold my letters or forbid me to have visitors.'

'In my own house young lady I may do anything I please.'

'Surely not when it concerns someone who is not a member of your family.'

'Even then. You are not of age and you came here under

my protection. As I see it it is my bounden duty to protect you from people like that young man.'

'You are not the guardian of my morals, sir.'

'I will make you sorry you said those words to me, Miss Chalfont. You will retire to your room now and you will not see Elizabeth again until you feel sufficiently cleansed and chastened. Under no circumstances will I allow my daughter's purity of mind to be contaminated.'

I stared at him in disbelief. I felt like calling him a humbug, a despicable hypocrite, but I wasn't sure. Until I was absolutely certain of my facts I could not speak. Gathering my shattered dignity, I stalked towards the door.

With my hand on the knob I heard him say, 'There will be no riding, Miss Chantry, I myself will ride with Elizabeth. And there will be no lessons with Miss Allinson. Am I understood?'

'Perfectly sir. Do I take it I am confined to my room or may I walk in the gardens? I can assure you that Mr Hardcastle will not be coming here again, he is returning to Sandhurst tonight.'

He did not deign to answer me, and with flaming cheeks and deep anger in my heart I ran up to my room. For the next few days I would have only my own company and although that did not worry me unduly the injustice of it made me wish I could leave Red Gables, never to return.

It was June, the sun was a golden glory and the scent of honeysuckle came through the open window, making my heart yearn for old innocent enchantments like picnics in the woods and roaming ancient bridle paths under a summer sky. Instead the next few days, or even weeks, were a punishment entirely out of equation with the crime, if seeing Alec had indeed been a crime. I was not to know how the events of the day would reflect upon what remained of my life at Red Gables.

CHAPTER EIGHTEEN

I cannot say that I missed Elizabeth's company overmuch. At her best she was agreeable and malleable, at her worst she was moody and apathetic. I was not going to miss the lessons either.

Every day I debated with myself how I should get away from Red Gables. My salary was paid until the end of the year so I was under an obligation to stay until then and my whole being recoiled from searching for work in Leeds where it was becoming increasingly difficult to find.

On my solitary walks I discovered the woods behind the house and I grew to love them: a shallow stream that bubbled and bounced between the stones, narrow sunlit paths to follow, and rabbits. I usually saw the tail end of them, white tails scuttering along the paths.

If I stood on the highest point I could see above the wall and I often saw children playing in the fields beyond. One day they waved to me enthusiastically and I waved back. They were only very young children but even this small diversion dispelled some of the isolation I was being made to feel.

It was late afternoon several days after my confrontation with Mr Chantry when I ran back to the house rather later than usual. I let myself in through the conservatory and here I encountered Jake the gardener. I smiled at him and he held out a beautiful begonia.

'This un's a rare beauty, miss, just come to 'er flowerin'.'

'She is beautiful Jake. I don't think I've ever seen one quite that colour before.'

'No miss, this un's new. Are yer goin' in the 'ouse, miss?'

'Yes Jake, is there something you want?'

'If yer see mi son Jimmy in there will yer tell 'im I'll soon be off 'ome. 'Ee took some plants to the drawin' room a while ago now an' the lad's no idea about time.'

'I'll find him Jake, I expect he's in the kitchens.'

I went first to the drawing room but there was no sign of Jimmy. I met Mary in the hall but she didn't know where he was.

'I 'aven't clapped eyes on 'im all afternoon.'

'Thank you Mary, he's probably gone to the stables.'

I was surprised by the sly amused look that came over her face and even more surprised by her next words. ''Ave yer tried the library miss, or one o' the rooms where yer might find Miss Elizabeth?'

I stared at her curiously for a moment, then turned away. Was the servant trying to tell me that Elizabeth and Jimmy were often to be found together? If so I wouldn't give her the satisfaction of thinking that I was surprised.

As I neared Elizabeth's door I heard voices. If I had heard her father's voice I would immediately have moved on, but it was Elizabeth's voice humming a tune and then Jimmy's guttural mutterings and inane laughter.

I knocked smartly on the door before flinging it open. Jimmy sat in the middle of her bed cross-legged, his eyes filled with glee as they rested on Elizabeth clad only in her frilly underskirt. She was dancing, twisting this way and that and moving her arms rhythmically to the tune she was humming.

Resolutely I slammed the door shut behind me. Elizabeth spun round, her eyes wild with terror, but Jimmy after the first shock merely rocked himself to and fro, laughing as before.

'Jimmy, your father is waiting for you in the conservatory. Go there at once,' I commanded.

He merely stared at me vacantly, his mouth open, and made no move. He was a tall fine-looking lad with a shock of silver-fair hair not unlike my own for colour. At first sight you would have thought him a fine specimen of young manhood until you became aware of the vacant blue eyes and the mouth falling loosely, stupidly open.

More firmly I repeated my request and he sluggishly rose. 'She were dancin' fer me, Miss Elizabeth were dancin'.'

'Yes, I know Jimmy but you must go before your father comes looking for you.'

'But she 'adn't finished, I wanted to see 'er finish 'er dance.'

I opened the door and watched him lumbering down the corridor muttering to himself.

Elizabeth, her expression sulky, reached for the dress which lay on the floor. 'Are you going to tell Father?' she asked fearfully.

'Of course not, but please don't ever do that again. You might do it once too often.'

'I don't know what you mean.'

'I think you do.'

'Well I don't care. It would serve my father right.'

'What, to be seduced by a boy who isn't quite normal? A boy who doesn't know from one moment to the next what he is doing!'

'It's no worse than being seduced by my father,' she snapped, her dark eyes blazing.

I stared at her stunned, then suddenly she crumpled to the floor, sobbing wildly. I gathered her into my arms. 'Oh Elizabeth, you don't know what you are saying, I'm not angry with you, I am only trying to protect you.'

'You don't believe me, do you Tessa? But it's true. Ever since I was twelve he's forced himself on me and there are times when he calls me Caroline. Why does he sometimes think I'm my mother?'

I didn't know what to do or what to say. I was only a few years older than this girl but I felt a million light years away from the things she was telling me and which my mind could barely accept. I had seen lust and depravity in my stepfather's house but this was something else, something so ugly my mind was refusing to take it in and all the time Elizabeth was babbling and sobbing out her hatred for the father I thought she had adored.

'Isn't there anybody you could tell?' I asked anxiously. 'Some older person who could help you?'

'Tessa, nobody must know, not ever. Promise you won't tell a living soul. Don't you see, all my life people would talk about me and point at me, and he would be punished, they'd probably put him in prison.'

'They would, but at least you'd be rid of him, he couldn't hurt you any more.'

'But he's my *father* Tessa, and when I was a little girl he was good and kind.'

For what seemed an age we sat together on the carpet with Elizabeth sobbing and my tormented thoughts trying in vain to find a solution. From the park I heard the sound of hoofbeats and carriage wheels and I knew he was returning home.

'Elizabeth, it's your father,' I urged fiercely, 'I must go, he mustn't find me here and you must compose yourself. If he sees you like this he will be sure something has happened.'

'I'll tell him tonight that I want you back Tessa, but you must promise me first that you won't say a word to a living soul. If you don't I shall jump through the window just like my mother did.'

I wanted to tell her that this was no time for melodrama but I could see she meant it. She was as distraught as her mother must have been on the day she killed herself.

'Elizabeth, I must go before he comes. Lock your door after me, with any luck he will think you are asleep.'

She nodded dully, and even as I ran to my room I heard his footsteps on the stairs, his rapping on her door, and his voice urging her to open it.

I felt sick and shaken. This man who liked to appear so moral, who was concerned that my innocent letters might bring an evil world within the radius of the prison he had built around us, who had questioned my suitability to be his daughter's companion because I had received Alec's kiss, was a monster. It was hypocrisy beyond belief, but it was cynical and clever hypocrisy because he was protecting himself. If Elizabeth learned nothing of the normal joys of life how would she be able to distinguish between right and wrong, between the normal and the immoral?

Elizabeth was a girl at a most vulnerable age, but how could I be sure that she was telling me the truth? In her loneliness wasn't it possible that she might fantasize about a lover, dramatize events because her life was so uneventful?

January couldn't come quickly enough for me.

It was several days after the scene I had witnessed in Elizabeth's bedroom and the day after I had been restored to riding and lessons with her. That afternoon she developed a chill which grew worse overnight and immediately the doctor was summoned. It was nothing worse than a bad chill but her father confined her to her room, and to my utter joy I was allowed to ride alone.

It was a treat to ride the horse to his full potential, galloping him across the park and jumping the privet fences, his long easy strides eating up the distance. I longed to take him through the gates and ride up to the fells. Poor horse, he was as much a prisoner as I was and he too was enjoying this unexpected chance to stretch his legs and to jump for joy. For most of the afternoon we stayed out, in spite of threatening clouds and the sharp feeling of rain in the air.

When eventually I returned to the stables I was surprised that no groom came forward to unsaddle him. He was sweating profusely so I set about unsaddling him myself. It was then that I heard low moans coming from the tack room, followed by the mutterings of the men.

I went into the tack room where the grooms stood looking down at a rough table where a man lay stretched out, moaning with pain. Because the man lay on his stomach I did not recognize him at first. His back was a mass of bright red weals standing out like bloody ribbons and the blood was dripping on to the rough worktop. Jake was bathing his wounds tenderly, his face set and angry. I recognized Jimmy by his shock of fair hair and by the pained anger on his father's face.

'But who has done this?' I asked one of the grooms.

'The master took a horsewhip to him, miss.'

'But why, what had he done?'

The young man lowered his head but Jimmy's father answered. 'The lad took a plant to Miss Elizabeth's bedroom, 'ee'd 'eard she were poorly. 'Ee's done nothin' wrong.'

Suddenly I became aware of a new presence in the room

and looking over my shoulder I saw my employer. The men retreated in a small group and only Jimmy's father stood near the boy.

As tenderly as any woman Jake gathered Jimmy into his arms and walked slowly towards the door, passing Mr Chantry without a glance while the men stood with bent heads, clutching their caps.

'Get back to your work,' he said sternly, 'there's been quite enough time wasted down here already.'

Slowly they shuffled past him, sullenly, their hatred so intense that I could smell it, but he seemed impervious.

'I was too severe,' he said to me. 'I should have realized the boy intended her no harm, but when I saw him bending over her I was beside myself with anger. I could not bear that fool, that simpleton to touch her.'

I didn't answer him, I was too angry. I made as if to walk past him but he said, 'Elizabeth will eat dinner in her room this evening, perhaps you will oblige me by dining with me downstairs.'

'As you wish, sir.'

'Promptly at seven then, Miss Chalfont.'

I changed for dinner early so I had time to go to Elizabeth's room before dinner.

She was on the window seat in her dressing gown, her dark hair released from its ringlets and hanging loose over her shoulders. Like this she seemed more adult but she was very pale and I suspected she had been crying.

'Do you know about Jimmy?' I asked gently.

'Yes, I saw it happen, right there on the path. Honestly Tessa I didn't ask him to come in here. He only brought me a plant.'

'The boy's back is in ribbons Elizabeth, that should warn you never to encourage Jimmy again. Another time your father might even kill him.'

I had told her in an unnecessarily brutal manner, hoping to make her see that she was playing with fire but all she said in reply was, 'Why are you dressed so early for dinner?'

'Your father has invited me to dine with him.'

She nodded, then brightening a little she said, 'I told you

my father would invite you back, I told him I needed you, that I wanted everything to go back to normal.'

Normal! When had anything in this terrible house been normal?

'Promise that you will lock your door and keep it locked unless it's one of the servants,' I urged.

'He will be so angry.'

'Elizabeth, promise me.'

I waited outside until I heard the key turn in the lock and only then did I walk downstairs.

For the main part we ate in silence. I was glad when coffee was served, and refused the brandy he offered.

'You should drink brandy, my dear, it is good for the digestion and only the best grapes are grown in the region of Cognac.

'By the way, how is my daughter's French, Miss Chalfont?'

'Not good Mr Chantry, but then neither is Miss Allinson's.'

'You don't think much of Miss Allinson, do you?'

'Not in comparison to the sisters at St Clare's.'

'But you do see that it would be quite impossible for Elizabeth to travel every day to St Clare's from here?'

'The convent is a boarding school, sir.'

'And then you would be out of a job, have you thought of that Miss Chalfont? You evidently don't know when you are well off. You have a beautiful house to live in, horses to ride, servants to wait on you and food set before you. Isn't that worth a great deal?'

'A very great deal, sir.'

'Then why are you rebellious?'

'It would be worth a great deal more if I did not feel a prisoner here, if I could move about freely and take Elizabeth with me. That I could receive my friends here and open my own mail.'

There, it was out. I expected his anger, perhaps even his dismissal but I was not prepared for his amusement. He threw back his head and laughed delightedly, and poured another brandy. 'I admire your spirit Miss Chalfont, but you are so very young, you know nothing of the evil and temptations in the world. I want only to protect you both until you are old enough to sift the good from the bad, the right from the wrong.'

I was aware that his speech was becoming slurred as he filled his glass yet again.

'You don't answer me, Miss Chalfont,' he persisted.

'I am nearly nineteen years of age sir, there are girls who are married at my age and bringing up children. I know right from wrong and I can differentiate between moral and immoral.'

'Oh to be so young and so sure,' he mocked. With a little bow in my direction he made his uncertain way towards the door, taking the brandy glass and the bottle with him. I knew what brandy did to a man, I'd seen my stepfather worse for drink and I feared for Elizabeth.

I went straight to my room, trying Elizabeth's door on the way. It was locked and there were no sounds from within.

It was dusk outside my window and the wind had risen, pointing to a wild and stormy night.

I washed and undressed, putting on my robe while I brushed my hair at the mirror. My hair needed cutting, it was very long now, lying in silver fair strands around my shoulders. I stared at my reflection with a strange curiosity. It was a woman's face that stared back at me. Almost overnight it seemed that my mouth had developed more passionate curves, my candid blue-grey eyes become more mysterious, and the rounded face that had always seemed so ordinary was now a perfect oval, shadowed and alluring.

I did not want to be a woman in this house, but then childhood had been no protection for Elizabeth.

I lay on top of the bed watching the play of the candle flame across the ceiling, and drifted off to sleep. I thought at first that it was the curtains billowing at the open window that woke me, and I rose hurriedly to close it.

It was then I heard the urgent tapping on a bedroom door and the deep murmuring of a man's voice. I opened my door to stand nervously listening in the darkness.

As my eyes grew accustomed to the gloom I saw a man at

Elizabeth's door and he was knocking again, this time almost shouting. 'Elizabeth, *open* this door. *Open it* or I shall break it in.'

In desperation I ran towards him, clutching at his arm, pleading with him, 'Mr Chantry, have you forgotten that Elizabeth is not well? Please go away.'

He stared at me through narrowed lids as though at first he didn't recognize me, and then to my horror his hand gripped my wrist, so tightly that I cried out with the pain of it.

He pulled me roughly towards my room while my fingers went numb from the pressure of his hand round my wrist. Brutally he flung me into the room and I stood swaying beside my bed, my eyes wide with apprehension, and for a moment he stared back at me and by the light from the candle now spluttering in its death throes I saw that his eyes were bloodshot, his mouth loose and trembling.

'Please Mr Chantry,' I gasped, 'please return to your room.'

He didn't move, and I went forward and gently closed the door in his face. But while my shaking fingers tried to lock the door it was suddenly flung open so violently it sent my sprawling, and then he was upon me, winding my hair round his fist until I cried out in pain, kissing my mouth. The smell of brandy sickened me, yet I could hardly breathe because of the hardness of his mouth on mine and I could taste blood where his teeth bit into my lips.

I was kicking wildly, my hands crushed beneath his weight. His hands were at the neck of my nightgown, pulling and tearing at it in a frenzy and I heard it tear, then his hands were on my body, rough and searching, and heaven help me my strength was leaving me. But now my hands were free and my fingers encountered the heavy candlestick. With a strength born of desperation I lifted it and brought it down on the side of his head. I heard him groan, and before he could summon his wits I brought it down again. This time I heard the sickening thud it made and I felt his hands relax so that I could wriggle out from under him. He lay very still.

My nightgown was torn from top to bottom and my hands were sticky with blood. My teeth were chattering until I could hardly hear myself think and he lay so still that only the occasional moan told me he was alive. Grabbing my robe I ran to the stairs. It was so dark I had to feel my way to the conservatory. Every sound, every creak made me stop with a thundering heart, terrified that he was lumbering after me, his eyes gleaming with madness.

My fingers were hurting as I struggled with the bolts on the conservatory door and when an owl hooted somewhere out there in the darkness a scream rose in my throat. At last I had the doors open and I took to my heels, and ran whimpering down the long drive towards the gates.

I was unaware of the wind striking cold through my flimsy robe. My feet too were bare and the ground cold, but I never paused. The night sounds, the wind and the tossing trees, the sudden lash of rain and the rustlings in the bushes did not deter me. I ran until my breath was coming in painful gasps and I had to stand holding on to the iron gates until I felt calmer.

Behind me the house was in darkness and the path was empty. The gates were locked and I skirted the wall until I found an old oak tree overhanging the wall.

Climbing the tree was no problem but there was a fair drop on the other side. It did however overlook a grassy banking and with a prayer I let go the branch and dropped, winding myself in the process. I lay still until I could get my breath back and the rain fell on my face, chilling me to the bone.

I cared nothing for the rain, I only knew that I was free. I did not even ask myself if the man I had wounded could be dead, nothing mattered but my freedom, and I set off down the country lane, glad of the solitary lamp that still burned. My nightgown and robe clung to my body damp and cold, but in the lamplight I could see the splashes of blood on my nightgown and I held up my hands so that the rain would clean them. Seeing the dark crimson stain, I asked myself if I could have killed him. And who would believe the story I had to tell? They hanged murderers, didn't they? But surely they wouldn't hang me, I was too young, and I had been fighting for my life and my innocence. But I wasn't a virgin! Oh surely I wouldn't be branded as a harlot and murderess?

Another heavy burst of rain sent me running towards the cottages. I went to the first one and beat upon the door and eventually I saw lamplight through an upstairs window and heard heavy footsteps on the stairs.

'Who is it?' a man's trembling voice asked. I beat on the door again and this time it opened to reveal a man and woman in their nightclothes.

'Why it's a lass,' the woman said in amazement, and after that I must have fainted because I next found myself lying on a horsehair sofa pulled up in front of the fire and the woman was chafing my hands.

''Urry up wi' that tea, Jack,' she called out, 'she's comin' round.'

The tea she poured out for me was so hot and sweet that it made me cough. I felt frustrated. I wanted the tea but it was too hot to drink and I was so thirsty. Tears of self-pity rolled down my cheeks and sensing my impatience she added cold milk to the brew and held it to my lips again.

'Yer safe now,' she said, 'my but yer didn't 'alf give us a fright. Where've yer come fro', lass?'

I was in no condition to tell them my story yet and she soon realized it. 'Yer can sleep on't couch,' she said practically, 'I'll cover yer wi' a blanket an' Joe'll put a bit more coal on the fire. Yer can tell us yer story in the mornin'.'

Their whisperings woke me the following morning, but I lay with my eyes closed.

'Joe, did yer see 'er 'ands, covered wi' blood they were an' there's more on 'er nightdress and it's ripped fro' top to bottom.'

'Ay well, she could 'a tumbled somewhere, but the lass were frightened out of 'er wits. P'raps we should tell the police.'

'Not till she's 'ad a chance to tell us 'erself what 'appened,' the woman said sharply.

At that I allowed my eyes to flutter open, meeting their concerned stares.

She set about making breakfast, and after we had eaten I told all the events of the previous night. They listened in silence, but now and again I could see strange looks pass between them. They went into the kitchen and I heard them whispering. Then the woman came back alone, saying, 'Joe 'as to get to work now, luv, but yer'll be all right wi' me. Wi've bin 'aving a little talk an wi've decided yer shouldn't stay 'ere too long in case they come lookin' fer yer. Mi daughter, our Lily'll be 'ere presently, yer can go back wi' 'er.'

'She won't mind?'

'Bless yer no miss, but Joe works on Chantry's land, he's a forester. We 'as to be careful. We'as to think about our bread an' butter.'

A strange feeling came over me, a warning that I was not safe yet, and seeking reassurance I asked, 'Do you know Mr Chantry well then?'

'Eh bless yer lass, nobody knows 'im well. E's allus bin a strange un, remote like, even as a youngster, an' I've never set eyes on that daughter of 'is. Well now, if yer'd like to come upstairs wi might find some clothes our Lily left behind. 'Er 'usband works at the big 'ouse too, groom 'ee is, you probably knows 'im.'

She found a blouse and skirt of Lily's and some not very exciting underwear, and they fitted me reasonably well. My hair was a bedraggled sight but after brushing it she lent me a long slide to hold it back from my face and I felt much more presentable.

The morning wore on but there was no sign of Lily and my anxiety returned. 'Does your daughter always come in the morning?' I asked.

'Well nearly allus, p'raps somethin' 'appened to prevent 'er, but she'll be 'ere presently.'

She confided to me that her name was Alice Jenkins and her son-in-law was called Michael Gee. When she described him I remembered him perfectly, a thin ferret-faced little man who could never quite look you in the eye, the one groom I had never really liked at Red Gables.

She seemed surprised when her husband arrived home soon after four and again I heard the whisperings in the kitchen which filled my heart full of dread. Suppose Chantry was dead and that I had killed him, suppose he was so badly

207

hurt he might die? All sorts of terrifying thoughts came into my head while they muttered to each other and I could stand it no longer. Taking my courage in both hands I walked into the kitchen.

They both spun round to face me and I said, 'Mrs Jenkins, I feel I shouldn't stay here, I am putting you both in a most embarrassing position and I have friends in Grindale, I could go there.'

'Nay lass, yer needn't do that,' Mr Jenkins said quickly. 'Mi daughter'll be 'ere later. I've told 'em about yer bein' 'ere.'

'Do you know what is happening at the house?'

'Only that it's shut up like a clam. The doctor were there this mornin' but since then there's not bin a soul, neither in nor out.'

Dusk came and I began to feel like a prisoner and that they were my jailers. I sat between them, my anxieties mounting, and I felt that they were listening for every sound along the lane. Once or twice she went to peer along the lane.

I watched the darkness creeping slowly across the fells and I knew that soon it would be completely dark and that it was not Lily they were waiting for. I had to get away, but I was no match for Joe Jenkins and his stout wife. So what I could not do by strength I must do by guile.

'I would like to wash before your daughter arrives, Mrs Jenkins, could I do so in the kitchen?'

'Ey lass, yer look clean and tidy as it is.'

'But I would like to look a little more presentable.'

She could see that I was adamant, but I couldn't stop her bustling into the kitchen ahead of me. She found me a clean towel and stood hesitantly until I said, 'I'm quite all right now Mrs Jenkins, I'll come back as soon as I've finished.'

There was something in my face, some expression she was not proof against, and reluctantly she shuffled back into the living room while I closed the door behind her.

As soon as she had gone I slipped through the back door and ran for the side gate. I was free, but even as I congratulated myself I heard two riders approaching.

Almost immediately the front door opened and Joe Jenkins hurried down the path.

I leapt into some bushes, and then I heard Chantry's voice. Peering through the gloom I saw him at the gate on his big bay horse. With him was the groom I recognized as Lily's husband. Mrs Jenkins came running from the house. 'She's gone Joe, she's gone through the back door.'

There was consternation and I heard Chantry exploding savagely, 'You fool Jenkins, you bloody fool! You had her, why couldn't you keep her?' The light streaming from the cottage door showed me the white bandage covering his head and the chilling anger on his face.

'We weren't to know she'd go like that sir,' Mrs Jenkins was saying. 'We couldn't hold 'er by force.'

'Those were my orders Jenkins, to hold her by force if you had to. How long since she went?'

'Only minutes sir, she can't 'a gone far.'

'Right Gee, you ride on down the lane and I'll ride back towards the house. If you see her keep her.'

Gee set off down the lane and Chantry said harshly, 'Have you any idea where she might have gone?'

'No sir, the lass were a stranger to us,' Mrs Jenkins said.

I blessed her at that moment. I had told her I knew people at Grindale but she had not told him I had mentioned them. Poor sad people, so dependent upon him for their livelihood they had been willing to hand me back to him for chastisement, and yet at the last moment she was trying to shield me.

I waited until the Jenkinses had returned to their cottage and until the hoofbeats receded in the distance, then I took to my heels and headed for the stile and the path that led across the fell.

The years when I had roamed the fells around Grindale came to my rescue now. I knew every twist and turn, every grassy knoll, as I made my way towards Grindale.

I stumbled on through the night, at one time passing close to a farmhouse where I was frightened momentarily by the barking of dogs, and then I came to the beck and knew that in minutes I would come to the stile that led into the churchyard at Grindale.

I knew there was a decrepit shed in the Elliotts' back garden where the old man had at one time kept his pigeons and I made for this.

The night seemed endless. I sat in the chair the old man had once used, and trembled with the memory of the hatred I had felt towards Chantry, my overwhelming need to punish him still because he had made me a fugitive – as though I were the culprit instead of he. If I went to the police would they believe me? They were clannish, these country people, they still believed in the old feudal system of an overlord and the allegiance of serfs to the great houses. Though in Grindale, fortunately, Chantry was not the overlord.

I watched the dawn creeping slowly across the hills. It came gently with delicate rose, turning to a soft silver grey like the breast of a pigeon and then the grey turned to gold and the sun came up scattering the early morning mist that hovered above the fells while from the old elms in the churchyard the rooks rose in a flurry of blue black feathers into the morning sky. Smoke was coming from cottage chimneys now and nearby a rooster crowed, making me suddenly aware how I had missed the normal sounds of everyday life at Red Gables: dogs barking, milk churns clanking and the closing of cottage doors as the men set out to their work in the fields.

I ran down the garden path, hoping the Elliotts would let me in before people came onto the lane. I knocked tentatively and almost at once there was Mrs Elliott, staring at me with her face smiling a welcome as she pulled me into her arms.

My eyes filled with tears and hurriedly she said, 'Nay lass, there's no call fer tears, yer welcome at any time. Sit yer down 'ere lass an' I'll see about breakfast. Look whose 'ere Dad, it's Tessa an' the lass looks frozen.'

It was the warmth of her welcome that made me cry, the assumption that I could take my place in her little home as though I had never been away from it.

Mr Elliott came in with more coal for the fire and I moved closer to it, glad of the warmth. Ignoring my tears he said,

'We allus keeps a fire goin', even i' summer. The old man feels the cold in 'is old bones, 'ee were eighty-two i' March.'

For the first time in months I enjoyed my breakfast without sitting under Miss Allinson's lofty stare and the knowledge that I would never have to sit through Elizabeth's painful inadequacies again.

'I'm off now lass,' Mr Elliott called from the door. 'I'll leave yer two to talk.

'Tell 'er what yer want 'er to know lass, she's a good sort but she 'as a tongue that's over fond o' waggin'.'

I realized I would have to be very careful. Mrs Elliott was indeed a dear soul but she loved a good gossip and heaven knows my story was enough to make her welcome in many a home for a considerable time.

So I told her about Miss Allinson's lessons which I had hated, about my letters and the replies I had never received, and Alec's visit which had been so bitterly frowned upon. Of Elizabeth's involvement with her father I never said a word but I did tell her something of his attack on me, blaming it on drink, and my escape.

'Yer'll be wantin' to stay 'ere until yer decides what yer wants to do, Tessa?'

'Yes please, Mrs Elliott, for a few days until I've thought things out.'

'Yer can 'ave yer old room luv. I reckon yer didn't sleep much last night.'

'Nor the night before. I seem to have been running for days, I can't ever remember feeling so desperately tired before.'

'Well then yer must go right upstairs and get into bed. And don't worry, I don't want payin' for anythin'.'

I lay on top of the bed and I was asleep as soon as my head touched the pillow. If I dreamed I was not aware of it, and I remembered nothing until Mrs Elliott was shaking me gently and telling me that supper was ready.

I felt peaceful and safe in the Elliotts' cottage but I knew it could not be for long, it was merely a respite before moving on. I found myself thinking increasingly about Elizabeth. I had left her at the mercy of her father, but how could I have done otherwise?

Even more than leaving Elizabeth I regretted leaving my mother's emerald pendant which I had promised I would never part with.

I was pensive over the supper table and Mrs Elliott's father said to me kindly, 'Don't be in any 'urry to move on Tessa, yer very welcome to stay 'ere as long as yer wants.'

I thanked him gratefully, but all that night and the next day I fretted and worried, my mind going round like a dog at a fair until in the end despair overtook me and I was back at the beginning again.

I can't remember when the thought first flashed into my mind, but as the days wore on it became a compulsion too strong to be ignored. Quite firmly I knew what I was going to do. It all seemed suddenly so simple, as though the answer had been staring me in the face for weeks but I had been too blind to see it. I would go to Glamara where there were people of my flesh and blood, and I would face that stubborn bitter old man who was my grandfather and hear him tell me in his own words whether I was welcome or not. Then another thought struck: suppose my grandfather was dead? Then how would my mother's brother and sister receive me?

When I told the Elliotts of my decision the old man said, 'It's easy to think yer 'ates somebody when they're miles away lassy, but when 'ee sees yer standin' in front of 'im as pretty as a picture, then 'ee'll bury 'is pride. Whatever yer mother did to 'im 'ee's no right to take it out on yer.'

'What shall I do if he won't have me at Glamara?'

'Yer'll face that problem when yer comes to it lass, but it won't be a problem, mark my words. No man is goin' to spurn 'is own granddaughter when she's there askin' fer 'is 'elp.'

'I haven't any money, I'm afraid I shall have to borrow my fare.'

'Oh well, yer can pay mi back out o' the money yer grandfather settles on yer.'

We laughed. It was easy to feel suddenly cheered by their kindness and certainty that all would be well, even when the doubts persisted when I found myself alone.

Chapter Nineteen

I bade the Elliotts a tearful farewell and her last words to me
were, 'Now don't yer be standin' any nonsense fro' that
grandfather o' yours.'

I smiled tremulously at her and her father pushed a
shilling into my hand and said, 'Get yerself a cup o' tea at the
station i' Leeds, lass, yer might 'ave a little while ter wait fer
the train.'

Although it was late summer it was a grey day with a
promise of rain in the air. They stood at the garden gate until
I reached the end of the lane when I turned to wave to them.
I was not looking my best. I was still wearing 'our Lily's' old
skirt and her cleanly washed blouse, and had borrowed Mrs
Elliott's oldest raincoat. On my head was a shapeless felt hat
resembling a souwester and I was carrying a canvas bag
holding a pile of sandwiches and the old man's too-large
umbrella – he had said he would never need it again as he had
no cause these days to go out in the rain.

I felt like a tinker, the hat completely covering my hair and
my face peeping out from under it like a pale flower.

At Leeds, instead of the cup of tea I purchased a map of
the area around Glamara and while I waited for my
connection I spread it out over my knees devouring it avidly.

At last the train arrived and I found a corner seat. Three
others were in the compartment: a young couple in the far
corner holding hands and an elderly plump woman opposite
me, who promptly produced a pile of sandwiches from a
cardboard box. I produced mine as well, and we chatted as
we ate. It was a surprise to me when she remarked, 'If yer
gettin' off at Lambreck luv yer'd best be collectin' yer things.
It's the next stop.'

My things! My canvas bag and my massive umbrella. It

was my thoughts I should be collecting, and quickly before the train pulled into the station.

It was a tidy station with troughs filled with flowers and the bankings which in some stations were covered with weeds had been closely mown. Only a handful of people had left the train and I followed them down the narrow lane that led into the main street. I stood for a few moments looking at the scene and it was as though I had known it personally instead of only from my mother's description. Market stalls stood in the centre of the wide cobbled street but they were empty today because it was not Saturday. The Chalfont Arms was newly painted, its small-paned windows reflecting the sunlight, its window boxes filled with petunias.

It was like so many other dales villages but I found myself looking for special things as though I had known it as a child. I knew the baker's shop and the smell of newly baked bread, the greengrocers', his boxes of fruit and vegetables encroaching on the pavement, and I knew the cottage gardens gay with flowers. There was the village green in front of the stone church with its square Norman tower, and there were still white bustling ducks on the stream.

In the centre of the green was the great gnarled oak tree dressed in full leaf and a group of old men sat on the round seat which encircled it. I walked slowly, savouring every moment, and then beyond the church where the road divided I took the left fork which climbed the hill towards the gates of Glamara. I thought about my mother, somehow expecting that at any moment she would come riding down the lane on her fine horse, watched by many admiring eyes because she would look so beautiful with her dark red hair and elegant riding clothes. I could imagine her expression if she could see me arriving at her old home a shabby and poverty-stricken homeless waif.

The great iron gates stood open and with a lump in my throat and tears in my eyes I looked at Glamara for the first time. The drive seemed to go on for ever through the great trees of the parkland so that the house seemed far away, and much of it was hidden when the drive seemed to bend and wind downhill.

I trudged on clutching my umbrella and canvas bag, my borrowed shoes pinching a little, but now I could see the mere shining blue and silver, and beyond it the dark pines. I could see the house with its turrets and domes, soft mellow stone with tall chimneys and great mullioned windows. Behind the house rose tall rugged crags, and then rising to its full glory the reach of Mickle Fell.

In front of the house was a wide terrace on which giant white urns were set, now bright with flowers. I knew that the gardens were at the side of the house so as not to interrupt the majestic park and view of the mere.

With all the courage I could muster I climbed the few shallow steps up to the terrace, wondering if anyone watched me from the windows and what they would think of the strange shabby figure that was me. How had I dared walk down that drive with such impertinence, that drive which had seen the arrival of carriages bringing elegant men and women to the grand balls, and once, for a long glittering weekend, George III.

I did not have long to wait after ringing the bell. I heard footsteps approaching, the bolts were drawn back and I was facing a tall severe man with iron-grey hair who eyed me with a frown and some curiosity.

'Yes, miss?' he said stonily.

'I wish to see Sir John Chalfont please.'

He stared at me in amazement, then said, 'I'm afraid that won't be possible, miss.'

'Then is there some other person I could see – Miss Henrietta Chalfont perhaps, or Mr Godfrey.

'My name is Tessa Chalfont, Sir John is my grandfather.'

'Your grandfather!'

'I am Diana Chalfont's daughter.'

He continued to stare as though he could hardly believe my words, then he stepped back so that I might enter.

'I will ask Miss Chalfont to see you, miss, if you will just wait here.'

He walked stiff-backed and pompous towards the back of the hall and I was glad to be left to look at the beautiful carved shallow staircase ascending from the hall in a long graceful sweep. The dark oak panelling was relieved by priceless oil paintings and now and again by weapons of war. In several alcoves I could see suits of old armour and there were carved chests and great bowls of flowers. I could imagine how the hall would glow when a fire burned in the colossal stone fireplace, and the perfume of pine logs filling the air.

After only a few minutes I heard the butler's footsteps returning together with others, this time the light quick footsteps of a woman and I recognized her immediately as the woman I had seen in the tea lounge in Leeds: Aunt Hetty.

She put on her glasses as she reached me and I made my eyes meet hers bravely. The butler stood behind her, waiting no doubt to eject me should I prove to be an impostor, but she turned to him saying, 'You may go Wilson, I will ring if I need you.'

Although she was so small I was again aware of her air of breeding and good taste. She wore a well-fitting tweed skirt and a soft beige cashmere twin set, a single row of pearls and pearl ear studs. She had none of my mother's vibrant beauty but she had a delicate pretty face, sweet and gentle, and when she smiled it was illuminated with a definite charm.

'We will go into the small drawing room,' she said, 'we shall not be disturbed in there. Perhaps you would like to take off your outdoor clothing.'

I was glad to discard the umbrella and canvas bag and if she was surprised at my curious garb she was far too well-bred to show it. I shook out my hair, and stood before her in Lily's clean shirt blouse and faded blue skirt.

She folded my raincoat and placed the other things upon it on a chair, saying, 'I will ask one of the maids to put these in the cloakroom after we have had a little chat.'

I followed her, all the time looking round me curiously so as not to miss anything. The room we entered was at the back of the house overlooking the rose garden and it was beautiful. I was immediately aware of soft shades of beige and rose and blue and I was invited to sit in a soft velvet chair so that I could see the gardens through the window behind her chair.

She was staring at me in a puzzled manner. 'Haven't I seen you before?' she asked suddenly.

'I saw you once in Leeds. I had tea at the same table as you and your friend.'

Her eyes cleared. 'Of course, I was sure that I should know you but I couldn't think how. You were alone that afternoon – where was your mother?'

'She had gone to the shops, I wondered what I should do if she came looking for me before you left.'

'You say my sister Diana is your mother?'

'Was my mother. She died more than a year ago.'

A shadow crossed her face and she said, 'Oh I am so sorry. Of course we had completely lost touch. Your grandfather was very bitter, he had worshipped her and I'm afraid he never got over it when she left in such a manner. I tried to persuade Father to forgive her but he was adamant. He wouldn't have any of her old friends here, not even Edward who had been her fiancé.'

'Edward came to Mother's funeral. She was killed in a hunting accident near Grindale.'

'When I last wrote to your mother she was living in London.'

'I left London when I was only four years old, we never returned there.'

'And your father, my dear? Wilson told me you had announced yourself as Tessa Chalfont but surely...'

'Nigel Lorival was already married when he took my mother away from Glamara. She didn't know, she believed she was truly his wife. He died before I was born.'

'Oh my dear, I fear you have had a very sad life, can you bear to tell me about it?'

'Yes I think so if you have the time to listen. It is a very long story.'

'How long is it since you have eaten?'

'I had some sandwiches on the train.'

'If you will just excuse me for a moment I will ask the housekeeper if we can have something in here and I'll see about a room being prepared for you.'

'You mean I shall be allowed to stay tonight?'

'My dear child, where else would you stay? I shall not be long.'

217

I went to the windows. Beyond the rose garden and above the dark green conifers I could see the distant blue of the lakeland hills. It was all so peaceful, the perfume of roses and the humming of bees, birdsong and the gentle stirring of the leaves on the giant copper beeches that edged the garden. The house was very quiet. I could hear no voices or laughter, and I dreaded the meeting which must come soon between myself and my grandfather.

Aunt Hetty returned with a bright smile. 'We are going to have tea in here Tessa, and later on this evening a meal will be served to you in your room.'

At that moment my heart sank. So I was not going to be treated like one of the family after all, I would be given a meal and a bed for the night and probably sent packing in the morning. Some of my fear must have shown in my face because she said quickly, 'The house will be full of visitors tonight Tessa, indeed I shall have to put you in the East Wing which is seldom used these days, but all the other bedrooms have already been spoken for. They will be arriving for dinner but I am sure I have time to hear your story before then.'

Tea was brought in by a fresh-faced country girl wearing a black dress, white apron and lace cap. My eyes lit up at the sight of freshly baked scones with cream and strawberry jam, a chocolate-covered cake and dainty sandwiches. I watched my aunt pour the tea into thin white and gold china cups and at her invitation I set to with relish. I hadn't realized I was quite so hungry.

'Now my dear,' my aunt began, 'do you feel able to tell me your story?'

'I may have to tell it more than once, do you think my grandfather should hear it first or are you going to tell him?'

'Your grandfather died three days ago Tessa, that is why the house will be filled with guests tonight – people and family who will have come to attend his funeral tomorrow.'

I stared at her aghast. I couldn't have arrived at a less opportune moment and yet I was also aware of a wild surge of relief: never to have to look in his bitter old eyes or see the withering look of distaste on his face, never to hear his voice lashing my mother's memory. He had gone for ever, and I was here at Glamara and there was nothing he could do to prevent it. Then another doubt came into my mind and voicing my fears I said, 'So my uncle, Mr Godfrey . . .'

'He is Sir Godfrey now, and yes this is his home. He will be back this evening and most of the family will be home for the funeral. Your Aunt Abigail is resting, she hasn't been too well recently and these last few days have been a particular trial to her?'

So I told her my story, our time in Grindale and my mother's marriage to Jack Bryant. I told her about my years at the convent and my time at the Chantrys' house and I told her everything without looking once at her face. I could not bear to see her expression when I told her why I had left my stepfather's house, or why I had fled from Red Gables. We sat for what seemed an eternity after I had finished the tale but when I finally looked up to my surprise she was dabbing at her eyes.

'Oh my poor child, if only I had known.'

'But you couldn't have done anything Aunt Hetty, you couldn't have made him forgive her.'

'No, I don't suppose so, but at least I could have sent her some money, discreetly without him ever finding out.'

'My mother had a great deal of his pride, perhaps they were too much alike.'

'Yes, there is a great deal in what you say, Tessa. He never loved me as he loved your mother, she was so beautiful and so vital and I was never jealous of her. I was glad for her to have the best of everything, the prettiest clothes, the finest horses, the most beautiful jewels, I merely basked in her reflection. When she went it seemed as though all the life had gone from Glamara, that it was a dead house. Bitterness entered my father's soul, he grew morose and difficult, and the older he grew the more difficult he became, until there were times when I thought I couldn't bear it a second longer. For a few days he would be contrite when he knew he had hurt me, and then he would forget and the old bitterness would take possession of him again.

'He locked her bedroom door and refused entry to any but

the servants who had to ask him for the key so that they could clean it. He kept it like a museum although she had taken everything she could conveniently carry when she left.

'In those early days I often heard him pacing about in her room as though some of her personality remained to taunt him, and then one night he had Godfrey take down all her portraits, and there were a great many of them. They were burned out there in the parkland and we had to stand and watch, not only the family but the servants too.

'You have different colouring but I see Diana in you, Tessa, that slender grace, her features and her voice with that special lilt in it that was always so attractive. . . .'

She fell silent for a little, then rousing herself asked, 'Have you no luggage at all dear?'

'No. I have only what I stand up in, and these are borrowed I'm afraid.'

'We shall have to find you some of Laura's then, you are about the same size. We will go to your room in the East Wing. I take it you will not wish to meet the rest of the family this evening?'

'Oh no Aunt Hetty, nor tomorrow either if it is my grandfather's funeral.'

'All the visitors will have gone tomorrow, there will only be family at the dinner table.'

'Will they be horrified do you think, suppose they won't accept me?'

'My brother will accept you willingly. He resented my father's bitterness towards your mother as I did. Abigail is a sweet dear soul, she will make you welcome here I know, and the boys too will not be averse to having a pretty cousin suddenly thrust upon them.'

'And Laura?'

'Laura has been spoiled, just as your mother was spoilt before her. At first she may resent you Tessa: the attention you'll receive, your beauty, a dozen and one things, but at heart she is a generous girl, when she is over her first antagonism she will find your story romantic instead of tragic, exciting rather than sad. You will become the intriguing young woman who might conceivably usurp the

220

place of Roxanne, her finishing school friend and present idol.'

Feeling more reassured I followed her small slender figure along several corridors until we came to another staircase equally charming, although not quite so spectacular as that in the main hall.

'I have brought you this way so as not to meet any of our guests or other members of the family, not because I am wishing to hide you my dear, but so that you will not be embarrassed.'

'Thank you, Aunt Hetty.'

'The East Wing overlooks the mere and many of the highest Pennine hills. The sun will have left that part of the house now but it is a charming room, not one of the largest but I feel sure you will be comfortable in it. But I am sure Godfrey will insist that you occupy your mother's old room when he knows you are here, Tessa. It is on the front of the house and very beautiful. We will leave you to decide.'

'I can't believe that I am really to stay here.'

'Haven't you always wanted to see Glamara, your mother loved it so?'

'All my life. I dreamed about it, yearned for it, but it was all so impossible. Now I'm afraid that for me it has been a last resort.'

'Well here we are, do you think you will be comfortable in here?'

I knew I would. It was a heavenly room with a soft beige carpet, and floral chintz at the window and covering the bed. The fire had been lit and a rose velvet chair had been set before it. There were large wardrobes, and a walnut period desk. My eyes lit up with pleasure and I murmured, 'Oh this is lovely, thank you so much.'

Aunt Hetty showed me the door which led into a pretty pink and white bathroom. My eyes shone as they beheld the soft pink towels and I suddenly longed for a bath. As if she read my thoughts Aunt Hetty said, 'By the time you have had your bath Tessa I will have found you a nightgown and some slippers, then you can either read or write letters until your evening meal arrives. I suppose you do have friends who would be glad to hear from you?'

I knew that I would write to Alex and to Susan and the Elliotts. The latter would be very anxious to know how I had fared.

'I can assure you nobody is going to prevent your letters going out, or withhold their replies.' There was a twinkle in her eye as she made this last remark and I knew I was going to love Aunt Hetty.

After I had bathed I found a soft woollen nightgown and a more summery affair in the bedroom, a quilted dressing gown and a pair of blue slippers only a little too large for me. I looked a different person after I had brushed my hair, with my skin glowing from the bath and my mind freed from immediate worries. The East Wing was too far away from the normal sounds of the house but then with something like shock I realized that somewhere in one of those rooms downstairs my grandfather lay dead, and it was natural that the house should be quiet out of respect for him.

It must have been then that the preposterous idea came to me. I wanted to see him. Hitherto he had been only an imagined figure, a vague shadowy individual born of my resentment, clothed with his bitterness. Now I had to look at him in the flesh despite the fact that he was dead. I knew that I could not go into that part of the house until the rest of them were in bed, even so I had never been more sure of anything in my life: I had to look just once upon the face of my grandfather.

Would the bitterness still be reflected on that cold set face, I wondered, or would death have removed for ever the antipathy that had coloured his life, and somewhere would he know that I was here at last in Glamara and there was nothing he could do to prevent it?

I wrote my letters and the long night wore on. I watched the sky change from blue to grey and then to a deep dark blue lit by stars and a full moon. I was glad, knowing that it would light my way through the unknown corridors.

Taking my courage in both hands I lifted the candlestick and left my room.

I had no difficulty in finding the second flight of stairs, my difficulties began when I reached the bottom and I took several wrong turnings before I reached the main hall. My heart was pounding now so that the candelabrum shook in my hand and the tightness in my throat was so intense I could scarcely breathe.

Suppose I should meet some member of the household crossing the hall, Sir Godfrey perhaps? How would he view a stranger wandering the rooms of his house carrying five tall candles in search of his dead father?

I met no one. The dancing light from my candles fell upon evil visors above suits of old armour, on portraits of long-dead Chalfonts, and on hunting scenes, but my eyes were drawn to one door, the door which I had seen Aunt Hetty and the butler glance at in a peculiar manner when I was admitted into the hall. He was in there. I felt sure of it and now I was becoming frightened, of the stillness and the silence, of the strange uncanny atmosphere the angel of death had laid upon the entire house.

The knob turned without a sound, and raising my candelabrum on high I went into the room, my mouth dry, my heart beating so wildly it seemed that I must suffocate. The coffin was laid on trestles and at both ends candles burned, so that the room was thrust into a new brilliance by the candles I carried. The lid of the coffin stood upright against the wall and over the face of the man in the coffin was a large silk handkerchief. Without hesitation I lifted it.

At that moment I was not afraid. I was staring at an old man with silver hair and moustache. His eyes were closed, his hands crossed upon his breast, and the face was peaceful. I had expected arrogance, even in death, stubborn pride and twisted hostility but this face was calm and gentle, as though death had erased old hatreds and memories. Death had come as a friend, releasing his tortured soul for ever from the agony of my mother's rejection.

I found to my astonishment that I no longer hated him. I understood him, his hurt pride and the feeling of betrayal that had made him want to punish her again and again. I too knew how to hate. I hated my stepfather and John Chantry, I would never forgive either of them – but then I had never loved either of them. For the first time I began to see that hatred where once there had been love was the most cruel of all.

At that same moment I sensed a presence in the room, that some other person stood behind me, their eyes boring into my back. I dared not turn my head. As calmly as I knew how I replaced the handkerchief over the dead man's face and walked quietly from the room.

PART THREE

CHAPTER TWENTY

It is strange to think that I have been two years at Glamara, two years to realize the fulfilment of an impossible dream for I love it as much today as I did in all those years when it was simply a name to an imaginative child. Since that morning when I sat on the window seat in the bedroom that was once my mother's and is now mine, watching the long procession of black funeral coaches pulled by black horses with purple plumes following my grandfather's coffin on its journey to the churchyard in Lambreck, my entire life has taken on a new meaning and a new and welcome stability.

There were problems, how could there not be, particularly with Laura who in those early days believed I had come from nowhere to steal what was rightly hers, including the affection of her family.

Looking back I know now that the first evening was the worst and I tremble a little when I remember how nervous I felt as I followed Aunt Hetty's neat figure into the drawing room. I was wearing one of Laura's less attractive evening gowns which she had been kind enough to place at my disposal, even though we had not as yet met. Shades of yellow had never become me, and this was a particularly insipid lemon which warred with my eyes and did nothing for my pale blonde hair.

Laura was much my size so the dress fitted me well enough and from the feel of the material and the graceful folds of the full skirt I knew that it had cost a great deal. I imagined that on a girl with Laura's vibrant colouring it would look quite beautiful.

Although there were only four people in the room three of them were men, all well over six foot in height, and to me the room seemed crowded. The eldest of the three stepped forward and took both my hands in his, standing for a few minutes looking down at me before he took me in his arms and I was surprised to see the gleam of tears in his eyes. As he held me against him I too became aware of a tightness in my throat and knew immediately why. He reminded me of my mother: the laughter lines at the corners of his mouth and his long cool stare, the set of his head on his broad arrogant shoulders. When he finally put me away from him he looked down at me with a twinkle in his eye, saying, 'You're not what I expected, Tessa. You have your own beauty, but by God you've got your mother's guts.'

'Because I came here, you mean?'

'Yes. It must have taken some doing. Weren't you afraid, child?'

'I was terrified. If you had rejected me there was nothing left. Would my grandfather have rejected me?'

'That we shall never know. He's gone now and taken the answer with him but from now on this is your home, Tessa. You're welcome at Glamara.'

'I should tell you that I haven't any money, I haven't even any clothes, but if I could just stay here for a little while until I can see my way ahead. . . .'

'You're asking for breathing space?'

'Yes that's it. I don't want to be an encumbrance, I'm capable of earning my own living but if I could just take a little time to sort things out, just a few . . .'

'Come and meet the others my dear, in a few days you shall tell me all about it and we'll decide then what form your future is going to take. This is my wife Abigail, she might like you to call her that, or Aunt Abigail, which ever you prefer.'

I never called her aunt but I warmed to her smile of welcome. She was not a beautiful woman but she had a plain sweet face, pale and delicate, and looking at her two strapping sons it seemed hardly believable that she could have produced such virile and handsome boys.

I was surprised to learn that they were twins and the surprise must have shown on my face because Adam hastened to explain that they were not identical twins.

'I'm the eldest by half an hour,' he said laughing, and

immediately Robert put in, 'But I'm the best-looking, it all depends what you're looking for.'

'I don't understand.'

Adam explained, 'Well that half hour means that I get all this one day.'

'While I get the freedom to leave all this behind,' Robert put in with a gay smile.

'Who could ever want to leave all this behind?' I murmured in amazement.

'That's only because it's all new to you,' Robert said. 'Glamara's like a strong drug.'

'Or a demanding passionate woman,' Adam interrupted him, 'so that you've always got to be asking yourself, "Dare I leave her, can I leave her?" then just when you think you've made your escape you realize how much you love her, that there's nothing like her and you have to come back.'

'I know what you mean, I always yearned after her just as my mother always yearned to come back to her....'

'But your mother was the only one who ever had the guts to get away.'

'She went away for all the wrong reasons, and when she had gone she found she couldn't get back.'

'Well, when I go it shall be for all the right reasons,' Robert said confidently.

'What will they be, I wonder?'

'Because the house belongs to Adam, because I'll be free to make my own mistakes. I say, you do ride I hope?'

'Yes. Oh it must be lovely to ride around here, all the time I was walking up that long drive I was thinking how exciting it would be to gallop a horse across the parkland and up into the fells.'

'Tomorrow morning then, right after breakfast,' Adam said before his brother could ask me.

'Don't let the boys monopolize you Tessa,' Abigail called to me from her seat before the fire.

I took my place beside her and my heart lifted at the warmth I felt in the presence of these people who were my family. As if to put me completely at ease the talk became

229

general. It was country talk such as I had often heard in the West Riding and I felt at home in it. I looked round the charming room, appreciating the glow of firelight on polished walnut. Showy chrysanthemums vied with red autumn leaves in a large oriental vase, and I wished I could have looked more closely at the figurines in porcelain and jade and at the priceless paintings.

In the massive mirror above the ornate fireplace were reflected the long rich velvet drapes at the windows and my feet sank into the incredible thickness of the Chinese carpet, its exquisite delicate colours vying with the oriental richness of its design.

This was a house furnished by generations of Chalfonts to be loved and treasured until time itself ceased to exist. As Robert had said, one day this house and everything in it would belong to Adam, but none of us would be able to escape ever from the spell its beauty had laid upon us.

My thoughts were interrupted by Sir Godfrey asking impatiently, 'Where is that girl? Why is it that we always seem to be waiting for Laura? I'll give her five minutes, if she's not down then we start dinner without her.'

Abigail laughed gently. 'You know what girls are like dear, she'll be here soon.'

She turned to me saying, 'Laura has been away at school for so long she is finding it very exciting now that she can wear her own clothes instead of those the school dictated. She knows you are here, I'm sure she's looking round for something particularly pretty to make an impression on you.'

Robert and Adam chortled. 'We all know what Laura's about, Mother,' Adam said. 'She's looking round for something to make Tessa feel pea-green with envy.'

A vague anxiety passed over me, particularly when her father, now thoroughly exasperated, rang the bell pull near the fireplace, and on the arrival of the butler instructed him that we were ready to eat dinner.

'Very well sir,' the butler said, then we formed a small procession and followed him from the room. My uncle went first after offering his arm to his wife, then followed Adam with Aunt Hetty and Robert gallantly offered his arm to me.

Laura appeared several minutes later and I drew in my breath sharply at my first sight of her. For one blinding moment I could have believed that it was my mother who stood with the light shining on her dark mahogany hair, tall and slender, in a dress of rich emerald-green watered silk.

I realized almost at once that she was like my mother only in colouring. Laura had a pretty pert face, although at that precise moment it was undeniably sulky. Meeting her father's scowl of annoyance she hurried to the table and took her seat beside Adam and across from me.

'Now perhaps we can begin dinner,' Sir Godfrey said sharply. 'Why are we always waiting for you, my girl?'

'I'm sorry Father, I couldn't find my shoes, not the right ones for this dress.'

'And what about that dress?' he said. 'Isn't it a bit too soon after your grandfather's funeral to be seen wearing that particularly vivid colour? Something more subdued would have been more appropriate, including something more suitable for your cousin.'

'Oh Father, I've been wearing subdued colours too long as it is.'

'No doubt, but the fees were not subdued were they, and it had to be Switzerland. You wouldn't even listen to anything else, remember?'

'I'll change it if you don't like it, Father,' she cajoled him gently, and I could see that however cross he might be with her he adored her. Laura was the apple of his eye and as my eyes met hers across the table I felt her resentment, not particularly against me, but against anyone who might take some of her father's affection away from her.

I smiled in the face of her cold stare and immediately Sir Godfrey said, 'This is your cousin Tessa who is coming to live here. I expect you two girls to be friends, you're much of an age, you'll probably find you have a lot in common.'

'I already have friends, I expect she does too,' Laura said ungraciously.

'You'll be living here in the same house, you can have whatever friends you like out of it, but within these walls you'll be friends. I want no upsets within my own home.'

He looked first at me then at Laura. Her face was mutinous but in spite of the chill which seemed suddenly to have descended on my life I smiled at her. 'I hope we shall be friends Laura, it's so wonderful to have a girl cousin so near to my own age.'

'Your male cousins would do you more good,' Adam interposed dryly but his father silenced him with a look.

'Tessa spoke to you Laura, have you nothing to say in reply?' Sir Godfrey said, eyeing her sternly.

She tossed her head in a gesture reminiscent of my mother in one of her more petulant moods. 'We shall have to see how much we have in common,' then more conciliatorily, 'I see the dress fitted you.'

'Yes. I had to shorten it a little. Thank you so much for lending it to me.'

'Aunt Hetty didn't tell me you were fair. I expected you to have red hair.'

The meal progressed normally, with Laura speaking mostly to her mother while I chatted to Aunt Hetty. The men seemed to have accepted that Laura and I would be friends, and would have been surprised if they could have known how I doubted their expectations.

Friendship between Laura and myself would be an uphill climb but I resolved that it would not be on my account that it failed. I would do nothing to offend her and although I wanted their affection, even craved for it, I would let them all see that I wanted nothing from any of them that they were not prepared to give.

I was amazed how quickly the villagers in Lambreck accepted me and news got around quickly that Diana Chalfont's daughter had arrived in their midst. They spoke to me in the shops and bobbed quaint country curtseys when I met them in the lanes around Glamara. And if they wondered why I wished to be known as Tessa Chalfont, Sir Godfrey told me, they would quickly understand that it was because I was prouder of that name than any my mother had seen fit to provide me with.

I had been at Glamara almost a month when my uncle asked me to follow him to his study. I was surprised to find my old luggage standing on the floor. In answer to my curious look he said, 'Check that everything's there, Tessa. I had my lawyers write to Chantry, in fact I threatened him direly if he didn't return your belongings intact and at once.'

He stood over me while I checked. I was glad to have my own clothes once more. I had been wearing Laura's unwanteds and several others I had purchased locally, but now at least I would have my own skirts and blouses. I had outgrown my party dresses.

Nothing seemed to have been omitted and yet there was a doubtful frown on my face until my uncle went to his desk and pulled out a small package.

'Is this what you are looking for?' he said, holding out the velvet box which I instantly recognized.

Lying in their satin bed were the gold chain and exquisite emerald. I looked up at him with shining eyes and he smiled. 'I remember the night my father gave that pendant to your mother. She was wearing a gown exactly the colour of the stone and he was standing there near the window watching her delighted face. She turned round so that he could fasten it behind her neck and when the light caught the stone the entire room seemed to flash with green fire. What a night that was. We danced until dawn, with every young feller in the Riding queuing up to dance with Diana. Proud as a peacock my father was. Poor man, he was not to know that that was the last night she would ever dance in this house.'

His face was sad, reflective, then he turned to me with a visible effort to return to the present. 'There's not much there in the way of clothes, Tessa.'

'No, I didn't need many clothes. I was Elizabeth's companion, and the clothes I had were ample for my needs.

'I'm desperately worried about Elizabeth Chantry. Shouldn't she be protected against her father, surely there is something we can do to get her away from Red Gables?'

'We must tread very carefully here, Tessa. I have spoken to the chief constable who knows Chantry as well as anybody knows him. He has always been a strange remote man, completely withdrawn from the community, a man who has never entered into the life of the villagers. If the police go to the house and openly accuse Chantry of incest and he and his daughter deny it, where does that leave you?'

'It seems incredible that we can do nothing.'

'We can leave matters to the police. They have been alerted so it's out of your hands. I'd rather it remained that way.'

It was unsatisfactory but I saw the logic of his arguments and I too was unsure of Elizabeth's reliability.

'Forget the past and its turmoils Tessa, you are here with us at Glamara and you are very welcome.

'And we'd better come to some arrangement now, Tessa, I can't have my niece going round the village dressed like one of the servants much longer. I propose to give you an allowance, the same as I give Laura though I've no doubt you'll spend it more wisely. That girl costs me a packet, I can tell you, but it's my own fault, I've spoilt her.'

'I can't possibly allow you to treat me like Laura, she's your daughter, I'm only your niece, and one you didn't bargain for.'

'And why do you suppose I'm twice as wealthy as I would have been if your mother'd been less foolish? I came in for more of the old man's wealth and now I propose to settle what your mother should have had on you. I'll set up a trust fund to handle it wisely for you and you'll receive a monthly allowance to spend on things like clothes and such.'

I sat down weakly on the edge of a chair. I had not expected such generosity in my wildest dreams but he seemed to think nothing of it and was busy embroidering on his plans for my welfare. 'You must ask Hetty to take you up to London, although Abigail assures me she can find everything she wants in York or Harrogate.'

'I don't know what to say, I hadn't expected such kindness.'

'Well then, the less said about it the better. I'll speak to Hetty, she'll enjoy a trip to London, you can see some of the shows, visit the shops. You can stay in the town house in Belgrave Square or you can stay in some hotel. Hetty likes hotel life, which is pretty ridiculous when I pay a staff of servants to look after the house there. You'll be a nice change

234

from some of Hetty's old cronies.'

'Like Gertrude,' I couldn't resist saying mishievously.

He raised his eyebrows. 'You mean you've actually met Gertrude?'

'I saw them together in Leeds, she's totally unlike aunt Hetty.'

'She is that. A very formidable woman Gertrude and yet they've been friends from girlhood. For all Gertrude's domineering ways you'd hardly believe she married a man who's never worked a day since. A charming wastrel he is, you'd have thought Gertrude would have had her head screwed on tight enough and yet she fell for Horace Chorlton.'

'Perhaps that domineering manner is only a façade.'

'Perhaps it is, but I can tell you this lass, I wouldn't like to tangle with Gertrude in one of her more opinionated moods.'

We chuckled together about Aunt Hetty's friend and remembering Laura I said, 'Do you think Laura would like to come to London with us?'

'She's off to the South of France with Roxanne and Sir Julian soon. Didn't I just say that girl was costing me a fortune?'

He was smiling so that I didn't think he begrudged Laura's call upon his purse strings too much.

'Let us get the girl off to France and then up you go to London with Hetty. That reminds me, you should have a maid, Laura won't want you sharing hers but she's for ever telling me that all young ladies of quality have their own maids these days.'

'Oh Uncle Godfrey, I don't want a maid, I wouldn't know what to do with one, I can dress myself and look after my clothes.'

'Well if you change your mind I'm sure one of the young housemaids could do with a change.'

I had often imagined spending money on beautiful things without having to count the cost, now here I was in London's famous fashion houses. With Aunt Hetty I looked at silk and satin, crêpe de chine and chiffon. We watched tall sinuous mannequins parade in exquisite creations, dragging priceless furs behind them, and I tried on hats – hundreds of hats, so that in the end I was completely mesmerized.

'How do I know what I shall need?' I asked Aunt Hetty in dismay. 'Shall I be going to balls and concerts? Will there be garden parties and what shall I need for race meetings?'

'Now that Laura is home there will certainly be balls,' she advised me, 'and a great many people will be invited. You must have a friend you wish to invite, Tessa.'

I immediately thought of Alec as Aunt Hetty went on, 'The last I heard she was trying to inveigle her father into presenting her at court. He's strongly against it, though. It would mean us spending a lot of time in London and Godfrey hates London, he's never happy away from the country and he regards the presentations as "the silly season", little less than cattle markets. No doubt you'll hear a lot more about it when we return home.'

In the end I decided on three ball gowns: in white chiffon, orchid pink, and blue the colour of my eyes. They were all gowns for the grand occasion and I wasn't too sure that I was being sensible. With them I chose shoes and evening bags, and velvet cloaks with luxurious fox collars. Then there were the afternoon gowns and the morning gowns, the less formal party dresses and the country tweeds and cashmeres. Possibly my favourite purchase was a new riding habit in such a fine black material it felt like silk to the touch although it was in fact pure wool broadcloth.

I was reluctant to show the family my purchases, feeling sure they would frown on my extravagance, but Abigail and the boys enthused about them, while my uncle looked on complacently.

Laura was still in Nice but her letters to the family were filled with stories of balls and dinners, invitations to lunch or dine on yachts anchored in the harbour, and race meetings. It appeared she had a string of young men all in love with her.

'What is Roxanne like?' I once asked Aunt Hetty.

'Very beautiful and no doubt a big responsibility for Sir Julian, who is comparatively young. You'll meet them soon,

I know Abigail and Godfrey intend to invite them here when they return from the continent.'

Adam saw Roxanne as a bewitching creature, a goddess he had placed on a pedestal and worshipped from afar, but Robert described her as a self-opinionated minx who needed a slap now and again.

'I don't know if all that means you don't like her, or you like her too well,' I retorted, laughing at his blushing face.

'Liking her too well wouldn't do a bit of good, she's eyes for nobody except Julian.'

'But Julian's her guardian.'

'That's what makes it so ridiculous.'

Robert didn't want to talk about Roxanne but Adam was prepared to talk about her all the time, her beauty, her grace, her conversation.

'Isn't there some boy she is fond of?' I asked him.

'Boys don't have much chance against Julian,' he answered somewhat grumpily.

Abigail, with her customary generosity, described her as an enchanting creature with a quicksilver wit and an exotic alien beauty that men found irresistible.

King Edward VII died in the early part of May and immediately the court went into mourning. Although Godfrey regretted the death of the King he was delighted that there would be no 'silly season', and in its place he decided he would hold a splendid ball for Laura at Glamara. When she arrived home from her holiday in France he put the idea to her. 'Invite all those dizzy young friends of yours, it's one way of showing them that you're not exactly a pauper and your father's prepared to spend a bit of money on you without putting you up to the highest bidder.'

Laura was not displeased. Glamara was a show place and well she knew it and immediately she set about deciding what she would need to wear to outshine most of her friends.

'Why don't you show her what you bought in London?' Abigail suggested so I took Laura into my bedroom and spread my purchases on the bed.

'I suppose my father gave you the money for them,' she said a little sulkily.

'Yes. He was very generous, insisting because my mother never received any of Grandfather's money.'

'Well it was her own fault, wasn't it?'

'I suppose it was. You can't imagine how much you remind me of my mother. She was imperious and spoilt, accustomed to having her own way. That was why it was so terribly hard for her to come to terms with all that life did to her. I doubt if you will ever make her mistakes but you have all her inconsistency and arrogance.'

She stared at me in surprise, and then left without answering.

That evening she spent most of the time after dinner in trying to persuade her father to allow her to visit the fair which came yearly to a neighbouring village.

'Gracious girl, what's so marvellous about this country fair? The place'll be full of tinkers and horse thieves. If Adam or Robert'll take you, then you can go.'

Neither Adam nor Robert wished to go, but to her annoyance, Adam embroidered on the matter. 'It's a day out for the servants, lots of noise and sideshows, swings and gypsy fortune-tellers, then a roll in the hay with some local swain to round off the day. I can't think what's in it for you, Laura.'

'It's something to do,' she persisted. 'Gracious me what ever happens in the country, there are times when I think I might just as well be dead. Tessa's been here nearly six months and she's not been to a single dance or concert and now we can't even go to the fair in case we're contaminated with vice.'

'I wasn't aware that Tessa wanted to go to the fair,' her father said patiently. 'Are you partial to country fairs, Tessa?'

'I don't know, I've never been to one.'

'Well if the two of you want to go then you shall. Peters can drive you over in the trap and go back for you around four o'clock. I'll expect you to stay together.'

The day of the fair arrived with a fresh breeze coming right off the fells and a blue sky filled with golden splendour. I found myself wondering what I should wear – my new clothes were far too good and my old clothes not good enough. While I was going doubtfully through my wardrobe Laura came to see if I was ready.

'What does one wear for a country fair?' I asked, eyeing her pretty sprigged voile with its tiny bodice and full frilly skirt. With it she wore a wide-brimmed straw hat and I realized miserably that I possessed nothing like it.

'You'll have to wear something of mine.'

I thought I was now well blessed with clothes but I had seen nothing like Laura's collection. Without hesitation she went to the wardrobe and instantly laid her hands on four pretty dresses.

'Any one of these would suit you,' she said, 'please yourself.'

'Then I'd like to borrow this if I may,' I said, indicating a delicious pale blue voile sprigged with tiny sprays of white heather, and without further ado she selected the hat which went with it, a white floppy-brimmed one with blue streamers.

She eyed the finished result with her head on one side and with the utmost candour said, 'I suppose I wouldn't have minded you half so much if you hadn't been pretty. I don't want you stealing my admirers, so I'm just warning you to find your own.'

'I don't know any young men in these parts, which particular ones must I discourage?'

'Only one, that's Iain Gilmour. I'm willing to share the rest, but if Roxanne brings Julian to Glamara I'd advise you not to spend too much time in his company.'

'I shall probably invite Alec Hardcastle if nobody minds. He's a boy I knew in the West Riding.'

'Does he have any money?'

'I think his family is quite well off.'

'What does he do?'

'He's at Sandhurst.'

'Men can look positively divine in uniform, is he very handsome?'

'I suppose he is quite good-looking, he's very nice.'

'Are you terribly in love with him, have you had an affair?'

239

'How would you like it if I asked you such a question?'

'I wouldn't mind, it would depend on the man. Mother's terribly old-fashioned and Father can be stuffy. Did you and your mother live a terribly bohemian life?'

'No we did not,' I answered her sharply. 'My mother was always very strict where I was concerned. Didn't you say Peters would be waiting for us?'

Not at all put out by my sharpness she said, 'You really do look very nice Tessa, and there's no need to be so defensive. Cook's put a hamper up for us, chicken and pork pies, lots of cake and fruit. We can eat in the trap or we can take the hamper with us and picnic on the fells.'

We were both in high spirits as we ran down the stairs and out into the park. Peters assisted us into the trap and then we were off at a brisk pace. Laura seemed excited, sitting on the edge of her seat, her face rosy with delight at the prospect of the day ahead. I couldn't help wondering if she was expecting to meet somebody at the fair.

The fair was in a large field just off the main highway and before we reached it I could hear the music and see the roundabouts and marquees, and I too became enthusiastic when I saw the crowds in holiday mood. As Peters helped us down on to the grass he said, 'What time shall I be back for yer, Miss Laura?'

'Not before five Peters, there's so much to see and do.'

'Keep away fro' the tinkers miss, an' them mangy dogs o' theirs.'

Laura laughed delightedly. 'You sound just like my father.'

The hamper was fairly heavy so we set off across the field carrying it between us until Laura said, 'I don't much fancy carrying this thing all afternoon. What do you say we eat now and then we can leave the hamper somewhere in the hedgerow.'

I agreed, so we found a grassy bank above the path and opened the well-packed wicker box. Cook had provided a hearty repast and we ate enthusiastically. A shaggy mongrel came to sit on the path below us, eyeing our food with hungry brown eyes, and in spite of Peter's warning we tossed him pieces of chicken and ham which he ate ravenously. A poorly clad boy came with a rope which he fastened round the dog's neck and grinned at us, asking, ''Ave yer owt to spare i' that basket?'

He was a handsome boy about sixteen years of age, with a shock of dark curly hair and one thick gold earring. I had eaten quite sufficient and in a burst of generosity I said, 'You can have what's left, there's cake and pork pie.'

'You can have mine too,' Laura said to him, and immediately he scooped up the hamper and raced off, the dog yapping at his heels.

Some of Laura's excitement took hold of me as we arrived at the sideshows, listening to the barkers extolling the strangeness of the Dog with Two Heads and the Bearded Lady. I didn't want to look at them, I thought they were sad and for once Laura held the same views. Her pretty head was turning this way and that until I became convinced she was looking for someone or something and somewhat sharply I said, 'What are you looking for, Laura? You didn't just want to come to the fair to look at sideshows and watch the servants enjoying themselves?'

'I'm looking for the fortune-teller.'

'Fortune-teller!'

'Yes. My maid told me about her, all the servants have been to see her at one time or another, she's absolutely fantastic.'

'Surely you don't believe in such things.'

'I don't disbelieve when I know a lot of it comes true. Jenny for instance, she's one of the housemaids. Last year Gypsy Tara told her her father was going to die very suddenly and that one of her brothers would join the navy. Her father died only three weeks later and her brother did join the navy. Then there was Mrs Whitmore. She was told that her husband would have an accident and sure enough only a couple of days later he was kicked by a runaway horse and he hasn't worked a day since.'

'I'd rather not know such things.'

'She won't tell us anything like that. I want to know what sort of man I'm going to marry and if he has money. Roxanne had her palm read by a gypsy in Cheltenham and she told her she would have two husbands, one of them a man owning great estates.'

'And does Julian own great estates?'

'He has a beautiful house in London and another in the North Riding near Whitby. He has interests in shipping and he's very rich.'

'But that doesn't make him the man Roxanne will marry.'

'No, but I'll be surprised if she marries anybody else.'

By this time we had walked around the entire fairground and were approaching several tents and caravans at the edge of the field. The children running about the grass were dark and for the most part dirty, and the dogs looked savage. One old woman was stirring something in a large cauldron over a fire and another sat on the steps of her caravan smoking a clay pipe. They eyed us surlily and I hung back a little saying, 'I don't like it here, Laura.'

'Oh do come on Tessa, if the servants are not afraid to come here surely we shouldn't be. That's the caravan we want over there.'

The handsome dark gypsy woman standing at the caravan doorway wore a black, long-fringed shawl and round, heavy gold earrings.

'Are you going in first or shall I?' said Laura.

'You go, I'm not very sure that I'm going in at all.'

'Wait here at the bottom of the steps, nobody's going to harm you.'

The gypsy smiled, flashing white teeth with extensive gold fillings, and opening the door wider she invited Laura in.

It seemed an eternity of a wait, but I could hear the drone of the gypsy's voice and occasionally Laura's gentle tones. The boy we had seen earlier strolled over and with an impudent grin on his handsome swarthy face he said, 'Waitin' to 'ear yer future then.'

'I don't know, at the moment I'm waiting for my cousin.'

'She's good yer know, they come fro' miles to 'ear what she can tell 'em. Are yer afraid to know about the future?'

'I think perhaps we are not supposed to know.'

'Oh well, if yer frightened, yer'd best stay outside,' he

taunted, and that was the moment I decided I would go into the caravan and learn my fate.

Laura came out smiling and I imagined she had paid the gypsy amply because there was a satisfied smile on the woman's lips as she stepped aside for me to enter. The van was considerably larger than I had thought it would be, and it was surprisingly clean, with pots of geraniums on the window sill and polished brass and copper ornaments. She indicated a small table covered with a black velvet cloth on which reposed a crystal, and with some strong misgivings I sat opposite her.

She held out her hand. 'Yer'll cross mi palm wi' silver lass, then I'll see what's in front o' yer.'

She held my hand lightly, and with her other hand she delicately traced the lines across my palm.

'Yer've got an interestin' 'and luv, not like the other young lady who 'as a smooth passage through 'er life. Yer only young but already yer've 'ad yer fair share o' troubles and it's left yer wi' some bitterness in yer heart. Yer'll find out luv as the years come an' go that folk are not allus what they seem ter be an' yer'll 'ave need o' that special courage fer life's goin' to bring more than yer fair share o' problems.

'Yer 'ave two marriage lines but it's the second that'll bring yer greater 'appiness, afore that there be sorrow, heartache an' a lot o' despair.

'Yer'll luv somebody wi' all the passion an' feelin' yer capable of an' 'ee'll luv yer in return. That luv'll colour yer whole life an' yer must never be sorry it belonged ter yer for the luv that comes later'll be a different sort o' luv, it'll be more gentle, more easy, an' it'll grow wi' the years.'

'Then the first man I marry is going to die?' I whispered.

'Lovin', livin' an' dyin', it 'appens to us all, lass. There's different ways o' lovin' an' yer'll experience 'em all.

'Yer'll never be short o' money lass, yer days o' poverty 'ave gone fer good.'

She let go my hand and reached out for the crystal, which she stared into for several minutes before she spoke again.

'Yer a lass who allus tries to keep 'er promises. Yer'll not be sorry if yer keeps this one. Does yer know what I mean?'

'I'm not sure.'

'Yer've got it in yer to 'elp somebody and keep a promise at the same time. Think about it lass an yer'll know what I'm tryin' to say.'

I was thoughtful as I left the caravan but almost immediately Laura was at my side bubbling with excitement. 'Isn't she absolutely marvellous?' she enthused. 'She told me about things that had happened to me in Switzerland, and how could she possibly have known about those? She even told me that I would grow apart from Roxanne and we've been friends since we were small.'

I stared at her curiously. 'Wouldn't you mind about that?'

'It would depend upon the circumstances, but she said I would marry well and have lots and lots of money as well as two children. I asked her if I'd be in love with the man I married and what do you think she said, she said I was a girl who would love where it mattered most, what do you suppose she meant by that?'

'I should think it would be very nice to make a suitable marriage and be very much in love at the same time.'

'Then it must be Iain Gilmour. I've always been in love with Iain and my parents would be delighted if I got him, he comes from a very acceptable family and I should think he's quite fond of me.'

'Do you know that for sure?'

'He always comes to see me when he's at home, as a matter of fact I'm probably the first person he comes to see and he's always the first one to put his name on my dance card. He's up at Cambridge studying law, but you'll meet him when he comes home for the holidays.'

'What did she tell you? Did she say if you'll marry and what sort of a man he'll be?'

'Yes I shall marry.'

'Somebody you already know?'

'She didn't say.' I decided to be discreet about the things the gypsy had told me.

'Well,' she said impatiently, 'she must have told you something else.'

'She was very insistent that I kept a promise I had made to

somebody and the only person I can think of is Annie.'

'Annie! Who is Annie for heaven's sake?'

I spent the next hour telling Laura about Annie, trying to make her see the poverty in which she lived, the hopelessness of her future until in the end Laura was caught up with enthusiasm.

'What can you hope to do for her, give her money?'

'No, money isn't the answer. She needs work in the country where she can get her health back. I was thinking about Annie when I saw your father's servants so happy and so well.'

'Country folk don't take kindly to city girls coming to steal their jobs. Do you want this Annie as a personal maid?'

'No, Annie would be absolutely lost in such an occupation. She did all the rough work in my stepfather's house, scrubbing floors and cleaning out grates, Glamara must have servants who do that sort of work.'

'Oh yes, we have scullery maids and such, but you'd really need to see Cook, she's responsible for girls who do that sort of work. Why don't you send for Cook after dinner, she'd know if there is anything.'

'I couldn't possibly send for Cook.'

'Well of course you could, it's no use asking Father, he'd say right away that you should bring Annie to Glamara, and then there'd be whisperings among the servants and one or two of them could make it very uncomfortable for her.'

I saw the logic of her argument but still I was troubled. I walked along in pensive silence until she said, 'Are you sure that gypsy woman didn't tell you anything else?'

'She told me I'd never be short of money again.'

'Well there you are then, you're obviously going to marry a rich man. I wonder if it's this Alec of yours?'

I spoke to Cook in the morning room. There was a surprised though slightly wary expression on her round, apple-cheeked face as I spoke of Annie. I knew she did not take kindly to my suggestion.

'Well,' she said reluctantly, 'we are goin' to be short of a kitchen maid shortly. 'Ow soon can yer get 'old of Annie?'

We arranged on a fortnight, and I told her, 'I'm sure you won't regret it. And please make the others see that this isn't going to be the start of a lot more girls coming from the city, it's only just this one girl.'

'I'll do mi best, miss, an' if I do 'ear about any of 'em snubbin' 'er they'll 'ave me to reckon with.'

Laura was eager to find out how I had fared with Cook. As soon as I told her I would have to go to Leeds to find Annie she stated her intention of accompanying me.

Chapter Twenty-One

I dressed in navy blue with a white organza collar on my jacket and a pretty boater surrounded by a white organza ribbon with a bow hanging from the back. It looked businesslike but it was also very smart and suited my pale gilt hair and English complexion. I didn't want to dress overwhelmingly for our visit to Annie's home, so I was rather dismayed to see Laura dressed both expensively and extravagantly. A small grey hat decorated with osprey feathers sat on her red curls, her fine woollen suit was in the same pale grey and there was an arctic fox collar round her neck. Her elegant beauty would stand out like a beacon in the streets where we would be going.

I felt some misgivings. 'Are you really sure you want to come with me, Laura? You'd be much better occupied looking round the city shops.'

'Of course I want to come with you. I'm very interested in poor people, I'd like to see how they live and what their houses are like.'

'I wonder if you're interested in them for the right reasons?'

'Really Tessa there's no call for you to sound so superior, I'm every bit as kind-hearted as you are. We surely don't need to dress in sackcloth and ashes to demonstrate our feelings for them.'

'I suppose not.'

'Well come along then, let's get it over with, oh and by the way I've booked for a show tonight. I saw it in London and it's absolutely divine, I can easily see it again and you will love it.'

We walked quickly away from the main shopping streets and as the streets grew narrower and meaner the old feeling of bitterness crept into my heart. Laura was looking round her with interest.

'Gracious me, does Annie live here?'

'No. It's much worse where she lives. Please Laura, try not to show how terrible you think it is.'

'It is terrible, but they must know that without seeing it on my face.'

Just then two boys came running down the street, their clothing dirty and tattered, and Laura shrank against the wall. Impatiently I took hold of her arm and pulled her along the footpath. Meanwhile the streets grew meaner and the women standing at their doors eyed us with surly reserve.

Laura stopped in her tracks, eyeing me stonily. 'How far have we to go? It's terrible here, we should go back at once. Surely you could send her a letter and ask her to come to the hotel.'

'I told you not to come Laura, I knew what it would be like.'

'Any minute now one of those dreadful women is going to rip the clothes off our backs and the men will be worse. Do come back Tessa, you can't do any good here.'

'I've come so far Laura I am not going back until I've seen Annie. You can please yourself.'

I marched on relentlessly and after a few moments I heard her footsteps running after me. Her face was sulky but I couldn't go back. If I did I doubted if I would ever find the courage to walk those streets again.

At last we came to the street where Annie lived in the centre of a block of two-up and two-down cottage houses. The road was unpaved, the flagged footpath sunken in places and hazardous to our high heels.

We looked at each other outside the peeling front door and I could see the fear in her eyes which made me suddenly contrite. I reached out and took her hand in mine. After all what had Laura had to do with poverty? What she was seeing this afternoon could only have emerged from her most terrifying nightmare.

'This is the house, Laura,' I said gently. 'Please don't be afraid, you will not be harmed.'

She lifted her head proudly saying, 'I'm not afraid, I just want to get it over and done with so that we can go back.'

I nodded reassuringly then I knocked on the door. It was opened by a little girl of about six or seven wearing a dirty apron. The saucer-blue eyes in her pinched face stared at us in surprise.

'Is your mother in?' I asked her with a smile of reassurance.

The child didn't answer but continued to stare at us and then from inside the cottage a woman's voice said, 'Who is it, Mary? Ask 'em to wait a minute.'

We waited several minutes and still the child stared at us in the open doorway, then a woman came to the door with a child in her arms. I had seen Annie's mother only once, during a band concert in the park, but I would not have recognized her in this gaunt, pale-faced woman who stared at us with hostile, hollow eyes.

'You probably don't remember me,' I began tentatively, 'my name is Tessa Chalfont. I would very much like to see Annie.'

'She's at work.'

'When will she be home?'

'About six o'clock.' Then curiosity got the better of her. 'What are yer wantin' our Annie fer?'

'I would like to offer her work.'

'She 'as work, she's at Bryant's mills.'

'But she gets such terrible asthma, the job I am offering her is in the country where she would be so much better.'

'We needs the money she gets fro' Bryant's, her father's bin out of a job nigh on three years now.'

'I'm sorry. May I tell you about the work I have found for Annie?'

'Yer'd best come in then.'

We followed her and I saw Laura flinch. The flag floor of the parlour was bare except for a rag hearthrug. A meagre fire burned in the grate and in front of it stood a heavy armchair and an old rocking chair.

A wooden cradle occupied one alcove and a tall wooden cupboard reached from the floor to the ceiling in the other. A white scrubbed table occupied the middle of the room and overall there was a strong smell of carbolic soap.

Annie's mother laid the baby in the cradle while the little girl hovered round her skirts, continuing to stare at us.

'Where is this job?' the mother inquired.

'At my uncle's house in the North Riding.'

'An 'ow about 'er money? We can't do without that.'

'She would be able to send money to you I'm sure, and you would know she was being well fed and cared for.'

She was still doubtful, and while we waited in an uncomfortable silence we heard uneven footsteps outside and the sound of men singing raucously. Her face paled, then she hurried to the door.

'So yer 'ere at last,' she said. 'We've got visitors waitin' to see yer.'

A shabby man came in. His eyes were bloodshot and even from across the room I caught the unwashed beery smell on his person.

His eyes narrowed and he leered, 'Well who 'ave we 'ere, two more hoity-toity women tellin' yer 'ow to bring up the bairns. Why don't yer bring out the beggin' bowl then.'

'They're 'ere to offer our Annie a job in the country,' his wife said sharply.

He leered right into Laura's face and she backed away so sharply he grinned, enjoying her discomfort. 'Job! What sort of a job?'

'In service. Some big 'ouse in the North Ridin' where these ladies live.'

'An' what makes 'em so anxious to find our Annie work? She 'as work, an' she's needed 'ere.'

Ignoring him I appealed to Annie's mother. 'Please do what you can to persuade Annie to take this employment. I've written the name of our hotel on this piece of paper.'

He snatched the paper before his wife could take it, and flung it into the fire. 'Our Annie stays 'ere i' Leeds where she belongs. Folk i' your walk o' life don't come round offerin' work to the likes of us unless there's someat at the back of it. Now yer'd best be on yer way an' I don't want to see either of yer around 'ere again.'

He flopped down into the armchair and closed his eyes. In just a few seconds he started to snore noisily.

'We must go, Tessa,' Laura insisted, 'we can do no good here. You've done your best.'

She was right. I had tried but we had met only prejudice and hostility. I could only look at Annie's mother helplessly and follow Laura.

We were halfway down the street when she came running after us. 'I'm right sorry yer 'ad to meet 'im when'ee were drunk, miss. 'Ee's not a bad man, just filled wi' despair at not knowin' what's goin' to 'appen to us.'

'If he didn't drink so much you'd have more money for the children,' I ventured.

'I know, but that's all 'ee's got, the pub an' 'is mates. I'll talk to our Annie, I'll persuade 'er she must go to the country, yer can leave 'er ter me.'

I hunted in my bag to find my diary and a pen. 'I'll write all the directions down for you, the time of the train from Leeds to Lambreck. And tell Annie I'll meet the train. I shall expect her a week on Sunday and I want you to give her this money for her fare. Please don't worry about her, she'll be happy at Glamara and she'll not forget to send you whatever she can afford.'

She took the money and pushed it into the pocket of her apron. 'I'll keep it 'idden away miss, if 'ee gets 'is 'ands on it it'll be spent at the pub. Annie'll be on that train, I promise yer.'

I thanked her warmly, and to my surprise Laura opened her purse and handed her a pound note saying, 'Don't let him get his hands on this either. Spend it on the children.'

I was glad to return to Glamara, to the peace of the rolling hills and the warm honesty of the good earth, to Aunt Hetty's endless preoccupation with her embroidery silks and Abigail's gentle doe eyes following Godfrey with silent adoration, and her horror when Laura described our adventure in the back streets of Leeds.

Now between Laura and me there was a camaraderie we had not known before. We rode together across the low rolling fells and we sat in each other's bedrooms telling stories of our childhood. Laura was convinced that Annie would not arrive on the following Sunday and as the days passed I came halfway to believing her. It was therefore with some trepidation that I drove the trap to meet the train on Sunday afternoon.

Annie stepped gingerly from the train to stand looking small and forlorn at the end of the platform. I waved my arm and she hurried towards me, hampered by a large newspaper parcel. I looked at her pale pinched face with dismay. She seemed to have shrunk. The lustre had gone out of her hair and her thin arms and legs seemed like picking sticks, they were so thin.

'Have you been ill?' I asked her gently.

'Oh no miss, except fer mi asthma, but I reckon it'll be better here.'

She trotted beside me to the trap and I was surprised how small she seemed. I spread a warm rug over our knees and with a word to the pony we were clattering across the cobbled square. She looked around her with interest and I was glad to see a certain excitement.

'I allus wanted to work in the country, I couldn't believe it when mi mam said you'd remembered me.' She fished in her pocket and held out a little silver and some copper. 'This is yer change fro' what yer left wi' mi mam.'

'No Annie, you must keep it.'

'But it's four and sixpence miss, yer can buy a lot wi' four and sixpence.'

'Then *you* shall buy something, Annie, there must be many things you need.'

'Thank yer miss, if yer sure I could buy somethin' fer mi mam and send it to 'er.'

I pulled up the pony so that we could sit looking across the parkland to where the house stood impressively in the distance with the sunlight gilding the warm stone and lighting up the windows and turrets, and Annie gasped with admiration.

'Oh Miss Tessa, it's a fairytale palace, like somethin' the sleepin' beauty might 'a lived in. It's so big, are there an awful lot o' folks livin' there?'

'There are, but there are more servants than family, then there are the men who work on the estate and the grooms who look after the horses. You will be part of all those people, Annie.'

She was silent as we drove along the long drive up to the house and I sensed she was completely overawed by her surroundings.

'I'll drive the trap into the stables, Annie, and then I will take you to the kitchens myself and introduce you to Cook and the others.'

'They won't think I'm 'avin' any favouritism, miss?'

'They might, but I don't intend that you should go there on your own, that would be too overwhelming.'

An air of peace pervaded the kitchens. Cook was asleep in her rocking chair in front of the fire. The housekeeper was sitting at the kitchen table with the newspaper and from next door I could hear much giggling from a group of girls. There was no sign of the butler.

The housekeeper looked up with some surprise when we entered and putting on my most charming manner I led Annie forward, saying, 'This is Annie, Mrs Graves, she has come here to be a scullery maid under Cook. She once worked for my mother in Leeds.'

Annie had not forgotten her quaint curtsey and the housekeeper eyed her over closely, not missing a single item from her darned cotton gloves to her worn but well-polished shoes.

'You can leave the girl with me then,' the housekeeper said stiffly. 'Cook will see to it that she knows her duties and she'll find there's plenty to do in a house of this size.'

'Annie isn't afraid of hard work, but I should like it to be known that I want her to be happy here. She will not expect any sort of favouritism simply because I am responsible for bringing her here, but she will look for friendship and kindness from the rest of the servants.'

'You can leave things in my hands Miss Tessa, there will be no cause for complaints.'

I smiled my thanks, then turning to Annie I said, 'Welcome to Glamara Annie, I hope you will be very happy here.' Then I left the kitchens for the realms above.

I had only just reached my room when Laura was there asking eagerly, 'Well did she arrive?'

'Yes.'

'Gracious me, I doubt if I'd be so willing to work for the gentry if I lived like those people live.'

'It isn't our fault they live like that, and Annie is wise enough to know it. Now, I can see you have something to tell me. What is it?'

'The ball father promised is to take place just before Christmas, here at Glamara! I was too young to attend the last one but I saw people arriving from all over the country. There were gorgeous gowns and jewels, and plants and flowers. And for this one there will be a Christmas tree and the hall will be decked with holly. You must invite Alec, he sounds divine, and you must have had girlfriends in Leeds.'

'There was only Susan I really cared about.'

'Then you must invite her. Let them see Glamara and make them all pea-green with envy.'

'Oh Laura!'

'When Alec sees you looking beautiful in a real ball gown, surrounded by all this, he'll propose on the spot. What will you wear?'

'I haven't had time to think about it, probably the white chiffon.'

The white chiffon with its trail of silk gardenias from

shoulder to hem was the sort of dress I had always dreamed about but never expected to own.

'Well of course, isn't that just the thing, terribly virginal and bridal. I shall wear my jade-green taffeta, red hair and jade go so beautifully together.'

I knew this was true. Mother had always looked her most beautiful in jade.

'Don't wait until the last minute to write to that Alec of yours,' was her parting shot. 'If you had any sense you'd invite him to spend a weekend here and then he would know what to expect.'

There was some truth in this. I had written to tell Alec I was at Glamara but I had told him very little about the house or my connection with the Chalfont family. He would be completely overawed by a house that could comfortably accommodate Briarcrag in the West Wing.

I decided to write to his mother enclosing a letter which I hoped she would forward to Alec. By this time he would probably have joined a regiment.

A week later I received a reply from her indicating that Alec was now a subaltern with the Royal Horse Artillery stationed on the Northumbrian coast and my letter had been sent to him there.

Her letter was full of news. Mr Hardcastle was a prospective Liberal candidate for Grindale and the surrounding district. He seldom had time to visit the mills in Leeds now but he had very able managers to handle his affairs which were running like clockwork. Joan was spending Christmas in Cheltenham and Susy had taken to horses and was turning out with the hunt on Boxing Day. As for Mrs Hardcastle herself, she was the chairwoman of the local Rose Society, had taken up the breeding of field spaniels and was much in demand as a judge of the breed.

I remembered Madge Hardcastle the first time I saw her, a big-boned red-faced woman who wanted desperately to learn all the social graces and speak the Queen's English.

Well, the Hardcastles had made the best of the attributes the Lord had given them, and later that evening when I told Godfrey about them he endorsed my admiration.

Both Godfrey and Abigail thought it a good idea to invite Alec to spend a weekend at Glamara now, well before the ball. Surprisingly however Aunt Hetty seemed not so sure.

'He's the first boy you have really known, Tessa, you should not become too committed until you have met other young men.'

'There's no harm in inviting the lad for a weekend, Hetty, and Tessa needn't be in his company all the time he's here. Does he ride?'

'Yes Godfrey, he rides very well.'

'Well then, the hunt meets on Saturdays so he can ride as our guest. We can invite people over and I expect he'll be quite happy for you to show him the estate and the village. You can invite young Gilmour over, Laura.'

Alec accepted my invitation instantly, and the following weekend he arrived driving a noisy, small and ramshackle two-seater which my uncle looked at with disgust since he deplored motor cars and stuck doggedly to horse-drawn vehicles.

To say Alec was overwhelmed by the size and majesty of Glamara would be an understatement. He stared with awe at the great mullioned windows, and the turrets rising symmetrically into the frosty air.

'You don't mean to say all this parkland belongs to Glamara?' he asked in astonishment.

'Yes, the mere and the forest too, as far as your eyes can see.'

'Gracious Tessa I had no idea it would be like this. I can understand your need to come here.'

'I was desperate when I came, Alec, and I had no means of knowing if they would take me in. Perhaps if my grandfather had been alive it would have been another story.'

'It's jolly nice of them to invite me for a weekend.'

'And for the ball, I hope you'll be able to come.'

'I'll move heaven and earth to come Tessa.' He put his arms around me and drew me into an ecstatic embrace.

The weekend was a success. I liked Iain Gilmour, who was a tall gangling boy with a shock of sandy hair and an infectious sense of humour. I had thought he would be very

255

sophisticated and something of a snob because Laura enthused so endlessly about superior people, consequently I was agreeably surprised.

He got along with Alec famously and we went everywhere together which gave me little opportunity to be alone with Alec. This was a relief to me and an annoyance to Alec who, I am sure, had believed we would take up our association exactly as we had left it.

On the second evening he waylaid me leaving my room and I felt convinced that he had been waiting for me.

'Tessa, I've got to see you alone, do we have to be with your cousin all the time?'

'You like them don't you?'

'Well yes, of course I like them, but I've come to be with you. Can I come to your room tonight?'

'No Alec, I'd rather you didn't, things are different here.'

'Why are they different, you love me don't you? If you don't why did you invite me?'

A sharp anger passed over me. 'I didn't invite you here so that we could sleep together,' I snapped. 'If you really loved me you wouldn't expect it, and although it happened once, I won't let it happen again until I'm sure.'

'Sure! Sure about what?'

'That I love you Alec.'

'But I thought you did love me. I love you, heaven knows I've told you often enough. I'll speak to your uncle, ask him if we can get married. My army pay isn't much as yet but the old man would be generous and you have your own money now. We'd get by, please say yes, Tessa.'

'I don't want you to speak to my uncle yet. Alec, please believe me when I say that I care very much for you, but we were thrown together before we ever had a chance of meeting other people. I don't want to marry you because we are having an affair, I want to marry you because I love you and I don't want you to marry me because you think it's your duty.'

'I'm not interested in other girls.'

'Have you met many of them?'

'Some. Sisters of boys I was at school with. I'm invited to the homes of brother officers and they have sisters and girlfriends. I know my own mind Tessa, there's not one of them I prefer to you.'

'Well I haven't met anybody I can compare you with. Alec, why don't we pretend we've just met so that we can really get to know one another as adults? There are so many things I love about you, your humour, your enthusiasm, your kindness. Why don't we simply enjoy being together, and perhaps I'll find I can't live without you.'

He had a hurt, sulky, little-boy look that made me suddenly feel so much older. I linked my arm through his and squeezed it against me. 'Darling Alec, please don't be cross, I just want us to be sure, and we *are* so young. We have all our lives before us.'

I had never known him be out of countenance for long, and now I watched his smile return, and he kissed me lightly.

'My father said I'd find out sooner or later that women were unpredictable, I never expected to find that you were. All right my love, have it your way, but I can't wait until Christmas before I see you again.'

'My uncle says you can come whenever you have a free weekend and I'll write often. Perhaps Laura would spend a weekend with me near your camp.'

'I've seen enough of Laura for one weekend thank you, I'd have to take the two of you out.'

'Then you must come here. Thank you for being so understanding, Alec, I'm sure neither of us will be sorry.'

'He's nice, your Alec,' Laura said as we walked back along the drive after waving the two men goodbye.

'Yes he is, very nice,' I agreed.

'Are you in love with him, Tessa? Do you want to marry him?'

'I'm not sure, Laura, not nearly as sure as your wanting to marry Iain.' I wanted to be sure, but I was so soon a woman, so late a child. I wanted his admiration, his friendship, but trying to see any future for us was like looking through a veil into great uncertainty. I had read about love, thought about love. Now I had his assurances of love in every letter and in every look, but I felt there should be more, that it was all too easy.

I had thought love would be a great towering emotion that would give me no peace, that it would fill my entire being with joy and power and tenderness, and somehow I felt cheated.

I felt cheated when I watched Abigail worshipping Godfrey with her eyes, with every inflection of her voice, fussing about him when he came in cold and wet after a day visiting his tenants or riding his big bay stallion behind the hounds over fells white with frost. Once she said to me in her low, gentle voice, 'We like Alec very much Tessa, he cares a great deal for you.'

'Yes, I believe he does Abigail.'

'But you are not sure how much you care for him?'

'Marriage is such a commitment, it would be terrible if either of us met somebody we care for even more. I sometimes wonder if we might drift into marriage without either of us knowing....'

'I understand you, Tessa. I loved Godfrey when I was just a shy little girl living with ageing parents over at Netherfield. His father used to bring him to see us often because we were old friends of the Chalfonts and I used to wish I was bigger and stronger so that I could cope with all his adventures. He met all the county's beautiful women and I was so sure he would find one of them to marry, but Godfrey is indolent. He knew I adored him and he loves to be adored. I have been a very fortunate woman.'

'Have you been happy, Abigail?'

'Blissfully happy, Tessa. I gave him the sons he wanted and later we had Laura. I know that women look at Godfrey and he is flattered by their attention but I know that he thinks of me with special warmth because I am his wife.'

When I didn't speak she smiled rather sadly, saying, 'That wouldn't be enough for you, would it? You are your mother's daughter and you have great beauty. I wouldn't like you to throw the real thing away for something more exciting, only to find you have made a terrible mistake.'

'I will remember your words Abigail, and when you know me better you will see that I am not really like my mother at all. I watched her make a second mistake and that is why I have to be sure.'

'Then you must take your time my dear, you are very young and so is Alec. Besides, Godfrey isn't too happy about his army career.'

I looked at her in surprise. 'But Alec always wanted to join the army. He has a commission and he is very ambitious to do well.'

'And I am sure he will, my dear. Don't take any notice of what I said, Godfrey is too close to the land, he doesn't see beyond it.'

I was thoughtful as I left her. The world was full of trouble spots: the North West Frontier, Africa, the Sudan. Alec had enthused about the life we could live in India and had painted a glamorous picture of regimental balls and fashionable soirées without thought of the dangers he might encounter. I was not afraid of danger. If I loved Alec I would follow him to the moon if need be, but the uncertainty persisted.

Aunt Hetty was the next one to pose her questions. 'Are you and Alec going to announce your engagement at the ball, my dear?' she asked with a smile on her pert little face.

'We haven't talked as far as that, Aunt Hetty.'

'He is very much in love with you, dear.'

'Yes.'

'And you?'

'I love him, Aunt Hetty, but I don't know yet if I am in love with him.'

'I loved somebody once, oh I was only in my twenties at the time and I could have married him but I couldn't decide in a hurry and he too was in the army and going abroad. I let him go without accepting him and he was killed in the Sudan.'

How would I feel if the same thing happened between Alec and me?

At the end of November, Abigail began to have doubts about the suitability of any of her evening gowns for the ball, and Laura was openly scathing about them. 'I don't know why my mother always wears the most unsuitable colours. She looks positively frightful in puce, and lavender is for old ladies. She should wear something to brighten up her colouring, heaven knows she doesn't make the best of what she has.'

Later, over dinner, Laura said, 'I hope you are not going to wear that awful plum-coloured thing, Mother, it's old-fashioned and the colour doesn't suit you.'

Abigail's pale face flushed and somewhat sharply Adam said, 'Are you suggesting Mother dresses like Lady Franklin?'

'Heavens no, *she* dresses like a seventeen-year-old, I just want Mother to be a bit more adventurous. After all she is the hostess, so why shouldn't she try to look the part?'

'Your mother knows she can go out and buy anything she likes,' Sir Godfrey said firmly. 'Why don't you go with her into York and help her to choose something?'

'I haven't time before the ball, Iain's family have invited me to spend a few weeks with them, besides she won't find much in York, she always goes to the same shop and they always trot out the same disasters.'

'I'll go with you if you like Abigail,' I put in quickly, believing that this time Laura had gone too far.

'If Tessa is willing to go with you then you must go up to London,' Sir Godfrey decided. 'Spend a few days there, I'll inform the servants in London to expect you.'

'Would you mind Tessa?' Abigail asked tentatively.

'Of course not, I shall enjoy it.'

We spent four days in London and I encouraged Abigail recklessly. Her taste in colours was not my own. She looked at maroon and the dreaded puce until I had to literally drag her away and encourage her to look at soft blues, delicate peach and apricot, and doubtfully she murmured, 'But Tessa, don't you think they are too young for me? I am forty-four, I wore these colours when I was twenty.'

'But they *suit* you, Abigail. You are not old so why should you dress old?'

260

'Laura will be furious with me I know if I buy one more dress in puce.'

'Then you should try this one,' I said, holding up a creation in pale green. 'You have pretty colouring and a lovely complexion and this colour would do wonders for your hair and eyes.'

Her eyes were brown, and her light brown hair was so fine she tended to wear it taken back from her face and severely fastened with slides or hairpins. I encouraged her to have it cut and styled and I watched carefully how it was done so that I could instruct her maid when we returned.

Against her better judgement she settled for the green and against my better judgement she bought another in plum in case Godfrey didn't like the green.

I enjoyed those few days with Abigail. We went to two plays and she enjoyed taking tea in Fortnum and Mason's or at one of the fashionable hotels.

'I don't mind staying at the house, Tessa, but there I don't really *see* anything, we might just as well be at Glamara. When we go to the hotels or the shops we can see the people and I love to look at what they are wearing,' she confided.

The day before we returned to Glamara she decided she would like tea at the Dorchester. Wrapped in our furs we set off through the park at a brisk pace. Our cheeks were glowing when we finally arrived at the hotel and the hot perfumed air met us as we entered the foyer.

'I'd like a table where we can see everything,' she whispered and I couldn't help smiling at the little-girl excitement on her face.

As soon as we had settled ourselves at the table she said, 'I've just had an idea, Tessa, for the theatre this evening we should have some flowers. Would you like to go to the florist and ask her to make up two sprays? We can pick them up on our way out.'

'What had you in mind, Abigail?'

'Something that will go nicely with light brown I think, and you choose something to suit your gown.'

I intended to wear a coral-pink dinner gown so I chose

261

roses in the same colour, but for Abigail I chose orchids which I knew would give her nondescript gown the sophistication it lacked.

As I re-entered the lounge I was surprised to see a man standing at our table in conversation with Abigail. She was chatting with unusual animation. She turned to me with a bright smile, saying, 'Tessa, this is Sir Julian Telford, Roxanne's guardian. This is my niece Tessa Chalfont, Sir Julian.'

He took my hand in his and bowed politely. I was aware of his eyes looking into mine, and a devasting smile that brought the warm colour to my cheeks. He was without question the most attractive man I had ever met. Taller than average, he had the lean lithe grace of a panther, with hair as shining and blue-black as a raven's wing. Surprisingly his eyes were as steely blue as my own, and in that moment when he smiled down at me with casual charm I was appalled at the heady attraction he surprised in me.

'Have you settled down at Glamara, Tessa?' he asked, using my first name easily.

'Yes thank you, it is very beautiful.'

'Yes indeed. Well, I will say goodbye now, and I shall look forward to seeing you again in December.'

I watched him walk away with mixed emotions, while Abigail busied herself pouring the tea. I had never believed those stories of people who looked at each other for the first time and discovered an attraction so intense they never overcame it. Now it had happened to me. I judged him to be about thirty-five, a man of the world, sophisticated and assured, while I was only just finding my feet in an adult world. It was mad, indescribably foolish.

I became aware of Abigail chattering beside me. 'How nice to see Julian. I always find him very charming.'

'I wonder why he isn't married. Do you suppose he is waiting for Roxanne to grow up?'

'Oh no, I'm sure he's not. I have heard certain things but with Roxanne one can never be sure if they are true, she's such a romanticizer.'

'What sort of things have you heard?' I asked curiously.

I had to know. Everything about this man was suddenly important to me.

'Well, we know that his mother was Spanish, I believe it is because of that that he now finds himself Roxanne's guardian. Her father and Julian were first cousins. He is a very wealthy man. I have been to his home near the coast – it's very beautiful, but such a wild unfriendly coast, although Julian doesn't seem to find it so.

'Apparently when he was very young he fell in love with a dancer. Both his grandfathers objected to her, though she was very beautiful and extremely talented. They spent some time together touring Europe and they were involved in a bad motor accident which permanently injured the girl. Julian was driving the car at the time. She lives very quietly now in France. Julian supports her and from time to time goes to visit her. He has never loved anybody else, nor will he. That is the story as Roxanne told it to Laura. I can't say how much truth there is in it.

'Of course Julian *does* visit France two or three times a year, but when he comes to Glamara the talk is all of sailing and hunting. Julian is very good at keeping matters on an impersonal footing.'

How I resented that beautiful woman who had danced her way into Julian Telford's life. I was amazed at the intensity of my feeling for this man I had barely met. There was danger for me in our meeting in December, danger to my heart and my peace of mind. And then I was remembering Alec's face, boyish and sunny, filled with enthusiasm for our future together, and at that moment I resolved that I would not put my heart or my common sense in danger. I would tell Alec at Christmas that I would marry him.

The resolve was firmly in my mind when we went to pick up our flowers. The florist who handed them to us in exquisitely wrapped boxes said that Sir Julian Telford had paid for them and hoped we would accept them with his best wishes for a very pleasant evening.

While Abigail enthused over his generosity I ached with a new and frightening desire.

CHAPTER TWENTY-TWO

There was so much to do in those last few days before the ball. The autumn weather had lingered on and it was hard to believe that Christmas was only days away. Excitement gripped the entire household from Sir Godfrey down, and the servants went about with smiles, hurrying about their duties as though their lives depended on it.

A gigantic Norwegian spruce was placed in the hall and all the family took part in decorating it. Adam and Robert teased Aunt Hetty unmercifully as she struggled to reach the branches, until Adam lifted her bodily regardless of her screams of protest. It was well into the afternoon when we had finished and Abigail said, 'Will one of you go down to the kitchens and tell Cook we would like our tea in the drawing room? I asked her to hold it up until we had finished decorating the trees.'

'I'll go,' I called cheerfully, hurrying away.

I had never seen such preparation, with the kitchen tables piled high with the produce needed for the next few days. Cook was in her element, issuing instructions right, left and centre while the maids scurried round.

'I 'aven't seen yer these last few weeks Miss Tessa, but I just wanted yer to know that lass fro' Leeds is comin' on champion. She's a worker, I'll say that fer 'er,' she said. 'She's in the scullery peelin' potatoes, yer can 'ave a word with 'er, but only five minutes mind.'

'Thanks Cook, I promise, only five minutes.'

Annie's face lit up when she saw me. She was surrounded by pails and potatoes, but I was glad to see the rosy colour in her cheeks. The pinched look of poverty had gone.

'Cook says we can have five minutes together, so we will have to be quick. Are you happy here Annie?'

'Oh yes miss I *am*, I've never bin so 'appy.'

I laughed. 'What, with all those potatoes to peel?'

''Onest I don't mind a bit, 'specially when they're for the grand ball tomorrer night. The butler sez we can take it in turns to watch the guests arrivin' fro' the second-floor winder.'

'Has everybody been kind to you here, Annie?'

'Well they were a bit quiet like at first, but I gets on wi' 'um well enough now. I works 'ard an' Cook's praised me up a bit.'

'You see Annie, things are improving. One day you'll be able to go to Leeds to see your family.'

'P'raps a shall. Amy Garret is leavin' in the New Year an' Cook says a could get the under 'ousemaid's job if a works 'ard.'

'I suspect you are becoming very ambitious, Annie,' I laughed.

'I wants to be a lady's maid Miss Tessa, but not just anybody's. I wants to work fer you. Yer knows I'd foller yer to the ends o' the earth, nobody's bin as kind ter me as you 'ave.'

I could feel the salt tears pricking my eyes. She was so overwhelmingly honest, her devotion so absolute, I wasn't sure I could ever live up to the pedestal she had placed me on. . . .

On the day of the ball I was aware of a tremendous excitement like no other I had ever known. Julian would be coming, and I needed to see if that mad treacherous attraction for him was with me still; if it was then I was not yet ready for marriage to anybody.

Immediately after lunch I donned a warm coat and with a scarf over my head I set off across the frozen park with two of the dogs for company. I was near the drive when I recognized Alec's car coming towards me and the cheerful tooting on the horn. I ran towards him and in spite of the size of the car he made room for me and the two dogs, with the smallest sitting on my knee whilst the bull mastiff squeezed into the luggage space.

'You'll catch your death walking out here in this weather,' he said sternly, the tone belied by the affection in his eyes.

'There's so much going on at the house, Alec, I've been busy all morning and I needed some air.'

'I hope I'm not the first to arrive.'

'No, some of them came yesterday, and I must warn you one of them is a retired general with little or no time for modern warfare.'

'General who?'

'Sir Bertram Robertson. I sat next to him at dinner last night and he was very interested in you. He knows your father, incidentally.'

'What did you tell him about me?'

'That you were in the Royal Horse Artillery and that you liked horses. He seemed to think you had enthused a little too much about army life overseas.'

'Oh, what did he have to say about that?'

'He pointed out his wife as an example and compared her to an old prune.'

'Every bit the gallant officer and gentleman.'

'I rather think she got her own back later when she told him the port was bad for his liver.'

We laughed merrily together. It was easy to laugh with Alec, easy and natural and exactly as I laughed with Adam and Robert.

'Don't your parents mind you being away for Christmas, Alec?'

'No, I promised to be with them in the New Year and they are expecting you too Tessa. I hope you'll come.'

'When in the New Year?'

'New Year's Day actually. They are giving us as much leave as possible, we're being posted to Ireland in January.'

'Oh Alec, that's terrible, there's always such trouble in Ireland.'

'It *is* terrible when I was expecting something a little more exotic like India or the Far East. I couldn't expect you to come to Ireland with me, you'd be better off here, although it would be good for your complexion, all that rain. They tell me that's why it's so green.'

I smiled but didn't comment. Alec took it for granted that we would marry.

We saw nothing more of each other until afternoon tea was taken in the drawing room and here I only had time to introduce him to the guests already present before it was time to greet new arrivals and dress for the ball.

For a little while I sat in my dressing gown where from the window seat I could look down the drive where assorted vehicles were already meandering up to the house. My mother had told me how from this same window seat she had sat as a girl watching the arrival of her father's guests and I could imagine I heard her low honeyed voice still, describing the events of times long gone.

I could hear guests' laughter as they entered the house while footmen and other servants hurried to park their vehicles. Some had come in carriages others in motor cars, and many of the cars had to be pushed because the servants didn't know how to drive them. Horse blankets and fodder were provided and I marvelled anew at the thought that had gone into organizing tonight's event.

I did not expect to see anything of Laura's maid – she would be kept far too busy attending to Laura's needs – but I had never found my hair difficult to arrange.

It was so wonderful to step into that exquisite gown with its trail of silk gardenias. My shoulders rose from the wide neckline like creamy satin, the tiny waist and long flowing skirt emphasized my slender figure, and I seemed to acquire a new grace. I knew that I was beautiful, from my silver-fair hair to the white satin slippers hidden beneath the hem of my gown. It was not my mother's vibrant loveliness that stared back at me from the long cheval mirror, but a more delicate, more subtle beauty. I decided against wearing the emerald, it was too exotic for the virginal beauty of the gown, so I wore the simple gold cross and chain I had been given as a girl and the gold earrings Aunt Hetty had bought for me in London. I had dressed my hair high at the front, allowing one thick curl to fall forward over my shoulder, and I knew the style suited me.

The hall was crowded with people laughing and talking, all of them with glasses in their hands. A huge log fire burned in the massive stone fireplace and the Christmas tree was alight with candles. Vying with the dark evening dress of the men there were others in bright hunting pink and many of the women wore sparkling tiaras. I paused halfway down the stairs when Alec, looking unbelievably handsome in his uniform, bounded up to greet me. Then most of them were looking at us, smiling indulgently, admiringly at two young people in the prime of their youth and beauty who they believed were devastatingly in love.

I was deliriously happy as we waltzed under the crystal chandeliers in the perfumed beauty of the ballroom. It didn't matter that outside in the dark night it had started to snow, I was in love with the music, the atmosphere, and as Alec's face laughed down into mine I believed I was in love with Alec too.

I loved them all. Abigail looking happy and pretty in her new green gown, and Aunt Hetty waltzing with Robert – who lifted her off her feet at every corner to the delight of all those looking on and to her consternation. Godfrey stood with his cronies in a corner of the hall, and soon they were singing hunting songs well away from the music in the ballroom, and Abigail looked on indulgently if not a little doubtfully.

My dance card was full although Alec's name figured more prominently than the rest. I danced with Adam and Robert. I even danced with old General Robertson who marched me up and down as if we were on the parade ground and who held me so tightly I could hardly breathe. I danced with Iain Gilmour while Laura danced with Alec, and I thought how lovely she looked in her jade dress which complemented so exquisitely her burnished hair.

The ball had been in progress for quite some time when a hush descended suddenly and looking round at hearing Alec's quick intake of breath I saw Roxanne for the first time and Julian for the second.

They stood on the steps leading down to the ballroom. A tall slender girl with raven-dark hair and a golden beautiful face above a gown as brilliant as a scarlet poppy which swirled and shimmered around her slender form as if it had a life of its own, she was very conscious of the picture she presented. But the man at her side captured all my attention and for the second time I was aware of feelings so alien they left me breathless. I had been waiting for this moment all my life, it seemed, as though nothing that had happened before or anything in the future had any meaning.

I remember Roxanne's cool stare as we were introduced and the limp offering of her hand, but then my hand was enclosed in Julian's warm grip and he was smiling down at me with that devastating charm.

'I'm afraid we are very late,' he said, 'but the roads are treacherous across the Whitby moors.'

'Oh Julian you should have come much earlier,' Abigail said, 'the weather has been beautiful until today.'

'Unfortunately I had business which kept me near the coast. We have arrived safely so all we need do now is enjoy ourselves. I suppose your dance cards are already full?'

'Oh we'll change them around,' Laura said. 'Roxanne, you can steal Iain and I'm sure Tessa won't mind lending Alec to you for a few dances, and Julian can take their places.'

Alec was enthusiastic in the ballroom but Julian was graceful. Dancing with him was a combination of skill and elegance and we danced without speaking, although occasionally when others came too near he held me close and when my eyes met his he smiled.

I was bemused, yet distrustful of this strange and rare emotion that gripped me. When I was not dancing with Julian I watched him with others – Laura, Abigail, Aunt Hetty – and Roxanne. With his dark hair as shining as her own, they were like two people modelled from the same piece of clay, and I imagined it was their Spanish blood which made them seem so alike.

By the end of the evening I was wishing they had not come. Before they entered the ballroom I had been a girl completely happy at her first ball, now I was a woman suffering the first searing hurt of an impossible love.

It was impossible. For one thing Julian Telford was at least fifteen years my senior. No doubt he had loved many beautiful sophisticated women and there was that one woman, now an invalid, whom he loved above all others.

As I stood at the edge of the ballroom waiting for Robert to bring me a drink I became aware of the general's voice chatting to people nearby.

'That young whippersnapper is having the time of his life, and the girls are falling for his uniform just as they always did.'

I looked up startled to see Alex dancing by with Roxanne, looking into each other's eyes, he slightly bemused, Roxanne admiring and flirtatious.

'Isn't he engaged to Godfrey's niece?' a stout woman sitting with Lady Robertson asked.

'They're not engaged yet.'

'Waltzing about in his pretty uniform, it's uniform of a different sort he'll be wearing before long or I'm very much mistaken,' the general snapped. 'I don't trust that Kaiser fella, he's power mad and he's jealous of us. Mark my words, we're in for trouble with Germany in the not too distant future.'

'I've not heard any such views expressed elsewhere,' said another man.

'Sir Julian Telford can tell you something about the keels being laid in the shipyards to outmatch the Germans who are busy building up their fleet.'

Robert came back carrying two glasses and when we were out of earshot I told him what I had overheard about trouble in Europe.

'Don't take any notice of the general, Tessa, he's an old warmonger, he'd love there to be a war so he could get back into harness.'

'But he's too old.'

'He's also very experienced. He's in the territorials like my father, if there was a war tomorrow they'd both be called on.'

'And you would have to go too, and Adam.'

'And what about your Alec, already up to the eyes in it?'

'I suppose Julian would have to go as well.'

'He's already in the Royal Naval Reserve so he'd go immediately. But what are we talking about war for? We're here to enjoy ourselves. You shouldn't listen to the general, he's never happier than when he's talking about war in some part of the world.'

So we danced and forgot about war and I danced the last waltz with Alec and we laughed in spite of the general's cynical eyes watching us round the room.

A sudden thaw had removed every trace of snow by the following morning and over breakfast Godfrey announced that there would be a deer stalk, with the honour of the kill going to the only man in uniform – who happened to be Alec. Alec was thrilled by the prospect but I refused to go with him. I had seen the deer roaming the park, beautiful graceful animals with gentle brown eyes behind incredibly long lashes, the stags proud and noble, the young ones remarkably tame. Godfrey had explained to me that from time to time the deer needed to be culled for the good of the herd, but I failed to understand why one of them had to die simply to provide a day of sport and so that Alec could show off his marksmanship.

They set out accompanied by a fair number of the women guests, including Laura and Roxanne. Feeling thoroughly sickened, I donned my riding habit, intending to ride in the opposite direction to that taken by the deer stalkers.

The day was fresh and as I rode towards the lower slopes of the fells I was surprised to see another rider climbing the hill ahead of me. He was on a black horse which I recognized as Godfrey's and I halted to watch them racing back down the slope, taking the stone wall skilfully. It was no novice who rode Emir with such natural grace.

I waited near the gate which led into the lane, knowing that the rider would stop there in case people were walking along it. The horse had already slowed to a canter as they approached it.

I had no difficulty in recognizing the rider, and waited for him. Then we were riding side by side and I hoped he would think my blushing face was on account of my exertion in riding with the wind in my face.

'Were you on your way back to the stables, Sir Julian?'

'Not necessarily, we could continue on to the moors if you like, and please Tessa there is no need to call me *Sir* Julian.'

I was glad that I rode my horse with confidence and as if he recognized my pleasure he said, 'Have you always ridden, Tessa? I ask because I believe you have only recently come to live at Glamara.'

'My mother taught me when I was very young. For a time there was no opportunity but now I ride whenever I can.'

'I too, we have moors as wild if not wilder than these round my house near the coast. When I was a small boy I rode for miles across my grandfather's lands near Seville.'

'I had almost forgotten you are half Spanish.'

'My mother was Spanish. I spent a lot of my time there when I was a boy.'

'You did not want to go out with the shooting party?'

'I prefer riding up here on the fells, deer stalking is not my idea of spending a pleasurable afternoon. You too decided not to take part.'

'Yes. This morning one of those gentle beautiful creatures was roaming happily with the herd, tonight it will be dead and for no real reason except that the Lord of the Manor fancies venison.'

He laughed. 'I can see you feel they are guilty of a very despicable act.'

'Don't you?'

'My grandfather bred bulls for the bull ring. I never thought much about their slaughter until I was about ten years old. A young bull calf had become tangled in the thorn bushes and the men had to rescue him. They brought him down to the house in a covered cart and being curious I opened the canvas to look at him. He was only a few weeks old, and when I opened the flap a ray of sunlight entered the darkness and there he was trying to capture it on his tiny horns. I was enchanted, and suddenly very sad. You see Tessa, I knew what his future would be. One day that bull would enter the bull ring to the sounds of cheers and martial music, the matador would strut and pose, the girls would fling their posies, but no matter how well he fought, no matter if he killed a dozen matadors, the bull would die, weakened by the spears in his side, his heart filled with blind rage and despair. Then his body would be harnessed behind two horses and dragged ingloriously from the ring while the crowd went mad with adulation for his slayer.'

'You hate all blood sports?'

'Most of them. I hate prolonged butchery in the name of sport.'

'Roxanne has gone on the shoot.'

'Of course. Her father was my cousin, he had few tender feelings towards the bulls bred for the ring.'

'As her guardian you have not been able to influence her?'

He looked at me with a wry smile. 'I was twenty-three when I became Roxanne's guardian and she was already eight years old. If I had been married or if she had been a boy it would have been easier, but although she was malleable and obedient I felt that Roxanne had never been a child, that perhaps I have never really understood her.'

'She does not ask for your advice?'

'No. Sometimes I give it and it is unacceptable. As the years pass I give it less and less.'

'Will you remain her guardian until she marries?'

'Or until she is twenty-one, which ever comes first.'

'She is very beautiful. I don't think I have ever seen anyone so beautiful.'

'Yes she is beautiful. There are times when I look at that lovely face and wonder what goes on behind it. What does she think about, what does she feel? Is she capable of love and tenderness, or are her passions destructive and punishing?'

I looked at his dark face uncertainly. It was pensive, his thoughts turned inward, until suddenly he turned his head and smiled, a smile so sweet and embracing my heart leapt in response.

'I have heard something of your story from Laura,' he said. 'I think she was resentful of your appearance at Glamara. I hope you have now become friends.'

'We are better friends than we were several months ago. I can see how difficult it must have been for Laura to accept me, after all none of them had even known of my existence until the day I arrived.'

'One day you shall tell me about your life before you came here. I was watching you last night in the ballroom. Time has not quite banished the shadows from your eyes, or is it that you cannot quite believe your present good fortune?'

'I do think about the past and I am grateful for the present. I'm not sure what I was thinking about last night when you caught me looking so pensive.'

'And I am told you are soon to announce your engagement to that nice young officer.'

I raised my eyes to search his face. He was looking at me gravely, expecting an answer, but I had none for him. Instead I pointed down the hill towards the house where a weary procession was wending its way back, carrying with them the body of a deer.

'Well,' he said, 'it looks as though we shall have our venison. Perhaps we should ride back to meet them.'

We rode swiftly, jumping the narrow streams and low stone walls and arriving in the parkland just as they were walking the last half mile towards the house.

Alec greeted me exuberantly. 'Right between the eyes Tessa, first shot,' he said gaily.

Godfrey remarked, 'You should have been there to see it, Tessa, this lad of yours'll do well in an emergency.'

Laura was hanging on Iain's arm but Roxanne was eyeing me, not entirely pleased at seeing Julian and me together.

'I didn't know you and Julian had decided to go riding,' she said shortly.

'We met on the fells. I recognized the horse but not the rider.'

'Oh, Julian doesn't mind whose horse he rides, if he can't ride his own.'

I sensed her anger but I said nothing more and soon retired to my bedroom. I was still in my slip searching for my gown when there was a tap on the door and Laura and Roxanne entered.

They were already dressed, Laura in a pale green creation that suited her colouring, while Roxanne wore black. It suited her remarkably well, and was relieved by a most exotic collar of coral and turquoise which she explained was Spanish.

They perched on my bed unceremoniously while I stepped into my dress and Laura said, 'Why don't you wear one of your new dinner gowns?'

'This *is* one of my new gowns.'

'I'm not sure I like you in that shade. Was Mother with you when you bought it?'

'No, Aunt Hetty.'

'Oh well, neither of them is exactly a fashion plate.'

I began to think they had entered into a conspiracy to make me feel disenchanted with my appearance when Roxanne said, 'I believe your mother had red hair Tessa, wouldn't you have liked it too?'

'Yes, when I was a little girl I was always sorry mine wasn't red.'

'Oh well, I suppose you are a traditional English rose. I'm not nearly so unusual when I visit my father's family in Spain.'

'Don't you think Julian is absolutely *devastating*, Tessa?' Laura said archly.

'He's very good-looking.'

Roxanne laughed. 'Oh, Julian is accustomed to all the girls going ga-ga over him. They follow him about and tell him all sorts of confidences but he is quite immune to their blandishments, he is even immune to mine.'

'Does that worry you Roxanne?' I couldn't resist snapping.

'As a matter of fact it does. I hate to see him all moody and miserable. Perhaps he'll go to France soon to cheer himself up.'

I didn't speak, pretending to be busy searching for my earrings but Roxanne went on undeterred. 'Don't you think it's absolutely terrible for a man so handsome and virile to waste his life caring for a woman who can never be a wife to him? She's a complete invalid you know, it's not as though they can even have an affair.'

'Well that's it,' I said brightly, 'I'm ready now. Shall we go down?'

'When are you going to announce your engagement?' she asked as we walked along the corridor.

'I don't know.'

'I understand Alec is going to Ireland almost immediately.'

'Yes.'

'I have friends in County Antrim. I do so love Ireland, all that lovely coastline and their horses are quite the best in the world. I always hunt when I'm in Ireland, it is so much less inhibited.'

'I've never been there.'

'You must go while Alec is there. You won't mind if I look him up will you?'

'Of course not, it would be a pity to be in Ireland and not see a friend.'

'You sound remarkably sure of him.'

'No, I wouldn't say that.'

Laura was looking decidedly uncomfortable and I was glad. She deserved to be discomfited, and I took my place at the dining table without a second glance at either of them. I was sitting beside the general, who immediately dug me in the ribs with his elbow and said, 'Good shot that young feller of yours made this afternoon, Tessa. Why weren't you there to see it?'

'I went riding on the fells.'

'Not fond of blood sports then?'

'Not particularly.'

'Still you should have seen that shot, right between the eyes. Good man to have on a safari, or a battleground.'

Across the table my eyes met Julian's and he smiled. Almost immediately I was aware of Roxanne's long cool stare and I shivered in spite of the warmth of the room. Perhaps I should have heeded the warning note that crept into my heart but I had no means of knowing then what fate would do to any of us. Outwardly we were a gathering of family and friends eating dinner in a country house presided over by a genial host, but there were undercurrents round that table I was only distantly aware of.

There was something about Roxanne that frightened me even then when we hardly knew each other. I was sure she could be an implacable enemy if her desires were thwarted. Now, sitting between Godfrey and Iain, she was using her beauty and her wiles to charm them both. Iain's young face was bemused. He had not yet learnt how to tease and flirt, and it was Godfrey who was responding to her coquettish behaviour with heavy-handed flattery. There was a sulky expression on Laura's face and Abigail seemed more concerned with her daughter's annoyance than with her husband's attempts at flirtation.

Alec on my right seemed unaware of the atmosphere as he chatted to the general about his life in the army, and since I was sitting between them all I could do was get on with my meal and answer occasional questions.

Julian seemed cynically amused, but whether with Roxanne and Godfrey, the general and his questions, or the guests generally I did not know. Occasionally his eyes would meet mine and I hoped the treacherous colour would not reach my cheeks in case it was that which brought the amusement into his eyes.

In later years when I thought about that evening I wondered if that was when it began. There we all sat like pawns upon a chessboard, to be moved and mated and slain, and I wondered if fate already sat back complacently, waiting for the next act in the drama of our lives to unfurl.

After dinner we all moved to the music room and Abigail asked Julian to play the piano for us. He played well, music that swept melodiously round the room, filling my heart with unexplained longings and a vague remote sadness.

Roxanne leaned across the grand piano watching his hands on the keyboard and when he had finished she went to sit beside him and they played together as they must often have done before, their fingers responding beautifully, ecstatically, as though they belonged together. And while they played once again her eyes met mine, triumphantly assured.

'Have you no accomplishments Tessa?' she asked. 'Perhaps it's your turn to entertain us now.'

'I love music but I never learnt to play the piano.'

'Well Laura did and she hated every minute of it. Can't I persuade you to at least play something for us?' she went on, switching her gaze to Laura.

'How could I possibly play anything after Julian? My mother will sing for you if you like.'

Julian turned to Abigail. 'Yes, come and sing for us Abigail, you have a lovely voice.'

She chose one of Grieg's sweet haunting songs and it was true her voice was lovely. It was not a voice to fill a large concert hall but she had had some early training and it filled the music room, tenderly and with great pathos, for the song spoke of the summer that was dying.

We tried to encourage her to sing again but the general was snoring in his chair, much to Lady Robertson's annoyance. 'Bertie wake up,' she said, prodding him energetically. 'I declare you haven't heard a note. We all have to listen while you fight your old wars over again, surely you can keep awake long enough to absorb a little culture.'

'A nightcap, General?' Godfrey inquired, lifting up the decanter from a side table.

'Whisky, my dear feller.'

'A small one,' put in his wife, to be rewarded by a martial scowl.

As we crossed the hall and moved towards our rooms the general took hold of my arm and in a voice audible to all said, 'Make up your mind quickly to marry this young feller, Tessa, or at least set his mind at rest before he ships off to Ireland.'

Alec squeezed my hand and Roxanne cried, 'Oh yes, we must have something to celebrate and what better thing than an engagement? Don't you agree, Julian?'

'Perhaps Tessa would prefer to celebrate her engagement when it doesn't vie with Christmas,' he replied dryly.

'Oh but a Christmas engagement would be lovely, Alec will never have an excuse to forget an anniversary. Christmas morning would be splendid, when everybody is handing out presents.'

How insistent she was, and the others, as if caught up by her enthusiasm, added their persuasions to hers. Now Alec was standing with his arms around me laughing, with delight, caught up by the moment, and Godfrey was saying,

'Yes by God, let us celebrate it on Christmas morning, there's surely no better time.'

And when all the excitement and the laughter had died down I was only aware of Julian's voice saying, 'You will have to celebrate without me, Godfrey, I must return home tomorrow. But of course Roxanne may stay as long as she wishes.'

At the top of the stairs he shook Alec's hand and then mine and with a courteous inclination of his head he said, 'I hope you will be very happy Tessa. Perhaps the next time we meet you will be a married lady.'

I stared into his face, so grave, so serious and it was as though icy fingers held my heart in a grip of steel. If we had been alone I would have thrown my arms around him and held him close. As it was he released my hand and turning away he left me without a second glance, while I stared after him, my entire being filled with utter desolation.

I slept badly. I told myself that I was a stupid fool: he had given me absolutely no cause to think he cared anything for me at all, he had merely been charming and polite. Julian was an obsession that I had to erase out of my heart and my life, never to think of again.

Roxanne had professed great interest in my engagement to Alec but she was not there to join in the celebrations, she had left Glamara with Julian. When Laura came to my room to tell me they had gone we stared at each other with mutual feelings of cynicism.

'I don't care if she never comes here again,' she stormed. 'She was hateful because you went riding with Julian and she made me hateful too.'

'Why has she the power to make you hateful to anyone? Surely you're not afraid of her?'

'She was always like that at school. If she disliked anybody she could be vile and she could make me vile too. If I didn't do as she wanted she would make friends with somebody else and they would all ignore me.'

I thought about Marylee, but Marylee had been a pinprick compared to Roxanne with her power to manipulate and use people.

'I can't think many of the girls would really like her.'

'No, but you couldn't ignore her, at least they all wanted to be her friend because she was so beautiful and she was such an exciting person to be with. Do you know she actually had an affair with a young matador who went to her great-grandfather's place to select bulls for the bull ring in Madrid? And it was so different to have a guardian like Julian instead of ordinary parents like mine. If you were friends with Roxanne you got invited to marvellous places and when Julian came to the school all the girls fell in love with him.'

'Including Roxanne?'

'Especially Roxanne.'

'In spite of the affair with the matador?'

'Oh that was nothing. Roxanne said it was experience for the time when Julian realized he was in love with her. It was all terribly exciting and you can see for yourself nothing ever *really* happens at Glamara.'

I went to the wardrobe and took out the Christmas presents I had been about to wrap when she came into the room.

'Do we put our Christmas presents round the tree until Christmas morning or do we distribute them this evening?'

'Oh, round the bottom of the tree with the others.'

'What about the servants?'

'Well mother and father go down to the kitchens on Christmas morning and the butler lines them all up to receive a present according to the work they do. You needn't worry that they're forgotten and none of them will expect anything from the rest of the family. You surely haven't been buying presents for the servants?'

'Only for Annie.'

'She's only a scullery maid, for heaven's sake!'

'I knew her before she came here and I don't suppose there'll be anything for her from home.'

I had seen it in a shop in London, a small print showing a rough sea dashing against cliffs, threatening to overturn the tiny boats tossing about in the harbour and with a wild and stormy sky overhead.

'If you give it to her in front of the other servants they won't like it,' she warned.

I decided to take Annie's print down to Cook and I found her in her kitchen. I showed her the print and asked her advice about when it should be given.

'Just put yer card inside and wrap it in fancy paper and I'll give it to Annie when there's nobody about. There's bin nothin' for Annie fro' Leeds, nothin' except a letter.'

'No, I don't suppose they have anything to spare and I think Annie understands very well.'

'Ay well, she's bein' promoted in the New Year to under housemaid, that'll please 'er an' she deserves it. Is it true that yer'll announce yer engagement on Christmas morning, Miss Tessa?'

'Yes, but we are not planning to marry for some time. He is going to Ireland for a couple of years. Probably we shall think about it then.'

'And do 'is family know about the engagement?'

'Yes, they are delighted. We are spending New Year with them at Grindale.'

'An' so they should be, capturin' a beautiful young lady like yerself, Miss Tessa, and with a dowry fit fer a princess an' this beautiful 'ouse to get married from.'

I could have talked to Cook for hours, but Laura came looking for me, putting her bright head round the door and calling, 'Alec's been looking all over for you, Tessa, he says he hasn't seen you today at all. When I get engaged I'll be with him every minute until he slips that ring on my finger.'

Alec looked cross but after we had been walking in the fresh breeze for some time he recovered his habitual good humour.

'When I didn't see you I wondered if you'd changed your mind about our getting engaged, Tessa. You haven't, have you?'

'Of course not, but I'm glad it's to be just family instead of all those people the other evening.'

'I would have liked my parents to be here. They're so pleased. As a matter of fact your uncle suggested sending for them but it was a bit short notice.'

281

'I don't think your mother was too happy with our friendship at one time.'

'Probably because we were too young, it was never because she didn't think a lot about you, or your mother.'

I didn't argue with him but I could have done. In those days I hadn't been the fiancée she wanted for her son. Now things were different. I pulled myself up sharply, afraid of the cynicism that coloured most of my thoughts these days, wondering if she had gone for ever, that girl with the wide honest eyes who looked at people and life in full expectation that they and it would play fair.

CHAPTER TWENTY-THREE

And so it was that Christmas morning Godfrey announced my engagement to Alec Hardcastle.

Our good health was drunk both in the dining room and in the servants' hall, and we went with Abigail and Godfrey when they took the servants' presents so that they could add their congratulations to the family's.

Annie greeted us with her quaint little curtsey and as we spoke to other of the servants I could see her watching Alec covertly as if she needed to reassure herself that he was right for me.

They went up one by one to receive their presents and I saw that Annie's was a fairly large oblong box which I took to be the expensive chocolates Abigail ordered regularly from York. She would never before have received such a present.

Later as we circulated round the room Annie sidled up to me, saying, 'The picture were lovely, Miss Tessa, I'll treasure it for the rest o' mi life.'

By this time Alec had reached our side and I said softly in his ear, 'This is Annie, Alec. Do you remember my telling you she worked at the Bryant house in Leeds?'

He took Annie's hand and looked down into her blushing

face. 'I do remember, dear. This is a big improvement to your last post, Annie.'

'That it is sir.'

I drew him gently away in case the other servants thought Annie was coming in for too much attention, and he whispered, 'That was a very nice thing, to bring Annie here.'

'I had to do it, Alec, I couldn't bear to think of her existing in that terrible environment.'

'Is there anybody as nice as you, I wonder?'

'Of course there is, only you are prejudiced.'

So, Christmas in the year nineteen hundred and twelve passed happily and peacefully and in the new year we went to Grindale to see Alec's parents.

They received me warmly and I knew that they were pleased for both of us as were the Elliotts when I went to their cottage, taking Alec with me.

I felt a different person from the girl who had grown up in Grindale. Now I was financially secure – and secure too in Alec's love. I greeted old friends and those others who had not been so friendly with a serenity I could not remember ever having felt as a girl and we were fêted and made much of. Something of the old reserve remained, but I was stern with myself. It was useless to nurse bitterness about old slights that were best forgotten. I could not live in the past and it was better if I tried to forget it.

On the seventh of January I drove Alec to the station along remembered lanes whose hedgerows were white with frost. The train was not due for several minutes and I watched him walking back from the booking hall looking handsome and absurdly young in his uniform: his face smiling under his peaked cap, his leather riding boots under his white trench coat polished and shining in nut-brown leather. For the first time a lump came into my throat at the thought of him going away, and when he took me in his arms the tears were rolling slowly down my cheeks.

'Good gracious girl, there's nothing to cry about,' he said gently. 'With a bit of luck I'll be home on leave soon and the troubles have died down a bit recently. It's not as though I'm going to war, love.'

283

'I know, it's just that I don't want you to go at all.'

'Well don't send me off with tears in your eyes, and write often. I'll be living for your letters.'

'I will, oh I will.'

He held me close to him and kissed me longingly then the train was thundering into the station. He held my hands until the train began to move, then I was running beside it until it gathered speed and he was swept out of sight.

The following day I returned to Glamara and Robert cheered me up by allowing me to learn to drive his two-seater, a rather more opulent contraption than Alec's. Laura too was having driving lessons and we vied with each other for the praise of Adam and Robert, which was rare in coming.

I enjoyed driving and if they withheld their praise both Laura and I thought it was because we were learning far too well, and their masculine pride was affronted at our handling of anything mechanical and therefore something entirely from a man's world. When Godfrey witnessed our prowess, however, he bought two small cars – one for each of us – which we drove with increasing skill over the winding narrow roads of the North Riding, and even into the more adventurous lanes of neighbouring Cumberland.

In the summer Laura announced her engagement to Iain Gilmour and there were further celebrations, then almost immediately she departed with Iain and his parents on a cruise that would take them to the Far East and Australia where Iain's father had business commitments.

On the morning she came to say goodbye to me I was surprised when she hugged me warmly. 'I shall miss you, Tessa. I'm sorry we weren't friends right from the outset.'

'It's how we've finished up that matters.'

'You'll write and tell me everything, won't you?'

'There won't be much to tell.'

'Oh, *you* know, with the gossip – who's going to marry who and who is ending an affair. I haven't heard from Roxanne, though I did write to tell her of my engagement.'

'Perhaps she's abroad.'

'That wouldn't surprise me, but Julian sent me silver so he must have told her.'

'Maybe she's jealous.'

'How could she be with all the men she's supposed to know?'

'Well if Julian couldn't understand her, what hope have you got?'

'You got quite friendly with Julian, didn't you Tessa? Even after I told you to be careful. I would be afraid to get on the wrong side of Roxanne.'

'Well I don't suppose I shall be seeing much of her, or Julian either.'

'And you are safely engaged to Alec which is a very good thing if you ask me.'

She embraced me once more and then I stood at my window to watch them driving away. It would be quiet at Glamara without Laura. Adam and Robert were busy on the estate and when they were not they went off to race meetings or to friends who lived in different parts of the country, where they could hunt with meets over different terrain.

Godfrey too was rarely around during the day and Abigail was engaged in her regular round of good works throughout the district. I was much on my own. I accompanied Aunt Hetty when she went into the village to buy embroidery silks and we would have tea in the teashop opposite the inn.

Most afternoons I rode alone, setting my horse in the direction of the fells for I enjoyed jumping the stone walls and the little streams that came tumbling down the hillside. I rarely met a single person, but when I reached the lane early one afternoon I was surprised to see another horseman approaching. He rode slowly, a lumpy stout gentleman slumped in the saddle, allowing his horse to amble up the lane at his own speed. I recognized General Robertson immediately and imagined that once he had ridden his horse with great aplomb and daring as a young subaltern, while now in his middle age he seemed hardly to care how he rode. I smiled to see him straighten up in the saddle, urging his surprised horse on with some of his old fervour when he spotted me.

'Hello there mi dear, is your uncle at home?'

'He was in his study when I left the house. Would you like me to ride back with you?'

'That's right, keep an old man company. I don't get to ride with many pretty girls these days.'

My horse fell into step beside his and immediately his talk turned to Alec. 'Heard from that young fella of yours? Ireland isn't it?'

'Yes. He writes whenever he can, usually about twice a week.'

'And hating every minute of it I shouldn't wonder. You can't even begin to respect a faceless enemy.'

'Respect? An enemy?'

'Well yes m' dear. Somebody you know you're at war with, who meets you face to face, him with his army and you with yours. It's not like that in Ireland, you don't know who your friend is.'

'Alec doesn't say anything about the troubles, they've been there so long one begins to accept them until something terrible happens and we are all filled with revulsion.'

'Of course, and if we hit back it's us who are the murderers, with the gunmen treated like martyrs. I tell you Tessa, the Zulus in Africa were more honest foes than that rabble across the Irish sea.'

'You dislike the Irish, General.'

'Nay lass I love 'em. Some of my best friends are Irish but it's this element in their midst that I despise so much, and it's this wonderin' if the people you like most are harbouring them. The sooner your young feller comes back from there the better.'

By this time we were riding across the parkland and he turned to me with a smile, saying, 'A few years ago I'd have challenged you to a race across the park, but it's doubtful now if mi old horse could rise to the occasion.'

'Have you had him long?'

'I had him in Africa against the Boers and in the Sudan, he's done his share of fighting if he never does any more, and we're both too old to be called into action for the next lot.'

'The next lot?'

'Take no notice of an old soldier, Tessa. Clara says all I

286

think about is war, old wars and imagined ones. You enjoy yourself and don't you spend all your young life waitin' for that young feller to come back, there's some mighty pretty colleens in Ireland.'

That night over dinner I repeated our conversation to Godfrey. 'What do you suppose he means about the next one?' I asked him curiously.

'He thinks there's going to be trouble with Germany. It's one of his pet theories, he's had it for years.'

'Do you agree with him?'

'Well I've got to admit I don't like the way things are going. The Kaiser's a bit of a madman and I believe he's wanting to extend his empire. To do that he's got to take what doesn't belong to him and to protect ourselves we might have to step in and stop him.'

'That would mean war?'

'Yes Tessa, that would mean war.'

'Oh Godfrey, surely it's not going to come to that. Aren't there enough intelligent people here and in Germany to clamp down on his ambitions?' Aunt Hetty said, while one look at Abigail's pale face told me she was thinking of her sons.

'Sometimes intelligence isn't enough Hetty, not when it's met with blind egotism.'

'Well do let us stop talking about war Godfrey,' Abigail said sharply.

'All right mi dear, now what would you like to talk about? There's racing at York this weekend, how do you fancy going over there? I could write to Johnny Bainbridge to see if he'll put us up for a few days.'

'Oh I don't think so dear, but perhaps Tessa would like to go with you.'

In answer to his inquiring look I nodded happily. 'I'd like that very much Godfrey, I love racing.'

It was so easy to fill my days with pleasures of this sort because in Yorkshire race meetings were a way of life and practically every week meetings were held somewhere in the vicinity.

Over the years since I left Leeds I had kept up a

correspondence with Susan Latchford but we had never suggested visiting each other, so I was very surprised to receive an invitation to spend a long weekend in Leeds at the beginning of June. Susan was to become engaged to John Prescott, a nephew of the Prescott family, and since he was an orphan their engagement party was to be held at the Prescott house in Leeds.

Susan and her father met me at the station and immediately we both exclaimed upon the changes that time had wrought in our appearance. I had always considered Susan a pretty girl, but now she was also elegant in pale grey and violet, and throwing her arms around me she embraced me warmly.

'Tessa you look marvellous, and so grown up.'

'Well of course we are, and you look marvellous too and very elegant.'

After I had admired their new motor car we drove through the streets of Leeds which seemed to me remarkably unchanged, and later while I unpacked Susan came to sit in my room, exclaiming rapturously over my silken underwear and my clothes.

'When shall I meet your fiancé?' I asked.

'This evening. He's still in university studying to be a vet. He's hoping to get a practice somewhere in the area. I do wish Alec could have come with you, it must be horrible having him in Ireland, one hears such terrible things.'

The Prescott house could quite easily have been accommodated in a corner of Glamara, and yet as we approached it on that beautiful June evening with the sun warming its mellow Pennine stone, I thought it looked particularly beautiful. It was one of those country manor houses that England delights in. Surrounded by formal gardens and beautiful trees, with lawns as smooth as velvet and with the doors flung wide so that people could move on to the terrace, it presented a delightful picture of charming hospitality, borne out by the warmth of their welcome.

Sir John Prescott was a past Lord Mayor of the city and I knew well his reputation as a caring and generous factory master. Lady Prescott was a pretty woman, delicately made, with soft silver hair and a sweet smile.

'I expect you young ones will want to dance later on,' she said, smiling, 'but for the older ones we have invited artists to sing and play for us so I must ask you to bear with us in the earlier part of the evening.'

We took our places in the drawing room after I had been introduced to Susan's fiancé, an extremely personable young man with a close-clipped moustache, and a Yorkshire accent which he was trying desperately hard to disguise.

I enjoyed music at all times, and I listened appreciatively as one after another talented local artists sang for us: Victorian ballads, and duets from popular musical comedies and operettas.

It was during a lull that I noticed a young man standing near the wall who was staring unashamedly in my direction. Every time I allowed my eyes to wander round the room he was still watching me and Susan whispered in my ear, 'You've made a hit Tessa, he's not taken his eyes off you the entire evening.'

'Who is he?'

'Lionel Prescott, the elder of the Prescott boys. He's very nice, what a pity you're engaged.'

'I wish he wouldn't stare at me, it's embarrassing.'

I was introduced to Lionel Prescott over supper. He was good-looking without being strictly handsome, and as he took my hand and bowed formally over it he said, 'Haven't we met before? I know that sounds like a cliché but I'm sure I've seen you somewhere, perhaps when you were at school in Leeds.'

'You may have seen me in the area, I lived in one of the houses across from the park.'

'Are you staying here long?'

'Only for the weekend.'

'But you'll come again?'

'I don't know, it will depend how soon my fiancé gets leave from Ireland.'

I couldn't miss the expression on his face, disappointment, regret, and then almost immediately we were speaking of ordinary things as he escorted me to the terrace where his younger brother was setting up his gramophone and other young people were standing nearby choosing records.

I enjoyed Lionel's company and as the evening progressed I danced with him again and again. He was charming without being studied, he was interesting without being pompous, and I liked his sense of humour. I danced with other young men, but it was always Lionel I returned to. During a foxtrot which I danced with his younger brother, Alexander said, 'My brother's been looking at you all evening. Are you going to put him out of his misery and go out with him?'

'I'm sorry Alexander, I don't think my fiancé would like it.'

'Oh gosh, missed the boat again has he?'

'Does he always?'

'Well no, he's never been a great one for the girls, always too studious, not like me.'

'You mean you like the girls too well?'

'I suppose so. My father's threatened to cut my allowance if I bring just one more home before I pass my finals.'

'He's probably quite right.'

Just then I found my dress tugged at and turned to see Marylee smiling at me as though we had always been the best of friends. 'Hello Tessa, I heard you would be here tonight. How are things in the North Riding?'

'The same as ever, Marylee, how are you?'

'I'm fine. We passed close by your house on the way to Scotland last summer, I almost called to see you.'

I smiled but offered no comment or invitation and after we had danced on Alexander said, 'We've all met Marylee. I take it your house is something of a show place, otherwise I doubt if she'd have been interested.'

'Considering we never got on at school I can't see why she wanted to look me up.'

'Well if you give her any encouragement you'll have a guest on your hands for life.'

Just then there was some consternation among people standing in the gardens and looking down towards the city where we could clearly see a red glow in the sky.

The older people were flocking out of the drawing room. Lady Prescott came towards our group.

'Something is wrong in the city,' she exclaimed, 'and the Jeffersons haven't arrived. They must have been held up somewhere down there.'

The blaze seemed to be spreading, and then we could clearly see the headlights of a car climbing the hill towards the house. With a sigh of relief Lady Prescott said, 'This must be the Jeffersons.'

The car stopped and a man and woman in evening dress half ran from it towards the terrace. The woman looked frightened and they were both evidently excited. As they came into the light I could see blood on the man's cheek and on his wife's arm, and she was trying to shake particles of glass from her hair.

Lady Prescott took the woman's arm and led her towards the house while Mr Jefferson stayed to tell his story, holding a handkerchief to his bleeding cheek.

'They've gone mad down there,' he cried. 'They've barricaded the mill owner and his office staff inside the offices and set fire to the mill. They're breaking windows and tearing up fences, they were setting fire to the gates when we were there.'

'Where, which mills?' somebody cried.

'Bryant's mills. The streets and all along the canal banking are filled with men, woman and children, somebody is going to get killed before the night is out. When we tried to get through somebody hurled a paving stone and it shattered a side window. That is where we got these cuts. It could have been worse.'

Sir John joined us. 'The police are already there and the fire engines are trying to get through. I'm going down there, I'll try to talk a bit of sense into them.'

'They're in no mood to listen,' Mr Jefferson warned. 'Why not let the police deal with it?'

'No, damn it, some of those people used to work for me. Come with me, Lionel, I might need you.'

I ran after Lionel and took hold of his arm. 'Are you sure it is Bryant's mills?'

'They must be, Jefferson knows them.'

'Please Lionel, let me come with you.'

'That's impossible, Tessa. You saw what happened to Mrs Jefferson.'

'I don't care, I must see for myself what is going on.'

He stared at me and something of my desperation must have got through because he got hold of my arm and dragged me towards the house. 'Be quick and get your coat, my father will be waiting.'

I sat in the back seat, my eyes straining to where the sky was a big red glare and the sparks were flying in all directions. I did not see how those poor houses could possibly escape and long before we reached the area the ash was falling on the windscreen, the smell of burning timber was choking me and my eyes smarted from the smoke. The fire engines could not get near because of the men, women and children who stood arm in arm across the road, their faces filled with anger and determination to hold their ranks against all comers.

Some of the men had clambered on walls and shed roofs, while others had armed themselves with stones and pieces of timber. There were several fires but it was the boiler yard which posed the greatest problem. With its vast bank of coal it was now an inferno and people were being beaten back by the flames, their screams vying with the crackling of burning timber.

They came towards the car, staring at us with hate-dazed eyes, and then over the clamour one man's voice shouted, 'It's Sir John Prescott and his lad.'

He pushed his way to the car and Sir John let down his window so that they could speak.

'It's Saunders, isn't it,' he said, and the man nodded.

'Yer'd best stay in yer car sir, the mob's wild.'

'How did it start? Lionel asked.

'Bryant sacked two men and refused their wages. One o' the men 'as a sick wife an' 'ee were needin' that money. I've never seen owt like this, the rest of 'em just walked out an' went in a body to Bryant's office. He wouldn't see 'em, then when they persisted he went outside wi' 'is office staff an' turned the fire 'oses on the workers. I'm feared fer the 'ouses, they're nobbut hovels but at least it's a roof over their heads.'

Just then could be heard the insistent honking of a horn. A taxi drew up alongside us and a woman ran screaming from it towards the office block in spite of the mob who caught at her clothing and rained blows upon her head.

I recognized her immediately by her vivid red har, and in confirmation the man at the window said, 'That's 'is fancy woman.'

It was the women who were screeching obscenities at her, tearing at her clothing, her hair, any part of her person they could lay their hands on.

'Can't we do something?' I cried, 'they'll kill her.'

'Yer musn't leave the car, miss, she mun fend for 'erself.'

In spite of the mob by this time she had reached the office and knelt on the road, pounding at the door.

'If she thinks 'ee's goin' to put 'is life i' danger by comin' down to open it fer 'er she's sadly mistaken,' Saunders said. 'He'll let 'er die out there wi'out liftin' a finger.'

The police and firemen were pushing a way through the crowds and we saw them lift Mrs Howlett and carry her back to a police van. Her face was grey, her hair a sad and bedraggled mass, blood oozed from a cut on her head and her eyes were swollen.

The office block was broken into and presently three men were brought out, with the police fighting every inch of the way to get them to the van unscathed.

I recognized Bryant's squat, bloated figure as the mob howled derision, and then to add to the confusion the hosepipes began playing on the houses nearest to the canal which were in the greatest danger.

'We must try to get back Lionel,' Sir John was saying, 'we can do no good here, even if they would listen to us. Come to see me in a few days Saunders, we might have something for you.'

The man touched his cap and we were allowed to pass through the crowd which parted sullenly, although I saw several of the men take off their caps in respect. We drove in silence and I sat huddled in my corner, my thoughts in the past, glad that my mother wasn't alive to witness her husband's degradation.

It seemed that every light burned in Susan's house as we approached it and the family were out in the garden staring down the road. Susan rushed towards me, crying, 'Tessa, was it terrible down there?'

I nodded wordlessly. I turned to say goodnight to Sir John and found Lionel behind me. Taking my hand he said seriously, 'Goodbye Tessa, take a good look in the mirror when you get inside. At least we were able to provide you with a little excitement during your weekend in Leeds.' Then he was getting back into the car and I was watching its tail lights departing.

Something nagged at me even as I told the Latchfords what we had seen, and later when I beheld my blackened face and sooty hair in my bedroom mirror. It was just as I was drifting off to sleep that I sat up sharply with a terrible thought: I had not told Lionel Prescott why I had wanted to drive into the city with him, that it was because Jack Bryant was my stepfather, and now he would think I was just a girl looking for excitement, any excitement, however disastrous it might be for a great many people.

I felt unreasonably sorry that I hadn't made my position clear and, although it was doubtful that we would ever meet again, I hoped Susan would tell him why her friend had been more than interested in the downfall of Jack Bryant.

CHAPTER TWENTY-FOUR

I had hoped that Alec would be able to come home to attend Laura's wedding in the autumn of 1913 but it was not possible. It was almost a year since I had seen him and there were times when I found myself struggling to remember how he had looked on that occasion. I was better at remembering Alec as a boy I had teased and laughed with during our schooldays than Alec as the man I would one day marry.

Godfrey was disgruntled. 'Surely the army can spare him for a couple of days,' he grumbled, 'after all one man's absence will neither make nor break matters in Ireland.'

'Perhaps there are problems we don't know about,' I said, 'I'm sure they don't tell us everything that goes on.'

'I've a good mind to write to his commanding officer,' Godfrey said testily.

'Alec wouldn't like you to do that. He's very disappointed not to be coming, and I don't think asking for any sort of favouritism would be to his advantage.'

'No, perhaps not. Oh well, Laura's wedding will take place whether he condescends to join us or not. You'll have to make do with one of Iain's friends as an escort.'

Laura was too enchanted to be put out about anything. Alec's absence barely raised an eyebrow but I was touched when she invited me to be her chief bridesmaid.

'I thought you would want Roxanne,' I said uncertainly.

'I don't expect she'll even come to the wedding. She hasn't written for ages and I don't know where she is. Julian is coming, and he doesn't know where she is either.'

'But he's her guardian.'

'Not any more he isn't, you forget she's over twenty-one and I bet he's pleased about that.'

'How many bridesmaids will you have, then?'

'I would really like another two so I shall have to ask the Gervase girls. I'm not too keen, though. Monica was a distinct roly-poly the last time I saw her and Agnes has a decided squint. I did so want my bridesmaids to be pretty. You will look lovely in whatever I decide to put you in but I'm not happy about the others.'

'How long since you saw them?'

'Oh they were only schoolgirls, the families are close friends. What colour would you like to wear?'

'Nothing yellow, please.'

'Mm, I remember that yellow thing of mine you were

wearing the first night we met. You looked positively frightful.'

'Thank you very much.'

'Well, haven't you just said yellow wasn't your colour? What do you say to ruby? A dark rich ruby velvet made in the Tudor style, with ermine muffs and ermine on your headdresses. Mother will probably be wearing that terrible puce she's so fond of.'

'You're quite wrong about that.'

'What then?'

'I shan't tell you, but you'll be agreeably surprised.'

The next weeks were hectic. There were drawings to be looked at, materials to be chosen, and then a great many fittings before Laura was finally satisfied in her role as bride of the year.

The day of the wedding dawned misty as befits a November day, but as the morning progressed the clouds lifted and a watery sun shone in a pale, colour-washed sky.

The men looked handsome and debonair in their formal morning dress and Laura hugged her mother delightedly when she saw her looking pretty and elegant in peach lace, her large hat decorated with peach silk roses to match the flowers pinned on her gown. Aunt Hetty had chosen her favourite shade of soft brown, neat and restrained, her well-cut jacket having a luxurious collar of sable. Leaving for the church with Adam and Robert, they were a very elegant foursome.

Laura looked beautiful and ethereal in rich bridal satin and lace, her frothy veil held in place with a Tudor headdress of seedpearls and diamante. The long embroidered train seemed to go on for ever as I followed her into the church.

She had changed her mind about the ruby velvet for me and instead I was attired in royal blue, my hands warm in a tiny ermine muff, my Tudor headdress decorated like the bride's. The vibrant colour set off my delicate colouring. The two other bridesmaids wore ruby, and Laura had been relieved to see that the puppy fat had gone and the squint was less pronounced. We were much of a height and as the bridal procession entered the church there were gasps of admiration from the villagers and the servants from Glamara who sat in the pews behind the family and their guests. I kept my eyes on Sir Godfrey and Laura as they made their dignified passage down the aisle of the old stone church and I listened to the profound words of the marriage service with a strange sense of detachment, unsure if I was quite ready to say them with any real sense of meaning.

As I came out of church on Robert's arm he whispered, 'Your turn next, Tessa.'

I didn't speak, favouring him only with a small swift smile, and he said gently, 'You're not sure are you, Tessa?'

'No, perhaps not.'

'You'll feel differently when you see him again, it is this separation which is so punishing.'

'I hope so. It's all going to be so different when Laura's gone.'

'Of course, much more ordered and peaceful, meals will be eaten promptly and mother will be able to relax and wear the colours she likes instead of the ones Laura likes.'

'You are really very fond of Laura, Robert, you don't mean half the things you say.'

'Yes I am fond of her, but I *do* mean all the things I say. I hope I'll be able to get out of these uncomfortable clothes as soon as she's gone. There's nothing planned for this evening.'

'Are all the guests going after the reception?'

'I should imagine so, I always feel that weddings fall a little flat when the main participants have gone.'

The reception took the form of an elaborate buffet where people circulated to their heart's content, standing in groups, eating and drinking. I stood close to Robert, not daring to move in case I encountered Julian's dark eyes watching me across the room. I had not seen him, but his expensive present was on display, a silver rose bowl and two magnificent candelabra. The card with them was from Julian and Roxanne, but I was sure she had had no part in either choosing or helping to pay for them.

The speeches were made, the toasts were drunk and then I was upstairs helping Laura into a green georgette dress and the beige mink coat her father had bought her, joking that, thank heavens, it was the last article of clothing he could in all honesty be expected to provide.

She looked enchanting, and throwing her arms around me she said, 'Thanks for all you've done Tessa, it was a lovely wedding, wasn't it?'

'Yes, quite perfect.'

There were tears in her eyes as she picked up her gloves. 'Now that I'm really leaving Glamara I suppose I'm going to miss it, but it's going to be heavenly living in the south. We shall only be twenty-five miles from London. Think of it Tessa, all those lovely shows and nightclubs if we feel like it, you can keep your rugged splendour, give me civilization. Now come down into the hall, I'm going to throw my bouquet and you should be the one to catch it.'

I stood with the crowd while Laura stood on the stairs taking careful aim in my direction. The flowers fell into my arms naturally and the guests laughed while General Robertson said in a jocular voice, 'The flowers have got it right for once, Tessa's next on the list.'

We stood in the early dusk until Iain's car disappeared along the drive. Guests were soon saying their farewells and then for the first time I saw Julian, speaking to my aunt and uncle. The strength of my feelings was so potent I felt suddenly weak and vulnerable.

He turned and our eyes met. My heart thumped sickeningly as he came towards me, stopping to speak to one or two people who greeted him on the way.

I despised the treacherous trembling of my body which made me feel gauche and stupid, but surely no other man of my acquaintance walked with quite that long lean grace, or captivated with his charm while remaining strangely aloof.

He took my hand in his and bowed gravely over it, then he smiled down into my upturned face and I was staring at him, as though I was trying to memorize every feature, every fleeting expression while he chatted naturally and easily about Laura's wedding.

He would never know the effort it cost me to respond to his conversation normally and naturally, and only when I watched him walking away did I realize that neither of us had mentioned Alec or Roxanne.

I had called him Sir Julian and he had not objected, placing me immediately at a distance. Oh, it was so strange how I remembered those foolish small things as if they were important, reading into them a significance they did not possess. That night as I lay in bed watching the drifting shadows on the ceiling I could have wept with chagrin at my youth and inadequacy. Julian was a man of the world. He must have guessed that I was infatuated with him, he would be amused, perhaps even a little flattered that on so short an acquaintance he had the power to leave me tongue-tied and dismayed.

I firmly resolved that in the morning I would write Alec a long letter telling him how much I missed him and that I wanted him home very soon. I hoped I might begin to see my infatuation for Julian as the hopeless thing it was and, although I carried out my resolution faithfully the following morning, it did nothing to help. It was still Julian's face I saw most clearly in every waking moment and perhaps even more realistically in my dreams.

As spring followed winter my life seemed to have taken on a monotonous simplicity which often made me feel that I was living in limbo, hanging suspended awaiting some momentous event to shatter the gentle pattern of my life.

One thing did occur in April which hardly seemed to touch me at the time but which was to have an essential bearing on what came later. Sir Edward Chalmers died from a massive heart attack. Godfrey broke the news to us over dinner that night and while the family expressed its concern he said, 'I shall have to go over to Easdale for the funeral, he was a constant visitor at this house in the old days although we haven't seen much of each other in recent years.'

'I will go with you, Godfrey,' said Aunt Hetty.

'I would like to come too, if I may,' I said earnestly. 'He came to my mother's funeral and brought his son. I shall be very unobtrusive but I would like his son to know that I was there.'

The tiny village church was thronged and I watched

curiously as Richard and his mother followed Sir Edward's coffin up the aisle. Sir Edward's widow was pale but tearless, her thin sharp features cold and unattractive in her mourning apparel, and she leaned heavily on her son's arm. Richard too was pale, but composed, his thin shoulders already bowed under his grief and the responsibility his father's death had suddenly thrust upon his shoulders.

Easdale Hall was large, its surrounding park and land almost as vast as Glamara's, and the tenants filled the church to overflowing. Most of them would already be wondering what changes would come to pass now that a young man held the reins. I knew from my years at Grindale that Sir Edward had been respected whilst his wife was generally disliked. Now I felt convinced Richard would find himself too close to his mother, and without Sir Edward's help and advice, at a great disadvantage.

I stood back from the crowd around the open grave but where I could still hear the words of the funeral service. When it was over they gathered in small groups, no doubt expressing their condolences, and slowly I walked through the churchyard so that I need not speak or even be seen by any of those present, many of whom I had recognized.

A little way from the path a girl knelt to arrange flowers in a stone urn on what appeared to be a new grave and there was something in her pose that seemed familiar. She was dressed in black. The flowers at last to her liking she gathered the cut stalks into a little parcel and rose to her feet, then she turned and I realized with surprise that it was Elizabeth Chantry.

I went forward to meet her, taking her hand in mine and saying, 'Elizabeth, how nice to see you.'

Her eyes flew open in surprise, then snatching her arm away she cried, 'How dare you speak to me, how dare you come to look at my father's grave!'

'I'm sorry Elizabeth, I didn't know your father was dead. I am with my aunt and uncle at Sir Edward's funeral.'

She made as if to push past me, her face angry, a dull flush colouring her cheeks, and nonplussed I said, 'Elizabeth, why are you so angry? Surely you must know why I left your house, it wasn't because I wanted to leave you.'

'I know why you left, my father told me. You threw yourself at him, told him that you loved him, and when he told you to pull yourself together you threatened to leave us. He let you go though, didn't he? He didn't try to stop you?'

'But that wasn't the truth, Elizabeth.'

'My father never lied to me. All that cant about being virtuous, all that advice you gave me about being careful with that poor idiot boy when you were planning on seducing my father. I hate you Tessa Chalfont, I'll hate you as long as I live.'

I stepped back and allowed her to pass, shaken by her anger, but there seemed no point in arguing. Then she came back and with her face close to mine she hissed, 'I wonder what your fine friends would think if I told them how you behaved in my father's house, standing there so calmly as though you had nothing to be ashamed of.' She turned and made as if to walk towards the mourners but I caught hold of her arm and spun her round. I was as angry now as she and in a low voice which I was trying hard to control I said, 'If you say just one word about me to those people there I shall tell them what your father did to you, constantly and criminally while you were still a child and living under his protection. Do you seriously think I would love a man like that? I thought he was a monster.'

'My father never did anything to me.' Her voice was shaking and she was very frightened.

'Then, Elizabeth, you are a liar just as your father was a liar.'

The funeral party was moving towards us now and although she stood beside me uncertainly I knew that I had won. With one more look of bitter hatred in my direction she took to her heels, along the path and out through the lych gate. There was no time to draw my veil before Richard recognized me. He came to my side, raising his hat.

'Thank you for coming,' he said simply. 'I saw that your aunt and uncle were here and I looked for you. Why did you come?'

'As a mark of respect, because you and your father came to my mother's funeral.'

301

'Not for any other reason?'

I looked at him helplessly. 'Isn't it enough that we came?' I murmured uncertainly.

'It is enough that you came. You're the one I care about.' Then with a brief smile he left me and hurried after his mother.

I was to spend the following weekend at Briarcrag with Alec's parents and I hoped his mother had heard from him by this time. She had been anxious the last time we had spoken on the telephone, and since his letters to me had been more spasmodic of late, I had little comfort to offer her.

'How long is it since you heard from Alec?' Abigail asked one evening, and I had to admit that it was several weeks.

Godfrey looked up sharply, saying, 'Damn it, there's no pitched battles in Ireland, so why doesn't he write? Either there's something going on that we don't know about or there's trouble in another direction.'

'What sort of trouble?' Adam asked. 'You mean there's another girl?'

'Of course not, I mean enemy trouble. Robertson was over last night, he's convinced we're for it, and before very long.'

'Robertson's not the only person who thinks so,' Robert said. 'As soon as there's something definite we might as well join up, no point in waiting until we're called up.'

'What is all this stupid talk of joining up?' Abigail cried. 'I can't stand this continual talk about war?'

In spite of Godfrey's warning look Robert said, 'Well, there's a new spring to old Robertson's step these days, if you ask me he's already riding that charger and leading his men into battle. Poor old chap, the nearest he'll come to the battlefront is some comfy chair in Whitehall.'

'That's probably where I'll end up too,' Godfrey put in sharply, 'but we're the ones with the experience, not you young pups hardly washed behind your ears.'

'It's the young pups who'll be doing the fighting,' Robert observed.

'Nor can you put old heads on young shoulders, more's the pity,' his father snapped.

As I drove to Grindale on Saturday morning that conversation was churning over and over in my mind. It was now three weeks and four days since I had received Alec's last letter, and in that I had sensed an undercurrent.

I reached Briarcrag and joined Mrs Hardcastle in time for afternoon tea. 'Joe won't be in until dinner,' she informed me. 'He had to go over to Leeds this morning, something's brewing but I don't know what.'

I asked her pointedly if she had heard rumours of unrest abroad from Mr Hardcastle, but she seemed not to know what I was referring to and I quickly changed the subject. I had no wish to alarm her, particularly as she had not heard from Alec.

'I'm vexed with him,' she said angrily. 'He knows I worry about him, I didn't want him to go to Ireland, I'd rather he'd have gone anywhere but there. They don't seem to care who they hurt or kill. I can't see any end to the troubles.'

'Perhaps none of them are allowed to write if something new is afoot,' I said in what I hoped was a conciliatory manner. 'I am sure Alec will write when he is able.'

'Why he ever wanted to go into the army is a mystery. It's all wrong that Joe has had to appoint managers to look after the mills when we have a son who could have taken over. Joe's getting too old to worry about his business, and you'll see, it'll be the children of his managers who'll come in for all we've worked for instead of Alec and the girls.'

'Oh surely not. They must get something from all their father's hard work even though they are not connected with the mills.'

'I sometimes think Alec doesn't deserve anything. He went off into the army without a thought for us, and the girls are getting that hoity-toity they'll like as not marry men who think of nothing but riding horses and living like gentlemen.'

I didn't argue with her. She had so wanted to be a gentlewoman, now it seemed she was quarrelling with the results. Her daughters were growing away from her and I wished fervently that Alec would write soon to end her worrying.

The weekend was not a great success. Every day I spent at

Briarcrag brought too many memories of other years and even at mealtimes I was aware of undercurrents. I believed Mr Hardcastle had worries he was loath to communicate to his wife, and my presence only emphasized Mrs Hardcastle's annoyance with her son.

It was early evening when I returned to Glamara to find that the general and his wife were guests for dinner. The men sat over their port for so long that Abigail became fidgety and Lady Robertson said, 'They'll be discussing the news from abroad, Bertie doesn't like it.'

'News, what news?' Abigail cried.

'Surely you've heard about the assassination of Archduke Franz Ferdinand and his wife in Sarajevo. Now Austria and Serbia are at war and Bertie says it'll spread, we'll be in it before we know where we are.'

'I can't see for the life of me what the assassination in Bosnia has to do with us,' Abigail said, but her voice trembled pitifully, and Lady Robertson looked up with concern.

'Don't worry your head about it my dear, Bertie's a warmonger, always has been. It's his training, you know.'

At last the men joined us and Robert suggested a rubber of bridge.

Relieved we settled down to play. I partnered Adam but I played badly, my thoughts on other things. I found myself constantly apologizing until in the end he said, 'Wake up, Tessa, this isn't like you.'

'Perhaps I'm not really in the mood after all.'

'Oh well, we'll finish this rubber and then we'll call it a day. You've been living it up during your weekend at Briarcrag, you haven't said much about it.'

'It was very nice.'

I did not miss the sharp look he gave me while making myself concentrate sternly on the cards in my hand.

'You are not letting this talk of war worry you, I hope,' Aunt Hetty said, 'I'm sure nothing is going to happen.'

My eyes again met Adam's but I failed to read any reassurance in them.

It was the following Saturday morning when I heard

Alec's voice on the telephone and with my voice faint with relief I said, 'Alec, where are you? It's been ages since I heard from you.'

'Yes I know, I'm sorry Tessa. When can we meet?'

There was something in his voice, a hesitancy, a remoteness so at variance with his usual buoyancy, and the first faint trickle of disquiet made me suddenly silent.

'Tessa,' his voice came more urgently. 'Can you hear me, when can we meet?'

'Where are you?'

'At Briarcrag, I arrived last night.'

'Couldn't you have let me know when you were coming home?'

After a brief silence his voice was cautious. 'There wasn't much time, I'll explain when I see you.'

'Come over as soon as you like, Alec. How long is your leave?'

'Very short, I shan't be able to stay. Will you meet me in the village?'

'Don't you want to come up to the house?'

'I want to see you alone, Tessa, you know how difficult it is with all the family there. Meet me in that little teashop, three o'clock or thereabouts. Please say you'll be there.'

'Well of course I'll be there, what do you expect?'

'Until then Tessa.'

He was gone. I replaced the receiver thoughtfully. This Alec had been a stranger, not even Ireland could account for the change in him. I found myself trembling with a desperate, unaccountable fear.

I set out shortly after two, walking briskly, wearing a blue tweed suit and sweater and with a tam-o'-shanter on my head sporting a huge knitted bob. The outfit was becoming and I knew the colour suited me, all the same I was miserable. I had never before felt this uncertainty about Alec, he had always been so predictable, so utterly safe, now it was as though I was on my way to meet a man I had never really known.

It was so wrong of Alec to say he would meet me in the teashop. It was Saturday afternoon and crowded with shoppers. I was fortunate to find a table for two against the wall where others would have difficulty in hearing our conversation. It was almost four o'clock when Alec arrived, breathless and apologetic.

'Gosh Tessa, I am sorry but I got stuck behind a convoy of army vehicles, it was impossible to get past them.'

'I suppose if the general had seen them he would say it was a sure sign of war,' I said, smiling. 'I didn't order until you came, what would you like?'

'Oh, any old thing. Tea and cakes if that'll suit you.'

When I looked back on that afternoon I remembered most the stained tablecloth and the waitress who clattered crockery and cutlery on to the table.

Alec's impish, boyish smile had gone and in its place was a worried maturity. He seemed reluctant to talk and believing I knew the reason for his reluctance I said, 'You are trying to tell me that there is going to be a war and that you will have to go away,' I prompted him.

He looked up startled, then as though he physically gathered his courage together he said, 'I think there will be a war, Tessa, but there's something more.'

'More than war?'

'I'm afraid so.'

At that moment I felt so much older than he sitting embarrassed and contrite like a little boy who had been caught with his fingers in the candy jar.

'You've found somebody else, Alec. I've heard how pretty the Irish colleens can be.'

He looked up startled. 'Oh Tessa,' he murmured miserably, 'I'd have given anything for this not to have happened but I couldn't help it. I love you Tessa, I'll always love you, this is different.'

'I know. You love me but you're not in love with me.'

It was amazing how well I understood how he felt, for hadn't that been how I had loved Alec until I realized how much more I loved Julian?

'Tell me about her,' I said, placing my hand over his.

'That's the horrible part about it,' he said, 'you already know her.'

'I know her!'

'Roxanne.'

I stared at him in both anger and dismay. Immediately I saw it all. Roxanne had gone to Ireland deliberately to steal Alec from me and the hatred I had felt for her at our first meeting surged over me so that if I had had her there before me I would have raked my fingers across that too perfect face.

'She was staying with some friends quite close to where we were stationed, they were Julian's friends actually, but she visited them often. I thought she was in love with Michael, he was the son of the family but apparently not, they were just friends.'

He looked up at me hoping for questions but I sat silent. I had no intention of helping him.

'The family invited a party of officers to dinner one evening, and later to a ball they were giving.'

'At Roxanne's instigation, I have no doubt,' I murmured caustically.

'They were very kind Tessa. After all it wasn't much fun being stationed in Ireland and most of us jumped at any chance we had of forgetting why we were there. Roxanne stayed most of the summer and I don't think for a moment either of us wanted it to happen, it just did.'

'You fell in love.'

'Yes. Tessa, I've told you, I love you very dearly but I can't live without Roxanne, she's a fever in the blood, a song in the heart, can't you understand?'

'Oh I do, I understand very well. I hadn't realized what a lyrical turn of speech you possessed, that's all.'

'You're angry Tessa, and rightly so, but don't blame all this on Roxanne. I'm just as much to blame as she is. When we realized what had happened she said she was leaving Ireland, that she wouldn't see me again, but it was too late for that. We knew then we couldn't live without each other.'

'Where is Roxanne now?'

'At Briarcrag. I wanted my parents to meet her. We intend to marry as soon as possible so it had to be like this.'

'And have your parents accepted it?'

'They will. It will be hard for them at first, they were always so fond of you Tessa, but even my mother could see that Roxanne is something special, she's beautiful and cultured, it's not as though I have come home with any sort of girl. Roxanne wanted to come with me today, she said we should see you together but I insisted in coming here alone. She's driving around in the car somewhere, no doubt feeling very miserable and upset.'

He blushed furiously at the cynical raising of my eyebrows.

'Tessa, please don't hate us. One day when you find somebody you can love there's no reason under the sun why we can't all be great friends. Roxanne is a wonderful person, you could love her as I love her.'

'In the meantime, Alec, I suggest you go to meet her. It would be impolite to keep somebody who means so much to you waiting.'

I don't remember what else we said to each other before we went our separate ways. I walked briskly along the village street and it was only when I reached the narrow road leading up to Glamara that I slowed my steps. There were tears on my cheeks but they were tears of anger rather than regret, tears for the memories that had fled into a mist of bitterness and resentment.

I had almost reached the gates when I saw Alec's two-seater. It was parked on the road and Roxanne sat at the wheel watching me approach. I wanted to ignore her, to walk past with my head in the air, but I knew that she would regard this gesture as immature and petty so I made myself approach the car, staring at her in silence so that I was rewarded when her eyes were the first to look away.

'Tessa, we are both miserable over what has happened, believe me we didn't mean it to be like this,' she said earnestly.

'But didn't you go to Ireland with all this in mind, Roxanne?'

'But the boys there are so lonely, I thought they would be glad of a little gaiety. Alec and I were friends then, nothing more.'

'Alec tells me you are to be married quite soon.'

'Yes. There may be trouble in Europe and if he has to go away we didn't see why we should wait.'

'No of course not. What has Julian had to say about your marriage?'

For a brief moment only I saw her eyes narrow and a strange glitter made them seem as green as a cat's, then in a light voice she said, 'Well after all, I am over twenty-one, and Julian's guardianship is at an end.'

'But he will be concerned, surely.'

It was still there, that tantalizing half smile, and I wished fervently that I had not mentioned Julian.

'If Julian hadn't been quite so besotted with Carmelita you could have consoled him. You would have liked that, wouldn't you Tessa?'

'Why should Julian need consoling?'

'So, the kitten has claws,' she sneered. 'Poor Tessa, you are not Julian's type unfortunately. I know the sort of woman he admires and she is not in the least like you.'

I turned to walk away. I was seething with anger and resentment. At that moment I could have shaken her as I had once shook Marylee, and with a far greater rage.

'I'm sorry about Alec,' she called after me, 'I hope in time we can all be friends.'

I turned to stare at her.

'How can we ever be friends, Roxanne? You came to Glamara determined to dislike me and now you have succeeded in hurting me,' I said bitterly.

She sat with her hands resting on the wheel, her eyes on the road ahead, and then without even looking at me she said. 'One day you will hurt me and to a far greater extent than I have hurt you.'

'How will I hurt you, how do you know?'

'A gypsy told me years ago in Seville.'

'You surely don't believe in such rubbish.'

'Oh but I do.'

Something in her face drew me back to the car. Her green eyes held mine and I could no more have moved away than a tiny bird could have flown away from a snake.

'She told me that one day a woman would come into my life with silver-fair hair and eyes as blue as an alpine lake and steal what was mine.'

'But it is you who have stolen from me.'

She smiled a little at that, a smile of unconcern. 'She told me there was love and hate and death in my hand and this woman would be concerned with all three. When I met you I knew you were that woman, and the next day when I saw you out riding with Julian I hated you as much as I loved him. Death is something else.'

I stared at her appalled. 'How can you talk of loving Julian when you are to marry Alec?'

She threw back her head and laughed, then as I was about to turn away she said, 'Who knows what the next few years will bring, particularly if there is war? One day Tessa, you'll see, the things the gypsy told me will come true.'

Almost before I was aware of it she had started the car and it raced away, leaving me staring after it.

Chapter Twenty-Five

As I drove home to Glamara on an early September evening it seemed incredible that England had been at war with Germany for over a month. In France men were dying in rat-infested trenches and yet here in this peaceful corner of Yorkshire the corn was ready for harvesting. Over the park the scent of woodsmoke drifted sharply pungent.

The hills, the land, the perfect symmetry of the house remained unchanged but not so the lives of Glamara's people. Robert and Adam were now subalterns finishing their training in a camp somewhere in Sussex, and Godfrey had been called to the War Office so he was living at the London house. Glamara was a house of women, for most of the men had already been called to the colours and in the

roads and lanes throughout the dales ponies and horses had
come into their own again.

Much of the parkland was already under the plough and
Abigail and Aunt Hetty had been quick to organize the
village women and the servants into teams of helpers who
knitted socks and pullovers, balaclavas and warm gloves.
They rolled bandages and baked cakes and biscuits and every
day there was a procession arriving to sit with Abigail in the
ballroom which had now been turned into some form of
workroom.

They came early and left late, and one day I suggested to
Abigail that when the winter came it would be too much to
expect them to trail the long distance up to the house when
we could conveniently drive down to the village hall instead.
She had seemed not to like this idea – somehow it robbed
Glamara of its part in our activities – and I did not press the
matter, but I knew I would be driving Godfrey's old chaise
and would be responsible for the shopping and for conveying
the helpers.

Laura came back with her little boy, expecting to stay for
the duration of the war. Her husband was already in France.
But she hated the quiet of Glamara and quickly returned to
the outskirts of London where she said she felt nearer to her
husband.

Strange as it may seem I still visited the Hardcastles at
Briarcrag for the odd weekend. Madge Hardcastle did not
get on with her daughter-in-law and saw her seldom, the last
time being just before Alec was sent to the front.

'I made every effort,' Mrs Hardcastle said sharply. 'I
didn't want him to have her but there was no way I was going
to lose my son for any girl. She refused to meet me halfway.
We weren't good enough for that hoity-toity little minx.
Besides, she's foreign. She doesn't like this and she doesn't
like that. Even the horses weren't good enough for her to ride
and they've cost Joe a fortune.'

'Perhaps in time you'll come to like her. Is Alec happy?'

'If he isn't we'll be the last to know.'

I couldn't resist asking if they had met Sir Julian, and the
answer I got was that Sir Julian was in the Royal Navy and

already at sea, a fact that gave me a certain amount of comfort. Even if he was in danger at least he wasn't with Carmelita.

I was filled with admiration for Abigail, who looked so frail yet worked her fingers to the bone on every war effort which occurred to her until Aunt Hetty remonstrated with her sharply, saying she would be fit for nothing when Godfrey came home on leave, and he would be angry to see how thin and delicate she had become.

'I must do *something* Hetty,' Abigail answered. 'My two boys are out there and if none of our efforts reach them at least some mothers' sons are going to benefit.'

She had a portion of the parkland cleared for keeping chickens and ducks and the eggs they laid went into baking cakes which were packed into crates and sent off to the Red Cross. There were many occasions when I found myself working side by side with Annie who was now an upper housemaid and inordinately proud of the fact. She still had ambitions of becoming my maid but I explained that it was unthinkable for any of us to have a personal maid when so many girls were being called upon to do war work, and she would be far more useful helping to run the house.

She had grown taller over the years and filled out considerably until now she was a comely girl and no longer the victim of cruel asthmatic attacks.

I was amused to find that some of the younger girls were putting messages in their parcels and indeed one or two of them resulted in meetings and blossoming romances.

'Isn't there some young man you would like to write to?' I asked Annie one afternoon when we were busy sorting through piles of hand-knitted garments. She blushed a bright red and dived deeper into the box. 'There must be somebody,' I insisted, 'all the boys who have gone from the village as well as from the house, isn't one of them worthy of a letter from you?'

'I writes to George occasionally, an' I 'ad a letter fro' Wills, one o' the grooms.'

'And who exactly is George?'

'E's Cook's nephew, she introduced mi to 'im last time 'ee

came to see 'er. Ee's all right, but there's nowt goin' on between us. I 'ardly knows 'im but 'ee asked mi to write an' I promised.'

'You did quite right Annie. One day you must get married and have children, that is the right vocation for you.'

Her mouth set mutinously. 'I'm not so sure I want to get wed, Miss Tessa, I saw some rotten marriages when a were livin' i' Leeds, it were allus the woman who suffered when there were no money comin' in.'

I hated it when Abigail's eyes scoured the newspapers day after day when news of those who had been killed or wounded were reported. There were pages of them now, and there were many times when we recognized a name: a family friend, a boy from the village or a servant from the house. Both Adam and Robert were in Flanders and day by day I watched helplessly as Abigail's skin tightened on her cheeks and her eyes became pools of despair.

'She's working herself into a nervous breakdown if she continues like this,' Aunt Hetty complained. 'I've tried reasoning with her, I've told her how the boys and Godfrey would hate to see her wearing herself out. Abigail has always put all her eggs into one basket and made idols of those she loves.'

In the quiet of my room I too scanned the daily newspapers for the Fleet too were suffering casualties in the Atlantic.

Godfrey came home for Christmas in 1916 and miraculously the two boys got leave, before the big push, as they called it. If there was a frantic note to our enforced gaiety who can blame us when the news from France had been so bad? We welcomed the New Year with a strange recklessness, as though it could be our last.

At the beginning of February I was walking from the chicken run to the house in the late afternoon. The winter sky was red and there was promise of snow in the air. It was bitterly cold and looking down the drive my heart missed a beat at the sight of a boy in post-office uniform riding his bicycle towards me.

I walked swiftly to meet him. His hands were encased in

thick woollen gloves so that he had difficulty in extracting the telegram out of his satchel while I chafed with impatience at his slowness. At last he handed me the telegram which was addressed to Lady Chalfont. I thrust it deep inside my pocket of my coat and ran to the house. I went in search of Aunt Hetty and when I held out the telegram her face drained of colour. 'What are we to do, Tessa? We must give it to her but I am so afraid.'

'Couldn't we telephone Godfrey?'

'The telegram is addressed to Abigail, it would mean our opening it first and one never quite knows how she will take things. Let us wait until after dinner.'

None of us had any appetite, Abigail because she was unwell and Aunt Hetty and myself because of the terrible task facing us. We had moved to the drawing room when Abigail said, 'Is something wrong? You were both very quiet over dinner.'

Aunt Hetty opened her bag and took out the telegram, handing it without speaking to Abigail who recoiled from it as though the envelope had a life of its own.

'It is bad news, I know it. I haven't slept for days, I knew something was wrong with one of my boys, perhaps both. I always knew, even when they were children.'

With shaking fingers she took out the telegram, then with a little cry she crumpled among her cushions in a dead faint. Aunt Hetty hurried with smelling salts and I ran to pick up the telegram.

The news was terrible. Captain Adam Chalfont had been killed in action and Captain Robert Chalfont was wounded and was in a field hospital.

I passed the telegram to Aunt Hetty and watched helplessly as her face crumpled with distress. She had loved both the boys dearly and so had I, but now I could only sit miserably by while she devoted all her attention to Abigail.

The days and weeks that followed were terrible for everybody. It was heartbreaking to see Abigail struggling to fulfil her everyday duties. We had had no further news of Robert in spite of Godfrey's efforts to discover his whereabouts and how badly he was injured.

The nights were the worst when we three women sat at the dinner table trying to converse, when the eyes of the servants who waited on us stared sadly when the food was returned to the kitchens barely touched.

How slowly the fingers moved on the marble clock on the mantelpiece in the drawing room, and I grew to dread the sound of Aunt Hetty's knitting needles clicking mercilessly on while Abigail stared into the fire. There were nights when I lay awake listening to Abigail's feet padding past my room, then after a while I would hear her overhead, pacing backwards and forwards. I did not know which I dreaded most, those plodding footsteps or the long silences before she returned to her room in the first light of dawn.

Finally I told Aunt Hetty about her nightly wanderings and that night after dinner she faced Abigail.

'If you go on like this you will disintegrate into some sort of semi-invalid. You have one son who needs you and will soon be coming home. What will he say if he sees you looking like a ghost?'

Abigail looked at her plaintively. 'Robert will understand that I am suffering for the loss of Adam. He will not expect me to behave differently.'

'Adam is in the hands of God, Robert is still with us. He too will be sad at losing Adam but he will make an effort not to show it because of you. Don't you think you could make a similar effort?'

That night Aunt Hetty and I searched out Abigail and we found her in the old nursery above my room, rocking herself to and fro in the wooden rocking chair, holding one of the children's favourite toys. She seemed not to care as we led her back to her room, but in the morning Aunt Hetty resumed her attack.

'You are wallowing in self-pity, Abigail,' she said sharply. 'You are not the only woman to have lost a son, there are thousands of women losing husbands, sons and fathers. If they all went on like you the war might as well be lost.'

'I'll try Hetty, I will try,' Abigail wailed pitifully.

'Look at that little Mrs Cookson in the village, she's lost two brothers, and a husband. She has one child and another

315

on the way, don't you think she's in a far worse plight?'

'I didn't know she had lost her husband,' Abigail said, some semblance of interest creeping into her expression.

'Well she has, and those two nice brothers who used to work in the stables here. Now this morning you must let old Will drive you over to the Cosgroves', it's cold but you'll be all right with a rug over your knees.'

Abigail demurred but Aunt Hetty was adamant, so that we shortly saw Abigail setting off in the chaise.

'Now then Tessa, you and I are going up to the nursery to tidy it up,' Aunt Hetty said briskly. 'We can't do much about the big stuff but the smaller things we can sort out.'

'Won't Abigail mind?'

'Probably, but we can't have her sitting up there night after night nursing old toys.'

We packed the toys into large wooden crates from the attics, but the large rocking horse and the doll's house had to remain as we were quite unable to move them.

There were children's books too, masses of them, and I returned to one of the attics to find another crate. My eyes were drawn to a large panelled oak chest and curiosity got the better of me. It was not locked and I opened it gingerly.

Tissue paper covered the contents but without hesitation I removed it and took out the most beautiful, ethereal gown I had ever seen. The ivory Chantilly lace swept from a tiny seed-pearl-trimmed body into long sweeping folds ending in a train several yards long, and I held it against me, bemused by the scent of lavender.

A sound at the door made me turn round quickly to find Aunt Hetty looking at me with a strange expression.

'Oh Aunt Hetty, I shouldn't have been so curious. Is it your gown?'

'It was your mother's but she never wore it. I can't even begin to tell you why I kept it. Father said everything that might remind him of her must be burned, but he forgot this dress and I hid it away. Her veil is in there also.'

There were yards of it, and a headdress of orange blossom and tiny seed pearls. The orange blossom had been preserved almost in a mummified state in its lacy bed, but now the petals began to fall. Facing the discarded mirror propped on one wall I placed the veil on my head, and it seemed that I faced a fairy figure, insubstantial as a dream, with a haunting, elusive beauty.

Aunt Hetty's cheeks were wet with tears, and tremulously she said, 'When you came here Tessa I was glad I had kept this dress, imagined you would want to wear it on your wedding day. You said so little about your broken engagement, and then so many other things happened and the moment was gone when we could have discussed it.'

'I was so angry, Aunt Hetty. More angry than hurt, I think. If it had been any other but Roxanne I could have wished Alec well, but Roxanne set out deliberately to take Alec away from me. I was never sure that we were right to get engaged, but you heard Roxanne doing her level best to push us together, and then for her to set herself out to break us up seemed like wanton cruelty to me. I hurt for the loss of Alec's friendship rather than his love, and I cannot think that she will make him happy.'

'I have that feeling too. I have known Roxanne since she came here as a little girl years ago. It was always Roxanne who suggested their naughty schemes and Laura who got punished for them.

'She was vindictive as a child but I can't think for the life of me what you could have done in the small time you knew her.'

'I rode with Julian on the afternoon they went deer stalking, I don't think she was terribly pleased about that. But how could she possibly believe there was anything serious between us?'

'Roxanne was a great romancer, a devious romancer. Perhaps it's just as well that you have no further contact with her or with Alec. When you fall in love, Roxanne will be safely out of the picture.'

Together we folded the gown and veil and replaced them in the chest and closed the lid.

'If I ever fall in love I'll remember it's here,' I said.

'You must fall in love Tessa. Don't be like me, a fussy old maid and everybody's favourite aunt. But don't be like

Abigail either. She doesn't just love her menfolk, she worships them. Such adoration should only be given to Almighty God, ordinary human men will always fall a little short, I think.'

I laughed at her determined little face. 'Oh Aunt Hetty, I love the things you say, you're always so logical, some man missed a treasure when he missed you.'

She blushed and snapped back at me smartly, 'Well I was a treasure to my father but he never thought so, I fetched and carried for him all my life but at night when he stared into the fire it was your mother he was thinking of, not me.'

Abigail never did refer to the toys and after a few days she ceased to visit the nursery. We heard that Robert had been removed to a hospital in Sussex suffering from concussion, shrapnel wounds and a broken leg, and after a few days we were delighted when he was moved to a convalescent home just outside Harrogate, where we could visit him.

Abigail and Aunt Hetty visited him almost at once and when they returned Aunt Hetty told me that he was very cheerful, though hobbling about on crutches.

'Did he mention Adam?' I asked.

'Yes. He saw Adam fall and was rushing to attend to him when a shell hit a building and the masonry fell on top of him. When he came round he was in a field hospital and he learned later that Adam had been killed. The boys were very close, and he is guarded when he talks about his brother, perhaps because his mother was there, I don't know.'

'I'd like to see him.'

'He asked about you Tessa, why don't you go tomorrow?'

Robert greeted me with obvious delight. He kissed me warmly, saying, 'I'll do better than that when I get out of this plaster. Just say that's to be going on with.'

I laughed at his high spirits. 'I'll contain my soul in patience, then. How long do you suppose you'll be here?'

'Until they've patched me up for front-line duty again.'

'Oh Robert no, you can't possibly be expected to go back there.'

'You'll see my girl, if things go on as they are they'll be

recruiting schoolboys, old men and the permanently crippled.'

'The news is bad, isn't it?'

'Yes, it couldn't be worse. But don't look so downcast Tessa, we'll lick 'em yet. Have I ever told you a lie?'

Amused, I remembered all the tantalizing little fables he had told me, things that were never meant to be taken seriously, and knowing that I was remembering he dissolved into laughter. When the nurse came in with cups of tea he held out his hand to her, saying, 'Look what a treasure they've given me, they can't have known my bad reputation.'

'I should get away while the going is good,' I warned her, smiling.

She dimpled prettily. She was a dark-haired Irish girl, as fresh and wholesome as country butter and it was obvious she thought a lot of her good-looking patient and he of her.

He said, 'Her name's Moira Callahan, did you ever hear anything more perfectly Irish? She's a grand girl, comes from County Clare.'

The nurse helped Robert to sit up among his cushions and I noticed how she avoided his laughing eyes before retreating with a blushing face.

'You shouldn't embarrass the poor girl,' I admonished him. 'You're in no condition to flirt.'

'I've made her a promise too, Tessa. I'll do better when I'm fully recovered. I hope she doesn't object to waiting. By the way, Father came to see me yesterday, will you tell Mother?'

'He came here and yet he didn't visit us!'

'There was a reason for that. Roxanne was with him. He met her in London and naturally he told her about Adam and me. She asked if she could come to see me, so what could he do but bring her?'

I was silent for so long that he reached out and took my hand in his. 'I'm sorry about Alec. I suppose you hate him like hell?'

'I didn't hate him when he told me what had happened, I don't hate him now. I could never hate Alec, we've been friends too long, but I don't love him either, sometimes I don't think I ever did.'

'I don't think you did, you were just two kids thrown together by circumstances and other people's interference.'

'Yes, particularly Roxanne that Christmas at Glamara.'

'I agree. Well, they're married. She's living somewhere in London and Alec's at the front. I asked her why she didn't live at Briarcrag for the duration but she pulled a face and said she wouldn't be found dead in Yorkshire. I can see problems ahead for both of them if Alec gets out of this lot.'

Then to change the subject Robert said, 'There's a friend of yours in a private ward here: Sir Richard Chalmers.'

'Richard is in here?'

'Yes. Pretty badly smashed up I hear. I believe it was touch and go at one time but he's on the mend now. I don't suppose he'll ever be fit for much, his injuries were too severe.'

'Oh dear, I am so sorry. Is he allowed visitors?'

'His mother comes every day, stays about fifteen minutes then goes. He'll not get much joy out of her visists, her face is enough to turn the milk sour. Father went along to see him but he hardly got a good afternoon out of Dora. She was always a peculiar woman.'

'Did you know her well?'

'No, but one can't help hearing what other people thought of her. Edward never looked happy and she seems to have kept Richard under her thumb most of his life.'

My mind went back to the day of the point-to-point meeting and Richard's unhappy boy's face when he apologized for his mother's behaviour. I didn't want to meet her, but I wanted to see Richard. His future prospects seemed grim to say the least.

'Would you mind if I left a few minutes early so that I can call in to see him?' I asked Robert hopefully.

'Of course not, but you'll come again soon won't you, Tessa?'

'I'll come very soon.' I reached over and kissed him, then with a little wave I left him and went in search of Richard's room. I inquired from a nurse if I could see him for a few minutes, surprised when she asked if I was a relative.

'No, just an acquaintance. My cousin Captain Chalfont told me he was in here.'

'Well perhaps five minutes, then. His mother's been and gone, but she doesn't like him to have visitors, she says they tire him.'

'I won't stop more than five minutes I promise, but I thought it might cheer him up a bit.'

'I'm sure it will, poor boy he needs cheering up and that's a fact.'

She indicated his door. I knocked tentatively and a voice told me to enter. He was lying propped up against his pillows, his face was grey with pain, and he seemed many years older than at our last meeting.

I smiled at him, and suddenly I saw the warm colour flow into his cheeks and his eyes open wide with surprise.

'Hello Richard, I didn't want to leave without seeing you.'

He struggled to sit up among his pillows but flopped back, and I hurried forward to settle them around him.

'Don't try to sit up on my account,' I said smiling down at him. 'Robert told me you were here, you are feeling much better I hope?'

'Actually no. I still feel pretty rough. They tell me I'm better but it's a slow process. I *am* glad to see you, Tessa.'

'Is there anything you would like the next time I come to see Robert?'

'My mother never brings books or magazines, she says they will tire my eyes. But I could do with something to read.'

'Will your mother object if she sees you with them?'

'I'll take jolly good care she doesn't see them, one of the nurses will hide them away until she's gone.'

I smiled doubtfully. It seemed strange to me that a man of twenty-five or so should be so dependent upon his mother's whims and fancies, or her likes and dislikes, but obviously Richard had been too long under her thumb and now he was too weak to fight her influence.

We talked about normal ordinary things, the weather and the countryside, dogs and horses and, although I purposely refrained from referring to his injuries, when I was leaving him he said, 'I'm sorry to be such an old crock, Tessa.'

'You mustn't worry, you won't always be a crock.'

'That's just it, I shall never be completely well again.'

'Have the doctors told you that?'

'They have hinted at it but my mother told me I mustn't expect miracles. They tell me I shall never be able to walk without a stick, both my legs were badly crushed, in fact from the waist down I'm less than a man.'

'Oh Richard I am sorry, but they can do such marvellous things in hospitals these days, perhaps you are being pessimistic.'

'I don't think so. You'll come again won't you. I've told you the worst, we need never refer to it again.'

'I'll come whenever I can Richard, though I don't suppose your mother would approve.'

'I don't see why not, neither of us is to blame for the past.'

It was true, but all the same I did not think Richard would tell her of my visits.

Robert improved rapidly and soon he was walking in the grounds without the aid of his stick, plaguing the nurses with his teasing and flirting with most of them. Richard too was improving slowly so that now he sat in a chair by the window with a rug over his knees and looked forward eagerly to my visits when I took him books, and magazines like *Country Life* and *Field Sports*.

He looked dismayed when I told him that Robert was being sent home for a few days before rejoining his regiment.

'Does that mean you won't be coming here again, Tessa?'

'I will come to see you if you would like me to.'

'Gracious yes, what would I do if you stopped coming? You've got me sane these last few weeks. Alec Hardcastle doesn't know what a lucky chap he is.'

I stared at him in surprise. Of course Richard didn't know anything about the ending of my engagement to Alec, and in a small matter of fact voice I told him what had happened.

He listened without interrupting and when I had finished I was surprised at his strangely contented smile. Taking hold of my hand he said, 'You *have* got over it though, haven't you, Tessa? You're not still hurt by it.'

'No of course not. Alec and Roxanne are married, there wouldn't be any point in continuing to be hurt about something so irrevocable.'

'You would be hurt if you still loved him.'

'Yes, so I mustn't still love him. I'm settling down to being an old maid very nicely, thank you.'

'You'll never be an old maid Tessa, you're far too beautiful and much too nice. If I thought there was any danger of that I'd marry you myself.'

We both laughed at his words but there was no laughter in his eyes, instead there was an intensity that brought the warm colour into my face, leaving me embarrassed and perplexed.

Was I wrong to see so much of Richard? I knew he admired me and had done so ever since our first meeting, now I was remembering how his eyes lit up when I entered his room, how they lingered on my face as if he would hold the memory of it sacred and alive until our next meeting.

I liked him immensely, I admired his courage in the face of great pain, and it was evident we liked the same things. He loved country life in the dales as I did, walking the fells with the wind in his hair and the rain soft against his face. Then I saw the bitterness when he told me he would never ride his horse again along the old country bridle paths.

His mother's visits depressed him utterly and once I saw her leaving, a haughty pale-faced woman with tightly compressed lips and an arrogant air. It was little wonder his nurses referred to her as 'the duchess' and resented her as a domineering busybody.

I began to worry about Richard. I did not want him to love me when there could be nothing more between us than warm friendship. I had a dream of the man I wanted to marry that refused to go away, a dream which I was sure was destined to remain unfulfilled.

But returning to Glamara a week later, after visiting Richard, all thoughts of love or friendship were instantly driven from my mind when Aunt Hetty told me that Abigail had suffered a stroke. Hetty had been trying all afternoon to

323

reach Godfrey, both at the War Office and his London house. Robert had returned to his regiment the day before, and Abigail's distress at losing him again so soon had in all probability brought on the stroke.

I tried all evening to reach Godfrey without avail so it was decided that I should journey up to London the following morning with an urgent plea that he return home at once.

'What did they say at the War Office?' I asked Hetty curiously. 'Surely they should know where you could find him.'

'They don't tell you anything Tessa, I probably spoke to the office boy anyway and all I got was that Sir Godfrey was away for several days.'

'What did they say at the house?'

'It was Roberts. He simply said Sir Godfrey was away. If Godfrey is on leave he should be with his wife at Glamara. Heaven knows where he spends his time, it certainly isn't here.'

'Perhaps he's away on some hush-hush matter concerning the war, in which case we can expect them to be discreet.'

'I suppose so but I am very worried, Tessa. Abigail has always been so frail. And how many times have we seen Godfrey during the past three years? You don't mean to say he can't get away some time, other people do.'

London was more crowded than I had ever seen it, mostly with men in uniform. The Chalfonts' town house looked exactly the same as always: brasses brightly polished, long net curtains sparkingly clean, stone steps well scrubbed.

Roberts, the elderly butler, opened the door, eyeing me uncertainly from his tall thin height. 'Why Miss Tessa,' he exclaimed, hovering doubtfully on the step.

'Aren't you going to invite me in, Roberts?'

There was a leather suitcase in the hall and with a great feeling of relief I turned to Roberts, saying, 'My uncle is back then?'

'Yes miss, this morning.'

'Will you please tell him I am here, I'll go into the drawing room.'

There was something reluctant about his attitude, but

why? I was merely making a request to see my uncle, and he must have realized it was important.

There were flowers in the drawing room, long-stemmed dark red roses and white carnations on a small table near the window. I stared at them curiously. Only a woman could have arranged them with such perfection and yet I had not heard that such a treasure was employed at the London house. Indeed Abigail had said that there were only Roberts and his wife there now.

I should have known in that moment, but my mind was on other matters, and in the next moment Godfrey came in, tanned and smiling, greeting me with a warm embrace though his eyes were strangely wary.

I explained the reason for my visit quickly, and he frowned. 'Is she very ill?' he demanded quickly.

'The doctor says with rest she should recover but it only happened yesterday, it will take time. When will you be able to come?'

'Not today I'm afraid, but definitely first thing in the morning.'

'I was thinking in terms of the morning too,' I said, indicating my overnight case.

He appeared nonplussed and I stood hesitantly waiting for him to tell me to take my things upstairs and at least to offer me some refreshment, but instead he walked slowly towards the door muttering for me to wait where I was.

I settled down to wait, but I was hungry, I had eaten nothing since breakfast and it was now after three. I knew the house, surely I could find my own way up to the bedrooms. It was from outside the master bedroom that I heard voices: my uncle's and a woman's, arguing. Turning on my heel I started to creep downstairs. Just then the door opened and my uncle appeared on the threshold, his face reddening furiously when he saw me.

'I was looking for somewhere to put my case,' I explained, but then the door behind him opened wider and I stared in disbelief at Roxanne in a delicate pink negligée, her black hair in great waves around her shoulders.

I looked from her to my uncle, seeing the shamed look on

his face but on hers only a strange, triumphant smile.

'You haven't chosen a very opportune time to call,' she said, smiling as though I had interrupted a village tea party.

'Get back into the room,' Godfrey muttered, his face black.

'Very well darling, heaven knows I have no wish to receive a lecture from Tessa. Don't forget we are dining out.'

The door slammed behind her and Godfrey followed me back into the drawing room.

'I'm sorry Tessa, I didn't intend you to see Roxanne here.'

'I'm sure you didn't.'

'You don't understand.'

'I think I understand very well, Godfrey.'

'I said you didn't understand and no more do you. It's not that I care for Abigail any less.'

'You mean it's all right as long as she doesn't know?'

'No damn it, that's not at all what I mean. Tessa, she bewitches me, she's like no other woman I've ever known, I can't get her out of my mind unless I have her. How can I expect you to understand?'

'Oh, but I do understand. She's a fever in the blood, a song in the heart.'

'What are you talking about?'

'I'm sorry Godfrey, you evidently don't have Alec's poetical turn of phrase when he described Roxanne to me. However I get the gist of it. I'll find somewhere else to stay tonight, I wouldn't like to put you to any inconvenience.'

'You can stay here, Tessa.'

'I wouldn't dream of staying under the same roof as Roxanne. I'll probably see you on the first train home in the morning. And your secret is safe with me: Abigail has enough misery in her life just now, your infidelity would probably kill her.'

I walked quickly in the direction of the park, the fallen leaves crunching under my feet, surprised that the light was fading. For a few minutes I sat on a bench while I tried to catch my breath. A woman came to sit beside me, a newspaper clasped tightly in her hands. She appeared distressed, and my own problems seemed less important when I saw the tears rolling down her face.

'Can I help you?' I asked her gently.

'Nobody can help me,' she said, turning a tearful gaze upon me. 'I've just heard that my husband's been killed.' She got up quickly and thrust the newspaper into my hands. 'Every day there's more,' she said, her voice rising hysterically. 'There's thousands that'll never be coming back.'

She left me quickly, her feet making no sound as she hurried across the grass.

My eyes were inescapably drawn to the page listing casualties, and at once one name leapt at me: Captain Alec Hardcastle, killed in action.

I have no memory of how long I sat there until I suddenly became aware of the cold. I jumped to my feet and walked quickly along the path. I walked unseeing, unheeding like a dead thing, numbed and without feeling, and as I walked along the road people jostled me and stared but I had no thought for them. As I crossed the road I was suddenly aware of shouts and the screech of brakes and tyres, but I had no thoughts for my own safety, and then above me the Dorchester Hotel loomed in the dusk.

I stood inside the door looking round the scented foyer, surrounded by the hum of conversation, laughter and warmth. I sank gratefully into the first seat I could find.

I couldn't believe that Alec was dead, Alec my dear friend, Alec who had charmed me with his boyish laughter and his endless enthusiasms. I caught sight of myself in a mirror opposite and gasped a little that this windblown wide-eyed girl could be me. I had lost my hat but I tried to smooth my hair into some semblance of order. I was still clutching my overnight case and my handbag but I had no idea of the time or where I was going to spend the night. All I knew was that Alec was dead, killed in France while his wife slept in the arms of my uncle.

I looked longingly towards the tea lounge realizing that I was so hungry that my hands were trembling. I decided I would order tea and then think what I must do.

Choosing a table near the wall I looked round the room

and then my heart gave another lurch. Against the far wall a naval officer sat talking to a woman and the profile he turned towards me was Julian's. The woman was hidden from me by a potted palm, and I could see only an elegant grey skirt and grey shoes, and her long white hands.

My eyes looked hungrily at his profile, severe and perfectly proportioned. He was smiling a little as he listened to her, and then he laughed, and with a sickening feeling in the pit of my stomach I leapt up to rush from the room. Unfortunately at that moment a waiter was making his way past my table with a loaded tray and I collided with him, and the tea things were everywhere. I felt that all London must have heard the noise and clatter and with my face burning I helped him to collect the scattered things on to his tray, then I took to my heels.

I felt my arm taken in a firm grasp and found Julian looking down at me, his eyes filled with amusement. 'So it *is* you Tessa, upsetting the decorum of the Dorchester's tea lounge. What are you doing in London?'

I stared up at him completely tongue-tied, then gathering my scattered wits I said as haughtily as I knew how, 'I'm only here until tomorrow morning, I didn't see the waiter.'

His mouth twitched at the corners and I felt he wanted to laugh but instead he said, 'Are you staying in Belgrave Square?'

'No. I don't know where I'm staying yet.'

He raised his eyebrows. 'You mean you have nowhere to stay?'

Annoyed by the incredulity in his voice I snapped, 'No, my visit was arranged suddenly.'

'Why?' he persisted.

'Because Abigail has been taken ill and I wanted to find Godfrey.'

'And did you find him?'

'Yes, we are travelling north in the morning.'

'Then why aren't you at Belgrave Square?'

'It wasn't convenient.'

I wanted to tell him, I wanted to fling the answer at him in

328

a way that would shake that superior smiling face, but I couldn't do it. If he didn't know Roxanne after all these years why should it be left to me to tell him, besides he was probably more interested in returning to his companion who was proving so amusing.

I was hurt and miserable and suddenly his face became grave and taking my arm he propelled me towards the reception desk.

'I know most of these people are looking for accommodation but we are leaving here tonight, I will ask if you can have my room.'

'Really Sir Julian, that isn't necessary, something will turn up.'

'Don't be silly Tessa, nothing is going to turn up. Your innocent faith that Destiny will suddenly take you under her wing is very touching but quite impractical. Now will you come with me and leave matters in my hand.'

The desk clerk argued that there were people waiting but Sir Julian was firm, and because of his long association with the hotel I was informed that the room was mine for one night.

'If you would like to return to the tea room, Tessa, I'll clear my things out.'

'Thank you,' I murmured, 'you've been very kind.'

'I am invariably kind to waifs and strays and young ladies who set about knocking waiters over.'

He was regarding me with a half smile and my heart lurched sickeningly. I was wishing I didn't find him so devastatingly attractive, and that the smile which robbed his face of its accustomed severity was not so powerfully sweet. I could feel my face blushing uncomfortably under his regard, and when my eyes met his again I sensed a puzzlement in them as though he intended to question me further. Instead he said, 'I hope Abigail is not seriously ill.'

'I'm afraid she is, she has had a stroke.'

His face registered sympathy. 'But she will recover I hope?'

'We all hope so.'

329

'I have a few days' leave but it may not be possible for me to come over to Glamara. However I intend to write to Godfrey as soon as I can.'

'He will be pleased to hear from you, Sir Julian.'

'Leave is not very frequent I'm afraid, but I feel sure we will meet again very soon Tessa. Perhaps not this time as I shall be very busy, but in the near future I hope.'

'Yes Sir Julian, perhaps we shall.'

I offered my hand which he took formally in his, then after favouring me with a quite piercing glance he left me. I paused to watch his tall slender figure walking towards the lifts, as though I would imprint it upon my heart for all time, then I turned away.

The table where he had been sitting with his companion was now empty and I supposed she had gone up ahead of him. I ached to know who she was and if they had been staying at the Dorchester together. It seemed on that day that all my innocence had gone for ever and that I would never be able to trust again.

On entering the room which had been Julian's I looked around expectantly but the room stared back impersonally. I imagined I could smell a woman's lingering perfume and I flung open the windows in spite of the chill wind that billowed into the room.

I slept badly. All night long I thought of Julian and some woman making love on that bed, lying in each other's arms, fulfilled and contented, while in that other bedroom in Belgrave Square Godfrey and Roxanne would be spending their last night together before he returned to Glamara. Julian might be in love with Carmelita, but he could not be expected to live like a monk because love between them was impossible. There had been no doubt that he had been amused and delighted by his companion of the afternoon.

Godfrey was at the station before me, pacing the platform and occasionally looking towards the barrier. 'You've cut it a bit fine, Tessa. Where did you stay, by the way?'

'I met Sir Julian at the Dorchester, he was just leaving so I got his room for the night.'

'Wasn't he curious as to why you were not staying at the house?'

'Yes, I told him it wasn't convenient.'

In the train I felt nervous under his regard, and for want of something better to say I said, 'Sir Julian said he would be writing to you. He was sorry to hear about Abigail.'

'I expect he was, they always got along together. Did you mention Roxanne to him?'

'If you mean did I tell him where she was and who she was with, no I did not.'

'I'm grateful to you for that Tessa.'

'I told you yesterday that your secret was safe with me. I suppose she has left Belgrave Square now?'

'She is returning home later in the day.'

'There will be no good news waiting for her.'

'What do you mean?'

'Alec is dead. I read his name in yesterday's casualty list.'

'Oh my God!'

He looked shocked and bewildered, like a man suddenly faced with more tragedy than he knew how to handle, and I had no mercy. I wanted him to be hurt, he deserved to be hurt and so did Roxanne, but I had the feeling that he would suffer more than she. Roxanne only suffered when happenings inconvenienced her, other people's pain left her untouched.

Aunt Hetty greeted us with relief and the news that Abigail had had a further stroke and was now dangerously ill. Abigail did not know Godfrey when he reached her bedside although she stared at him unseeing before she lapsed once more into unconsciousness. That was the last time she opened her eyes, three days later she was dead and Godfrey was locked in his study to suffer alone.

The disenchantment with a world that had seemed so dear and familiar was complete. I had loved Glamara and all those who lived under its roof now only Aunt Hetty was left to reassure me that once there had been warmth and love and laughter in a world grown suddenly grey and cruel.

As we followed Abigail's coffin down the long drive I was

331

remembering watching my grandfather's funeral from my bedroom window, alone and forlorn, and afraid of the future. Then when the future came it had been so wonderful it had exceeded my wildest dreams. I began to cry, not just for Abigail but for my dreams that had been shattered and for a love that could never be mine.

Julian had sent flowers but could not attend the funeral because his short leave was over.

I continued to visit Richard at the nursing home. He was walking in the grounds now, hobbling round painfully on two sticks and he was quickly tired. He surprised me one day by saying, 'My mother knows you are visiting me.'

'Doesn't she mind?'

'I have made her see how much your visits have meant to me, and you have done nothing to make her dislike you. She always cared for my father more than he cared for her, and she blamed your mother. When we saw your mother that morning at the point-to-point meeting my father's face changed, I knew he still loved her. My mother saw it too, that is why she was so rude to you both.'

'What a disaster it all was, Richard. I'm glad your mother knows I come here, I hated deceiving her.'

'I'd like you to meet. Why not come a little earlier next time, who knows perhaps you could be friends? My mother has very few friends.'

I knew Richard loved me. Every glance, every moment we touched, however fleetingly, I could tell he loved me by the sudden trembling of his hands. His nurses greeted me with smiling faces and sympathetic eyes and I know he talked about me to them.

My meeting with his mother was not the peaceful acceptance I had hoped for. She was just leaving his room when I arrived armed with magazines and flowers from Glamara. I smiled at her shyly, but immediately eyeing the magazines she snapped, 'Now I know why Richard is complaining of eye strain. Did he ask for those?'

'They help him to pass the time, Lady Chalmers.'

'He should rest his eyes. You know, Richard, that the doctor said your eyes were affected. It was the blast, you know,' she said, turning to me. 'It is kind of you to visit him Miss Chalfont, but too much reading and too many visitors are not good for him.'

'Mother, please don't interfere,' Richard cried with some degree of anger. 'I look forward to Tessa's visits, heaven knows I'm bored to tears with nothing to do. I've been here too long as it is. I will speak to the doctor when next he comes.'

She looked at me with hostile eyes and pursed lips, and I felt her antagonism, she did not need to put it into words. She seemed disinclined to leave us together but Richard's sulky face and my discomforture sent her away with a look of resigned annoyance.

'Your mother doesn't like my being here,' I said to him unhappily.

'Tessa please, if you stop coming I think I shall go mad. It is only you who has kept me sane all these long months. Mother will change when she sees how sweet you are and how good you are for me.'

I didn't agree with him but I reverted to my later time and in the weeks that followed I met her only once in the corridor, when she acknowledged my presence with a polite nod and distant smile.

In France the tide was slowly turning in our favour and now that America had entered the war hearts were suddenly lighter. Although there was still a long way to go and still a lot of suffering to be endured it seemed that at last victory was within sight.

Robert was still with his unit in Berkshire and had not as yet been detailed for overseas service, consequently he managed to get home on leave from time to time although we had not seen Godfrey since Abigail's funeral. In Leeds Susan had given birth to her first child, a little boy, and I was invited to attend his christening and stay with her for a few days. She called him Mark, and he was a lovely child so that we all adored him. It was so comforting to be able to talk to a woman of my own age and now that I was no longer expected to live in that dismal house across the park I was seeing Leeds in a new light.

Susan's husband was serving in France but she remained touchingly convinced that he would return to her unscathed. He had been wounded in the early stages of the war, and when fully recovered had returned to the front. Susan maintained that lightning never struck twice in the same place and went about her life serenely smiling.

There were new curtains at the windows of the house across the park and fresh paint on the woodwork, and when I remarked on this to Susan she told me that Jack Bryant had died in the spring, a grossly dissipated man, his business in ruins, and completely friendless apart from Mrs Howlett, who in spite of his constant abuse had stayed to care for him.

The house had been sold and I hoped she managed to get her hands on anything that could be salvaged from the wreck of both their lives. She had been more sinned against than sinning, and I remembered how honest she had been about returning my mother's possessions.

I was glad to hear that she was now respectably married to a grocer and living in Bradford where she was a model of decency.

I was sad to learn that the Prescotts' younger son had been killed in the battle of the Somme. Lionel Prescott was serving with the Royal Navy and it was well over twelve months since Susan had seen him.

'He asked if I ever saw you Tessa,' she said smiling, 'I rather think Lionel was quite taken by you.'

'I hope you told him why I was so anxious to go down to the Bryant mills during the riot.'

'Yes, and he understood perfectly. He's nice Tessa, when the war is over and Lionel comes home you should spend some time here, who knows, something might come of it.'

I smiled at her idea of matchmaking.

It was late afternoon when I returned to Glamara and immediately I was aware of voices raised in anger coming from Godfrey's study. Aunt Hetty met me in the hall, tearful and agitated.

'Whatever is going on?' I asked her.

'Godfrey and Robert are here, they arrived last night and

they have been quarrelling ever since. Come into the drawing room.'

I followed her obediently.

'Godfrey informed us last night that he has decided to remarry.' Her voice was flat and matter of fact but her eyes were angry, her small form bristling with annoyance. 'He is marrying Roxanne.' She was staring at my face, waiting for it to register all the horror and dismay I was feeling, but when I showed nothing she snapped, 'I must say you don't seem very surprised, Tessa.'

'When are they getting married?' I asked.

'Almost immediately. They are marrying by special licence in London, with Abigail and Alec hardly cold in their graves. They will live at the London house until the war is over and then presumably they will return here.'

'If he brings her here what will you do, Aunt Hetty?'

'This is my home and no Roxanne is going to move me out of it, even if she is Lady Chalfont. I shall travel more, I shall stay with friends for weeks instead of days, but I shall come back here, never fear. It is what is going to happen to *you* that is more important. I am sure you will not wish to remain at Glamara with Roxanne as its mistress.'

'No, obviously I shall not want to remain here, but I have time to think about it. There will be a solution somewhere. What do you suppose Robert will do?'

'He is threatening to go abroad after the war is over and settle there. He will never accept Roxanne.'

'I hadn't thought Robert would be so hostile, he has always seemed so easygoing.'

'That was when life was normal and good here Tessa, it has all changed now and we are not prepared for it or willing to settle down under it. You will see, you and Robert will leave here but I'm an old maid with nowhere else to go and no real desire to accommodate them both by leaving.'

I hugged her. 'Oh Aunt Hetty, it is all going to be so terrible. In time you will hate being here and that might force you to leave.'

Her face puckered into grief. 'Why has Godfrey done this to us, Tessa? Anybody but that girl I could have stood, but after what she did to you I can't understand my brother at all.'

'Love makes us do strange things, Aunt Hetty.'

'Is Roxanne capable of love do you think, or does she merely wish to become Lady Chalfont and the mistress of Glamara? My brother is a fool, he's far too old for her, in no time at all he'll be the laughing stock of the county.'

'We don't know that, Aunt Hetty.'

'It doesn't require much imagination to know what will happen, though.'

The rest of that week was one I wish to put behind me, never to be resurrected. Meals were taken in tight-lipped silence on Robert's part and florid displeasure from Godfrey. Aunt Hetty picked at her food like a little bird and I tried to make some sort of conversation without success. I was relieved when Robert returned to his regiment and Godfrey to London without speaking to each other.

I caught Aunt Hetty in tears a day or so later. 'Robert says he is never coming back to Glamara, Tessa. He told me just before he left.'

'But he will own all this one day, how can he not come back?'

'He says after the war he will emigrate, I haven't the slightest idea where, and he meant it.'

'Time will mellow Robert's anger, I feel sure.'

'Robert is a lot like his grandfather. Adam was a gentler more forgiving boy. My father never forgot or forgave as you well know, and nor will Robert. I doubt if he will ever set foot in this house again.'

'What about Glamara?'

'Robert always said he was glad the title was going to Adam and not to him. Even now when the title *will* go to him nobody can force him ever to come back here.'

Nothing at Glamara was the same, it seemed as though Roxanne's shadow cast a cloud over servants and family alike. I caught Cook dabbing her eyes several times and Annie said to me, 'What'll you do Miss Tessa, when Sir Godfrey brings 'is new wife up 'ere?'

'They won't be coming for some time, Annie.'

'But will yer stay on 'ere Miss Tessa, after what she did ter yer?'

'I very much doubt it Annie, but I have made no plans as yet.'

'When yer leaves Miss Tessa, I leave. She's trouble Miss Tessa, I can see it comin'. She's 'armed yer once and she'll do it again if she gets a chance.'

'Why do you say that Annie? You don't know her.'

'I've seen 'er. She's beautiful like that Jezebel in the Bible, an' I reckon she's just as wicked.'

I smiled a little at her vehemence. I did not believe that Roxanne could ever harm me again. By the time they took up residence at Glamara I would be gone and our paths would never cross again. That is what I believed would happen. How could I have known how prophetic Annie's words were?

PART FOUR

CHAPTER TWENTY-SIX

Godfrey and Roxanne were married quietly in London at the end of April and set up home in Belgrave Square.

Halfway through May Godfrey arrived at Glamara to await the arrival of Roxanne's portrait which he had had specially painted to hang in the hall alongside Abigail's.

Aunt Hetty remonstrated forcibly with him saying it should be placed elsewhere, it was sacrilege to hang it next to Abigail so soon after her death.

Godfrey was furious. He did not care what people said or thought about him, he and Roxanne were married and it was nobody's business but his. In the end however Abigail's portrait was removed to a corridor while Roxanne's took pride of place in the hall.

After he had gone I stood below it looking up at the dark beautiful face. Her long white hands held a long-stemmed rose, and the scarlet lips curved passionately in the creamy oval of her face. Her blue-black hair fell to her shoulders, held back on one side by a jewelled comb. She was too exotic for Glamara, she did not belong.

I poured out my woes to Richard on every visit and he listened sympathetically.

'I expect I'll soon be leaving here,' he surprised me by saying. 'The doctors have told me there is nothing more they can do for me, and that I am as well as I shall ever be.'

My heart filled with pity. He was so brave, accepting it without complaint, but I could only guess at his chagrin and pain when he was alone.

'I shouldn't be bothering you with my problems Richard when you have so many of your own,' I said unhappily.

'Have you thought what you will do?'

'I don't seem able to think. I shall leave Glamara of course but where I shall go I have no idea. I have enough money to

341

buy a house anywhere in England so I am really very fortunate, thanks to Godfrey. It's just that I shall hate leaving old friends and Glamara itself. I have loved the house so long.'

'Is there no man you want to marry, Tessa?'

'No. I don't think that is the answer Richard.'

'It could be.' He was staring at me intently.

With a little smile I tried to treat his words lightly. 'Surely it would be unfair to marry anybody simply to get away.'

'It would be unfair for me to ask you to marry me when you can see I am less than a man, but it would solve a lot of your problems, Tessa.'

'I am very honoured Richard, but don't you think marrying you would create a great many new ones?'

'I don't understand.'

'Your mother most of all.'

'She would have to accept it Tessa. I shall have no children to come after me and I shall not live a long and healthy life. The doctors have given me five or six years, no more. It is cruel of me even to think that you would want to spend those few years with me.'

I was overwhelmed with pity but when he saw the tears in my eyes he said firmly, 'Please Tessa, I couldn't bear to have you cry over me. But will you think about it? You can fill my days with so much joy and when it is all over you will still be young. Forget about my mother for the time being.'

'I can't forget about her Richard. She would rather you married anybody but me and resenting me like she does it would be cruel of you to place us in such a predicament.'

'Why should it be a predicament at all? My mother would leave the hall and take up residence in the lodge house. I know she would prefer to live in something smaller. You need never see her unless you wanted to.'

'That would be a most unnatural arrangement.'

'But why? I could visit her, you need never go with me. Besides, in time she would care for you as I do, knowing that it is thanks to you that my remaining years were being made so contented.'

'We don't know that Richard, you are only surmising that

I will make you contented, I could actually make you feel very frustrated...'

'And inadequate,' he finished for me. 'I am aware of that, but I love you Tessa, I've loved you since that morning I saw you at the point-to-point meeting. You had so much grace and you were surrounded by so much resentment from all those people who were determined to look down on your mother.'

I didn't know what to say. When I thought about marriage I thought about passionate love and children, not constant caring for an invalid husband, and yet Richard was my dear friend and in a way I did love him, but I pitied him far more.

'Think about it Tessa, please, and don't be afraid to say no when the time comes, I shall understand and it will not harm our friendship.'

I warmed to him more than I had ever done, holding my face against his and feeling him suddenly stiffen in my arms, then relaxing visibly as I moved away. At that moment I knew he was afraid of me, afraid of the passion I aroused in him, a passion which must remain for ever unfulfilled, and I knew that if I married him I would have to live with that. Surely such a marriage could be death to both of us.

I kept Richard's proposal to myself. Each day I thought about it more and more and yet I was no nearer a decision.

Richard believed I was wavering, and he followed up his proposal by telling me that he had talked it over with his mother and she had agreed to take up residence in the lodge house, nor had she been averse to the prospect of having me as a daughter-in-law. A situation which I must confess filled me with surprise.

It seemed to me that fate was conspiring to push me into the marriage.

At the beginning of July Godfrey brought Roxanne to Glamara. It appeared she was tired of the London round and craved for country air and horse riding. Aunt Hetty pointed out with some relish that most of our horses were serving with the cavalry in Flanders, leaving only placid elderly ones in the stables but Roxanne seemed unperturbed.

'I am not wishing to hunt,' she said calmly, 'I merely feel I

343

would like to ride in the country again. I'm sure Godfrey will make some enquiries about finding a suitable mount for me.'

Roxanne had arrived wearing an expensive silk suit, with mink ties thrown carelessly around her shoulders, elegant and smart. As we sat over afternoon tea I couldn't help but think what a charming picture she presented with her slender legs encased in pure silk and her narrow exquisite shoes. I felt countrified and dowdy beside her and yet there was something about me which provoked her antagonism.

'You rushed off so quickly the last time we met,' she said. 'Where on earth did you manage to find a room?'

'I was very fortunate. I met Sir Julian in the Dorchester and I was able to take his room since he was leaving.'

She laughed her low lilting laughter, and a mischievous smile settled on her face, 'I can well imagine Julian rushing back to Carmelita, she is living in Yorkshire now you know. You would like her Tessa, she's very lovely – and talented too before she had her accident.'

I said nothing but busied myself pouring out a second cup of tea, and all the time I was aware of her eyes watching me, willing me to carry on the conversation. Instead I said, 'I am going to see Richard this afternoon Aunt Hetty, I doubt if I shall be back for dinner.'

'A new admirer Tessa?' Roxanne asked.

'An old friend, Sir Richard Chalmers.'

'I've met him, a tall shy boy, a little bit gawky, but of course it was years ago, I suppose he's grown up quite handsome.'

'He has been wounded, he is in a nursing home at present.'

'I can see you as a ministering angel Tessa, but be careful, you surely don't want him to get too fond of you, it would be so awful to have a wounded hero for a husband.'

I knew that I had to get away from Glamara quickly, I could not live in the same house as Roxanne with her airy taunts and sly allusions to Julian and the woman he loved.

'Oh well,' she said at last, 'I suppose I'd better unpack. I didn't bring a maid but I expect there is one here.'

'There isn't. Laura took her maid with her and all the younger servants have been called away for war work.'

'Surely not *all* of them?'

'Well there's Annie, the upper housemaid. They didn't take her because she has a history of asthma. But she's had no training as a lady's maid and I doubt if she'd like the position anyway.'

'Gracious me, things have changed. I'm so sick of this war, it's spoiling all our lives. I'll have a look at this Annie of yours, she might do at a pinch.'

As I left the drawing room I met Annie in the hall hurriedly wiping her hands on her apron.

'Lor' Miss Tessa, 'er Ladyship's asked mi to 'elp with 'er unpacking, what shall I do? I can't work fer 'er Miss Tessa, I'll leave first, I'll go back to Leeds and look for war work.'

'Don't do anything right now Annie, things will sort themselves out. She will soon get tired of life in the country.'

Just then Roxanne came down the stairs. There was an angry frown on her face and seeing Annie she snapped, 'I asked you to come to my room five minutes ago girl, what have you been doing?'

Annie gave me a sorrowful look then ran up the stairs following in the wake of Roxanne's slender, straight-backed figure.

Richard was waiting for me in the hospital garden and as soon as I saw him I knew he had some news for me.

'I thought you had decided not to come Tessa, you're late.'

'I know, Roxanne arrived unexpectedly and Godfrey has left her at Glamara until she grows tired of it.'

'And how has it been?'

'Oh it's early days yet, but it's no use Richard, I can't stay there, I have to get away.'

'Does that mean that you have decided against marrying me?'

I looked at him helplessly, unsure.

'You can't even stand me for five or six years, Tessa?'

His face was sad. I sensed his lonely yearning, his need to have me love him and heaven help me I was not proof against it. He had been hurt enough. I did not know then how much my need to get away from Glamara influenced my decision, I only know that I promised to marry him at the earliest possible moment and then he told me that he was leaving the nursing home in the morning.

'You must come up to the hall Tessa, you'll need to see what changes you need to make.'

'I don't want to make changes Richard, it's your home and you will want it to stay exactly as it is. Are you quite sure your mother will be happy living at the lodge house?'

'We haven't talked about it recently, but I am sure everything will be all right. Do you want a big church wedding?'

'Heavens no, I want it to be as quiet as possible.'

We were to be married in the little church where Sir Edward had been buried. Aunt Hetty gave me her views on the morning of the wedding as I struggled into the blue crêpe-de-chine dress I had chosen.

'This wedding is most ill advised Tessa, you are marrying an invalid whose mother hates you behind that cold set mask she calls a face. You are deliberately throwing your life away.'

'Richard will be kind, Aunt Hetty, and I shall have to show his mother that I am a good wife to him. Don't worry, everything will be all right.'

'I do worry. You should be marrying a virile man who can give you children, not that pale unhappy man who already bears the mark of martyrdom.'

'I'll write often Aunt Hetty, and you must come to stay with us. I'm taking Annie with me, I suppose you know that.'

'Well you will need all the devotion you can get with Dora Chalmers as your mother-in-law. It's getting late, we had better go, Tessa.'

Godfrey and Roxanne were back in London and Robert was waiting for us in the hall, and he came immediately to my side saying, 'You look lovely Tessa, I should be marrying you myself.'

The little church within a stone's throw of Easdale Hall was crowded with villagers and the estate tenants. There were few personal guests and I was struck by the silence as we came out of church. For the main part the villagers stared at us solemn and surly, and I became nervous as we made our way along the narrow path in the churchyard.

Richard walked gamely on his two sticks but I could not take his arm and once, when I almost stumbled near the gate, it was Robert who came to my aid. Lady Chalmers' face was inscrutable. She passed between the waiting villagers, some of whose families had been tenants on the estate for generations, with an unsmiling face, pale and drawn, acknowledging nobody.

The wedding breakfast too was not a jubilant affair. It was eaten in the great oak-panelled dining room but there were none of the jovial speeches from old friends and family, indeed only the vicar expressed his rejoicing that the Lord of the Manor had come home at last and found himself a bride.

Richard and I spent three days in York, wandering among the ancient cobbled streets where the buildings seemed almost to meet over our heads, but Richard soon tired. While I roamed round the minster he sat quietly in one of the pews until I returned to him. Although I could manage the days, the nights were the worst when I lay alone in my solitary bed, listening to Richard's hesitant footsteps pacing the room next to mine, or moaning with pain when he couldn't sleep.

I knew this would be the pattern of my married life and the sooner I accepted it the happier I would be. All the same when I saw other couples walking arm in arm or standing in the parks wrapped in each other's arms I made myself talk blithely and nonsensically about the first thing that came to my mind. I don't think for one moment he was fooled.

On Saturday morning we returned to Easdale Hall and my spirits sank as we drove along the curving drive towards the great stone hall surrounded by tall beeches. The heavy oak door was closed, and not a face looked out of the windows to see our arrival. Richard opened the door but it was his mother who came to meet us in the hall as though she had been waiting there all morning, wearing funereal black which she had not set aside since her husband's death, and without a smile. She allowed me to kiss her cold cheek briefly although she said not a word to either of us.

'It is kind of you to be here to welcome us,' I heard myself saying hesitantly.

'I have decided against taking up residence at the lodge

347

house, at least for the time being. I have spoken to the doctor and he advised against it, Richard. He said there would be days when you will need a great deal of help and Tessa may not be able to manage without me.'

I stared at her with dismay and Richard too frowned, his face flushed with annoyance. 'There *are* the servants Mother, and I have Flanagan my batman to help me.'

'You have a wife and a mother Richard, it would be wrong to put your problems on Flanagan's shoulders. I'm not saying he mustn't stay but there are other tasks he could perform, particularly in the stables.'

'He is my batman mother, I will tell Flanagan what his duties are and where.'

Red spots of colour burned her cheeks but she raised her head proudly, surveying her son with mounting irritation.

'Very well Richard, but remember I am only trying to do the best I can for both you and your wife. It is no use closing your eyes to the fact that you are an invalid and will remain so. If you have told Tessa otherwise then you have misled her.'

'Tessa knows what I am Mother, now I would like to go up to my room, I am very tired.'

He moved slowly towards the stairs and I followed him, then he turned to his mother, asking in a resigned voice, 'Have you decided which rooms Tessa and I are to occupy, Mother? You appear to have made all the other arrangements.'

She bit her lip angrily. 'I thought you would prefer to stay in your own room with all your familiar things around you. I have given Tessa the blue room at the front of the house. It gets the evening sun and the views are nice.'

Richard was not pleased. I could tell by his moroseness as he climbed the stairs. I went with him into his room where we found Flanagan already unpacking his suitcase although I had not seen it taken from the car. He was a short cheerful Irishman with merry twinkling eyes and I warmed to him instantly in that cold dark house.

I saw Richard settled into his room and then picking up the smallest case I went along to mine. It was large, with a dressing room and bathroom leading off it. Like the rest of the house I had seen so far it appeared dark and unwelcoming. The carpet was a dull blue-grey and the curtains and bedhangings were also in blue with splashes of grey and a little yellow. I hated it on sight. If this house had truly been my own I could have made the room more cheerful but it could never be my home. Richard's mother had laid her stamp firmly on every room and in the weeks and months that followed I knew there would be times when our swords would clash, while there would be others when for the sake of peace and quiet I would acquiesce.

At eight o'clock the three of us sat down to dinner but it was Richard's mother who sat at the head of the table and Richard at the other end, while I sat in the middle, so far apart conversation was difficult. The butler and one girl served the food, which I found tasteless and unappetizing. Richard toyed with it petulantly, until in the end his mother snapped, 'I can see you have no appetite Richard, you are obviously tired after those three days in York.'

I forced myself to eat every morsel, and then to ease the conversation I said, 'Can you tell me if Annie has arrived yet from Glamara, Lady Chalmers?'

'Annie?'

'Yes, Tessa's maid,' Richard said.

'We can surely do without maids in wartime, Tessa.'

'Nevertheless Annie has left Glamara to come here with me. She is capable of other duties and is a willing and efficient worker.'

'Most of our young servants were called up at the beginning of the war and the girls were placed on ammunitions, how have you managed to retain the services of a maid through the war years? The girl looked perfectly well and able to do some more useful work.'

'So Annie did arrive, Lady Chalmers?'

'I told her we had sufficient servants for our needs and I believe the butler sent her away.'

'He sent Annie away! But that is monstrous, the girl works for me, she has given up her position at Glamara, she will have nowhere to go. You had absolutely no right to take

349

matters into your own hands and send her away.'

'I may do what I like in my own house, let me remind you of that.'

'But not with my servant, Lady Chalmers. I want us to be friends since we are expected to live under the same roof but I will not be treated like a child who does not know her own mind. Let me remind you that I am your son's wife and that he is now the head of this house.'

The mask slipped from her face for the first time and pure and bitter hatred leapt out of her dark eyes. 'And that is the only reason you married him isn't it? To be the mistress of Easdale Hall, a position your mother aspired to also. Well you have satisfied your ambition but it is a very hollow victory. You have no real husband and there will be no children.'

She rose stiffly and stalked from the room while I was left shaking with anger, then at the sight of Richard's shattered face I felt a wave of pity and I rushed to take him in my arms.

For the first time he drew away from me, holding himself stiff, saying in a muffled voice, 'Ask Flanagan to take me to my room. I will not inflict my company on either of you again today.'

'Richard, please don't take any notice of your mother. She hates me, that is why she is saying these things, but it shouldn't make any difference to us.'

I was worried about Annie. She had little self-confidence, and to have been so ignominiously sent away would have been crushing. I hoped she would have had the sense to return to Glamara. On the other hand she could have returned to Leeds, and I did not think I could face searching for her in those narrow dismal streets.

I did not want to telephone Aunt Hetty, who would only start to worry about me, so as a last resort I telephoned Cook, instantly relieved to hear her warm country voice assuring me that Annie was there.

'Bless yer Miss Tessa she came back the same night, in tears she was, thinkin' yer didn't want 'er, but I said it's not like Miss Tessa to go and do a thing like that, just wait 'ere a while and yer'll be 'earin' from 'er, I said.'

'Oh Cook, I am glad. There was some terrible misunderstanding here, I should have told Lady Chalmers that I was expecting Annie.'

'Are yer still wantin' 'er, Miss Tessa?'

'Oh yes I do want her, and as soon as possible. If she will let me know the time of her train I will arrange to meet her.'

'She's gone to church this mornin'. Her Ladyship's still in London and yer aunt's visitin' friends. I 'ates all this quiet, I do, but I'll get Annie to write ter yer as soon as she gets 'ome.'

My relief was enormous. I needed Annie at Easdale, not as a personal maid but because she might be my only friend.

The events of our homecoming night were repeated in a hundred different ways. My mother-in-law no longer tried to hide her antagonism and under her influence Richard became distant and querulous.

The constant inactivity depressed me. I had imagined it would be like Glamara with the villagers and the people from the hall participating in all manner of things in aid of the war but apart from church on Sunday morning we had no contact.

As they had done at our wedding they stared at us in surly silence. When I suggested some sort of contact Lady Chalmers stared at me as though I had taken leave of my senses.

'You are surely not suggesting that I invite those people *here*? I send money in aid of the war effort. You are not at Glamara now, and the sooner you realize it the sooner you will feel like settling down here.'

'I have settled down, Lady Chalmers, but I am bored with all this inactivity.'

'Speak to the vicar, perhaps he will find you something to do. I daresay he will feel your boredom childish and hard to understand, since you have an invalid husband to care for.'

'His batman does far more for him than I do – at his request, I might add.'

'If you want something to do outside your duties as a wife you might attend to the flowers. Your mother had a great flair for frivolity. Perhaps you have inherited her talent.'

'I find this constant reference to my mother very wearing,

Lady Chalmers. Whatever bitterness you felt for her should not be visited on me.'

'Bitterness! I felt no bitterness against your mother, I disliked her. She hurt Edward so terribly that he never got over it.'

I was so unreasonably angry I could have struck her, and I wanted to wipe that self-righteous expression from her haughty face.

'Would you have preferred it if my mother had not gone away? If she had not been so foolish you would not occupy the position you have today. Sir Edward would have married her, not you.'

The mask was stripped from her face, leaving it naked in its bitterness, so that I felt appalled at what I had said. Drawing herself up to her full height and clothed in her tattered pride she swept from the room leaving me miserably contrite.

'That was cruel,' said Richard from the doorway, sitting in the wheelchair he used frequently now.

'I know, it was unforgivable, but day after day she taunts me about my mother and a past that I can know nothing about. I have stood enough, Richard. Things would have been different if she had gone to live at the lodge house.'

'You should have known she was sensitive where Father was concerned.'

'I did know, but I am sensitive too. Oh Richard, what is she doing to us? We used to be able to talk together and have our own little jokes, now we rarely see each other and she is always there when we do.'

'She is older than you are Tessa, you should learn to get along with her. She could be a good friend to you.'

I stared at him dully. How could Richard be so obtuse? But I was to learn more and more each day that where his mother was concerned that was exactly what he was.

Knowing that Richard could no longer ride, I had not even visited the stables, but now without consulting him I donned my riding habit immediately after breakfast. There were only two horses in the stables, one of them an elderly placid gelding called Ross and the other Richard's horse, a large chestnut hunter, lively and sadly in need of exercise. I was surprised to find Flanagan cleaning out his stable and when he saw me his eyes lit up.

'Are you thinkin' of ridin' him then, Milady? Old Ross'll not take kindly to a saddle now he's in retirement, but this feller'll give ye a good ride. I offered to give 'im some exercise but the major said to wait a while. He won't moind if ye ride him Oi'm sure.'

Richard was becoming increasingly unpredictable, but the longing to ride the horse was more powerful than my fear of Richard's reactions.

'What is his name?' I asked, watching the little man busy fixing the saddle and tightening the girth.

'Oi calls him Sandy, but Sir Richard never loiked that. His real name's Shamara.'

I smiled, fondling the horse's smooth neck. 'I shall call him Shamara. If I give him his proper name perhaps my husband will allow me to ride him regularly.'

'Just so, Milady. Now off you go and enjoy yerselves.'

Once I was in the saddle I felt a different person. I was Tessa Chalfont again, with the wind in my hair and a fast horse under me, the short grass flying under the horse's hooves. As we rode across the park I could feel the sparkle coming back into my eyes and the colour into my cheeks long before we reached the gates.

I pulled the horse up as we reached them and we rode at a more leisurely pace along the village street. There were people working in their gardens who stared at me in surly silence, and when I smiled at them and wished them good day they merely touched their caps or curtsied but their expressions never altered.

They were respectful but behind their respect was a deep-rooted and sullen distrust and I wished I knew the reason for it. I could feel their eyes staring after me, boring into my back like a stiletto, and my nervousness communicated itself to the horse who started to prance and cavort. I was relieved to see a familiar figure walking quickly down the street, with his long black cassock flapping round his ankles. I rode to the vicar's side, glad to see a friendly face in that most unfriendly street.

'Good morning. Am I able to persuade you to call at the vicarage for coffee?' he smiled.

'Coffee would be very nice but I am riding Shamara without my husband's permission so I don't want to keep him out too long.'

'Surely you don't need his permission, Tessa? I would think he would be grateful to you for giving the horse some exercise.'

'It is something I wouldn't like to take for granted.'

'I understand. Have you settled down at the hall?'

'Yes, but I do wish there was more for me to do. Isn't there something connected with the church, some committee I could sit on where I could meet the villagers and work side by side with them? I don't mind what it is as long as it benefits the war effort.'

His face was doubtful and I sensed a vague embarrassment in his manner so that I asked sharply, 'Why is everybody so unfriendly in the village, Vicar? It is something I have not been accustomed to.'

'The villagers are not unfriendly, my dear, but they live in great awe of the people at the hall. They don't believe that you are people like they are.'

'But whyever not? People can't help where they are born, it shouldn't make any difference.'

'I can see you have had a very enlightened upbringing Tessa, but Sir Edward was always very remote. He was a good employer but he rarely mixed with the people and as he grew older he grew even more withdrawn. Sir Richard was invariably with his mother when they rode through the village and Lady Chalmers has always been a person who cannot give of herself.'

He looked at me doubtfully as though he had said too much and I embarrassed him further by saying, 'You do not think the villagers would take kindly to my joining them, Vicar?'

'It would not be a very good idea, Tessa. They would be awkward and embarrassed by your presence, and you would very soon wish to be elsewhere. I know these people, they are good, honest and hard-working but they are rigid in their adherence to the old class system.'

'I am sorry you cannot help me with my dilemma.'

'These are early days, Tessa, give yourself a little time.'

'Time is the only thing I seem to have.'

As we were saying our farewells a pony and trap came from the churchyard, driven by my mother-in-law. She acknowledged our presence by the merest inclination of her head and drove swiftly onwards.

'I really must get back,' I told the vicar regretfully. 'I did not want my husband to know about my riding his horse from anybody but myself.'

I urged the horse to a trot while in front of me a group of villagers shooed their children out of the street, staring at me with hostile eyes.

I left Shamara in Flanagan's care and hurried towards the house where Richard met me in the hall. His face was flushed and there was a high-strung tension about him as he hobbled towards me on his sticks.

'Who gave you permission to ride my horse?' he asked, and I recoiled at the venom in his voice.

'I didn't know I needed permission, Richard. I ride perfectly well, you know that I was not likely to do the horse an injury.'

'The horse has a history of vice you wouldn't know about.'

'I saw no sign of it Richard, he behaved beautifully.'

I had to be so careful not to look at him with pity. He resented that I was able to ride the horse he loved when he never could. It was sad and childish to accuse the horse of a vice he did not possess.

'Darling, I *must* do something, if I don't I shall go mad in this house. Your mother orders the meals and chooses the food we eat. Even the flowers I arrange are of her choosing, now I am told I must not ride your horse when I am perfectly capable of handling him.'

He said nothing but remained staring at me dully, until his eyes wavered and with a little hope I pressed on, cajoling and desperate.

'Have you forgotten how we talked in the nursing home, how you promised that we would be together to live our lives in peace? Can you honestly say any of it has been like that or if it will ever be any different?'

'My mother considers it her duty to stay with us.'

'No Richard, I don't believe that. Your mother is on a crusade to destroy us. She is trying to make you resent me and you are listening to her. Do you want her to drive me away? How can I ever have any faith in the promises you made me?'

'I don't know what it is you want, Tessa.'

'And yet it is very simple, Richard. I want us to live our married life without interference, I want you to trust me, but more than anything else I want to have some useful life of my own, to feel this house is my own and ride Shamara without facing your resentment every time.'

'And then you will come back to your helpless log of a husband who will be expected to sit meekly in his chair waiting for you.'

'Richard, you were as you are now when I married you, you know I have never complained, nor shall I.'

'I can't order my mother to go.'

'No, it is too late for that, but please don't order me to be *less* than your mother. If you forbid me from every joy my heart holds dear we shall not grow closer together, you will merely succeed in destroying me. I will not be destroyed without a fight Richard, I will leave you first.'

His eyes opened in shocked surprise, and then his face crumpled into distress and with a little cry of pity I took him in my arms. I felt that it was a child I was embracing, a sad miserable child, and my heart ached with the pity of it all. I should not pity my husband, it was no substitute for love.

The next few weeks were more congenial, as though he had at last come to terms with his disability and accepted that I must live my life to the limits of my youth and strength. I rode Shamara every day now, over the fells or through the villages near the hall. I called on old friends in Garsdale and Grindale and took tea at the vicarage, but between Lady Chalmers and myself there was no affinity.

She sensed the new camaraderie between her son and me, and I felt she was merely biding her time. Yet I gave her the benefit of the doubt by asking her advice on many matters. She gave it grudgingly, but it seemed to satisfy Richard.

Prayers were said now for the ending of the war, and victory hymns rang out across the velvet lawns round the stone church. The news from France was increasingly good as the German army was scattered and in full retreat.

For myself I felt that there was no victory, for we had all been the losers. So many of the boys I had known would never be coming back to the land fit for heroes and I developed a strange cynicism. The high-flung speeches, the victory marches meant nothing when compared to the loss of millions of young lives, and I wondered increasingly what it had all been for. Alec was dead and Richard was a hopeless cripple, Adam and Abigail both dead, and at Glamara Roxanne's portrait looked down upon the hall with proud confidence.

I tried not to think about Julian. After the war he would be coming back to Carmelita and I was dismayed to find that the mere thought of it caused me acute pain. Surely I was not going to be a slave to the memory of Julian for the rest of my life?

Susan and her son Mark came for a visit that summer. The enchanting baby had turned into a sturdy toddler and as we fished in the stream that ran through the grounds or rode along the country lanes in the trap I felt happier than I had for months.

It was several days before I sensed a withdrawal in Richard, a strange resentment in his dealing with the child. I felt angry with myself when I realized that Mark's presence at Easdale brought home to Richard more sharply his own limitations. When he saw me with Mark, romping in the grass, or even sitting with him curled up against me looking through his picture books, Richard's face told me that he could not bear to watch us.

Susan too noticed and one evening when she came into my room to chat as she invariably did, she said, 'Perhaps it is time for us to go home Tessa, any day now Mark's father should be returning and I feel we should be there to welcome him.'

'But the war isn't quite over yet, Susan, and he won't be home immediately.'

'No, but we need to get ready for him.'

'It's Richard isn't it? I was hoping you hadn't noticed. I think he resents Mark because we will never have a child. I only hope he doesn't think I have invited you here to taunt him.'

'Oh surely he wouldn't think that!'

'He might if his mother has put the suggestion in his mind.'

'You're not happy are you, Tessa? I thought Lady Chalmers was going to live at the lodge house.'

'She changed her mind. Perhaps you *should* return to Leeds, I hope your visit hasn't been spoiled.'

'No of course not, and you must come to see us soon and stay for a little while. It would do you good to get away, go to a few concerts and the cinema.'

'Perhaps before the end of the summer.'

'Yes, that would be lovely.'

I was careful not to hold Mark too close or too long when we said our farewells and after they had gone I could almost feel Richard's relief.

'Children can be so disruptive,' his mother said, 'the child is in danger of being spoilt.'

'Perhaps that is natural,' I retorted. 'Susan has had to be both father and mother since Mark was born. His father will soon be home, I'm sure he will be delighted with his son.'

'Well of course,' she snapped waspishly, 'what father isn't?'

'Other people's children are less trouble than one's own,' I said lightly, smiling at Richard to assure him that that was what I truly believed, but his face remained enigmatic and he went into the library without another word.

I wished Lady Chalmers had friends she could visit if only for a few days but she showed no inclination to leave Easdale for a holiday of any kind. When I suggested it she merely raised her eyebrows, saying, 'I prefer the country to the sea, and where could I go that is more beautiful than here?'

'Perhaps nowhere,' I agreed, 'but a change of scenery could be very beneficial.'

'I do not feel the need for a change, Tessa, but if you wish to go away you must do so, Richard and I will be perfectly happy together.'

'I would not dream of going away without Richard.'

'Well I doubt if he would wish to accompany you, he is happier here where there are no people to stare at him or comment on his disability.'

'People are not generally so unkind.'

'Perhaps not in so many words, but my son is sensitive.'

I made no more suggestions that any of us left Easdale although I knew it would have suited her admirably if I had taken advantage of Susan's invitation. Also I yearned for Glamara and the dark beauty of the rolling hills, but I closed my heart to it.

On a cold November morning the Armistice was signed in a quiet railway siding in France and slowly over the weeks that followed the men were drifting back to the farms and villages. Bells were rung and prayers of thanksgiving were spoken in churches throughout the land, but at Easdale Hall the only difference the ending of the war brought was the return of some of the house servants and a more clinical cleanliness to the austere rooms.

The men who had worked as grooms before the war were no longer required, and I ached to see their downcast faces and hunched defeated shoulders when they were told. I almost knew their thoughts. They had fought for those long desperate four years only to be thrown on the scrap heap when they returned. It was all so different from the things they had been promised. They had been told they would be heroes, but now here they were without work and little prospect of any.

The grass grew long in the parkland and there were unweeded paths and straggly branches, but when I commented on this to Lady Chalmers I was informed in no uncertain manner that expenses needed to be curtailed. She had lost money in investments overseas and since Richard

359

was unable to attend to the estate she needed to employ others to do things for her. Accountants for instance, and an estate agent would have to be appointed, all costing money.

I busied myself weeding the paths and borders while Flanagan cut out the dead branches, but the task was enormous and would easily have employed half a dozen men quite comfortably. My hands grew rough and calloused from the tough weeds and I became ashamed that anybody should see them. Saddened, I was rapidly coming to the conclusion that my mother-in-law enjoyed austerity and the chance it gave her to complain.

The months wore on, snow fell and frost lay thick across the fields. In the villages the faces of the people remained unhappy and pinched. They remained unfriendly and I seldom rode through the lanes now but confined my outings to the low fells where I could follow well-worn bridle paths.

I cannot recall when I first began to notice a worsening in the sullen resentment of those who lived near the hall, but on the rare occasions when I rode into the village they stood in tight little groups, muttering. Sometimes the men took up belligerent attitudes at the edge of the road but it was the women who frightened me most by their angry scowls and threatening gestures.

I told Richard nothing of this, I was too afraid he would prevent my riding his horse anywhere at all, and Flanagan shook his head sadly when I complained to him.

'Aw sure an' they resent yer, Milady, an' them with no money comin' in an' you riding about on that fine horse of yours. I should keep away from the village if I were you, until it all blows over loike.'

'I've done nothing to offend those people, Flanagan, I'd like to get to know them better, besides I don't want them to suppose I'm afraid.'

'It moight be that ye need to be a bit more afraid of 'em, one day they moight do ye some injury.'

'Oh surely not.'

'Well Oi'm not so sure, just you be very careful, Milady, and don't give 'em cause to get too near to ye. It's nothin' you've done, to be sure, but there's somethin' afoot. They even give me the cold shoulder when I goes down to the pub for a glass of ale.'

It was only a few days later when I was invited to the vicarage for tea and I went gladly, riding Shamara down the narrow lane, avoiding the looks cast in my direction.

I heard the hiss of a stone flying past my head to be followed by another which struck Shamara sharply on his cheek. Terrified, the animal reared up, his front legs thrashing the air, and it took all my skill to remain in the saddle. A man stepped from the crowd that had now gathered around me, and disregarding the thrashing hooves he took hold of the bridle, his red angry face leering up at me while a youth standing beside him threatened me with a stone.

'Next time yer Ladyship it'll be a bigger stone, we don't want yer sort ridin' in the village.'

I was carrying a whip which I very much felt like using, but I curbed my anger. 'Please let go of my horse, I intend to ride on.'

'Oh no yer don't, yer can ride back where yer've come fro', I'm warnin' yer, if yer comes into't village again yer'll know about it.'

I stared at him long and hard but then I became aware of shouts coming from somewhere along the street and I had never been more glad to see the vicar – approaching at a run with Flanagan bringing up the rear.

'Let the horse go, Burgess! What is the matter with you all? Lady Chalmers has done nothing to deserve such a reception.'

'She's done nothin' fer us either, she's one o' them livin' like kings while the rest of us are starvin',' Burgess retorted, but by now Flanagan had hold of the bridle and was talking to the horse in his soft Irish brogue and I could feel Shamara's body relaxing.

'Come now,' the vicar said calmly, 'nobody in the village is starving.'

'Does 'er Ladyship live wi' a 'ole big enough to 'ouse a bullock in 'er roof? We've eaten nowt but tatties for weeks an' we 'as little 'uns riddled wi' rickets an' 'oopin' cough through lack o' nourishment. Mi 'usband worked at the 'all, an' a good workman 'ee was too, now the squire don't even want ter see 'im after three year in the trenches.' She was a woman of about forty with grey grizzled hair and a thin, pinched face. An older woman spoke sharply. ''Er 'usband doesn't care. 'Ee's not like 'is father, an' that old mother of 'is 'ud wipe us off the face o' the earth if she could.'

I listened in dismayed silence. I had seen grim poverty in the city but there was something about these country folk that brought to my mind all the terrible stories I had ever read about the feudal system, when the lord of the manor had all the light and music in the world and the peasants on his land starved.

An old man came forward and the others parted to let him pass as though he might be some person of influence in the village. As he neared the flank of my horse he took off his cap and I found myself looking at a fine lined face, and although his eyes were shrewd they were not unkind.

'It's true what they're sayin', Milady, but they had no call to throw stones at yer 'orse. Yer young fools, yer could 'a killed 'er if 'ee'd toppled over an' fallen on top of 'er. If he'd taken off down the road she'd never 'a pulled 'im up. Yer goin' about things the wrong way, yer young 'ot 'eads. Act first, think after, that's what yer doin'.'

'What other way is there?' a woman demanded.

'Yea, tell us that,' another cried. 'Mi 'usband's bin up ter the 'all five times but all 'ee ever sees is that chap i' the black suit who sez Sir Richard can't be disturbed.'

'Ay. It'd do Sir Richard more good to get off 'is backside an' see fer 'isself 'ow we're livin'.'

I spoke to the man. 'My husband was badly injured in the war, it is quite impossible for him to walk round the estate. Have you spoken to his mother?'

This was met by hoots of derisive laughter but ignoring it, the old man spoke directly to me.

'Like a said yer Ladyship, I don't 'old wi' 'em throwin' stones at yer 'orse or takin' their spite out on yer, but Sir Edward'd turn over in 'is grave if he could see the state o' his tenants' cottages.'

'What is your name?' I asked him.

'Joe Butterfield, ma'am. I worked for the Chalmers for nigh on fifty years. I knew Sir Edward's father an' 'is father afore 'im. We've gone through some 'ard times but it were never as bad as now.'

'You say your houses are in need of repair?'

'Some of 'em are past repairin'. There's 'oles in the roofs lettin' the rain in. They're that damp it's little wonder the bairns are fit for nowt.'

'Will you show me your cottages.'

They looked at one another uncertainly then one man said, 'Why don't she see 'em, she'll know then we're tellin' no lies. Yer can see mine ma'am.'

Flanagan helped me down from the saddle and accompanied by the owner of the cottage and the vicar I set off up the path. I was agreeably surprised to see that the interior was scrupulously clean, if barely furnished and shabby.

Halfway up the steps to the bedroom I became aware of a strong musty smell and I could see the paper hanging off the walls. I stared round in appalled silence. Although it was summer and there had been a dry spell for several weeks, there was a dankness in the dark discoloured rugs and the walls where the evidence of damp had not dried out.

The tenant showed me cracks in the ceiling, and his wife said, 'It's that cold in the winter we 'as to sleep with our coats on, an' last year mi old mother got pneumonia an' died.'

'I keeps patchin' things up,' the man said, 'but timber costs money an' last winter we only 'ad enough to buy food and pay the doctor's bills.'

'Is this one of the worst cottages?' I asked hopefully.

'Bless yer no, ma'am, this is one o' the best. Yer should see Bessy Turner's cottage an' 'er wi' a bairn an' two little girls.'

'I would like to see that one.'

Bessy was outside the cottage and as we walked down the lane I tried to guess her age. She was painfully thin but there was a wistful prettiness about her which I found appealing. Her faded gingham dress hung on her angular limbs and had seen much washing but there was a coltish grace about her figure as she strolled beside me. Her hair was fair and fine, but she had it scraped back from her face and caught by a slide and I believed it could look so pretty if she allowed it to frame her face.

She pointed to a row of four cottages. 'Mine's the end 'un,' she explained, and a little girl ran from the gate and hid her face shyly in her mother's skirts, occasionally peeping at me with wide saucer-blue eyes and I smiled at her, asking, 'What is your name?'

She was too shy to answer, and her mother said, 'It's Lucy, ma'am. I 'ave another little girl but she's livin' over at Settle wi' 'er grandmother, that 'elps us out a bit.'

'You have a baby too, I believe?'

'Yes ma'am, our Sam. 'Ee's just gettin' over bronchitis an' 'oopin' cough. Right poorly 'ee's bin but the doctor sez 'ee thinks 'ee's on the mend now.'

The cottage was pretty from the outside. Like all the others it was built from Pennine stone and the garden had been lovingly tended, but as soon as I entered the living room I could smell the musty dampness, so overpoweringly strong it gripped my throat. I could feel poverty physically in the threadbare pieces of carpet and peeling walls, and the girl clutched my arm and pointed to the sagging ceiling.

'There's a big 'ole in the roof an' when the rain comes it falls through on to't bedroom floor, that's why this ceilin's like it is.'

She was interrupted by a fretful wail from the corner of the room where a roughly made wooden cradle was standing, and going to it immediately she took out a baby wrapped in a pathetic bundle of old blankets.

She rocked the child in her arms making soothing noises but he coughed cruelly until an older woman turned back the blanket and stuck a dummy in his mouth.

I could see the child's face now, pathetically wizened like the face of an old, old man, and red and angry with coughing. His hair was scant, and I suspected scurvy.

'How old is your baby?' I asked her gently.

'He's sixteen months old, ma'am, but 'ee's not comin' on like ee should.'

I turned away in case she should see my shocked

expression. I couldn't help comparing this sad child to Susan's little boy who at two years old was running about on plump sturdy legs, his face rosy with health.

My heart ached with pity, but there was anger too. I had seen poverty before and much of that had been the fault of my stepfather. This time I was learning that they blamed my husband's family for it.

Outside the cottage Flanagan helped me to mount my horse and I addressed my words to Joe Butterfield who stood at the back of the crowd. 'Mr Butterfield, I will speak to my husband this evening about what I have seen today. I am sure he will be as disturbed as I have been.'

'Will 'ee give us work?' a man said. 'Wi don't want 'is pity.'

'Please leave things in my hands, I will do all I can.'

The old man nodded. 'That's fair enough, Milady.'

I thanked him with a smile, then turning to the youth who had thrown the stone at my horse I said sternly, 'I hope you will never do anything so foolish again. Quite apart from the injury you might have caused to me it was cowardly to shy a stone at an innocent animal.'

The boy shuffled his feet and looked down at the ground. Wheeling my horse round, I left them, with Flanagan walking beside me.

'Are ye thinkin' the major'll do somethin' for the villagers then, Milady?'

'I hope so Flanagan, if he doesn't then I certainly will.'

As we entered the gates he asked anxiously, 'Will you not be mentioning the horse, Milady?'

'The horse, Flanagan!'

'Yes Milady. The major's only waitin' for an excuse to stop you ridin' him, and didn't he nearly throw you? He'll either stop you ridin' him or worse.'

'What could possibly be worse than that?'

'He once threatened to 'ave the horse shot, that were in one of 'is black moods, afore he got resigned to you ridin' him.'

I stared at him in horrified surprise. 'Surely my husband wouldn't do such a wicked thing. He loves Shamara.'

'Yes Milady, he does, but he loves him like a favourite toy he's grown too old to play with, and he can't abide to see anybody else get pleasure from it. Perhaps it reminds 'im o' the days when he could ride. It's 'ard fer us to understand Milady, us being fit and well loike, but Oi hopes you won't mention the horse.'

'Of course I won't mention him.'

He smiled, well satisfied. I dismounted outside the hall, leaving Flanagan to return the horse to the stables. His words about Shamara troubled me. I had known that Richard suffered black moods and I understood them, what I hadn't known was that he could be vindictive enough to vent his spite on a horse he had once loved.

I was dreading the evening ahead of me. I intended to speak to Richard after dinner but we were never alone, his mother was always with us, working on her tapestry or writing the day's events in her diary. I often wondered what she found to write about for her days were a monotonous round of exactly the same thing. Every morning she interviewed the housekeeper about the meals, and later the butler as they wrestled with the housekeeping accounts. When she did not drive down to the churchyard to lay fresh flowers on Sir Edward's tomb, she was in the greenhouses attending to the orchids which were her only hobby.

It was a hobby I could not understand, for what had those strange exotic flowers to do with my plain unfashionable mother-in-law? Roses I could have understood. Geraniums would have been perfect, but not those alien, often bizarre tropical flowers that reminded me quite amazingly of Roxanne.

CHAPTER TWENTY-SEVEN

After dinner that day I wracked my brains trying to think of a suitable opening to tell Richard about the afternoon's events.

He sat in his favourite chair in front of a fireplace filled with plants and I was wishing we had a fire, for the evening was chilly. His head was buried in his newspaper, while in and out went my mother-in-law's needle in the tapestry firescreen she was working on. My opportunity came when she put her tapestry on one side and took up her diary, remarking that there were several days to enter.

'What ever do you find to put in your diary?' Richard asked curiously. 'The days are too monotonous and unvaried.'

When she didn't answer I said, 'My day wasn't monotonous Richard, I met some of your tenants and saw into their cottages.'

He looked up in surprise and although Lady Chalmers didn't raise her head she sat with her pen stilled.

'You say you went into their cottages?' he asked, staring at me in surprised amusement.

'Yes. I was invited to the vicarage and on my way I met a group of your tenants who asked to speak with me.'

'Why would they do that?'

'Richard, their cottages are in a terrible state. There are holes in most of the roofs and the walls are so damp the wallpaper is peeling. There are sick children in those cottages and I saw a baby with whooping cough who looked more like an old man than a baby. They are living on what they can grow and the men have no work. This is a terrible homecoming for men who have spent the last four years in the trenches.'

'Why did they take you to see those things?' Lady Chalmers asked. 'What do they expect you to do about them?'

'They hoped I would tell Richard. He owns those cottages and is responsible for making them habitable. They had every right to complain and I suppose when they saw me the opportunity seemed a good one.'

'I knew this would happen, seeing you riding day after day past their homes on your fine horse and in your impeccable riding clothes, you were an affront to those people who have nothing.'

'I am not the cause of their having nothing, nor of the state of their cottages. It is disgraceful that people should be living in homes not fit for farm animals. Their cottages were clean, God knows how they have the incentive when the buildings are practically falling down.'

'Don't you know girl that we too are suffering the effects of the war? There are things that need attention here but where is the money to pay for them?'

'We are not living in poverty. If there are things needing attention on the estate why can't some of those men be given work?'

'No doubt they prefer to stand about bemoaning their lot instead of doing something practical like putting their homes to rights.'

'That is an unreasonable thing to say. To put things to rights they need materials, where would the money be coming from? Not from their landlord, apparently.'

'Why haven't they been here to see me instead of accosting my wife?' Richard demanded.

'They have tried to see you, several times, but the butler told them you couldn't be disturbed. I tell you Richard, those people are desperate, if something isn't done soon and before the winter starts we could have deaths on our hands and I very much fear their anger would make them desperate.'

'I never heard anything more ludicrous!'

'It isn't ludicrous. One old lady has already died from the effects of last winter in those damp dreary rooms and now a child is ill and unlikely to get much better unless something is done quickly. I promised I would talk to you tonight Richard, if only you could see those cottages for yourself.'

'That is quite impossible,' his mother snapped. 'He can barely walk through the house.'

'Then if he can't see them for himself he should take my word for it. The tenants said the cottages would never have been allowed to get into such a state in Sir Edward's time.'

A dull flush coloured her cheeks and angrily she retorted, 'In my husband's time we had more money and the villagers more sense. They would never have dared to accost me in the street, but then I never irritated them by parading my wealth.'

'Tessa is not visiting the village wearing jewels and sables, Mother, she is only accepting an invitation to take tea at the vicarage,' Richard said sharply and I gave him a smile of gratitude.

'Nevertheless,' his mother retorted, 'those people associate a fine horse and a lady rider with considerable means.'

'Richard, what are you going to do for those people? I told them I would speak to you and they have a right to an answer.'

'I can answer for Richard. Much of his money, like mine, is tied up in shares which we would be foolish to sell at this moment. We cannot afford more workpeople on the land and the tenants should be encouraged to undertake their own repairs.'

Ignoring her I said, 'Richard, is that your answer also?'

'I employ an estate agent, I will consult with him before I agree to do anything about the cottages,' he answered.

In the next breath his mother said, 'This is really none of your concern, Tessa. I would appreciate it if you would leave matters regarding the estate in my son's hands, or mine.'

I sprang up in sudden anger. 'If nothing is done regarding those cottages very quickly then I shall use my own money to make them habitable. I am Richard's wife and whether you like it or not the mistress of this house. When they plead with my husband they plead with me and I will speak to the estate agent myself if necessary.'

With my head held high I walked out of the room and up to my bedroom. I was trembling with distress. What had happened to the friendship and affection Richard and I had shared? Those weeks when I had visited him at the nursing home had been warm and gay with our laughter, now thanks to his mother's presence in the house there was only bitterness and insecurity between us.

I had never told Richard that I loved him, he had not asked for my love, only my care and tenderness, and I had been prepared to give these in full measure. Now between us was an ever-widening gulf and I could see no prospect of it closing, not with Lady Chalmers under the same roof.

By making him a good wife I had hoped to come closer to

his mother so that one day she would forget the past in realizing that fate had sent me to make atonement for old griefs, but now I knew that the bitterness was too deep and I had been foolishly naïve to believe it could ever be otherwise. As long as she lived she would resent and oppose me.

I paced my bedroom floor in a mood of rage and helplessness until at last I heard Richard and his mother going to their rooms. I heard her door close and knew that for several moments Richard stood outside his room looking in the direction of mine before I heard the soft closing of his door.

I waited until I heard Flanagan go downstairs then I went to Richard, knocking on his door as I always did and remaining outside until I heard his surprised voice telling me to enter.

He was sitting in his dressing gown, where the lamplight could fall on the book in his hands. His face was grey and careworn and a sudden rush of pity made me go to him quickly, placing my arm around his shoulders, my face close to his. Immediately I felt his withdrawal, as I always did when I touched him.

He feared the passion I aroused in him as much as his own inadequacy, so that any display of affection on my part had to be stifled in case he should think I desired him. I had to be so careful to maintain some sort of normality between us, and now indicating the book on his knee I asked lightly, 'Isn't that rather small print to be reading in this dim light?'

'I wasn't reading Tessa, I doubt if I could get interested in it anyway tonight.'

'What is the matter with us Richard, what is this distance that prevents us talking to each other these days?'

'I wasn't aware of any distance Tessa, it is late and I am tired, that is all.'

'It isn't in the least late my dear, and we must talk. Surely even you must see that talk is becoming increasingly impossible when your mother is always with us.'

'Why do you resent her so much? This is her home too Tessa.'

'I don't want to talk about your mother, Richard, that isn't why I came here. I want to talk about the cottages and what we can do to help the tenants.'

'Tessa, it isn't your affair.'

'But it has been made my affair. Why won't you discuss it, why must you behave as if I were merely a nuisance interfering with something that didn't concern me? Why must it always be you and your mother, never you and your wife?'

He looked at me in brooding silence while I faced him, taut and vulnerable, pleading for the support he seemed unable to give. 'The estate agent will take care of things, that is what I pay him for.'

'But when? Oh Richard, if you could have seen that baby, more like a wizened little monkey than a child, you would have felt pity for them too.'

'I will speak to him in the morning when he comes up to the hall to see my mother. Nothing can be done before then so won't you please return to your room Tessa, and I will tell you tomorrow what we have decided.'

'Why is it always your mother the estate agent comes to see, why can't you do anything without her being involved? Are you the master here or is it your mother?'

His face flushed angrily and for a moment I feared I had said too much, then the anger died out of it to be replaced by resignation. 'I had always understood that my father would leave my mother well provided for but that the bulk of his money would come to me to administer the estate. However, he died before he could make the necessary arrangements and now I am in the situation where the bulk of my father's estate is managed by my mother. She promised to have it legally transferred to me after the war but when I came home injured I was too ill to keep her to that promise and now it is never mentioned. My mother likes to hold the purse strings, she will remain reluctant to have things changed.'

I stared at him in disbelief. 'So her money pays for the food we eat and the servants wages and her money that will ultimately have to be spent on repairing those cottages?'

'Yes.'

'In that case Richard you need not speak to the estate agent in the morning, I will spend my money on the repairs. It will give me a purpose in life, provide me with some pleasure in contributing to other people's welfare and an opportunity to earn my keep.'

I saw him wince but I didn't care. At that moment I was too angry, too humiliated, and if there was appeal in his sombre eyes I was too hurt to see it.

I arrived late at the breakfast table hoping that Lady Chalmers might have breakfasted early but she was still there, opening her mail and barely taking time to nod to me coolly before continuing to read her letters. I said as calmly as my courage would allow, 'Richard and I talked about the cottages last night and we decided that I would have the repairs carried out at my expense. Do you think I should consult the estate agent or a builder?'

I was rewarded by seeing her eyes grow hard and the colour creep into her thin scrawny neck.

'The estate agent must be consulted. It would be totally wrong to call in an outside builder and open everybody's mouth.'

'You would be happier if they thought the instructions had originated from you or Richard?'

'It would be more diplomatic.'

'Very well then. You can rest assured nobody outside this house will ever know that it is my money we are using. I would not dream of allowing the tenants to know that both my husband and his mother had been reluctant to help them.'

She stared at me long and hard but I went on calmly eating my breakfast, determined not to let her see the terrible resentment in my eyes should they meet hers across the table.

I had had little contact with Alan Frobisher the estate agent except for an exchanged smile or formal greeting, and he seemed surprised when I entered his office that morning. He jumped up and pulled up a chair for me.

He was a man of medium height, with a plain open face and eyes that smiled and were piercingly blue. I guessed him to be in his early forties but he might have been younger. He invariably wore riding breeches and a checked hacking jacket around the estate and I had been told he had served in the yeomanry as a captain. He came originally from Lincolnshire, and I liked his firm handshake and his businesslike approach to the reasons for my visit.

I explained quickly about the state of the cottages and he agreed that he had seen for himself the need for repairs but that his hands had been tied when faced with Lady Chalmer's insistence that other matters came first.

'Have we her permission to go ahead with repairs?' he asked warily.

'Of course, I wouldn't have come here otherwise.'

'But it is only recently she refused to speak about them, I wonder what made her change her mind.'

'Possibly because they accosted me yesterday in the high street. They were very angry, Mr Frobisher. I'm sure Lady Chalmers doesn't want the tenants to become so frustrated they start attacking us whenever we go into the village.'

'Indeed no. You were attacked then?'

'Not exactly, but I was aware of their anger and I understood it when I saw their miserable dwellings. How soon can the work start?'

'As soon as possible, Milady.'

'Can work be found for some of them on the project?'

'I don't see why not, if it is only labouring.'

'Then I think you should try. Work for those people is almost as important as getting their roofs repaired.'

'Leave things with me and I will report to you as soon as I am ready to start. Do I need to speak to Lady Chalmers do you think?'

'No, but I think my husband might like to be consulted from time to time. It is sad that he will not be able to see the cottages for himself.'

That was the beginning of an interest that went on through the summer until the first chill winds swept down the fells and invaded the park as I rode Shamara towards the village. I was greeted with smiles of welcome now and was touched by small gifts that were presented to me – home-made jams and lemon curd, scones and cakes, and from Joe Butterfield a bunch of his prized chrysanthemums.

A warm friendship had grown up between Alan Frobisher and me. I liked his sense of humour, and his disciplined attention to detail while under his guidance the cottages took on a new aspect. Roofs and walls were strengthened and the men took pride in working on their homes and being paid for doing so. The cottages became homes to be proud of.

The baby who had looked so ill was now running about on legs that were becoming increasingly stalwart and his sister ran to me with eyes shining merrily in greeting. What was more important however was the new purpose I felt in life and I worried increasingly about what I would do when the work was completed. I regaled Richard each night with news of the transformation while his mother sat grim-lipped and silent with antagonism etched deep on her face.

On the day that the work was finally completed Alan Frobisher and I were invited to a party in the village hall to commemorate the event.

Alan said, 'Do you think Sir Richard would like to take part, Milady? I could ride back and ask him if you like.'

'Oh I do think that is a lovely idea, I'm sure he will come.'

It was wonderful to see them all sitting down at long wooden tables in the village hall, their faces shining with happiness, while the tables groaned under the fare I had contributed.

For over an hour I responded to the smiles and talk that went on around me but my eyes were constantly trained on the door where at any moment I expected Alan Frobisher and my husband to enter, but then my hopes began to waver as the fingers on the clock moved round and Joe Butterfield shook his head doubtfully, putting my fears into words.

'It don't look as though anybody's comin' fro' the 'all then.'

'There's still time Joe, my husband isn't able to do anything in a hurry.'

He continued to shake his head and just then Alan Frobisher entered the room alone. He shook his head at the question in my eyes, and seeing Joe next to me he said lightly, 'Sir Richard's not well enough to come down, Milady, he sends them all his best wishes and hopes to see the cottages for himself very soon.'

He conveyed Richard's supposed good wishes to the villagers who stood and offered up a toast for his health and complete recovery.

Taking Alan aside I whispered, 'What really happened, Alan?'

'Lady Chalmers said there would be too much noise and neither of them were prepared for it.'

'And my husband?'

His honest wholesome face looked strangely troubled and he shook his head doubtfully. 'I don't know, Milady. He didn't speak to me, it was almost as though he resented me but I can't for the life of me think why.'

'His illness makes him depressed, so that he sees problems where there aren't any, and I fear his mother doesn't help matters. She is constantly reminding him of his disabilities, which makes him feel more inadequate than he really is.'

It was the first time I had ever mentioned the situation between us but I felt so alone and troubled, and the concern in Alan Frobisher's face made me feel I could trust him.

'Don't let it spoil your night, we are here to enjoy ourselves, remember,' he said quietly.

I smiled at him tremulously, then as the music started up he asked me to dance. He was not a brilliant dancer but I suddenly realized how wonderful it was to dance again and how much I had missed it. I was still young enough to take pleasure in whirling round the room to the strains of the village band, even if they were often out of tune.

It was almost eleven and I was dancing round energetically in the arms of one of the villagers when I became aware of a hushed silence and looking up I was amazed to see Richard in the doorway with Flanagan beside him. Richard was leaning heavily on two sticks and his eyes burned into mine with a hostility that took my breath away.

We continued to stare at each other in the same uncomfortable silence for several moments and I was suddenly aware of people searching for their coats and beginning to drift out of the room, looking at my husband oddly and almost fearfully as they went.

Gathering my scattered wits I ran to his side and said as cheerfully as I knew how, 'Why Richard you came, how absolutely splendid. But why did you leave it so late?'

He stared at me without smiling. 'Get your coat, I've come to take you home.'

'But you needn't have bothered darling, Alan would have taken me home.'

'I'm sure he would but I am here to take you home myself, now please get your coat.'

Sensing that something was terribly wrong Alan Frobisher came to my side saying, 'The party's almost over, sir, you should have come down earlier.'

Richard didn't even look at him so that Alan stood flushed and silent. I hurried to retrieve my coat. People were looking at me curiously, but I made myself smile, waving to them gaily, saying what a wonderful party it had been and wishing them well in their pretty homes.

My husband had already turned away and then Flanagan went to assist him while I walked behind with Alan. When we reached the car I shook hands with him formerly and in a voice which Richard could plainly hear I said, 'Thank you Alan for all you have done. It has been a lovely party, hasn't it?'

'Yes indeed, Milady.'

We drove in silence back to the hall and those villagers we passed on the street only looked at the car curiously and in silence. I felt so angry I could have quarrelled with him then but I maintained a stony silence because of Flanagan's presence. When he deposited us at the hall I stormed into the house before either of them, my head held high. I faced Richard in the hall while Flanagan hurried up the stairs, almost falling over himself in his haste to leave us alone.

'How dare you humiliate me in front of all those people? I'm not a child to be told I must be home before eleven, you had absolutely no right to behave so inconsiderately,' I stormed.

'I have the right of a husband who is being deceived by his wife with one of his paid servants.'

'What *are* you talking about?'

'You and Frobisher. Do you think I haven't eyes in my head? Do you suppose I don't know what has been going on between you these past months?'

I stared at him speechlessly, in an astonishment so intense I had no immediate words to refute his statement, and then anger overcame me, anger so passionate I could have struck him.

'Are you mad? Do you seriously believe that Alan Frobisher means anything to me beyond that I trust him and regard him as a friend and helpful employee of yours?'

'Tessa, I'm not blind,' he said wearily. 'Don't you think I haven't noticed the change in you these last few months. You've been more like the Tessa I used to know, with your eyes shining and laughter on your lips, and it is surely not because a few cottages were being repaired. My mother noticed it too, she warned me weeks ago about what was happening.'

'But of course she did. She probably told you I was exactly like my mother before me. Well I'll tell you why I went off with a new degree of happiness and it had nothing at all to do with Alan Frobisher, although I like him very much and you too should know that he is a good and sincere man. I was happy because for the first time since I entered this house my life had a purpose. I no longer had to behave like a stupid doll who was expected to have no thoughts of my own and no initiative to change things. How dare you chastise me like a backward child, and with something so outrageous that it doesn't deserve an answer? Why don't you confront Alan Frobisher with your suspicions? Let him see what a foolish man you are, a man who listens to his mother until there isn't a thought in his head that she hasn't put there.'

I took to my heels and ran upstairs. Dora Chalmers stood at her bedroom door and it was clear that she had heard everything.

I knew that in the morning I would have to get away

somewhere to think things out. I couldn't go to Glamara, not with Roxanne watching me with those mocking amused eyes of hers, so I would go to Leeds. Perhaps Susan would have me for a few days.

I was up very early and after throwing a few things in a suitcase I crept downstairs. I would tell Richard where I was going but I did not want to face him or his mother until I was in a calmer frame of mind. Shrugging my arms into an old trench coat I let myself out of the house. There was a new autumnal chill in the air as I trudged across the damp grass towards the stables and over the fells the mist hung low. Early as I was Flanagan was at the stables before me and as I went to stroke Shamara's neck he came up to me with a dismal frown.

'They've offered the horse to the ridin' stables at Garsdale, Milady. Sure an' I only heard it miself in the village pub yesterday, an' them not sayin' a word to me who's looked after him since the day I came 'ere and afore that in France.'

I stared at him in disbelief. 'I can't believe Sir Richard would do such a thing without telling either of us. He loves Shamara.'

'Well I reckon he has. Diabolical it is, a lovely horse like this bein' ridden by amateurs. Oi don't really know what's 'appenin' any more, but if things go on as they are it's home to old Oirland I'll be goin' afore I'm much older.'

'You would leave, Flanagan?'

'Oi would, Milady. Oi told Sir Richard Oi'd stay as long as he wanted me but I reckon he don't need anybody as long as he has 'is mother.'

When I didn't speak he went on, 'It's 'er Ladyship that's done this. What's she got against yer, Milady? Instead of hatin' you she should go down on her bended knees and thank the good Lord that he found a woman like you willin' to marry him.'

I looked at Flanagan helplessly, but ignoring his words I said practically, 'How soon is he sending Shamara to the riding stables?'

'He's asked them to be makin' an offer for him, if the offer's right he'll go. Yer can bet yer last half-crown that the offer'll suit her Ladyship jest foin. Oi tell you Milady, if that 'orse goes Oi goes too.'

'What would you do, Flanagan?'

'Mi father were a blacksmith in County Wicklow an Oi always worked with 'orses. Oi'll get a job there never fear, an' Oi can't say Oi'll be sorry.'

'I'm going to Leeds for a few days, Flanagan, so don't do anything in a hurry. How can I get in touch with you without any of the servants knowing?'

'Oi'm always down at the pub at lunch toime, Milady, Oi'll write the number down for you. Ask for me and don't you be tellin' the landlord who you are. Anythin' he knows an' the entire village knows it in less than an hour.'

'I'll remember.'

'Will you be saying anything to the major, Milady?'

'Not just yet, Flanagan. I will wait until the time is right.'

I could tell he was enjoying the conspiracy and as I walked briskly back to the hall my heart was filled with determination that I would move heaven and earth to prevent Shamara going to Hugh Mallory's riding stables. I would not allow Richard's mother to defeat me on this.

I went directly to Richard's room. He was still in bed with his breakfast tray lying untouched across his knees, looking grey and careworn. I could tell he had slept badly, all the same I steeled my heart against pity and the sudden look of alarm that crossed his face.

I decided not to mince words. 'I am going away for a few days, Richard, I'm not sure for how long. Perhaps to Susan's if it is convenient.'

'Why?'

'Surely you don't need to ask that question. If I stay here after last night's episode I shall explode. I need to think Richard, about us and about our marriage. I'll let you know when I expect to return.'

I didn't attempt to either kiss him or take his hand, but after a long hard look I left him alone.

In my room I found Annie looking askance at my half-filled suitcase. 'Yer goin' away, Miss Tessa?' she said in some dismay.

'Only for a few days, Annie. I'm going to Leeds, would you like to visit your family?'

Her face lit up with that sudden sweet smile that made her seem almost pretty. 'Oh yes Miss Tessa, I'd like to see mi mam. They've moved into a little terraced 'ouse in a better district, I'd like to see it, 'er letters are full of it.'

'Very well then, I'll finish packing and meet you downstairs. Flanagan's brought the car to the front door, so do hurry Annie.'

She was out of the door almost before I had finished the sentence and I heard her feet running frantically along the corridor and the door leading to the servant's quarters slam shut behind her. Ten minutes later I was driving swifly towards the gates with Annie sitting excitedly beside me, and both of us feeling like a pair of caged birds which had suddenly been released into the sunlight.

We called for coffee at a hotel where I could telephone Susan. I was glad to hear her voice exclaiming warmly, 'But of course you must come here, Tessa, we'll be delighted. Is everything all right?'

'There are problems, Susan, but they'll keep until we meet. I'm on my way, I shall be there in about an hour.'

As the car ate up the miles into the city I found myself remembering the Mother Superior's words in what seemed like another world: that one day I might be glad of Susan's friendship which I was then so anxious to disparage.

All my life had been change, and as I drove along the familiar roads of the city I had the strangest feeling that my life would soon be changing again, but whether for good or ill I did not know. My fate was hidden from me but as I revelled in my newfound freedom the feeling was taking shape that I could never go back to a life in that dark inhospitable house presided over by a woman who hated me as desperately as she had once hated my mother.

Richard didn't need me. I bore his name yet I was not a real wife to him, he neither needed my heart nor my body, he didn't even need my friendship. I had married him in the belief that I would make the rest of his life bearable, that even if I could not give him back his health and vigour I could at least try to substitute them with tenderness and warmth. Well, I had failed, and now the kindest thing I could do was to get out of his life so that he need not be tortured by groundless suspicions, or that other more insidious torture, of longing to possess me when the passion of love had been denied him.

It was a neat terraced house Annie's family had removed to in a far better area. Iron railings enclosed a small neat garden, woodwork was freshly painted and there were gay cotton curtains.

Her face beamed with delight when she saw it. 'Will yer not come in Miss Tessa and have a look round?'

'They're waiting lunch for me Annie, but on the way back I would love to see it. Shall we say a week today?'

'That would be luvely, an' don't yer go an' worry about them back at Easdale. I 'ates 'er I do, wi' 'er long doleful face an' 'er pernickety ways.' She collected her suitcase and after a gay wave walked happily up the path to her father's house.

The sheer normality of Susan's lifestyle was like a breath of clean moorland air. They had moved into a large comfortable house where her husband could keep half the downstairs rooms as part of his practice, which was considerably large since he was the only veterinary surgeon on that side of the city. There was a big rambling garden with a swing for young Mark and it seemed to me that there were dogs of all shapes and sizes, as well as two fat tabbies.

Meeting her husband again I liked him more and more. John was several years older than Susan but I liked his straight eyes and attractive, one-sided smile. Most of all I liked the obvious wellbeing and happiness of this little family. Lunch was a pleasant meal and we laughed often in spite of the thoughtful glances I often surprised on Susan's face.

John went off to visit some of the farms in the vicinity, and Mark was spending the afternoon with his grandparents.

Susan said quietly, 'What's wrong, Tessa?'

Even then I found it hard to tell her about the misery of my life at Easdale and was about to wave it aside with airy inconsequence, but my unhappiness was too new and too raw. I found myself telling her everything, about my mother-in-law's intense dislike and Richard's unwarranted suspicions.

She listened quietly and when the sorry tale was told she said anxiously, 'You can't go on living there, Tessa, it will destroy you.'

'If I am not already destroyed, yes it will.'

'Why does Lady Chalmers stay with you if she dislikes you so intensely?'

'I think that the only pleasure she gets from life is seeing me looking increasingly unhappy, knowing that she is destroying things for us.'

'That is sadistic.'

'I know. My mother-in-law is often sadistic and I think it is too late for Richard to change. She has controlled his life for too long. Now that Richard is an invalid she wants him entirely to herself. That is why she refused to go to the lodge house, why she will do everything in her power to make my life so miserable I can no longer live there. I won't let her destroy me Susan, and I know the things she will say about me if ever I leave my husband. My reputation won't be worth a fig.'

'I think you've already made up your mind to leave him.'

'I don't see anything else for it, but I have something to take care of before I do.'

'What is that?'

'Richard's horse Shamara. I love him, Susan. Now Richard has offered Shamara to riding stables, which means that if I stayed with him even the one small pleasure of riding Shamara would have gone.'

'He couldn't stop you buying another horse, though.'

'No, perhaps not, but I know the Mallory stables and Shamara is a thoroughbred. How could I let him go to end his days as a shabby hack? Besides there's Flanagan, Richard's batman. He went to Easdale to care for him and he would willingly stay there but he too isn't popular with Dora and he says if Shamara goes, he'll go.'

'So, if she gets rid of Flanagan and you go too she really will have Richard to herself. What do you suppose she'll do then, she can't look after Richard single-handed?'

'She would bring in a paid nurse. She's threatened to do that several times when she's been displeased with Flanagan. A paid nurse would be in her employ, Flanagan was never that and even I couldn't be classed as her servant.'

'Can I help in any way? John might know if somebody in the vicinity is looking for a good mount.'

'That was what I was hoping, either that or some way of keeping him myself.'

'You could stay with us until you've sorted things out.'

'Thanks Susan, but I need to get right away. If Richard knows I am here he will think my absence is only temporary. I thought tomorrow I would visit one or two estate agents to see if they know of any property some distance away which would suit me.'

'Until you really know what you want Tessa, why don't you go to the cottage? We bought it when Mrs Haworth died.'

'The cottage?'

'Yes, you remember, we used to holiday there year after year. It's a smallholding actually. There's stabling for at least two horses and a small flat over the stables. It was a labour of love furnishing the cottage and the views are wonderful.'

'But won't your parents want it, or even you and John? It sounds perfect to me.'

'Now that it belongs to us we somehow don't go there so often. Besides, we never go there in the wintertime. I should tell you that the north-east coast is wild but incredibly beautiful. The house is about half a mile from the coast.'

'Oh Susan it sounds absolutely perfect.'

'If Richard has offered the horse to stables how are you going to have him?'

'He's asked the stables to make him an offer. I can exceed whatever Hugh Mallory offers and Richard needn't know who's buying him. But we'll need to find him a stable until I'm ready to take him.'

'I'll ring Lionel Prescott, I'm sure he'd take Shamara until you're ready.'

My heart felt lighter than it had done for months. It

seemed that suddenly I had a host of friends all willing to help me and although there was still the trauma facing me of telling Richard I was leaving him permanently, I had somewhere to go.

Lionel Prescott came to the house for dinner and I explained about the horse but not about my intention of leaving my husband. Susan and John left us alone to talk about the stabling, and meeting his questioning grey eyes I realized I would have to tell him something of the truth.

He listened quietly then surprised me by saying. 'You are thinking if you leave Richard now he will come to his senses and realize he must choose between you and his mother?'

'It's a ridiculous choice to ask him to make and I'm not even sure if he is capable of throwing off the fetters he has known all his life. I have been told that he cannot expect to live a long life, and I had so hoped to make what he had left happy and contented. None of it has been like that.'

'Will he do nothing to prevent your leaving him?'

'There is nothing he *can* do Lionel. He will not ask his mother to leave us in peace and I cannot live under the same roof as Lady Chalmers, so what else is there?'

'I don't know, Tessa. I have never been utterly and entirely possessed. I'll gladly take the horse until you are ready to receive him. How do you propose to get him here?'

'I have to telephone Flanagan tomorrow. He will know how much Hugh Mallory has offered for the horse and I propose to cap it.'

'Surely not in your name?'

'Of course not, I shall have to think up a fictitious one.'

'I will get my accountant to write to Richard. I could say I had heard he had a horse for sale and ask how much he would accept for him. I should think your husband would take the highest bid.'

I thanked him warmly, and for the first time in many months I slept long and dreamlessly in the pretty room that looked out across the moors surrounding the city.

Next lunchtime I telephoned Flanagan at the village inn but immediately I heard his voice I knew that all was not well.

384

'There's big trouble Milady, 'er ladyship's insistin' that the 'orse goes as soon as possible. It's me she's wantin' to get rid of an' Oi'm not one to stay where Oi'm not wanted.'

I explained rapidly about Sir Lionel's offer, and his voice brightening considerably he said, 'Oi can borrow old Jarvis's horse box, Milady, there'll be no problem about takin' the 'orse to Leeds.'

'Flanagan, if I can take Shamara with me would you be willing to work for me?'

There was a pause at the other end of the line and I waited breathlessly for his answer.

'Take 'im with you, Milady? Will you be leaving Easdale then?'

'Yes Flanagan, but that is between you and me of course.'

'Of course Milady. Where would you be goin'?'

'I've got a temporary place until I find something better. There are stables with a flat over, and there would be plenty of work for you. I believe it is a smallholding, chickens and a big garden.'

'Would you be there on your own, Milady?'

I laughed. 'Why no Flanagan, your reputation would be quite safe. There is a housekeeper and I shall be taking Annie with me, that is if she'd come of course.'

'Oh she'll come, no doubt about that, Milady, and so will Oi.'

'Oh Flanagan that's wonderful, now all that remains is for Sir Lionel to press home his offer. I will telephone you again tomorrow, I should have some news for you then.'

There were still many problems ahead, but my heart felt surprisingly lighter than it had for a long time, and more particularly when Sir Lionel came to tell us that Richard had accepted his offer for Shamara. I could well imagine Hugh Mallory's chagrin at the loss of the horse but Flanagan's delight was so obvious I laughed with him over the telephone.

I arranged that he should bring Shamara to Leeds the following day and I couldn't stifle my sharp elation that in this one instance I had beaten my mother-in-law at her own game.

Matters had moved so quickly over the last few days it seemed almost impossible to believe that Shamara was safely installed in Sir Lionel's stables and Annie and I were driving back to Easdale Hall. Flanagan had already given his notice.

It was one of those mellow golden days of early autumn when the sun hung low in a cloudless sky and the scent of woodsmoke drifted lazily across the fields. The birds were gathering before they swept away on their long journey to warmer lands and the hawthorn bushes were laden with red and shiny berries.

I was not looking forward to the task ahead of me but nor had I any regrets. I had tried and failed, and I could not think that Richard would grieve over my departure. His mother would feel only elation.

The house stood dark and forbidding as always, and I couldn't help wondering if it would have presented quite that aspect if my mother had had a hand in its image.

'Pack everything you wish to take away, Annie,' I cautioned her, 'and then go to my room, I shall want you to help me pack. There are some things I brought from Glamara that will want careful wrapping.'

I watched her hurry towards the servants' quarters then I squared my shoulders and went to Richard's room. I found him sitting in his chair looking out across the gardens to the woods beyond.

I had thought at first that he was asleep until I saw his hand wearily press his forehead as though he had a headache. At that moment I could have hurried towards him, to lay my cool hand on his throbbing head and place my cheek next to his, but I steeled myself to ignore his distress. At the slight noise made by the door closing he turned and saw me.

There was no smile of welcome as we stared into each other's eyes, then I took my seat across from him and it was there in the light I saw for the first time the wariness in his expression and the appeal I must ignore.

'How are you, Richard?' I asked gently.

'As you can see Tessa, much the same. Flanagan is not here any more. I have a male nurse, a very competent man who has worked in a hospital. He knows exactly how to handle me.'

'I'm glad.'

There was a long uncomfortable silence and then firmly, cruelly perhaps, I said, 'Richard, I cannot stay in this house any longer, I am leaving you.'

His face flushed angrily, and he snapped, 'I suppose you are going to Frobisher.'

'Of course not, how could I when he lives at the end of your garden?'

'Frobisher has gone, my mother dismissed him.'

'Richard, you are a fool. There was nothing between Alan Frobisher and me and it is disgraceful that you have allowed your mother to sack him. He was a good man, I only hope he gets something better soon and with people who are able to appreciate his worth.'

His face was flushed and hostile, and I could not tell if he believed that I did not know where Alan Frobisher had gone.

'I am leaving you because I can no longer bear your suspicions or your mother's interference. I shall remember that once we were close to each other, Richard, and I hope that your health will improve.'

'I have no intention of divorcing you, Tessa.'

'I have not asked for a divorce Richard, nor do I want anything from you.' I bent down and quickly brushed his cheek with my lips, then without a backward glance I left him.

Annie and I packed quickly and in silence, and then we carried the cases downstairs towards the door. It was Annie's little gasp that made me look round to find my mother-in-law standing stiffly in the centre of the hall.

'Hurry Annie, take these two cases to the car, I will bring the others,' I said urgently.

'You are going away again?' Lady Chalmers demanded sharply.

'I am going away for good,' I answered, and she was not quick enough to hide the sudden gleam of satisfaction that came into her eyes.

'I have told Richard that I am leaving him but I am not expecting him to divorce me. He does not seem unduly distressed and I am sure you are intensely gratified.'

'My son is too ill to concern himself with the trauma of divorce proceedings but I do not suppose it will prevent your finding some man to care for you. It was never any problem to your mother.'

No power on earth could have made me leave without making a retort capable of wiping that self-satisfied cynical smile off her thin lips. I looked at her levelly, then in a voice that was quiet with venomous anger I said, 'You have no idea how much I pity you. It must have been terrible to live with a man all those years and know that he loved another woman. I am not surprised that it has left you with so much bitterness. I hope you feel that you have got your revenge even when it has taken its toll on the life of your son.'

I left without looking at her again. I was shaking as I stepped behind the wheel and the scalding tears filled my eyes and rolled down my cheeks. It seemed to me at that moment that my life was over, I was twenty-five years old and felt I might just as well be dead.

CHAPTER TWENTY-EIGHT

It was raining on the day Annie and I arrived at the smallholding at the edge of the windswept Whitby moors, a chill misty rain that hid the view of the sea and turned the rain-washed countryside into a kaleidoscope of gentle colour.

As I drove into the yard behind the cottage the door opened and a plump rosy-cheeked woman bustled out, holding a raincoat over her head.

'My but yer've brought some rain wi' yer, ma'am,' she said, but her smile was warm and from inside the kitchen came the appetizing smell of cooking. Flanagan was the next to appear, a broad smile illuminating his face as he reached for the luggage.

'Well here we are Milady, settled in nice an' homely. It's a nasty day but tomorrer could be jest as different.'

'Did Shamara settle in well?'

'Roight as rain Milady, as if he'd bin 'ere all his life. Oi rode 'im across the fells this mornin', like a young 'un he went, lovin' every minute of it.'

'I'm glad. Are your quarters comfortable?'

'That they are. Very snug Oi am up there with mi own fireside an' a comfortable bedroom. Mi auld father'd say Oi'd fallen on mi feet an' no mistake.'

I laughed, suddenly feeling more carefree than I had felt in weeks.

'Yer'll 'ave somethin' ter eat afore yer unpacks, I 'ope,' Mrs Cross said, 'I've set the table in the livin' room, there's a good fire an' yer'll see 'ow cosy it is when the curtains are drawn shuttin' out the rain.'

'I suppose you have a lot of rain along this coast?' I asked her.

'Nay ma'am, we don't fare too badly fer rain, cold it is on this side o' the Pennines, it's wetter on't other side. Yer don't know this part o' Yorkshire I take it?'

'Not well at all.'

''Ow long are yer expectin' ter stay 'ere, ma'am?'

'Until I can find something suitable, I shall start looking immediately. I don't suppose you know of anything nearby?'

'There's nothin' nearby but if yer goes into Whitby one o' the estate agents might know o' somethin'.'

All the time we had been talking she had been bustling round in her kitchen, basting a joint of lamb and stirring something that smelled absolutely delicious.

Annie and I dined together in spite of her protestations that she would eat in the kitchen. The meal was excellent and the room was warm and comfortable in the glow from the fire and the lamps hidden beneath rosy shades.

The wind had got up and we could hear it moaning around the house, but I settled down to write to Aunt Hetty. I felt that at last she had a right to know something of my unhappiness during the last few months, and where I was hiding myself.

I sat staring into the fire, my pen idle in my hands. Over the rain I could hear a long mournful sound repeating itself as the minutes ticked away. I went into the kitchen to ask Mrs Cross what it was.

'Why ma'am that be the foghorn comin' fro' the cliffs. It'll be goin' all night an' until the mist clears, is it goin' to keep yer awake?'

'I doubt it, now that I know what it is.'

The kitchen was now clean and sparkling and Mrs Cross sat at the table with her knitting.

'Have you always lived in these parts?' I asked her.

'Mostly i' these parts. Wi 'ad a little cottage in't village an' mi 'usband worked at Moorcliff. Gardener 'ee were.'

Moorcliff! Where had I heard that name before? It eluded me and yet I was so sure I had heard it somewhere, but then Mrs Cross was saying, 'It's funny 'ow yer life changes, me an' Jack were right 'appy in our little cottage. It's a good job yer can't see into the future, I reckon.'

I smiled, bidding her goodnight and saying it had been a long day. There was a fire in my bedroom and I lay in bed listening to the rain and the sound of the foghorn, thinking about the gypsy who had once told my fortune and Laura's at the country fair. She had been uncannily right about a great many things.... I drifted gently into sleep, then suddenly came wide awake.

Moorcliff! I knew the name now. It was the name of Sir Julian's house and with my heart beating painfully against my ribs I asked myself savagely if I hadn't left one trauma behind only to be faced with another I had not bargained for.

My sleep had been plagued by dreams, only Moorcliff became Glamara and as I ran down the long drive with my hands outstretched, looking for Julian, the house changed yet again and became Easdale Hall with dark shrouded windows and the aura of death all around me.

I lay for a few moments in that half state between waking and sleeping, then curiosity overcame me with an urgent desire to look out of my window at what lay beyond.

It was one of those soft autumn mornings which often follow a period of rain. The sun touched on dry, golden-coloured leaves clinging tenaciously to trees and shrubs which leaned away from the sea as though it was their enemy and the moorland their friend. The house was set back from the road, connected to it by a narrow lane, and the road wound towards the cliff edge.

The morning sun sparkling on the waves turned them into shifting patterns of silver. I looked in vain for signs of another dwelling. The cottage was built on a mound so that the views were magnificent, but the lie of the cliffs was so tortuous that other houses could easily be nestled in bays and inlets hidden from us.

I was about to turn away when below me the door opened and Annie ran out into the garden. It was only seven o'clock by my watch but there was Annie doing a little dance like some Grecian nymph, her rusty-coloured hair flaming in the wind, possessed of an unexpected grace and that strange elusive beauty I sometimes surprised in her.

I did not want her to see me watching her but my heart lifted. There was so much joy in her, so much elation that at long last she was looking at the sea, that I felt at least some good had come from the troubled pattern of my life.

There was no sign of her exhilaration when she served my breakfast a little later. Her unruly hair was once more confined and she wore a clean white apron over her plain black dress.

'Are you going to eat breakfast with me?' I asked her.

'No Miss Tessa, I 'ad it in the kitchen wi' Mrs Cross. I don't want to be treated any different than 'er, I'm yer servant Miss Tessa, not yer friend.'

'But you *are* my friend Annie, my very good friend.'

'That I am ma'am, but I'm not yer friend like Miss Susan, an' if yer don't mind I'd like the difference to be made plain.'

'Very well Annie, you are my servant and my friend if that is how you want it.'

'I do Miss Tessa, I really do.'

'Have you seen the sea?'

'Oh yes, lovely it is. I wants to see it when it's rough like

391

that little picture you bought me.'

'The sea can be very cruel Annie, it can take lives. I like it as it is today, gentle and benign and blue.'

'It's like life, isn't it Miss Tessa? Sometimes it can be real cruel, then just when yer think it's all 'opeless it's calm like the sea.'

I stared at her for a moment, thinking again how astute she could be. There was so much more to Annie than the quaint awkward exterior most people saw, something as elusive and fleeting as her rare moments of beauty.

'I am going into Whitby this morning Annie. You should come too, if you are to know your way around these parts. I am going to the estate agents, we shall have to find somewhere to live before the Latchfords need this house again.'

'Yer really want's to live i' these parts then?'

'I don't know. Perhaps we should get right away from Yorkshire, after all there are other beautiful places with a warmer climate.'

Her face was doubtful and with some asperity I said, 'Did you never learn that poem at school Annie, "What do they know of England who only England know"? Well it's the same with Yorkshire. We only know Yorkshire, perhaps we would appreciate it more if we got to know some other part of England.'

She picked up her tray with a little shake of her head and retreated to the kitchen, and I was sorry for my outburst, unable to analyse the reason for it.

She sat beside me in the car, grimly correct in her shapeless black coat and her black felt hat pulled down firmly over her hair, the epitome of servile competence, and I felt faintly aggravated at her insistence in keeping herself firmly behind that narrow line that separated class from class. So extraordinarily English and so instilled into every one of us.

She did unbend a little as we drove along the cliff top where we could see the lie of the road twisting and bending until we came at last to the ruined abbey on the hillside overlooking the little town and the sea.

I was given a list of likely properties as far up as Redcar in the north and Filey in the south, and during the following days I looked at several, choosing them always south of Whitby as though afraid to venture further north. When I rode Shamara we confined our rides to the moors and the coast line south. It was as though I dare not risk looking at Moorcliff in case I aroused all the old longings that had tormented me since the first day I saw Julian.

Strangely enough it was Annie who first saw the house.

I was tired, I seemed to have tramped miles through rooms, upstairs and downstairs in innumerable houses but finding nothing I couldn't live without. I sat in front of a blazing fire leafing through the lists, feeling unusually lethargic and wishing I had someone I could discuss things with.

When Annie brought my coffee I asked her to sit down opposite me, and when she remained standing I very crossly snapped, 'For heaven's sake Annie do sit down, you make me feel nervous hovering like an avenging angel. Let me tell you what I have seen.'

She duly sat down on the edge of a chair, and ignoring her uncomfortable posture I ran through the prospects. 'I'm fed up with looking at houses,' I said firmly, 'I suppose one or two of these would be suitable with my own furniture and ornaments around me, but I'm not at all sure.'

'They're all south of 'ere though, why don't yer look north Miss Tessa?'

'What do you know about the north Annie?'

'Well ma'am, I does a lot o' walkin' an' I gets the bus that goes all along the coast, then I gets off when I 'as a mind to and walks back. It's lovely, so wild and beautiful an' I thinks I've found one o' them little harbours like that in mi picture, an' there's a big 'ouse just like one o' them castles in a fairy story. I went right up to the gates one day just to take a peep inside. Mrs Cross says 'er 'usband used to do a bit o' gardenin' there only the garden's all rocks wi' just heather an' thrift 'atween 'em.'

'The house is called Moorcliff.'

'Moorcliff, that's right Miss Tessa. Mrs Cross said it were an old derelict castle till the gentleman as bought it started puttin' it to rights. There were a lady sittin' in the garden when I looked through the gates. It were warm in the sun an' the 'ouse is right on the cliff top.'

'I can see it's caught your imagination, Annie.'

'Yes, it's beautiful, just like Glamara's beautiful. I never thowt much of Easdale Hall.'

'I could have made it beautiful Annie, I just wasn't given the chance.'

'No Miss Tessa, a could see that fer miself. Why don't yer ride Shamara to the top o' the fell, yer can see the 'ouse fro' there. I'd like yer to see it, Miss Tessa.'

'I might do that tomorrow, Annie.'

I sat daydreaming after she had left me, thinking about the house which Julian had so lovingly restored, and the lady who sat in the garden looking out over the sea. Did Carmelita love it too? I wondered, or did she hate the chill winds that swept in from the sea and hunger longingly for the sunshine of distant Spain or France?

Next morning I rode Shamara across the long low moor that swept northward, with the sea ever shimmering in the east, and it was only when we reached the edge of the cove that I paused to look across the cliff top to where Moorcliff stood indomitable and enchanting on the point.

The windows caught the gleam of sunlight so that for a moment it seemed that the rooms behind them were on fire, and the ancient stone was warm and rosy in the morning light. There was a symmetry about the turrets and bastions which spoke to me of sterner days when the castle had withstood the tumult of ancient wars, but there was enchantment in the way it blended with the rocky coast and the wild sweep of moorland.

As I rode back along the cliff top I began to imagine what life might be like in that house with Julian, and unbidden the tears rose into my eyes so that impatiently I brushed them away, urging Shamara forward, diminishing my heartache in the speed of his flying hooves.

That night I made a decision I would look no more at properties in the North Riding of Yorkshire, instead I would think about Cumberland and the haunting beauty of the

lakes, or better still Warwickshire in whose gentle countryside memories would cease to plague me and old desires
would die a natural death.

The morning was clear and fine and gave little inkling that
by noon the mist would have descended upon the moors so
densely that I would find myself hopelessly lost. I had no
excuse, I should have known how treacherous the moors
could be, how suddenly the mist could obliterate landmarks,
bringing with it icy moisture that clung to one's clothing and
skin, chilling to the marrow.

I had been so wrapped up in my immediate problems I
had failed to see the ominous signs. It came down so quickly
that I sat motionless on Shamara's back, my heart filled with
dismay, and I knew that we dare not move from the path for
fear of becoming hopelessly lost, or even caught in some
morass from which we would be lucky to escape.

I dismounted offering words of comfort to Shamara,
feeling him shivering against me, both of us wallowing in
misery.

I had no means of knowing where the coast lay, or indeed
how far we had ridden because my thoughts had been on
other things. There was nothing for it but to remain exactly
where we were until the mist lifted and I hoped and prayed
this would be before darkness. I had known the mist linger
on for days around Glamara, I could only hope that here so
close to the sea it would soon disperse.

The time seemed to pass so slowly. I sat on a rock beside
the path while Shamara champed the harsh moorland grass
which I felt convinced would hurt his mouth and provide
little nourishment.

Darkness came and I went to stand close to the horse so
that we could each derive a little warmth from the other. It
seemed to me that the horse and rider came suddenly out of
nowhere until they were almost on top of us, and the horse
was wheeled so sharply that he reared up on his haunches
with a shrill whinny of protest. Then the rider said angrily,
'What the hell are you doing out here on a day like this, who
are you?'

A torch was shone into my face and I covered my eyes,

blinking in its bright light, then I heard the laughter in the voice that I recognized. 'I meet you in the lounge of the Dorchester without a bed for the night, and now here you are lost in the middle of nowhere. What shall I do with you?'

I was angry that it was Julian who had found us but my heart was hammering so hard I had no words to answer him with, and getting down from his horse he said, 'I suppose you are chilled to the bone. How long have you been out here?'

Finding my voice at last I stammered, 'Since this morning, there was no mist then.'

'Gracious me, girl, you should know about moors, you saw the signs. Why didn't you get back to where you had come from?'

'It was too late, the mist came down before I realized it and I didn't want to take the wrong direction. What are *you* doing out in it?'

'I'm going home. I know these moors like the back of my hand and I can rely on my horse. Here, get up on your horse and I'll take your bridle. Where are you going?'

'I'm at the smallholding called Rowans, do you know it?'

'Yes, I didn't know there was anybody there except Mrs Cross.'

'The house is owned by Mr Latchford and the Latchfords are friends of mine.'

'I see. And are you there on your own?'

'No I have Annie my maid with me, and Flanagan who cares for the horse. There's Mrs Cross too, of course.'

'Your husband is not with you?'

'No.'

'Whatever brings you to the north-east coast so late in the year? You would have found it far prettier in the summertime and a good deal less treacherous. I think perhaps I should take you straight to Moorcliff, you can telephone Mrs Cross from there.'

'I would really much rather go straight home if you don't mind, I can find my own way from Moorcliff along the top of the cliff.'

'With your penchant for doing the unexpected you would probably end up by falling over the cliff. And since you know

Moorcliff is my house, why haven't you been to see me?'

'I haven't been here very long and I've been busy since I arrived.'

'Busy?'

'Yes, seeing estate agents. Rowans is only on loan to me, I need to find somewhere to live.'

'I see, or rather I don't see. I heard your husband was an invalid, does this mean that he has since died?'

'No, I have left him.'

There was silence and I ached for him to ask me why, for what sort of a woman would leave an invalid husband? He was silent however and after a bit he started to ask about Aunt Hetty and Godfrey. I was surprised that he did not mention Roxanne.

'I suppose you know Robert is in South Africa?' I asked him.

'Yes, I hear from him occasionally, doing very well too from his letters.'

There were lights now through the gloom and I recognized them as the lights along the road. Here near the coast the mist was not so thick and we were able to gallop the few miles side by side.

Even in this half light I was aware of his superb grace. He rode as though he and the horse were one, his dark clear-cut profile complementing the big black horse. The old magic was with me still and I wondered why it should be that this man I had known so long but knew so little kept me chained to him by bonds as light as silk yet as inflexible as steel.

There was consternation at the Rowans. Annie was in tears while Flanagan and Mrs Cross stood in the gardens looking towards the cliffs, with the lights from the house streaming out behind them. Annie came running towards us, stumbling over the uneven ground, the tears streaming down her face while she cried, 'Oh Miss Tessa, we've bin that worried, wherever 'ave yer bin?'

'I'm quite safe Annie, Sir Julian found me and brought me back.'

Annie treated us to one of her quaint curtseys and Flanagan took hold of the bridle, looking a shade more interested in the welfare of the horse than my own.

Julian refused to take some refreshment.

'I must get back to the house, they will be concerned if I do not arrive home soon.'

'Of course sir,' she said, 'Lady Chalmers will want a hot bath and a good hot meal I'm sure, Annie and I'll go and attend to it.'

They left us together. His grey eyes were amused as they looked down into mine and I was very aware of the unfortunate picture I presented with my damp hair and the wet riding habit that clung to my skin uncomfortably.

His eyes were sombre and no longer amused and I could feel the warm blood suffusing my cheeks until I inwardly squirmed with impatience at my powerlessness to appear before this man wearing the veneer of sophistication I had acquired over the years. With Julian I was still the young Tessa who had accepted his praise of her horsemanship with all the delight of a puppy anxious to please.

I had been engaged to one man and married to another and yet I could not look at Julian without the insidious ache in my heart and the mad desire to throw myself into his arms and tell him with all a young girl's insecurity that I loved him, that as long as I lived I would never love anybody else.

He dismounted and took my hand. 'I hope you will be able to dine with us one evening Tessa, I will telephone you.'

It was the 'us' that brought sanity back and I heard my voice saying coolly, 'Thank you Sir Julian, that would be very pleasant.'

'Why are we so formal?' he said with that maddening half smile. 'Once upon a time you called me simply Julian.'

'I can't remember, would you prefer it?'

'Of course, otherwise I shall call you Lady Chalmers. I shall take pleasure in dining with Tessa as an old friend. I doubt if I would derive the same pleasure from dining with Lady Chalmers who is a complete stranger.'

'Then I shall certainly call you Julian. Thank you for coming to my assistance today, I shall be careful to watch for signs of mist when I ride on the moors again. Goodnight.'

I watched him ride into the gloom, only turning away

when horse and rider were shrouded in the floating mist. As I walked back to the house I made a solemn vow that I would find a house miles away from Moorcliff, and quickly so that I would have a good excuse not to accept his invitation to dine.

I waited impatiently for replies to letters I had sent to estate agents in Penrith and Warwick, and meantime confined my rides on Shamara to the cliff tops near Whitby, but I listened to Mrs Cross's talk of Julian.

'I think 'ee's only 'alf English ma'am, half Spanish or Italian he is, but I'm not sure which. 'Ee's very 'andsome, I'll not deny that.'

'I believe his mother was Spanish.'

'Is that so. Funny yer should 'a known 'im afore yer came 'ere.'

'Yes, his ward was at school with my cousin. They visited my uncle's home quite often at one time.'

'Miss Roxanne were a right little madam, pretty as a picture an' wi' all the confidence in the world. 'Ee used to take 'er abroad, but when she were 'ere they used to ride along the cliff top, natural like. I loved watchin' 'em. Just the way you ride ma'am, as though yer've allus bin used to 'orses.'

This I felt was praise indeed and I rewarded Mrs Cross with a warm smile and a comment I was ashamed to put but couldn't help.

'It is a very large house for Sir Julian to be living in alone.'

'That it is, an' Miss Roxanne doesn't seem ter come 'ere these days, an' Sir Julian doesn't travel abroad like 'ee once did.'

'Is he alone there now?'

'Well there's some as sez 'ee is an' others as sez 'ee isn't. I believe there 'as bin a lady stayin' at Moorcliff but I don't know if she's still there.'

A whole week passed and Julian didn't telephone and I began to think that he had changed his mind, or perhaps Carmelita wanted no intrusion into their private happiness. I had begun to convince myself that this was indeed the case when he telephoned one afternoon while I was out.

Mrs Cross gave me the message as soon as I returned. 'I

didn't rightly know what to say ma'am, so he's pickin' yer up at seven-thirty.'

By half past five I had begun to panic. I needed to have my hair done but there wasn't a hairdresser within miles and I hadn't looked at my dinner dresses since I arrived, indeed they were pushed to the back of the wardrobe behind tweed skirts and woollen sweaters.

It was Annie who shampooed my hair, coping with its fine silken fairness and twisting and teasing it into a style a fashionable hairdresser would not have been ashamed of.

'Annie you've done wonders with it,' I exclaimed delightedly, 'where did you learn to manage hair like this?'

'I told yer Miss Tessa, I used ter watch Miss Laura's maid an' Lady Abigail's. I've allus bin good with 'air. 'Ave yer decided which dress ter wear?'

'No, either the jade or the black, I think. Black suits me.'

'Black yer can wear fer a funeral an' it's not a funeral yer's goin' to. I allus liked that bright blue dress.'

'Don't you think it's a little bit too bright for a small dinner party?'

'No, not many folk can wear that blue, but it brings out all the colour in yer eyes. Wear that one Miss Tessa, ter please me.'

So I wore the blue, deceptively simple in heavy georgette, fitting my slender figure with exquisite grace, my only ornament the two strands of pearls Richard had given me as an engagement present.

'Perhaps I shouldn't wear these,' I said to Annie unhappily, 'I have other necklaces.'

'Why shouldn't yer wear 'em? They were given ter yer afore it all went sour, Miss Tessa.'

'They've lost none of their lustre. I once read that pearls could lose their lustre if they were worn by some people.'

'Like that poor man's mother fer instance, she'd 'a turned the milk sour an' no mistake.'

I laughed, feeling a little light-headed suddenly when I thought of the evening in front of me and my meeting with the woman Julian loved.

A final look in the mirror told me that perhaps Annie was

right about the dinner gown, it did light up my face and complemented my fair hair and grey-blue eyes.

Julian came promptly at seven-thirty and as I sat beside him in the big car the road opened up before us like a ribbon of silver with the full moon gleaming on the water and Moorcliff rising on the point like some fairy castle. The setting was romantic and I was very aware of his slender hands on the wheel and his nearness.

There were lights in the downstairs rooms and one upstairs, and I wondered if that room upstairs belonged to Carmelita and what she would be wearing for dinner. I imagined her as some fairy-tale dancer, as ethereal and enchanting as Roxanne had described her, the sort of woman a man would love desperately, bewitched by a charm that was alien and different. A woman who could float round the rooms of Moorcliff on angel feet, delicately poised and with a body as enchantingly graceful as a swan's.

All these things I was thinking as Julian led me through a courtyard I viewed with awed admiration. It was tiled in colours as charming and subtle as those in an old master and a short staircase ascended from it to a little balcony and a doorway which led under an arch into the house. The balustrade was of exquisitely sculptured iron and in the middle of the courtyard a fountain played. It was a tiny bit of old Spain set in the midst of the wild moors of Yorkshire and I exclaimed with delighted surprise at its originality.

'It was the Spanish coming out in me,' Julian said, smiling and pleased with my appreciation. 'Sometimes it does in quite unusual ways. I saw the possibilities here and so an ancient Spanish courtyard became a feature. I am glad that you like it.'

Indeed the hall too seemed to have captured all Julian's memories of a youth spent in his grandfather's house near Seville. Spanish banners were hung above the gallery that ran round it and in the alcoves were suits of old Spanish armour while beautiful rugs gave colour to the dark floor. The chandeliers too were in intricately wrought Toledo steel and on the walls were old weapons.

Julian indicated a large portrait and I was struck by its

401

beauty and how perfectly it blended with the rest of the decor. It was the portrait of a lovely woman: dark, with a pale oval face framed by a black lace mantilla over a jewelled comb.

'She's beautiful,' I murmured.

'My mother. My grandfather had that portrait painted the year of her marriage. I have only just acquired it, until now it was on the wall of his house near Seville.'

'It is right in this setting.'

'Yes, I believe it is.'

The dark eyes in the portrait looked down into mine. She had the same exotic beauty as Roxanne without her restlessness and her eyes were brown, not jade. I was reluctant to move on. I took pleasure in looking for Julian's face in the beautiful face of his mother, but the likeness was elusive and Julian's blue-grey eyes were entirely English.

Lightly he touched my hair and smiled, his dark sweet smile. 'I was thinking how different you are Tessa, both so beautiful, and yet that silver-fair hair and those English eyes might look incongruous in a hall devoted to my memories of Spain.'

I was glad of the subdued lighting which hid my blushing face, and taking my elbow lightly he indicated that we should move on. I was surprised by the drawing room for it seemed that in just a few seconds we had moved from Spain into the delicate charm of an English home. It could well have been one of the rooms at Glamara with its delicate chintzes and watercolours. I felt at home in it, it was the sort of room I had known for most of my life and at that moment I believed it represented the side of Julian I knew best, instead of that other dark alien Julian whom Roxanne and Carmelita would know.

While he poured sherry I studied the room closely. It echoed his good taste in porcelain and furniture. There were photographs on the china cabinet and I longed to look at them but I stayed where I was in case he might think me too curious.

'This reminds me of the drawing room at Glamara,' I said.

'I thought you might think so. Whenever I visited

402

Glamara I used to wish the house was mine. I had never thought I might settle down in Yorkshire, I had a house in Richmond in those days, but somehow I began to see Yorkshire as the only place where I wanted to live permanently. I loved its great open spaces and the beauty of the dales and I started to look for a suitable house. This place was really almost a ruin but on closer inspection I began to see its possibilities. There were times when I thought I had taken on too much. Time dragged and there were constant interruptions caused by bad weather and winter storms but at last it took shape, and I have been happy with the results. I have shipping interests in Hull so it is not too remote, yet remote enough to distance me from the world's hurly-burly.'

'I know exactly what you mean. I am happier in the city these days than I ever was before but I am always glad to return to the peace of the countryside. I suppose I am a country girl at heart.'

He smiled, then consulted his watch. 'I told them we would dine at eight-thirty Tessa, I hope you have a good appetite.'

'Are we dining alone?'

'No. I have a guest. I think you will like Carmelita, she is a charming woman.'

My heart sank rapidly, but I made myself press on. 'Has she been staying with you long?'

'Since just before the war started. I was lucky to get her out of France when I did, if I had left it another month it would have been impossible.'

'Yes of course.'

'Ah, here she is,' he said as the door opened, then he rose quickly and went to meet her.

I was totally unprepared for the woman he brought forward to meet me for she was nothing at all like the Carmelita of my imagination. She was small and silver haired, with a calm beautiful face and her proportions were slight and graceful although she leaned heavily on two sticks.

Julian said, 'Tessa, this is Carmelita Alvariz, I have told her a great deal about you.'

She took the seat next to me and extended a slender almost

transparent hand which I took in mine. I felt strangely confused. This woman was nothing at all like the picture Roxanne had painted of her, for one thing she must be several years older than Julian, and Roxanne had led me to believe that she was a gay gypsy creature who had danced into his life and kept him chained where no other woman could ever find an entry.

She was charming, speaking with a slight foreign inflection that was very attractive. 'Julian tells me you are staying near here, Lady Chalmers, does that mean that you are thinking of settling in this part of Yorkshire permanently?'

'I am looking at properties here and elsewhere. Would you please call me Tessa?'

She smiled. 'But of course, I should like that and you must call me Carmelita. I shall miss Yorkshire when I return to France, but I must see if my house is still there and I fear I have already overstayed my welcome.'

'You are returning to France?' I asked aware of the surprise in my voice.

'Yes of course. I have no excuse to remain here any longer now that the war has been over almost a year. I hope to find things unchanged but one cannot be sure.'

My confusion placed me at a great disadvantage and as Carmelita and Julian chatted normally together I stayed silent in an endeavour to collect my scattered thoughts. A butler came to announce that dinner was served and we made our way slowly into a darkly panelled dining room where the table sparkled with glass and silver and a large bowl of crimson roses.

I know that the meal was beautifully cooked and served, but I was so confused by my thoughts that half the meal was over and I could not have said what we had eaten. Gradually I relaxed but there were times when Julian looked at me curiously and I felt sure he had observed my preoccupation. I hoped he did not think I was ungracious or unappreciative of his efforts to entertain me.

We took our coffee in the drawing room and later Carmelita asked him to play the piano for us.

'Julian plays so beautifully, I shall miss his music when I

return home,' she said, smiling at me gently. 'Are you musical Tessa?'

'I'm afraid not, but I love it. I only wish I *could* play something.'

'I too am no performer, but there is music in my soul.'

He played for over an hour, and I ached with loving him as his slender fingers roamed across the keys and the lamplight fell in his dark shining hair, throwing into sharp relief the severity of his profile, a severity that could so instantly be relieved by the amazing sweetness of his smile.

At just after eleven o'clock there was a slight tap on the door and a dark slender girl entered, going immediately to Carmelita who smiled at her with something like relief, and I noticed that she seemed tired. Her face had become pale and she leaned heavily on the girl's arm as she rose.

'This is Inez my maid and companion,' she said, smiling at me. 'She knows it is past my bedtime. I hope you will excuse me Tessa.'

'Yes of course Carmelita, you should have said if you were tired.'

'It is the flesh that is weak, my dear. I love hearing Julian play and yet I am aware of my limitations.'

She held up her face so that Julian could kiss her cheek. 'I think I shall rest tomorrow Julian, you will understand?'

'Of course my dear, I shall be away until the evening anyway.'

We watched her making her painful way towards the door, pausing occasionally before she felt able to move on, the girl walking beside her solicitously.

Julian replenished my glass then took the chair opposite mine, looking at me keenly over the rim of his glass. 'Why were you so surprised by Carmelita, Tessa? She was evidently not what you expected.'

'I had heard she had been injured in a road accident, but I did not know how badly.'

'But that was not all?'

'No. I thought she would be younger, a great deal younger.'

'You mean you were led to believe she was younger, young

405

and beautiful and astonishingly graceful as a dancer should be.'

'Well yes...' I said unhappily.

'And that I was desperately in love with her and she with me.'

'Something like that,' I murmured miserably.

He was watching me with a frown, his eyes narrowed and gleaming, and I did not know if he was angry with me or with the stories I had listened to.

'And what other incredible tale did my ward conjure up to assure you of my commitment to Carmelita?'

'She said you were driving the car that crashed, injuring Carmelita. Julian, how much of it is true?'

'Hardly any of it, my dear. It is strange how one can stay on a course almost parallel with the truth and yet remain so totally at variance with it. When I was six years old Carmelita was sixteen. Her father was one of the stewards on my grandfather's ranch and she used to come up to the big house with her mother who worked there as a maid. My grandfather wanted me to breed bulls while I wanted to be a musician, her father wanted her to marry her cousin who owned a café in Seville and she wanted to be a dancer. Carmelita and I had a lot to say to each other in those days.

'When the gypsies came to Seville to dance in the streets on the day of the big bull fights Carmelita ran away to join them. I didn't see her for years, but when at last I did go back to Spain for a holiday at my grandfather's home she had been taken up by an impresario and had become famous. She danced in all the best nightclubs and theatres, her picture was pasted alongside those of the heroes of the bull ring.'

'And then you fell in love with her?' I prompted.

'How obsessed you are by the idea of love, Tessa. No, I did not fall in love with her, by that time I knew that my future would be here in this country and she was married to a Spanish nobleman who treated her cruelly and who was driving the car in which she was injured. He was drunk, he was also killed in the crash.'

'But...'

'But what Tessa?'

'Why should Roxanne lie about it, why did she lie to me?'

His eyes were filled with a strange amusement, then in a voice that was almost weary he said, 'It was hard to be the guardian of a girl who considered herself to be in love with me and with a singleness of purpose that defied description.

'I thought Roxanne would grow out of it, I knew that girls often got fixations about older men they believed they were in love with and for years Roxanne had tried to make me jealous, with her teachers, her music master, her tennis coach, then I began to see her in a new light as she grew older. There was a terrifying determination about her, a power to destroy not only herself but other people also. I distanced myself from her as often as was possible but she had been placed in my care and it wasn't always easy. She was only a schoolgirl when I saw the willpower behind the naïvety, the malevolence behind the sweetness, the unlovely behind that all-too-perfect face.'

'But why did Roxanne lie to me, why did she always seem to want to hurt me?'

He looked at me curiously, his eyes sombre, then in a voice deceptively light he said, 'I often asked myself that question, when she married that boy Alec and later when she married Godfrey Chalfont and became the mistress of Glamara. Had Roxanne seen something I had failed to see, did she know me better than I knew myself?'

'I don't understand.'

'And yet it is not so difficult Tessa. Until you suddenly decided to marry that boy who was so easily stolen by Roxanne you were available and I found you more than a little appealing.'

'I didn't know, how could I?'

'I wonder if there will ever be a time when I find you heart-whole and unhampered by men who want to marry you or others you feel you must marry in order to comfort their remaining years.'

'Why are you laughing at me?' I demanded, stung by the amusement in his eyes and the laughter in his voice.

'Am I laughing at you Tessa? I shouldn't be, I should be justifiably angry with you.'

'Angry?'

'Yes. Why did you marry that boy who can never be a proper husband to you, to bury yourself in that mausoleum with a mother who resented you from the outset, why did you ever listen to Roxanne?'

I stared at him helplessly, confused and bemused by the turn our conversation had taken and in a small voice I asked, 'How do you know so much about me and my marriage?'

'Your aunt told me and Roxanne told me her garbled version of the event.' His smile was bleak as he said, 'I suppose Roxanne told you that I was accustomed to girls falling in love with me, accustomed and amused by it.'

I nodded helplessly.

'I thought as much,' he said. 'Roxanne liked to picture me as a gay Lothario who went about breaking hearts because in her foolishness she believed I had broken hers. My dear Tessa I would have been terrified of the passions in Roxanne's heart, they are destructive and punishing, there was never any danger that I would respond to them.'

The amusement had left his face and we stared at each other for a moment unsure and waiting, then lightly and to my utmost consternation he said, 'Come with me, Tessa, and I will show you over the house.'

I followed him willingly enough, but I couldn't understand why one moment we were discussing emotions dangerously intimate and the next we were walking round the rooms of Moorcliff looking at pictures and the restoration of rooms that had once lain in ruins.

We climbed up the stone steps in an old tower and from the top we could look out across the sea and listen to its roar as it fell in great crashing waves on the rocks below.

'It's beautiful,' I murmured, 'but it's frightening too.'

'Yes, but tonight you are seeing it in one of its more benign moods. There are times when it is terrifying, when the entire house is filled with the sound of its anger.'

'I think I might be afraid at such moments.'

'But not if you were not alone.'

'No, perhaps not. Julian, who was that woman I saw in the Dorchester. It wasn't Carmelita?'

For a moment he stared at me uncomprehending, then he smiled, his eyes filled with amusement. 'My dear, if you hadn't been in such a hurry to rush from the room causing that poor waiter to drop his tray you would perhaps have seen that there were three of us. I was with a brother officer and his wife.'

I could feel the warm red blood suffusing my face and throat but when our eyes met I surprised, after the amusement passed, a strange intensity in his gaze.

He took my arm lightly as we walked down the shallow uneven steps, and in a conversational voice he said, 'Next week I am taking Carmelita home to France, I am not sure how long I shall be away.'

'Perhaps by the time you return I shall have found somewhere permanent to live.'

We did not speak again until we reached the warmth of the drawing room where he added logs to the already glowing grate, then for a few moments he stood looking down into the flames which danced and teased his profile into sharp relief and I stared at him fiercely as though I would instil the memory of him into my heart for all eternity.

Quite suddenly, as though he had made up his mind about something he had been thinking of all evening, he said, 'Why don't you come to France with me, Tessa? We could see Carmelita installed in her home and then we could go on to Spain. I don't suppose you have ever seen the grapes ripening on the vines or the dry plains shimmering under the heat of the sun with the snow-capped Sierras in the distance.'

I stared at him in disbelief, but to follow up his words he said, 'You have no idea how bitter the winters can be along this coast.'

'You don't mean it,' I blurted out, watching his face for the return of amusement.

'When you know me better Tessa you will know that I rarely say things I don't mean.'

'But Julian I am married, people will talk, they will say horrible things about us, you can't want that to happen.'

'My dear Tessa I don't give a damn what people say and you shouldn't either. I know that you are married, a few words mumbled over a prayer book. That doesn't make a marriage, a marriage is what comes after, the caring and the loving. Surely you don't feel married.'

'No, no I don't. Oh Julian, I want to come so much but I'm afraid.' We stared at each other for a long moment, unsure and waiting, then with a little cry I ran towards him and threw myself into his arms.

I had never been kissed until Julian kissed me, never felt such sweet joy as the passion he aroused in me or known that hands could be so gentle and fulfilment so complete.

It would have been the same wherever it happened, in the heather where the fells sloped down to the sea, or the caves, shining and wet beneath the cliffs, but it happened before a fire blazing in the hearth of a formal drawing room and the joy was the same. I only knew that at last I was a woman with the man I loved held in my arms, his skin warm and moist against mine, his eyes dark with passion as our bodies moved rhythmically towards their climax. When it came I buried my head in his shoulder, my entire being burning with the power of giving, the unbridled elation that at last the man I had loved for so long lay in my arms, a willing partner in the passion we had shared.

As I lay quietly in his arms watching the play of firelight on the ceiling it seemed that we existed alone in a world devoid of every living thing and it was only later as I sat before the mirror in my bedroom at the Rowans that sanity suddenly made me see how impossible it all was.

I looked at my hair hanging in great waves around my shoulders and I shivered in the chill room, pulling the robe closer round my shoulders. 'Come with me to France,' he had said, but how could I escape so lightly from the conventions we had sworn our lives to? As I paced my lonely floor I thought of Richard, and of how eagerly his mother would embrace my infidelity. I thought about Aunt Hetty and Susan, and then I thought about Annie. What would I tell Annie with her upright moral little soul, so dedicated to what was right and what was wrong?

I didn't sleep. Before it was properly light I was walking backwards and forwards on the cliff top, my heart longing for

Julian, my sanity telling me that even to think we could be together was living in a fool's paradise.

Annie came out to feed the seagulls and seeing me pacing alone on the cliff top she ran to my side. 'Lord Miss Tessa, but yer did give me a fright, what are yer doin' out 'ere afore it's properly light?'

I suddenly found myself shivering, and with consternation in her eyes she said, 'Come inside Miss Tessa, yer as cold as ice.'

Was there accusation in her voice? I allowed her to pull me towards the house and I watched dully as she laid a match to the fire in the tiny sitting room while she bustled about setting the breakfast table.

Now and again I felt her eyes upon me but my misery was too complete to care. I wanted to be with Julian more than I had ever wanted anything in my entire life, but how was it going to be possible? Even as she placed a steaming cup of coffee before me she said accusingly, 'Yer were late 'ome Miss Tessa, I waited up fer yer till long after twelve, an' I didn't sleep a wink until I 'eard Sir Julian's car outside the 'ouse. What time was it Miss Tessa?'

'I don't know Annie, it was probably late.'

'Did yer enjoy yer evenin' then?'

'Yes thank you Annie.'

Her eyes constantly rested on me, and in some aggravation I said, 'I don't want anything to eat Annie.'

I felt instantly contrite when I saw her pained expression. 'I'm going upstairs Annie, perhaps I'll ride this morning before it starts to rain.'

'Yer shouldn't Miss Tessa, it's that cold an' the rain looks like it'll come any minute. Flanagan'll exercise the 'orse.'

'I'll ride him myself Annie, I need to go somewhere to think and I can't think in this house with you constantly telling me I can't do this or that.'

I felt wretched. I didn't want to hurt Annie but apart from my memory of love I was beginning to realize that nothing was solved.

It was cold and fresh on the moors but by urging Shamara on to a gallop across the short grass I felt my body growing

411

warmer and my spirits rose. It was only when we reached the summit of the fell and I could look down at the tall chimneys of Moorcliff that they plummeted again into the depths of despair.

Suppose I went with Julian to France, what prejudice would I face when I returned? In the society in which we lived men were strangely immune from the consequences of transgression, and I was after all a married woman who had deserted an invalid husband.

Julian was a bachelor, a wealthy handsome bachelor who would hurt no one by loving me, while I would be classed as the scarlet woman following in the footsteps of a mother whose reputation had not been entirely blameless. Oh I could see the expressions on the faces of those self-righteous matrons as they discussed us over their tea cups and the whispered accusations at hunt balls and race meetings. I must have been mad ever to say I would go with him to France, and yet my willing treacherous body longed for him as it would go on longing for him across the years.

I felt the first spots of rain against my cheeks, and saw the grey breakers dashing on the rocks below and the dark circling clouds lowering on the purple moors. Then I heard the sound of another rider approaching and saw Julian urging his big black horse towards me.

He stared at me with sombre eyes, then dismounting he came to my side, helping me down until I stood within the shelter of his arms.

'I should have kept you with me,' he said, 'I should have known how you would torture yourself when you had time to think.'

With the tears streaming down I sobbed out my fears. 'Oh Julian they would torture us, crucify us with their accusations, I can't come with you, it's impossible.'

He held me tenderly, whispering words of love, kissing my eyes and my mouth, and I clung to him helplessly. 'Tessa, do you care more about what people say about us than you care for me?'

I stared at him, the denial sharp on my lips, then he stifled my words of protest with his kiss, and when he released me he said firmly, 'You will come with me to France, Tessa, and when we return you will live with me at Moorcliff. I love you, I want you for my wife but it isn't possible yet. Whenever it is, those people who had the most to say will be the first to forget. Now return to the house and get out of those wet clothes, I don't want an invalid on my hands when we drive into the sunshine.'

I clung to him, reluctant to find myself alone again with a heart full of doubts, but he helped me up on to Shamara's back, holding the reins and looking up at me with a face filled with resolve. 'I shall be away for the rest of the day Tessa, I have business to attend to in Hull, and I shall make arrangements for our journey. I want no more arguments when I return, do you understand?'

I nodded mutely. I could no longer argue with Julian, his resolve was my resolve, and I knew now that for good or ill we would be together until one or both of us died. I halted my horse at the fork in the path where Julian would leave me to ride down to Moorcliff, and as he brought his horse to stand beside mine he took my hand once again in his and looked deep into my eyes.

'You will promise me Tessa, no more heart-searching, no more doubts or misgivings, not if you love me.'

'I do love you Julian, I can't bear to think about those long wasted years when I thought you could never love me.'

For a moment he held my hand firmly in his, then apparently satisfied he smiled and let it go. 'I'll see you in the morning Tessa. If the weather is decent we'll ride together, if not I'll bring the car round and we can drive out somewhere for lunch. Around ten o'clock shall we say?'

'Yes Julian, I'll be ready.'

He waited while my horse picked its way along the narrow path that led to the road at the bottom of the moor, and when we reached it I turned. He stood where I had left him, then with a wave of his hand he urged his horse down the hill and he was lost to sight.

That afternoon I busied myself going through my wardrobe. I was not sure I had suitable clothes for France or Spain for I had lived my life close to the soil of the dales and

413

had dressed accordingly. Tweeds and twin sets, trench coats and stout walking shoes, even my evening gowns had been bought years before, for when had we ever entertained at Easdale? I stared at them in dismay wondering if there would be time to go into Harrogate or York before we left.

After a small tap on my door Annie came in, eyeing the things on my bed curiously. 'Why are yer sorting through yer clothes when yer've found nowhere ter go yet?'

I stared at her for a few moments, unsure of how I was going to tell her about my future plans, then making up my mind that I should speak swiftly and without subterfuge, I said firmly, 'I am going away for a few weeks or months with Sir Julian, Annie. I'm not quite sure just now how long we shall be away.'

'Yer mean just yer an' Sir Julian, Miss Tessa, nobody else?'

'Well we are taking Sir Julian's visitor back to her home in France, then we are going on to Spain for a while.'

'That means just yer and Sir Julian?'

'Yes Annie, just the two of us.'

She opened her mouth to speak then thought better of it, and with a murmured, 'I'll go an' see ter yer tea Miss Tessa,' she went out of the room.

I was trembling with suppressed anger. Damn her virtuous moral little soul, I thought savagely, then felt immediately ashamed. I mustn't blame Annie who loved me and looked up to me, but if Annie could look at me with hurt surprise, how much more vindictive would others be?

I squared my shoulders and made myself walk downstairs, adopting an unconcerned attitude. Annie hovered over me, pouring my tea and at times looking at me anxiously and expectantly although as yet I could tell her nothing further.

I spent the long evening trying to read, plagued by Annie's resentment, and retired early. Quite deliberately I lingered over my toilet the following morning so that I could eat breakfast hurriedly without having to look into her searching eyes.

Julian came for me promptly at ten and I know she watched us through the sitting room window as we drove away. The rain soon ceased and before us stretched the promise of one of those rare autumn days I loved. The earth smelled sweet after the rain and we followed the road northwards through stone villages and where the sea swept invitingly round sheltered sandy bays. Through ancient towns watched over by ruined castles and old abbeys, where market days were jostling bright and quiet country roads led over wild moorland where the only sound was the weird cry of the curlew, the only signs of life the sheep sheltering beneath the towering crags.

Julian told me that all arrangements had been made and we would be leaving in five days. When I told him I was troubled about clothes he merely smiled saying, 'You can buy others in France, Tessa, you will need something for the sun which will still be reasonably hot there. Ideally you should buy things abroad, the shops in England will be preoccupied with winter clothes.'

I listened to his low voice extolling the virtues of the long tree-lined roads and the sunlight shining on red-roofed old towns of ancient chateaux rosy pink in the sunset and great bunches of purple grapes ripening on the hillsides.

That night I ate dinner with Julian and Carmelita. She seemed to have recovered from her weariness and she added to Julian's tales of the beauties of the countryside around Bordeaux and the valley of the Gironde.

'You are glad to be going home?' I asked in some surprise.

'But of course, I am glad to be going home to the sun but I am sorry to be leaving my good friend here. Not nearly as sorry now that I know I am leaving him in your hands, my dear.'

I blushed, aware of her dark eyes resting on my face, warm and gentle, and while Julian went down to the cellar for another bottle of wine she said softly, 'You will love him very dearly Tessa, I know, and he is a man who needs love, perhaps more than most.'

'Why is that Carmelita?'

'He did not have a happy childhood in that great house with a grandfather who asked more than that small boy was prepared to give. His mother was always delicate and his father was one of those unimaginative Englishmen who hide always behind a veneer of impartiality, even coldness.'

'I see.'

'And then when he was still very young that impossible child was handed into his care and being Julian, he tried to steer her life into honourable and correct channels. I could have told him then that he would fail. That too-beautiful child with her passions and her needs. I used to warn him against her, but he only laughed, saying she was only a child. A more devilishly disturbing child I could not imagine.'

'You did not like Roxanne, Carmelita?'

'I did not like Roxanne any more than I liked her father before her. I was only twelve years old when that man broke into my bedroom in my father's house and seduced me. I was too afraid to tell my father, or indeed to tell anybody, and as the years passed he took me again and again, in my room or in the fields, whenever he could lay his hands on me.'

I stared at her with horror-filled eyes. 'Does Julian know? Didn't you tell your father?'

'It might be difficult for you, an Englishwoman, to understand. We were nothing. Peasants. The Montoros prized their cows more highly than they prized the people who worked on their land. The bulls are for the bull ring, but the courage and stamina that makes a bull worthy of the skill of the matador comes from the cows. No, I could not have told my father who depended on the Montoros for our food, his pay and the tumbledown shack we lived in.

'Julian believes I ran away from my father's house because I did not want to marry my cousin. It is only a half truth. All my life I wanted to dance. I danced before the workers round the camp fires in the evenings, that was my dream, but most of all I ran away from Carlos Montoro. If I hadn't I would have killed him.'

'But so many years have passed, hasn't it been possible to tell Julian since?'

She shrugged her slender shoulders, gracefully, elegantly, and at that moment I could see the dancer in her.

'Our lives changed. The gypsies who took me with them when they left Seville were kind to me and eventually I was

416

noticed and realized my dream. Julian only came back to Spain on rare occasions to see his grandfather. In every respect he became the Englishman his father wished him to be. You will have heard how Roxanne's parents died, but to make Julian responsible for their child's welfare, for her entire future was an imposition entirely deplorable.'

'Is it because of the father that you hated the child so much?'

'I tried not to hate her. I looked for her mother in that beautiful child but all I saw was her obsession with Julian, her torturing jealousy – of me, of any woman he met socially. If she can destroy things for you she will do so.'

'Even now when she is married to Godfrey?'

'Your uncle is a stepping stone in a succession of stepping stones. No doubt that boy she married was another one, but Roxanne's ultimate goal has always been Julian. You must not underestimate Roxanne, Tessa. She is capable of coming here with a smiling face and all the graciousness of your dearest friend, but she has the heart of a viper.'

I stared at her, afraid and fascinated by the picture she was painting of Roxanne, and she went on, 'How long do you think you will be able to keep your secret from her, Tessa? Your family will have to know where you are and believe me Roxanne is capable of anything.'

I could not believe that Roxanne could harm me. Carmelita was dramatizing her potential for evil simply because she had suffered at the hands of Roxanne's father, but when I was about to say as much she clutched my hand, saying, 'Hush Tessa, no more now, Julian is coming back.'

As I listened to them chatting normally about the journey we were to take my thoughts were miles away. I wondered what Roxanne would do when she knew that I was living with Julian. I could see Roxanne's eyes filled with mocking amusement, feel the hatred behind the smiling façade of that too perfect face. . . . Then my eyes met Julian's and he smiled, lifting my spirits with a sudden tenderness.

Julian was not Alec to be beguiled and flattered. Roxanne had never been a song in the heart or a fever in the blood to Julian, she had merely been an encumbrance thrust upon him too suddenly and tragically at a time in his life when he should have been gay and carefree. Roxanne would not be able to harm me now. Julian would know how to stand between me and her so that I need not be afraid of her ever again.

After dinner I telephoned Susan to ask if they would be wanting the cottage in the next few months but she assured me it would be Easter before they even thought of going there.

'Haven't you managed to find something yet, Tessa?' she asked.

'Not yet, but I am going abroad for a few months and I would like to leave Annie and Flanagan at the cottage until I return.'

Her voice was filled with surprise. 'Did you say abroad Tessa, isn't that a little sudden?'

'Yes, very sudden and I can't explain on the telephone. I'll be in touch as soon as I come back.'

'Are you going alone?'

'No. I'm sorry to be so vague but you'll understand eventually.'

'Don't worry about the cottage then, Mrs Cross will be glad of Annie's company during the winter. Why aren't you taking Annie with you?'

'It isn't possible, Susan.'

'Oh very well, I won't ask any more questions, I'll contain my soul in impatience.'

I laughed a little, then wished her a hurried goodbye.

Ahead of me lay the task of talking to Annie and I was not looking forward to it. The opportunity came the following afternoon, when I suggested that Annie and I should take tea together in the sitting room. She seemed reluctant and I knew she was always uncomfortable when we dined together, watching me carefully before picking up a fork or a knife, then copying the way I cut a sandwich or ate a pastry. Her reluctance on this occasion stemmed from something besides her table manners and I believed it was because she was afraid of hearing more about my wanton descent into depravity.

It was only after we had eaten that I said, 'Annie, this is a good opportunity for us to have a little chat about the future.'

She started to collect the china on to a tray and made as though to carry it into the kitchen. More nervous than I, she did not want to hear what I had to tell her.

'Leave the tray, Annie. Sit there in front of the fire and listen very carefully, it concerns your future as much as mine.'

She sat uncomfortably on the edge of her chair, her hands clenched tightly in her lap, not looking at me. Her face was pale and I could see that she was trembling.

I spoke to her gently, hoping that she would recognize the appeal in my voice.

'The Latchfords are not requiring the cottage until Easter at the earliest, and I expect to be back long before then. Mrs Cross and Flanagan will both be here. Do you wish to stay here with them?'

'I don't rightly know, Miss Tessa. I'll 'ave nothin' to do 'ere wi' yer gone.'

'I'm only one person, Annie. You can help Mrs Cross care for the cottage and you can take care of the money. I will leave enough for your wages and Flanagan's, and enough for Shamara's keep. Mrs Cross I will pay separately.'

She looked down at her hands twisting together in her lap, and helplessly I went on, 'If you do not wish to remain here you can return to Glamara.'

'I couldn't go back to Glamara, Miss Tessa, and them all wonderin' why I'm back an' where yer are. When yer comes back, Miss Tessa, will yer go on lookin' fer somewhere fer us to live together like afore?'

'No Annie, I shall go to live at Moorcliff with Sir Julian. I am hoping you will come with me but if you feel that is impossible I shall try to understand.'

'Oh Miss Tessa,' she wailed, 'I can't bear ter think yer'll be livin' like mi aunt an' that Jack Bryant. Everybody talkin' about 'em an' callin' 'er all sorts o' names. I'd die if I ever 'eard 'em sayin' such things about yer.'

I stared at her appalled. The comparison was too incongruous for words and yet I should have known that in

Annie's rigid little soul there was no difference between us. I said nothing but one look at my angry face brought her kneeling on the rug at my feet.

'Forgive me Miss Tessa, I knows yer not really like 'em but it won't stop folk thinkin' yer are. Do yer 'ave to go an' live together, why can't yer just love 'im an' stay apart till yer can marry 'im?'

'If you ever fall in love Annie, you'll know why. I can't wait for Richard to die, we must be together now while we are still young, not wait for some vague impossible future that could find us bitter and empty because we have waited too long.'

I rose, looking down at her bent head. 'If you are not here when I return Annie I shall be sad but I shall understand. I don't want you to stay with me when it is against your conscience and I shall always think about you and hope life is kind to you.'

The great tears rolled down her face. In the quiet of my bedroom I wept too, for Annie and my lost innocence, but most of all because marriage with Julian was not possible and I so yearned to be his wife and bear his children.

When I spoke to Flanagan I quickly discovered he had no reservations. He would have his beloved horse to care for and enough money to spend at the races and his visits to the pub. There would too be the advantage of Mrs Cross's cooking and his comfortable rooms above the stable.

When I informed him that he would be bringing Shamara to Moorcliff after we returned from Spain and that there would be a cottage for him close by he betrayed not the slightest surprise. Flanagan was a survivor. He was unconcerned what the gentry were about, they had their ways and he had his.

Mrs Cross seemed not to view my fall from grace with Annie's disapproval. She admired Julian and made no bones about telling me how kind he had been to her when her husband died. 'Life's short,' she said sagely. 'Yer wise to take yer 'appiness while yer can, ma'am.'

The next few days saw me packing, and the morning at last arrived when all that remained was for me to say farewell to

Annie. I could tell she had been crying but I tried not to notice as I handed her a sum of money.

'I have made arrangements with the bank manager in Whitby to take care of any bills that may come in Annie. If you need money for other things he has my authorization to see that you get it. You will be quite comfortable here with Mrs Cross and she is glad to have you.'

'Yes Miss Tessa.'

'If you want to go home for Christmas you must do so.'

'Yes Miss Tessa.'

I felt irritated by her terse answers. I tried to put myself in her place, to feel as she felt. She had joined her life to mine without fear or favour, and I had disappointed her. With sudden warmth I put my arms round her and kissed her cheek. 'Annie, please don't look so woebegone. I'm so happy and you are spoiling things for me.'

She sniffed dejectedly.

'Is it that you don't like Sir Julian?'

Her eyes opened wide at that and the denial came quickly. 'Oh no Miss Tessa, it's not that at all. I do like 'im, I likes 'im a lot, I just wish yer were 'is wife, that's all.'

'I shall be one day, Annie. I shall be his wife and you shall stay with me and look after our children. Isn't that what you want?'

'I 'opes yer'll wait to 'ave children till yer wed, Miss Tessa.'

I didn't answer her. Whenever I thought about marriage the waiting seemed interminable but it was not in me to hope for Richard's death.

I was glad that at that moment I heard Julian's voice in the hall. At the door I turned and looked back at her. 'Take care,' I said, smiling, but although she looked at me long and hard she didn't answer. As we drove away from the house Mrs Cross and Flanagan waved to us from the garden but there was no sign of Annie. Then I glimpsed her staring from my bedroom window and for a few moments some of the joy disappeared from the day.

That night was the start of our life together, and as I lay in Julian's arms warm and tranquil after love I could hear the sea crashing on the rocks below Moorcliff while a full moon sailed high in the dark blue sky.

I knew that when we returned this would be how it would be night after night, listening to the sea and the sound of his quiet breathing, seeing the seasons come and go, the spring tides and the autumn gales, the dark moors covered with mist or purple with heather and I sighed with contentment, praying that something so perfect would last.

CHAPTER TWENTY-NINE

It was mid morning when we left Carmelita's villa on the banks of the Gironde with the big car eating up the miles as we followed the wide sweep of the river towards Bordeaux.

For almost three weeks we had enjoyed the slow pattern of life along the river, the pastel villas, the great chateaux, and the miles of vineyards that covered the gently sloping hills. In that time we had seen Carmelita pick up the threads of her life. She had wept a little when we said our goodbyes, holding Julian close and saying in a trembling voice, 'Thank you dear friend for everything you have done for me, been to me. I doubt if I shall ever see you again.'

He laughed at her fears, saying in a light voice, 'But of course you will see me again, whenever we grow tired of rain and icy winds.'

When she embraced me she whispered, 'Make him happy, Tessa, but remember my warning.'

'Please, Carmelita, you are frightening me, it is not like you to be so pessimistic.'

'I did not live with the gypsies all those years without learning some of their perceptions.' She took both my hands in hers and stared down at them, opening my palms so that the lines showed up clearly.

When she looked up at last her eyes were bleak, and

harshly I cried, 'What did you see Carmelita, why are you looking at me like that?'

'It is nothing, nothing at all. I am a fool to worry about things that will never happen. Now go off on your holiday.'

Reluctantly I withdrew my hands and then Julian was waiting for me and with a gay wave I ran towards him. She stood in her garden until our speeding car was hidden from view, while all I could think of was that we were together at last in the mellow autumn sunshine. Beside me Julian sat handsome and tanned, his smile incredibly sweet when for a moment his eyes left the road to smile into mine.

I, who had spent nearly all of my life in England's largest county, where dull leaden skies are more familiar than the sun, grasped the sunshine of Spain with total joy.

I knew now what they meant when they talked about castles in Spain, there were so many of them, and beautiful cathedrals, their stone warmed by the sun as we swept south through Valencia and into Andalusia.

This was the Spain of my dreams, the Spain beloved of the Moors who had left their architecture with its beautiful filigree for ever captured in the ruins of the Alhambra at Granada, yet strangely overpowered by the Sierra Nevada, the highest mountains in Spain.

For hours we wandered through the beauties of the Alhambra and the gardens of the Generalife and my entire being was so uplifted the gypsy quarter of Granada came almost as an anti-climax. We sat for a while listening to their music and watching the grace of their dances, and I thought of the young Carmelita who went with them willingly, imbued with delight at the colour and fire of their dancing.

After the entertainment Julian handed them a sum of money and when he spoke to them effortlessly in their own language they laughed like delighted children.

Andalusia was the province of Julian's childhood, embracing cities I had always dreamed of like Seville and Cordoba, Granada and Cadiz. I began to keep a diary which made Julian smile a little. 'Why worry your head about these old cities, Tessa, when you will find the road that winds over the Sierra Morena through the olive groves to Seville more enchanting?' he said, teasing me with his smile.

It was in Seville where I saw shadows cross his face and I realized that many of his memories were bitter. Crowds filled the sun-baked streets and groups of gypsies wandered across the squares, singing and dancing for the amusement of those who lined the streets in a festival mood.

'Why are there so many people here?' I asked curiously. 'Is it some religious festival?'

'Rather the reverse, I fear. It is the day of the Corrida de Toros, the bull fight.'

At his words I could feel it, the frantic excitement, the cruelty and the stench of death. The overpowering expression of man's domination over lesser creatures, finesse over brute strength, the bewilderment of a dazed and tortured animal, his angry glazed eyes roaming over a wildly cheering crowd eager for his death, and then when it came it would either be swift and sure if the matador was skilful, or prolonged and agonizing.

I felt Julian's hand tightening round mine and his voice was very gentle. 'Don't think of it Tessa, think of something else instead.'

With an effort I dragged my unwilling thoughts away from the bull ring, asking instead, 'Do you intend to visit your grandfather's ranch, Julian?'

'I think not. He is dead and I have only distant relatives on the estate. I think instead we should see all we want in the city, then we should drive through the mountains to a place I know for dinner. We can drive down to Cadiz from there.'

Behind the main streets and squares of Seville the lanes were deserted, and so narrow the sun barely reached the pavement. Together we marvelled at the cool beauty of the quiet courtyards in the Alcazar and at a small café within its shadow we sat drinking iced sherry in long rose-coloured glasses.

'This is really the best time of the year to see it,' Julian explained. 'In the summer the heat is cruel and the great plains beyond the city are a sun-baked desert. Has it been anything like your imagined idea of it?'

What had I imagined Seville would be like? I knew that it

was here that Drake and other famous pirates singed the King of Spain's beard, that Seville oranges were bitter and only suitable for marmalade. I had read that in Holy Week the processions were wonderful to behold and that at night men sang in whitewashed taverns while the women wore very long full skirts and mantillas and were beautiful and graceful.

When I said all these things to Julian he seemed amused. 'It is also true that many of the women are extraordinarily fat and there is always something a little disappointing about the reality.'

'Then what is it about your Spain that makes it so very different?' I demanded to know.

'For one thing it has little to do with tourists but everything to do with her music, her strong heart beating beneath the olive groves and the high sierras. I have found Spain changed, which I suppose was inevitable, after all it is more than twenty years since I was last in Seville. I very much fear that one day nationalism will be doomed and cosmopolitanism will take its place.'

'Perhaps you shouldn't have come back here?'

'If I had come back alone I think I would have been sad, as it is I am seeing Spain with your eyes and finding it as enchanting and beautiful as you do.'

'And I think you are saying that just to reassure me that you are enjoying yourself.'

'Oh but I *am* enjoying myself. Long golden days when I can see your eyes filled with wonder and long nights when I can make love to you and feel your heart filled with contentment.'

He was playing with my hair, twisting it round his fingers, and I laughed, enjoying his touch against the nape of my neck.

'Your hair is almost silver, Tessa, the sun has bleached it. Will the gold ever come back do you think?'

'Of course, when we return to the wind and the rain. I wish we could just go on like this for ever.'

'Now you know you don't mean that. After a few months of this you will long for the sound of the sea and the wild beauty of the dales. Besides, you will be missing Shamara and Annie.'

'I'm not so sure about Annie.'

He smiled. 'Annie will forgive you, hasn't she built her life around you?'

'But suppose she's gone? I can't help worrying.'

Talk of Annie was disturbing me and taking something precious from the day, and recognizing it Julian said gently, 'Do you want to go home, Tessa?'

'I don't care what Annie thinks about me, I was right to come with you. Julian, if only you knew how long I have been in love with you, how I agonized when I thought you loved Carmelita, how I tramped my bedroom at Easdale longing for you.'

He laughed, then pulling me to my feet and holding me within the circle of his arms he said, 'We'll make other journeys into the sun, Tessa, tomorrow we'll go home and put an end to all your doubts and worries.'

The nostalgic journey into Julian's past was over. We were going home to the vagaries of the English winter but Spain would be with me always in Julian, the fire and the passion, the amusement in his dark eyes and the cool remote profile like those I had seen in portraits on old castle walls.

Driving up from the south coast on a mid December afternoon with the rain pattering on the windows and the scent of the English soil all around us was an unexpected joy. I had thought I would miss the sunshine of Spain but in actual fact I had had a surfeit of sun and I had found the nights after the heat of the day excruciatingly cold.

It was late afternoon when we came at last to the dark Pennine hills, shadowed by drifting clouds and the wide turbulent rivers that ran north and east towards the sea. I sat forward in my seat, my eyes drinking in the frosty patchwork fields bordered by low stone walls, the scattered homesteads and crumbling abbey walls, the tall cathedral spires across the hedgerows and winding roads crossing moors as barren and undulating as the grass on the dunes near Moorcliff.

Julian smiled his slow sweet smile and for a moment I rested my head against his shoulder.

'You're glad to be going home?' he asked gently.

'Yes, I feel that this is really the beginning of our life together. I shall have to learn something about the work you do, your business trips and all those other mundane things in your life that I know nothing about. Julian, have you really thought how little I do know about you? But I'm glad we're rich. You needn't smile, I've spent a lot of my life being poor.'

'Why don't you think about all the things we have in common, like horses and dogs and music? I'm not so sure about sailing. Do you like sailing, Tessa?'

'Sailing!'

'Why yes. It is one of the joys of my life. I have a lovely little yacht in the harbour a few miles from the house, you'll see it soon.'

'The only sailing I have ever done was on the channel ferry and the sea was as calm as a millpond.'

He laughed. There were so many things I needed to discover about Julian. I looked at his remote profile under cover of the closing darkness but his eyes were on the road. He had switched on the car's headlights and before us the road opened up like a golden ribbon as it swept across the moors towards the sea.

I waited two whole days before I went to the Rowans, two days to unpack and settle into my new home, two days to acquaint myself with the house and its servants as well as the dogs who greeted us rapturously. There were three of them: Minstrel the black labrador who was twelve years old, with failing eyesight and a touch of arthritis; Buster the English bull terrier, his small piggy eyes filled with mischievous humour, tough and resilient, built to fight and survive; and the dog I thought of as mine, Jasper, the black cocker spaniel with gentle brown eyes and silken coat, and long curling ears which he always seemed in danger of tripping over. Right from our first meeting Jasper adopted me and Julian laughed, calling him a turncoat, just like a fickle woman.

Jasper accompanied me on the morning I walked along the cliff top to the Rowans. Long before I caught sight of the house I began to have doubts. Would Annie still be there, still trying to hide the disappointment she had found so difficult to hide before we went away?

I heard a shout from the direction of the house and looking up I saw Annie running towards me as fast as her legs could carry her, waving her arms enthusiastically, then she was upon me and although I could see the tears in her eyes her smile was warm before she threw her arms around me and held me close.

'Oh Miss Tessa, I'm that glad yer back,' she cried breathlessly. 'Why've yer come back so soon, didn't yer enjoy it then?'

'I loved it Annie but I was homesick, thinking about you and settling down in our new home.'

'But yer'll be 'ere all through the winter when yer could 'a bin sittin' in the sun.'

I linked my arm through hers, giving it a little squeeze. 'I know, but think how I would have missed the snow and the ice and the long lovely evenings in front of the fire.'

She was eyeing the dog cautiously and I said, 'This is Jasper, Annie. Why don't you make friends with him?'

Mrs Cross was already at the gate and I hurried forward to greet her.

'My, ma'am, but yer do look well, it's easy ter see the sun's bin shinin' on yer.'

'Yes, a little too powerfully some of the time. How are you Mrs Cross?'

'Well enough, ma'am. Annie 'ere looked after me very well when I 'ad the flu an' Flanagan were good wi' the fires an' shiftin' the snow.'

Just then Flanagan appeared from the stableyard, beaming with pleasure, and taking his hand I said, 'It's easy to see you've weathered the winter well. How's Shamara?'

'He's waitin' for you, Milady, an' haven't Oi been tellin' 'im all mornin' that you were back? That's a nice little dog you've got there an' no mistake. Used to see spaniels in Oirland wi' gamekeepers, hunters they are.'

'Well I'm afraid Jasper is simply a family pet.'

How easily the word family came to my lips. I thought of Julian as my husband and that one day we would be a family,

428

but if Mrs Cross and Annie thought my use of the word unseemly their expressions didn't change.

I went with Flanagan to look at Shamara and as I fondled his face he nuzzled my shoulder gently.

'He's beautiful, Flanagan, you've looked after him so well.'

'Oi loves that 'orse, Milady, an' Oi thinks he loves me, at least he should for all the toime Oi spend with 'im.'

A cup of coffee was waiting for me in the familiar parlour and Mrs Cross asked, 'When will yer be wantin' Annie up at Moorcliff, ma'am?'

'How about tomorrow, Annie? But if you like you can walk back with me and take a look at your room this afternoon.'

Her eyes lit up when she saw her bedroom and particularly the view from the window. 'Oh Miss Tessa it's beautiful, an' so close ter the sea. I'd like our Mary an' mi mam ter see this, like somethin' in a palace it is.'

'Well not quite Annie, but it is very nice.'

'Are the other servants in this part o' the 'ouse then?'

'No, you're the only one up here, but you are going to be my maid. Now come with me and take a look around the house.'

She exclaimed with delight at the beautiful curved staircase which swept up from the hall, and when she saw the drawing room she cried, 'Oh Miss Tessa it reminds me of Glamara.'

'Sir Julian loved Glamara, I think he deliberately copied the decor of a great many of the rooms. Now you must see the inner hall.'

Her eyes opened wide at the many varieties of tropical wood, intricately carved, the elegant tiles and wrought iron, but most of all at the fountain cascading over the marble steps, its spray falling on the plants which grew around the exquisitely proportioned pool.

'Oh Miss Tessa, it's beautiful . . . That lady i' the picture i' the hall, Miss Tessa, didn't she remind yer a little bit o' Miss Roxanne?'

For a moment I stared at her in shocked surprise. Of course. Julian's and Roxanne's mothers were sisters, there was bound to be a family resemblance and yet I had been strangely unaware of it until now.

'I suppose you're right Annie, perhaps there is a family resemblance but I can't say it was very evident to me.'

'It's there Miss Tessa, I don't rightly know where but I noticed it the moment a clapped eyes on it.'

I had opened the outside door and we were standing on the path looking down the drive.

'I'll come for you in the morning Annie, about ten.'

Minstrel and Jasper followed her as far as the gate but when I called to them they immediately came back to my side. There was no sign of Buster, who went off on his own excursions, to the dismay of the local cat population.

For a long time I stared at the portrait of Julian's mother and the longer I stared the more I became aware of her resemblance to Roxanne. They both had the same creamy oval face, although in this portrait the mantilla hid her dark hair while Roxanne allowed hers to flow around her shoulders in shining blue-black waves, or in the evenings piled on top of her exquisitely poised head and held in place by jewelled combs.

Their eyes were not the same colour but their shape was the same, slightly slanting under delicately arched brows. Roxanne's mouth was wide and passionate while this woman's mouth had a wistful curve to it and there was no mockery in her expression, unlike the amused cynicism that was never far from Roxanne's eyes.

I was still looking at it when Julian came into the hall. 'Why are you suddenly so interested in my mother's portrait, Tessa?'

'I never realized it before but she is extraordinarily like Roxanne.'

'I have never thought so.'

'But the shape of their faces, their eyes, don't you see it now?'

'Roxanne's eyes are green like a cat's. I used to tease her about it. My mother's eyes were hazel and their mouths are not at all the same. A vague family resemblance perhaps, nothing more.'

As I walked with him up the shallow stairs with his arm around my waist I was remembering the first time I had seen Julian and Roxanne and I had thought then how beautiful they both were, dark and lithe and incredibly graceful. I looked up suddenly to find his eyes upon me, grave and a little curious and he said, 'You were not happy to find some fleeting resemblance to Roxanne in my mother's portrait, Tessa.'

'No.'

'But why ever not?'

'I'd rather she looked completely different.'

I sounded so infantile, so incredibly naïve, and although his smile was gentle I had the feeling that he thought so too.

'You must try to forget the past, Tessa. I'm not asking you to forget that Alec was your friend. So Roxanne stole your friend and she has usurped Abigail's place in Godfrey's affections. Does it really matter? They are nothing to do with us.'

'But they are, Godfrey is my uncle and she is your cousin. Suppose they decide to visit us?'

'We make them welcome, we let them see that we are happy together, and nothing in the world is going to change that. They will be guests in our house Tessa, we must make sure that nothing from the past can spoil things and create a bad atmosphere.'

When I didn't speak he gave me a little shake, kissing the top of my head and saying, 'You haven't said anything, Tessa.'

'If they come here I'll try very hard, Julian, but I hope very much that they won't come. I'm not very good at pretending.'

'But you will for all our sakes?'

I nodded, and again he kissed my hair and held me close, then swiftly changing the subject he said, 'I spoke to Flanagan. He is bringing Shamara up to the stables first thing in the morning.'

'Did he say if he was looking forward to living here?'

'He didn't say, but I gather that he will be happy wherever the horse is.'

I laughed, my good humour restored, and Julian said, 'Did Annie say anything about your aunt's visit?'

I stared at him in surprise. 'Why no. You mean that Aunt Hetty came here?'

'No, to the Rowans I believe.'

'But why didn't Annie tell me?'

'No doubt she will. I expect she was far too excited by your homecoming, it slipped her memory for the time being.'

'Julian, how could Aunt Hetty slip anybody's memory?'

'My dear I don't know, but you will be able to ask her tomorrow. Don't look so tragic darling, I can't believe you're frightened of Aunt Hetty as well as Roxanne.'

'I'm not afraid of her, I'm just anxious to know why she came.'

'I told you you should have written to tell her exactly what was happening, she was bound to be worried about you and sending her postcards from Spain wouldn't exactly alleviate her concern. She obviously needed to know why you were in Spain and with whom. Darling Tessa, in time everybody has to know and that includes Roxanne and Godfrey and that unhappy husband of yours. His mother too, I might add.'

I wondered if I would ever be able to keep anything secret from Julian, my fears, my doubts, my imaginings. We were home and I had the feeling that all sorts of people would descend upon us, shattering our privacy, our togetherness. I went to stand at the window of our bedroom looking out to where a sea fret rolled in dismally, chilling the air with its vapour, hiding the sun. I shivered, feeling suddenly cold and Julian came to put his arms around me as though aware of the doubts coursing through my mind.

Raising my arms round his neck I buried my face in his shoulder, and in a small voice I pleaded, 'Make love to me Julian, now, so that I don't have to think about Aunt Hetty or anybody else.'

He laughed, the amused teasing laughter that I loved, then he picked me up in his arms and carried me to the bed, undressing me with gentle efficient hands, kissing me with warm tenderness until the tenderness became passion and I cried out with the frantic urgency of wanting more.

CHAPTER THIRTY

How beautiful was that long bleak winter that will stay in my heart to warm other winters which hold their sadness. It seemed then that my world was complete as I rode with Julian in the early morning mist or across the moor with the sun setting in a great red ball, leaving the sky flaming with crimson. Then there were the long winter evenings with the fire blazing and the glow from the lamps falling on polished walnut and rich velvet drapes, evenings when we came to know each other with a warm tenderness, and nights when I would lie in his arms listening to the sea pounding mercilessly on the rocks below the house and the wind moaning like a banshee over our heads.

Annie took up her life at Moorcliff with a happy acceptance I had never expected and Flanagan too seemed happy by the sounds of the melodious Irish songs issuing from the stables. In the early days he had been wary of Buster, the bull terrier with small wicked eyes and questing nose, but suddenly they were the best of friends. I never quite knew how Flanagan accomplished this but at lunchtime and in the evenings they would sidle off together across the cliffs, the stocky Irishman and the white dog with his ungainly gait looking so much a pair that Julian and I laughed at the similarity.

In more ways than one Buster adopted Flanagan. He spent most of his time around the stables and made short work of the vermin which always appeared where there was grain. I suspect there were nights when Flanagan encouraged him to sleep at his cottage and one morning when I saw them entering the stables together Flanagan said slyly, 'Didn't Oi foind him in the kitchen this mornin', Milady, an' me not knowin' he'd followed me home.'

Flanagan knew all right but we put no constraints upon

433

Buster. He was an independent dog with none of the adoring ways of Minstrel or Jasper and Flanagan with his free and easy lifestyle suited him admirably.

When I asked Annie about Aunt Hetty she seemed momentarily embarrassed. ''Ow did yer know, Miss Tessa?' she asked in some dismay.

'Flanagan told Sir Julian. Annie why didn't you tell me?'

'I meant to tell yer when yer were settled in proper, Miss Tessa.'

'How did she know where to find you?'

'She got the address fro' Miss Susan. My but she asked some questions, an' me tryin' not to tell 'er the truth. I thought that ought to come fro' you, Miss Tessa.'

'You told her I had gone abroad with Sir Julian though.'

'She guessed as much, but I told 'er you'd taken Sir Julian's friend 'ome to France.'

'And I wrote to her from Spain so she will have a very good idea what the situation is.'

'She will that, Miss Tessa. She were all prim an' proper like a little neat bird, but I could tell she were puttin' two an' two together.'

'And not liking it one litle bit.'

'I don't know, Miss Tessa.'

I believed that Annie could have told me more and when I said as much to Julian he merely smiled, saying, 'Aunt Hetty will descend upon us one of these mornings and make her disapproval plain.'

Aunt Hetty didn't visit us, instead she wrote long letters filled with recrimination and demanding explanations for my conduct. She told me that she had little time for the world as it was becoming, the lack of decorum, the constant seeking after pleasure. 'Young people have absolutely no thought for anything beyond themselves,' she wrote. 'I had thought it would be so different when the war was over.'

When I showed her letter to Julian he remarked wryly, 'What she doesn't realize is that it was the young people who fought the war, they know better than most how transient life can be.'

I brooded over her letter for several days before I sat down to answer it. I told her the truth, that we loved each other and hoped one day to marry, in the meantime it was our wish to live together regardless of what people thought. Without Julian life would be nothing, with him it was everything. I told her that until now I had never been alive, but I asked her to think kindly of me and forgive me if she could.

She wrote back saying that she would tell nobody of my fall from grace but she would pray for me.

Dear Aunt Hetty, how her world had changed. Adam was dead and Robert was farming somewhere in South Africa. Laura seldom visited Glamara now that Roxanne had married her father and I was living with a man I was not married to. I could imagine how earnestly she prayed for us all.

I was surprised how well Annie learned. She borrowed books from the library and struggled determinedly to read them, occasionally asking me the meaning of words and their pronunciation. She had her unruly hair cut and she watched me applying my make-up with avid interest. I corrected her speech at her own request and I marvelled how this girl who had had little formal education applied herself so diligently to improving herself.

I gave her underwear and clothes which I had grown tired of, not clothes I would have worn in the evening or even in the afternoons, but sensible skirts and sweaters, and even Julian remarked on her appearance.

I discovered that she worshipped him in a quiet way, and when he smiled at her or spoke kindly her face would light up with colour and Julian too remarked at the elusive beauty which momentarily illuminated her face.

Spring came bringing with it high tides and gales and then suddenly summer was with us. The wide golden beaches were thronged with holidaymakers and so too were the narrow hilly streets of Whitby. In spite of all this new activity however there were vast stretches of the North Riding lonely and undiscovered and quiet harbours known only to the local people and the fishermen. It was in one of these tiny harbours that Julian kept his yacht.

I had discovered that I loved sailing and my face grew rosy

and tanned as it had in Spain and there was nothing I liked better than cresting the waves with the wind in my hair and the spray against my face. Julian was delighted with my enthusiasm and I made friends with the fishermen and many of the men who worked on the boats.

We were leaving the harbour one day when an old man came up to us. His face was burned a bright brick-red and there were wrinkles round his deep blue eyes from staring at the sea in the bright sunlight.

''A've bin meaning ter ask yer, Sir Julian, but it's a right pity ter see that yacht lyin' idle all summer, isn't the young lady interested in sailin' now?'

'I don't know, Fairbrother, but I'll make some inquiries.'

'Well one or two visitors were askin' about it. I know it belongs to Miss Roxanne, where might she be livin' then?'

'Over at Wensleydale. If she does intend to keep her perhaps she could be moved to one of the lakes, they would be more convenient than here.'

'It's a shame sir to see 'er lyin' idle. I'd buy 'er miself if I 'ad the brass.'

'Well she doesn't belong to me so I have no power to part with her. I'll give it some thought.'

'Thank ye sir. I reckon yer comin' on apace, Milady. Yer enjoyin' sailin', I can tell.'

'Very much, better than I ever thought I would.'

'Ay well, the sea's a hard taskmaster. Yer knows it best when the sun's shinin', but yer'll never forget it when yer sees it in a fury. It'll toss these little boats about as though they were cockleshells. Ask Sir Julian, it's monny a one 'ee's had broken up on the rocks 'ere when the gales come.'

I looked up at Julian. 'I didn't know, he didn't tell me,' I said, and Julian smiled.

'No,' he said gently. 'When the gales do come you'll see for yourself. One grows to love a boat, it's tragic to see her broken up on the rocks like so much matchwood and in so short a time.'

He took my arm as we bade the old sailor goodbye. All I could think about was that Julian would have to approach

Roxanne about the yacht's future and the fear that she would visit us soon deepened. At the top of the hill where the car was parked we could look down at the boats in the harbour and I asked, 'Which one is Roxanne's?'

He pointed to a white yacht anchored near the harbour wall, her sails furled, a trim little vessel that had obviously been well cared for.

'I gave her to Roxanne on her eighteenth birthday and she christened her *Catrina*. She was fond of sailing and became quite an expert. People change, Tessa, no doubt she now has other interests and will want to part with the yacht.'

'When will you know?'

'I'll telephone her in the morning.'

'Perhaps she'll come here.'

'Perhaps. Darling, don't mind so much, she's got to know about us one day, the sooner the better I think.'

'I can't believe Aunt Hetty would tell her.'

'It doesn't matter, Tessa. My duty to Roxanne is over, I do not have to account to her for my actions. I did not interfere with hers even when I thought them deplorable.'

At the end of October he had to go up to London to attend a conference, and although he invited me to go with him the dates tied with an invitation from Susan to visit them.

We had so much to talk about and since I had feared that Susan and her husband would be appalled at my lifestyle, I was relieved to see that they were not. Susan was so happy in her own marriage she was generous enough to want the same happiness for me.

She startled me on the second day by producing an invitation card which she tossed across the breakfast table. It was from the convent, for the retirement presentation to the Mother Superior. I looked across at Susan in some surprise.

'I didn't think nuns ever retired,' I said. 'In any case she always seemed so old.'

'She's almost seventy, but I agree she seemed like seventy to me then. You will come with me, Tessa?'

'I don't see how I can go, Susan, there'll be too many people asking questions. You know what it's like when you meet people you haven't seen for years, all of them wanting to know if you're married, where you are living and how many children you have.'

'You'll know how to answer questions like that, after all I'm your friend and I've only just been told. It's nobody's business, Tessa.'

'I know, but I'll feel like a scarlet woman in those hallowed halls.'

'What rubbish. You're more married to Julian than you ever were to Richard. Please come, Tessa. You liked her, surely it isn't too much to ask you to go to her farewell party and wish her well.'

Her pleas wore me down and in the end I said I would go. It was then that some perverse feeling of defiance made me dress for the occasion in my most fashionable gown. It was in fine black wool, deceptively simple and very expensive. With it I wore a small black cocktail hat, silver mink ties around my shoulders and expensive high-heeled black court shoes. When Susan saw me she laughed delightedly.

'Tessa you look so much like the femme fatale I've always read about, but so very elegant you make me feel like a country bumpkin.'

I looked at Susan in her beige tweed suit and sensible shoes with feelings of misgiving, but when she saw the doubt in my face she laughed. 'You look beautiful Tessa, I dress for the life I lead, there's no reason for you to turn up looking like a country vet's wife. When Marylee sees you she'll be pea-green with envy.'

'I haven't worn this dress since we were in London. We live very quietly Susan, in fact most days I wear the same sort of clothes you are wearing now.'

'All the more reason for you to cut a dash today then. I can't wait to see some of their faces.'

'How is Marylee?'

'She married Ronald Sorrell, a solicitor. You can't mention a committee that Marylee doesn't sit on. Her husband's a city councillor and she's a magistrate so you could say she's arrived.'

It was evident that the presentation was going to be well

attended. Cars lined the long road outside and filled the courtyard of the convent. As we walked through the gardens I looked around curiously. Nothing seemed changed, except for the addition of a swimming pool behind the tennis courts.

'Do you know what they have bought the Mother Superior?' I asked Susan.

'Books I believe. Some that she particularly asked for.'

'I should contribute but who can I ask?'

'Oh ask Marylee, she handles everything.'

The main hall was crowded, and we had to stand at the back of the hall while the presentation was made by the Lord Mayor. A pile of expensive leather-bound volumes lay on the table in the centre of the dials and the Lord Mayor handed the Mother Superior an illuminated scroll depicting the sum total of her service to the girls she had cared for over the years.

I listened to her voice which seemed hardly changed, a low lilting voice which still bore a trace of Irish and which could be surprisingly authoritative when the occasion demanded it. Then we stood in a long queue waiting to file past the dais to shake her hand.

She greeted every person there with great charm and patience and when it came to my turn her faded blue eyes lit up with pleasure.

'Why, Tessa Chalfont, how glad I am to see you here and how kind of you to come when I am sure there are more pressing demands on your time.'

My smile faltered. I wondered what demands she was referring to and how much she knew about my life since I left the convent. In a few seconds we had passed on and, still bemused, I was following Susan in the direction of the library.

There was a small queue in the library in front of a table at which three women sat handing out tickets.

'What do we want tickets for?' I asked Susan.

'Tea I suppose. Do you recognize Marylee?'

She had changed considerably from the rather pretty slender girl I remembered. She had grown considerably stouter or so she appeared, in floral chiffon and a large flower-bedecked hat. On her ample bosom fell several rows of pearls, and a vast cameo decorated one shoulder. In the split second her eyes fell on me I was convinced she took in everything I had on, and she recognized me instantly.

As she gushed over me her eyes were everywhere, on the mink ties and the two rows of pearls around my throat, on the absurdly expensive hat and the too-high heels on my fashionable black shoes, holding my gloved hand for a great deal longer than was absolutely necessary.

'Why Tessa Chalfont, I didn't think you lived anywhere in the vicinity, I haven't seen you for years. Didn't you go to live somewhere in the dales?'

I smiled, feeling Susan's small shove in the middle of my back.

'Of course that was ages ago,' she went on. 'I suppose you are married now, but you're not back in Leeds surely?'

'No.'

'Where are you living now?'

'On the coast, north of Whitby.'

'Really. Now I wonder why I had the idea you lived somewhere in the West Riding?'

I smiled politely, inwardly squirming at her questions.

'I expect you'll be staying for tea. Are you staying with Susan?'

'Yes. I haven't paid my contribution to the Mother Superior's present, I should like to do so.'

'Well how funny you should come along right now. A group of the old girls are wanting to give her something a little more exciting than those old books she asked for. We know she likes pictures and there is one she particularly admired in an exhibition. We thought we'd like to give her that but it is frightfully expensive and we haven't nearly enough. We might have to put it out for other donations but your bit will certainly help.'

'How much does the picture cost?'

'Nearly five hundred pounds. We've chipped in thirty pounds each, but as you can imagine many of the girls haven't married as well as I have and even Susan's husband is feeling his way. Veterinary surgeons don't make fortunes.'

'How much exactly are you short for the picture?'

'Two hundred and fifty pounds, we might have to change our minds about the picture.'

I wrote out a cheque for the entire two hundred and fifty pounds. It was an act of bravado, but in some strange way it was in payment for all that I had suffered at Marylee's hands in the days when I had very little. I signed my name Tessa Chalfont and handed her the cheque.

'You intend to give all this?' she asked in amazement.

'Yes. I would like her to have that picture, she has had so few of life's frivolities. At seventy years of age I feel she deserves them.'

'You have signed your maiden name.'

'I know. The account is in my maiden name. You will have no difficulty with the cheque.'

She was still staring at it as though she could hardly believe her eyes and with a brief smile I passed on after taking a ticket from the outstretched hand of one of the other women who gazed at me curiously, her eyes wide with suppressed excitement.

Susan's eyes danced with laughter. 'You enjoyed that, didn't you Tessa?'

'Yes. It was ridiculous and ostentatious but I wanted the Reverend Mother to have her picture.'

Susan stopped for a word with an acquaintance, but I was glad to move out into the gardens. So many memories came crowding in one after the other as I stood pensively in the sheltered garden and I did not hear the Reverend Mother's silent tread. It was only when she spoke to me that I came out of my reverie to find her faded blue eyes regarding me kindly.

'I was hoping I might find you out here Tessa,' she began, 'the rooms are too crowded for much conversation.'

'What will you do when you leave this lovely place?' I asked her curiously. 'Somehow I had never imagined you would retire.'

She laughed. 'My dear, teaching nuns like teachers generally have their limitations, I have done very well to go on so long. I shall go back to my old order in County Clare. It is not at all stringent and I shall have my own little room where I may have the things I love around me. I have done my duty to the world, the rest of my life will be relatively peaceful and largely devoted to God.'

'I hope you will be very happy, Reverend Mother. I am sure you will often think of us all.'

'Oh yes, I shall be doing that more often than you realize, and some of my girls I shall think of more than the others. You are one of those girls, Tessa.'

'Why is that?'

'Because there was always something about you that seemed to invite tragedy, perhaps because you loved so intensely and suffered so terribly. It seemed to me that fate called upon you to bear so much while you were still too young. I heard that you had married and that your poor husband was an invalid. Is it too much to hope that his health is improved?'

'I'm afraid not, Reverend Mother.'

'My dear child, that is an ordeal in itself. It was very noble of you to take on such a burden.'

I felt the hot stinging tears in my eyes and I hunted hurriedly in my bag for a handkerchief while she stared at me with sudden consternation.

'Oh my dear,' she said gently, 'I shouldn't have spoken of it at this time, now I have upset you.'

With a degree of desperation I said, 'It isn't in the least like you suppose, and I can't allow you to think I am some sort of heroine who is deserving of your sympathy. I married Richard when I didn't love him but we were friends and I wanted to be a good wife to him and bring some sort of tenderness into the years remaining to him. The marriage didn't work out. I was very unhappy and I was not making him happy either. I left Richard in the care of his mother, I haven't seen him since.'

She stared at me sadly and when she didn't ask questions I went on, 'I am living with somebody else, somebody I have loved for a long long time, so you see I am not a very good woman, I am what most people would call an unrepentant sinner.'

'I doubt if I could ever think of you as that Tessa.'

'That is because you are good and charitable, the rest of the world would think on very different lines.'

'You say you love this man dearly?'

'Very dearly. I am happy with him, more happy than I have ever been and if you were to tell me that my immortal soul is for ever damned because of him I do not think it would matter.'

'My child I am not too interested in perfection. The perfect beings of this world have no need of my prayers. I suppose one day you and this man hope to marry?'

'Yes, but that would be after Richard's death, and I could not wish him to die simply to accommodate our desires.'

'I shall pray for you Tessa. I shall pray that one day there will be peace and happiness in your life. And thank you my dear for being so open and frank with me. It took a great deal of courage I think, and now let us go into the dining hall and see if there is anything left for us. From the looks on those hungry young faces I very much fear most of the food will have gone.'

'A cup of tea is all I ask, I am not very hungry.'

'Nor I. Cucumber sandwiches I find particularly indigestible and I have never had a sweet tooth. You came with Susan Latchford? Susan was always a very nice girl, I am glad you have kept up your friendship.'

'I have you to thank for that. There was a time when I was so ready to discard it but you cautioned me that the time would come when I would need a friend. I have needed friends so many times.'

She smiled. 'I wish I could say that all my girls learned their lessons with such humility.'

Immediately we entered the dining hall she was met by a crowd of people all wishing to speak to her and after bidding her goodbye I hurried on to find Susan.

'I see you've been talking to the Mother Superior,' she greeted me. 'You look a bit upset, I suppose she's wormed it out of you?'

'No, I told her of my own free will. I could not have her regarding me as some sort of martyr, tied to a helpless invalid.'

'Did you expect to shock her?'

'No, only to disillusion.'

'In your absence Marylee has been asking all sorts of questions. Who your husband is, what he did for a living, was he very rich, he certainly must be for you to be wearing such clothes. You can imagine the sort of things she wanted to know.'

'I hope you didn't satisfy her curiosity.'

'She was duly impressed when I told her you were married to a baronet.'

'Oh Susan, even when we're not even living together.'

'Well you're living with another one and I didn't give her an inkling of either of their names. How Marylee would have loved to capture Lionel Prescott and how very hard her mother tried. Lionel was always too hard a nut for Marylee to crack.'

'You know Susan, you are becoming increasingly malicious with your advancing years. Do you think we might go now? I can see Marylee bearing down on us with a great look of determination and I couldn't bear another inquisition from her.'

We left hurriedly, escaping by the skin of our teeth and only because Marylee was accosted by one of the nuns.

I was glad I had agreed to attend the function with Susan, I tried not to live in the past, but some of the memories the day had evoked had been happy ones even if others had not. I had been shown compassion and humanity by a woman I had the utmost admiration for and she had promised to pray for me.

A pale watery sun was shining as I set out on my journey home, my heart warm and secure in the knowledge that soon Julian and I would be together again at Moorcliff.

Although it was now my home it had not become part of me as Glamara was. I loved it because Julian's personality was stamped upon it, but so much of Roxanne still existed at Moorcliff. Her bedroom overlooked the moors and the sea and there were many of her books on the library shelves.

My anticipation was all for Julian, if I had been driving home to a fisherman's cottage my joy would have been the same, and as I travelled the last few miles I increased my speed although I knew he would not as yet have arrived.

I was therefore agreeably surprised to find his long black tourer outside the front door and my heart lifted and began to race as it always did prior to our meeting.

I heard voices coming from the side of the house and went towards them. Julian was standing chatting to a man I had never seen before, a thickset young man wearing country tweeds. I thought that Julian's face looked concerned.

They both turned when they heard my footsteps and Julian smiled and held out his hand. 'Tessa, this is George Longton, our veterinary surgeon. It's a good thing I came home a little early.'

'Is something wrong, one of the horses?'

'No, it's old Minstrel, I'm afraid he's had a heart attack.'

'Oh no, is he going to be all right?'

'Not this time Tessa, I'm afraid he's dead.'

My heart felt like lead when I thought about the beautiful faithful old dog and Julian's arm came round me and held me close. 'He was very old, Tessa, and I'm surprised he went on as long as he has. George said he couldn't have suffered, it was practically instantaneous.'

I nodded mutely. I had loved Minstrel, he had followed me about the house with devoted loyalty, suffering the boisterous playfulness of Jasper and the wicked pranks of Buster philosophically, but Minstrel had been Julian's dog and I knew how much he would be missing him.

'I know where there's a young pup about four months old,' the vet told him, 'golden retriever he is, he'll be a big dog one of these days.'

'I'd like to see him,' Julian said.

'I'll bring him in the morning, sir,' the vet said, then wishing me good afternoon he walked briskly towards his car.

'Can you really replace Minstrel so soon?' I asked Julian unhappily.

'I'm not replacing him Tessa, I never shall, this puppy will be a new dog, a new personality.'

It was an unhappy homecoming for both of us. I was soon

445

to learn however that it was not entirely on account of Minstrel's death.

We took our coffee into the drawing room and although I leafed through a magazine I could feel Julian's eyes on me. When I looked up he smiled but I could tell that he had something on his mind.

'Is something wrong Julian, something besides Minstrel?'

As though he had suddenly made up his mind he looked frankly into my eyes and said, 'You are not going to like this, Tessa, but there was nothing I could do about it. Your uncle and Roxanne are coming here tomorrow.'

My eyes opened wide with shocked dismay. 'Why, when did they decide? Oh Julian do they have to come?'

'I'm afraid so. I wrote to Roxanne about the yacht and they have elected to come over and see to it personally. I can't prevent them from coming, this after all was her home and there are probably several things of hers that are still here.'

'Do they know about us?'

'I don't know, your name wasn't mentioned by either Godfrey or Roxanne. You mustn't worry darling, they will have to know and the sooner the better.'

'Julian I'm afraid, I don't want anything to change, I want our life together to go on exactly as it has and I'm so very frightened that her coming here will change all that.'

'Be reasonable darling, how can it? She can't destroy anything for us. Aren't you endowing her with an importance she doesn't possess? This is your home Tessa, you will receive Roxanne and Godfrey as its mistress, and they will be your guests. If Roxanne cannot accept the situation then she will not be invited here again.'

I sat on the rug at his feet, leaning against him, feeling his comforting warmth and the light touch of his hand against my cheek. Julian was right and I was being stupid and fanciful. Roxanne had been infatuated with Julian when she was little more than a schoolgirl, the sort of infatuation many girls develop for older men, and no doubt she was now amused by it. That foolish girlish desire she had entertained for him must be put in its proper perspective, a schoolgirl crush, nothing more.

Then why didn't I believe it? Why did I keep remembering Carmelita's warning that I should ignore her smiling face and the charm that covered the insidious manipulations of a viper?

That night we made love with a passion and desperation so intense it seemed we had to experience in a single night all the joy and tenderness most men and women give to each other throughout a lifetime.

Long after he slept I lay awake listening to the sea rolling inwards across the rocks and before dawn the steady beating of rain against the window. Now and again the room was lit by flashes of lightning and in the distance the thunder rolled.

I dressed with more than my usual care the following morning and when Annie came in to put the room to rights she looked at me anxiously.

'Is it true Miss Tessa that Sir Godfrey and Lady Chalfont are comin' 'ere today?'

'Yes. I suppose they are talking about it downstairs.'

'Yes. The housekeeper was wonderin' if Lady Chalfont will be wantin' her old room or if she should give them a double room elsewhere.'

I stared at myself in the mirror. I didn't know and wished I had had the presence of mind to ask Julian. I deplored the fact that the room Roxanne had occupied as a girl was still considered her room.

'I will speak to the housekeeper Annie, will you ask her to see me in the morning room?'

She stared at my reflection, meeting my eyes. Annie had always known when something was troubling me. She thought however that it was the advent of my uncle which troubled me and I was not prepared to enlighten her.

'You mustn't worry Miss Tessa, Miss Hetty'll have told him about you and Sir Julian, if he was angry he wouldn't be comin'.'

After I had spoken with the housekeeper and advised her to prepare the double room overlooking the moor I decided to walk down to the stables. From inside the stableyard there was laughter and the excited barking of a small dog, followed by Buster's deeper more mature bark.

Julian and the vet stood in the yard with one of the grooms while Flanagan, and Buster with a restraining rope tied through his collar, stood a little way back watching the antics of a boisterous dog, barely half grown. When he saw me he ran towards me barking excitedly, his beautiful feathery tail waving enthusiastically, leaping up at me when I spoke to him, and Julian laughed.

'This fellow's in need of training,' he said. 'Have you thought of a name for him, Tessa?'

'You should choose his name Julian, he's your dog.'

'I think we'll call this fellow Honey. I was thinking of the colour of his coat.'

We all agreed that Honey suited the retriever admirably and with the choosing of a name he became our dog.

Honey was left with one of the grooms after Julian advised him to give the dog some initial training before he was to be allowed in the house, and particularly as we were expecting guests.

As we strolled back to the house I asked, 'Did they say what time they would be arriving?'

'Shortly after lunch although Roxanne was not the most punctual of persons. Maybe your uncle has rectified that particular flaw.'

I doubted very much that my uncle would have rectified anything. He had been besotted with his young wife. I found myself thinking about Abigail who had always been so painstakingly punctual. Did Godfrey ever compare the qualities of his first wife with the failings of his second, or did her youth and beauty compensate for the lack of Abigail's many qualities? Dear Abigail who had loved so selflessly, content and proud to be Godfrey's wife and the mother of his children.

It was almost four o'clock when a new sports model came up the drive and I saw that Roxanne was driving while Godfrey sat beside her, watching complacently as she pulled up at the entrance with something of a flourish.

Julian held out his hand to me. 'Perhaps we should go out to meet them Tessa, they are after all our first visitors.'

My heart was beating fiercely as I walked with him to the car and then Godfrey was kissing my cheek while Roxanne threw her arms rapturously round Julian's neck. The fact that they greeted me without surprise told me that they already knew I was living at Moorcliff and I felt a certain surprise that Aunt Hetty must have warned them of my presence. It was several days later when Roxanne told me that Aunt Hetty had delighted in telling her, showing her the postcards I had sent from Spain. Yet it all seemed out of character to me.

She laughed airily. 'Your aunt doesn't like me so it's no use making any secret of the fact that we don't get on.' She was watching my face closely, and when I didn't respond she went on , 'I'm sick of hearing what a good wife Abigail was, sick of hearing how well she was respected in the area. I'm Lady Chalfont now and the sooner she gets used to the idea the better for all of us.'

We were alone that afternoon. Julian had taken Godfrey on a tour of the house and gardens and as soon as they had gone out the old Roxanne was back, sarcastic, taunting although in the presence of the two men she was charming, entirely sweet in her manner towards me.

'I must say you have surprised me, Tessa,' she went on with that cool maddening smile. 'You were so angry at seeing Godfrey and me together in London and here you are actually living with Julian. Surely the circumstances are identical.'

'My uncle had a good marriage with a woman who adored him,' I retorted, 'the circumstances were entirely different.'

'But of course they would be, wouldn't they? I had the idea that your husband adored you and was entirely dependent on you.'

Stung to anger I snapped, 'Whatever the circumstances Roxanne, Julian loves me and I love him. One day we hope very much to marry but if that never becomes a possibility we shall stay together exactly as we are.'

I saw her eyes narrow until they seemed to gleam like a cat's eyes, like pieces of chipped jade. 'It all sounds terribly romantic but I know Julian a little better than you do. He will grow tired of you as he has grown tired of so many other women.'

'I don't believe you Roxanne, and I only need to tell him that you are upsetting me by remarks like these to make him ask you to leave.'

She laughed, but there was no real mirth in her laughter. For the first time I felt strong. There was nothing she could do or say to alter the fact that I had Julian's love and I knew then that every intimate look of love, every time our hands touched, every time she saw us bidding them goodnight at the entrance to our bedroom was like the twisting of a knife in her proud, envious heart.

Over the next few days there were other incidents destined to annoy me. She took to riding Shamara in the early morning when she knew I usually rode him myself. She would walk across the moors with Jasper, calling him to her side with enticing titbits so that one day Julian remarked, 'Why not ask Tessa if she would like to go with you, or are you trying to annex the dog's affections?'

Flanagan complained to me bitterly that she rode the horse too hard, so that he returned to the stables sweating profusely, and when I remonstrated with her she merely shrugged her elegant shoulders saying, 'He's in need of a good ride, you're too soft Tessa, with the horse, the dogs and with Julian.'

'And you Roxanne are abusing your position here as a guest.'

It was incredible how swiftly her moods could change when we were not alone, how affectionate, gay and witty she could be, how charming, joining Julian at the piano or chatting easily about people I had known around Glamara. All the time Godfrey watched her with loving indulgence and Julian with cynical scepticism, and my heart lifted when I realized he was never fooled by her duplicity.

She seemed strangely reluctant to make any decision about the yacht. From time to time she visited the harbour and went aboard her but I believed that as long as the yacht remained in the area the excuse was there for Roxanne to visit us. At times Godfrey would say they did not wish to overstay their welcome, that there were matters to attend to at Glamara and they should seriously think of returning home.

Always Roxanne prevaricated, accusing him of being ridiculously homesick, that he thought more of his old Glamara than of her, and telling me that she was bored with the country, that it was selfish of Godfrey to wish Aunt Hetty upon her and that if he wanted to return home he could do so and she would return later at her own time.

I was dreading that this might indeed happen, and Julian too became insistent that if she didn't want to decide about the yacht herself then she should leave matters in his hands.

I remember most the morning I ran into my bedroom intending to change out of my riding habit before lunch. I stopped short on finding Roxanne staring out of the window, from which she must have seen me riding Shamara.

She turned and with that slow tantalizing smile she said, 'I got bored, Godfrey has gone out with the dogs and heaven knows where Julian is.'

'Julian has gone north on business,' I snapped tersely.

She picked up one of my silver-backed hairbrushes then more irritably placed it back with the others. She was wearing riding breeches and a heavy pale blue sweater, with her dark hair tied back and held in a pale blue chiffon scarf.

'Are you intending to ride?' I asked her.

'I haven't made up my mind yet.'

'I don't want you to ride Shamara, I've already had him out and I don't like the way you ride him.'

She looked amused. 'I'll ride Caliph if I ride at all. I've been looking at your clothes. I like the sable coat, I suppose Julian bought that for you.'

'You had absolutely no right to look in my wardrobe, Roxanne. What are you doing here?'

'You seem to forget that this was once my home.'

'I haven't forgotten, but it is no longer your home, it's mine and you have no right in my bedroom.'

I walked past her and went into the bathroom, locking the door behind me, followed by her laughter. I bathed quickly and hurried into my room hoping to find her gone but she was still sitting where I had left her.

'Do you mind leaving now, Roxanne? I wish to get dressed,' I asked firmly.

'Go ahead, I can't think you're that modest,' she snapped back.

For a moment I stood hesitantly by the side of the bed, unsure how to treat this interloper, but she was looking round with amused contemplation.

'This is a beautiful room, isn't it?' she said conversationally. 'So spacious and calm, hardly evocative of the passion it must inspire. I used to imagine what it would be like sleeping in that bed, having Julian make love to me. It makes me very angry to think that it is you who sleeps in his arms every night.

'I hope you haven't forgotten what the gypsy in Seville told me, not now when everything is coming so true.'

'I'd be obliged if you didn't talk so much rubbish, Roxanne. You are making it come true by deliberately making yourself a part of my life. You didn't have to go after Alec, you didn't have to marry Godfrey.'

'And you didn't have to come here to live with Julian but you couldn't help yourself, could you Tessa? It's all to do with fate and now it only remains for death to separate us. Will it be your death Tessa, or Julian's or mine, I wonder?'

I stared at her in fascinated horror, then with a little cry I ran to the door and held it open.

'Please go Roxanne, it is hateful of you to frighten me like this. I want you and Godfrey to go home.'

She laughed, completely uncontrite. 'I'll go, but we shan't be going home, not yet awhile anyway.'

I stood on the landing watching her run lightly downstairs. She was singing softly to herself while I stood trembling, with my heart thumping painfully in my breast.

CHAPTER THIRTY-ONE

I believe that every minute of that day will be in my memory as long as I live. The weather had been deteriorating for several days with strong winds and sharp rainstorms, yet on that particular morning the sun shone, a sun that was too bright. Julian proclaimed over breakfast that it could not last.

All morning he worked over some papers in his study while Godfrey read the morning papers and Roxanne sat on the window seat staring out towards the sea. There was a strange restlessness about her, a feeling I had often surprised in Buster when, although lying quietly at my feet, his lead held loosely in my hands, his whole being was intent on some plan of his own, a desire to escape and go cavorting across the cliff in search of adventure. Roxanne's thoughts too were on other things, other plans entirely divorced from the quiet of the drawing room and more in keeping with the unpredictability of the threatening storm clouds.

I decided I couldn't sit there trying to interest myself in the morning papers, so I called to Jasper and taking a coat and tying a scarf over my head I set out across the cliffs in the direction of the village. The chill of the wind almost took my breath away, and even Jasper looked at me in some surprise, unsure that he would not rather have stayed in front of the fire.

We had not gone far when I was surprised to see Annie standing on the edge of the cliff looking out to sea with such an attitude of expectancy I joined her.

'What are you looking for?' I asked curiously.

She turned and I could sense a strange excitement about her. 'It's the storm, Miss Tessa, I can feel it coming.'

'Then you shouldn't be out here.'

'Oh Miss Tessa, it'll be just like that little picture you gave me an' I've never seen a storm afore, leastways not near the sea. I'm goin' down to the harbour where the boats are, just to see if it really is like the picture.'

'Oh Annie,' I snapped impatiently, 'you'd be much better indoors, I don't want you catching your death of cold.'

She stared at me doubtfully. There was a time when I would have laughed indulgently at her absurd longing to watch boats being storm-tossed on a raging sea, but today I felt irritated by her, even when I knew that it was not really Annie who was to blame for my ill humour.

I turned away to continue my walk towards the village and I suspected that she stared after me with an expression of hurt appeal in her eyes.

I was glad when Mrs Cross invited me in for coffee but agreed when she said, 'Don't think I wants yer to go, ma'am, but there's an almighty storm brewin' an' I think yer should get off 'ome afore it starts.'

Putting Jasper on his lead I set off towards home and met Flanagan and Buster on their way to their usual assignation at the village inn. But looking up at the sky Flanagan shook his head dismally. 'I reckon you'll jest about be getting back in toime, Milady, and Oi thinks we'd be more sensible if we walked back with ye.'

Buster sat with his ears laid back, his small eyes gleaming wickedly, and Flanagan said, 'Sure an' he doesn't loike this weather any more'n Oi do.' Without more ado he fell into step beside me while Buster ran on ahead wagging his whiplash tail enthusiastically.

Roxanne's car had gone and I selfishly hoped they would be out for lunch. I went to the study where Julian sat over his documents and after asking him if he was ready for lunch I said, 'Where are the others?'

'I have no idea, I haven't seen either of them since breakfast.'

'Roxanne's car has gone from the drive, they haven't chosen a very good day to go out.'

Julian seemed singularly uninterested in the whereabouts of his guests and I decided to leave him to get on with his work.

They had not returned when we sat down to lunch an hour later.

Julian smiled when I told him about Annie's excitement and her longing to see if the approaching storm matched the painting I had given her.

'She will find it more than comes up to her expectations,' he said. 'I have seen some terrible storms along this coast, today's will be no exception.'

We were at the coffee stage when Godfrey appeared full of apologies. 'I'm sorry about this, but Roxanne had made up her mind to go. I've left her down at the harbour, she said she wasn't hungry and I told her I'd drive back for her in about an hour.'

Julian stared at him askance. 'You mean to say she's actually gone down to the yacht on a morning like this?'

Somewhat resentfully Godfrey said, 'Well you have been going on to her about it for several days. She thought it was time she made her mind up.'

'She has had more than a week to make up her mind, why choose a day like this? Was she intending going to see Fairbrother?'

'She said she was going to look at the boat first.'

Julian's face darkened with anger, and Godfrey said sullenly, 'She seemed to know what she was doing and she wouldn't allow me to go with her.'

'Have you thought what would happen if she attempts to go on board? The yacht could break her moorings at any time, I've seen it happen a dozen times, a yacht of that size is little more than matchwood in a gale of this dimension.'

By this time some of Julian's urgency had communicated itself to Godfrey and I too had risen to my feet.

'Stay here Tessa,' Julian commanded. 'Of all the damned irresponsible things that girl has done, this is the worst.'

I ran to the window where I saw Julian's car moving swiftly down the drive. I was trembling with a fear I had never known before, fear of the storm and the unknown, fear that before the day was out some tragedy would touch all our lives and I ran upstairs to a window overlooking the sea.

I had seen storms in the dales when the thunder rolled round the fells and lightning lit up the sky, when the moorland grass rolled in waves and the pines tossed their feathery branches in the wind, but they had not been like this.

It had started to rain, great heavy drops that fell miserably from a purple sky and the thunder was matched by the angry roar of the sea. It crashed relentlessly on the rocks while the spray flew upwards, covering the garden with spume like drifting snow.

I stood for what seemed hours and although it was only early afternoon the sky was dark, while the wind howled around the house. Jasper sat trembling beside me, occasionally whimpering when the thunder crashed and I sat in a chair near the window, stroking his soft satiny coat, speaking to him gently.

How long I sat there I have no idea. The day was full of sound but it was all outside the house, inside it seemed that I was living in a vacuum, empty rooms in an empty house, and that in the morning it would lie in ruins like the shattered remnants of my life.

From out at sea there appeared other flashes of light and I could only think that somewhere a ship was in distress. I found myself praying for them, asking God to calm the storm and bring them safely to port.

I sat on in the increasing darkness feeling cold but with neither the will nor the energy to move. Suddenly Jasper ran barking at the door. I looked up expectantly but it was Annie who stood there with the rain dripping off her mackintosh and souwester, wild-eyed and fearful, and I knew that she was the harbinger of the news I had feared all afternoon. Annie who loved me and wanted only what was best for me, would she be the one to tell me that my life was ended?

I stared at her dully, while she, practical as always, said, 'Oh Miss Tessa you shouldn't be sittin 'ere in the cold.'

I didn't speak, but continued to stare at her. I rose to my feet and stood with my eyes searching her face, and seeing my distress she started to gabble incoherently in her haste to tell me her news.

'It's terrible Miss Tessa, an' the boat's cut loose. The master sent mi back to be with yer, God knows what they're goin' ter do, an' Miss Roxanne's on the boat an' Sir Godfrey nearly out of 'is mind down there.'

'Annie talk slowly, I can't understand while you're going on like that.'

'It's the boat, Miss Roxanne is on the boat an' she's tossin' about in the middle o' the 'arbour there like a little cockleshell. They say she'll break up afore they can do anythin' an' there's Sir Godfrey, frantic 'ee is an' Sir Julian's tryin' to get some 'elp.'

'What sort of help?'

'Well there's a lot o' the men there now, they did say it might mean gettin' a rope out to 'er. Oh Miss Tessa, we could see her Ladyship standin' on the deck wi' 'er 'air streamin' in the wind, she were laughin', she must 'a bin hysterical.'

I could imagine Roxanne laughing, at the storm, at the trauma she had brought into our lives, at Julian's anxiety to bring help. But who would take the rope I asked myself, even when the answer stared me in the face. Julian would not ask any of those men to do anything he was not prepared to do himself, he would think of their wives and their children, he would think of the girl who had once been put into his care, but would he for one desperate moment think of me?

I ran past her out of the room and down the stairs, and she came after me calling, 'Miss Tessa, where are yer goin', yer can't go down there, yer'll never stand up i' the wind an' Sir Julian'd be furious wi' me. He said I 'ad to come back ter be wi' yer an' I 'ad to keep yer 'ere.'

I turned to stare at her helplessly.

'Please Miss Tessa stay 'ere, I'll never be able ter look 'im in the face again if I lets yer go.'

'Annie I *can't* stay, I must go to him.'

She fussed over me while I thrust my feet into rubbers and my arms into an ancient mackintosh, then with a souwester covering my hair I ran towards the front door while she ran after me.

'Please Miss Tessa, wait for me, I'm coming with yer.'

'No you're not, Annie, go upstairs and get out of those wet

things. I can manage on my own and we'll want something when we get back.'

'But Miss Tessa!' she wailed but I was already out and running towards Roxanne's car which was standing on the drive. My relief was enormous when I found the keys in the lock. The wind was buffeting so strongly that it took all my concentration to keep the car on the road.

The storm was deafening and in the light from the head-lamps the driving rain lashed down in torrents. On every bend I could feel the tyres slipping and sliding and there were times when the force of the wind sent the car side-ways. Grimly I drove on until I could see the harbour wall where men and women were gathered, the women with saturated shawls on their heads, the men in dripping mac-kintoshes shining wet. They parted to allow the car through, staring at it with dull miserable eyes. As I left the car at the end of the wall the dull force of the gale hit me, whipping the door out of my grasp so that a man came forward, using all his strength to close it. I could hardly stand, so powerful was the wind, and another man took my arm.

'Yer can't go down to the 'arbour,' he said anxiously. 'Yer'll never stand on yer feet down there.'

'But I must go down, please don't try to stop me.'

I was struggling against his restraining hands and then from nearby I heard a voice saying, 'Let 'er be, I'll look after 'er Ladyship.'

It was Fairbrother. He took my arm and together, slipping and sliding and fighting the wind for every breath, we made our way down the slope towards the sea. I stared with incredulous horror at the sight which met my eyes.

Men were clustered on the lower harbour wall, twenty or thirty of them hanging on with grim determination to a rope fastened round Julian's waist, and Julian was standing on the deck of the yacht which was bobbing like a tiny cork on mountainous waves. I could see Roxanne clasped in his arms as he struggled to fasten the rope around her.

She was holding him fiercely, her long dark hair flying in the wind, and then she was fighting him with every breath in her body.

'My God,' the old man breathed, 'she's strugglin' wi' 'im, what's she about?'

At that moment the boat spun round and I could see her face. She was laughing wildly, hysterically, and then her eyes met mine and the laughter changed to triumph. Then a wave mightier than the rest swept her from his grasp and they were both struggling in the water with the yacht like a broken toy all around them. Then I could see them no more.

To my horror I saw the rope swept out of the hands of the men below me, pulling two of them into the waves, and all around me was sound, the storm, the wailing of the women and the shouts of the men. I could not see the far harbour wall because of the mountainous waves that covered it and soon what was left of the yacht had disappeared while the two helpless men were swept out in the wake of Julian and Roxanne. The others clustered helplessly against the wall, then with hunched shoulders and despairing eyes started to walk towards us.

One of them, meeting Fairbrother's eyes, shook his head dismally.

'Which two were it?' Fairbrother asked him.

''Awks an' Jenkins. We 'ad 'im, we 'ad 'em both, what did she want to fight 'im fer? Hysterical thet's what she were, 'ee'd got the rope round 'er, God knows why she fought 'im.'

I watched them climb sorrowfully up the slope and Fairbrother turning to me said, 'There's nothin' else ter be done tonight, Milady, yer'd best get back to the 'ouse.'

'You mean we're just going to leave here, that we're not going to try?'

'Ma'am, two good lads 'ave lost their lives as well as Sir Julian an' the girl, we can't risk more. Yer saw what 'appened, like a wild thing she were. It were just as if she wanted ter die but she wanted 'im to die with 'er. I'm not makin' much sense ma'am, but we've lost four ... Oh we'll search, we'll search as soon as we're able.'

I stared at him, my eyes wide with horror, and he went on. 'It might be days Milady, weeks. I've known men be washed up as far north as Berwick an' as far south as Grimsby after such a storm.'

I sank back against the wall. I couldn't be hearing aright. He couldn't be talking about Julian who only a few hours before I had been facing across the luncheon table, seeing his sweet remote smile as we spoke about Annie, seeing his face darken with anger when Godfrey told him where Roxanne had gone.

Like a wounded animal I wanted to run away and hide but I willed myself to act with a courage I did not feel.

'I must find my uncle, Fairbrother. Have you seen him?'

'Ay, the poor gentleman, 'ee were watchin' wi' the crowd fro' the top wall.'

Together we fought our way back along the slope, while Fairbrother between gasps was saying, 'My but she were 'allus an 'andful, Miss Roxanne. Rode that 'orse of 'ers as though the devil 'isself were after her, sailed that boat i' all sorts o' weather. She were nobbut a little 'un when Sir Julian took charge of 'er but she allus wanted 'im after she were old enough ter want anybody. Well I reckon she's got 'im, but it's taken death to make 'im 'ers.'

I turned to stare at him, at his old weather-beaten face with the rain pouring from his souwester, his deep blue eyes filled with compassion, and with my heart filled with anger I gasped, 'Not even in death will she have him, not if there's any justice in heaven.'

He nodded, his eyes filled with pity, then taking my arm again he said, 'Come ma'am, we must get yer back to the 'ouse an' out o' this storm.'

The crowd had struggled back from the wall, leaving Godfrey alone, oblivious to the driving rain and the spray that covered him. He stared at me without recognition for several seconds, then dully he said, 'She's gone Tessa, both of them gone, tossed about like two rags dolls in the sea.'

It was an old man who stared at me, an old man with tortured eyes and trembling mouth, and taking his arm I said, 'Come with me, we can't do anything here.'

Like a child he allowed me to lead him back along the wall while the crowd watched silently. He seemed like a child as I held the car door open so that I could manoeuvre him into the front seat.

I heard women sobbing as they watched us drive slowly between their ranks, and strangely I felt their sympathy, it seemed to reach out to me invisibly. But Godfrey sat staring stolidly in front of him, oblivious to everything except his own personal loss.

When we reached the house the doors were flung open and servants came out to assist Godfrey from the car. Annie's tears mingled with the rain on her cheeks.

'Oh Miss Tessa, yer should never 'a gone out.'

'Don't fuss Annie, my uncle must go to bed at once, he's soaked to the skin.'

'I'll see to him, Milady,' the butler said.

'Yer should get ter bed yerself, Miss Tessa,' Annie said quickly.

'Annie I don't want to go to bed, you surely can't think that I would sleep. I think that I shall never sleep again.'

I did change out of my wet things into a warm robe but I couldn't bear to stay in the bedroom I had shared with Julian. Instead I returned to the drawing room where Annie had stoked up the fire and where a tray lay waiting for me. I was not hungry but I took the hot milk and whisky she offered, then I sat back with closed eyes, not wanting to talk, locked in my own private misery, oblivious that Annie sat opposite me so that I was surprised much later to find her watching me across the hearth with her face swollen from weeping.

I looked at the clock for I had no idea of the time, time seemed to be something that had ceased to exist since I watched Julian and Godfrey leave the house in the early afternoon. Now I saw that it was almost two o'clock, and overhead the thunder still rolled and the rain battered the window.

'Annie it's late, you should be in bed.'

'I couldn't leave yer 'ere on yer own, Miss Tessa. I could 'ave another room got ready fer yer.'

'No Annie, I'd rather stay here. Please leave me, I'd rather be alone right now.'

'Yer won't do anythin' silly Miss Tessa?'

I stared at her anxious face. Did she really think I was

going to throw myself off the cliff top? I loved Julian, I would go on loving him as long as I lived, but I would not insult his memory by joining him and Roxanne in a watery grave.

'Go to bed Annie, I won't do anything silly.'

She went reluctantly and I switched off the lights and sat in the glow of the firelight, listening to the storm. Misery encompassed me like a shroud but in spite of it eventually I must have closed my eyes because when I awoke the dawn was slowly creeping in the room and I was aware of the silence, a silence that shouted at me after the clamour of the night before. Then it all came back to me and with the memory of it the tears came and I gave myself up to the blessed abandonment of grief.

It was still only a little after six o'clock when I pulled back the drapes. Incredibly the sea was calm. The waves rolled in across the bay, gentle benign waves that caressed the sand and there was a glow in the sky which heralded the rising sun.

The storm was over, but with its passing passed joy and love and all my hope for the future. My dearest love had gone, so how could I ever again feel tenderness and completeness? I too was a dead thing, an empty shell. In those moments I believed I would never again know joy or happiness, that my life was ended, as surely as if I too had been swept away by the storm.

Annie came with coffee before it was properly light and I knew that she too had been awake for most of the night. Her eyes were puffy from too much weeping and I could feel them watching me furtively for signs of the breakdown she was convinced must come.

Grimly I held my emotions in check with an unnatural calmness. I made myself go through the motions of everyday living, bathing and dressing, brushing my hair and applying my make-up, aware that next to the bathroom was the room I had shared with Julian, the bed we had slept in and where we had made love.

His dressing gown lay over the arm of a chair, his slippers lay beneath it. On the dressing table lay a pair of gold cuff links and the book he had been reading lay open on the bedside cabinet.

I made myself sit at the breakfast table, toying with a slice of toast, opening my mail, laying Julian's mail beside his plate, but it was a false normality, and Annie who waited on me knew it also.

The house was coming to life. Fires were being laid, I could hear a vacuum cleaner, and in the gardens the barking of young Honey and the deeper more resonant barking of the bull terrier.

When my uncle joined me I could hardly believe that this was the same man whose laughter had filled the hall of Glamara after a day on the hunting field or during one of the balls Abigail so loved.

We eyed each other in silence, he unable to understand why his young wife had elected to die, and I hating her because she had cost Julian his life. He knew that any effort on his part to excuse Roxanne would be turned aside scornfully. As long as I lived I would hate her and never forget that look in her eyes before the final wave claimed them. I had little patience with his grief. How dared he grieve for a woman who had embraced death with such fervour? To me Roxanne was little better than a murderer.

He too toyed with his breakfast, drinking several cups of coffee but ignoring the food.

'Perhaps we should go down to the harbour,' he volunteered after an interminable silence.

'We can do nothing there, I prefer to wait until there is news.'

'I might be able to help.'

'How can you possibly help? There are boatmen searching the area, we should leave it to the professionals.'

He stared at me pitiably but I refused to show sympathy. At that moment there was none in me, my heart felt as hard, as cold and unrelenting as stone. After breakfast I tried to get interested in the newspaper. As yet the tragedy had not been reported in its full implications and I was glad of that. Godfrey wandered out into the garden and I watched from the window as he pottered dismally along the paths. We could not bear to sit together with me hating and reproachful and he like a lost soul asking questions to which there were no answers.

It was late morning when a police car turned in at the gates and I waited with bated breath while a servant answered their pounding on the front door. They addressed their words to Godfrey. Roxanne had been his wife, I have no idea in which category they placed me although they were respectful and the inspector eyed me with some admiration when I was able to make decisions that Godfrey shied away from.

They had both been found, Roxanne washed up on the beach a few miles to the north, Julian caught up on the rocks below Staithes. We were asked to accompany them and I could see Godfrey visibly shrink away from the ordeal. Without this confirmation I believed he had cherished hope that somewhere, somehow his wife would be safe. Now all hope was gone. I trembled to think what I would have done if Roxanne had survived and Julian had been lost, for I knew in my innermost heart that I would have killed her.

We went with them, sitting at the back of the police car, none of us speaking. The sun shone on the sweep of golden sand and tall cliffs, and on the sea sparkling silver, as unruffled as a placid lake.

Below us on the sands we could see crowds, the police keeping them back from the two still figures lying on the sand, and my heart gave a terrifying lurch, to be replaced by amazement at the noise that was all around us.

'What is it?' I whispered urgently.

'Bells ma'am,' the inspector said, 'church bells, they always rings 'em after a tragedy. I thinks it's barbaric but it's not meant to be, it's meant to be a sign of respect for the dead and sympathy for the living.'

I held my hands over my ears but the clamour went remorselessly on and I have no idea what was said to me as we left the car. Godfrey hung back, his face crumpled like a small boy's, and resolutely I took hold of his hand and pulled him after me.

Without the warmth in his eyes and the tenderness in his voice it was not Julian that I looked at, but rather a stranger, a remote pale stranger with a blue bruise on the side of his

464

face, the dark lashes brushing his cheeks.

It could have been a cold marble statue lying on the sand, not the man I had loved whose charm had embraced me like a cloak, whose remote sweet smile had the power to bring me trembling to his side. I watched them cover his face, knowing that I would never see him again. Beside me Godfrey wept like a child. I turned away, I did not want to look at Roxanne, but I inquired if they had found the two other men who had been washed into the sea.

'Not yet Milady,' the inspector said, 'we're still searchin'.'

It seemed that the next few days belonged to some other person as I went through the ritual of speaking to vicars and lawyers, morticians and people who had known Julian and respected him, but it was Godfrey who appalled me most by his insensitivity.

'They should be buried together in the churchyard here,' he stated as though he had already made up his mind. 'Roxanne spent most of her young life here and they died together, I see no point in taking her to Glamara.'

Incensed I turned on him angrily. 'I will not allow your wife to be buried beside Julian! How dare you even suggest it?'

He stared at me surprised and I realized that even in his grief Godfrey was incapable of seeing how bitterly I resented all mention of Roxanne, or how fiercely I blamed her for Julian's death.

'But Tessa, it is the simplest solution, when I spoke to the vicar he agreed with me.'

'It has nothing whatsoever to do with the vicar. Roxanne was your wife, she must be buried in the Chalfont tomb. I will not have her buried here, wild horses wouldn't make me.'

I was adamant and in the end he realized he would have to take his wife's body back to the dales. I have no doubt that many of those concerned thought that I was hard, that I was so eaten up with bitterness even death had no power to erase it.

It was over at last and they had all gone, people I knew

465

and people I didn't. Julian had been laid to rest beside his parents in the quiet churchyard of the old Saxon church he had known as a boy.

I had thought Godfrey would never forgive me my bitterness against his wife, but as the days passed we drew closer together as in the old days and on the morning he left for Glamara I wept a little. It seemed that with Godfrey's going went all the familiar, solid and stable qualities in my life.

The servants at Moorcliff were kind but they had been Julian's servants, only Annie and Flanagan belonged to me and in some way I felt they were both being made aware of their separateness. It was Annie who put it into words when she said, 'Shall we be looking for somewhere to live again Miss Tessa, an' will it be round 'ere?'

I had no answer for her until I had seen Julian's lawyer and he was due at the house two days after the funeral. We dined together and if there was a certain constraint between us I felt it was because I was not Julian's wife and he knew nothing of the circumstances that had brought us together.

In the drawing room he seemed happier to fiddle with his papers than make conversation, and I sat with my coffee, my thoughts turned inwards, waiting for him to break the silence. At last he cleared his throat and I looked up quickly.

'Lady Chalmers, are you aware of any of the details of Sir Julian's will?'

'No, we never discussed it. We were both young, neither one of us expected to die quite so soon.'

'No, no of course not. Sir Julian was always very practical, he hated loose ends. Sir Julian has left most of his considerable wealth to you, Milady. He left one hundred and fifty thousand pounds to Lady Chalfont, but in the event of her death before yours the money would automatically come to you. He has left several bequests, to servants, to hospitals in the area and to charities. Apart from these Milady you will be the recipient of nine hundred thousand pounds.'

I stared at him in disbelief. I had had no idea of Julian's real wealth. I thought quickly about the night I had made him smile by saying I was glad we were so rich. Now I would willingly give away every single penny for just one more night in his arms.

'He never mentioned his plans for this house in the event of his death?' the lawyer went on.

'No. It was our home and we did not speak of the death of either of us.'

'No, of course not, then I must tell you that Sir Julian has left the house as a home for sick and ageing seamen who are alone in the world. This means Milady that you will not be able to stay here for any length of time. Sir Julian has arranged for me to set up a fund for the employment of nursing staff, he has also instructed that any of the servants wishing to remain here may do so. You Milady are to be allowed to take any article of furniture, indeed anything you wish from the house before it is handed over to the trustees.'

'I intend to leave here as quickly as I possibly can. I could never have stayed on in this house where we were so happy. Julian would know that.'

'Yes, I am sure he would. There is the question of the horses Milady, have you thought what you will do about them?'

'One of the horses is mine, I brought him here, and Caliph I intend to keep also.'

'Have you any idea where you will go?'

'In the long term no, perhaps to my uncle's house until I have had time to sort myself out.'

He nodded sympathetically. 'It will take time, one doesn't get over such a tragedy quickly. There is one other matter Milady. Sir Julian's yacht was damaged in the storm but only very slightly. Do you wish it to be sold?'

'No. I will ask Mr Fairbrother to repair it, then I rather think Sir Julian would wish him to keep it.'

The lawyer raised his eyebrows. 'It is worth a considerable amount of money, are you sure that would have been his wish?'

'I am quite sure. Fairbrother loved the yacht and cared for her.'

'Very well Milady, I will make all the necessary

arrangements to have the yacht transferred into Fairbrother's name. She will be an expensive toy for a man in his position.'

'He is the sort of man who should have her, not some dilettante who would merely employ a man like Fairbrother to sail her. I will see that he has sufficient means to repair the yacht and look after her.'

I felt faintly irritated by the lawyer's supposition that because of his social standing Fairbrother was being handed too much, but I was remembering the old man's exhausted and bedraggled condition on the night of the storm.

The lawyer finally departed and I settled down to read the list of beneficiaries amongst the servants.

The bequests were more than generous, from the butler down to the youngest kitchenmaid. None of the grooms or the gardeners had been forgotten, even Flanagan was to receive two hundred pounds, and my eyes flew open wide at the sum left to Annie. Five hundred pounds, to Annie it would be a fortune, more than she could expect to earn in a lifetime, and I was not surprised when later that night she burst into torrents of tears when I told her about the legacy.

'Oh Miss Tessa, what shall I do wi' all that money? Why should 'ee leave all that ter me?'

'Because he wanted you to have it Annie, and one day when you marry you will be glad of it.'

'Eh, I shan't marry, Miss Tessa, not ever. I'll stay wi' you an' look after yer.'

Her face lit up when I told her that I proposed to go back to Glamara.

'Will it be fer good, Miss Tessa?'

'I don't think so Annie, just for a time perhaps, long enough to lick my wounds and sort myself out.'

'Oh Miss Tessa it'll be grand ter see them all again, an' you'll 'ave yer aunt, an' yer loves it so. Will Flanagan be comin' with us?'

'I hope so. I shall take Shamara and Sir Julian's horse, and of course there are the dogs.'

Although Jasper was my dog he had been wandering round the house like a lost soul, sitting close to me so that I could feel his plump shivering body against my legs, occasionally whimpering with distress, and I knew that he was missing Julian and that in his doggy soul he knew tragedy had entered our lives and that I too was suffering.

I took to walking on the cliffs with Jasper and Honey, who was now growing up rapidly and becoming less adventurous and far more decorous.

Fairbrother was so overwhelmed when I told him about the yacht that he wept quite openly, promising to look after the boat and that as long as he lived it would be Sir Julian's boat and he only the keeper of it.

Flanagan received the news of his legacy with some surprise, but he was happy about the horses and Buster, and the idea of taking up employment at Glamara was received with satisfaction.

'Are you going to invest it Flanagan?' I asked him, thinking I might be of some help.

'Why no Milady, it's thinkin' I am of taking a holiday in the old country, jest a week or two. Oi'd like 'em to see me all dressed up in mi country tweeds wi' the jingle o' money in mi pockets an' a job to come back to. Oi'm not interested in mi old age ma'am, the good Lord'll look after mi when the toime comes.'

PART FIVE

CHAPTER THIRTY-TWO

I could not bear to stay on in the beautiful bedroom overlooking the sea and transferred for the time that was left at Moorcliff into another room.

I felt ill, suffering between bouts of extreme depression and activity when I set about packing trunks with my clothes and the few things I decided to take with me from the house. These were mostly articles of china and jade, and one or two small pictures Julian and I had bought together.

I had long letters from Aunt Hetty urging me to arrive at Glamara quickly, letters in which she said Godfrey seemed morose and crotchety and spent most of his time outdoors on the estate in spite of the increasing cold.

I told the lawyer that it was my intention to leave Moorcliff at the end of November, exactly one month after Julian's death and he seemed surprised. When I told him what I had taken from the house he said, 'I would have thought you would have taken far more Lady Chalmers, there must be many things which would have reminded you of Sir Julian.'

I stared at him, then in some exasperation snapped, 'I do not need material things to remind me of Sir Julian, if I did I would strip the entire house.'

I asked my uncle if Flanagan could take up residence in a cottage on the Glamara estate at once, and receiving a reply in the affirmative I watched him depart, driving a horsebox containing Shamara and Caliph and with Buster beside him on the driver's seat.

Two days later the staff collected outside the house to say goodbye and as I walked along shaking each one by hand several of the women were in tears and one or two of the men were close to them.

It was mid morning and before me stretched the long drive across the northern moors and through the dales. I had asked the lawyer to dispose of my car, deciding to keep Julian's which seemed far more adequate for our luggage, as well as Honey and Jasper.

Annie looked at me anxiously as I took my place beside her. 'It's a long journey, Miss Tessa,' she said doubtfully. 'Are yer goin' to be able to drive all that way?'

I smiled at her concern. 'I'm glad to be leaving, if it was twice the distance I could face it.'

Before we turned out on to the road I stopped the car and we looked back at the house. For a few moments misery engulfed me. Such a little time we had had together. That I would never in this life see Julian again brought the hot stinging tears to my eyes and the pain in my heart was like a stabbing.

Annie sat silent while I composed myself and we spoke little on that long drive through the cold wind and the darkening moors, with the rain pattering against the windows. Above us two curlews circled lazily, their sad lonely cries filling the morning with pain, echoing the anguish in my heart and the aching desolation which I believed would be with me for always.

As we drove at last through Lambreck I could sense Annie's excitement as she sat forward to peer through the windscreen. I was thinking about all those long years when I had longed for Glamara and how I had asked it to shelter me in moments that were desperate and filled with pain. I was remembering the night I crept down the stairs to stand staring at my grandfather's cold white face on the night before his funeral.

There were so many memories crowding in on me as we drove those last few miles. It seemed to me that Glamara had been a rock to cling to in all the traumatic moments of my life, but there had been none that required so much under-standing or so much benediction as the one that brought me to her now. Here at Glamara I had accepted Alec's desertion and Roxanne's treachery. It was from this house that I had gone on my wedding day and I was remembering too those other nights when the wind had sighed yearningly through the trees outside my window, as yearningly as I had longed for Julian even then.

Now, all I asked from Glamara was that it would afford me some breathing space, some passing comfort in which to allow me to build some sort of future.

Long before we reached the front entrance the doors were flung wide and Aunt Hetty and several of the servants were rushing out on to the drive.

In the next few moments I was held in her embrace while all around me dogs were barking, Jasper and Honey and the dogs who had run out of the house. Suddenly Cook was there and the housekeeper, the butler was helping Annie with the luggage and there were cries of 'Welcome home Miss Tessa', and even Annie was smiling at their greeting and then Godfrey was there, taking my hand and looking down into my eyes, earnestly, sadly before he put his arms around me and held me close. I had come home.

If I had returned to Glamara in the summertime I would have known the benison of her gentleness, but I had returned in the winter when the dark brooding hills frowned ominously as they circled the house. I had come back expecting to be confronted by old memories but nothing was the same. Godfrey was glad I had returned but I felt an invisible barrier between us.

He knew that I blamed Roxanne for Julian's death and because she had been his wife he believed that I blamed him also. I tried to banish this belief by seeking him out on the estate so that we could ride or walk together, but in those early days although he greeted me affectionately he seemed to prefer to ride or walk alone.

'Give him time Tessa,' Aunt Hetty said, 'you know he loves you dearly.'

'Oh Aunt Hetty, I hate her still, she's taken Julian and now her shadow lies between Godfrey and me.'

Her portrait had gone from the hall and in its place hung a dark oil painting of a Scottish loch surrounded by heather-clad hills. It was no doubt priceless but distinctly dismal and I asked Aunt Hetty why Godfrey hadn't put Abigail's portrait in its original place.

'I didn't interfere, Tessa. He's put Roxanne's portrait in his study and I was worried at first in case he spent hours sitting in there alone just looking at it but strangely enough he seldom goes in there.'

'Aunt Hetty I could not allow Roxanne to be buried with Julian, I hope you understand.'

'Of course, and I too have tried not to be bitter. Death does not kill love, my dear, so how can it kill hate?'

'Did you try to like her?'

'How could I? She was the talk of the neighbourhood with her men friends, I sometimes wondered why Godfrey tolerated it, he must have known.'

'She had men friends round here?'

'Oh yes. Jeffrey Denton for one and he with a young wife of only eighteen months. She wasn't very selective, some of them were young, others older than Godfrey. She showed me the presents they bought her as though she was proud of them and friends I had known over the years didn't call any more. Even the villagers talked and the servants started to leave.

'I chastised her about her behaviour more than once but she only laughed, telling me I was a silly jealous old maid whom no man had ever looked at twice. If I didn't like her behaviour then nobody was keeping me here. But I was brought up in this house and Godfrey is my brother. No little harlot like Roxanne was telling me to leave it.'

'Was it you Aunt Hetty who told her I was with Julian?'

She blushed, momentarily discomfited. 'I *had* to tell her, Tessa. She was taunting me, telling me about her lovers since she married Godfrey, and others when she was married to Alec. Then she said if she couldn't have Julian she didn't care who she slept with and God help me I found pleasure in telling her it was you Julian loved.'

'And then?' I prompted her.

'She didn't believe me until I showed her your postcards from Spain. After that she ran wild, she couldn't contain her anger or her jealousy and Julian played into her hands when he wrote to her about the boat. Godfrey told her to sell it, but she must go over to the coast to see it. She pestered his life out with stories of how she loved sailing, how she couldn't bear to part with it and at last he gave in to her. You know the rest, Tessa.'

She started to cry and I watched helplessly while her small body seemed wracked with sobbing. 'It's all my fault,' she moaned, 'she would never have known if I hadn't told her.'

'She would have found out sooner or later, Aunt Hetty, it wasn't something we could keep secret for ever.'

'Perhaps not dear, but you had so little time. She's dead and I can't forgive her, any more than you can.'

I seldom went into the village but when I did I was touched to see how the villagers greeted me with shy smiling faces and warm words of welcome. I doubted if they knew anything about my life since I left Glamara because the servants jealously guarded all matters surrounding the family.

I shall always remember the day I faced Aunt Hetty over coffee cups in her favourite sitting room with the rain pattering against the window and the light from the fire touching on a bowl of bronze chrysanthemums and giving a glow to the silver coffee set.

I had delivered my bombshell and now watched the changing expressions on her face, bewilderment and doubt, pain and sorrow before the tears rolled down her cheeks and she sobbed into the ridiculous handkerchief she fished out of the pocket of her cardigan.

'Are you sure Tessa?' she whispered at last.

'Yes I am quite sure Aunt Hetty.'

'Oh Tessa, what are people going to say? It is more than a year since you left Richard. What are you going to do?'

'You are surely not suggesting that I have my baby adopted, Aunt Hetty?'

'I don't know what I am suggesting, I'm too upset. It's not as though Julian is here to take care of you, that would have been different, you'd have been over at the coast and nobody round here would have known anything about it.'

'Well Julian isn't here and my baby is going to be all I shall ever have of him.'

'I can't imagine what your uncle is going to say.'

'I shall tell him in due course Aunt Hetty, I won't leave it to you to tell him.'

'And the servants. You don't care, Tessa?'

'No Aunt Hetty, I'm very much afraid I don't care what anybody says, and if I am going to become an embarrassment to you I will look for somewhere to live some distance from here. I am a very rich woman, my child will lack for nothing and I shall love him enough for both of us.'

'Oh Tessa you can't go away from here, I didn't mean that.'

'Aunt Hetty I love you very dearly but there is no reason for you to feel embarrassed on my account. This is your home and you have lived among these people all your life. You understand their narrowness, their ideas of what is proper and what is wrong, I will not let you suffer for anything I have done. I will find somewhere to live and I will take Annie with me. You will be very welcome to visit us whenever you feel like it.'

The tears started afresh and I put my arms round her. 'Please don't cry, Aunt Hetty, this isn't a tragedy to me, I want this baby more than anything in the world, it's as though something has come out of a great aching void to bring solace into my life. Don't spoil this moment for me by your tears, share some of my joy instead.'

She continued to sob however, and with a little sigh I left her alone. That night I told Annie and was amazed to see the sudden joy light up her face.

'Oh Miss Tessa I'm glad, an' I 'opes it's a boy I do. A boy who looks like Sir Julian an' who grows up just like 'im. I knows a lot about babies, mi mother 'ad enough of us 'eaven knows.'

I was glad at least that Annie had received my news with enthusiasm, and later I told my uncle. He seemed at first not to take it in, then he said abruptly, 'Do you intend to keep the child, Tessa?'

'Of course.'

'It's a hard world for a woman bringing up a child alone.'

'I have sufficient means, my child will lack for nothing.'

'I wasn't meaning material wealth, you should remember how your mother was made to suffer at the hands of society.'

'I do remember, I shall never forget it but times are changing, Uncle. I shall call myself Mrs and nobody will ever know the true story.'

'I'm afraid you won't find it quite so simple my dear, there will be schooling, you'd be surprised what details they want to know before a child's allowed in school.'

'By that time I hope the world will have become a little more compassionate uncle, at least towards my child.'

'Well it's your bed mi dear an' I reckon you'll have to lie on it. You know you can depend on me for any help you want.'

I reached up and kissed his cheek. 'I know I can Uncle Godfrey, but I won't ask for anything and I won't embarrass you by remaining. I shall look for a place of my own some distance from here.'

'That you won't. You'll stay here where you belong, such nonsense, what'll you do on your own with no family behind you?'

I was so touched I felt the tears spring to my eyes and embarrassed he said, 'Whoever expected you to leave Glamara? It wasn't Hetty was it?'

'No Uncle Godfrey it was entirely my idea, but Aunt Hetty would be hurt by the scandal and I wouldn't like that.'

'This family will stand together. It was rocked by Roxanne's behaviour. Don't look so surprised Tessa, I knew all about that. I also knew she was besotted with Julian and he never gave her any cause, whatever she asked you to believe.'

'How could you bear to see her behaving so badly, how dared she do it to you?'

'It was my punishment for being such a God-damned fool. I fell in love with a beautiful face and body, I failed to see the ugliness underneath. You know Tessa I loved Abigail even though she was as homely as a pumpkin, but she was pure gold underneath and she loved me so much there were times when I felt suffocated by it. I could have loved her more if I'd let myself, but instead I fell in love with a pretty face and forgot my wife's more sterling qualities. It happens to a lot of us and most of us don't learn before it's too late.'

He left me shaking his head solemnly, and I watched him go with eyes filled with warmth and pity.

The days passed and no more mention was made of my leaving Glamara but that was not to say I had given up the idea. I had only to look at Aunt Hetty's dismal face to spur me to make inquiries from various estate agents in the Cotswolds and further south.

There were days when I felt lethargic, when I found the idea of food nauseating but Annie cajoled and bullied me into eating.

'Surely yer don't want yer child to be a weak little thing wi' no stamina,' she would scold. 'Mi mother wouldn't eat when she 'ad our Joe an' look at 'im, poor little thing. 'Ee's that stunted at the side o' the others, 'ee looks as though a puff o' wind'd blow 'im over.'

Convinced by her description of Joe I made myself eat but I had little appetite.

Aunt Hetty was starting to fuss too. 'You're so thin, Tessa,' she said, 'are you sure you are eating enough?'

'Quite sure Aunt Hetty, Annie stands over me to make sure I'm eating.'

'I must say Godfrey has taken the news of your pregnancy very well, much better than I thought he would.'

'Yes, he was very kind.'

'I hope you have given up those foolish ideas you had of leaving here Tessa,' she added, and I couldn't help smiling to myself when I recalled how she had welcomed those foolish ideas in the first days after I had told her about the baby.

'Aunt Hetty, I can't go on staying here for ever. One day this will be Robert's house. I want my child to grow up in his own home, although as yet I don't know where it is going to be.'

I remember the morning I took stock of myself for the first time since Julian's death. It was Annie who sparked it off.

'Miss Tessa, you don't look nothin' like yerself any more,' she admonished me. 'You don't bother with yer 'air an' you've all them beautiful clothes that yer never even wear.'

'I don't care about clothes any more Annie, there's nobody to care what I look like now.'

'Oh but there is Miss Tessa, there's yer aunt and uncle, and there's all the servants who sees yer everyday. In time there'll be the baby, surely you'll want your baby to be as proud of the way yer looks as you were of yer mother. However unhappy she was she allus looked beautiful.'

I stared at her in hurt surprise. 'Oh Annie, that isn't fair.'

'No I don't suppose it is, but I hates ter see yer goin' about like a pale little ghost. Yer can't 'ave 'im back and he'd 'ate to see yer the way yer are now, yer nothin' like the girl 'ee loved an' that's a fact.'

After she had left me I looked in the mirror. She was right. My hair that had always seemed so shining and silvery fair was now scraped back from my face in an unbecoming bun, revealing my thin pale face and the dark circles round my eyes. I reached up and released it from the restraining hairpins and it fell around my face which immediately took on a softer aspect, disguising the sharp angular planes of my face that were now so evident.

The thick tweed skirt and fawn sweater were unattractive, and yet my wardrobe was filled with clothes. I rummaged through them and came across a skirt Julian had loved to see me in, a soft blue mohair that made my figure seem more rounded, as did the soft blue sweater I selected. The change in my appearance was so startling that Annie's eyes lit up with delight when she came back to apologize for her remarks.

'You were quite right Annie, I looked terrible. It would have grieved Julian to see me looking like that. Aunt Hetty was probably thinking what you were thinking.'

'She'll be glad to see yer more like yerself, Miss Tessa, when she comes back.'

Of course. Aunt Hetty and Godfrey had gone to pick up a puppy from one of our neighbours. Her little dog had died and this puppy was to be his replacement, although I knew she still mourned for the dog who had been her companion for so long.

The housemaid who was lighting the fire in the morning room had not been at Glamara long, and she could barely conceal her surprise at my changed appearance. I settled down in front of the fire to write letters but was disturbed a few minutes later by another housemaid informing me that a gentleman was asking to see me. Surprised, I asked her who he was.

'Sir Richard Chalmers, Milady.'

I stared at her in shocked surprise, feeling the blood drain from my face and a sudden faintness take hold of my limbs. Richard here! Anger encompassed me. Had he come now to offer me that divorce he had denied me before, now when it was too late, now when Julian was dead, now when I was alone and my child would have no father?

The girl was staring at me and gathering my scattered wits I said as calmly as I could, 'Show Sir Richard in here.'

After she had gone I went to the brandy decanter and poured a small measure into one of the glasses, drinking it quickly to give me the courage I needed to meet Richard face to face.

I heard his sticks, and then we were staring at each other across the room and I recognized my own voice inviting him to sit near the fire. In that first instant I saw the greyness in his face, its thinness and the silver wings at his temples. He leaned heavily on his two sticks and seemed to have great difficulty in lowering himself into the chair so that instinctively I went forward to help him.

I had thought to see hostility in his eyes but there was none, only a great kindness, and unbidden the treacherous tears rose into my eyes and rolled unashamedly down my cheeks.

'Tessa I'm sorry,' he said gently, 'I wanted to come before but I wasn't sure how you would receive me.'

I stared at him doubtfully. 'You're sorry about Julian? Then you knew?'

'Yes. Roxanne told me. She took great delight in telling me, I have her letter here.'

I watched him take out his wallet from which he extracted a folded sheet of pale peach notepaper which he passed over to me. How she must have hated me to pen that letter telling my husband where I was living and with whom. She wrote to Richard as a friend, to prove to him how worthless I was, how well rid of me he was and I handed the letter back to him with shaking fingers.

'Richard, I'm sorry you had to find out like that, but I loved Julian and I never said I loved you. I wanted us to be happy together, I tried very hard to make it worthwhile, but almost from the outset our marriage was doomed.'

'And I was stubborn and difficult, and as time passed I saw how badly I had let you down. You're so thin Tessa, have you been ill?'

'No, just desperately unhappy. How have you been Richard?'

'Some days better than others. My heart isn't up to scratch and of course I can't get about much, but one mustn't complain. A great many men didn't come back at all.'

There was silence between us while he looked down at his hands and I found myself wondering why he had come. I was calmer now, the constraint between us had gone and I could feel something of the old comradeship. At last he looked up, staring straight into my eyes and I was aware of his earnestness.

'I'm not much good with words Tessa, but I want you to come back to me. I had to come in person, a letter wouldn't have done.'

I stared at him in disbelief, not even sure if I had heard aright, but he was saying, 'I don't expect you to make up your mind right away, but perhaps we could talk about it a little.'

'Richard I don't know what to say. I haven't heard from you or seen you for over a year and in that time a great many things happened to me. I lived with a man I loved, ecstatically, devotedly, and I still love him even though he is dead. I know that in time the pain will lessen but that it will ever go away completely I don't know. Besides I do not think I could ever return to your home to live the sort of existence we had before, it is unthinkable. Richard, shouldn't you be hating me, resenting me for living with Julian when I was still your wife? Can you really bear to take me back?'

483

'I could never hate you Tessa, and I know we could never go back to the sort of life we had before. My mother is no longer at the hall, she has gone to the lodge house where she promised to go before we married. She made your life at Easdale unbearable and I realized too late how you suffered because she was eaten up with an old bitterness. I should have been a bulwark you could lean on, instead I was a straw in the wind.'

I didn't speak, and when I was silent for so long he said, 'It is I who should ask your forgiveness Tessa, for my selfishness, my thoughtlessness, but if I had been all you expected of me you would never have left me and you would perhaps never have known that happy time with Julian.'

He took my silence for a sign that I was thinking over his proposal but instead I shook my head sadly. 'I can't come back to you Richard, not now. I am going to have a child, Julian's child. It would be heartless and cruel to expect you to cherish another man's child, I am not so insensitive.'

Not in the least disconcerted he said calmly, 'It would be your child Tessa, *our* child, and I would care for you both. Surely life with me would be preferable to life on your own with a child to bring up? He would bear my name and there would be nobody to say he wasn't ours, nobody to *dare* to say he wasn't ours.'

'There would be your mother, Richard. She knows we could never have children, she would know the child wasn't yours, she would never let me forget it.'

'My mother will know when to keep silent. Our relationship hangs on a very fine thread and I cannot think she wishes to lose me entirely. Mother will have the sense to know that any further interference in our lives would sever that thread.'

He was looking at me with so much appeal in his tired eyes I did not know what to say. I needed time to think, time to accept all the implications life with Richard would mean, and to encourage me further he said, 'Why not give it a try Tessa? You can always leave again if things don't work out.'

I smiled a little at that. He made me sound like a butterfly on the constant lookout for pastures new but I respected the logic of his remark. I need never again live where I didn't want to live, I need never again be made miserable because of envy or bitterness, I was my own woman and Julian's money had made it possible, but was money enough?

I had to think about my child in a world filled with prejudice and intolerance. Memories of my own childhood were still fresh in my mind and in the twenties a child could still be made to suffer for the transgressions of its parents.

I could go back to living with Richard and my child would bear his name. Perhaps between us would grow that old comradeship and trust we had lost, and once again I could help him to bear the pain his war injuries had laid upon him. I didn't know how much we still had to give each other or even how much I could trust him to honour his part of the bargain after he had let me down so abysmally before.

As though he knew some of the doubts passing through my mind he urged, 'Tessa, please come back, I have made you promises I would rather die than break. You owe it to yourself and to Julian's child, if I let you down a second time I shall not deserve to keep you.'

'I need to think Richard, did you expect me to make up my mind immediately?'

'No. I thought you might want to discuss it with your uncle and aunt.'

'I feel that I should.'

'Will you write to me then, or better still visit me?'

'Yes I promise.'

He rose unsteadily and grasping his sticks made his painful way to my side. 'Can you bear to return to such an old wreck, Tessa, or am I being mad to expect it?'

'You are not being mad, Richard, I had not thought to find such kindness. It is a long way back to the West Riding, will you not stay and eat lunch with us?'

'No thank you Tessa, I will stop off somewhere on the way back. I'd prefer you to talk to your relatives without any persuasion on my part. Don't make me wait too long for your answer.'

I walked with him to the door and then his chauffeur came forward to assist him into the car. I stood watching it down the long drive before I went back into the house.

I sat staring into the fire for a long time after he had gone. Could I really bear to go back to that cold dark house with his mother's taste, or the lack of it, evident in every room? Could I bear to drive past the lodge house, seeing her eyes peering through the window, meeting her along the roads or in the village, when she knew that my child was not Richard's? I could understand the resentment she would feel, but whether she liked it or not I was still Richard's wife.

I heard Aunt Hetty and Godfrey return and from the excited barking of a puppy I knew she had made her choice. She came immediately into the morning room carrying him, a tiny bundle of tan and fawn, bright brown eyes inquisitive, a gay bundle of mischief and Jasper ran barking to greet them.

'Isn't he adorable,' Aunt Hetty enthused, 'and so intelligent, I shall call him Rusty, it's the colour of his coat.'

'He'll be spoilt to death.'

'How nice you look, Tessa, I was wondering when you'd start to take a little interest in your appearance.'

'Annie bullied me into it and as things have turned out I'm rather glad I made the effort.'

'Why, have we had visitors?'

'One visitor. Richard has been to see me.'

She stared at me speechless for several moments, then briskly she said, 'I'll take the puppy down to the kitchens, he's very young, I'm not sure if he's completely house trained. I shall be back in a moment.'

How she must have hurried to the kitchens. She was back in minutes still wearing her tweed pull-on hat and gaberdine raincoat.

'What brought Richard here?'

As briefly as possible I related the events of the morning and she sat listening without comment until the tale was told.

'What answer did you give him?' she demanded.

'I told him I would think about it carefully and discuss it with you and Godfrey.'

'Tessa, you can't possibly go back to the sort of life you had at Easdale before, it is unthinkable. Dora will not have changed, if anything she will have become far more bitter and disruptive. It is quite impossible for you two to live under the same roof and Richard should be made to realize it.'

'He does realize it Aunt Hetty, his mother has gone to the lodge house.'

'But she is on the estate, you will probably see her every day; besides there is the question of the child.'

'That is what concerns me most. Richard has promised that the child will have his name and will be brought up as his own. He seemed happy about the baby, complacent. Richard likes children, it was a bitter blow that he could never have any of his own.'

'And do you think his mother doesn't know that? How will she react to having another man's child being brought up as her grandson? My dear girl, she will spread it far and wide that the child isn't her son's.'

'And Richard will dispute it, or he will separate himself completely from his mother which is something she would hate.'

'You are seriously thinking about this proposition aren't you, Tessa? And ignoring its implications. Is that wise of you?'

'I'm not very sure about what is wise and unwise any more, Aunt Hetty, but I do remember my own childhood without a father to take care of us. The children of some of my mother's oldest friends called me a bastard. I was never invited to their parties or their homes, I was only tolerated at the riding stables. My child will be rich but I don't want money to buy friendship, I want my child to be welcomed, to have an honoured name and a stable background. I could not wish my childhood on anybody, the slights and hurts, the degradation, and I could not bear the same sort of treatment my mother had to suffer.'

'It is a great pity you didn't think of all these obstacles before you conceived this baby, my dear.'

'It didn't matter, Aunt Hetty. I had Julian then, and one day we would marry. Great heavens, never in a thousand years did I expect Julian to die.'

'You realize it is a decision you must make on your own, Tessa. Neither Godfrey or I can make it for you.'

'I know. I shall talk to Godfrey after lunch but I expect his reaction will be the same as yours. Aunt Hetty, if I could just go on living here at Glamara, existing from day to day with the future shut out and unimportant, I would welcome it, but it isn't possible. I have to rebuild my life and Richard has held out a helping hand which I cannot afford to disregard.'

She looked at me sadly, then I saw her face change and I knew that she had accepted it. Godfrey too would accept it, I would always be welcome here but I had to find my own destiny, live my own life.

CHAPTER THIRTY-THREE

Before Christmas I was back in my old bedroom at Easdale Hall with Annie as my maid. Flanagan was back above the stables, both the horses were in their stalls, and the retriever and Jasper were at the house while Buster remained with Flanagan. I was touched by Richard's attempts to make the house look welcoming. There were flowers in every room and bright log fires. There was even a Christmas tree in the hall.

The rooms seemed singularly devoid of furniture, and Richard explained that his mother had taken much of it and that I could refurnish Easdale Hall to my own taste. This I enjoyed doing. There were new drapes at the windows and polished walnut furniture replaced the traditional dark oak and mahogany. I ordered crystal chandeliers for the hall and over the staircase and new carpeting for many of the rooms. I was extravagant but I spent my own money and Richard appeared delighted with the results.

The servants were glad to see me back and I was agreeably surprised to see a new contentment on their faces and a new pride in the furnishings and trappings I had installed.

Lady Chalmers had gone to spend Christmas in some hotel on the south coast, and I was glad that we did not have to meet so soon.

Richard was kind and solicitous as he had been before we married and although there were hundreds of times I ached for Julian I knew I had done the right thing.

Another moment of joy came when we attended morning service at Christmastime, and the villagers came forward in their dozens to greet us. They welcomed us both, and I was glad to see that Richard was taking an interest in his tenants and in the village generally.

During the next few months I filled my days with plans for the future. Annie overwhelmed me with gifts of baby clothes until I insisted on purchasing the wool she made up into exquisite matinée jackets and warm vests, so tiny they could have fitted a doll.

'All the servants are that glad about the baby,' she said. 'Cook says it's bin a long time since there were a child in this 'ouse.'

'Have they shown surprise that I am expecting a baby, knowing how badly crippled Sir Richard is?'

'Why no Miss Tessa, they're just that glad fer both of yer.'

'I wonder what Richard's mother is thinking?'

'I saw 'er in the village yesterday. She hasn't changed any, Miss Tessa, she still looks that haughty and proud. I 'opes she doesn't come 'ere pokin' 'er nose into things.'

'She must have heard about the baby?'

'I suppose so. Don't yer go worryin' yer 'ead about Lady Chalmers, she can't hurt yer ever again. Sir Richard'll see to that.'

Aunt Hetty visited us for several days at the beginning of May armed with warm woollen shawls for the baby and a cradle draped in pretty primrose-sprigged voile. When I remarked on her extravagance she said, 'The cradle was in the attic at Glamara, I simply had it draped in a different colour.'

'I'm so glad you kept the cradle Aunt Hetty, it's beautiful. I wonder what other treasures you have stored away in those attics at Glamara.'

'I was brought up to be thrifty, after all there is no point in throwing good articles away, one never knows when they will come in useful,' she said tartly.

I loved having her, and she got along well with Richard.

'Why isn't my mother more like her?' he said after she had left. 'My mother was never one for showing affection, she treated me like a possession instead of a child, any affection I ever had came from my father and if he displayed it when she was around she was jealous.'

'What a destructive emotion jealousy can be,' I mused, 'and usually there is so little cause for it. Your mother must have made herself quite ill from imagining slights that were never intended.'

'Yes, but what was much worse, she put a wedge between my father and me and between my father and herself.'

'What has she had to say about the baby, Richard?'

'Nothing, absolutely nothing. I can't think she will remain silent, Tessa, but I can handle my mother now, you must not let her worry you.'

'She will be thought of as the child's grandmother, we must include her in anything we plan.'

'Yes, well I suggest we meet that fence when we come to it. She will say nothing publicly, she is too jealous of the Chalmers' good name.'

'And I have done nothing to maintain it.'

'You did everything to maintain it in the face of considerable opposition. If my mother becomes obstreperous she will be made to see that.'

'Oh Richard, I just want to have my baby and a whole lot of peace. I want us to live together like a family, a happy family.'

'But these last few months Tessa, you have been happy here?'

'Yes Richard, as happy as I can expect to be yet. You have been so terribly kind, so considerate, and I love you very dearly.'

'Love without passion. A friend for a friend?'

'Perhaps, but then you are a friend, Richard, my very good friend.'

490

He was relying on me more every day. His eyesight was not good and he liked me to read to him, from the newspaper and field magazines, sometimes from a novel he was enjoying, and there were days when he suffered blinding headaches that left him tired and drained.

I admired him so much, his courage and his dependability, but it gave me pleasure to help him and he was so very grateful. This was how I had first imagined it would be.

It was assumed by the entire household that my son was born prematurely at the end of June, an assumption strengthened because I had a fall coming down the stairs which brought on the birth.

It was not an easy birth. I was slight and he was a large beautiful child, but whatever pain I suffered was forgotten the moment I held him in my arms. He cried so seldom that I slept peacefully in the large bedroom overlooking the park, but I knew that Annie vied with the baby's nurse until I remonstrated with her sharply.

'Please Annie, leave the baby to the nurse, there will be all the time in the world for you to care for him when she has gone.'

''Ow long's she stayin' 'ere then?' she asked morosely.

'For three months, that is all.'

'We didn't really need 'er at all, Miss Tessa, I reckon I knows just as much about rearin' babies as she does.'

'I daresay, but why don't you look after me and leave the baby to his nurse?'

Richard was enchanted with him, gazing into his cradle with rapt admiration and making all the appropriate fatherly noises which made us all smile. I did not gather strength as quickly as I should have done (though the child thrived by leaps and bounds) and there were times when I was alone when I wept a little, thinking how Julian would have adored his son.

It was two weeks later when Richard's mother came to see me. I was resting in front of an open window on a warm sunny day filled with the sound of birdsong. The baby asleep in his cradle by my side and occasionally I looked down at him as proud and contented as a mother cat with her kitten.

She came unannounced and I did not hear her until her shadow fell across the cradle, and I looked up startled.

She stood looking down at the child expressionlessly, then said coldly, 'It would appear I must congratulate you, Tessa.'

I looked at her uncompromising face doubtfully, and she went on, 'Oh, not on the birth of the child, but on your cleverness in making my son accept him as his own, and gulling everybody else into accepting that my stricken crippled son is capable of fathering the heir to Easdale.'

I stared at her cold angry face glaring at the child sleeping so peacefully, and this time there was no disguising the hatred in her narrowed eyes or the menace in her clenched hands.

With a little cry I lifted him into my arms, holding him against me as though to shield him from this avenging witch about to lay a curse on his innocent head.

Richard came into the room, taking in the situation at a glance, and said sternly, 'What are you doing here, Mother? If I had known you wished to see the child I would have sent a car for you.'

'I am quite capable of walking that small distance, Richard, I merely wished to keep up the illusion that the child is yours and that his grandmother should call to see him.'

Richard frowned, but determined to keep the peace he said equably, 'Well now that you have seen him, don't you think he's a fine little chap?'

'Babies look much the same at that age. It is not like you to be so besotted with anything.'

'Perhaps I am entitled to be besotted with my first son.'

She stared at him contemptuously. 'Your *first* son Richard! Will there be others then? It will be interesting to know who your wife will select to father the next one – a groom perhaps, or your chauffeur?'

Richard's face darkened and grew cold, then he walked slowly to the door and flung it open. 'I must ask you to leave us, Mother. It has taken you seven months to set foot in this house, another seven months would be too soon.'

She left, her head held high, not looking at either of us, and

Richard closed the door sharply behind her.

I was trembling as I laid the child back in his cradle and Richard looked at me across the room with dark, pain-filled eyes. 'I'm sorry Tessa, I had no idea she would come here.'

'She frightens me, Richard. She hates me so much, so intensely, I am afraid she would harm the child if she had the chance.'

'She will not come into this house again, I promise you.'

I felt shaken by the encounter, and to change the subject Richard said, 'Have you thought what you want to call him?'

'I think that is something we should decide together. Would you like me to call him Richard?'

'As one of his names perhaps, I am sure you will want another one to be Julian.'

'I have been thinking about it carefully during the last few days. I think I would like to call him Adam, it would please Godfrey who has always been very good to me. Suppose we call him Adam Julian Richard?'

His face flushed with pleasure, and so my son was christened on a mellow golden day in late August in the tiny village church, watched by most of the villagers. I asked Susan and her husband John to be godparents and if it was noticed that the child's grandmother was not present nobody mentioned it.

Both Godfrey and Aunt Hetty were delighted by our choice of names, particularly when I told them he would be known as Adam Chalmers.

I was touched by the gifts the villagers gave to me: mittens and bootees, little matinée jackets and soft woollen toys; in return Richard gave the two children who had been born closest to Adam a gift of money.

The years of Adam's babyhood passed quickly, and Adam grew strong and sturdy, with dark shining hair and that sweet remote smile, Julian's smile, that still had the power to stir my heart with a remembered pain.

A new estate agent had been appointed during my absence and I met him one morning when he came up to the house to consult Richard about some matter. His name was Simeon Ellis and he was a slender, very dark man, small in stature and with dark beady eyes in a swarthy face. I did not take to him, nor to the way he eyed me boldly. When we met on the estate, though he was civil enough there was insolence in his small bow and even in the way he said, 'Good day, your Ladyship.'

I began to understand this dislike when I saw him leaving the lodge house on several occasions, and once I saw him standing in the village lane chatting to my mother-in-law. Although I bade them good afternoon only the man acknowledged me and I passed by with heightened colour and a feeling of deep resentment.

I said nothing of my dislike to Richard, but I determined to see for myself that his orders were carried out by visiting the estate office two or three times a week. Ellis didn't like it, and on one occasion after I inquired why the perimeter wall hadn't been restored he said irritably, 'Sir Richard gave me no instructions to attend to that, Milady.'

'But it's crumbled to a dangerous degree,' I retorted. 'Does my husband know about it?'

'He knows, but I can't tell Sir Richard how much money he has to spend on the property, there's more than the perimeter wall needing attention.'

That afternoon I made it my business to walk round the estate and the outside of the house. I was soon convinced that it needed a fortune spending on it – there was rotting woodwork and crumbling masonry everywhere. I had spent my own money lavishly on making the interior warmer and more attractive as a home, but I had believed the building itself to be Richard's concern. Now I realized something would have to be done urgently.

When I approached him about it he seemed so irritated I decided the time was not opportune, and as his condition worsened I knew I could not possibly have workmen tramping in and out of the house or hammering on the walls when he suffered his blinding headaches.

Flanagan was a tower of strength, since Richard had long since dispensed with the male nurse his mother had brought in. When I asked him why Richard said sharply, 'The fellow reported to my mother every day, I felt stifled by him. Besides I didn't want him here when you came back.'

The thing that delighted me most was that Richard and Adam adored each other. They spent hours over picture books and jigsaw puzzles, while it was left to me to educate Adam into the more manly pursuits like riding his pony, walking in the fells and learning to swim. Once as we walked the dogs near one of the reservoirs he caught sight of a boat and I saw his eyes light up with pleasure and I found myself praying silently, Oh no Adam, please, not sailing! I couldn't bear it, and walked swiftly on so that he had to run to catch up with me, staring into my face doubtfully, unsure why I was so troubled.

I saw the deterioration every day in Richard's health and one day on a rare occasion when he went into the garden I saw him poke at a piece of stonework with his stick, sending it crumbling on to the path. I knew that he too was worried about the state of the house but he made no mention of it to me.

One day stands in my mind more than any other. He had been ill for most of the night and I cautioned Adam to be quiet around the house, finally sending him down to the stables where he kept his pet rabbit and where Topsy our black cat had given birth to four adorable kittens.

I went to sit with Richard in the morning room, more than ever aware of the tiredness round his eyes. Gently I asked him if he was feeling better, and his reply startled me for he had never been given to self-pity.

'Don't look for miracles, Tessa, there are none for me. I try not to think of it, and yet when I am alone at night I hear quite distinctly the slow, inevitable footfalls of Death.'

I stared at him in shocked surprise and his small sad smile sent me hurrying to his side. I held him against me, aware of his wasted frame beneath the veneer of clothing.

'Richard, I should have known what it was like for you to be alone, I have been so incredibly selfish. Would you like me to move in with you?'

He shook his head emphatically. 'No Tessa, that is the last

thing I want. My dear I do have some pride you know, I would not like you to see me when I become a craven coward.'

'I don't believe it, you could never be that.'

'I very often am, my dear.'

'But I must do something to help you. I hate feeling inadequate, helpless.'

'You help me more than you know, Tessa, and when I'm not eaten up with self-pity I believe our life together is good, it restores my self-respect. Don't look so worried, Tessa, I'm feeling particularly low today, you'll see how I can bounce back after a good night's sleep.'

That night I was determined he would sleep and insisted that he take one of his sleeping tablets. Surely enough, the following morning found him considerably more cheerful, either that or he was putting a brave face on things.

When Adam was five years old Richard decided he would rent a house near the sea for the summer, but seeing my doubtful face he changed his mind. Those traumatic gales on the Yorkshire coast were still too vivid in my memory. They made me afraid, particularly for my son with his passion for boats of any kind. He had begun to cut pictures out of magazines, and sticking them enthusiastically on his bedroom walls, and while other children loved stories about animals and knights in shining armour, my son cried out for stories about ships and the sea.

We were offered a delightful cottage on the shores of Lake Derwentwater. My fear of the water did not extend to the lakes although I did admit they could be dangerous to a small boy who loved boats, but when I saw the cottage I immediately fell in love with it.

The views across the lake to the mountains were magnificent and the cottage was a joy – low-ceilinged, with dark oak beams and wide window sills on which pots of geraniums bloomed. The days were filled with sunshine from early morning until dusk. The garden ran down to the lake, where there was a boat house and a tiny cabin cruiser cared for by an old man whose brown wrinkled face and bright blue eyes reminded me of Fairbrother.

Adam loved that boat and we spent long hours cruising between the wooded islands, finding places where we could picnic, where the willows dipped their branches into the lake, and where we could watch the swans gliding peacefully in the shallows. At other times we would drive over the mountain passes towards other lakes, more remote and wilder, and always the dark forests of evergreens filled the air with their clean fresh scent.

To my great joy Richard seemed so much better in those weeks we spent in Cumberland. With our departure from Easdale he seemed to shed a great many worries, colour came back into his cheeks, he walked less painfully and discovered a new zest for living. We all adored the cottage and there were many times when I wished with all my heart that it was our permanent home, that we did not have to go back to that great house with its ill-fitting windows and draughty corridors.

The evenings were so quiet we could hear the silence, broken only by the occasional croaking of frogs or the plop of fishes, the far-off barking of a fox or the lazy hooting of an owl. As the days shortened and the evening came earlier the cottage took on a new delight. The lamps were lit and log fires blazed on the hearth. Long country twilights were shut out by heavy drapes, and we spent our evenings listening to music or reading, long after Adam had been put to bed.

There were nights when I found myself thinking, this is what it must be like to be old, with only time's golden memories to intrude into the sameness of each day. And then with a feeling of shocked surprise I would think, but we are *not* old, how can we bear to think like old people, behave like old people? We were living in limbo, divorced from time and space, and yet that summer was a magical time.

On one such evening Richard looked at me with gentle concern. I sat curled up in an armchair with a book on my knees but I had not been reading for some time. I smiled, wondering how long he had been watching me.

'You were miles away Tessa, but I almost knew what you were thinking. That we could spend evenings like this when we are eighty at least.'

'Of course not.'

'Oh yes, my dear. You have slowed your steps to match mine when they should run and dance and look for adventure.'

'Richard I'm a grown woman not a young girl, and I've had all the adventure I can handle. Contentment is something to be prized.'

'Of course it is, but contentment is for the old and you are not old Tessa. I hate to see those beautiful eyes filled with despair and sudden longing.'

'Now you really are wrong, Richard. There is no despair in my heart. If there are times when I am quiet, don't you ever find yourself remembering old times, other places and people you have loved? But there is no despair.'

'Not even in remembering Julian? You can tell me, Tessa, it doesn't hurt me any more.'

I sat thinking quietly for several minutes. How could I make him believe that my heart no longer felt saddened with despair, that time, that magical healer, had worked its magic, without destroying the memories? Then the lines of a poem, written by Emily Brontë flashed into my mind and in a quiet voice I quoted them to Richard.

There should be no despair for you,
While nightly stars are burning;
While evening pours its silent dew,
And sunshine gilds the morning.

There should be no despair, though tears,
May flow down like a river,
Are not the best beloved of years
Around your heart for ever?

'Who wrote that?' he inquired. 'I don't ever remember hearing it before?'

'Emily Brontë wrote it and there must have been many times when she knew despair living in a bleak vicarage surrounded by dark forbidding moors, with an ageing father obsessed with rigid principles, a drunken brother and two sisters as dogged as she was by ill health.'

He nodded and I was glad that the tenor of our conversation had changed. It was stimulating to talk to Richard about literature and poetry. He had a bright alert mind unimpaired by his ailing body.

The long summer passed into autumn and still we lingered on in Cumberland, all of us imbued with a desire to stay away from Easdale for as long as possible.

It had to come though, that moment of parting. The days were growing shorter and I realized that I would have to be the one to decide when we should go back. It was Adam, playing with the dogs in the garden, who made me make the decision. We had to think seriously of a preparatory school for him and he must soon be made to realize that life was not all play, that there were sterner things in store. Consequently on a misty day at the end of October we returned to the West Riding.

There was silence in the car as we drove up to the house. Adam sat behind with the dogs but he had been fast asleep for some time.

I wondered if my face looked as bleak as my heart felt. Richard placed his hand over mine, his smile warm and understanding. 'I know you didn't want to come back here Tessa, but I promise we'll do something about the house. You've done so much already.'

'I loved that cottage, we were so happy there.'

'I know, Tessa, but this is my home, it's been in my family for centuries and one day I want it to belong to Adam.'

'But Richard, haven't you thought that there may be somebody with a better right to it?'

'Nobody has a better right to it than my son, and Adam is my son, I have that right Tessa.'

I nodded. 'Yes Richard, you are the only father he has ever known and he loves you. I think you have that right.'

'Then we'll make it beautiful for Adam, a place he'll be proud to bring his wife to one day. We'll start in the spring when the weather gets better.'

CHAPTER THIRTY-FOUR

Life at Easdale slipped into its familiar pattern. Adam and I walked in the park with the dogs and in the frosty mornings we rode, often accompanied by Flanagan on Caliph. Adam adored Flanagan, who entertained him with stories of his army days and his life in Ireland before the war. He learned to imitate Flanagan's brogue, and I watched Adam grow tall and beautiful and so terribly like Julian.

In the evenings Richard and I went over brochures about preparatory schools and public schools until my head spun.

'Surely you must have some preference?' he asked me encouragingly.

'No I haven't. I'd like his first school to be somewhere close so that we can go to speech days and other functions, but I'm far more worried about the public school.'

'Why not send him to my school? I was at Sedbergh and I was always reasonably happy there. I'm not saying I did much for the school but I like to think it did a great deal for me. If you agree, Tessa, we should put his name down as soon as possible.'

A preparatory school was found which was prepared to take him when he was seven and I was surprised to find that Adam showed little distress when I informed him that he would be going away from home and only coming back to us for the school holidays.

'Don't you mind, darling?' I asked him.

'Not really, Mother, I don't like Easdale. Why couldn't we have stayed on at the cottage?'

'Because it wasn't our home. Easdale will be yours one day, Adam, try to learn to love it.'

'Mother, who is that old lady who stares at me through the window of her house when I go walking in the park? Sometimes she shakes her fist at me.'

'Ignore her then, she has no right to shake her fist at you.'

'But who is she?'

'She's an old lady who isn't very well. Try not to go near the lodge house when you play in the park and don't look at the windows if you can help it. She will soon grow tired of shaking her fist at you if she sees you're not interested.'

Richard's mother had not set foot in the house since the day she came to see the baby, and if Richard called to see her I never knew. Once or twice I had seen one of our servants leaving the lodge house – Mrs Pearce, who had worked for Lady Chalmers' family before she married Sir Edward. I felt that it was unfortunate that one of our servants was probably tittle-tattling between the two houses and said as much to Richard.

'The next time I visit my mother I'll ask her if Mrs Pearce cannot be employed at the lodge house. If they are so close she should welcome it.'

I was not really surprised that I heard no more about the removal of Mrs Pearce. I said nothing to Richard, but it was obvious to me that his mother did not wish to employ Mrs Pearce. On the contrary, she preferred having a spy in the enemy camp, so to speak.

It was only two weeks to Christmas and I made sure that every room in the house was warm, with bright log fires burning in every grate. Richard hated the cold and it was bad for him. I could not bear to see his thin pinched face, and more and more as the days passed I looked for signs of deterioration in his condition, relieved when I did not find any.

It was time to do my Christmas shopping, and I asked Richard, 'Have you thought what I can get for you?'

He smiled, that particularly sad smile which seemed more pronounced than ever these days. 'There's no point in getting me anything that might last.'

'Oh Richard I wish you wouldn't say things like that, it makes me so unhappy.'

He leaned over and gently kissed my cheek.

'Don't be unhappy Tessa, I'm not.'

It was the week before Christmas and Adam and I had

been into the forest behind the house. We returned armed with bunches of holly, bright with red berries and pine cones. We had spent all morning decorating the tree and even Richard had helped until he grew tired of standing.

Adam rushed towards the drawing room to show Richard the fruits of our excursion. It felt luxuriously warm in the hall and I looked round me with pleasure, at the pretty tree with its gay baubles and the great brass bowl filled with copper beech and yellow chrysanthemums. Easdale could never be Glamara, but at least I was slowly converting it into a home I could be proud of. I caught sight of my reflection in the huge mirror over the fireplace and I went right up to it to look closer.

In the years since I returned to Easdale I had recovered some of my lost beauty but it was a more mature beauty which faced me now. My pale hair framed my face, lending a new enchantment to my wide blue-grey eyes with their dark-ringed pupils. The wistful curve of my mouth had not changed but my slender figure had developed a new maturity like the blossoming of a rose.

I knew that if I wore my more glamorous clothes I could be beautiful but then with a wry smile I turned away. There would never be an occasion to wear glamorous clothes at Easdale. They belonged as securely in my past as the sea breaking against the rocks on the Costa Brava and Julian's dark eyes smiling into mine above his glass of sangria.

Just then the drawing room opened and Adam came running towards me, his face puzzled, hurt.

'What is it darling?' I asked gently.

'It's Father. Mother, why doesn't he speak to me or look at me? I touched his hand but it's so cold and he didn't even open his eyes.'

An icy feeling took hold of me, but I said, 'Go down to the butler's pantry, Adam, and ask him to come to me in the drawing room, then ask Annie to give you some tea.'

'But I want Father to see the holly.'

'We don't want to wake him up if he's sleeping, do we? We can show him the holly when it's all arranged in the dining room. Now hurry.'

It was only when I heard the door which led below stairs close behind him that I entered the drawing room.

Richard was sitting in his favourite place in front of the window. One of his sticks lay at his feet and his hands hung unnaturally at his sides. His head had fallen forward and long before I reached him I knew that he was dead. Then the butler was beside me, shaking his head dismally.

'The master's dead, Milady, there's nothin' anybody can do for him now.'

'Will you telephone for the doctor? And please ask Annie to keep Adam out of here,' I asked him.

He was gone, my dear good friend, and once more I was alone. He had told me so many times that one day this would happen, but now I could not believe it. I stood staring at him, unable to see his face, and but for the unnatural fall of his hands I could have thought that he was sleeping, that at any moment he would open his eyes and speak to me.

I had lived with the idea of Richard's death for so long; now that it had actually happened it seemed like some sort of anti-climax, but fiercely I told myself that I should not mourn for him. He would not want that. He had walked with pain for so long, death had dogged his footsteps every hour of every day, and now he was at peace.

How did one talk to a child about death? How was it possible to explain to my son that the father he had loved had left us for ever, that from now on there would be just the two of us, that we would never see Richard again.

He listened to me quietly and I was not sure how much he understood until he asked, 'Was that why Father wouldn't speak to me, Mother, was it because he was dead?'

'Yes Adam, that was why.'

'But he was still there, sitting in his chair like always.'

'Yes darling, but that wasn't really your father, that was only what was left of him. You see darling he was really very very tired, and when we are ill and old our spirit shuffles off this mortal body as if it were an old overcoat we don't want to wear any more. What you saw this afternoon was the old overcoat your father had grown very tired of and now he is free and at peace.'

'But why can't we see him, why has he gone so far away?'

'Because God needs him far more than we do. It doesn't mean he has ceased to love us Adam, just that the time had come for him to go.'

'Does that mean that one day you will have to go too, Mother?'

'Yes darling, but it is nothing to be afraid of. In time God will come for us all.'

'Did he come for Tiger then?'

'Yes, Tiger and all the other animals you love will have a place in heaven. You are the man of the house now, Adam, you will have to look after me and Annie and all the other servants, and from now on they will call you Sir Adam just like they called your father Sir Richard.'

'This house will be so big Mother, can't we go back to the cottage near the lake now?'

'No darling. This house is your home, your father would want you to love it and care for it just as his family have cared for it for centuries. You shall help me to make it beautiful.'

'As beautiful as Glamara?'

'We can try.'

I listened to his prayers, to the long list he asked God to bless, of people and animals, and then fiercely I had to hold back my tears as he concluded with, 'Please God, if you really don't need my father after all, will you send him back to us?'

I waited while he drank his milk and settled down under the bedclothes, and it was only much later when I looked at him before going to bed that I discovered that his cheeks were stained with tears.

Later that evening after everybody had come and gone I left the house and set off quickly down the drive. I had never set foot in the lodge house but I wanted to tell Richard's mother myself about the death of her son and the arrangements for his funeral.

The house was in total darkness apart from the glow of firelight from a downstairs room, and although I knocked nobody came. Hesitantly I tried the knob and it opened to my touch. I was afraid to take a step into the blackness in case I bumped into furniture or knocked something over. I stood quite still until through a chink in the door on my right I could see a faint glow which told me this must be the room with the fire.

Opening the door quietly, at first I thought the room was empty, and then I saw Dora in a chair before the fire, looking into the flames, immobile and oblivious to my presence. I had no wish to startle her by switching on the light, so I went forward and touching her arm gently I said, 'Lady Chalmers, it's Tessa.'

She looked up at me, and even in that moment I saw the narrow glitter of hatred in her eyes and in a voice as cold as ice she said, 'You've come to tell me my son is dead. I already know.'

'I couldn't come any earlier. Would you mind if I put on the light?'

When she didn't answer me I hunted round and switched on a lamp beside her chair. She did not invite me to sit down, and I continued to stand looking down at her, at her thin grey hair drawn tightly back into its unbecoming bun, at her angular face stamped with bitterness, and the thin clawlike hands twisting and turning in her lap.

It was impossible that I should be expected to talk to my mother-in-law as though I were a stranger, and I pulled a chair forward so that we faced each other across the hearth.

I told her how I had found him and the arrangements that were made for his funeral. It was to be in the family vault where the Chalmers had been buried for generations in the village churchyard, and I said I would send a car to bring her up to the house on the morning of the funeral.

'I shall make my own way to the funeral of my son,' she snapped tersely. 'I do not intend to join the formal mourning party.'

'You mean you prefer to let everybody see how far we are estranged, that not even at your son's funeral can you bear to be with me or my son?'

'That is exactly what I mean. Don't think I don't know how you have worn my son down with your gadding about, all those months in the Lake District sailing with that boy, never being allowed to rest, amusing that brat of yours so that you could do exactly as you liked. He was a nursemaid to that child, looking after him while you went off in that car of yours day after day. He needed rest, to sit quietly like he did when I was at the hall, not that tearing about all over the place looking for something to amuse you and that boy. But for you my son would still be alive.'

I stared at her askance, then rose to my feet with the realization that we had nothing more to say to each other.

It was only when I reached the door that she said, 'You think you've won don't you, Tessa Chalfont? You think you are going to go on living at Easdale as though you've every right to it, that I'm going to watch you act the great lady up at the hall while that bastard son of yours becomes Sir Adam Chalmers just like you always wanted.'

Standing over her I did not raise my voice but my eyes burned down into hers and my words fell like chips of ice even on my own ears.

'I am not interested in anything you say or think. You tried to spoil my life with Richard once and you succeeded until he saw you for what you are, a foolish desperate old woman eaten up with bitterness, unloved by your husband and your son because of something in *you*, not because of anything I have ever done or said to make Richard hate you. If my son remains here at Easdale as Sir Adam Chalmers it is because Richard wished it, and willed it. Nothing you can say or do will alter that fact.'

'We will see about that.'

'Very well. If it gives you so much satisfaction you must do what you can to destroy us, but I warn you Dora, I was prepared to be your friend, but I can be a merciless and implacable enemy.'

I left her, rushing towards the hall until my breath came painfully and I was dimly aware of the scalding tears coursing down my cheeks, and I could not have said if they were tears of anger or of sorrow.

They came from all over the West Riding to Richard's funeral, and as I looked back from the big black car at the upstairs windows I could see Adam's face peering dimly through the glass. I had left him with Annie and I was glad of

Aunt Hetty's presence beside me and Uncle Godfrey sitting morosely facing me as we drove to the churchyard.

Richard's mother came alone, driving the trap she always used in the village lanes, and immediately I was aware of the whisperings around us and anxious looks cast in her direction by family and servants alike.

I saw that Mrs Pearce moved to stand beside her, staring at me stolidly, her red bovine face almost defiant.

I had made arrangements for luncheon to be served at the hall for the mourners. The vicar asked, 'I suppose Lady Chalmers will be lunching at the hall, Milady?'

'I very much doubt if she would come, Vicar, but you have my permission to invite her.'

He stared at me doubtfully. 'I notice she came to the church on her own. My dear, isn't this a time for forgetting old scores, forgiving old foes?'

'I agree with you, Vicar. It seems Lady Chalmers has other ideas.'

He looked at me sorrowfully and I turned away to join Aunt Hetty on the path leading to the gates.

'How dare she make it so obvious that you and she are not friendly,' she said angrily. 'Opening everybody's mouths, making an issue of it.'

'Aunt Hetty, the villagers know we haven't been friendly for years, they would expect her to do what she did.'

'Well I hope you and Adam are coming back with us. I don't like to think of you staying on here with that woman living on your doorstep.'

I smiled down at her. 'This is my home, Aunt Hetty, I can't spend all my life running back to Glamara every time fate deals me a poor hand.'

'Well, come for Adam's sake if nobody else's.'

'I think we should stay on here for a while before we even think of taking a holiday. Perhaps we'll come in the spring.'

After luncheon Godfrey too endorsed her invitation but I gave him the same answer.

'I have to get accustomed to the idea of being alone Uncle Godfrey, of feeling Easdale is my home.'

'There are some people who might say Dora has every

right to feel aggrieved, Tessa, if she should talk about Adam's paternity.'

'I know. Godfrey, I didn't ask for this. I'd far rather come back to Glamara with you and never set eyes on Easdale again, but Richard wanted it. He became the father Adam never had, they adored each other and I almost believe Richard thought he was Adam's father. I don't care about the title, I don't care about anything the Chalmers family can do for me, you know that, but I do care about Richard's wishes, and he left the hall to Adam. These last few years were as happy as he knew how to make them, he was kind and considerate and he was very forgiving.'

'If he'd been so kind and considerate in the first place you'd never have gone to live with Julian or borne his son,' he said gruffly.

'I know, and I would have missed so very much, Godfrey. In a very perverse way I have Richard to thank for that time I spent with Julian.'

'Women's logic is incomprehensible to me,' Godfrey said, but he was smiling a little. 'You'll come to us in the spring, Tessa? It's a lonely house with just Hetty and me.'

'I'll come. Doesn't Robert say if he intends to come over?'

'Never. It seems as if he's forgotten everything he ever knew about Glamara and England.'

I stood at the door to watch the last car sweeping down the drive. I heard Adam's footsteps running across the hall and next moment he had run straight into my arms. He felt so warm and confiding, his sturdy legs pressed against my knees, his rounded arms round my neck, his cheek against mine, and over his head I smiled into Annie's eyes as she stood holding a tea tray.

'Join me, Annie,' I urged her gently, 'I know you don't like doing so but this is a rare occasion.'

'I don't want the others ter think I'm curryin' favour, Miss Tessa. They all 'ates Mrs Pearce fer that, I don't want 'em to think the same about me.'

'I'm sure they won't, Annie. After Christmas is over I must speak to the housekeeper about Mrs Pearce, there's something about that woman I don't like.'

She nodded. 'Yer does well not to trust her, allus down at the lodge house she is, carryin' tales like as not.'

We said little about Richard's funeral in front of Adam, and I was pleased to see that his appetite seemed unimpaired as he tucked into scones and strawberry jam.

Richard's lawyer arrived two days after the funeral armed with several bulging files and wearing a woebegone expression. He spread his files out across the library desk and I sat opposite waiting until he had drunk two cups of coffee and sorted out his papers.

One of the servants came to add more coal to the fire and shivering a little he said, 'This house must need a great deal of heating, Lady Chalmers.'

'Yes, and the windows fit badly and need replacing. It is a draughty house.'

He was looking at me with a degree of sympathy I had not associated with his prim and proper exterior. 'I'm afraid I have no good news for you. Did Sir Richard ever discuss his financial affairs with you?'

'No, and I never asked him.'

'Not even in connection with the house?'

'He intimated that perhaps in the spring we would be able to have some work done on it.'

He sighed. 'These files, Lady Chalmers, are filled with correspondence exchanged between Sir Richard and his mother over the past six years. As you are probably aware Sir Edward died so suddenly that he had not had sufficient time to put his house in order. In normal circumstances his wife would have received a generous allowance and the bulk of his estate would have come naturally to his only son and heir.'

He looked at me to see if I would comment but I remained silent.

'Lady Chalmers always vowed she would make matters right when Sir Richard returned after the war, but when he was invalided out of the army his mother did nothing about the will, maintaining that her son would never marry, least of all have children, and since he would spend the rest of his life in her care matters should be left in her hands.

'When he married I urged her to redress the situation but

some perverse feelings of her own made her very stubborn and she adamantly refused to sign over to Richard the sums of money he was entitled to.

'At first he wrote to his mother in reasonable terms asking for what was rightly his, but recently the correspondence became more acrimonious and it had reached the state where I was seriously considering urging him to sue his mother in open court.'

'You are telling me, Mr Darnley, that there is no money. Will you tell me what there is?'

'There is Easdale Hall, and several small investments which mount to very little left directly to Sir Richard by his grandfather. I'm sorry to be the one to give you this news, Lady Chalmers. I know nothing of the quarrel between Sir Richard and his mother, but a grandchild often brings people together. In this case it will be the grandchild who suffers most. Will you be able to keep this place on?'

He was looking round the room with a frown, seeing the patches of damp around the windows and the mould on the carpet near the skirting board.

'My husband wanted Adam to live here, he wanted us to love it as he loved it. Something will be done to preserve it.'

'It will take a great deal of money.'

'I know.'

I rose and held out my hand which he took in a sympathetic grasp.

'I could advise you to sue Lady Chalmers, not for yourself, but on behalf of your son.'

I shook my head. 'Thank you Mr Darnley, I shall manage.'

I accompanied him to the front door then slowly returned to the hall where I stood gazing up at the dark panelled walls. I could smell the mustiness, and the unbidden tears rolled unchecked down my face.

Julian had left Moorcliff to ailing sailors but he had made me a rich woman. Now it was going to take a considerable amount of that money to restore this house I hated into some semblance of a home.

The days of Christmas came and went. Rain pelted from leaden skies all through Christmas Eve and on Christmas morning we drove to church along flooded roads. A watery sun came out on our way back, and then Adam and I sat down to eat lunch in solitary state in the vast dining room.

The holly we had gathered looked pretty in a chased copper bowl, but already the berries were drying. The tinselled tree gave a new air of festivity to the hall and Adam asked curiously, 'When will you give the servants their presents, Mother?'

'Immediately after lunch, dear. We will invite them to the hall and the butler will call out their names and you shall hand the presents round.'

'Is that what they did at Glamara?'

'Something like that.'

'Will Annie be there, and Flanagan?'

'Of course, and they will all eat Christmas dinner together downstairs and pull their crackers.'

'But we have to eat alone?'

'Yes dear. Another year perhaps we might go to Glamara.'

He remained silent after that. He had Julian's reserve, the detachment I had so often struggled against in his father, a detachment I was reluctant to intrude upon in my son.

The ceremony of handing out the Christmas presents went smoothly and Adam played his part with surprising maturity. The young housemaids bobbed their little curtseys and the men smiled and took Adam's outstretched hand, looked on by a benevolent butler. It was only when they came to Mrs Pearce that I sensed something antagonistic in her attitude.

Her large peasant's face did not smile, nor did she curtsey. That I didn't mind, after all Adam was only a small boy, I didn't expect grown men and women to fawn over him, but there was something cynical in the way she looked at him, a vague air of resentment which she failed to hide.

Later while the servants sat in the kitchens to enjoy their Christmas meal Adam and I walked to the stables. The horses were pleased to see us, accepting the titbits we offered gently, nuzzling my shoulder.

'Didn't you feel like riding your pony today, Adam?' I asked him.

'Not today, Mother, he should have a holiday on Christmas Day.'

'Now why didn't I think of that?' I asked smiling.

As we walked back Adam said, 'Will that old lady be spending Christmas all by herself, Mother?'

I looked at him startled, then pity overwhelmed me. I would have been prepared to invite Dora to eat with us but she had slammed the door firmly in my face. It seemed that we were two women destined to stay apart, both lonely, both too proud to bridge our differences.

'Perhaps she likes to be alone, Adam, no doubt Mrs Pearce will be spending the evening with her.'

'I don't like Mrs Pearce, and she doesn't like me.'

'Whatever makes you think that?'

'It's true, Mother. She was with that old lady one day when she shook her fist at me, then they both laughed.'

'Was Flanagan with you?'

'Yes.'

'What did he have to say?'

'He said she was a noisome old biddy who was off her head.'

I smiled, turning my head away so that he would not see my amusement. I could well imagine Flanagan's thoughts on my mother-in-law but I said quickly, 'Ignore her, darling, don't give her cause to think you are being insolent by staring at her.'

'Is she really off her head, Mother?'

'She is probably a little strange.'

'My father used to visit her, I've seen him going into the house. Why was that when she doesn't like me and never comes to see you?'

'He visited her out of a sense of duty, Adam, because she is old and because it was expected of him.'

He digested this information quietly and I was glad when he didn't pursue the conversation. I re-endorsed my decision however, that I would speak to the housekeeper about Mrs Pearce immediately the holidays were over.

Unfortunately other matters proved far more demanding. On New Year's Day the wind started to blow from the east, bringing driving snow, and long before nightfall it covered the park like a blanket. The wind moaned round the house with undiminished fury for three long days. It rattled the windows and brought down long pieces of guttering as well as two tall chimney stacks which crashed through the roof on to the attics above the library. The draughts were everywhere, finding chinks in the ill-fitting windows.

Well supplied with logs, fires burned cheerfully in every grate in the house but they did not have the power to remove the chill and in the evenings we sat wrapped in woollen cardigans listening to the wind echoing in the chimneys and the staccato tapping of icy hail against the windows. I could settle to nothing and the servants too went about their work with red noses and pinched unhappy faces.

Although I wrapped Adam up warmly he complained that his bedroom was cold and when the wind veered round the smoke billowed back down the chimney and into the room. Annie's chilblains returned. I saw her trying to hide her hands and on examination I was appalled at the swollen red lumps on every finger.

I began to hate the house, particularly after the day I sat before the fire helping Adam with one of his jigsaw puzzles. Suddenly he screamed and my eyes followed his pointing finger towards the window and the two blurred white faces peering in. I sprang up and drew the drapes sharply to cut out the malignant staring faces, amazed that they had braved the walk across the frozen park to find some misplaced enjoyment from staring in at us.

That night I sent for the housekeeper, wishing fervently that I had done so before. Surely Mrs Pearce couldn't expect to stay in my employment after that episode.

She stood before me with tight-lipped expectancy as she always did when she thought I had a complaint about one of the servants or their work.

When I spoke of Mrs Pearce, however, her face relaxed and she said quickly, 'I'd be glad to see her go, Milady, she's a disruptive influence in the servants' quarters, always complainin', always trying to stir things up among the younger servants.'

I told her about the afternoon's occurrence and she sniffed disdainfully. 'She's always down at the lodge house, Milady, I can't see why she doesn't go to work down there, except that she'd have no tales to go running with.'

'I'm reluctant to take anybody's livelihood away from them, but I don't want her here any more, and if my mother-in-law thinks so highly of her then she should be given the chance to employ her.'

'She already does employ her Milady, it's you who's paying her wages, that's all.'

'Do you wish to tell her or would you rather I did it?'

'The butler'll do it, Milady, no doubt he'll take great satisfaction from it.'

It was Annie who told me she had left with bad grace, accusing the housekeeper and butler of plotting against her but assuring all of them that she would get her own back, Lady Chalmers would see to that.

I felt miserable about the episode, indeed I felt miserable about the whole wretched environment and like Adam I was wishing we lived in some cosy cottage far away from Easdale where the rooms were small and cosy and where the wind didn't echo like a banshee around and through the house.

I could not remember a winter like that one. The snow lasted until the end of February and the vista of rolling moorland covered with snow seemed like an arctic landscape, particularly when Flanagan and Adam decided to erect great shapes resembling polar bears out of the snow. The boy was happiest outdoors when he was well wrapped up against the elements and away from the insidious draughts.

Annie informed me that the servants were well accustomed to the bad winters and their effect on the house. 'They say it'll all end when the weather gets better, Miss Tessa.'

'I dare say it will Annie, but in the meantime we are suffering.'

'I'm getting used to it now. I'm readin' better an' I'm speakin' better, don't you think so Miss Tessa?'

'Yes Annie, I had noticed, you are doing very well.'

514

'The servants are teasin' me about it, they say I'm aimin' to be somethin' I'm not. It's not that, I just want to talk proper, like a real lady's maid should.'

I smiled at her gently. Once or twice I had caught her reading some of Adam's early educational books. I had managed to find a private tutor for him, a shy earnest young man who battled up the drive every morning and returned in the late afternoon to the village where he lived with his mother.

At the end of February the weather began to abate somewhat and I occupied my time wandering around the house trying to assess all the work that it needed. I decided it would cost a fortune to make it right, and with repairs in mind I spoke to the butler.

'Why was it ever allowed to get into such a state?' I asked him curiously.

'Sir Edward seemed to lose interst in the house, Milady. In later years he seemed lethargic about most things and her Ladyship made the decisions.'

'This house seems to be suffering from the fact that no decisions were made. Could the local builders undertake all the work required here?'

'I doubt it Milady, there's only old Mr Parsons and his two sons. They're good enough when it comes to repairing cottages, but a place of this size is another matter.'

'Well we should put some work Mr Parsons' way, perhaps you would ask him to come up to see me.'

The result was that three building firms moved in at the end of February and the house resounded with the noise of their chisels and hammers while week after week I handed out money for materials and the men's wages.

Half way through March Aunt Hetty descended upon us for a few days, surveying the alterations and repairs with stunned dismay. .

'It is quite disgraceful that you are having to pay for all this, Tessa, what were the Chalmers family doing all these years to let it get like this? And why should you spend the money Julian left you on this monstrosity?'

'It isn't a monstrosity, Aunt Hetty, it just isn't Glamara.

I'm trying to turn it into something worthwhile, something Richard would have wanted for Adam.'

'Then Richard should have seen what needed doing to it,' she snapped acidly.

'Poor Richard had quite enough to think about. I blame Dora for much of this, but I'd rather do it all myself than have her living here and interfering. It's bad enough having her at the end of our drive. She comes peering through the windows from time to time, either her or that woman Mrs Pearce.'

'Can't you put a stop to it?'

'I don't see how, apart from calling in the police, and I don't want to do that.'

'I've a good mind to give her a piece of my mind.'

I smiled at her indignation. She looked so much like a pugnacious little bird in defence of her young that I said, 'Ignore her Aunt Hetty, that is the advice I have given Adam and it seems to make her crosser than any confrontation would do.'

At the end of five days she left, saying that I should pull myself together, do something about my appearance and spend some money on myself instead of lavishing everything on the house.

She had only been back at Glamara two days when I received a long letter from Godfrey intimating that I should scrutinize the bills carefully, or send them to him for his accountant to deal with. I wrote back reassuring him that he need not worry, and hoping he would come as soon as the repairs were finished to view the transformation.

It was Easter when we went to visit Susan in Leeds, and both Adam and I were looking forward to the change of scenery.

Susan exclaimed with dismay over my appearance. 'Tessa, what *have* you done to yourself? You look even worse than you did after Richard died, you are far too thin and your hair needs something doing to it.'

'Well I've been caring for it myself, there didn't seem much point in looking glamorous when the rooms were falling to pieces round our ears.'

'Well, you will have to do something while you're here. You need some fashionable clothes, as we shall be socializing. While you're here we are going to the shops and the theatres, and we are going to the Lord Mayor's Ball next Friday. Right after lunch we are going into the city and we are going to find you a ball gown.'

'But I'm still in mourning.'

'All right, a black ball gown. You look lovely in black Tessa, with your blonde colouring.'

I couldn't argue with Susan. She swept me along in her wake and all afternoon we shopped until my feet ached and I begged to be allowed to sit down somewhere and drink tea.

An appointment was made to have my hair done on the afternoon of the ball and then I bought black evening shoes and an evening bag before we visited the most exclusive gown shop in the city.

'I can't afford to shop here,' Susan remarked, 'much as I would love to, but I shall enjoy seeing what they have to show you.'

'I'm not very sure that I can afford to shop here either,' I complained. 'I need to start thinking about Adam's school fees and the house has taken a small fortune.'

'You are still a wealthy woman, Tessa. Make the most of yourself, set out your stall as Marylee used to say.'

'What do I need to set out my stall for?'

'You're still young and very beautiful in spite of looking so plaintive. The world is full of eligible men and you have to think about the future.'

'Susan, the last thing I want is an eligible man.'

'Well, we will see, but don't run away with the idea that your life is over, it isn't. Adam needs a father's influence. However good you are as a mother you can't make up for the loss of a father in his life.'

'That is no reason for me to go looking for a husband. I prefer to let life take its course.'

'Well naturally, that is how it should be, but there's no point in burying yourself miles from anywhere and looking as though you didn't care.'

By this time we had reached the first floor of the dress

salon and a willowy brunette had come forward to appraise us critically, no doubt taking in my unfashionable coat and shoes and Susan's sensible tweeds.

'My friend Lady Chalmers would like to see some of your evening gowns,' Susan said shortly. 'She is a widow so perhaps you have something in black to show her.'

The assistant's expression had undergone a remarkable change, no doubt at hearing my title, and effusively she ushered us towards small gilt chairs placed around a dais at the end of the room.

'Would you be interested in white or purple which are second mourning colours, you understand?'

'I would prefer black,' I answered her. White would look far too virginal and I always associated purple with older people.

The first gown we were shown was a creation of white lace, far too bridelike so that even Susan said, 'You couldn't possibly wear that, Tessa.'

The next gown was in a deep violet and far too old for the model, who was about my age. I was beginning to think we were going to be unlucky when a girl emerged wearing a long black evening gown. She was blonde, with colouring not unlike my own, and the black velvet fell away from her shoulders into a tiny bodice and long sweeping skirt, beautiful and dramatic, the grace of the skirt moulding her figure as I knew it would mould mine. Its only decoration was the band of dark sable round the neckline and edging the wide medieval sleeves which fell away from the model's arms to display their slenderness.

I knew that this was my gown and I knew it would fit me beautifully. Even the assistant and the models gasped with surprised delight when I decided to try it on and, although the price was wickedly expensive, I was urged by Susan to pay it.

I can't say that I didn't get pleasure from dressing for the Lord Mayor's Ball. It seemed so long since I had worn a ball gown, and memories came crowding back of dancing with Alec and the Chalfont boys under the chandeliers at

Glamara, dancing with Julian under a sky ablaze with stars on a night fragrant with oleanders, a night made for lovers.

I was glad of the sable stole I had had the foresight to bring, and looking at my reflection my heart lifted as it had not done for many months.

The wide neckline complemented my slender throat and creamy satiny shoulders. My only jewellery was the long diamond earrings Julian had given me on our last Christmas together, and the diamond brooch at my breast. Only a few months before I had been content to grow old, saddened and often lonely, with all passion spent and love something barely remembered, as elusive as a faded dream. Now I realized that I still had youth and beauty, and unbidden old desires were rekindled, and memory, heedless of time and place, was once more at my side.

Susan gasped with delight when she saw me. 'There,' she said, 'what did I tell you, Tessa? You'll be the belle of the ball.'

'I probably won't dance a step, I've forgotten how.'

Adam and Mark gazed at us in wide-eyed wonder when we presented ourselves for inspection a little later. Susan was wearing a pale apricot which suited her tawny colouring, so different from my nordic fairness, and her husband John, out of his country tweeds, looked remarkably handsome. He took hold of her arm and squeezed it affectionately.

'We don't make a bad-looking couple, do we Tessa?' he said, laughing.

'No indeed, you make a very handsome couple.'

'You shouldn't pander to his vanity, Tessa, more often than not I see him covered with dog hairs and smelling of stables.'

If anybody had told me that one day I would feel a stranger in a crowd of people bent on enjoying themselves I wouldn't have believed them, but that was how I felt when we entered the ballroom. We spoke to groups of people as we circled the room, to women who appraised me and men who showed their obvious admiration, to older people who looked on me benevolently and younger people who admired me, but when the music started I urged Susan and John to dance while I found a chair placed unobtrusively behind a potted palm.

I adored music, my feet tapped under cover of my gown, and I could barely prevent my fingers beating out the tempo on my knee. Susan and John returned to my side, and when the music struck up again she insisted that John and I dance together.

How could I ever have thought that I had forgotten how to dance? I loved every moment as I whirled round the room in John's arms, I wanted the music to go on for ever, disappointed that we were whirling to a stop at the end of the dance.

'You dance beautifully, Tessa, I might have known you would. Now where is that girl, it rather looks as though she found herself a partner,' John said, his eyes scanning the room for his wife.

Several minutes later Susan joined us, pulling Lionel Prescott by the hand.

'Look what I've found,' she laughed, 'hiding at the back of the room where Nancy Lister couldn't see him.'

'Oh surely not,' John laughed, 'whatever is wrong with poor Nancy?'

'Nothing except that she chatters too much, she's another Marylee.'

Lionel invited me on to the floor. He danced well and I gave myself up again to the sheer joy of dancing to a good orchestra on a splendid floor.

'You're enjoying this Tessa, how long is it since you've danced?'

'Too long I'm afraid. Dancing was something I never thought about when Richard was alive, for obvious reasons.'

'So there is a whole gap in your life when doing things you loved had to be stifled?'

'Yes, but there were other things to take their place.'

For a time we danced in silence, and when I looked up he smiled at me, a smile that was warm and sympathetic.

'It's nice to see you again Lionel, you are one of those nice people one doesn't see for ages and then when we do meet it might have been only yesterday when we were together.'

'Like an old armchair or overcoat you mean?'

'Of course not.'

'Just somebody it's comfortable to be with then?'

'Something like that.'

'So your marriage worked and you have a son, Tessa,' he said gently.

'Yes. Adam. He's almost five.'

'Gracious me, is it so long since we drove into Bryant's mill yard to break up that fracas? You've changed very little, Tessa.'

'You should have seen me when I arrived in Leeds. My hair was a mess and I had nothing fit to wear for this ball, now I'm beginning to feel glad I made the effort.'

'You have always looked very beautiful to me, Tessa.'

He was looking down at me with obvious sincerity, and I found myself blushing under his steady regard.

'Will you ride with me tomorrow, Tessa? If the weather is decent I'll pick you up about two o'clock.'

'I'd like to check with Susan first, if she doesn't mind then I'd love to ride with you.'

Susan made no protest and while the men chatted she said softly, 'Lionel's always admired you Tessa, aren't you glad you came?'

'Very glad, I haven't forgotten how to dance after all.'

It seemed so long since I had laughed with the sheer joy of being alive, of moving my limbs in time to the music, of seeing admiration in the eyes of a man and I danced and danced until people began slowly to drift away from the ballroom, and only a few of us had the energy to enter into the intricacies of the Lancers, and even fewer when the last waltz was played at three o'clock.

I lay awake for a long time, the music still in my ears, the movements of the dance alive in my limbs, too exhilarated to sleep. It was a wild and heady intoxication. Even the haunting memories of Julian and the more sober ones of Richard had no power at that moment to dispel my joy in the evening. I knew that when I returned to Easdale the old familiar problems would be back with me, but tonight at least

521

I could relive my youth and the joys associated with it.

I was waiting for Lionel immediately after lunch, attired in riding breeches and hacking jacket, pleased that the day was fresh and sunny and looking forward to riding along bridle paths that led up to the fells above the sprawling city. The horses were fresh and delighting in the exercise and we spoke little as they picked their way through shallow streams and along ancient byways where once the pilgrims had walked on their way to the abbeys, and then we were on the fells where we could let our horses have full rein, galloping them joyously in the wind that swept down from the summit.

We paused at last to look down on the city and Lionel pointed out different landmarks. Since the ending of the war the city seemed to have spread in all directions and now there were suburbs of wide avenues and newer more spacious houses. Where some of those narrow dismal streets had lain like a blot on the city there were now open spaces where the old houses had been taken down. Lionel told me they would be converted into play areas for the children or new factories and schools would be built there.

'I used to hate this city when I lived in my stepfather's house,' I told him. 'I yearned for the country where the poverty never seemed so terrible. Those poor people with their thin pinched faces, and the children running about in rags waiting for their fathers to leave the public houses. I'm glad things are changing, those streets were an insult to humanity.'

'Change doesn't happen overnight, Tessa, there is still a lot to be done. The war was a terrible thing, but while men were being slaughtered in the trenches this city and many others were becoming more affluent. Employment was at its most fruitful, weaving cloth, making uniforms and all the other things associated with war. It won't last of course, but that affluence has made us see nobody should ever again be expected to live on starvation wages and in squalor.'

'You say it won't last Lionel, you mean there will still be unemployment, hardship even?'

'Unemployment will come, I'm afraid, as machines take

the place of men and women, but it must not go hand in hand with the loss of self-respect.'

I warmed to Lionel Prescott, seeing him as a caring compassionate man, and I welcomed his friendship. I knew that he admired me, it was there in his eyes when they met mine, in his protective charm and the warmth of his smile, but I was not ready for anything beyond that.

Whenever I thought of Richard it was with a feeling of peace. He had walked with death for so long and now his suffering was over, and I had done my best to make his last few years gentle and worthwhile. Julian had been different, with his vitality and the passion he had brought into my life. His death had been a wanton waste, a terrible sin that still had the power to fill my heart with anger and grief.

'I wonder what you are thinking of to bring that look of despair into your eyes?' he said gently.

I looked up at him, startled. 'I'm sorry Lionel, I was thinking about something that makes me very unhappy, I shouldn't spoil our time together by reliving sad memories. Shall we ride back or is it too soon?'

'We'll go back another way. Tell me about your son, Tessa, am I going to meet him?'

'I would like you to meet him.'

'I suppose Richard was very proud of him?'

'They were very fond of each other, I was glad about that, it made things so much more bearable.'

He didn't speak for a little while then he said, 'When you speak of Adam and Richard you sound almost surprised that they should have been so fond of each other.'

I had not meant to even hint that there were problems in Richard's relationship with Adam, there was no reason why I should say anything to Lionel or indeed to anybody. As far as the world was concerned Adam was Richard's son, and yet I felt the need to tell Lionel the truth, even when I was unsure how he would react to it.

He was looking at me expectantly and I knew that my face was troubled, and misunderstanding my doubts he said, 'I suppose Richard wondered how you would cope alone with a child to bring up, perhaps he would have preferred not to have had children under the circumstances.'

We had reached a curve in the hillside where a glade of beech trees swept down into a valley. Stone cottages sheltered under the crags, their gardens gay with spring flowers, and turning to Lionel I said, 'Can we stay here a little while and rest the horses?'

'Of course, it's a good idea.'

He dismounted and came to lift me down, so that for a moment I was held close against him, then with a little smile he released me and leaving the horses to champ the fresh grass we went to sit on a low stone wall.

I sat pensive and quiet, and he seemed reluctant to intrude upon my thoughts although from time to time I felt his eyes upon me. I knew that if I told him the truth I would disappoint him yet again. I had not forgotten the night I went with him to the riot in the city and the look on his face when he left me because he thought I had merely been anxious to experience the excitement of the moment. How much more might I disappoint him now?

'Did Susan never tell you anything about my life after you were kind enough to stable Shamara for me?' I asked quietly.

'She told me you were living on the coast north of Whitby but that is all. I assumed Richard had had the courage to leave his mother in the West Riding and join you there.'

When I didn't immediately answer him he said, 'How long were you alone before he joined you, Tessa?'

'He didn't join me. It was some time later that I went back to Richard, after I went back to Glamara in fact.'

'You stayed on at the Latchfords' cottage for some time then?'

'For a short while, then something happened to change my entire life, something I can hardly believe even now. I left that cottage to live with somebody else, a man I had been in love with for a very long time. We couldn't marry because Richard was so ill, I couldn't bother him with divorce proceedings. It didn't matter, it wasn't important.'

When he didn't speak I went on with an empty sinking feeling in my heart, sure that every word I uttered was driving another wedge between this man and myself, but now that I had started I had to go on. Not even to save our friendship could I pretend to be something I was not.

'We were blissfully happy together, both of us very sure that one day we would marry and have the children we both longed for, but Julian was drowned during one of the terrible gales on that coast. My uncle's second wife was drowned with him, indeed Julian had gone to try to save her, but they both perished. I wanted to die too, Lionel, there seemed to me no point in living after Julian died, but I know now that one doesn't die from a broken heart. Then I realized that I was going to have a child, Julian's child.

'I was living at Glamara with my aunt and uncle and one morning Richard came to see me. He had known about Julian for some time and he knew all about the tragedy. He asked me to return to him, and even after I told him about the child it made little difference, he still wanted me to go back to him.

'I like to think that in those few years we built something good together and when Adam was born he adored him right from the start. They were father and son, happy in each other's company, and Adam took Richard's name and is heir to his property. That was Richard's wish, not mine.'

'He must have loved you a great deal Tessa?'

I nodded, aware of the tightness of tears in my throat.

He was so quiet, looking down the valley towards the city with narrowed eyes, thinking his own intimate thoughts and after a while I stood and moved towards the horses.

'Perhaps we should get back, Lionel,' I said, and without speaking he rose to his feet and assisted me into the saddle.

As I looked down on him from my horse I said gently, 'Poor Lionel, it seems I am destined to disappoint you, but if we are to be friends it must be on my terms, for what I am, not what you suppose me to be.'

He smiled. 'It took a lot of courage to tell me all that, Tessa.'

'Yes, I'm very much afraid that it did.'

As we rode back we spoke of ordinary things far divorced from the turmoils of my life, and if I felt surprise that he did not refer to them I kept our conversation light and ordinary since he seemed to prefer it that way.

We left the horses with their groom then drove to Susan's house. The children had not as yet arrived back from her mother's house and he refused the tea that was offered, saying he had to put in an appearance at the mill.

As Susan and I drank tea in the lived-in drawing room where a fat tabby slept on a chintz-covered chair and two canaries sang happily in a cage near the window I told her that I had told Lionel my story.

'Whatever made you do that just yet?' she said, troubled. 'He admires you so much Tessa, I expect this afternoon's been like a slap in the face to him.'

'I had to tell him now, Susan. If I had let our friendship continue so that he grew more fond of me, how could I ever have told him then? Don't you think it would have been like a death blow to him later?'

'I don't know, but I do know Lionel. He's not had a great deal of experience with women, he never seems to have had the time, but I do know he likes you. Being a widow, having a son would have been no problem, but the rest . . .'

'I agree, and now I am going to collect my son and my luggage and go home. The world is full of nice young women who will jump at Lionel Prescott, and who have no skeletons in their cupboards, no searing love affairs and no regrets or punishing memories to ever come between them.'

'Perhaps he'll talk to me about things,' she said hopefully. 'I'll be able to put him right on a whole lot of scores.'

'Better leave things as they are Susan, it's all too soon and I'm simply not ready for another relationship yet.'

'He's not just somebody you've met last night Tessa, he's an old friend, for heaven's sake.'

'He's not even that, Susan. He never knew me when I was growing up in this city although I'd heard plenty about the Prescotts. I've met him very seldom and that is what counts, not the number of years I've known him. Let it be Susan, I expect in time Lionel will at least respect me for telling him my story. It would have been so easy not to tell him, so much easier to pretend that there were no shadows in my past, but there should be honesty between friends.'

'Oh you and your wretched honesty. Just when I thought at last things were going right for you and I had brought it about.'

I went over to her and kissed the top of her head. 'I'll go upstairs and pack, Susan.'

'You're really going tomorrow?'

'Yes, I think we should. I dread all the things that will be waiting for me at Easdale.'

'When are you coming again?'

'Next time you are coming to us. I had thought we might rent the cottage again this year, Mark would love it in Cumberland. If you get the chance why don't you all join us there?'

'Perhaps we will,' she said thoughtfully. I could tell her thoughts were still on my afternoon with Lionel and I guessed she would have plenty to tell John when he returned home that evening.

I had only half done the packing when Adam rushed into the bedroom and seeing the suitcases his eyes opened wide with dismay. 'Mother, we're not going home are we?'

'I'm afraid so darling, your pony will be missing you, don't you want to see him again?'

'The pony's all right Mother, he's got the other two horses and Flanagan is looking after him. I like it here, and I don't like it at Easdale. Why can't we stay, just a little bit longer!'

It would have been so easy to agree, but I knew that I would only be delaying the moment when we must go back, so I said firmly, 'You promised not to be difficult when we must return to Easdale, Adam. I have a lot to see to there, besides I was thinking we might go to the cottage in the Lake District before the summer was over, and perhaps Mark and his parents will be able to join us there.'

His face brightened. 'When, Mother, when can we go there?'

'I don't know yet, but as soon as I can get things sorted out at home.'

'I must tell Mark!' Like a flash he had gone and I heard him running along the passage and down the stairs, then the barking of the dogs as the door slammed behind him.

I sat on the edge of the bed, deep in thought. It was going to be increasingly difficult bringing up a boy single-handed, particularly a boy with Adam's high spirits and wilful exuberance. School would help considerably but there were things even a school couldn't teach him. Squaring my shoulders I made myself resume my packing, determined not to give way to self-pity or that other more destroying emotion, despair.

CHAPTER THIRTY-FIVE

On my return to Easdale, there were tenants to interview, most of them with complaints, and the vicar came to welcome me back but after two cups of tea his conversation turned to his views on his leaking church roof and an estimate he had received for its repair which was well outside the fund he had available.

Flanagan too had a complaint. 'Lady Chalmers has taken to lookin' into the stableyard, Milady, and what moight she be worryin' her head about, an' her with never a thought on horse ridin'. Oi don't loike 'er down there, Milady, an Oi don't loike that Mrs Pearce who peers through the windows. Damned cheek that's what it is, an Oi thinks yer Ladyship should be tellin' her about it.'

'If I see her doing it I shall certainly say something.'

'Thank you, Milady. Oi 'ad to have the vet to Buster, sick he were, the vet said he must have picked something up. Oi keeps him on a leash now, Milady, Oi don't like him running loose, particularly near the lodge house.'

I looked at him sharply. 'What are you implying, Flanagan?'

'Sure and Oi'm not implying anything Milady, but Buster's on a lead now when we walks down the drive an' Oi'd advise you to do the same with the other two.'

After he had gone I looked through the windows disconsolately. There were builders' vans parked at the side of the house as well as a great deal of their material, and from the regions above I could hear knocking and the sound of men's voices.

That afternoon Adam and I walked down to the stables where Adam greeted his pony ecstatically and I went to look at Buster, who sat in his basket a more subdued and much thinner dog. He wagged his long whiplash tail at me but stayed in his basket. I said to Flanagan, 'He's not much like himself. Does the vet say he's going to be all right?'

'Oi reckon so Milady, wicked it is to put poison down for animals to pick up. Oi gave that Mrs Pearce a piece of mi moind but she said they'd seen rats about an' were only lookin' after themselves.'

'So it was poison, Flanagan. What did the vet say?'

'Told me to keep 'im on a tight rein, but Buster don't loike that. Why shouldn't the dogs roam about their own grounds Milady, it's unnatural to 'ave to keep 'em tied up.'

I turned away and was walking thoughtfully towards the house when I saw Mrs Pearce. Standing still I watched her antics with mounting distaste.

She slipped quietly along the paths, then bending low crept close to the windows of the house, staring in unashamedly when she saw there was nobody in the room. White-hot anger took hold of me and I hurried across the grass, my feet making no sound, until I stood behind her. 'What are you doing here, Mrs Pearce?'

I had the satisfaction of seeing her jump several inches in the air before she turned to face me, her face red as beetroot, her small puffy eyes startled and a little afraid. 'I was lookin fer 'Arris the builder Milady, 'ee said a could find 'im 'ere today.'

'There is no need for you to look through the windows Mrs Pearce, it is most disconcerting. If you want to see Mr Harris then I suggest you arrange for him to call at the lodge house. I've seen you looking through the windows before, I can't think you have been looking for Mr Harris on every occasion.'

She lowered her scarlet face, then with a distorted curtsey she scuttled away.

I felt troubled by the encounter, and vexed with myself for feeling troubled. Mrs Pearce was a woman of low intelligence, but I had not been mistaken about the cunning in her narrow eyes or that vague air of insolence.

Easdale did nothing for my peace of mind. I would never be entirely happy in the house and the knowledge that Adam hated it made matters worse. How I longed for Glamara, and yet I was reluctant to take up Aunt Hetty's urgent requests for us to visit them. I had to make myself find some sort of contentment in a house where my son was master. One day it would belong to Adam's children, surely I was not going to allow Dora Chalmers and her familiar, Mrs Pearce, to spoil our future in the house.

I saw Flanagan strolling across the grass with Buster on a lead. He stopped and spoke to the dog, patting his head gently. Buster was not happy, he had always been a dog who liked to roam freely, small gleaming eyes alive with curiosity, his long white nose twitching with excitement, now he sat disconsolately on the grass, still painfully thin after his ordeal, and again I was troubled.

I felt that this house was death to all of us, including the animals, and the sensation of impending doom sent me hurrying to join Flanagan.

Picking up on my mood, he said, 'It's a great pity you and the boy 'ave to go on livin' here at Easdale, Milady, aw sure an' ye've done nothin' to deserve 'er Ladyship hating you loike she does.'

'There are times when it frightens me, Flanagan.'

'When they starts takin' their malice out on dumb animals, it frightens me too, Milady.'

We walked in silence for several minutes until we could see the lodge house through the trees and I asked him curiously, 'Are they having some building work done, do you know?'

'I'm not sure but I have seen Harris goin' in an' out these last few days, and more particularly when you were away, Milady.'

'It would be interesting to know why he goes there. They

are taking a very long time over the repairs to Easdale, I'm sure the work should have been finished long before this.'

'Do you never take a look around, Milady?'

'I know nothing about building repairs Flanagan. I thought it better to let the men get on with their work without any interference from me, now I'm not very sure that was a good decision.'

'You be takin' a look around Milady, and foind out what's bin done and what needs to be done. Sure an' Harris moight be as honest as St Patrick himself, or he moight just not be.'

I nodded briefly and left him to go on with his walk. Resolutely I walked round the house, looking up at the windows. There were so many of them which had been replaced and which would all need painting, but there were others still in their original state. Just then I saw Harris coming towards me, and on the spur of the moment I asked, 'How long do you expect to be here, Mr Harris? The repairs seem to be going on a very long time.'

'There were a lot to be done Milady, an' we've bin waiting for material an' the better weather.'

'I can appreciate that. Perhaps you will let me have your bill for what you have carried out up to now.'

'I 'aven't made it out yet, Milady.'

'Then will you do so?'

'When will yer be wantin' it then?'

'Tomorrow Harris. I think that will do very well.'

'I'll do mi best, Milady.'

'I'm sure you will. I don't want excuses Harris, just bring me the bill.'

He seemed ill at ease but I did not care. If there were discrepancies I wanted to know about them, and I also wanted to know what was happening at the lodge house which necessitated his constant attention.

The butler brought Harris's bill to the study the following day and I sat gazing at the enormity of it. I had known it would be extensive, but before I paid it I needed to assure myself of its authenticity. Consequently I rang for the butler after I had had time to study it thoroughly.

He stood in front of Richard's carved oak desk looking at me steadily, the epitome of the well-bred British servant, and though there were times when I believed I was surrounded by enemies and when I wondered whom I could trust apart from Annie and Flanagan, I realized I would have to trust Farrell. He was a long-standing servant, but could I be sure that his loyalty lay with me and not Dora? As though he sensed something of my doubts he prompted gently, 'Is something wrong, Milady?'

'How long have you worked for the Chalmers family, Farrell?'

'I was a footman here when Sir Edward's father was alive. It seems to me, Milady, that I had no life before I came to Easdale.'

'I'm sure it does. You will be very familiar with the layout of the house then, the number of rooms and the windows?'

If he was surprised he didn't show it. 'I may have forgotten one or two but it is a small matter to go round the house and count them. Would you like me to do that, Milady?'

I shuffled the bill in my hands. 'I have Mr Harris's bill for the windows and I would really like to know how many have been repaired and how many have been replaced. 'Will you check for me, Farrell?'

'I will check every room, and Mrs Roberts will come with me to double check.'

'Thank you Farrell. I shall do nothing with the bill until I hear from you.'

I felt that I was penny-pinching, and yet I had been put on my guard by the way Harris's eyes avoided looking into mine. Quite suddenly the weight of the responsibilities thrust upon my shoulders brought the stinging tears to my eyes. I was not equipped to deal with a house of this size with its crumbling walls and the damage that years of neglect had inflicted on it. I wished we could go away, find some small cottage where Adam and the animals could live unhampered by restraints put upon them because an old woman was so eaten up with bitterness she was prepared to do them harm.

Why didn't I move out and let Dora have Easdale? But she didn't want Easdale, she wanted to get rid of us. If she returned here after we had gone the house would be a wilderness in only a few years, the sort of wilderness it had become before I arrived with my youth, my patience and Julian's money.

Farrell came to the study the following morning with everything conscientiously written down in a small notebook. 'Including the attics Milady and the conservatory there are sixty-four windows in the entire house. All except eight have been replaced.'

'Replaced and not repaired?'

'Replaced Milady, only three have been repaired.'

'I see.'

I was looking down at the bill in my hand unhappily, and he prompted, 'I take it my figures do not correspond to those on Harris's bill?'

'No Farrell, the bill is for the replacement of sixty-four windows. No mention is made of repair and the five that have been left alone are not mentioned either. Will you ask Mr Harris to see me, there is something very wrong somewhere.'

I sat looking gloomily out of the window. In the distance I could see the chimneys of the lodge house and the suspicion that was born in me at that moment filled my heart with helpless rage.

Harris arrived promptly and stood in front of my desk twisting and untwisting the cap in his hands. His bill was spread out in front of me and although it was written indelibly on my mind I made a pretence of looking at it again in order to calm my racing heart.

'I am not sure if I agree with your figures, Harris, particularly the windows.'

'Oh, 'ow's that Milady?'

'We have sixty-four windows in the entire house, and your bill is for sixty-four replacements. Surely this can't be right? Three windows were merely repaired and five were left exactly as they were.'

His face took on a darker hue, and biting his lip nervously he said, 'Yer can see mi bills for materials if yer like, they don't lie.'

'I'm not suggesting that they do, but I am only prepared to

533

pay you for the fifty-six that were replaced and the three that were repaired. If sixty-four windows were delivered here then I suggest you obtain the money for the others from the person who ordered them, whoever it is.'

'She said there'd be no trouble Milady, she said it were all part an' parcel o' the 'all, jest like the farms an' the tenants' houses, she said.'

'Who said?'

'Lady Chalmers, Milady. She said the 'all 'ad allus paid for repairs at the lodge house.'

'I'm sorry Harris, you should have come to me before you carried out any repairs to the lodge house requested by my mother-in-law. I suggest you go down there and inform Lady Chalmers that I am not prepared to pay for her windows or indeed anything else she has asked you to do for her.'

'But suppose she won't pay, Milady? I can't afford to be the loser, I 'as men to pay an' a family to keep.'

'What do you do with any of your other customers who refuse to pay you?'

'I takes 'em to court Milady, I sues 'em.'

'Then I suggest you do exactly the same with Lady Chalmers. She is no different from the rest of them.'

He stared at me stolidly, then shaking his head he said, 'It's 'ard yer are, Milady. 'Er Ladyship told me as 'ow she'd 'ad to leave the 'all where she'd lived all 'er married life, an' 'er son that she idolized, just cause yer didn't want 'er 'ere. Now she's old an' ailin' an' yer won't even pay fer some new winders fer 'er 'ouse. Droppin' to pieces they were. I don't know 'ow yer can be so cruel, Milady, an' yer looks so nice an' behaves so gentle.'

I held out my hand. 'This is my cheque for everything you have done at the hall, apart from the windows we have just been discussing. My mother-in-law should not be discussing me with you, but if you are prepared to believe everything she has told you then perhaps it might be a good thing if you removed your workmen and your materials from here at once. Thank you for all that you have done. I hope you will be successful in your claim against Lady Chalmers.'

He went, muttering to himself, and I sat back in my chair, drained. I could not believe that I had been so rigid, so determined not to be coerced into paying for repairs I had not asked for. I knew there would be repercussions however and I did not have long to wait.

Simeon Ellis came to see me immediately after dinner, standing opposite my chair and holding out a long envelope. It was his resignation.

'I don't like my employers interfering with the way I run things on their land.'

'Perhaps it's as well I have interfered, Mr Ellis, otherwise I should have been paying good money for inferior workmanship, and for work on a property which does not belong to me.'

'Doesn't belong to you!'

'Yes. My husband signed the lodge house over to his mother for her lifetime and she in turn promised to keep it in good repair. Financially she was well able to do so.'

'Lady Chalmers made no mention of it to me.'

'There was no reason why she should, she did not employ you although there have been times when I have wondered whose orders you obeyed, hers or mine.'

'You'll have a job administering this estate without me, you'd have done well to take a leaf out of the old lady's book and been a bit nicer, Milady.'

'And you, Mr Ellis, will do well not to threaten me in my own house. I will pay you a month's salary and you can leave immediately.'

'I'm willing to stay the month,' he blustered.

'I wish you to go now, today if possible.'

I wrote out a cheque which I handed to him. He looked at it then without another word marched out of the room.

It was a fine morning at the end of July when I rode Shamara through the woods behind the house and up the old bridle track towards the hills. Racing the horse along the long low fell, I had no premonition of what this day had in store.

Unlike the terrible time on the Yorkshire coast when Julian lost his life, this day was fine and sunny. The air was

535

filled with the scent of clover and birds sang in the beeches. As I looked down on the village from the heights there was an air of peace pervading in every direction. Men were working in the fields, their brown backs bent in the sunshine, children ran and laughed in the gardens, and here and there a lazy column of smoke ascended from some kitchen fire.

There had been no more unhappy incidents, and I wondered if I could trust the lull in my mother-in-law's hostilities. In three days' time we were leaving for a month's holiday at the lakeland cottage and already Adam was counting the minutes, telling the dogs solemnly that they were going on holiday, filling Annie's mind with stories of the lake and the mountains, the boat, and the swans that came every morning for their breakfast.

Dark clouds began to gather before mid-day and then the wind rose, making it one of those freak days that descend upon the dales in high summer. Long before I reached the stables the rain came, driving straight down, glistening on the leaves of the trees, drenching the flowers so that they hung their heads dejectedly.

I left Shamara in Flanagan's capable hands, then I took to my heels and ran to the house, going upstairs immediately to get out of my wet things. Annie came in to help me off with my clothes and run a bath.

'Who'd 'ave thought the day'd turn out like this?' she complained, 'some o' the servants 'ave gone over to the fair at Garsdale, they'll be drenched to their skins they will.'

'I didn't know there was a fair at Garsdale.'

'Full of it they were, all gone off to see some fortune-teller. They wanted me ter go with 'em but I make nowt o' fortune-tellers, lot o' rubbish that's what it is.'

I didn't answer her. My thoughts were on that other summer's day a long time ago when Laura and I had sallied forth from Glamara on such an errand.

'Don't yer think so, Miss Tessa?'

'I don't know, Annie. A gypsy told my fortune once, and she was remarkably accurate.'

Her eyes opened wide. 'Really Miss Tessa, what did she tell yer?'

'She told me I would lose the man I loved and there would be much sadness for me before I saw my way clear ahead.'

'Well there 'asn't been all that much 'appiness goin' for yer, has there Miss Tessa? I wonder if it's the same woman the maids are 'opin' to see.'

'It's possible, she was a Romany. She was very good with my cousin Laura, and as things have turned out she was pretty good about my future too.'

'Did she tell yer you'd get married to Sir Richard?'

'I'm not sure after all this long time what she said exactly. I know she told me I'd lose the man I loved but in the end I would find happiness with somebody else.'

'I wonder who that's likely to be, Miss Tessa?'

'It's nobody, Annie. I don't think I want to get emotionally involved again, ever.'

'Oh but yer will, Miss Tessa. Yer still young and beautiful. Yer the sort a' woman a man looks at, not like me whose never likely to make a chap look twice.'

I laughed. 'That's because you don't look at *them*, Annie, you give the impression that you are so efficient and self-contained that any man would be superfluous in your life.'

'Do I really do that, Miss Tessa?'

'Yes Annie you do. Don't you ever want to get married and have a home of your own, and children?'

'I don't know. That'd mean leaving you an' I don't want that.'

I slipped my arms into a warm dressing gown and started to brush my hair. She was standing near the dressing table looking unusually pensive and I stopped my vigorous brushing to say, 'Annie, your life is your own, it doesn't belong to me or to Adam. On the day you come to tell me that you have fallen in love and want to get married you will make me very happy.'

'Yer won't mind mi leaving yer, Miss Tessa? Yer won't miss mi?'

'Oh Annie, I shall miss you terribly. There will be whole days when I shall wish you were back with me, but like us all, one day you must fly the nest and make your own life.'

'But this is my life, Miss Tessa.'

'No it isn't, Annie. The birds and animals make their babies go when the time comes, just as I know that one day Adam will leave me when he falls in love. I wouldn't want it any other way.'

'Some women are not happy wi' the men they marry.'

'I know, and I sincerely hope that will not be your misfortune. You're not a child any more Annie, you should be able to sort out the wheat from the chaff.'

'That I can Miss Tessa, an' when a looks around a finds some of 'em wantin'.'

I laughed, then she laughed too, and said, 'If yer goes down to the drawin' room I'll bring yer a cup of tea.'

'That will be lovely, just give me time to put on something respectable.'

Looking back on that day years later I could only feel astonishment that anything which started so normally could end so traumatically. For the rest of my life I believed I would distrust normality, look for hidden meanings and dangerous undercurrents.

As the day wore on the rain stopped, only the wind moaned mournfully around the house. Adam and I played numerous card games, but mostly he wanted to talk about the holiday ahead. When we had finally exhausted that subject we went on to talk about his preparatory school in September and I felt utterly disconcerted when he said happily, 'I shan't be here very much at all will I, Mother?'

'Oh darling, do you really hate Easdale as much as all that?'

'If we lived at the cottage always I wouldn't want to go away to school.'

'But because you live here you are looking forward to it, is that what you are saying?'

He looked at me unhappily, his beautiful boy's face strangely sad before he gave me his sweet remote smile, Julian's smile.

'I don't want to leave you Mother, or Annie and the animals, I just want to leave Easdale. Shall we always have to live in this house, even when I'm a man? Won't we ever be able to get away from it?'

'Your father was very proud that it would be yours one day, Adam.'

'I know, but he wasn't afraid of those two old women at the lodge house.'

I didn't know how to answer him. How could I tell my son not to mind when I minded them so dreadfully myself? He went to stare through the window at the dull grey day and the wildly tossing trees, then after a few moments he returned to sit at my feet.

'Will you be able to come and see me at school, Mother?'

'Of course, darling. There will be sports days and speech days when parents can visit. You will make friends that could last a lifetime.'

'Like you and Aunt Susan?'

'I hope so, Adam.'

After he had gone to bed I sat alone in the drawing room trying to read but for most of the time the book lay idle on my knees. The ferocity of the wind intruded into my innermost thoughts and for a long time I sat staring into the fire trying to make pictures in the coals as I had often done as a child.

When Annie came in with a cup of hot chocolate for me just after ten I brightened at the sight of her serene, smiling face. She seemed so happy and when I remarked upon it she said, 'I've just finished all mi packing, Miss Tessa, I'm that excited.'

'You will need something for all weathers Annie, the climate can be very changeable in the Lake District.'

'I know, Miss Tessa, Sir Adam's told me to take plimsolls fer sailin' an' walkin shoes for walkin'. I've packed the lot. Will ye 'ave room for all of 'em in the car, that's what I'd like to know?'

'Lots of room Annie, the luggage will go in the boot and Adam can sit behind with the dogs.'

She nodded happily.

'You can't wait to get away from here can you Annie, just like Adam?'

'It's the holiday I'm lookin' forward to, Miss Tessa, I never 'ad 'em as a child, it 'as nothin' at all to do wi' Easdale.'

She was lying. It had everything to do with Easdale, but

539

she didn't want to distress me by saying so.

I was tired when I went to bed but for a long time sleep eluded me. I had put out the light and although the house was quiet, outside the wind moaned and the branches of the trees tapped mercilessly against the windows. Occasionally flashes of lightning lit up the sky but the thunder seemed a long way off. Eventually I slept.

It can only have been apprehension that woke me. I looked at the clock beside my bed and the luminous figures told me that it was a little after two. The flashes of lightning seemed to have increased and occasionally the sky outside my room flamed bright red, and I could hear crackling sounds totally unlike the noise of the wind.

At first I felt no sense of danger, I simply lay still watching the flaming sky, then I could taste the acrid smoke burning in my throat and I jumped out of my bed and rushed to the window. There was smoke everywhere, deep impenetrable smoke, and then again the sky lit up and I could see the flames leaping and dancing, tearing at the trees, then I heard voices, men's voices and footsteps running madly beneath my window.

Snatching a dressing gown from my bed and thrusting my feet into slippers I rushed towards the door. Jasper lay there whining and from somewhere in the hall I could hear Honey barking. I ran out on to the landing where I could see into the hall below. At the sight of me Honey came bounding up the stairs, whining with distress now, and with the two dogs I ran to Adam's room, shaking him from a deep slumber, staring into his frightened eyes and urging him to put on his dressing gown and not be frightened.

My urgency compelled him to act swiftly, and gathering a blanket over my arm I raced with him along the corridor where the servants had gathered, the girls wide-eyed with terror, yet following me without question towards the back staircase. Smoke billowed from the hall and we could plainly hear the crackle of flames.

Most of them were in their nightclothes but there was no time to think of clothing, all I wanted was to get out into the night air. Just then the butler arrived, his eyes red rimmed from the smoke, his face blackened with soot.

'The fire's spread, Milady, we can't use the hall,' he said anxiously.

'I know, Farrell. Is everybody here?'

'I think so, Milady.'

'Where's Annie, has anybody seen Annie?'

'She were 'ere a minute or two since,' one of the maids said, and I looked round me helplessly unable to see her.

'You had better get out into the open air, Milady,' the butler urged. 'The smoke is terrible.'

It was in our throats, smarting in our eyes, but still I lingered, how could I leave without Annie, and seeing my hesitation he urged again, 'Don't worry, Milady, I'll find her, she can't be far away.'

Adam was coughing beside me, the tears streaming down his face, and gathering the servants together I herded them down the back stairs, already filled with smoke but where the flames had not yet penetrated.

Outside in the wind the girls huddled together and I told them to run towards the garages where they might find some sort of shelter. I wrapped the blanket round Adam and waited in the courtyard for the butler and Annie. After about five minutes he came out alone, spluttering from the smoke in his throat, his eyes red and inflamed. I pounced on him at once, demanding to know if Annie had escaped.

'I haven't seen her, Milady, one of the footmen said she ran back to her room, she was talking about some pictures she wanted to bring.'

I stared at him, appalled. Surely she couldn't have risked her life to bring that picture I had given her years before? Surely she must have found it and escaped while we were still waiting at the top of the stairs.

The butler was looking at me helplessly. 'We can't go back in there, Milady, the front of the house is completely alight. The fire engines are on their way.'

'Where did the fire start, Farrell?'

'In the stables Milady, it spread like lightning and the wind blew sparks towards the house.'

Adam's face was frightened now. 'Mother, the pony and

the horses, and the other animals!'

'Yes darling, Flanagan will be taking care of them, try not to worry.'

I had told my son not to worry but *I* was worried. I was thinking of Flanagan in his flat above the stables but most of all about Annie. Oh that foolish girl, to have run back for a picture of such little material value that it could have been replaced a dozen times.

'Go with Mr Farrell, Adam,' I ordered, 'and stay with him until I come for you.'

'But where are you going, Mother?'

'I'm going to the front of the house to see if I can find Annie and Flanagan. Stay with Mr Farrell, promise?'

He nodded miserably, and I said to Farrell, 'Don't let him out of your sight, and please take Honey. Jasper will come with me.'

Jasper trotted beside me, dejection apparent in every line of his sturdy body, occasionally looking up at me with sad brown eyes. I could feel the heat of the fire and from the drive I could look back at the house and see the flames leaping in every room. Most of the windows had gone and the flames leapt up to the attics. Then the roof too was alight, the air rent with the sickening crash of falling masonry.

The noise was terrible, the crackle of timber and the sound of the wind, the crashing of stone walls and the clanging of bells as three fire engines raced up the drive, then there seemed to be men everywhere, their shouts mingling with the disintegration of our home.

I have no idea how long I stood watching the end of Easdale before I saw Flanagan staggering towards me with Buster, a rope tied through his collar, his white coat sootied and grimed, and Flanagan's face blackened, his eyebrows singed, his eyes awash with smarting tears.

I ran towards him. 'Oh Flanagan, I'm so relieved to see you. The fire started in the stables I'm told?'

'Yes, Milady.'

We stared at each other and I was unable to put my question into words. He reached out and touched my hand.

'Don't worry, Milady, I got 'em out, the pony and Caliph are safe.'

'And Shamara?'

'He panicked Milady, I couldn't hold him. He tried to jump the wall but he was too frightened. He broke his back leg.'

'Oh, Flanagan!'

'He didn't suffer, Milady. Oi 'ad to shoot him.'

Tears filled my eyes. 'I don't know where Annie is, Flanagan. She ran back to get some wretched picture out of her bedroom. You haven't seen her, have you?'

'No Milady, Oi haven't. It's the wind that spread the fire, it couldn't 'ave happened on a worse night.'

'Have you any idea how it started?'

'No, but the fire people'll have a good idea when they've finished here.'

'Flanagan, will you have a look round for Annie? I'll go this way if you'll go that.'

He nodded and I continued my search. People were walking up the drive, villagers mostly, and grimly I found myself wondering how they would enjoy the spectacle. Half way down the drive I came across Caliph and the pony standing shivering beside the railings. Caliph came to me immediately, nuzzling my shoulder as I talked to him calmly, stroking his long satiny neck. He looked none the worse for his ordeal but the pony's tail was scorched and he seemed very nervous, his eyes wild, trembling under my touch.

Reluctantly I turned away to continue my search for Annie. I was desperately afraid of what I would be told and it seemed that by staying with the horses I would delay the moment as long as possible. However I had to face it, either that or the joy of knowing she was safe.

My feet felt cold from the wet grass and the dog shivering beside me reminded me that I was wearing only a thin nightgown under my summer robe.

'Come Jasper,' I said briskly as I turned to walk swiftly back along the drive. I had only gone a little way when I became aware of two darkly clad figures under the trees near the boundary wall and I paused, staring at them curiously. They had not seen me, but there was no disguising their expressions. They were watching the leaping flames and the crumbling house with glee, their faces alight with wonder, devoid of sorrow or horror, and as if they sensed my presence they turned to stare at me.

By right those expressions should have changed, they should have shown sympathy, compassion, but on one face there was only animal cunning and on the other elation and triumph.

I knew at that moment who had been responsible for destroying Easdale, whether or not I would ever be able to prove it. Such helpless rage filled my heart that I could have killed them both. I stood looking at them until first one and then the other looked away, then as if in defiance Dora Chalmers lifted her head and with her eyes gleaming balefully she said, 'That's going to be a fine house to hand down to your bastard son, Milady.'

I walked towards them and stood looking down on them, feeling suddenly very strong, 'I don't know whether you are evil or merely insane, but for tonight's work I'll see that you're put away where you can't do any more harm, ever.'

I turned to walk away and behind me there was silence, then above the clamour I suddenly heard Dora's laughter.

Oh my God, I thought helplessly, she must be insane to find amusement in all this.

Morning brought the full realization of all I had lost. Annie had died in the fire, the house had gone, and Shamara. What was left were the garages away from the house, and two of the kitchens swimming with water and smelling vilely, blackened with smoke yet offering some sort of shelter.

The servants had lost their livelihood as well as their home and bidding goodbye to Farrell and the housekeeper I shook my head sadly. 'I'm sorry I can't offer you renewed employment, you have all been wonderful but I have no home to go to as yet.'

'We realize that, Milady,' the butler said gently. 'Is there anywhere we can get in touch with you?'

'You can always write to me at Glamara in the North

Riding, if I am not there they will forward the letters. If I am ever looking for new servants, or if I find somewhere to live where I need you, perhaps you would consider it.'

'Oh yes Milady, these last few years since you came to live at Easdale have been happier ones for all of us. The house took on a new feeling, we were all aware of it. I'm sorry it has had to end like this.'

'Thank you Farrell, I appreciate it and if I can do anything for any of you, references, anything at all, please write to me.'

They stood in a forlorn group on the wet grass and my heart was filled with compassion for them. I told Farrell to take them into what was left of the kitchen while I looked round for the Police Inspector. I found him in earnest conversation with the Fire Chief but when he saw me he came immediately to my side.

'This is a bad business Milady,' he said earnestly.

'Yes, but right at this moment I am concerned about the servants. They too have lost everything and they are only wearing their nightclothes. Can something be done for them quickly?'

'What had you in mind Milady?'

'Well quite obviously they need clothes and somewhere to sleep. As soon as I can I will try to get some money to them but it's tonight I'm worried about.'

'How many servants are there Milady?'

'About ten I think. They are all house servants.'

'I'll get one of my men to take them in the van to the cottage hospital, they'll find beds there and we'll get on to the Red Cross with regard to clothing. Do any of them live round here Milady?'

'I believe two of the girls have relatives in the village but apart from that none of them are from these parts.'

'Leave things with me Milady, I'll get them fixed up in no time but how about yourself and the youngster ma'am?'

'I don't know, I'll think about us when I've seen the servants cared for.'

The black police van arrived minutes later and the servants were bundled into it immediately. In spite of their fears, some of the girls giggled at the sight of the Black Maria but

Farrell quelled their hysteria with a stern look. I watched the black van trundle down the drive and then quite suddenly I felt very vulnerable and alone.

We sat in the dismal kitchen, Adam, Flanagan and I, and with us sat three dejected dogs and one white rabbit, his fur blackened with soot. We had lost our home and all our belongings, I had lost a dear friend and a beloved horse and we had nowhere to go on that morning as we waited for the fire chief and the police to finish their inspection of what was left of Easdale. The morning papers would be full of the disaster and I found myself wondering what they would be thinking at Glamara, what Susan and John would be thinking in Leeds. The telephone wires were down and they would have no idea how many of us had survived.

The vicar and his wife came laden with baskets of food but the smoke had eaten into our throats so that most of it was tasteless. I thanked them warmly for their kindness and the vicar said, 'Of course my dear, you and the boy must come to us but we have no extra room for Flanagan and you will need somewhere for the dogs and horses.'

After they had gone Flanagan said, 'You mustn't be thinkin' of me Milady, Oi can shack down anywhere, Oi've done it before Oi can do it again.'

The police and the fire chief reported that the fire had been started deliberately. Then they started to probe, asking me if I had any suspicions. I was still seeing the look of triumph on Dora Chalmers' face, and filled with a great resolve I told them something of the events of the years I had spent at Easdale: my mother-in-law's growing bitterness, her resentment and her threats.

As the picture grew clearer the inspector said, 'Do I take it you are accusing your mother-in-law and her companion of setting the fire, Milady?'

'You say it was done deliberately Inspector, and I can think of only those two people who would have the nerve, the access and the resentment to do such a terrible thing. They have threatened me and my son, they have tried to antagonize the people of the village against me and over the years I have been a victim of Lady Chalmers' hatred, even when my husband was alive. I am accusing Lady Chalmers, Inspector, it is for you to prove I am right.'

Flanagan left to see to the horse and pony, and Adam and I stayed in the kitchen, oblivious of our appearance and the chill that invaded our bones. Adam seemed strangely calm and I hoped he wasn't suffering from delayed shock. I tried to keep calm myself. Tears would come later, but just then I had to be strong for the child's sake.

As if sensing something of my thoughts he said, 'We won't ever need to live here again, will we Mother?'

'No darling.'

'What will they do with the house, will it be pulled down?'

'Oh I do hope so, Adam. It is dangerous to leave it standing like this.'

'Can it be put right again so that we will have to come back here?'

'No, it is too badly damaged ever to be put right.'

He could not disguise the relief that shone on his face and putting my arms round him I said, 'You're glad aren't you Adam, you'd rather live anywhere than here?'

'Yes Mother, I didn't want there to be a fire and lose Annie and Shamara, I just wanted us all to be together a long way away from here. Why did those two old ladies set fire to it, was it to get rid of us?'

'I think so, Adam.'

'Why does Lady Chalmers hate us so much and why does she have your name, Mother?'

'She was your father's mother but they didn't get along together so she went to live at the lodge house.'

'Perhaps if she had lived at Easdale she wouldn't have set fire to it,' he surprised me by saying with a child's logic.

'Perhaps. Would you have liked her to live at Easdale?'

'Oh no Mother, I didn't even like her living at the lodge house.'

There was the sound of a car's engine from the courtyard and I went to the open doorway to see who our visitors were. I couldn't see the car but I heard footsteps approaching, stumbling at times over the rubble. I waited expectantly at the door and then my eyes opened in dismay as Lionel

Prescott rounded the corner of the house and stared at me with anguished eyes.

He quickened his step and took me in his arms, holding me against him so that I took comfort from the warmth of his body against mine, the gentleness of his embrace. Then catching sight of Adam staring at us with wide curious eyes he knelt down and brought Adam into his embrace.

Over Adam's head he said, 'It's reported briefly in the morning paper, Tessa. I suppose it's too soon to have the full story. Susan wanted to come with me but I dissuaded her, I was unsure what I would find.'

'Thank you for coming,' I said, then I began to tell him everything about the last traumatic hours, Annie and Shamara, the two dark figures in the park, and as I talked he watched me with mounting concern.

He said firmly, 'I am taking you and the boy back with me now, Susan is expecting you.'

'Lionel, I can't leave the area just yet, the police have asked me to stay close at hand.'

'But you can't stay *here*, Tessa.'

'I've been invited to stay at the vicarage for the next few days, but can you possibly find room for Flanagan and the horses? One of the local farmers would lend him a horse box, he just needs a roof over his head until I know where we go from here.'

'Of course Flanagan can come with me, and the horses. How about the dogs?'

'If you could take Buster and Honey, Jasper can come with me. I think he would fret without me.'

'What about clothes, Tessa? I suppose everything was destroyed?'

'Everything. I'll have to write to Aunt Hetty for some money and buy something in the village. We only have what we stand up in.'

'I'll bring something from Susan's, her clothes will fit you and you can get something for Adam in the village. How much money will tide you over for the time being?'

'I don't know, you've been too kind already.'

'Fifty pounds, a hundred. I'm not being kind Tessa, I'm being practical.'

'Fifty then, Lionel. They've taken the servants to the cottage hospital for the night but I should do something about getting money to them in the morning.'

'I'll drive round there now. I'll leave some money with your butler, he is with them I suppose?'

'Yes. I'm very grateful Lionel, and of course I'll repay you as soon as I can.'

He smiled deprecatingly and touched by his solicitude I began to feel an abiding gratitude that he had come to me at a moment when my faith in human nature had been at its lowest ebb.

With Flanagan's immediate future assured some of my worry passed, and we went with Lionel to the vicarage.

I gave the vicar's wife a sum of money and asked her to purchase underwear, a skirt and sweater from the village store, well aware that what they had would be distinctly unfashionable. Then Lionel himself set out to buy clothes for Adam. At least we would both look as though we belonged in the land of the living.

Catching sight of my reflection in the hall mirror, I gasped with dismay. My pale hair was blackened with soot, my eyes were red-rimmed and my dressing gown was covered with grime. What a dismal picture I must have presented to Lionel Prescott, who had never before seen me looking less than elegant.

It was early evening when he left for Leeds, and I thanked him warmly for all his care. He looked down at me with a strange expression in his eyes and I found myself blushing furiously under his regard. However much I had disappointed him by my past lifestyle there was no evidence of it in his expression. It was the look of a man who had a very special regard for the woman under his scrutiny. He did not attempt to kiss me, but instead he took my hand and pressed it gently, then he was gone.

We stayed in the vicarage, neither Adam nor I anxious to go out, bombarded with telephone calls from Aunt Hetty urging us to come at once to Glamara. I gave her the same answer I had given Lionel, that we could not leave the village until the inspector had finished with his inquiries, and these were taking longer than I had imagined.

I spoke to the headmaster of Adam's preparatory school explaining that it would now be after Christmas when he could start there, and he assured me that would be perfectly in order. Slowly matters were falling into place, but as yet the full enormity of all that had happened had not been felt. I had too much company with the vicar and his wife, and Adam kept very close to me, only taking time off to play with Jasper in the garden. When one of the village children looked through the gate he ran inside the house immediately, as if he was afraid of that child's face staring at him with undisguised curiosity.

I found myself wondering if Easdale had placed an indelible shadow on our future, on our association with other people, on our faith in God, but the vicar assured me our reaction was perfectly normal and only time would bring healing. I knew that he was right, time could bring solace if not forgetfulness. But how could I say what the experience had done to Adam?

He seemed singularly uncaring about our holiday in the Lake District and when I mentioned it he pondered a little then surprised me by saying, 'But it won't be the same without Annie, will it Mother? I was going to take her in the boat and in the forest, we were going to hunt for blackberries and watch the squirrels. Perhaps we could go there next year when I won't have promised all those things to Annie.'

I felt the tears gliding down my cheeks, and he came to put his arms around me. 'Why did she go back to the house, Mother, was it something very important?'

'She went back for a picture I once bought her, it wasn't a very expensive picture but she loved it.'

'What kind of a picture?'

'Oh just a picture of tiny boats bobbing about on an angry sea, I don't think she ever showed it to you.'

'Did you like it, would you have gone back for it?'

'No Adam, I didn't like it, I never wanted to look at it again.'

'Why? Wasn't it a nice picture?'

'Not to me darling, it reminded me too much of things I want to forget.'

At long last the police inspector came, informing me that he had questioned Lady Chalmers and her companion closely about the fire and in the end it was Mrs Pearce who had not proved clever enough to lie with any degree of effectiveness. Then my mother-in-law had disintegrated, laughing and crying, hysterical with bitterness, and giving herself away with every word and every gesture.

'The old woman's insane, of course,' he said, 'and Mrs Pearce has simply been a tool in her hands, too unintelligent to see that the old lady's hatred was pushing her into great wickedness while she, poor woman, only tried to ingratiate herself with some mistaken idea that she was being loyal to an old employer.'

'What will happen to them?' I asked, my hands clenched fiercely in my lap.

'We'll prosecute, Milady. But you can be sure they'll plead insanity. I should think both of 'em'll end their days in a mental institution, but that doesn't bring your house back or the girl who died in it.'

I sat thinking about Annie, and feeling no pity for the two women who had taken her life.

'Thank you, Inspector, for letting me know what has happened. Now I shall go home to Glamara. In all the traumatic moments of my life I have gone there and the house has been waiting, like a benediction almost.'

I decided that we would go to Glamara the following Saturday but when Godfrey stated his intention of coming for us I said there was no need. We had no luggage to speak of, apart from joint belongings which would easily fit into one small grip, so we decided that he would meet us at the station.

Later that evening Lionel telephoned, saying he needed to see me before I returned to the North Riding, so we arranged that he should come on Friday morning.

'Will he bring my pony back with him?' Adam asked with more interest in his voice than I had heard for days.

'Oh no I'm sure he won't. Flanagan will see to the pony, darling, I don't really know why Sir Lionel is coming.'

Adam was playing in the garden when Lionel arrived and I saw how eagerly he ran to the car before Lionel had had time to step out on to the drive. Then after Lionel had tousled his hair playfully they returned to the house laughing together, a scene so normal a casual onlooker would not have thought that tragedy had played any part in bringing them together.

Lionel greeted me naturally, taking my hand in his and smiling down at me. 'You're looking more like yourself, Tessa. How are you feeling?'

'I'm not sure, I walk and talk and eat, but sleep is something that eludes me.'

'Adam tells me you are all packed up for the journey to Glamara.'

'Packing up didn't take very long, we have what we stand up in plus the things we sleep in. I am wearing the very best the village could produce.'

He laughed. 'I have never seen you looking less than beautiful, and you *are* looking brighter. The clothes don't matter. You're off in the morning and your uncle is not coming for you?'

'No, it wasn't necessary. He will meet the train.'

'I will take you, Tessa. Indeed I insist on it.'

'Oh Lionel, no. You have done far too much already.'

'You think I should send you a bill, Tessa?'

His eyes smiled down at me and for the first time in days I smiled too, then more soberly I said, 'I hadn't expected such kindness, we are so very grateful.'

'The police notified Annie's parents of her death, Tessa, but I went round to see them myself.'

'There you see, how can I ever repay kindness of that sort? How did they take it?'

'Her mother wept a little, I think she cared very deeply, but for the rest of them, I came away feeling a little disgusted.'

'Why was that?'

'Her father's a loud-mouthed, overbearing ruffian. All he could talk about was that they hadn't been good enough for her since she went to work for the so-called gentry, that poor Annie had enjoyed playing lady bountiful merely to shame him.'

'That's monstrously unfair. She was so good to them, spending all her pocket money on them, particularly on Mary who did nothing to deserve it.'

'I met Mary: pretty, spoilt, obviously the apple of her father's eye.'

'Yes, Mary was always the pretty one. I remember that Annie was so proud of her sister's looks, she often said Mary was everything she was not. But Annie was worth a hundred of her sister. Wasn't Mary the least bit upset about Annie's death?'

'I doubt it.' He smiled wryly. 'She said Annie had promised her several trinkets and she wanted to know if they had all been lost in the fire.'

'Oh no!'

'Oh yes, my dear. Sister Mary is an obvious survivor.'

I felt saddened and sickened by their insensitivity and seeing my obvious distress he said, 'Don't let any of this worry you, Tessa. Annie was happy with you. Probably the only time she was ever happy was with you.'

We arranged for the morning's journey, and after shaking my hand and ruffling Adam's hair once more Lionel left us, walking swiftly towards his car, then with a brief wave he drove slowly out of the gate.

There was an unfamiliar warm feeling in my heart where before there had been icy calm, and for the first time since the fire I felt that I might sleep that night.

Then, in spite of grief, in spite of the indifference of Annie's family to her death and the callous wickedness of those who had taken away our home and robbed others of their employment, a vague intangible joy penetrated into that dead thing that was my heart. Tomorrow we were going home, back to Glamara and the peace of her rolling acres, to the dark beauty of the northern Pennines and the feathery branches of the pines tossing helplessly in the wind that swept down from the fells.

I was going back as I had always gone back to lick my wounds, to find new strength for whatever I must face in the future. Through all the changes of my life Glamara had been a rock I could lean on, a sanctuary from the storm, a safe haven in a changing world.

PART SIX

CHAPTER THIRTY-SIX

We spoke little on our journey north the following morning.

I was glad when Lionel took the road that led away from Easdale instead of the one that passed its gates. I did not wish to look on the burnt-out wreck of the hall, the hall that Richard had so wanted for Adam, but as we climbed the hill out of the village some strange compulsion made me ask Lionel to stop the car. He did not offer to come with me, nor did Adam, and I walked alone to a stile that separated the road from the fields. From the bottom step I was able to gaze down on the ruined walls and chimneys, at the churned-up parkland and all the devastation of Easdale, and a lump came into my throat. The hall had been Annie's funeral pyre, and Shamara's.

For a few minutes I gave myself up to the aching luxury of grief, then impatiently I brushed the tears away, and squaring my shoulders resolutely I returned to the car. Lionel didn't look at me but continued to gaze straight ahead, then putting the car into gear he drove quickly towards the river meandering like a shining ribbon in the distance.

It was late afternoon when we came slowly along the drive, with the towers of Glamara silhouetted against a flaming sky. Welcoming lights burned in many of the downstairs rooms although it was only sunset, and as we neared the front door it was flung open and lights streamed out on to us.

Godfrey was there and Aunt Hetty, the butler and the housekeeper came rushing out, footmen came to take my luggage and even Cook was there using her large white apron to wipe away her tears.

Godfrey embraced me in his usual hearty manner and then Aunt Hetty came to envelope me in her arms, while Adam was lifted shoulder high on Godfrey's shoulder and conveyed to the house, and all around us dogs jumped and barked, although Jasper stayed close to me as though to say he was my special dog.

I stayed with Adam while he ate his evening meal and until he fell asleep. Looking down on his sleeping face I could see the dark curling lashes against his cheek and the faint blue circles of anxiety that had not completely gone.

Later I sat down to dinner wearing a long dinner gown I had found in my wardrobe and which I had forgotten I had. It was not strictly fashionable, but the colour suited me and I was surprised how tightly I had to pull in the belt because of the weight I had lost since last I wore it.

Lionel was staying the night, indeed both Godfrey and Aunt Hetty refused even to contemplate his returning home before morning, and I looked round the room appreciatively. Tall candles filled the candelabras, shedding their radiance on shining glass and silver and a bowl of white roses. I ate my meal listening to Godfrey and Lionel discussing the virtues of Hereford cattle and their respective bloodstocks.

Occasionally I caught Aunt Hetty's eyes upon me, and now and again on Lionel, discerning and expectant, and Lionel charmed her as once Julian had charmed her.

After coffee Aunt Hetty suggested that I showed Lionel over the house.

'I'd like that very much,' he said. 'I remember seeing this house years ago when I came up here on a fishing trip. It was something that stuck in my mind, the beautiful scenery and this gracious house, so much a part of it. It is strange to think that I should now be dining here.'

'Hetty should go with you,' Godfrey said, smiling. 'She can tell you the life story of every one of those old Chalfonts you will see on the walls and in the long gallery, even to that small brat who looks the picture of mischief.'

'That was Sir Nigel Chalfont, the fourth baronet,' Aunt Hetty replied primly. 'He was a royalist and died serving the king. He turned out to be a very fine gentleman.'

'And a bit of a lad with the ladies I shouldn't wonder,' Godfrey retorted.

'How do you know that?' I asked him.

'Well one has only to look at the adult portrait of Sir Nigel Chalfont in the library. A very handsome lad with a roguish eye although Hetty's inclined to look at all our ancestors through rose-coloured spectacles. Myself I'm not an ancestor-worshipper.'

'And neither am I,' Aunt Hetty retorted, 'but one has to be kind to their memory, they are not here to speak for themselves.'

'And a right champion they have in you, m'dear. Now off you go Tessa, it'll be interesting to know what Lionel thinks of Glamara.'

He admired everything. Glamara was a show place to be proud of and I saw the delighted appreciation in Lionel's eyes as he viewed priceless pictures and pieces of porcelain, the luxury of oriental carpets and the exquisite sheen on valuable furniture.

'This must have been a treasure house of a place to grow up in,' he remarked appreciatively.

'Yes, it must have been,' I agreed.

'You didn't grow up here, Tessa?'

'No. My mother grew up here and she told me such stories about it. I was almost grown-up when I came to Glamara.'

'You love it of course?'

'Yes, I've always loved it. It seems to me that every catastrophe of my life has brought me back to it and Glamara has always been waiting to heal my wounds, restore my confidence. Perhaps she will do the same for me this time.'

'I'm sure of it, Tessa. Now who are these people? Godfrey I can recognize, but tell me about the lady and the children.'

'That is Abigail, Godfrey's first wife, and their three children, Adam who was killed in the war, Robert who lives abroad and Laura who lives in the south of England.'

'Is there a picture of Godfrey's second wife, or doesn't she merit a mention?'

'I believe he has her portrait in his study. Her name was Roxanne.'

I hadn't spoken her name for a long time and now it felt strange and alien on my lips so that I turned abruptly away and walked the length of the gallery, leaving him staring after me. I waited for him to join me, aware that he looked at me anxiously, but determined not to be drawn into talk of Roxanne I said brightly, 'I'll take you into the ballroom now, then after we've seen the music room we can rejoin the others.'

It had not been a good idea to bring Lionel round the house. The ballroom brought back too many memories, and when we entered the music room he walked immediately to the grand piano and ran his fingers lightly and appreciatively over the keys while I stared at him in dismay.

'You play, Lionel? I didn't know,' was all I could find to say.

'Not too well, I'm afraid. I love music and only wish I played better, but I seem to have very little time these days.'

'I'm afraid I don't play at all but I do love music.'

'It's a very fine instrument, somebody should play it often.'

'I believe Aunt Hetty keeps it regularly tuned. She looks after everything here quite magnificently, I don't know what Godfrey would do without her.'

'I take it this has always been her home?'

'Of course. She never married and even when Abigail was here she left a great deal to Aunt Hetty.'

'As the daughter of the house, of course?'

'Exactly.'

He looked down at me long and searchingly, then he surprised me by saying, 'There are so many undercurrents associated with the house Tessa, perhaps it wasn't such a good idea after all to bring me round.'

'The tour has created memories, that is all. It is strange but one goes away, thinks one has forgotten almost, and then the memories are back and so much more powerful than before. It makes me wonder if it is entirely wise of me to keep coming back to Glamara. Perhaps I would be better to make memories of my own in a house of my own, quite divorced from the past and the influence of others.'

'One day Tessa you *will* have a house of your own and you will create your own memories.'

'You sound very certain, Lionel.'

'I would like to be more certain.'

Our eyes met, and there was no mistaking his meaning, but it was too soon. I could feel my face colouring under his regard, then taking my hands he said, 'I shouldn't have said that, Tessa, I should give you more time. Of course you need time, but I am afraid of time, I am afraid it could make you forget me, find other escapes, other men to love you.'

'Oh Lionel, you talk as if I am forever on the lookout for men to love me. I have only ever loved one man in my life and he is dead. I was happy being loved, if I ever thought there was the slightest chance that I could find some of that happiness again I would welcome it, but I am not ready for it yet, if I ever shall be I don't know.'

'I'm not going to pester you, Tessa. But in twelve months' time I shall come back to Glamara. You may only wish to see me as a friend and I shall understand, I shall know as soon as I look in your eyes if we are ever intended to be more than friends.'

'Lionel, that is twelve months out of your life when you might begin to find happiness with somebody else. I have no right to expect that of you.'

'You are not expecting it, I am offering it.'

'And in the meantime we are not going to meet or speak on the telephone, not even write to each other?'

'I shall be out of the country a great deal of that time. I am going to America and Australia where I have business interests and it's for the best, Tessa. I want to give you time to come to terms with your life, to heal, and to decide what you want from it, what you want for Adam, and even if you can bear to start again and share it with me. In twelve months I promise you I shall be here, on this very day, and if it's no, your friendship will still be very dear to me. And if it's yes then I shall spend the rest of my life trying to make you happy.'

He didn't attempt to kiss me, he simply stood staring down at me, but there was no denying the sincerity in his voice and in his expression.

When we returned to the drawing room I thought Aunt Hetty looked at us expectantly, but Godfrey went immediately to the drinks cabinet and I returned to my chair and picked up a magazine. I hoped she would not see that my fingers were trembling or be aware that the magazine was merely a prop to cover my beating heart. Startled, I heard her say, 'Didn't I hear the piano, Tessa?'

'Yes. Lionel plays, but he tells me he is out of practice.'

'How nice. That piano hasn't been touched since Julian played. . . .'

Her voice faltered, and in some confusion she looked away and my eyes met Lionel's over her head. There was a warm understanding in his gaze, an understanding of her hesitancy and my pain. Oh dear Lionel, I like you so much, but it is too soon.

Life settled down to the pattern I had known in the past. The villagers of Lambreck knew of the burning of Easdale Hall and there was sympathy in their faces when we met on Sundays at the morning service and when we shopped in the village high street. Then the men would raise their caps respectfully and the women would curtsey for although such old-fashioned courtesy was fast dying out in other parts of the country, in Lambreck it was still very much in evidence.

Occasionally I lunched with Godfrey at the Chalfont Arms where we met friends who talked avidly about their horses, the race meetings and the local hunt meetings to the exclusion of everything else, and more and more I began to feel that I had never really been away.

Some of the flesh crept back on my bones and Adam grew so straight and tall I had seriously to consider the possibility that some of the school clothes I had bought for him would now be too small.

Godfrey was none too sure that Caliph was the horse for me to ride.

'He's too big for you, Tessa, he's a man's horse. Now why don't you have a look at that little mare Colonel Wyndham has for sale? She's a beauty.'

'I don't feel particularly out of place riding Caliph, after all he's not a lot bigger than Shamara.'

'He's a man's horse, Tessa.'

'Which means you would like him yourself, I suppose?'

He had the grace to look embarrassed, then he laughed a little. 'Well m'dear, I always had my eye on him and I'm thinking of retiring Major. I'll give you a good price for him Tessa, either that or I'll buy the mare for you.'

'You can have Caliph, Godfrey, I owe you far more already than I can ever repay, if he pleases you then I shall feel I'm paying you back a little.'

His obvious pleasure was reward enough and I knew Caliph would be in good hands.

Several weeks after my return to Glamara I was surprised to receive a letter from the solicitor who had handled my affairs in Whitby. With his letter he enclosed another which Annie had left in his keeping after she received Julian's legacy. As I stared at the envelope addressed to me in her rounded childish handwriting it seemed that Annie reached out to me from the other side of the grave, causing me to weep with renewed distress.

I was glad I was alone and I took out a single sheet of paper written on both sides with that familiar childlike scrawl:

Dear Miss Tessa,

I expects yer'll be surprised to get this letter but I never had any money afore, and when Sir Julian left me all that money I thought I should leave it right in case anything happened to me. I knows I'm young to think about dyin, but then Sir Julian were only young when he had to go.

I'd like mi mam to have mi money but I knows if I leaves it to her mi Dad'll ave it, every penny of it. Our Mary's like him, there'd be nothin left in next to no time, but I'd like her to ave mi jet beads and the gold locket mi gran left me.

I want's mi money to go to our Joe. He's lame an e's not had much of a life. Joe and me were allus the plain ones. The others used to laugh at us and treat us rotten but I reckon if Joe has a bit o money they'll ave to watch their step.

He's only fourteen Miss Tessa, but if I dies an I leaves mi money to you, I knows you'll see that Joe gets it when he's older.

I hopes you don't mind me botherin you with all this but I didn't know what to do. Course, if I lives to be old you'll never get this

563

letter an there won't be any need to trouble yerself about it.

Thank you Miss Tessa, I've allus loved yer, you knows that.

Annie

I wept long and bitterly after reading that letter, but at least I could now do something for Annie, if it was only carrying out her wishes. Joe was now twenty-one so I consulted Godfrey's accountants who wrote to him to tell him of his good fortune, and I asked them to let me know what Joe decided to do with his money.

'Do you ever hear from Lionel?' Aunt Hetty asked one day. 'I never hear you mention him.'

'No. He said he wouldn't write or telephone me, I haven't expected to hear from him.'

'Does that mean that he is uninterested or simply that he thought it was too soon?'

'He thought it was too soon. He said in twelve months' time he would come here to see me, but he could have changed his mind.'

'He doesn't seem like the kind of man who would change his mind about anything that was important to him. What will you tell him when he comes?'

'*If* he comes Aunt Hetty. I don't know, I'm not sure.'

'Life can be very lonely, Tessa, I know and I don't want you to be as lonely as I have often been.'

'But you haven't been unhappy, Aunt Hetty, there have been compensations.'

'I agree. There have been friends and Godfrey's family, but they are not like one's own children. Of course you have Adam, but he needs a father behind him, it isn't easy for a woman on her own to bring up a boy.'

'But I must be sure, Aunt Hetty. It is better to be on my own all my life than married to the wrong man. That can be a destroying thing and I can't risk another mistake.'

'Richard wasn't entirely a mistake?'

'I know, we just had a bad start, that's all.'

'What *are* you going to tell Lionel then? I don't believe you are even considering your answer, but time passes very

564

quickly and you can't afford to be cavalier about a man who professes to love you.'

'Oh Aunt Hetty, heaven forbid that I should ever be cavalier about Lionel. I just want to be left alone to make my own decisions so that I can't blame anybody else if they go wrong.'

It was the beginning of December when I heard from my solicitors that Lady Dora Chalmers had suffered a massive heart attack in the mental home where she had been living since the days after the fire, and three days later was dead.

I felt no sorrow, how could I? And yet there were times when I asked myself if I could have done more, then memories of our encounters reassured me that she had not wanted either my friendship or my respect.

It was Godfrey poring over *The Times* at the breakfast table who gave a low whistle. 'Your mother-in-law's will is in *The Times*, Tessa, do you want to know how much she's left?'

'Not particularly, Godfrey. I don't suppose it can have been much, she was always complaining about poverty.'

'Poverty! She's left more than eight hundred thousand to her two sisters to be divided equally. That'll be Gertrude and Alice I take it, Hetty?'

'Yes, there's only the two of them left, Gertrude's a widow and Alice married that farmer from Kirkby.'

'They have children, I suppose?'

'Children but no grandchildren, and not likely to have any since their children have all been married for years.'

'Mmm. Ironic isn't it that the money'll go out of the family one day then? I don't suppose you mind, Tessa?'

'Well of course I don't mind, I don't want Dora's money, I never did and I certainly don't deserve it and Adam isn't entitled to it. I'm only angry that she cried poverty and wasn't averse to using my money to pay for repairs to a house she had allowed to run down.'

'Edward had money of course, but Dora's father was an old skinflint. No doubt he left her plenty.'

I didn't care where she had got it from, Sir Edward, her father or anybody else, but I was resentful that she had watched me spending my money on a house which she set fire to almost immediately the repairs were completed. My anger must have registered on my face because Aunt Hetty said gently, 'Don't mind so much, Tessa, you're young and you have Adam, that foolish woman had very little.'

'It was her own fault she had so little, Aunt Hetty, hoarding all that money, not going anywhere or doing anything, allowing her home to fall to pieces round her shoulders without lifting a finger to repair it, forever worrying Richard by telling him how poor they were and how it was impossible for them to repair their tenants' houses. She allowed me to repair those cottages, and how she must have laughed, knowing the size of her bank balance, thinking what a fool I was.'

'She was always a strange woman,' Godfrey said, 'I was amazed when Edward married her, except that she was always about when he was there, waiting like a female spider to snaffle him up when your mother went off with Nigel. The poor chap was a sitting duck.'

I felt exasperated – with people's weaknesses, with their lack of nerve. Otherwise how could Edward Chalmers have allowed Dora to dominate his life as well as his home?

Some of my thoughts must have conveyed themselves to my aunt because she said, 'Edward simply didn't care, Tessa, he adored Diana and when she went it was as though the sun had gone out of his life, nothing else mattered, would ever matter again.'

'But what about Richard? Surely he should have cared for his son.'

'One would have thought so dear, but who can say what unhappiness he suffered? Some people can retreat into their inner selves so successfully nothing matters.'

I knew how easy it was to do that. I too could have grovelled in my grief, shut myself away, nursing it like a dead thing hanging round my neck, but I had to think about my unborn child. I hadn't known Adam then, I hadn't known how beautiful he would be, how adorable his smile, how I would love him, but Edward had known Richard, watched him grow up. I could find no excuse in my heart for Edward Chalmers. He had been less than a man to allow his wife to dominate his son as well as himself.

Winter came at last to the northern fells. Snow fell from leaden skies and the wind blew relentlessly so that the long evenings were a joy, with the thick velvet drapes drawn and log fires burning half way up the chimneys.

Christmas was not far off but when I thought of other Christmases I had spent at Glamara I felt strangely sad. Godfrey had hoped Laura would come north for Christmas but she wrote to say they had so many festivities already planned they didn't feel like travelling at that time. She did however invite him to spend Christmas with them.

He seemed to be thinking about it, but then at the last minute he decided the weather was too severe for much travelling about the country, and I think Aunt Hetty was relieved. At least there would now be four of us sitting down to dinner on Christmas Day.

We decorated the huge tree in the hall and brought in holly and mistletoe from the forest and on Christmas Day Aunt Hetty performed the ceremony of handing out presents to the servants.

Later we heard the sound of their laughter as we ate our meal upstairs and Adam said, 'They're having much more fun than we are, Mother.'

'Well there are a lot more of them, darling. Perhaps after we have eaten we'll go downstairs and watch them dancing. Would you like that?'

His eyes lit up and Aunt Hetty said doubtfully, 'You don't think your being there will spoil it for them, Tessa?'

'No, I'm sure it won't. We shall be very discreet.'

The dancing had already started when Adam and I crept down the stairs leading to the servants' quarters, and we sat on the stairs watching them, whirling round to the tunes played by one of the villagers on his accordion. Kitchen maids danced with footmen, the butler danced with Cook and the housekeeper, and the grooms danced with the housemaids. It was all so happy and informal I could feel my feet tapping in time to the music and then Flanagan stood in front of me saying, 'And will you be 'onourin' me with the next waltz, Milady?'

'Oh Flanagan, do you really think I should?'

'Oh yes, Mother, *please*,' Adam said. 'I want to see you dance.'

So I took the floor with Flanagan and for a few minutes we danced alone before the rest of them joined in happily enough.

I danced with Flanagan and another of the grooms, I danced with the butler and the footmen, and one of the young housemaids dragged Adam down the stairs and attempted to teach him the Military Twostep, and his eyes shone with laughter.

Later in the evening hot punch was handed round and toasts were drunk to honour the engagement of one of the housemaids and the under-footman. With sprigs of mistletoe young footmen chased after the girls, much to the butler's concern, and Cook came to sit beside me on the stairs, saying, 'We allus enjoys ourselves at Christmas, Milady, but it's upstairs where it's changed. There used to be such goings on with Master Robert and Master Adam and the next morning we'd all be agog with it downstairs. I don't suppose them days'll ever come back, p'raps not till Sir Adam's grown up.'

'That's a long time off, Cook.'

'I knows it is but there's only you as comes back to Glamara, Miss Laura's not interested any more and Mr Robert's away all the time. Yer aunt and uncle are growin' older, they'll 'ave little time for dancin'. I wonder what'll happen to the 'ouse in a few years' time?'

'You are surely not expecting it to change all that much, Cook?'

'Well why don't yer look back a bit, Milady, if yer do you must know how much it's changed since afore the war, it seems as though the life's gone out o' the house. The children an' all their friends, Sir Julian an' even Miss Roxanne. All gone.'

All gone! I stared at her with sad eyes and the tears were not far away.

'Oh Milady, I shouldn't be upsettin' yer wi' talk o' the past, but I keep rememberin' how things were. Why even

Annie danced 'er feet off that last Christmas she were 'ere. She 'adn't much idea about dancin' but between 'em they taught 'er, she were that happy.'

I felt suddenly completely sobered, and although the dance was still going on with great gusto and enjoyment I made my excuses that Adam and I must leave and rejoin the people upstairs.

In the drawing room Godfrey slept in his chair and Aunt Hetty worked on her tapestry, so that not wishing to disturb them Adam and I went into the morning room where we played card games until it was time for him to go to bed.

Later I told Aunt Hetty something of the festivities which were still going on. We could hear the music and laughter, and Godfrey, waking up suddenly, said, 'Where on earth is that infernal noise coming from?'

'The servants' quarters, it's their Christmas Day party.'

He grunted. 'Shouldn't it be coming to an end by this time? It's nigh on eleven.'

'Oh let them have their fun, there's not so much of it these days that we can afford to begrudge the servants.'

'How long did you stay down there, Tessa?'

'About two hours. I danced with Flanagan and the butler, and several young men who appeared out of nowhere.'

'Good for you my girl, and what did Adam do?'

'He watched, and learned a few steps. Two of the servants have got engaged so we drank a toast to their future in fairly powerful hot punch.'

'Mm. I've often suspected that my wine cellar was depleted, now I've got the proof.'

'Well of course you haven't, and don't you dare mention it.'

He grinned. 'What about a present for the happy couple, Hetty?'

'Well of course, what do you suggest?'

'China, linen. Heaven knows there's enough stuff in this house to set up a dozen homes.'

'I'll see about it tomorrow. Which of the girls was it, Tessa?'

569

'Agnes, the pretty housemaid, and one of the footmen, I'm not sure which one, they all look so much alike in their uniform.'

'We'll have a look in the linen cupboards tomorrow, Tessa, and you shall help me decide what to give them. Household linen is very expensive, particularly the good variety, and we have more than enough for our needs.'

I couldn't help thinking how different things were at Glamara than they had been at Easdale. Dora would never have given linen to any of her housemaids, it is even doubtful if she would have known about the engagement.

Later that night after the house was quiet I stood at my window looking out across the parkland. A blanket of snow covered the distant fells and they gleamed silver white under a full moon. There was frost on the conifers below my window and on the telephone wires, frost on the window sills and icicles hanging delicately from the lintels. It was so still and silent and so incredibly light I could see the track of a fox's footprints across the grass quite close to the house and in my heart I felt a deep penetrating sadness, a yearning for the past so incredibly potent that it brought the hot stinging tears into my eyes.

Shivering a little at the sight of the silver night, even though the room was warm and glowing from the fire in the grate, I was about to turn away when I saw in the distance a car approaching, its headlights lighting up the drive, startling an owl which flew off screeching into the night.

Who could possibly be calling just before midnight on Christmas Day? Surely not some late-night reveller hoping to extend his celebrations at Glamara? If so it was someone who did not know how much Glamara had changed. I rubbed the window where my breath had misted it. The car had come to a halt in front of the house and the lights were switched off, then I could dimly see a man climbing out of the driver's seat and I hurried down the stairs.

My heart was thumping madly as my fingers coped with the heavy bolts on the door, then flinging it open I looked out with the lights from the hall illuminating the drive. I had thought it might be Lionel, eager to see me and reluctant to wait any longer, but the man was holding the car door open for a passenger, and then he turned to the light. With a cry of joy I ran across the snow, oblivious of my fragile house slippers and the wind buffeting my velvet robe, then I was in his arms and I was laughing and crying with joy. It was Robert.

I stood back at last, and then for the first time I looked at his passenger. She stood watching us, smiling, and with a little laugh Robert held out his hand and brought her forward to meet me.

'Tessa this is my wife, Caroline this is my cousin Tessa. Now both of you come inside the house out of the cold.'

We half ran across the forecourt and then Robert was barring the great doors behind us and I was ruefully shaking the soft snow from my slippers.

'A glass of whisky is what you need, my girl,' Robert was saying with all his old authority and yet he looked round the familiar hall with the fire dying in the giant grate, and the tinsel-decked tree. There was a light in his eyes I rejoiced to see, a great joy that he was once more standing in his old home, and then Godfrey was there and Aunt Hetty, embracing each other, laughing and crying, and the dogs were barking round our feet and Adam stood sleepy-eyed half way up the stairs.

Soon the servants were awake and fires were being lit in bedrooms and we were in the drawing room drinking hot toddies while Aunt Hetty, practical as ever, insisted that we go to our beds, that there was all the time in the world to exchange news and confidences.

Once more in my room I added several logs to the fire, for sleep did not come for a long time. I was happy for the first time since the fire. Robert had come home of his own free will.

It seemed to me in the months that followed that my life away from Glamara had been a dream – a book I had read, a play I had seen, so alien that none of it had happened to me at all.

It was as if Robert had never been away. He and Godfrey were friends again without any recriminations, almost as though by mutual consent the past was to be forgotten and never referred to, and in Caroline I found a friend. She was gentle and sympathetic, we liked riding and walking and we had similar tastes in art and music and literature. Aunt Hetty was delighted by her and so too were the servants. She was undemanding and appreciative and when she confided to us that she was expecting her first baby in the early summer we were overjoyed.

In January Adam went away to school, somewhat reluctantly I fear, because Robert spoiled him terribly. In Robert he seemed to have found the father he had longed for, somebody who could go riding with him, take him fishing and enter wholeheartedly into all the boyish pursuits Richard had been unable to enjoy.

He took school in his stride. He wrote enthusiastically about the friends he had made and rather less so about his lessons, but when I drove to the school to bring him home for Easter I was amazed how much he had grown in stature and how mature he seemed.

One day Aunt Hetty said as she watched me staring wistfully after Adam and Robert as they set off across the park together, 'Adam needs a father, Tessa, what are you going to say to Lionel when he comes?'

'You seem very sure that he will come.'

'Have you spoken to Robert about him?'

'Yes, but you know Robert, he says I should snap him up quickly before anybody else does. He had the nerve to say it might be my last chance.'

She laughed. 'I hope you won't snap him up for that reason, Tessa.'

'Aunt Hetty, why was Robert so antagonistic towards Roxanne? It can't have been simply because she was taking his mother's place?'

'Have you asked him?'

'No, I don't think he wants to talk about the past, at least not where Roxanne is concerned.'

'I don't believe Robert would mind you knowing, not after what she did to you,' she mused.

I stared down at her curiously. She was watching Adam

and Robert intently but she was not seeing them, her thoughts were back in the past on some moment that had caused her great distress, then she started to tell me.

'You know how close Adam and Robert were. They were more than brothers, they were identical souls, and yet Adam was always the serious one, on the surface that is. It was Adam who cried when he had to go away to school, Adam who openly worshipped his mother, Adam who fell in love, Robert was the one who went to school without shedding a tear, who followed his father everywhere and who liked to flirt without ever being serious. Then one summer Laura brought Roxanne to Glamara.

'Roxanne was like no girl the boys had ever seen and Adam fell desperately in love with her. Of course Roxanne revelled in it. That Robert didn't follow Adam's example piqued her terribly and I could see her every day playing one off against the other. Then there was that terrible morning when she came into the drawing room with a torn dress and bruise on her arms, nearly hysterical. She said Robert had been trying to make love to her in the conservatory and she had had to fight him off. The fact that Robert denied it adamantly didn't satisfy his brother and later that day I found them fighting like wildcats in the stableyard. I didn't dare separate them so I threw a pail of water over the pair of them. They didn't speak to each other for weeks, even after Roxanne and Laura went back to Switzerland.'

'But when I came here they were friends.'

'Oh yes, this had happened a few years before you came here, Tessa. The next time Roxanne came she wasn't interested in either of the boys, she had set her heart on Julian. Adam and Robert cynically watched her trying to make him jealous by flirting with every young man who came to the parties here, and Julian watched just as cynically.'

'I'm glad I haven't spoken of her to Robert, Aunt Hetty, I never shall,' I said earnestly.

She nodded. 'Yes, I don't think her name will be spoken again in this house by any of us.'

CHAPTER THIRTY-SEVEN

Summer came, with long golden days and gentle misted mornings. I went with Adam during the long school holidays to Devonshire, staying at a delightful hotel Aunt Hetty had recommended, and although I asked her to accompany us she said, 'I'm too old to quicken my steps to match Adam's, Tessa. You'll enjoy it more without me.'

We did enjoy it, we sat in the sun and walked over the hills, we went to summer theatres and I put aside my aversion to sailing. Adam loved messing about in boats. It was something I had no right to destroy, a part of living Julian had bequeathed to him, and I discovered again how much I too loved sailing with the wind in my hair and the summer sea calm and benign around us.

Too soon those long summer days came to an end. Adam returned to school and I grew restless. I had had no word from Lionel and there were days when I found myself wondering if he ever thought about his promise to seek me out when the twelve months had elapsed. He lived a busy life, met a great many people, might he not regret a promise he had made in a moment of emotional tension to a woman who had too much forgetting to do?

Aunt Hetty watched me constantly across the breakfast table when I ate little, and one morning she said, 'You're worried in case he comes and you're worried in case he doesn't. Shouldn't you be making your mind up on what you want from the future?'

'It isn't that easy,' I snapped in reply.

'I'm reluctant to give advice where it's not wanted but something must be said. However much you mourn Julian he's gone, Tessa, and you can't have him back ever. Richard too has gone but you are still here and so is Adam. If Lionel Prescott sees in you the woman he wants then you should welcome him with open arms. He's attractive, he's charming and he is very nice, what more do you want in a man?'

'He's everything you say, Aunt Hetty, but do I have enough to give him? Can I give him the same sort of love I gave Julian, or even the sort of love I gave Richard?'

'You gave Julian all the love and desire you had in your young body, all the dreams and desires of your youth were centred in him, the love you gave Richard was one you could have given to any man who needed your care and your pity.'

'That isn't fair, Aunt Hetty.'

'Perhaps not, but it's true nevertheless. It has to be a very different type of love you give Lionel Prescott, it has to be mature and intelligent, Tessa, and even if you never reach the heights you will never plummet the depths with him. You could have a happy and very serene future with a man like that.'

'He may not come.'

'Perhaps not, and if he does it's my guess you won't be waiting on the doorstep for him. You'll be off in the park or over the fells and he'll no doubt have to come looking for you.'

'How well you know me, Aunt Hetty.'

'There's a lot of your mother in you, a lot of her pride and independence. Swallow a little of it, that's my advice.'

I don't know what I expected, that he would arrive on the doorstep before breakfast perhaps, but when he hadn't arrived by lunchtime I ate in a hurry, avoiding Aunt Hetty's amused eyes, then immediately afterwards I grabbed my camel coat and calling to the dogs set off across the park in the direction of the moors.

It was a warm fresh day and I walked briskly, following the footpath that led towards the fells, crossing the shallow stream by the stepping stones while the dogs splashed through the water, shaking themselves so enthusiastically my coat was splattered. From the top of the fell I could look down on Glamara, at the smoke rising lazily from the chimneys, at the men rebuilding a stone wall where it had crumbled and at two of the servants walking across the park on their afternoon off. It was all so normal, why was my heart palpitating nervously and why was I alternately excited and angry?

The heather and the bracken were past their best but still I lingered on the hillside watching the clouds scudding across the blue sky, listening to the wind sighing through the branches of the pines, then resolutely I called the dogs and set off back to the house.

I had almost reached the wall that separated the moorland from the park when I saw Lionel walking towards me and I paused, reluctant to go further in case our eyes met too soon and I would know immediately that everything had changed.

He held up his hand when he saw me on the hillside and he climbed swiftly while I went slowly forward to meet him. I had forgotten how charming his smile could be, how warm and uncomplicated, whereas Julian's smile had lit up his face with surprising sweetness, robbing it of that strange remoteness which had often made me feel that I did not really know him at all.

He came forward to meet me with outstretched hands, saying, 'Your aunt said I would probably find you up here, Tessa. I meant to come earlier but I loitered, I was afraid, a coward if you like.'

'You were afraid, Lionel?'

'Yes, in case you didn't want to see me.'

'I was afraid too, Lionel, in case you had changed your mind.'

He sounded surprised. 'But I promised, Tessa.'

'I know, but when you'd had time to think about it, perhaps.'

'You should have known I wouldn't change my mind.'

'Lionel, how could I?'

'It was impossible that I should change my mind about something so important as our future. Do we have a future together, Tessa?'

I did not ask him again if he was sure. I knew he had never been more sure of anything in his entire life, it was in the sincerity in his eyes, in the firmness of his handclasp, in the beginning of his smile which was all tenderness, all love.

We walked back to the house through a sudden shower of

rain, hand in hand like children, our hearts filled with hope and promise, and as we ran the last few yards towards the gardens the sun came out, gilding the beech leaves which were already glowing in their autumn colours of russet and gold, warming the mellow stone of the house, shining in the forest of window panes.

I had loved Glamara all my life and always when my heart was most burdened by sorrow, devastated by tragedy, I had found solace if not forgetfulness beneath its roof. Now, once again, I would be leaving Glamara to go with Lionel. I would be making promises that were binding to love and honour, to abide where he abides and make his people my people, but I shall come back, a slave to the strange impossible magic the house inspires in those who love her, aware that here as nowhere else I shall not be able to escape from the bitter-sweet memories of the past, the old tormenting passions of days that are gone.